The Victoria Reader

S. Ellis

The Victoria Reader

A Treasury of Timeless Stories

Edited by

MICHELE SLUNG

HEARST BOOKS
A DIVISION OF STERLING PUBLISHING CO., INC.
NEW YORK

Jacket design by Deborah Kerner, Dancing Bears Design
Jacket photograph by Caroline Arber
Tapestry: Courtesy of The Royal School of Needlework Collection, London, England
Book design by Celia Fuller

Library of Congress Cataloging-in-Publication Data
The Victoria reader : a treasury of timeless stories / edited by Michele Slung.
p. cm.
ISBN 1-58816-253-2
1. Short stories, English. 2. Short stories, American. I. Slung, Michele B., 1947–.
PR1309.S5 V53 2003
823'.0108--dc21

2002151922

10 9 8 7 6 5 4 3 2 1

Published by Hearst Books,
A Division of Sterling Publishing Company, Inc.
387 Park Avenue South, New York, N.Y. 10016

Victoria and Hearst Books are trademarks owned by
Hearst Magazines Property, Inc., in USA, and Hearst Communications, Inc., in Canada.

www.victoriamag.com

Distributed in Canada by Sterling Publishing
c/o Canadian Manda Group, One Atlantic Avenue, Suite 105
Toronto, Ontario, Canada M6K 3E7

Distributed in Australia by Capricorn Link (Australia) Pty. Ltd.
P.O. Box 704, Windsor, NSW 2756 Australia

Manufactured in China

ISBN 1-58816-253-2

CONTENTS

SOCIAL SITUATIONS

COMIC INTERRUPTIONS

LINGERING ENCOUNTERS

CHERISHED FABLES

FAMILY REVELATIONS

ROMANTIC EPISODES

FOREWORD

I RECENTLY FINISHED READING a short story in this collection. Or at least I thought I had finished—but it keeps on coming back, seeping into how I see things, sharpening the way I hear a difference between what people are saying and what they are feeling. It's as if a room I know well had suddenly acquired a new window. Just a glance at the contents of this intriguing anthology makes me eager for yet more unexpected windows.

The feeling of holding such adventures in my hands brings back the pleasure of my childhood trips to the library in our small Massachusetts town, where nothing much happened. The library was my escape. We were allowed to take only three books out at once, so the faster I devoured them the sooner I was back for more. I wasn't a very discriminating reader then (Nancy Drew mysteries were my favorites), but the habit persisted until adulthood, when I fell for what writers such as Fitzgerald, Wharton, and Pushkin had to tell me about the human heart and character. Funny, how reading can lead one on. For instance, it was my affection for Pushkin's short stories that led me to Russia in the 1980s to photograph the rustic manor he'd lived in, lovingly preserved—through all political upheavals—by the country that venerated him. The mere mention of Pushkin opened doors for me to undiscovered Russian houses.

Michele Slung, the editor and gatherer of this collection, has been delighting *Victoria* readers with her literary insights for a long time now. She is quite simply one of the best-read persons I've ever known, with a gift for bringing overlooked gems to light with the radiance of her enthusiasm. I sometimes suspect she's read everything—from mysteries to cookbooks to novels of manners—especially of the late nineteenth and early twentieth centuries. I also suspect that Michele has been quietly compiling this selection of favorite stories in her mind for years. And now we have it.

You hold a whole little library in your hands. Who knows where it will lead you?

—Margaret Kennedy
Editor in Chief, *Victoria* Magazine

INTRODUCTION

When I was growing up and reading had already become as important to me as breathing, certain wonderfully hefty volumes of short stories had what I soon recognized as a special aura. As anthologies—a literary term with its origins in the idea of "a garland of flowers"—many of these books were never *about* anything in particular, that is, they had no set theme. What they all had in common was a sense of open-ended promise, the equivalent of bookish infinity when compared to the lesser pleasures of more slender tomes.

The English writer A. C. Benson once said, "All the best stories are but one story in reality—the story of escape." Into these anthologies, then, one escaped—blissfully. But not just to exotic landscapes or enchanted worlds or into the midst of thrilling escapades or gallant deeds. One also escaped into the minds, hearts and spirits of people—sometimes ordinary, sometimes extraordinary—whose very tissue was the fiber of story-pages. Yet they were no less real for that!

The delights of such books—"treasuries," they were often aptly called, but sometimes garlands, too—are best described, I think, as cornucopian. For, with their lavish harvests of adventure and romance, realism and fantasy, sentiment and satire, humor and human drama, their riches—

amassed from the work of so many different authors—offered something for everyone.

I remember how excited I was each time to have a new collection in my possession. The sensation was akin to having an invitation to a carefully planned party, with the book's editor its beckoning host. Opening the volume, I would begin by exploring its table of contents for the reassuring presence of familiar names and tales. Then, heartbeat quickening, I'd go on to identify those stories and writers that were enticingly unknown.

Either way, what lay ahead was bound to be satisfying, as I loved as much to encounter old favorites as to discover new ones. And, of course, there were, from time to time, those odd, sneaky stories that wouldn't instantly reveal themselves as acquaintances but, instead, would wait until I was nose to nose with them, as it were, and just starting to experience *déjà vu.* Caught you! they then seemed to say, but I took it in good humor, feeling I'd been nabbed fair and square and never minding that I hadn't *thought* I knew them.

These anthologies, somehow, even seemed to smell different from other books. Could one hazard a guess that that singular effect might have been owing to the many flavors of literature contained inside them? I know, too, that, like many readers, I chose to wander through them in ways exactly tailored to my personal satisfaction. To read straight ahead, only occasionally skipping or deferring, was usually my choice. And, at the same time, it was important to give each author and creation their due, fixing in my mind as I went along a running ranking of those I was enjoying the most.

The heyday of such expansively conceived, thoughtfully assembled anthologies, packed so abundantly with memorable moments and characters, was in the era before television had worked its changes on the ways families entertain themselves. But, as a reader and longtime collector of stories—who believes that nothing has ever really taken their place—I recently began to realize how much I missed them and the magical invitations they extended. It was then I knew that I longed to have the opportunity to put together such a book myself, to be the one hosting the festivities this time around.

So, with Mark Twain in attendance, along with P. G. Wodehouse, John Buchan, Edith Wharton, John Galsworthy, Oscar Wilde, Sarah Orne

Jewett, Ellen Glasgow, H. G. Wells and twenty-one others, I'm requesting that you join us for what is, in fact, a celebration and not just a mere party.

I say that not only because *Victoria* would have it no other way, but also because by calling our book a "treasury," it makes it clear that we believe that, in publishing it, we are honoring a great tradition. Also, though most of the authors' names are celebrated ones, the majority of stories selected, I'm pretty certain, will strike readers as far less so. Thus, it seems safe to promise that the charms of surprise will figure in with all the other rewards of this brand-new, yet altogether classic collection.

Half a century ago the American popular novelist Kathleen Norris wrote, "Just the knowledge that a good book is waiting for one at the end of a long day makes that day happier." I like to think that anyone opening *The Victoria Reader* already agrees with her.

—MICHELE SLUNG

SOCIAL SITUATIONS

THE INCONSIDERATE WAITER

J. M. BARRIE

FREQUENTLY I HAVE TO ASK MYSELF in the street for the name of the man I bowed to just now, and then, before I can answer, the wind of the first corner blows him from my memory. I have a theory, however, that those puzzling faces, which pass before I can see who cut the coat, all belong to club waiters.

Until William forced his affairs upon me that was all I did know of the private life of waiters, though I have been in the club for twenty years. I was even unaware whether they slept downstairs or had their own homes; nor had I the interest to inquire of other members, nor they the knowledge to inform me. I hold that this sort of people should be fed and clothed and given airing and wives and children, and I subscribe yearly, I believe, for these purposes; but to come into closer relation with waiters is bad form; they are club fittings, and William should have kept his distress to himself, or taken it away and patched it up like a rent in one of the chairs. His inconsiderateness has been a pair of spectacles to me for months.

It is not correct taste to know the name of a club waiter, so that I must apologise for knowing William's, and still more for not forgetting it. If, again, to speak of a waiter is bad form, to speak bitterly is the comic degree of it. But William has disappointed me sorely. There were years when I would defer dining several minutes that he might wait on me. His pains to reserve the window seat for me were perfectly satisfactory. I allowed him privileges, as to suggest dishes, and would give him information, as that someone had startled me in the reading room by slamming a door. I have shown him how I cut my finger with a piece of string. Obviously he was gratified by these attentions, usually recommending a liqueur; and I fancy he must have understood my sufferings, for he often looked ill himself. Probably he was rheumatic, but I cannot say for certain, as I never thought of asking, and he had the sense to see that the knowledge would be offensive to me.

In the smoking room we have a waiter so independent that once, when he brought me a yellow chartreuse, and I said I had ordered green, he replied, "No, sir; you said yellow." William could never have been guilty of such effrontery. In appearance, of course, he is mean, but I can no more describe him than a milkmaid could draw cows. I suppose we distinguish one waiter from another much as we pick our hat from the rack. We could have plotted a murder safely before William. He never presumed to have opinions of his own. When such was my mood he remained silent, and if I announced that something diverting had happened to me he laughed before I told him what it was. He turned the twinkle in his eye off or on at my bidding as readily as if it was the gas. To my "Sure to be wet tomorrow," he would reply, "Yes, sir"; and to Trelawney's "It doesn't look like rain," two minutes afterward, he would reply, "No, sir." It was one member who said Lightning Rod would win the Derby and another who said Lightning Rod had no chance, but it was William who agreed with both. He was like a cheroot, which may be smoked from either end. So used was I to him that, had he died or got another situation (or whatever it is such persons do when they disappear from the club), I should probably have told the head waiter to bring him back, as I disliked changes.

It would not become me to know precisely when I began to think William an ingrate, but I date his lapse from the evening when he brought me oysters. I detest oysters, and no one knew it better than William. He has agreed with me that he could not understand any gentleman's liking them. Between me and a certain member who smacks his lips twelve times to a dozen of them William knew I liked a screen to be placed until we had reached the soup, and yet he gave me the oysters and the other man my sardine. Both the other member and I called quickly for brandy and the head waiter. To do William justice, he shook, but never can I forget his audacious explanation: "Beg pardon, sir, but I was thinking of something else."

In these words William had flung off the mask, and now I knew him for what he was.

I must not be accused of bad form for looking at William on the following evening. What prompted me to do so was not personal interest in him, but a desire to see whether I dare let him wait on me again. So, recalling that a caster was off a chair yesterday, one is entitled to make sure that it is on today before sitting down. If the expression is not too strong, I may say that I was taken aback by William's manner. Even when crossing the room to take my orders he let his one hand play nervously with the other. I had to repeat "Sardine on toast" twice, and instead of answering "Yes, sir," as if my selection of sardine on toast was a personal gratification to him, which is the manner one expects of a waiter, he glanced at the clock, then out at the window, and, starting, asked, "Did you say sardine on toast, sir?"

It was the height of summer, when London smells like a chemist's shop, and he who has the dinner-table at the window needs no candles to show him his knife and fork. I lay back at intervals, now watching a starved-looking woman asleep on a doorstep, and again complaining of the club bananas. By-and-by I saw a little girl of the commonest kind, ill-clad and dirty, as all these ragamuffins are. Their parents should be compelled to feed and clothe them comfortably, or at least to keep them indoors, where they cannot offend our eyes. Such children are for pushing aside with one's umbrella; but this girl I noticed because she was gazing at the club windows. She had stood thus for perhaps ten minutes when I became aware that someone was leaning over me to look out at the window. I turned round. Conceive my indignation on seeing that the rude person was William.

"How dare you, William?" I said, sternly. He seemed not to hear me. Let me tell, in the measured words of one describing a past incident, what then took place. To get nearer the window he pressed heavily on my shoulder.

"William, you forget yourself!" I said, meaning—as I see now—that he had forgotten me.

I heard him gulp, but not to my reprimand. He was scanning the street. His hands chattered on my shoulder, and, pushing him from me, I saw that his mouth was agape.

"What are you looking for?" I asked.

He stared at me, and then, like one who had at last heard the echo of my question, seemed to be brought back to the club. He turned his face from me for an instant, and answered shakily:

"I beg your pardon, sir! I—I shouldn't have done it. Are the bananas too ripe, sir?"

He recommended the nuts, and awaited my verdict so anxiously while I ate one that I was about to speak graciously, when I again saw his eyes drag him to the window.

"William," I said, my patience giving way at last, "I dislike being waited on by a melancholy waiter."

"Yes, sir," he replied, trying to smile, and then broke out passionately, "For God's sake, sir, tell me, have you seen a little girl looking in at the club windows?"

He had been a good waiter once, and his distracted visage was spoiling my dinner.

"There," I said, pointing out the girl, and no doubt would have added that he must bring me coffee immediately, had he continued to listen. But already he was beckoning to the child. I had not the least interest in her (indeed, it had never struck me that waiters had private affairs, and I still think it a pity that they should have); but as I happened to be looking out at the window I could not avoid seeing what occurred. As soon as the girl saw William she ran into the middle of the street, regardless of vehicles, and nodded three times to him. Then she disappeared.

I have said that she was quite a common child, without attraction of any sort, and yet it was amazing the difference she made in William. He gasped relief, like one who has broken through the anxiety that checks breathing, and into his face there came a silly laugh of happiness. I had dined well, on the whole, so I said:

"I am glad to see you cheerful again, William."

I meant that I approved his cheerfulness because it helped my digestion, but he must needs think I was sympathising with him.

"Thank you, sir," he answered. "Oh, sir! When she nodded and I saw it was all right I could have gone down on my knees to God."

I was as much horrified as if he had dropped a plate on my toes. Even William, disgracefully emotional as he was at the moment, flung out his arms to recall the shameful words.

"Coffee, William!" I said, sharply.

I sipped my coffee indignantly, for it was plain to me that William had something on his mind.

"You are not vexed with me, sir?" he had the hardihood to whisper.

"It was a liberty," I said.

"I know, sir; but I was beside myself."

"That was a liberty also."

He hesitated, and then blurted out:

"It is my wife, sir—"

I stopped him with my hand. William, whom I had favoured in so many ways, was a married man! I might have guessed as much years before had I ever reflected about waiters, for I knew vaguely that his class did this sort of thing. His confession was distasteful to me, and I said warningly:

"Remember where you are, William."

"Yes, sir; but you see, she is so delicate—"

"Delicate! I forbid your speaking to me on unpleasant topics."

"Yes, sir; begging your pardon."

It was characteristic of William to beg my pardon and withdraw his wife, like some unsuccessful dish, as if its taste would not remain in the mouth. I shall be chided for questioning him further about his wife, but, though doubtless an unusual step, it was only bad form superficially, for my motive was irreproachable. I inquired for his wife, not because I was interested in her welfare, but in the hope of allaying my irritation. So I am entitled to invite the wayfarer who has bespattered me with mud to scrape it off.

I desired to be told by William that the girl's signals meant his wife's recovery to health. He should have seen that such was my wish and answered accordingly. But, with the brutal inconsiderateness of his class, he said:

"She has had a good day; but the doctor, he—the doctor is afeard she is dying."

Already I repented my question. William and his wife seemed in league against me, when they might so easily have chosen some other member.

"Pooh! The doctor," I said.

"Yes, sir," he answered.

"Have you been married long, William?"

"Eight years, sir. Eight years ago she was—I—I mind her when . . . and now the doctor says—"

The fellow gaped at me. "More coffee, sir?" he asked.

"What is her ailment?"

"She was always one of the delicate kind, but full of spirit, and—and you see, she has had a baby lately—"

"William!"

"And she—I—the doctor is afeared she's not picking up."

"I feel sure she will pick up."

"Yes, sir?"

It must have been the wine I had drunk that made me tell him:

"I was once married, William. My wife—it was just such a case as yours."

"She did not get better, sir?"

"No."

After a pause he said, "Thank you, sir," meaning for the sympathy that made me tell him that. But it must have been the wine.

"That little girl comes here with a message from your wife?"

"Yes; if she nods three times it means my wife is a little better."

"She nodded thrice today."

"But she is told to do that to relieve me, and maybe those nods don't tell the truth."

"Is she your girl?"

"No; we have none but the baby. She is a neighbour's; she comes twice a day."

"It is heartless of her parents not to send her every hour."

"But she is six years old," he said, "and has a house and two sisters to look after in the daytime, and a dinner to cook. Gentlefolk don't understand."

"I suppose you live in some low part, William."

"Off Drury Lane," he answered, flushing; "but—but it isn't low. You see, we were never used to anything better, and I mind when I let her see the house before we were married, she—she a sort of cried because she was so proud of it. That was eight years ago, and now—she's afeared she'll die when I'm away at my work."

"Did she tell you that?"

"Never; she always says she is feeling a little stronger."

"Then how can you know she is afraid of that?"

"I don't know how I know, sir; but when I am leaving the house in the morning I look at her from the door, and she looks at me, and then I—I know."

"A green chartreuse, William!"

I tried to forget William's vulgar story in billiards, but he had spoiled my game. My opponent, to whom I can give twenty, ran out when I was sixty-seven, and I put aside my cue pettishly. That in itself was bad form, but what would they have thought had they known that a waiter's impertinence caused it! I grew angrier with William as the night wore on, and next day I punished him by giving my orders through another waiter.

As I had my window seat, I could not but see that the girl was late again. Somehow I dawdled over my coffee. I had an evening paper before me, but there was so little in it that my eyes found more of interest in the street. It did not matter to me whether William's wife died, but when that girl had promised to come, why did she not come? These lower classes only give their word to break it. The coffee was undrinkable.

At last I saw her. William was at another window, pretending to do something with the curtains. I stood up, pressing closer to the window. The coffee had been so bad that I felt shaky. She nodded three times and smiled.

"She is a little better," William whispered to me, almost gaily.

"Whom are you speaking of?" I asked, coldly, and immediately retired to the billiard room, where I played a capital game. The coffee was much better there than in the dining room.

Several days passed, and I took care to show William that I had forgotten his maunderings. I chanced to see the little girl (though I never looked for her) every evening, and she always nodded three times, save once, when she shook her head, and then William's face grew white as a napkin. I remember this incident because that night I could not get into a pocket. So badly did I play that the thought of it kept me awake in bed, and that, again, made me wonder how William's wife was. Next day I went to the club early (which was not my custom) to see the new books. Being in the club at any rate, I looked into the dining room to ask William if I had left my gloves there, and the sight of him reminded me of his wife; so I asked for her. He shook his head mournfully, and I went off in a rage.

So accustomed am I to the club that when I dine elsewhere I feel uncomfortable next morning, as if I had missed a dinner. William knew this; yet here he was, hounding me out of the club! That evening I dined (as the saying is) at a restaurant, where no sauce was served with the asparagus. Furthermore, as if that were not triumph enough for William, his doleful face came between me and every dish, and I seemed to see his wife dying to annoy me.

I dined next day at the club for self-preservation, taking, however, a table in the middle of the room, and engaging a waiter who had once nearly poisoned me by not interfering when I put two lumps of sugar into my coffee instead of one, which is my allowance. But no William came to me to acknowledge his humiliation, and by-and-by I became aware that he was not in the room. Suddenly the thought struck me that his wife must be dead, and I—It was the worst cooked and the worst served dinner I ever had in the club.

I tried the smoking room. Usually the talk there is entertaining, but on that occasion it was so frivolous that I did not remain five minutes. In the card room a member told me excitedly that a policeman had spoken rudely to him; and my strange comment was:

"After all, it is a small matter."

In the library, where I had not been for years, I found two members asleep, and, to my surprise, William on a ladder dusting books.

"You have not heard, sir?" he said, in answer to my raised eyebrows. Descending the ladder, he whispered tragically: "It was last evening, sir. I—I lost my head, and I—swore at a member."

I stepped back from William, and glanced apprehensively at the two members. They still slept.

"I hardly knew," William went on, "what I was doing all day yesterday, for I had left my wife so weakly that—"

I stamped my foot.

"I beg your pardon for speaking of her," he had the grace to say, "but I couldn't help slipping to the window often yesterday to look for Jenny, and when she did come, and I saw she was crying, it—it sort of confused me, and I didn't know right, sir, what I was doing. I hit against a member, Mr. Myddleton Finch, and he—he jumped and swore at me. Well, sir, I had just touched him after all, and I was so miserable, it a kind of stung me to be treated like—like that, and me a man as well as him; and I lost my senses, and—and I swore back."

William's shamed head sank on his chest, but I even let pass his insolence in likening himself to a member of the club, so afraid was I of the sleepers waking and detecting me in talk with a waiter.

"For the love of God," William cried, with coarse emotion, "don't let them dismiss me!"

"Speak lower!" I said. "Who sent you here?"

"I was turned out of the dining room at once, and told to attend to the library until they had decided what to do with me. Oh, sir, I'll lose my place!" He was blubbering, as if a change of waiters was a matter of importance.

"This is very bad, William," I said. "I fear I can do nothing for you."

"Have mercy on a distracted man!" he entreated. "I'll go on my knees to Mr. Myddleton Finch."

How could I but despise a fellow who would be thus abject for a pound a week?

"I dare not tell her," he continued, "that I have lost my place. She would just fall back and die."

"I forbade your speaking of your wife," I said, sharply, "unless you can speak pleasantly of her."

"But she may be worse now, sir, and I cannot even see Jenny from here. The library windows look to the back."

"If she dies," I said, "it will be a warning to you to marry a stronger woman next time."

Now every one knows that there is little real affection among the lower orders. As soon as they have lost one mate they take another. Yet William, forgetting our relative positions, drew himself up and raised his fist, and if I had not stepped back I swear he would have struck me.

The highly improper words William used I will omit, out of consideration for him. Even while he was apologising for them I retired to the smoking room, where I found the cigarettes so badly rolled that they would not keep alight. After a little I remembered that I wanted to see Myddleton Finch about an improved saddle of which a friend of his has the patent. He was in the newsroom, and, having questioned him about the saddle, I said:

"By the way, what is this story about your swearing at one of the waiters?"

"You mean about his swearing at me," Myddleton Finch replied, reddening.

"I am glad that was it," I said; "for I could not believe you guilty of such bad form."

"If I did swear—" he was beginning, but I went on:

"The version which reached me was that you swore at him, and he repeated the word. I heard he was to be dismissed and you reprimanded."

"Who told you that?" asked Myddleton Finch, who is a timid man.

"I forget; it is club talk," I replied, lightly. "But of course the committee will take your word. The waiter, whichever one he is, richly deserves his dismissal for insulting you without provocation."

Then our talk returned to the saddle, but Myddleton Finch was abstracted, and presently he said:

"Do you know, I fancy I was wrong in thinking that waiter swore at me, and I'll withdraw my charge tomorrow."

Myddleton Finch then left me, and, sitting alone, I realised that I had been doing William a service. To some slight extent I may have intentionally helped him to retain his place in the club, and I now see the reason, which was that he alone knows precisely to what extent I like my claret heated.

For a mere second I remembered William's remark that he should not be able to see the girl Jenny from the library windows. Then this recollection drove from my head that I had only dined in the sense that my dinner bill was paid. Returning to the dining room, I happened to take my chair at the window, and while I was eating a deviled kidney I saw in the street the girl whose nods had such an absurd effect on William.

The children of the poor are as thoughtless as their parents, and this Jenny did not sign to the windows in the hope that William might see her, though she could not see him. Her face, which was disgracefully dirty, bore doubt and dismay on it, but whether she brought good news it would not tell. Somehow I had expected her to signal when she saw me, and, though her message could not interest me, I was in the mood in which one is irritated at that not taking place which he is awaiting. Ultimately she seemed to be making up her mind to go away.

A boy was passing with the evening papers, and I hurried out to get one, rather thoughtlessly, for we have all the papers in the club. Unfortunately,

I misunderstood the direction the boy had taken; but round the first corner (out of sight of the club windows) I saw the girl Jenny, and so I asked her how William's wife was.

"Did he send you to me?" she replied, impertinently taking me for a waiter. "My!" she added, after a second of scrutiny, "I b'lieve you're one of them. His missis is a bit better, and I was to tell him as she took all the tapiocar."

"How could you tell him?" I asked.

"I was to do like this," she replied, and went through the supping of something out of a plate in dumb-show.

"That would not show she ate all the tapioca," I said.

"But I was to end like this," she answered, licking an imaginary plate with her tongue.

I gave her a shilling (to get rid of her), and returned to the club disgusted.

Later in the evening I had to go to the club library for a book, and while William was looking in vain for it (I had forgotten the title) I said to him:

"By the way, William, Mr. Myddleton Finch is to tell the committee that he was mistaken in the charge he brought against you, so you will doubtless be restored to the dining room tomorrow."

The two members were still in their chairs, probably sleeping lightly; yet he had the effrontery to thank me.

"Don't thank me," I said, blushing at the imputation. "Remember your place, William!"

"But Mr. Myddleton Finch knew I swore," he insisted.

"A gentleman," I replied, stiffly, "cannot remember for twenty-four hours what a waiter has said to him."

"No, sir; but—"

To stop him I had to say: "And, ah, William, your wife is a little better. She has eaten the tapioca—all of it."

"How can you know, sir?"

"By an accident."

"Jenny signed to the window?"

"No."

"Then you saw her, and went out, and—"

"Nonsense!"

"Oh, sir, to do that for me! May God bl—"

"William!"

"Forgive me, sir; but—when I tell my misses, she will say it was thought of your own wife as made you do it."

He wrung my hand. I dared not withdraw it, lest we should waken the sleepers.

William returned to the dining room, and I had to show him that if he did not cease looking gratefully at me I must change my waiter. I also ordered him to stop telling me nightly how his wife was, but I continued to know, as I could not help seeing the girl Jenny from the window. Twice in a week I learned from the objectionable child that the ailing woman had again eaten all the tapioca. Then I became suspicious of William. I will tell why.

It began with a remark of Captain Upjohn's. We had been speaking of the inconvenience of not being able to get a hot dish served after 1 A.M., and he said:

"It is because these lazy waiters would strike. If the beggars had a love of their work they would not rush away from the club the moment one o'clock strikes. That glum fellow who often waits on you takes to his heels the moment he is clear of the club steps. He ran into me the other night at the top of the street, and was off without apologising."

"You mean the foot of the street, Upjohn," I said; for such is the way to Drury Lane.

"No; I mean the top. The man was running west."

"East."

"West."

I smiled, which so annoyed him that he bet me two to one in sovereigns. The bet could have been decided most quickly by asking William a question, but I thought, foolishly doubtless, that it might hurt his feelings, so I watched him leave the club. The possibility of Upjohn's winning the bet had seemed remote to me. Conceive my surprise, therefore, when William went westward.

Amazed, I pursued him along two streets without realising that I was doing so. Then curiosity put me into a hansom. We followed William, and it proved to be a three-shilling fare, for, running when he was in breath and walking when he was out of it, he took me to West Kensington.

I discharged my cab, and from across the street watched William's incomprehensible behaviour. He had stopped at a dingy row of workmen's houses, and knocked at the darkened window of one of them. Presently a light showed. So far as I could see, some one pulled up the blind and for ten minutes talked to William. I was uncertain whether they talked, for the window was not opened, and I felt that, had William spoken through the glass loud enough to be heard inside, I must have heard him too. Yet he nodded and beckoned. I was still bewildered when, by setting off the way he had come, he gave me the opportunity of going home.

Knowing from the talk of the club what the lower orders are, could I doubt that this was some discreditable love affair of William's? His solicitude for his wife had been mere pretence; so far as it was genuine, it meant that he feared she might recover. He probably told her that he was detained nightly in the club till three.

I was miserable next day, and blamed the deviled kidneys for it. Whether William was unfaithful to his wife was nothing to me, but I had two plain reasons for insisting on his going straight home from his club: the one that, as he had made me lose a bet, I must punish him; the other that he could wait upon me better if he went to bed betimes.

Yet I did not question him. There was something in his face that—Well, I seemed to see his dying wife in it.

I was so out of sorts that I could eat no dinner. I left the club. Happening to stand for some time at the foot of the street, I chanced to see the girl Jenny coming, and—No; let me tell the truth, though the whole club reads: I was waiting for her.

"How is William's wife today?" I asked.

"She told me to nod three times," the little slattern replied; "but she looked like nothing but a dead one till she got the brandy."

"Hush, child!" I said, shocked. "You don't know how the dead look."

"Bless yer," she answered, "don't I just! Why, I've helped to lay 'em out. I'm going on seven."

"Is William good to his wife?"

"Course he is. Ain't she his missis?"

"Why should that make him good to her?" I asked, cynically, out of my knowledge of the poor. But the girl, precocious in many ways, had never had many opportunities of studying the lower classes in the newspapers, fiction, and club talk. She shut one eye, and, looking up wonderingly, said:

"Ain't you green—just!"

"When does William reach home at night?"

" 'T ain't night; it's morning. When I wakes up at half dark and half light, and hears a door shutting, I know as it's either father going off to his work or Mr. Hicking coming home from his."

"Who is Mr. Hicking?"

"Him as we've been speaking on—William. We calls him mister, 'cause he's a toff. Father's just doing jobs in Covent Garden, but Mr. Hicking, he's a waiter, and a clean shirt every day. The old woman would like father to be a waiter, but he hain't got the 'ristocratic look."

"What old woman?"

"Go 'long! That's my mother. Is it true there's a waiter in the club just for to open the door?"

"Yes; but—"

"And another just for to lick the stamps? My!"

"William leaves the club at one o'clock?" I said, interrogatively.

She nodded. "My mother," she said, "is one to talk, and she says to Mr. Hicking as he should get away at twelve, 'cause his missis needs him more 'n the gentlemen need him. The old woman do talk."

"And what does William answer to that?"

"He says as the gentlemen can't be kept waiting for their cheese."

"But William does not go straight home when he leaves the club?"

"That's the kid."

"Kid!" I echoed, scarcely understanding, for, knowing how little the poor love their children, I had asked William no questions about the baby.

"Didn't you know his missis had a kid?"

"Yes; but that is no excuse for William's staying away from his sick wife," I answered, sharply. A baby in such a home as William's, I reflected, must be trying; but still—Besides, his class can sleep through any din.

"The kid ain't in our court," the girl explained. "He's in W., he is, and I've never been out of W. C.; leastwise, not as I knows on."

"This is W. I suppose you mean that the child is at West Kensington? Well, no doubt it was better for William's wife to get rid of the child—"

"Better!" interposed the girl. " 'T ain't better for her not to have the kid. Ain't her not having him what she's always thinking on when she looks like a dead one?"

"How could you know that?"

" 'Cause," answered the girl, illustrating her words with a gesture, "I watches her, and I sees her arms going this way, just like as she wanted to hug her kid."

"Possibly you are right," I said, frowning; "but William had to put the child out to nurse because it disturbed his night's rest. A man who has his work to do—"

"You are green!"

"Then why have the mother and child been separated?"

"Along of that there measles. Near all the young 'uns in our court has 'em bad."

"Have you had them?"

"I said the young 'uns."

"And William sent the baby to West Kensington to escape infection?"

"Took him, he did."

"Against his wife's wishes?"

"Na-o!"

"You said she was dying for want of the child?"

"Wouldn't she rather die than have the kid die?"

"Don't speak so heartlessly, child. Why does William not go straight home from the club? Does he go to West Kensington to see it?"

" 'T ain't a hit, it's an 'e. Course he do."

"Then he should not. His wife has the first claim on him."

"Ain't you green! It's his missis as wants him to go. Do you think she could sleep till she knowed how the kid was?"

"But he does not go into the house at West Kensington?"

"Is he soft? Course he don't go in, fear of taking the infection to the kid. They just holds the kid up at the window to him, so as he can have a good look. Then he comes home and tells his missis. He sits foot of the bed and tells."

"And that takes place every night? He can't have much to tell."

"He has just."

"He can only say whether the child is well or ill."

"My! He tells what a difference there is in the kid since he seed him last."

"There can be no difference!"

"Go 'long! Ain't a kid always growing? Haven't Mr. Hicking to tell how the hair is getting darker, and heaps of things beside?"

"Such as what?"

"Like whether he larfed, and if he has her nose, and how as he knowed him. He tells her them things more 'n once."

"And all this time he is sitting at the foot of the bed?"

"'Cept when he holds her hand."

"But when does he get to bed himself?"

"He don't get much. He tells her as he has a sleep at the club."

"He cannot say that."

"Hain't I heard him? But he do go to his bed a bit, and then they both lies quiet, her pretending she is sleeping so as he can sleep, and him 'feard to sleep case he shouldn't wake up to give her the bottle stuff."

"What does the doctor say about her?"

"He's a good one, the doctor. Sometimes he says she would get better if she could see the kid through the window."

"Nonsense!"

"And if she was took to the country."

"Then why does not William take her?"

"My! You are green! And if she drank port wines."

"Doesn't she?"

"No; but William, he tells her about the gentlemen drinking them."

On the tenth day after my conversation with this unattractive child I was in my brougham, with the windows up, and I sat back, a paper before my face lest any one should look in. Naturally, I was afraid of being seen in company of William's wife and Jenny, for men about town are uncharitable, and, despite the explanation I had ready, might have charged me with pitying William. As a matter of fact, William was sending his wife into Surrey to stay with an old nurse of mine, and I was driving her down because my horses needed an outing. Besides, I was going that way at any rate.

I had arranged that the girl Jenny, who was wearing an outrageous bonnet, should accompany us, because, knowing the greed of her class, I feared she might blackmail me at the club.

William joined us in the suburbs, bringing the baby with him, as I had foreseen they would all be occupied with it, and to save me the trouble of conversing with them. Mrs. Hicking I found too pale and fragile for a workingman's wife. And I formed a mean opinion of her intelligence from her pride in the baby, which was a very ordinary one. She created quite a vulgar scene when it was brought to her, though she had given me her word not to do so, what irritated me even more than her tears being her ill-bred apology that she "had been 'feard baby wouldn't know her again." I would have told her they didn't know any one for years had I not been afraid of the girl Jenny, who dandled the infant on her knees and talked to it as if it understood. She kept me on tenter-hooks by asking it offensive questions, such as, " 'Oo know who give me that bonnet?" and answering them herself, "It was the pretty gentleman there"; and several times I had to affect sleep because she announced, "Kiddy wants to kiss the pretty gentleman."

Irksome as all this necessarily was to a man of taste, I suffered even more when we reached our destination. As we drove through the village the girl Jenny uttered shrieks of delight at the sight of flowers growing up the cottage walls, and declared they were "just like a music-'all without the drink license." As my horses required a rest, I was forced to abandon my intention of dropping these persons at their lodgings and returning to town at once, and I could not go to the inn lest I should meet inquisitive acquaintances. Disagreeable circumstances, therefore, compelled me to take tea with a waiter's family—close to a window too, through which I could see the girl Jenny talking excitedly to villagers, and telling them, I felt certain, that I had been good to William. I had a desire to go out and put myself right with those people.

William's long connection with the club should have given him some manners, but apparently his class cannot take them on, for, though he knew I regarded his thanks as an insult, he looked them when he was not speaking them, and hardly had he sat down, by my orders, than he remembered that I was a member of the club, and jumped up. Nothing is in worse form than whispering, yet again and again, when he thought I was not listening, he whispered to Mrs. Hicking, "You don't feel faint?" or "How are you now?" He was also in extravagant glee because she ate two cakes (it takes so little to put these people in good spirits), and when she said she felt like another being already the fellow's face charged me with the change. I could not but conclude, from the way Mrs. Hicking let the baby pound her, that she was stronger than she had pretended.

I remained longer than was necessary, because I had something to say to William which I knew he would misunderstand, and so I put off saying it.

But when he announced that it was time for him to return to London,—at which his wife suddenly paled, so that he had to sign to her not to break down,—I delivered the message.

"William," I said, "the head waiter asked me to say that you could take a fortnight's holiday just now. Your wages will be paid as usual."

Confound them! William had me by the hand, and his wife was in tears before I could reach the door.

"Is it your doing again, sir?" William cried.

"William!" I said, fiercely.

"We owe everything to you," he insisted. "The port wine—"

"Because I had no room for it in my cellar."

"The money for the nurse in London—"

"Because I objected to being waited on by a man who got no sleep."

"These lodgings—"

"Because I wanted to do something for my old nurse."

"And now, sir, a fortnight's holiday!"

"Good-bye, William!" I said, in a fury.

But before I could get away Mrs. Hicking signed to William to leave the room, and then she kissed my hand. She said something to me. It was about my wife. Somehow I—What business had William to tell her about my wife?

They are all back in Drury Lane now, and William tells me that his wife sings at her work just as she did eight years ago. I have no interest in this, and try to check his talk of it; but such people have no sense of propriety, and he even speaks of the girl Jenny, who sent me lately a gaudy pair of worsted gloves worked by her own hand. The meanest advantage they took of my weakness, however, was in calling their baby after me. I have an uncomfortable suspicion, too, that William has given the other waiters his version of the affair; but I feel safe so long as it does not reach the committee.

OUR CONSUL AT CARLSRUHE

F. J. STIMSON

DIED.—*In Baden, Germany, the 22d instant, Charles Austin Pinckney, late U.S. Consul at Carlsruhe, age sixty years.*

There: most stories of men's lives end with the epitaph, but this of Pinckney's shall begin there. If we, as haply God or Devil can, could unroof the houses of men's souls, if their visible works were of their hearts rather than their brains, we should know strange things. And this alone, of all the possible, is certain. For bethink you, how men appear to their Creator, as He looks down into the soul, that matrix of their visible lives we find so hard to localize and yet so sure to be. For all of us believe in self, and few of us but are forced, one way or another, to grant existence to some selves outside of us. Can you not fancy that men's souls, like their farms, would show here a patch of grain, and there the tares; there the weeds and here the sowing; over this place the rain has been, and that other, to one looking down upon it from afar, seems brown and desolate, wasted by fire or made arid by the drought? In this man's life is a poor beginning, but a better end; in this other's we see the foundations, the staging, and the schemes of mighty structures, now stopped, given over, or abandoned; of vessels, fashioned for the world's seas, now rotting on the stocks. Of this one all seems ready but the launching, of that the large keelson only has been laid; but both alike have died unborn, and the rain falls upon them, and the mosses grow: the sound of labor is far off, and the scene of work is silent. Small laws make great changes; slight differences of adjustment end quick in death. Small, now, they would seem to us; but to the infinite mind all things small and great are alike; the spore of rust in the ear is very slight, but a famine in the corn will shake the world.

Pinckney's life the world called lazy; his leisure was not fruitful, and his sixty years of life were but a gentleman's. Some slight lesion may have caused paralysis of energy, some clot of heart's blood pressed upon the soul: I make no doubt our doctors could diagnose it, if they knew a little more. Tall and slender, he had a strange face, a face with a young man's beauty; his white hair gave a charm to the rare smile, like new snow to the spring, and the slight stoop with which he walked was but a grace the more. In short, Pinckney was interesting. Women raved about him; young men fell in love with him; and if he was selfish, the fault lay between him and his Maker, not visible to other men. There are three things that make a man interesting in his old age: the first, being heroism, we may put aside; but the other two are regret and remorse. Now, Mr. Pinckney's fragrance was not of remorse—women and young men would have called it heroism: it may have been. As much heroism as could be practiced in thirty-six years of Carlsruhe.

Why Carlsruhe? That was the keynote of inquiry; and no one knew. Old men spoke unctuously of youthful scandals; women dreamed. I suspect even Mrs. Pinckney wondered, about as much as the plowed field may wonder at the silence of the autumn. But Pinckney limped gracefully about the sleepy avenues which converge at the Grand Duke's palace, like a wakeful page in the castle of the Sleeping Beauty. Pinckney was a friend of the Grand Duke's, and perhaps it was a certain American flavor persisting in his manners which made him seem the only man at the Baden court who met his arch-serene altitude on equal terms. For one who had done nothing and possessed little, Pinckney certainly preserved a marvelous personal dignity. His four daughters were all married to scions of Teutonic nobility; and each one in turn had asked him for the Pinckney arms, and quartered them into the appropriate check-square with as much grave satisfaction as he felt for the far-off patch of Hohenzollern, or of Hapsurg in sinister chief. Pinckney had laughed at it and referred them to the Declaration of Independence, clause the first; but his wife had copied them from some spoon or sugar bowl. She was very fond of Pinckney, and no more questioned him why they always lived in Carlsruhe than a Persian would the sun for rising east. Now and then they went to Baden, and her cup was full.

Pinckney died of a cold, unostentatiously, and was buried like a gentleman; though the Grand Duke actually wanted to put the court in mourning for three days, and consulted with his chamberlain whether it would do. Mrs. Pinckney had preceded him by some six years; but she was an appendage, and her husband's deference had always seemed in Carlsruhe a trifle strained. It was only in these last six years that anyone had gossiped of remorse, in answer to the sphinx-like question of his marble brow. Such questions vex the curious. Furrows trouble nobody—money matters are enough for them; but white smoothness in old age is a bait, and tickles curiosity. Some said at home he was a devil and beat his wife.

But Pinckney never beat his wife. Late in the last twilight of her life she had called him to her, and excluded even the four daughters, with their stout and splendid barons; then, alone with him, she looked to him and smiled. And suddenly his gentleman's heart took a jump, and the tears fell on her still soft hands. I suppose some old road was opened again in the gray matter of his brain. Mrs. Pinckney smiled the more strongly and said—not quite so terribly as Mrs. Amos Barton: "Have I made you happy, dearest Charles?" And Charles, the perfect-mannered, said she had; but said it stammering. "Then," said she, "I die very happily, dear." And she did; and Pinckney continued to live at Carlsruhe.

The only activities of Pinckney's mind were critical. He was a wonderful orator, but he rarely spoke. People said he could have been a great writer, but he never wrote, at least nothing original. He was the art and continental-drama critic of several English and American reviews; in music, he was a Wagnerian, which debarred him from writing of it except in German; but the little Court Theatre at Carlsruhe has Wagner's portrait over the drop-curtain, and the consul's box was never empty when the mighty heathen legends were declaimed or the holy music of the Grail was sung. In fiction of the earnest sort, and poetry, Pinckney's critical pen showed a marvelous magic, striking the scant springs of the author's inspiration through the most rocky ground of incident or style.

He had a curious sympathy with youthful tenderness. But, after all, as every young compatriot who went to Baden said, what the deuce and all did he live in Baden for? Miles Breeze had said it in 'Fifty, when he made the grand tour with his young wife, and dined with him in Baden-Baden; that is, when Breeze dined with him, for his young wife was indisposed and could not go. Miles Breeze, junior, had said it, as late as 'Seventy-six, when he went abroad, ostensibly for instruction, after leaving college. He had letters to Mr. Pinckney, who was very kind to the young Baltimorean, and greatly troubled the Grand Duke his Serenity by presenting him as a relative of the Bonapartes. Many another American had said it, and even some leading politicians: he might have held office at home: but Pinckney continued to live in Carlsruhe.

His critical faculties seemed sharpened after his wife's death, as his hair grew whiter; and if you remember how he looked before you must have noticed that the greatest change was in the expression of his face. There was one faint downward line at either side of his mouth, and the counterpart at the eyes; a doubtful line which, faint as it was graven, gave a strange amount of shading to the face. And in speaking of him earlier, you must remember to take your india-rubber and rub out this line from his face. This done, the face is still serious; but it has a certain light, a certain air of confidence, of determination, regretful though it be, which makes it loved by women. Women can love a desperate, but never begin to love a beaten, cause. Women fell in love with Pinckney, for the lightning does strike twice in the same place; but his race was rather that of Lohengrin than of the Asra, and he saw it, or seemed to see it, not. Still, in these times those downward lines had not come, and there was a certain sober light in his face as of a sorrowful triumph. This was in the epoch of his greatest interestingness to women.

When he first came to Carlsruhe, he was simply the new consul, nothing more; a handsome young man, almost in his honeymoon, with a young and pretty wife. He had less presence in those days, and seemed absorbed in his new home, or deeply sunk in something; people at first fancied he was a poet, meditating a great work, which finished, he would soon leave Carlsruhe. He never was seen to look at a woman, not overmuch at his wife, and was not yet popular in society.

But it was true that he was newly married. He was married in Boston, in 'Forty-three or four, to Emily Austin, a far-off cousin of his, whom he had known (he himself was a Carolinian) during his four years at Cambridge. For his four years in Cambridge were succeeded by two more at the Law School; then he won a great case against Mr. Choate, and was narrowly beaten in an election for Congress; after that it surprised no one to hear the announcement of his engagement to Miss Austin, for his family was unexceptionable and he had a brilliant future. The marriage came in the fall, rather sooner than people expected, at King's Chapel. They went abroad, as was natural; and then he surprised his friends and hers by accepting his consulship and staying there. And they were imperceptibly, gradually, slowly, and utterly forgotten.

The engagement came out in the spring of 'Forty-three. And in June of that year young Pinckney had gone to visit his *fiancée* at Newport. Had you seen him there, you would have seen him in perhaps the brightest role that fate has yet permitted on this world's stage. A young man, a lover, rich, gifted, and ambitious, of social position unquestioned in South Carolina and the old Bay State—all the world loved him, as a lover; the many envied him, the upper few desired him. Handsome he has always remained.

And the world did look to him as bright as he to the world. He was in love, as he told himself, and Miss Austin was a lovable girl; and the other things he was dimly conscious of; and he had a long vacation ahead of him, and was to be married late in the autumn, and he walked up from the wharf in Newport swinging his cane and thinking on these pleasant things.

Newport, in those days, was not the paradise of cottages and curricles, of lawns and laces, of new New Yorkers and Nevada miners; it was the time of big hotels and balls, of Southern planters, of Jullien's orchestras, and of hotel hops; such a barbarous time as the wandering New Yorker still may find, lingering on the simple shores of Maine, sunning in the verdant valleys of the Green Mountains; in short, it was Arcadia, not Belgravia. And you must remember that Pinckney, who was dressed in the latest style, wore a blue broadloth frock coat, cut very low and tight in the waist, with a coat-collar rolling back to reveal a vast expanse of shirt-bosom, surmounted by a cravat of awful splendor, bow-knotted and blue-fringed. His trouser were of white duck, his boots lacquered, and he carried a gold-tipped cane in his hand. So he walked up the narrow old streets from the wharf, making a sunshine in those shady places. It was the hottest hour of a midsummer afternoon; not a soul was stirring, and Pinckney was left to his own pleasant meditations.

He got up the hill and turned into the park by the old mill; over opposite was the great hotel, its piazzas deserted, silent even to the hotel band. But one flutter of a white dress he saw beneath the trees, and then it disappeared behind them, causing Pinckney to quicken his steps. He thought he knew the shape and motion, and he followed it until he came upon it suddenly, behind the trees, and it turned.

A young girl of wonderful beauty, rare, erect carriage, and eyes of a strange, violet-gray, full of much meaning. This was all Pinckney had time to note; it was no one he had ever seen before. He had gone up like a hunter, sure of his game, and too far in it to retract. The embarrassment of the situation was such that Pinckney forgot all his cleverness of manner, and blurted out the truth like any schoolboy.

"I beg pardon—I was looking for Miss Austin," said he; and he raised his hat.

A delightful smile of merriment curled the beauty's lips. "My acquaintance with Miss Austin is too slight to justify my finding her for you; but I wish you all success in your efforts," she said, and vanished, leaving the promising young lawyer to blush at his own awkwardness and wonder who she was. As she disappeared, he only saw that her hair was a lustrous coil of pale gold-brown, borne proudly.

He soon found Emily Austin, and forgot the beauty, as he gave his betrothed a kiss and saw her color heighten; and in the afternoon they took a long drive. It was only at tea, as he was sitting at table with the Austins in the long dining room, that some one walked in like a goddess; and it was she. He asked her name; and they told him it was a Miss Warfield, of Baltimore, and she was engaged to a Mr. Breeze.

In the evening there was a ball; and as they were dancing (for every one danced in those days) he saw her again, sitting alone this time and unattended. She was looking eagerly across the room, through the dancers and beyond; and in her eyes was the deepest look of sadness Pinckney had ever seen in a girl's face; a look such as he had thought no girl could feel. A moment after, and it was gone, as some one spoke to her; and Pinckney wondered if he had not been mistaken, so fleeting was it, and so strange. An acquaintance—one of those men who delight to act as brokers of acquaintances—who had noticed his gaze came up. "That is the famous Miss Mary Warfield," said he. "Shall I not introduce you?"

"No," said Pinckney; and he turned away rudely. To be rude when you like is perhaps one of the choicest prerogatives of a good social position. The acquaintance stared after him, as he went back to Miss Warfield himself. A moment after, Pinckney saw her look over at him with some interest; and he wondered if the man had been ass enough to tell her. Pinckney was sitting with Emily Austin; and, after another moment, he saw Miss Warfield look at her. Then her glance seemed to lose its interest; her eyelids drooped, and Pinckney could see, from her interlocutor's manner, that he was put to his trumps to keep her attention. At last he got away, awkwardly; and for many minutes the strange girl sat like a statue, her long lashes just veiling her eyes, so that Pinckney, from a distance, could not see what was in them. Suddenly the veil was drawn and her eyes shone full upon him, her look meeting his. Pinckney's glance fell, and his cheeks grew redder. Miss Warfield's face did not change, but she rose and walked unattended through the centre of the ballroom to the door. Pinckney's seat was nearer it than hers; she passed him as if without seeing him, moving with unconscious grace, though it would not have been the custom at that time for a girl to cross so large a room alone. Just then someone asked Miss Austin for a dance; and Pinckney, who was growing weary of it, went out on the piazza for a cigar, and then, attracted by the beauty of the night, strayed further than he knew, alone, along the cliffs above the sea.

The next day he was walking with Miss Austin, and they passed her, in her riding habit, waiting by the mounting stone; she bowed to Miss Austin alone, leaving him out, as it seemed to Pinckney, with exaggerated care.

"Is she not beautiful?" said Emily, ardently.

"Humph!" said Pinckney. A short time after, as they were driving on the road to the Fort, he saw he again; she was riding alone, across country, through the rocky knolls and marshy pools that form the southern part of Rhode Island. She had no groom lagging behind, but it was not so necessary then as now; and, indeed, a groom would have had a hard time to keep up with her, as she rattled up the granite slopes and down over logs and bushes with her bright bay horse. The last Pinckney saw of her she disappeared over a rocky hill against the sky; her beautiful horse flecked with foam, quivering with happy animal life, and the girl calm as a figure carved in stone, with but the faintest touch of rose upon her face, as the pure profile was outlined one moment against the sunlit blue.

"How recklessly she rides!" whispered Miss Austin to him, and Pinckney said *yes*, absently, and, whipping up his horse, drove on, pretending to listen to his fiancée's talk. It seemed to be about dresses, and rings, and a coming visit to the B—s, at Nahant. He had never seen a girl like her before; she was a puzzle to him.

"It is a great pity she is engaged to Mr. Breeze," said Miss Austin; and Pinckney woke up with a start, for he was thinking of Miss Warfield too.

"Why?" said he.

"I don't like him," said Emily. "He isn't good enough for her."

As this is a thing that women say of all wooers after they have won, and which the winner is usually at that period the first to admit, Pinckney paid little attention to this remark. But that evening he met Miles Breeze, saw him, talked with him, and heard others talk of him. A handsome man, physically; well made, well dressed, well fed; well bred, as breeding goes in dogs or horses; a good shot, a good sportsman, yachtsman, story-teller; a good fellow, with a weak mouth; a man of good old Maryland blood, yet red and healthy, who had come there in his yacht and had his horses sent by sea. A well-appointed man, in short; provided amply with the conveniences of fashionable life. A man of good family, good fortune, good health, good sense, good nature, whom it were hypercritical to charge with lack of soul. "The first duty of a gentleman is to be a good animal," and Miles Breeze performed it thoroughly. Pinckney liked him, and he could have been his companion for years and still have liked him, except as a husband for Miss Warfield.

He could not but recognize his excellence as a *parti.* But the race of Joan of Arc does not mate with Bonhomme Richard, even when he owns the next farm. Pinckney used to watch the crease of Breeze's neck, above the collar, and curse.

Coming upon Miss Austin one morning, she had said, "Come—I want to introduce you to Miss Warfield." Pinckney had demurred, and offered as an excuse that he was smoking. "Nonsense, Charles," said the girl; "I have told her you are coming." Pinckney threw away his cigar and followed, and the presentation was made. Miss Warfield drew herself almost unusually erect after curtsying, as if in protest at having to bow at all. She was so tall that, as Emily stood between them, he could meet Miss Warfield's iron-gray eyes above her head. It was the first time in Pinckney's life that he had consciously not known what to say.

"I was so anxious to have you meet Charles before he left," said Emily. Evidently, his fiancée had been expatiating upon him to this new friend, and if there is anything that puts a man in a foolish position it is to have this sort of preamble precede an acquaintance.

"An anxiety I duly shared, Miss Warfield, I assure you," said he; which was a truth spoiled in the uttering—what the conversational Frenchman terms *banale.*

"Thank you," said Miss Warfield, very simply and tremendously effectively. Pinckney, for the second time with this young lady, felt himself a schoolboy. Emily interposed some feeble commonplaces, and then, after a moment, Miss Warfield said, "I must go for my ride"; and she left, with a smile for Emily and the faintest possible glance for him. She went off with Breeze; and it gave Pinckney some relief to see that she seemed equally to ignore the presence of the man who was her acknowledged lover, as he trotted on a smart cob beside her. That evening, when he went on the piazza after tea, he found her sitting alone, in one corner, with her hands folded: it was one peculiarity about this woman that she was never seen with work. She made no sign of recognition as he approached; but, nonetheless, he took the chair that was beside her and waited a moment for her to speak. "Have you found Miss Austin?" said the beauty, with the faintest trace of malice in her coldly modulated tones, not looking at him. "I am not looking for Miss Austin," said he; and she continued not looking at him, and so this strange pair sat there in the twilight, silent.

What was said between them I do not know. But in some way or other their minds met; for long after Miss Austin and her mother had returned from some call, long after they had all left him, Pinckney continued to pace up and down restlessly in the dark. Pinckney had never seen a woman like this. After all, he was very young; and he had, in his heart, supposed that the doubts and delights of his soul were peculiar to men alone. He thought all women—at all events, all young and worthy women—regarded life and its accepted forms as an accomplished fact, not to be questioned, and, indeed, too delightful to need it. The young South Carolinian, in his ambitions, in his heart-longings and heart-sickenings, in his poetry, even in his emotions, had always been lonely; so that his loneliness had grown to seem to him as merely part of the day's work. The best women, he knew, were the best housewives; they were a rest and a benefit for the war-weary man, much as might be a pretty child, a bed of flowers, a strain of music. With Emily Austin he should find all this; and he loved her as good, pretty, amiable, perfect in her way. But now, with Miss Warfield—it had seemed that he was not even lonely.

Pinckney did not see her again for a week. When he met her, he avoided her; she certainly avoided him. Breeze, meantime, gave a dinner. He gave it on his yacht, and gave it to men alone. Pinckney was of the number.

The next day there was a driving party; it was to drive out of town to Purgatory, a pretty place, where there is a brook in a deep ravine with a verdant meadow-floor; and there they were to take food and drink, as is the way of humanity in pretty places. Now it so happened that the Austins, Miss Warfield, Breeze, and Pinckney were going to drive in a party, the Austins and Miss Warfield having carriages of their own; but at the last moment Breeze did not appear, and Emily Austin was incapacitated by a headache. She insisted, as is the way of loving women, that "Charles should not lose it"; for to her it was one of life's pleasures, and such pleasures satisfied her soul. (It may be that she gave more of her soul to life's duties than did Charles, and life's pleasures were thus adequate to the remainder; I do not know.) Probably Miles Breeze also had a headache; at all events, he did not, at the last moment, appear. It was supposable that he would turn up at the picnic; Mrs. Austin joined her daughter's entreaty; Miss Warfield was left unattended; in fine, Pinckney went with her.

Miss Warfield had a solid little phaeton with two stout ponies: she drove herself. For some time they were silent; then, insensibly, Pinckney began to talk and she to answer. What they said I need not say—indeed I could not, for Pinckney was a poet, a man of rare intellect and imagination, and Miss Warfield was a woman of this world and the next; a woman who used conventions as another might use a fan, to screen her from fools; whose views were based on the ultimate. But they talked of the world, and of life in it; and when it came to an end, Pinckney noted to himself this strange thing, that they had both talked as of an intellectual problem, no longer concerning their emotions—in short, as if this life were at an end, and they were two dead people discussing it.

So they arrived at the picnic, silent; and the people assembled looked to one another and smiled, and said to one another how glum those two engaged people looked, being together, and each wanting another. Mr.

Breeze had not yet come; and as the people scattered while the luncheon was being prepared, Pinckney and she wandered off like the others. They went some distance—perhaps a mile or more—aimlessly; and then, as they seemed to have come about to the end of the valley, Pinckney sat down upon a rock, but she did not do so, but remained standing. Hardly a word had so far been said between them; and then Pinckney looked at her and said:

"Why are you going to marry Mr. Breeze?"

"Why not?"—listlessly.

"You might as well throw yourself into the sea," said Pinckney; and he looked at the sea which lay beyond them shimmering.

"That I had not thought of," said she; and she looked at the sea herself with more interest. Pinckney drew a long breath.

"But why this man?" he said at length.

"Why that man?" said the woman; and her beautiful lip curled, with the humor of the mind, while her eyes kept still the sadness of the heart, the look that he had seen in the ballroom. "We are all poor," she added; then scornfully, "it is my duty to marry."

"But Miles Breeze?" persisted Pinckney.

The lip curled almost to a laugh. "I never met a better fellow than Miles," said she; and the thought was so like his own of the night before that Pinckney gasped for breath. They went back, and had chicken croquettes and champagne, and a band that was hidden in the wood made some wild Spanish music.

Going home, a curious thing happened. They had started first and far preceded all the others. Miss Warfield was driving; and when they were again in the main road, not more than a mile from the hotel, Pinckney saw ahead of them, coming in a light trotting buggy of the sort that one associates with the gentry who call themselves "sports," two of the gentlemen whom he had met at Breeze's dinner the night before. Whether Miss Warfield also knew them he did not know; but they evidently had more wine than was good for them, and were driving along in a reckless manner on the wrong side of the road. The buggy was much too narrow for the two; and the one that was driving leaned out toward them with a tipsy leer. Pinckney shouted at him, but Miss Warfield drove calmly on. He was on the point of grasping the reins, but a look of hers withheld him, and he sat still, wondering; and in a moment their small front wheel had crashed through both the axles and spider-web wheels of the trotting buggy. The shock of the second axle whirled them round, and Pinckney fell violently against the dasher, while Miss Warfield was thrown clear of the phaeton on the outer side. But she had kept the reins, and before Pinckney could get to her she was standing at her horses' heads, patting their necks calmly, with a slight cut in her forehead where she had fallen, and only her nostril quivering like theirs, as the horses stood there trembling. The buggy was a wreck, and the horse had disappeared; and the two men, sobered by the fall, came up humbly to her to apologize. She heard them silently, with a pale face like some injured queen's; and then, bowing to them their dismissal, motioned Pinckney into the phaeton, which, though much broken, was still standing, and, getting in herself, drove slowly home.

"She might have killed herself," thought Pinckney, but he held his peace, as if it were the most natural course of action in the world. To tell the truth, under the circumstances he might have done the same alone.

Then it began. Pinckney could not keep this woman out of his head. He would think of her at all times, alone and in company. Her face would come to him in the loneliness of crowds; the strong spirit of the morning was hers, and the sadness of the sunset and the wakeful watches of the night. Her face was in the clouds of evening, in the sea-coal fire by night; her spirit in the dreams of summer morns, in the hopeless breakers on the stormy shores, in the useless, endless effort of the sea. Her eyes made some strange shining through his dreams; and he would wake with a cry that she was going from him, in the deepest hours of the night, as if in the dreams he had lost her, vanishing forever in the daily crowd. Then he would lie awake until morning, and all the laws of God and men would seem like cobwebs to his sorrow, and the power of it freezing in his heart. This was the ultimate nature of his being, to follow her, as drop of water blends in drop of water, as frost rends rock. Let him then follow out his law, as other beings do theirs; gravitation has no conscience; should he be weaker than a drop of water, because he was conscious, and a man?

So these early morning battles would go on, and character, training, conscience, would go down before the simpler force, like bands of man's upon essential nature. Then, with the first ray of the dawn, he would think of Emily Austin, sleeping near him, perhaps dreaming of him, and his mad visions seemed to fade; and he would rise exhausted, and wander out among the fresh fields and green dewy lanes, and calm, contentful trees, and be glad that these things were so; yet could these not be moved, nor their destiny be changed. And as for him, what did it matter?

So the days went by. And Emily Austin looked upon him with eyes of limitless love and trust, and Pinckney did not dare to look upon himself; but his mind judged by daytime and his heart strove by night. Hardly at all had he spoken to Miss Warfield since; and no reference had ever been made between them to the accident, or to the talk between them in the valley. Only Pinckney knew that she was to be married very shortly; and he had urged Miss Austin to hasten their own wedding.

Emily went off with her mother to pay her last visit among the family, and to make her preparations; and it was deemed proper that this time Pinckney should not be with her. So he stayed in Newport five long days alone; and during this time he never spoke to Miss Warfield. I believe he tried not to look at her; she did not look at him. And on the fifth night Pinckney swore that he must speak to her once more, whatever happened.

In the morning there was talk of a sailing party; and Pinckney noted Breeze busying himself about the arrangements. He waited; and at noon Breeze came to him and said that there was a scarcity of men: would he go? Yes. They had two sailboats, and meant to land upon Conanicut, which was then a barren island without a house, upon the southern end, where it stretches out to sea.

Pinckney did not go in the same boat with Breeze and Miss Warfield; and, landing, he spent the afternoon with others and saw nothing of her. But after dinner was over, he spoke to her, inviting her to walk; and she came, silently. A strange evening promenade that was: they took a path close on the sheer brink of the cliffs, so narrow that one must go behind the other. Pinckney had thought at first she might be frightened, with the rough path, and the steepness of the rocks, and the breakers churning at their base; but he saw that she was walking erect and fearlessly. Finally she motioned him to let her go ahead; and she led the way, choosing indiscriminately the straightest path, whether on the verge of the sea or leading through green meadows. A few colorless remarks were made by him, and then he saw the folly of it, and they walked in silence. After nearly an hour, she stopped.

"We must be getting back," she said.

"Yes," said he, in the same tone; and they turned; she still leading the way, while he followed silently. They were walking toward the sunset; the sun was going down in a bank of dense gray cloud, but its long, level rays came over to them, across a silent sea. She walked on over the rugged cliff, like some siren, some genius of the place, with a sure, proud grace of step; she never looked around, and his eyes were fixed upon the black line of her figure, as it went before him, toward the gray and blood-red sunset. It seemed to him this was the last hour of his life; and even as he thought his ankle turned, and he stumbled and fell, walking unwittingly into one of the chasms, where the line of the cliff turned in. He grasped a knuckle of rock, and held his fall, just on the brink of a ledge above the sea. Miss Warfield had turned quickly and seen it all; and she leaned down over the brink, with one hand around the rock and the other extended to help him, the ledge on which he lay being some six feet below. Pinckney grasped her hand and kissed it.

Her color did not change at this; but, with a strange strength in her beautiful lithe figure, she drew him up steadily, he helping partly with the other hand, until his knees rested on the path again. He stood up with some difficulty, as his ankle was badly wrenched.

"I am afraid you cannot walk," said she.

"Oh, yes," he answered; and took a few steps to show her. The pain was great; but she walked on, and he followed, as best he could, limping. She looked behind now, as if to encourage him; and he set his teeth and smiled.

"We must not be late," she said. "It is growing dark, and they will miss us."

But they did not miss them; for when they got to the landing place, both the sailboats had left the shore without them. There was nothing but the purple cloud-light left by this time; but Pinckney fancied he could see her face grow pale for the first time that day.

"We must get home," she said, hurriedly. "Is there no boat?"

Pinckney pointed to a small dory on the beach, and then to the sea. In the east was a black bank of cloud, rifted now and then by lightning; and from it the wind came down and the white caps curled angrily toward them.

"No matter," said she; "we must go."

Pinckney found a pair of oars under the boat, and dragged it, with much labor, over the pebbles, she helping him. The beach was steep and gravelly, with short breakers rather than surf; and he got the bow well into the water and held it there.

"Get in," said he.

Miss Warfield got into the stern, and Pinckney waded out, dragging the flat-bottomed boat until it was well afloat. Then he sprang in himself, and, grasping the oars, headed the boat for the Fort point across the channel, three miles away. She sat silently in the stern, and it was too dark for him to see her face. He rowed savagely.

But the wind was straight ahead, and the sea increasing every moment. They were not, of course, exposed to the full swell of the ocean; but the wide sea-channel was full of short, fierce waves that struck the little skiff repeated rapid blows, and dashed the spray over both of them.

"Are you not afraid?" said he, calmly. "It is growing rougher every minute."

"Oh, no, Mr. Pinckney," said she. "Pray keep on."

Pinckney noticed a tremor of excitement in her voice; but by a flash of lightning that came just then he saw her deep eyes fixed on his, and the pure white outline of her face undisturbed. So he rowed the harder, and she took a board there was and tried to steer; and now and then, as the clouds were lit, he saw her, like a fleeting vision in the night.

But the storm grew stronger; and Pinckney knew the boat that they were in was not really moving at all, though, of course, the swash of the waves went by and the drifted spray. He tried to row harder, but with the pain in his ankle and the labor he was nearly exhausted, and his heart jumped in his chest at each recover. "Can you not make it?" said she, in the dark; and Pinckney vowed that he could, and set his teeth for a mighty pull. The oar broke, and the boat's head fell rapidly off in the trough of the sea. He quickly changed about his remaining oar, and with it kept the head to the wind.

"We must go back," he said, panting.

"I know," said she. The windstorm was fairly upon them; and, in spite of all his efforts, an occasional wave would get upon the beam and spill its frothing crest into the boat. Pinckney almost doubted whether it would float until it reached the shore; but Miss Warfield did not seem in the least disturbed, and spoke without a tremor in her voice. The lightning had stopped now, and he could not see her.

He had miscalculated the force of the wind and waves, however; for in a very few minutes they were driven broadside back upon the beach, almost at the same place from which they had started. Miss Warfield sprang out quickly, and he after, just as a wave turned the dory bottom upward on the stones

"They will soon send for us," he said; and stepping painfully up the shore, he occupied himself with spreading her shawl in a sheltered spot for them to wait in. She sat down, and he beside her. He was very wet, and she made him put some of the shawl over himself. The quick summer storm had passed now, with only a few big drops of rain; and the moon was breaking out fitfully through veils of driving clouds and their storm-scud. By its light he looked at her, and their eyes met. Pinckney groaned aloud, and stood up. "Would that they would never come; would God that we could—"

"We cannot," said she, softly, in a voice that he had never heard from her before—a voice with tears in it; and the man threw himself down at her feet, inarticulate, maddened. Then, with a great effort at control, not touching her, but looking straight into her eyes, he said, in blunt, low speech: "Miss Warfield, I love you—do you know it?"

Her head sank slowly down; but she answered, very low, but clearly, *yes.* Then their eyes met again; and, by some common impulse, they rose and walked apart. After a few steps, he stopped, being lame, and leaned against the cliff; but she went on until her dark figure was blended with the shadows of the crags.

So, when the boat came back, its sail silvered by the moonlight, they saw it, and, coming down, they met again; but only as the party were landing on the beach. Several of the party had come back; and Mr. Breeze, who was among them, was full of explanation how he had missed the first boat and barely caught the second, supposing that his fiancée was in the first. An awkward accident, but easily explained by Pinckney, with the sprain in his ankle; and, indeed, the others were too full of excuses for having forgotten them to inquire into the causes of their absence together.

Pinckney went to his room, and had a night of delirium. Toward morning, his troubled wakefulness ended, and he fell into a dream. He dreamed that in the centre of the world was one green bower, beneath a blossoming tree, and he and Miss Warfield were there. And the outer world was being destroyed, one sphere by fire and the other by flood, and there was only this bower left. But they could not stay there, or the tree would die. So they went away, he to the one side and she to the other, and the ruins of the world fell upon them, and they saw each other no more.

In the morning his delirium left him, and his will resumed its sway. He went down, and out into the green roads, and listened to the singing of the birds; and then out to the cliff-path, and there he found Miss Warfield sitting as if she knew that he would come. He watched her pure face while she spoke, and her gray eyes: the clear light of the morning was in them, and on the gleaming sea beyond.

"You must go," said she.

"Yes," he said, and that was all. He took her hand for one moment, and lifted it lightly to his lips; then he turned and took the path across the fields. When he got to the first stile, he looked around. She was still sitting there, turned toward him. He lifted his hat, and held it for a second or two; then he turned the corner of the hedge and went down to the town.

Thus it happened that this story, which began sadly, with an epitaph, may end with wedding bells:

MARRIED. *At King's Chapel, by the Rev. Dr. A—, the 21st of September, Charles Austin Pinckney to Emily, daughter of the late James Austin.*

THE LADY AND THE FLAGON

ANTHONY HOPE

THE DUKE OF BELLEVILLE—which name, by the way, you must pronounce by no means according to its spelling, if you would be in the fashion; as for Belvoir is Beevor, and Beauchamp is Beecham, even so on polite lips Belleville is Bevvle—the Duke of Belleville shut the hall door behind him, and put his latchkey into the pocket of his trousers. It was but ten in the evening, yet the house was as still as though it had been two in the morning. All was dark, save for a dim jet of gas in the little sitting room; the blinds were all down; from without the villa seemed uninhabited, and the rare passerby—for rare was he in the quiet lane adjoining but not facing Hampstead Heath—set it down as being to let. It was a whim of the Duke's to keep it empty; when the world bored him, he fled there for solitude; not even the presence of a servant was allowed, lest his meditations should be disturbed. It was long since he had come; but tonight weariness had afflicted him, and, by a sudden change of plan, he had made for his hiding place in lieu of attending a Public Meeting, at which he had been advertised to take the chair. The desertion sat lightly on his conscience, and he heaved a sigh of relief, as, having turned up the gas, he flung himself into an armchair and lit a cigar. The Duke of Belleville was thirty years of age; he was unmarried;

he had held the title since he was fifteen; he seemed to himself rather old. He was at this moment yawning. Now when a man yawns at ten o'clock in the evening something is wrong with his digestion or his spirits. The Duke had a perfect digestion.

"I should define wealth," murmured the Duke, between his yawns, "as an unlimited command of the sources of ennui, rank as a satirical emphasizing of human equality, culture as a curtailment of pleasures, knowledge as the death of interest." Yawning again, he rose, drew up the blind, and flung open the window. The summer night was fine and warm. Although there were a couple of dozen other houses scattered here and there about the lane, not a soul was to be seen. The Duke stood for a long while looking out. His cigar burned low and he flung it away. Presently he heard a church clock strike eleven. At the same moment he perceived a tall and burly figure approaching from the end of the lane. Its approach was slow and interrupted, for it paused at every house. A moment's further inspection revealed in it a policeman on his beat.

"He's trying the windows and doors," remarked the Duke to himself. Then his eyes brightened. "There are possibilities in a door always," he murmured, and his thoughts flew off to the great doors of history and fiction—the doors that were locked when by all laws human and divine they should have been open, and the even more interesting doors that proved to be open and yielded to pressure when any man would have staked his life on their being bolted, barred, and impregnable. "A door has the interest of death," said he. "For how can you know what is on the other side till you have passed through it? Now suppose that fellow found a door open, and passed through it, and turning the rays of his lantern on the darkness within, saw revealed to him—"Heavens!" cried the Duke, interrupting himself in great excitement, "is all this to be wasted on a policeman?" And without a moment's hesitation, he leaned out of the window and shouted, "Constable, constable!"—which is, as all the world knows, the politest mode of addressing a policeman.

The policeman, perceiving the Duke and the urgency of the Duke's summons, left his examination of the doors in the lane and ran hastily up to the window of the villa.

"Did you call, sir?" he asked.

"Don't you know me?" inquired the Duke, turning a little, so that the light within the room should fall on his features.

"I beg your Grace's pardon," cried the policeman. "Your Grace gave me a sovereign last Christmas. The Duke of Belle-ville, isn't it, your Grace?"

"You will know," said the Duke patiently, "how to pronounce my name when I tell you that it rhymes with 'Devil.' Thus: 'Devvle, Bevvle.'"

"Yes, your Grace. You called me?"

"I did. Do you often find doors open when they ought to be shut?"

"Almost every night, your Grace."

"What do you do?"

"Knock, your Grace."

"Good heavens," murmured the Duke, "how this man throws away his opportunities!" Then he leaned forward, and laying his hand on the policeman's shoulder drew him nearer, and began to speak to him in a low tone.

"I couldn't, your Grace," urged the policeman. "If I was found out I should get the sack."

"You should come to no harm by that."

"And if your Grace was found out—"

"You can leave that to me," interrupted the Duke.

Presently the policeman, acting on the Duke's invitation, climbed into the window of the villa, and the conversation was continued across the table. The Duke urged, produced money, gave his word to be responsible for the policeman's future; the policeman's resistance grew less strong.

"I am about your height and build," said the Duke. "It is but for a few hours, and you can spend them very comfortably in the kitchen. Before six o'clock I will be back."

"If the Inspector comes round, your Grace?"

"You must take a little risk for twenty pounds," the Duke reminded him.

The struggle could end but one way. A quarter of an hour later the policeman, attired in the Duke's overcoat, sat by the kitchen hearth, while the Duke, equipped in the policeman's garments, prepared to leave the house and take his place on the beat.

"I shall put out all lights and shut the door," said he. "The window of this kitchen looks out to the back, and you will not be seen. You will particularly oblige me by remaining here and taking no notice of anything that may occur till I return and call you."

"But, your Grace, if there's murder done—"

"We can hardly expect that," interrupted the Duke, a little wistfully. Yet, although, remembering how the humdrum permeates life, he would not pitch his anticipations too high, the Duke started on the expedition with great zest and lively hopes. The position he had assumed, the mere office that he discharged vicariously, seemed to his fancy a conductor that must catch and absorb the lightning of adventurous incident. His big-buttoned coat, his helmet, the lantern he carried, his deftly hidden truncheon, combined to make him the center of anything that might move, and to involve him in coils of crime or of romance. He refused to be disappointed although he tried a dozen doors and found all securely fastened. For never till the last, till fortune was desperate and escape a vanished dream, was wont to come that marvelous Door that gaped open-mouthed. Ah! The Duke started violently, the blood rushing to his face and his heart beating quick. Here, at the end of the lane most remote from his own villa, at a small two-storied house bright with green paint and flowering creepers, here, in the most unlikely, most inevitable place, was the open door. Barred? It was not even shut, but hung loose, swaying gently to and fro, with a subdued bang at each encounter with the doorpost. Without a moment's hesitation the Duke pushed it open. He stood in a dark passage. He turned the glare of his bull's-eye on the gloom, which melted as the column of light pierced it, and he saw—

"There is nothing at all," said the Duke of Belleville with a sigh.

Nor, indeed, was there, save an umbrella rack, a hat stand, and an engraving of the Queen's Coronation—things which had no importance for the Duke.

"They are only what one might expect," said he.

Yet he persevered and began to mount the stairs with a silent, cautious tread. He had not felt it necessary to put on the policeman's boots, and his thin-soled, well-made boots neither creaked nor crunched as he climbed, resting one hand on the balustrade and holding his lantern in the other. Yet suddenly something touched his hand, and a bell rang out, loud, clear and tinkling. A moment later came a scream; the Duke paused in some bewilderment. Then he mounted a few more steps till he was on the landing. A door to his right was cautiously opened; an old gentleman's head appeared.

"Thank heaven, it's the police!" cried the old gentleman. Then he pulled his head in and said, "Only the police, my dear." Then he put his hand out again and asked, "What in the world is the matter? I thought you were burglars when I heard the alarm."

"Your hall door was standing open," said the Duke accusingly.

"Tut, tut, tut! How very careless of me, to be sure! And I thought I locked it! Actually open! Dear me! I'm much obliged to you."

A look of disappointment had by now spread over the Duke's face.

"Didn't you leave it open on purpose?" he asked. "Come now! You can trust me."

"On purpose? Do you take me for a fool?" cried the old gentleman.

"A man who leaves his door open on purpose may or may not be a fool," said the Duke. "But there is no doubt about a man who leaves it open without a purpose," and, so saying, the Duke turned, walked downstairs, and, going out, slammed the door behind him. He was deeply disgusted.

When, however, he had recovered a little from his chagrin, he began to pace up and down the lane. It was now past midnight, and all was very quiet. The Duke began to fear that Fortune, never weary of tormenting him, meant to deny all its interest to his experiment. But suddenly, when he was exactly opposite his own house, he observed a young man standing in front of it. The stranger was tall and well made; he wore a black cloth Inverness, which, hanging open at the throat, showed a white tie and a snowy shirt front. The young man, however, perceiving him, turned to him and said:

"It's very annoying, but I have lost my latchkey, and I don't know how to get into my house."

"Indeed, sir?" said the Duke sympathetically. "Which is your house?"

"This," answered the young man, pointing to the Duke's villa.

The Duke could not entirely repress a slight movement of surprise and pleasure.

"This your house? Then you are—?" he began.

"Yes, yes, the Duke of Belleville," interrupted the young man. "But there's nobody in the house. I'm not expected—"

"I suppose not," murmured the Duke.

"There are no servants, and I don't know how to get in. It's very awkward, because I'm expecting a—a friend to call."

"With my assistance," said the Duke deferentially, "your Grace might effect an entry by the window."

"True!" cried the young man. "Bring your lantern and give me a light. Look here, I don't want this talked about."

"It is a matter quite between ourselves, your Grace," the Duke assured him, as he led the way to the window.

"By-the-by, you might help me in another matter if you like. I'll make it worth your while."

"I shall be very glad," said the Duke.

"Could you be spared from your beat for an hour?"

"It might be possible."

"Good. Come in with me, and we'll talk it over."

The Duke had by this time opened the window of his villa; he gave the young man a leg-up, and afterwards climbed in himself.

"Shut the window again," commanded the stranger. "Oh, and you might as well just close the shutters."

"Certainly, your Grace," said the Duke, and he did as he was bid.

The young man began to move round the room, examining the articles that furnished the side tables and decorated the walls. The Duke of Belleville had been for a year or two an eager collector of antique plate, and had acquired some fine specimens in both gold and silver. Some of these were now in the villa, and the young man scrutinized them with close attention.

"Dear me," said he in a vexed tone, as he returned to the hearth. "I thought the Queen Bess flagon was here. Surely I sent it here from the Belleville Castle!"

The Duke smiled; the Queen Bess flagon had never been at Belleville Castle, and it was now in a small locked cabinet which stood on the mantelpiece. He made no remark; a suspicion had begun to take shape in his mind concerning this strange visitor. Two thousand seven hundred and forty guineas was the price that he had paid for the Queen Bess flagon; all the other specimens in the little room, taken together, might be worth perhaps a quarter as much.

"Your Grace spoke of some other matter in which I might assist you?" he suggested, for the young man seemed to have fallen into a reverie.

"Why, yes. As I tell you. I expect a friend; and it looks very absurd to have no servant. You're sure to find a suit of dress clothes in my bedroom. Pray put them on and represent my valet. You can resume your uniform afterwards."

The Duke bowed and left the room. The moment the door closed behind him he made the best of his way to the kitchen. A few words were enough to impart his suspicions to the policeman. A daring and ingenious scheme was evidently on foot, its object being the theft of the Queen Bess flagon. Even now, unless they acted quickly, the young man might lay hands on the cabinet in which the treasure lay and be off with it. In a trice the Duke had discarded the police uniform, its rightful owner had resumed it, and the Duke was again in the convenient black suit which befits any man, be he duke or valet. Then the kitchen window was cautiously opened, and the policeman crawled silently round to the front of the house; here he lay in waiting for a summons or for the appearance of a visitor. The Duke returned immediately to the sitting room.

On entering, he perceived the young man standing in front of the locked cabinet, and regarding it with a melancholy air. The Duke's appearance roused him, and he glanced with visible surprise at the distinguished and aristocratic figure which the supposed policeman presented. But he made no comment and his first words were about the flagon.

"Now I come to remember," said he, "I put the Queen Bess flagon in this cabinet. It must be so, although, as I have left my key at my rooms in St. James' Street, I can't satisfy myself on the point."

The Duke, now perfectly convinced of the character of his visitor, waited only to see him lay his hands on the cabinet. Such an action would be the signal for his instant arrest. But before the young man had time either to speak again or to put out his hand toward the cabinet, there came the sound of wheels quickly approaching the villa. A moment later a neat brougham rolled up to the door. The young man darted to the window, tore open the shutters, and looked out. The Duke, suspecting the arrival of confederates, turned toward the cabinet and took his stand in front of it.

"Go and open the door," ordered the young man, turning round. "Don't keep the lady waiting outside at this time of night."

Curiosity conquered prudence; the Duke set more value on a night's amusement than on the Queen Bess flagon. He went obediently and opened the door of the villa. On the step stood a young and very handsome girl. Great agitation was evident in her manner.

"Is—is the Duke here?" she asked.

"Yes, madame. If I lead you to the sitting room, you will find him there," answered the Duke gravely; and with a bow he preceded her along the passage.

When they reached the room, the lady, passing by him, darted forward and flung herself affectionately into the young man's arms. He greeted her with equal warmth, while the Duke stood in the doorway in some natural embarrassment.

"I escaped so successfully!" cried the lady. "My aunt went to bed at eleven; so did I. At twelve I got up and dressed. Not a soul heard me come downstairs, and the brougham was waiting at the door just as you said."

"My darling!" murmured the young man fondly. "Now, indeed, is our happiness certain. By tomorrow morning we shall be safe from all pursuit." Then he turned to the Duke. "I need not tell you," said he, "that you must observe silence on this matter. Oblige me now by going to my room and packing a bag; you'll know what I shall want for two or three days; I can give you a quarter of an hour."

The Duke stood in momentary hesitation. He was bewildered at the sudden change in the position caused by the appearance of this girl. Was he assisting, then, not at a refined and ingenious burglary, but at another kind of trick? The disguise assumed by the young man might have for its object the deception of a trustful girl, and not an abduction of the Queen Bess flagon.

"Well, why don't you obey?" asked the young man sharply; and, stepping up to the Duke, he thrust a ten-pound note into his hand, whispering, "Play your part, and earn your money, you fool."

The Duke lingered no longer. Leaving the room, he walked straight, rapidly, and with a firm tread, upstairs. When he reached the top he paused to listen. All was still! Stay! A moment later he heard a slight noise—the noise of some metal instrument turning, proceeding from the room which he had just left. The Duke sat down on the landing and took off his boots. Then with silent feet he crept cautiously downstairs again. He paused to listen for an instant outside the sitting room door. Voices were audible, but he could not hear the words. The occupants of the room were moving about. He heard a low amused laugh. Then he pursued his way to the hall door. He had not completely closed it after admitting the lady, and he now slipped out without a sound. The brougham stood in front of the door. The Duke dodged behind it, and the driver, who was leaning forward on his seat, did not see him. The next moment he was crouching down by the side of his friend the policeman, waiting for the next development in the plot of this comedy, or crime, or whatever it might turn out to be. He put out his hand and touched his ally. To his amusement the man, sitting there on the ground, had fallen fast asleep.

"Another proof," mused the Duke in whimsical despair, "that it is impossible to make any mode of life permanently interesting. How this fellow would despise the state of excitement which I, for the moment, am so fortunate as to enjoy! Well, I won't wake him unless need arises."

For some little while nothing happened. The policeman slept on, and the driver of the brougham seemed sunk in meditation, unless, indeed, he also were drowsy. The shutters of the sitting room were again closely shut, and no sound came from behind them. The Duke crouched motionless but keenly observant.

Then the hall door creaked. The policeman snored quietly, but the Duke leaned eagerly forward, and the driver of the brougham suddenly sat up quite straight, and grasped his reins more firmly. The door was cautiously opened: the lady and the young man appeared on the threshold. The young man glanced up and down the lane; then he walked quickly toward the brougham and opened the door. The lady followed him. As she went she passed within four or five feet of where the Duke lay hidden. And, as she went by, the Duke saw—what he half-expected, yet what he could but half-believe—the gleam of the gold of the Queen Bess flagon, which she held in her gloved hands.

As has been hinted, the Duke attached no superstitious value to this article. The mad fever of the collector had left him long ago; but amidst the death of other emotions and more recondite prejudices there survives in the heart of man the primitive dislike of being "done." It survived in the mind of the Duke of Belleville, and sprang to strong and sudden activity when he observed his Queen Bess flagon in the hands of the pretty unknown lady.

With a sudden and vigorous spring he was upon her; with a roughness which the Duke trusted that the occasion to some extent excused, he seized her arm with one hand, and with the other violently twisted the Queen Bess flagon out of her grasp. A loud cry rang from her lips. The driver threw down the reins and leaped from his seat. The young man turned with an oath and made for the Duke. The Duke of Belleville, ignoring the mere prejudice which forbids timely retreat, took to his heels, hugging the Queen Bess flagon to his breast, and heading, in his silk socks, as hard and as straight as he could for Hampstead Heath. After him pell-mell came the young man, the driver, and the lady, amazed, doubtless, at the turn of events, but resolved on the recapture of the flagon. And just as their figures vanished round the corner, the policeman rubbed his eyes and looked round, exclaiming, "What's the row?"

In after days the Duke of Belleville was accustomed to count his feelings as he fled barefooted (for what protection could silk socks afford?) across Hampstead Heath, with three incensed pursuers on his track, among the keenest sensations of life. The exhilaration of the night air and the chances of the situation in which he found himself combined to produce in him a remarkable elation of spirits. He laughed as he ran, till shortening breath warned him against such extravagant wasting of his resources; then he settled down to a steady run, heading across the Heath, up and down, over dip and hillock. Yet he did not distance the pack. He heard them close behind him; a glance round showed him that the lady was well up with her friends, in spite of the impediment of her skirts. The Duke began to pant; his feet had grown sore and painful; he looked round for a refuge. To his delight he perceived, about a hundred yards to his right, a small and picturesque red-brick house. It was now between one and two o'clock, but he did not hesitate. Resolving to appeal to the hospitality of this house, hoping, it may be, again to find a door left open, he turned sharp to the right, and with a last spurt made for his haven.

Fate seemed indeed kind to him; the door was not only unbarred, it stood ajar. The Duke's pursuers were even now upon him; they were no more than five or six yards behind when he reached the little red-tiled porch and put out his hand to push the door back.

But at the same instant the door was pulled open, and a burly man appeared on the threshold. He wore a frock-coat embellished with black braid and a peaked cap. The Duke at once recognized in him an inspector of police. Evidently he was, when surprised by the Duke's arrival, about to sally out on his round. The Duke stopped and, between his pants, made shift to address the welcome ally; but before he could get a word out the young man was upon him.

"Inspector," said the young man in the most composed manner, "I give this fellow in charge for stealing my property."

"I saw him take the tankard," observed the driver, pointing toward the Queen Bess flagon.

The lady said nothing but stood by the young man, as though ready with her testimony in case it were needed.

The Inspector turned curious eyes on the Duke of Belleville; then he addressed the young man respectfully.

"May I ask, sir, who you are?"

"I am the Duke of Belleville," answered the young man.

"The Duke of Belle-ville!" cried the Inspector, his manner showing an increased deference. "I beg you Grace's—"

"The name," said the Duke, "is pronounced Bevvle—to rhyme with devil."

The Inspector looked at him scornfully.

"Your turn will come, my man," said he, and, turning again to the young man, he continued: "Do you charge him with stealing this cup?"

"Certainly I do."

"Do you know who he is?"

"I imagine you do," said the young man, with a laugh. "He's one of your own policemen."

The Inspector stepped back and turned up the gas in his passage. Then he scrutinized the Duke's features.

"One of my men?" he cried. "Your Grace is mistaken. I have never seen the man."

"Yes, yes," cried the young man, and, in his eagerness to convince the Inspector, he stepped forward, until his face fell within the range of the passage light. As this happened, the Inspector gave a loud cry:

"Hallo, Joe Simpson!" And he sprang at the young man. The latter did not wait for him: without a word he turned; the Inspector rushed forward, the young man made for the Heath, and the driver, after standing for a moment apparently bewildered, faced about, and made off in the opposite direction to that chosen by his companion. The three were thirty yards away before the Duke of Belleville could realize what had happened. Then he perceived that he stood in the passage of the Inspector's house, alone save for the presence of the young lady, who faced him with an astonished expression on her pretty countenance.

"It is altogether a very remarkable night," observed the Duke.

"It is impossible that you should be more puzzled than I am," said the young lady.

"Excuse me," said the Duke, "but you run very well."

"I belonged to my college football club," said the young lady modestly.

"Precisely!" cried the Duke. "I suppose this door leads to our good friend's parlor. Shall we sit down while you tell me all about it? I must ask you to excuse the condition of my feet."

Thus speaking, the Duke led the way into the Inspector's parlor. Placing the Queen Bess flagon on the table, he invited the lady to be seated, and took a chair himself. Perceiving that she was somewhat agitated, he provided her with an interval in which to regain her composure by narrating to her the adventures of the evening. She heard him with genuine astonishment.

"Do you say that you are the Duke of Belleville?" she cried.

"Don't I look like it?" asked the Duke, smiling, but at the same time concealing his feet under the Inspector's dining table.

"But he—he said he was the Duke."

"He said so to me also," observed the Duke of Belleville.

The lady looked at him long and keenly; there was, however, a simple honesty about the Duke's manner that attracted her sympathy and engaged her confidence.

"Perhaps I'd better tell you all about it," said she, with a sigh.

"Not unless you desire to do so, I beg," said the Duke, with a wave of his hand.

"I am nineteen," began the lady. The Duke heaved an envious sigh. "I live with my aunt," she continued. "We live a very retired life. Since I left college—which I did prematurely owing to a difference of opinion with the Principal—I have seen hardly anyone. In the course of a visit to the seaside I met the gentleman who—who—"

"From whom we have just parted?" suggested the Duke.

"Thank you, yes. Not to weary you with details—"

"Principles weary me, but not details," interposed the Duke.

"In fact," continued the young lady, "he professed to be in love with me. Now my aunt, although not insensible to the great position which he offered me (for of course he represented himself as the Duke of Belleville) entertains the opinion that no girl should marry till she is twenty-one. Moreover, she considered that the acquaintance was rather short."

"May I ask when you first met the gentleman?"

"Last Monday week. So she forbade the marriage. I am myself of an impatient disposition."

"So am I," observed the Duke of Belleville, and in the interest of the discussion he became so forgetful as to withdraw his feet from the shelter of the table and cross one leg comfortably over the other. "So am I," he repeated, nodding his head.

"I therefore determined to live my own life in my own way—"

"I think you said you had been to college?"

"Yes, but I had a difference of—"

"Quite so. Pray proceed," said the Duke courteously.

"And to run away with my fiancé. In pursuance of this plan, I arranged to meet him tonight at his villa at Hampstead. He sent a brougham to fetch me, I made my escape successfully, and the rest you know."

"Pardon me, but up to this point the part played by the flagon which you see on the table before you is somewhat obscure."

"Oh, when you'd gone to pack his things, he took out a curious little instrument—he said he had forgotten his key—and opened the cabinet on the mantelpiece. Then he took out that pretty mug and gave it to me as my wedding present. He told me that it was very valuable, and he would carry it for me himself, but I declared that I must carry it for myself or I wouldn't go. So he let me. And then you—"

"The whole thing is perfectly plain," declared the Duke with emphasis. "You, madame, have been the victim of a most dastardly and cold-blooded plot. This fellow is a swindler. I daresay he wanted to get hold of you, and thus extort money from your aunt, but his main object was no other than to carry off the famous cup which you see before you—the Queen Bess flagon." And the Duke, rising to his feet, began to walk up and down in great indignation. "He meant to kill two birds with one stone!" said he, in mingled anger and admiration.

"It is pretty!" said the young lady, taking up the flagon. "Oh, what is this figure?"

The Duke, perceiving that the lady desired an explanation, came and leaned over her chair. She turned her face up to his in innocent eagerness; the Duke could not avoid observing that she had very fine eyes.

Without making any comment on the subject, however, he leaned a little lower and began to explain the significance of the figure on the Queen Bess flagon.

The Duke has been known to say that, in a world so much the sport of chance as ours, there was no reason why he should not have fallen in love with the young lady and offered to make her in very truth what she had dreamed of becoming—the Duchess of Belleville.

Her eyes were very fine, her manner frank and engaging. Moreover the Duke hated to see people disappointed. Thus the thing might just as well have happened as not. And on so narrow a point did the issue stand that to this day certain persons declare that it—or part of it—did happen; for why, and on what account, they ask, should an experienced connoisseur (and such undoubtedly was the Duke of Belleville) present a young lady previously unknown to him (or, for the matter of that, any young lady at all, whether known or not known to him) with such a rare, costly, and precious thing as the Queen Bess flagon? For the fact is—let the meaning and significance of the fact be what they will—that when the young lady, gazing fondly the while on the flagon, exclaimed, "I never really cared about him much, but I should have liked the beautiful flagon!" the Duke answered (he was still leaning over her chair, in order the better to explain and trace the figure on the flagon):

"Of him you are well rid. But permit me to request your acceptance of the flagon. The real Duke of Belleville, madame, must not be outdone by his counterfeit."

"Really?" cried the young lady.

"Of course," murmured the Duke, delighted with the pleasure which he saw in her eyes.

The young lady turned a most grateful and almost affectionate glance on the Duke. Although ignorant of the true value of the Queen Bess flagon, she was aware that the Duke had made her a very handsome present.

"Thank you," said she, putting her hands into the Duke's.

At this moment a loud and somewhat strident voice proceeded from the door of the room.

"Well, I never! And how did you come here?"

The Duke, looking round, perceived a stout woman, clad in a black petticoat and a woolen shawl; her arms were akimbo.

"We came in, madame," said he, rising and bowing, "by the hall door, which we chanced to find open."

The stout woman appeared to be at a loss for words. At length, however, she gasped out:

"Be off with you. Don't let the Inspector catch you here!"

The Duke looked doubtfully at the young lady.

"The woman probably misunderstands," he murmured. The young lady blushed slightly. The Inspector's wife advanced with a threatening demeanor.

"Who are you?" she asked abruptly.

"I, madame," began the Duke, "am the—"

"I don't see that it matters who we are," interposed the young lady.

"Possibly not," admitted the Duke, with a smile.

The young lady rose, went to a little mirror that hung on the wall, and adjusted the curls which appeared from under the brim of her hat.

"Dear me," said she, turning round with a sigh, "it must be nearly three o'clock, and my aunt always likes me to be in before daybreak."

The stout woman gasped again.

"Because of the neighbors, you know," said the young lady with a smile.

"Just so," assented the Duke, and possibly he would have added more, had not the woman uttered an inarticulate cry and pointed to his feet.

"Really, madame," remarked the Duke, with some warmth, "it would have been in better taste not to refer to the matter." And with a severe frown he offered his arm to the young lady. They then proceeded toward the doorway. The Inspector's wife barred the passage. The Duke assumed a most dignified air. The woman reluctantly gave way. Walking through the passage, the young lady and the Duke found themselves again in the open air. There were signs of approaching dawn.

"I really think I had better get home," whispered the young lady.

At this moment—and the Duke was not in the least surprised—they perceived four persons approaching them. The Inspector walked with his arm through the arm of the young man who had claimed to be the Duke of Belleville; following, arm-in-arm with the driver of the brougham, came the policeman whose uniform the Duke had borrowed. All the party except for the Inspector looked uneasy. The Inspector appeared somewhat puzzled. However he greeted the Duke with a cry of welcome.

"Now we can find out the truth of it all!" he exclaimed.

"To find out the truth," remarked the Duke, "is never easy and not always desirable."

"I understand that you are the Duke of Belleville?" asked the Inspector.

"Certainly," said the Duke.

"Bosh!" said the young man. "Oh, you know me, Inspector Collins, and I know you, and I'm not going to try and play it on you any more. But this chap's no more the Duke than I am, and I should have thought you might have known one of your own policemen!"

The Inspector turned upon him fiercely.

"None of your gab, Joe Simpson," said he. Then turning to the Duke, he continued, "Do you charge the young woman with him, your Grace?" And he pointed significantly to the Queen Bess flagon, which the young lady carried in an affectionate grasp.

"This lady," said the Duke, "has done me the honor of accepting a small token of my esteem. As for these men, I know nothing about them." And he directed a significant glance at the young man. The young man answered his look. The policeman seemed to grow more easy in his mind. "Then you don't charge any of them?" cried the Inspector, bewildered.

"Why, no," answered the Duke. "And I suppose they none of them charge me?"

Nobody spoke. The Inspector took out a large red handkerchief and mopped his brow.

"Well, it beats me," he said. "I know pretty well what these two men are; but if you don't charge 'em what can I do?"

"Nothing, I should suppose," said the Duke blandly. And, with a slight bow, he proceeded on his way, the young lady accompanying him. Looking back once, he perceived the young man and the driver of the brougham going off in another direction with quick furtive steps, while the Inspector and the policeman stood talking together outside the door of the house.

"The circumstances, as a whole, no doubt appear peculiar to the Inspector," observed the Duke, with a smile.

"Do you think that we can find a hansom cab?" asked the young lady a little anxiously. "You see, my aunt—"

"Precisely," said the Duke, and he quickened his pace.

They soon reached the boundary of the Heath, and, having walked a little way along the road, were so fortunate as to find a cab. The young lady held out her left hand to the Duke: in her right she still grasped firmly the Queen Bess flagon.

"Good-by," she said. "Thank you for the beautiful present."

The Duke took her hand and allowed his glance to rest for a moment on her face. She appeared to see a question in his eyes.

"Yes, and for rescuing me from that man," she added with a little shudder.

The Duke's glance still rested on her face.

"Yes, and for lots of fun," she whispered with a blush.

The Duke looked away, sighed, released her hand, helped her into the cab, and retired to a distance of some yards. The young lady spoke a few words to the cabman, took her seat, waved a small hand, held up the Queen Bess flagon, kissed it, and drove away.

"If," observed the Duke with a sigh, "I were not a well-bred man, I should have asked her name," and he made his way back to his house in a somewhat pensive mood.

On reaching home, however, he perceived the brougham standing before his door. A new direction was thus given to his meditations. He opened the gate of his stable-yard, and, taking the horse's head, led it in. Having unharnessed it, he put it in the stable and fed and watered it; the brougham he drew into the coach-house. Then he went indoors, partook of some brandy mixed with water, and went to bed.

At eleven o'clock the next morning Frank, the Duke's man, came up to Hampstead to attend to his Grace's wants. The Duke was still in bed, but, on breakfast being ready, he rose and came downstairs in his dressing-gown and a pair of large and very easy slippers.

"I hope your Grace slept well?" said Frank.

"I never passed a better night, thank you, Frank," said the Duke as he chipped the top off his egg.

"Half-an-hour ago, your Grace," Frank continued, "a man called."

"To see me?"

"It was about—about a brougham, your Grace."

"Ah! What did you say to him?"

"I said I had no orders about a brougham from your Grace."

"Quite right, Frank, quite right," said the Duke with a smile. "What did he say to that?"

"He appeared to be put out, but said that he would call again, your Grace."

"Very good," said the Duke, rising and lighting a cigarette.

Frank lingered uneasily near the door.

"Is anything the matter, Frank?" asked the Duke kindly.

"Well, your Grace, in—in point of fact, there is—there is a strange brougham and a strange horse in the stables, your Grace."

"In what respect," asked the Duke, "are the brougham and the horse strange, Frank?"

"I—I should say, your Grace, a brougham and a horse that I have not seen before in your Grace's stables."

"That is a very different thing, Frank," observed the Duke with a patient smile. "I suppose that I am at liberty to acquire a brougham and a horse if it occurs to me to do so?"

"Of course, your Grace," stammered Frank.

"I will drive into town in that brougham today, Frank," said the Duke.

Frank bowed and withdrew. The Duke strolled to the window and stood looking out as he smoked his cigarette.

"I don't think the man will call again," said he. Then he drew from his pocket the ten-pound note that the young man had given him, and regarded it thoughtfully. "A brougham, a horse, ten pounds, and a very diverting experience," he mused. "Yes, I am better in spirits this morning!"

As for the Queen Bess flagon, he appeared to have forgotten all about it.

EXPIATION

EDITH WHARTON

"I CAN NEVER," said Mrs. Fetherel, "hear the bell ring without a shudder."

Her unruffled aspect—she was the kind of woman whose emotions never communicate themselves to her clothes—and the conventional background of the New York drawing room, with its pervading implication of an imminent tea tray and of an atmosphere in which the social functions have become purely reflex, lent to her declaration a relief not lost on her cousin Mrs. Clinch, who, from the other side of the fireplace, agreed, with a glance at the clock, that it *was* the hour for bores.

"Bores!" cried Mrs. Fetherel impatiently, "If I shuddered at *them,* I should have a chronic ague!"

She leaned forward and laid a sparkling finger on her cousin's shabby black knee. "I mean the newspaper clippings," she whispered.

Mrs. Clinch returned a glance of intelligence. "They've begun already?"

"Not yet; but they're sure to now, at any minute, my publisher tells me."

Mrs. Fetherel's look of apprehension sat oddly on her small features, which had an air of neat symmetry somehow suggestive of being set in order every morning by the housemaid. Someone (there were rumors that it was her cousin) had once said that Paula Fetherel would have been pretty if she hadn't looked so like a moral axiom in a copybook hand.

Mrs. Clinch received her confidence with a smile. "Well," she said, "I suppose you were prepared for the consequences of authorship?" Mrs. Fetherel blushed brightly. "It isn't their coming," she owned—"it's their coming *now.*"

"Now?"

"The Bishop's in town."

Mrs. Clinch leaned back and shaped her lips to a whistle which deflected in a laugh. "Well!" she said.

"You see!" Mrs. Fetherel triumphed.

"Well—weren't you prepared for the Bishop?"

"Not now—at least, I hadn't thought of his seeing the clippings."

"And why should he see them?"

"Bella—*won't* you understand? It's John."

"John?"

"Who has taken the most unexpected tone—one might almost say out of perversity."

"Oh, perversity—Mrs. Clinch murmured, observing her cousin between lids wrinkled by amusement. "What tone has John taken?"

Mrs. Fetherel threw out her answer with the desperate gesture of a woman who lays bare the traces of a marital fist. "The tone of being proud of my book."

The measure of Mrs. Clinch's enjoyment overflowed in laughter.

"Oh, you may laugh," Mrs. Fetherel insisted, "but it's no joke to me. In the first place, John's liking the book is so—so—such a false note—it puts me in such a ridiculous position; and then it has set him watching for the reviews—who would ever have suspected John of knowing that books were *reviewed?* Why, he's actually found out about the clipping bureau, and whenever the postman rings I hear John rush out of the library to see if there are any yellow envelopes. Of course, when they *do* come he'll bring them into the drawing room and read them aloud to everybody who happens to be here—and the Bishop is sure to happen to be here!"

Mrs. Clinch repressed her amusement. "The picture you draw is a lurid one," she conceded, "but your modesty strikes me as abnormal, especially in an author. The chances are that some of the clippings will be rather pleasant reading. The critics are not all union men."

Mrs. Fetherel stared. "Union men?"

"Well, I mean they don't all belong to the well-known Society-for-the-Persecution-of-Rising-Authors. Some of them have even been known to defy its regulations and say a good word for a new writer."

"Oh, I dare say," said Mrs. Fetherel, with the laugh her cousin's epigram exacted. "But you don't quite see my point. I'm not at all nervous about the success of my book—my publisher tells me I have no need to be—but I *am* afraid of its being a *succès de scandale.*"

"Mercy!" said Mrs. Clinch, sitting up.

The butler and footman at this moment appeared with the tea tray and when they had withdrawn, Mrs. Fetherel, bending her brightly rippled head above the kettle, continued in a murmur of avowal, "The title, even, is a kind of challenge."

"*Fast and Loose,*" Mrs. Clinch mused. "Yes, it ought to take."

"I didn't choose it for that reason!" the author protested. "I should have preferred something quieter—less pronounced; but I was determined not to shirk the responsibility of what I had written. I want people to know beforehand exactly what kind of book they are buying."

"Well," said Mrs. Clinch, "that's a degree of conscientiousness that I've never met with before. So few books fulfill the promise of their titles that experienced readers never expect the fare to come up to the menu."

"*Fast and Loose* will be no disappointment on that score," her cousin significantly returned. "I've handled the subject without gloves. I've called a spade a spade."

"You simply make my mouth water! And to think I haven't been able to read it yet because every spare minute of my time has been given to correcting the proofs of 'How the Birds Keep Christmas'! There's an instance of the hardships of an author's life!"

Mrs. Fetherel's eye clouded. "Don't joke, Bella, please. I suppose to experienced authors there's always something absurd in the nervousness of a new writer, but in my case so much is at stake; I've put so much of myself into this book and I'm so afraid of being misunderstood... of being, as it were, in advance of my time... like poor Flaubert... I *know* you'll think me ridiculous... and if only my own reputation were at stake, I should never give it a thought... but the idea of dragging John's name through the mire...."

Mrs. Clinch, who had risen and gathered her cloak about her, stood surveying from her genial height her cousin's agitated countenance.

"Why did you use John's name, then?"

"That's another of my difficulties! I *had* to. There would have been no merit in publishing such a book under an assumed name; it would have been an act of moral cowardice. *Fast and Loose* is not an ordinary novel. A writer who dares to show up the hollowness of social conventions must have the courage of her convictions and be willing to accept the consequences of defying society. Can you imagine Ibsen or Tolstoi writing under a false name?" Mrs. Fetherel lifted a tragic eye to her cousin. "You don't know, Bella, how often I've envied you since I began to write. I used to wonder sometimes—you won't mind me saying so?—why, with all your cleverness, you hadn't taken up some more exciting subject than natural history; but I see now how wise you were. Whatever happens, you will never be denounced by the press!"

"Is that what you're afraid of?" asked Mrs. Clinch, as she grasped the bulging umbrella which rested against her chair. "My dear, if I had ever had the good luck to be denounced by the press, my brougham would be waiting at the door for me at this very moment, and I shouldn't have had to ruin this umbrella by using it in the rain. Why, you innocent, if I'd ever felt the slightest aptitude for showing up social conventions, do you suppose I should waste my time writing 'Nests Ajar' and 'How to Smell the Flowers'? There's a fairly steady demand for pseudo-science and colloquial ornithology, but it's nothing, simply nothing, to the ravenous call for attacks on social institutions—especially by those inside the institutions!"

There was often, to her cousin, a lack of taste in Mrs. Clinch's pleasantries, and on this occasion they seemed more than usually irrelevant.

"*Fast and Loose* was not written with the idea of a large sale."

Mrs. Clinch was unperturbed. "Perhaps that's just as well," she returned, with a philosophic shrug. "The surprise will be all the pleasanter, I mean. For of course it's going to sell tremendously, especially if you can get the press to denounce it."

"Bella, how *can* you? I sometimes think you say such things expressly to tease me; and yet I should think you of all women would understand my purpose in writing such a book. It has always seemed to me that the message I had to deliver was not for myself alone, but for all the other women in the world who have felt the hollowness of our social shams, the ignominy of bowing down to the idols of the market, but have lacked either the courage or the power to proclaim their independence; and I have fancied, Bella dear, that, however severely society might punish me for revealing its weaknesses, I could count on the sympathy of those who, like you"—Mrs. Fetherel's voice sank—"have passed through the deep waters."

Mrs. Clinch gave herself a kind of canine shake, as though to free her ample shoulders from any drop of the element she was supposed to have traversed.

"Oh, call them muddy rather than deep," she returned; "and you'll find, my dear, that women who've had any wading to do are rather shy of stirring up mud. It sticks—especially on white clothes."

Mrs. Fetherel lifted an undaunted brow. "I'm not afraid," she proclaimed; and at the same instant she dropped her teaspoon with a clatter and shrank back into her seat. "There's the bell," she exclaimed, "and I know it's the Bishop!"

It was in fact the Bishop of Ossining, who, impressively announced by Mrs. Fetherel's butler, now made an entry that may best be described as not inadequate to the expectations the announcement raised. The Bishop always entered a room well; but, when unannounced, or preceded by a low church butler who gave him his surname, his appearance lacked the impressiveness conferred on it by the due specification of his diocesan dignity. The Bishop was very fond of his niece, Mrs. Fetherel, and one of the traits he most valued in her was the possession of a butler who knew how to announce a bishop.

Mrs. Clinch was also his niece; but, aside from the fact that she possessed no butler at all, she had laid herself open to her uncle's criticism by writing insignificant little books which had a way of going into five or ten editions, while the fruits of his own episcopal leisure—"The Wail of Jonah" (twenty cantos in blank verse), and "Through a Glass Brightly"; or, "How to Raise Funds for a Memorial Window"—inexplicably languished on the back shelves of a publisher noted for his dexterity in pushing "devotional goods." Even this indiscretion the Bishop might, however, have condoned, had his niece thought fit to turn to him for support and advice at the painful juncture of her history when, in her own words, it became necessary for her to invite Mr. Clinch to look out for another situation. Mr. Clinch's misconduct was of the kind especially designed by Providence to test the fortitude of a Christian wife and mother, and the Bishop was absolutely distended with seasonable advice and edification; so that when Bella met his tentative exhortations with the curt remark that she preferred to do her own house cleaning unassisted, her uncle's grief at her ingratitude was not untempered with sympathy for Mr. Clinch.

It is not surprising, therefore, that the Bishop's warmest greetings were always reserved for Mrs. Fetherel; and on this occasion Mrs. Clinch thought she detected, in the salutation which fell to her share, a pronounced suggestion that her own presence was superfluous—a hint which she took with her usual imperturbable good humor.

II

Left alone with the Bishop, Mrs. Fetherel sought the nearest refuge from conversation by offering him a cup of tea. The Bishop accepted with the preoccupied air of a man to whom, for the moment, tea is but a subordinate incident. Mrs. Fetherel's nervousness increased; and knowing that the surest way of distracting attention from one's own affairs is to affect an interest in those of one's companion, she hastily asked if her uncle had come to town on business.

"On business—yes—" said the Bishop in an impressive tone. "I had to see my publisher, who has been behaving rather unsatisfactorily in regard to my last book."

"Ah—your last book?" faltered Mrs. Fetherel, with a sickening sense of her inability to recall the name or nature of the work in question, and a mental vow never again to be caught in such ignorance of a colleague's productions.

" 'Through a Glass Brightly,' " the Bishop explained, with an emphasis which revealed his detection of her predicament. "You may remember that I sent you a copy last Christmas?"

"Of course I do!" Mrs. Fetherel brightened. "It was that delightful story of the poor consumptive girl who had no money, and two little brothers to support—"

"Sisters—idiot sisters—" the Bishop gloomily corrected.

"I mean sisters; and who managed to collect money enough to put up a beautiful memorial window to her—her grandfather, whom she had never seen—"

"But whose sermons had been her chief consolation and support during her long struggle with poverty and disease." The Bishop gave the satisfied sigh of the workman who reviews his completed task. "A touching subject, surely; and I believe I did it justice; at least so my friends assured me."

"Why, yes—I remember there was a splendid review of it in the *Reredos*!" cried Mrs. Fetherel, moved by the incipient instinct of reciprocity.

"Yes—by my dear friend Mrs. Gollinger, whose husband, the late Dean Gollinger, was under very particular obligations to me. Mrs. Gollinger is a woman of rare literary acumen, and her praise of my book was unqualified; but the public wants more highly seasoned fare, and the approval of a thoughtful churchwoman carries less weight than the sensational comments of an illiterate journalist." The Bishop bent a meditative eye on his spotless gaiters. "At the risk of horrifying you, my dear," he added, with a slight laugh, "I will confide to you that my best chance of a popular success would be to have my book denounced by the press."

"Denounced?" gasped Mrs. Fetherel. "On what ground?"

"On the ground of immorality." The Bishop evaded her startled gaze, "Such a thing is inconceivable to you, of course; but I am only repeating what my publisher tells me. If, for instance, a critic could be induced—I mean, if a critic were to be found, who called in question the morality of my heroine in sacrificing her own health and that of her idiot sisters in order to put up a memorial window to her grandfather, it would probably raise a general controversy in the newspapers, and I might count on a sale of ten or fifteen thousand within the next year. If he described her as morbid or decadent, it might even run to twenty thousand; but that is more than I permit myself to hope. In fact I should be satisfied with any general charge of immortality." The Bishop sighed again, "I need hardly tell you that I am actuated by no mere literary ambition. Those whose opinion I most value have assured me that the book is not without merit; but, though it does not become me to dispute their verdict, I can truly say that my vanity as an author is not at stake. I have, however, a special reason for wishing to increase the circulation of 'Through a Glass Brightly'; it was written for a purpose—a purpose I have greatly at heart—"

"I know," cried his niece sympathetically. "The chantry window—?"

"Is still empty, alas! And I had great hopes that, under Providence, my little book might be the means of filling it. All our wealthy parishioners have given lavishly to the cathedral, and it was for this reason that, in writing 'Through a Glass,' I addressed my appeal more especially to the less well-endowed, hoping by the example of my heroine to stimulate the collection of small sums throughout the entire diocese, and perhaps beyond it. I am sure," the Bishop feelingly concluded, "the book would have a widespread influence if people could only be induced to read it!"

His conclusion touched a fresh threat of association in Mrs. Fetherel's vibrating nerve centers. "I never thought of that!" she cried.

The Bishop looked at her inquiringly.

"That one's books may not be read at all! How dreadful!" she exclaimed.

He smiled faintly. "I had not forgotten that I was addressing an authoress," he said. "Indeed, I should not have dared to inflict my troubles on anyone not of the craft."

Mrs. Fetherel was quivering with the consciousness of her involuntary self-betrayal. "Oh, Uncle!" she murmured.

"In fact," the Bishop continued, with a gesture which seemed to brush away her scruples, "I came here partly to speak to you about your novel. 'Fast and Loose,' I think you call it?"

Mrs. Fetherel blushed assentingly.

"And is it out yet?" the Bishop continued.

"It came out about a week ago. But you haven't touched your tea and it must be quite cold. Let me give you another cup."

"My reason for asking," the Bishop went on, with the bland inexorableness with which, in his younger days, he had been known to continue a sermon after the senior warden had looked four times at his watch, "—my reason for asking is, that I hoped I might not be too late to induce you to change the title."

Mrs. Fetherel set down the cup she had filled. "The title?" she faltered.

The Bishop raised a reassuring hand. "Don't misunderstand me, dear child; don't for a moment imagine that I take it to be in any way indicative of the contents of the book. I know you too well for that. My first idea was that it had probably been forced on you by an unscrupulous publisher. I know too well to what ignoble compromises one may be driven in such cases!" He paused, as though to give her the opportunity of confirming this conjecture, but she preserved an apprehensive silence, and he went on, as though taking up the second point in his sermon: "Or, again, the name may have taken your fancy without your realizing all that it implies to minds more alive than yours to offensive innuendoes. It is—ahem—excessively suggestive, and I hope I am not too late to warn you of the false impression it is likely to produce on the very readers whose approbation you would most value. My friend Mrs. Gollinger, for instance—"

Mrs. Fetherel, as the publication of her novel testified, was in theory a woman of independent views; and if in practice she sometimes failed to live up to her standard, it was rather from an irresistible tendency to adapt herself to her environment than from any conscious lack of moral courage. The Bishop's exordium had excited in her that sense of opposition which such admonitions are apt to provoke; but as he went on she felt herself gradually enclosed in an atmosphere in which her theories vainly gasped for breath. The Bishop had the immense dialectical advantage of invalidating any conclusions at variance with his own by always assuming that his premises were among the necessary laws of thought. This method, combined with the habit of ignoring any classifications but his own, created an element in which the first condition of existence was the immediate adoption of his standpoint; so that his niece, as she listened, seemed to feel Mrs. Gollinger's Mechlin cap spreading its conventual shadow over her rebellious brow and the *Revue de Paris* at her elbow turning into a copy of the *Reredos.* She had meant to assure her uncle that she was quite aware of the significance of the title she had chosen, that it had been deliberately selected as indicating the subject of her novel, and that the book itself had been written in direct defiance of the class of readers for whose susceptibilities he was alarmed. The words were almost on her lips when the irresistible suggestion conveyed by the Bishop's tone and language deflected them into the apologetic murmur, "Oh, Uncle, you mustn't think—I never meant—" How much farther this current of reaction might have carried her the historian in unable to compute, for at this point the door opened and her husband entered the room.

"The first review of your book!" he cried, flourishing a yellow envelope. "My dear Bishop, how lucky you're here!"

Though the trials of married life have been classified and catalogued with exhaustive accuracy, there is one form of conjugal misery which has perhaps received inadequate attention; and that is the suffering of the versatile woman whose husband is not equally adapted to all her moods. Every woman feels for the sister who is compelled to wear a bonnet which does not "go" with her gown; but how much sympathy is given to her whose husband refuses to harmonize with the pose of the moment? Scant justice has, for instance, been done to the misunderstood wife whose husband persists in understanding her; to the submissive helpmate whose taskmaster shuns every opportunity of browbeating her, and to the generous and impulsive being whose bills are paid with philosophic calm. Mrs. Fetherel, as wives go, had been fairly exempt from trials of this nature, for her husband, if undistinguished by pronounced brutality or indifference, had at least the negative merit of being her intellectual inferior. Landscape gardeners, who are aware of the usefulness of a valley in emphasizing the height of a hill, can form an idea of the account to which an accomplished woman may turn such deficiencies; and it need scarcely be said that Mrs. Fetherel had made the most of her opportunities. It was agreeably obvious to everyone, Fetherel included, that he was not the man to appreciate such a woman; but there are no limits to man's perversity, and he did his best to invalidate this advantage by admiring her without pretending to understand her. What she most suffered from was this fatuous approval; the maddening sense that, however she conducted herself, he would always admire her. Had he belonged to the class whose conversational supplies are drawn from the domestic circle, his wife's name would never have been off his lips; and to Mrs. Fetherel's sensitive perceptions his frequent silences were indicative of the fact that she was his one topic.

It was, in part, the attempt to escape this persistent approbation that had driven Mrs. Fetherel to authorship. She had fancied that even the most infatuated husband might be counted on to resent, at least negatively, an attack on the sanctity of the hearth; and her anticipations were heightened by a sense of the unpardonableness of her act. Mrs. Fetherel's relations with her husband were in fact complicated by an irrepressible tendency to be fond of him; and there was a certain pleasure in the prospect of a situation that justified the most explicit expiation.

These hopes Fetherel's attitude had already defeated. He read the book with enthusiasm, he pressed it on his friends, he sent a copy to his mother; and his very soul now hung on the verdict of the reviewers. It was perhaps this proof of his general inaptitude that made his wife doubly alive to his special defects; so that his inopportune entrance was aggravated by the very sound of his voice and the hopeless aberration of his smile. Nothing, to the observant, is more indicative of a man's character and circumstances than his way of entering a room. The Bishop of Ossining, for instance, brought with him not only an atmosphere of episcopal authority, but an implied opinion on the verbal inspiration of the Scriptures and on the attitude of the Church toward divorce; while the appearance of Mrs. Fetherel's husband produced an immediate impression of domestic felicity. His mere aspect implied that there was a well-filled nursery upstairs; that his wife, if she did not sew on his buttons, at least superintended the performance of that task; that they both went to church regularly, and that they dined with his mother every Sunday evening punctually at seven o'clock.

All this and more was expressed in the affectionate gesture with which he now raised the yellow envelope above Mrs. Fetherel's clutch; and knowing the uselessness of begging him not to be silly, she said, with a dry despair, "You're boring the Bishop horribly."

Fetherel turned a radiant eye on that dignitary. "She bores us all horribly, doesn't she, sir?" he exulted.

"Have you read it?" said his wife, uncontrollably.

"Read it? Of course not—it's just this minute come. I say, Bishop, you're not going—?"

"Not till I've heard this," said the Bishop, settling himself in his chair with an indulgent smile.

His niece glanced at him despairingly, "Don't let John's nonsense detain you," she entreated.

"Detain him? That's good," guffawed Fetherel. "It isn't as long as one of his sermons—won't take me five minutes to read. Here, listen to this, ladies and gentlemen: 'In this age of festering pessimism and decadent depravity, it is no surprise to the nauseated reviewer to open one more volume saturated with the fetid emanations of the sewer—'"

Fetherel, who was not in the habit of reading aloud, paused with a gasp, and the Bishop glanced sharply at his niece, who kept her gaze fixed on the teacup she had not yet succeeded in transferring to his hand.

"'Of the sewer,'" her husband resumed; "'but his wonder is proportionately great when he lights on a novel as sweetly inoffensive as Paula Fetherel's *Fast and Loose.* Mrs. Fetherel is, we believe, a new hand at fiction, and her work reveals frequent traces of inexperience; but these are more than atoned for by her pure fresh view of life and her altogether unfashionable regard for the reader's moral susceptibilities. Let no one be induced by its distinctly misleading title to forego the enjoyment of this pleasant picture of domestic life, which, in spite of a total lack of force in character drawing and of consecutiveness in incident, may be described as a distinctly pretty story.' "

III

It was several weeks later that Mrs. Clinch once more brought the plebeian aroma of heated tramcars and muddy street crossings into the violet-scented atmosphere of her cousin's drawing room.

"Well," she said, tossing a damp bundle of proof into the corner of a silk-cushioned bergère, "I've read it at last and I'm not so awfully shocked!"

Mrs. Fetherel, who sat near the fire with her head propped on a languid hand, looked up without speaking.

"Mercy, Paula," said her visitor, "you're ill."

Mrs. Fetherel shook her head. "I was never better," she said, mournfully.

"Then may I help myself to tea? Thanks."

Mrs. Clinch carefully removed her mended glove before taking a buttered tea cake; then she glanced again at her cousin.

"It's not what I said just now—?" she ventured.

"Just now?"

"About *Fast and Loose*? I came to talk it over."

Mrs. Fetherel sprang to her feet. "I never," she cried dramatically, "want to hear it mentioned again!"

"Paula!" exclaimed Mrs. Clinch, setting down her cup.

Mrs. Fetherel slowly turned on her an eye brimming with the incommunicable; then, dropping into her seat again, she added, with a tragic laugh: "There's nothing left to say."

"Nothing—?" faltered Mrs. Clinch, longing for another tea cake, but feeling the inappropriateness of the impulse in an atmosphere so charged with the portentous. "Do you mean that everything *has* been said?" She looked tentatively at her cousin. "Haven't they been nice?"

"They've been odious—odious—" Mrs. Fetherel burst out, with an ineffectual clutch at her handkerchief. "It's been perfectly intolerable!"

Mrs. Clinch, philosophically resigning herself to the propriety of taking no more tea, crossed over to her cousin and laid a sympathizing hand on that lady's agitated shoulder.

"It *is* a bore at first," she conceded; "but you'll be surprised to see how soon one gets used to it."

"I shall—never—get—used to it—" Mrs. Fetherel brokenly declared.

"Have they been so very nasty—all of them?"

"Every one of them!" the novelist sobbed.

"I'm so sorry, dear; it *does* hurt, I know—but hadn't you rather expected it?"

"Expected it?" cried Mrs. Fetherel, sitting up.

Mrs. Clinch felt her way warily. "I only mean, dear, that I fancied from what you said before the book came out that you rather expected—that you'd rather discounted—"

"Their recommending it to everybody as a perfectly harmless story?"

"Good gracious! Is *that* what they've done?"

Mrs. Fetherel speechlessly nodded.

"Every one of them?"

"Every one."

"Phew!" said Mrs. Clinch, with an incipient whistle.

"Why, you've just said it yourself!" her cousin suddenly reproached her.

"Said what?"

"That you weren't so *awfully* shocked—"

"I? Oh, well—you see, you'd keyed me up to such a pitch that it wasn't quite as bad as I expected—"

Mrs. Fetherel lifted a smile steeled for the worst. "Why not say at once," she suggested, "that it's a distinctly pretty story?"

"They haven't said *that?*"

"They've all said it."

"My poor Paula!"

"Even the Bishop—"

"The Bishop called it a pretty story?"

"He wrote me—I've his letter somewhere. The title rather scared him—he wanted me to change it; but when he'd read the book he wrote that it was all right and that he'd sent several copies to his friends."

"The old hypocrite!" cried Mrs. Clinch. "That was nothing but professional jealousy."

"Do you think so?" cried her cousin, brightening.

"Sure of it, my dear. His own books don't sell, and he knew the quickest way to kill yours was to distribute it through the diocese with his blessing."

"Then you don't really think it's a pretty story?"

"Dear me, no! Not nearly as bad as that—"

"You're so good, Bella—but the reviewers?"

"Oh, the reviewers," Mrs. Clinch jeered. She gazed meditatively at the cold remains of her tea cake. "Let me see," she said, suddenly; "do you happen to remember if the first review came out in an important paper?"

"Yes—the *Radiator.*"

"That's it! I thought so. Then the others simply followed suit: they often do if a big paper sets the pace. Saves a lot of trouble. Now if you could have got the *Radiator* to denounce you—"

"That's what the Bishop said!" cried Mrs. Fetherel.

"He did?"

"He said his only chance of selling 'Through a Glass Brightly' was to have it denounced on the ground of immorality."

"H'm," said Mrs. Clinch, "I thought he knew a trick or two." She turned an illuminated eye on her cousin. "You ought to get *him* to denounce *Fast and Loose*!" she cried.

Mrs. Fetherel looked at her suspiciously. "I suppose every book must stand or fall on its own merits," she said in an unconvinced tone.

"Bosh! That view is as extinct as the post chaise and the packet ship—it belongs to the time when people read books. Nobody does that now; the reviewer was the first to set the example, and the public was only too thankful to follow it. At first people read the reviews; now they read only the publishers' extracts from them. Even these are rapidly being replaced by paragraphs borrowed from the vocabulary of commerce. I often have to look twice before I am sure if I am reading a department store advertisement or the announcement of a new batch of literature. The publishers will soon be having their 'fall and spring openings' and their 'special importations for Horse Show Week.' But the Bishop is right, of course—nothing helps a book like a rousing attack on its morals; and as the publishers can't exactly proclaim the impropriety of their own wares, the task has to be left to the press or the pulpit."

"The pulpit?" Mrs. Fetherel mused.

"Why, yes. Look at those two novels in England last year."

Mrs. Fetherel shook her head hopelessly. "There is so much more interest in literature in England than here."

"Well, we've got to make the supply create the demand. The Bishop could run your novel up into the hundred thousands in no time."

"But if he can't make his own sell—"

"My dear, a man can't very well preach against his own writings!"

Mrs. Clinch rose and picked up her proofs.

"I'm awfully sorry for you, Paula dear," she concluded, "but I can't help being thankful that there's no demand for pessimism in the field of natural history. Fancy having to write 'The Fall of a Sparrow,' or 'How the Plants Misbehave'!"

IV

Mrs. Fetherel, driving up to the Grand Central Station one morning about five months later, caught sight of the distinguished novelist, Archer Hynes, hurrying into the waiting room ahead of her. Hynes, on his side, recognizing her brougham, turned back to greet her as the footman opened the carriage door.

"My dear colleague! Is it possible that we are traveling together?"

Mrs. Fetherel blushed with pleasure. Hynes had given her two columns of praise in the *Sunday Meteor*, and she had not yet learned to disguise her gratitude.

"I am going to Ossining," she said smilingly.

"So am I. Why, this is almost as good as an elopement."

"And it will end where elopements ought to—in church."

"In church? You're not going to Ossining to go to church?"

"Why not? There's a special ceremony in the cathedral—the chantry window is to be unveiled."

"The chantry window? How picturesque! What *is* a chantry? And why do you want to see it unveiled? Are you after copy—doing something in the Huysmans manner? 'La Cathédrale,' eh?"

"Oh, no," Mrs. Fetherel hesitated. "I'm going simply to please my uncle," she said, at last.

"Your uncle?"

"The Bishop, you know." She smiled.

"The Bishop—the Bishop of Ossining? Why, wasn't he the chap who made that ridiculous attack on your book? Is that prehistoric ass your uncle? Upon my soul, I think you're mighty forgiving to travel all the way to Ossining for one of his stained-glass sociables!"

Mrs. Fetherel's smile flowed into a gentle laugh. "Oh, I've never allowed that to interfere with our friendship. My uncle felt dreadfully about having to speak publicly against my book—it was a great deal harder for him than for me—but he thought it his duty to do so. He has the very highest sense of duty."

"Well," said Hynes, with a shrug. "I don't know that he didn't do you a good turn. Look at that!"

They were standing near the bookstall and he pointed to a placard surmounting the counter and emblazoned with the conspicuous announcement: "*Fast and Loose.* New Edition with Author's Portrait. Hundred and Fiftieth Thousand."

Mrs. Fetherel frowned impatiently. "How absurd! They've no right to use my picture as a poster!"

"There's our train," said Hynes; and they began to push their way through the crowd surging toward one of the inner doors.

As they stood wedged between circumferent shoulders, Mrs. Fetherel became conscious of the fixed stare of a pretty girl who whispered eagerly to her companion. "Look, Myrtle! That's Paula Fetherel right behind us—I knew her in a minute!"

"Gracious—where?" cried the other girl, giving her head a twist which swept her Gainsborough plumes across Mrs. Fetherel's face.

The first speaker's words had carried beyond her companion's ear, and a lemon-colored woman in spectacles, who clutched a copy of the "Journal of Psychology" in one drab cotton-gloved hand, stretched her disengaged hand across the intervening barrier of humanity.

"Have I the privilege of addressing the distinguished author of *Fast and Loose*? If so, let me thank you in the name of the Woman's

Psychological League of Peoria for your magnificent courage in raising the standard of revolt against—"

"You can tell us the rest in the car," said a fat man, pressing his good-humored bulk against the speaker's arm.

Mrs. Fetherel, blushing, embarrassed and happy, slipped into the space produced by this displacement, and a few moments later had taken her seat in the train.

She was a little late, and the other chairs were already filled by a company of elderly ladies and clergymen who seemed to belong to the same party, and were still busy exchanging greetings and settling themselves in their places.

One of the ladies, at Mrs. Fetherel's approach, uttered an exclamation of pleasure and advanced with outstretched hand. "My dear Mrs. Fetherel! I am so delighted to see you here. May I hope you are going to the unveiling of the chantry window? The dear Bishop so hoped that you would do so! But perhaps I ought to introduce myself. I am Mrs. Gollinger"—she lowered her voice expressively—"one of your uncle's oldest friends, one who has stood close to him through all this sad business, and who knows what he suffered when he felt obliged to sacrifice family affection to the call of duty."

Mrs. Fetherel, who had smiled and colored slightly at the beginning of this speech, received its close with a deprecating gesture.

"Oh, pray don't mention it," she murmured. "I quite understood how my uncle was placed—I bore him no ill will for feeling obliged to preach against my book."

"He understood that, and was so touched by it! He has often told me that it was the hardest task he was ever called upon to perform—and, do you know, he quite feels that this unexpected gift of the chantry window is in some way a return for his courage in preaching that sermon."

Mrs. Fetherel smiled faintly. "Does he feel that?"

"Yes; he really does. When the funds for the window were so mysteriously placed at his disposal, just as he had begun to despair of raising them, he assured me that he could not help connecting the fact with his denunciation of your book."

"Dear Uncle!" sighed Mrs. Fetherel. "Did he say that?"

"And now," continued Mrs. Gollinger, with cumulative rapture—"now that you are about to show, by appearing at the ceremony today, that there has been no break in your friendly relations, the dear Bishop's happiness will be complete. He was so longing to have you come to the unveiling!"

"He might have counted on me," said Mrs. Fetherel, still smiling.

"Ah, that is so beautifully forgiving of you!" cried Mrs. Gollinger enthusiastically. "But then, the Bishop has always assured me that your real nature was very different from that which—if you will pardon my saying so—seems to be revealed by your brilliant but—er—rather subversive book. 'If you only knew my niece, dear Mrs. Gollinger,' he always said, 'you would see that her novel was written in all innocence of heart'; and to tell the truth, when I first read the book I didn't think it so very, *very* shocking. It wasn't till the dear Bishop had explained to me—but, dear me, I mustn't take up your time in this way when so many others are anxious to have a word with you."

Mrs. Fetherel glanced at her in surprise, and Mrs. Gollinger continued with a playful smile: "You forget that your face is familiar to thousands whom you have never seen. We all recognized you the moment you entered the train, and my friends here are so eager to make your acquaintance—even those"—her smile deepened—"who thought the dear Bishop not *quite unjustified* in his attack on your remarkable novel."

V

A religious light filled the chantry of Ossining Cathedral, filtering through the linen curtain which veiled the central window and mingling with the blaze of tapers on the richly adorned altar.

In this devout atmosphere, agreeably laden with the incense-like aroma of Easter lilies and forced lilacs, Mrs. Fetherel knelt with a sense of luxurious satisfaction. Beside her sat Archer Hynes, who had remembered that there was to be a church scene in his next novel and that his impressions of the devotional environment needed refreshing. Mrs. Fetherel was very happy. She was conscious that her entrance had sent a thrill through the female devotees who packed the chantry, and she had humor enough to enjoy the thought that, but for the good Bishop's denunciation of her book, the heads of his flock would not have been turned so eagerly in her direction. Moreover, as she entered she had caught sight of a society reporter, and she knew that her presence, and the fact that she was accompanied by Hynes, would be conspicuously proclaimed in the morning papers. All these evidences of the success of her handiwork might have turned a calmer head than Mrs. Fetherel's and though she had now learned to dissemble her gratification, it still filled her inwardly with a delightful glow.

The Bishop was somewhat late in appearing, and she employed the interval in meditating on the plot of her next novel, which was already partly sketched out, but for which she had been unable to find a satisfactory dénouement. By a not uncommon process of ratiocination, Mrs. Fetherel's success had convinced her of her vocation. She was sure now that it was her duty to lay bare the secret plague spots of society, and she was resolved that there should be no doubt as to the purpose of her new book. Experience had shown her that where she had fancied she was calling a spade a spade she had in fact been alluding in guarded terms to the drawing room shovel. She was determined not to repeat the same mistake, and she flattered herself that her coming novel would not need an episcopal denunciation to insure its sale, however likely it was to receive this crowning evidence of success.

She had reached this point in her meditations when the choir burst into song and the ceremony of the unveiling began. The Bishop, almost always felicitous in his addresses to the fair sex, was never more so than when he was celebrating the triumph of one of his cherished purposes. There was a peculiar mixture of Christian humility and episcopal exultation in the manner with which he called attention to the Creator's promptness in responding to his demand for funds, and he had never been more happily inspired than in eulogizing the mysterious gift of the chantry window.

Though no hint of the donor's identity had been allowed to escape him, it was generally understood that the Bishop knew who had given the window, and the congregation awaited in a flutter of suspense the possible announcement of a name. None came, however, though the Bishop deliciously titillated the curiosity of his flock by circling ever closer about the interesting secret. He would not disguise from them, he said, that the heart which had divined his inmost wish had been a woman's—is it not to woman's intuitions that more than half the happiness of earth is owing? What man is obliged to learn by the laborious process of experience, woman's wondrous instinct tells her at a glance; and so it had been with this cherished scheme, this unhoped-for completion of their beautiful chantry. So much, at least, he was allowed to reveal; and indeed, had he not done so, the window itself would have spoken for him, since the first glance at its touching subject and exquisite design would show it to have originated in a woman's heart. This tribute to the sex was received with an audible sigh of contentment, and the Bishop, always stimulated by such evidence of his sway over his hearers, took up his theme with gathering eloquence.

Yes—a woman's heart had planned the gift, a woman's hand had executed it, and, might he add, without too far withdrawing the veil in which Christian beneficence ever loved to drape its acts—might he add that under Providence, a book, a simple book, a mere tale, in fact, had had its share in the good work for which they were assembled to give thanks?

At this unexpected announcement, a ripple of excitement ran through the assemblage, and more than one head was abruptly turned in the direction of Mrs. Fetherel, who sat listening in an agony of wonder and confusion. It did not escape the observant novelist at her side that she drew down her veil to conceal an uncontrollable blush, and this evidence of dismay caused him to fix an attentive gaze on her, while from her seat across the aisle Mrs. Gollinger sent a smile of unctuous approval.

"A book—a simple book—" the Bishop's voice went on above this matter of mingled emotions. "What is a book? Only a few pages and a little ink—and yet one of the mightiest instruments which Providence has devised for shaping the destinies of man... one of the most powerful influences for good or evil which the Creator has placed in the minds of his creatures...."

The air seemed intolerably close to Mrs. Fetherel, and she drew out her scent bottle, and then thrust it hurriedly away, conscious that she was still the center of unenviable attention. And all the while the Bishop's voice droned on....

"And of all forms of literature, fiction is doubtless that which has exercised the greatest sway, for good or ill, over the passions and imagination of the masses. Yes, my friends, I am the first to acknowledge it—no sermon, however eloquent, no theological treatise, however learned and convincing, has ever inflamed the heart and imagination like a novel—a simple novel. Incalculable is the power exercised over humanity by the great magicians of the pen—a power ever enlarging its boundaries and increasing its responsibilities as popular education multiplies the number of readers.... Yes, it is the novelist's hand which can pour balm on countless human sufferings, or inoculate mankind with the festering poison of a corrupt imagination...."

Mrs. Fetherel had turned white, and her eyes were fixed with a blind stare of anger on the large-sleeved figure in the center of the chancel.

"And too often, alas, it is the poison and not the balm which the unscrupulous hand of genius proffers to its unsuspecting readers. But, my friends, why should I continue? None know better than an assemblage of Christian women, such as I am now addressing, the beneficent or baleful influences of modern fiction; and so, when I say that this beautiful chantry window of ours owes its existence in part to the romancer's pen"—the Bishop paused, and bending forward, seemed to seek a certain face among the countenances eagerly addressed to his—"when I say that this pen, which for personal reasons it does not become me to celebrate unduly—"

Mrs. Fetherel at this point half-rose, pushing back her chair, which scraped loudly over the marble floor; but Hynes involuntarily laid a warning hand on her arm, and she sank down with a confused murmur about the heat.

"When I confess that this pen, which for once at least has proved itself so much mightier than the sword, is that which was inspired to trace the simple narrative of 'Through a Glass Brightly'"—Mrs. Fetherel looked up with a gasp of mingled relief and anger—"when I tell you, my dear friends, that it was your Bishop's own work which first roused the mind of one of his flock to the crying need of a chantry window, I think you will admit that I am justified in celebrating the triumphs of the pen, even though it be the modest instrument which your own Bishop wields."

The Bishop paused impressively, and a faint gasp of surprise and disappointment was audible throughout the chantry. Something very different from this conclusion had been expected, and even Mrs. Gollinger's lips curled with a slightly ironic smile. But Archer Hynes's attention was chiefly reserved for Mrs. Fetherel, whose face had changed with astonishing rapidity from surprise to annoyance, from annoyance to relief, and then back to something very like indignation.

The address concluded, the actual ceremony of the unveiling was about to take place, and the attention of the congregation soon reverted to the chancel, where the choir had grouped themselves beneath the veiled window, prepared to burst into a chant of praise as the Bishop drew back the hanging. The moment was an impressive one, and every eye was fixed on the curtain. Even Hynes's gaze strayed to it for a moment, but soon returned to his neighbor's face; and then he perceived that Mrs. Fetherel, alone of all the persons present, was not looking at the window. Her eyes were fixed in an indignant stare on the Bishop; a flush of anger burned becomingly under her veil, and her hands nervously crumpled the beautifully printed program of the ceremony.

Hynes broke into a smile of comprehension. He glanced at the Bishop, and back at the Bishop's niece; then, as the episcopal hand was solemnly raised to draw back the curtain, he bent and whispered in Mrs. Fetherel's ear:

"Why, you gave it yourself! You wonderful woman, of course you gave it yourself!"

Mrs. Fetherel raised her eyes to his with a start. Her blush deepened and her lips shaped a hasty "No"; but the denial was deflected into the indignant murmur—"It wasn't *his* silly book that did it, anyhow!"

COMIC INTERRUPTIONS

THE £1,000,000 BANK NOTE

MARK TWAIN

When I was twenty-seven years old, I was a mining-broker's clerk in San Francisco, and an expert in all the details of stock traffic. I was alone in the world, and had nothing to depend upon but my wits and a clean reputation; but these were setting my feet in the road to eventual fortune, and I was content with the prospect.

My time was my own after the afternoon board, Saturdays, and I was accustomed to put it in on a little sailboat on the bay. One day I ventured too far, and was carried out to sea. Just at nightfall, when hope was about gone, I was picked up by a small brig which was bound for London. It was a long and stormy voyage, and they made me work my passage without pay, as a common sailor. When I stepped ashore in London my clothes were ragged and shabby, and I had only a dollar in my pocket. This money fed and sheltered me twenty-four hours. During the next twenty-four I went without food and shelter.

About ten o'clock on the following morning, seedy and hungry, I was dragging myself along Portland Place, when a child that was passing, towed by a nursemaid, tossed a luscious big pear—minus one bite—into the gutter. I stopped, of course, and fastened my desiring eye on that muddy treasure. My mouth watered for it, my stomach craved it, my whole being begged for it. But every time I made a move to get it some passing eye detected my purpose, and of course I straightened up, then, and looked indifferent, and pretended that I hadn't been thinking about the pear at all. This same thing kept happening and happening, and I couldn't get the pear. I was just getting desperate enough to brave all the shame, and to seize it, when a window behind me was raised, and a gentleman spoke out of it, saying:

"Step in here, please."

I was admitted by a gorgeous flunkey, and shown into a sumptuous room where a couple of elderly gentlemen were sitting. They sent away the servant, and made me sit down. They had just finished their breakfast, and the sight of the remains of it almost overpowered me. I could hardly keep my wits together in the presence of that food, but as I was not asked to sample it, I had to bear my trouble as best I could.

Now, something had been happening there a little before, which I did not know anything about until a good many days afterward, but I will tell you about it now. Those two old brothers had been having a pretty hot argument a couple of days before, and had ended by agreeing to decide it by a bet, which is the English way of settling everything.

You will remember that the Bank of England once issued two notes of a million pounds each, to be used for a special purpose connected with some public transaction with a foreign country. For some reason or other only one of these had been used and canceled; the other still lay in the vaults of the Bank. Well, the brothers, chatting along, happened to get to wondering what might be the fate of a perfectly honest and intelligent stranger who should be turned adrift in London without a friend, and with no money but that million-pound bank note, and no way to account for his being in possession of it. Brother A said he would starve to death; Brother B said he wouldn't. Brother A said he couldn't offer it at a bank or anywhere else, because he would be arrested on the spot. So they went on disputing till Brother B said he would bet twenty thousand pounds that the man would live thirty days, *any way,* on that million, and keep out of jail, too. Brother A took him up. Brother B went down to the Bank and bought that note. Just like an Englishman, you see; pluck to the backbone. Then he dictated a letter, which one of his clerks wrote out in a beautiful round hand, and then the two brothers sat at the window a whole day watching for the right man to give it to.

They saw many honest faces go by that were not intelligent enough; many that were intelligent, but not honest enough; many that were both, but the possessors were not poor enough, or, if poor enough, were not strangers. There was always a defect, until I came along; but they agreed that I filled the bill all around; so they elected me unanimously, and there I was, now, waiting to know why I was called in. They began to ask me questions about myself, and pretty soon they had my story. Finally they told me I would answer their purpose. I said I was sincerely glad, and asked what it was. Then one of them handed me an envelope, and said I would find the explanation inside. I was going to open it, but he said no; take it to my lodgings, and look it over carefully, and not be hasty or rash. I was puzzled, and wanted to discuss the matter a little further, but they didn't; so I took my leave, feeling hurt and insulted to be made the butt of what was apparently some kind of a practical joke, and yet obliged to put up with it, not being in circumstances to resent affronts from rich strong folk.

I would have picked up the pear, now, and eaten it before all the world, but it was gone; so I had lost that by this unlucky business, and the thought of it did not soften my feeling toward those men. As soon as I was out of sight of that house I opened my envelope, and saw that it contained money! My opinion of those people changed, I can tell you! I lost not a moment, but shoved note and money into my vest-pocket, and broke for the nearest cheap eating-house. Well, how I did eat! When at last I couldn't hold any more, I took out my money and unfolded it, took one glimpse and nearly fainted. Five million dollars! Why, it made my head swim.

I must have sat there stunned and blinking at the note as much as a minute before I came rightly to myself again. The first thing I noticed, then, was the landlord. His eye was on the note, and he was petrified. He was worshipping, with all his body and soul, but he looked as if he couldn't stir hand or foot. I took my cue in a moment, and did the only rational thing there was to do. I reached the note toward him, and said carelessly:

"Give me the change, please."

Then he was restored to his normal condition, and made a thousand apologies for not being able to break the bill, and I couldn't get him to touch it. He wanted to look at it, and keep on looking at it; he couldn't seem to get enough of it to quench the thirst of his eye, but he shrank from touching it as if it had been something too sacred for poor common clay to handle. I said:

"I am sorry if it is an inconvenience, but I must insist. Please change it; I haven't anything else."

But he said that wasn't any matter; he was quite willing to let the trifle stand over till another time. I said I might not be in his neighborhood again for a good while; but he said it was of no consequence, he could wait, and, moreover, I could have anything I wanted, anytime I chose, and let the account run as long as I pleased. He said he hoped he wasn't afraid to trust as rich a gentleman as I was, merely because I was of a merry disposition, and chose to play larks on the public in the matter of dress. By this time another customer was entering, and the landlord hinted to me to put the monster out of sight; then he bowed me all the way to the door, and I started straight for that house and those brothers, to correct the mistake which had been made before the police should hunt me up, and help me do it. I was pretty nervous, in fact pretty badly frightened, though, of course, I was no way in fault; but I knew men well enough to know that when they find they've given a tramp a million-pound bill when they thought it was a one-pounder, they are in a frantic rage against *him* instead of quarreling with their own nearsightedness, as they ought. As I approached the house my excitement began to abate, for all was quiet there, which made me feel pretty sure the blunder was not discovered yet. I rang. The same servant appeared. I asked for those gentlemen.

"They are gone." This in the lofty, cold way of that fellow's tribe.

"Gone? Gone where?"

"On a journey."

"But whereabouts?"

"To the Continent, I think."

"The Continent?"

"Yes, sir."

"Which way—by what route?"

"I can't say, sir."

"When will they be back?"

"In a month, they said."

"A month! Oh, this is awful! Give me *some* sort of idea of how to get a word to them. It's of the last importance."

"I can't, indeed. I've no idea where they've gone, sir."

"Then I must see some member of the family."

"Family's away too; been abroad months—in Egypt and India, I think."

"Man, there's been an immense mistake made. They'll be back before night. Will you tell them I've been here, and that I will keep coming till it's all made right, and they needn't be afraid?"

"I'll tell them, if they come back, but I am not expecting them. They said you would be here in an hour to make inquiries, but I must tell you it's all right, they'll be here on time and expect you."

So I had to give it up and go away. What a riddle it all was! I was like to lose my mind. They would be here "on time." What could that mean? Oh, the letter would explain, maybe. I had forgotten the letter; I got it out and read it. This is what it said:

You are an intelligent and honest man, as one may see by your face. We conceive you to be poor and a stranger. Enclosed you will find a sum of money. It is lent to you for thirty days, without interest. Report at this house at the end of that time. I have a bet on you. If I win it you shall have any situation that is in my gift—any, that is, that you shall be able to prove yourself familiar with and competent to fill.

No signature, no address, no date.

Well, here was a coil to be in! You are posted on what had preceded all this, but I was not. It was just a deep, dark puzzle to me. I hadn't the least idea what the game was, nor whether harm was meant me or a kindness. I went into a park, and sat down to try to think it out, and to consider what I had best do.

At the end of an hour, my reasonings had crystallized into this verdict.

Maybe those men mean me well, maybe they mean me ill; no way to decide that—let it go. They've got a game, or a scheme, or an experiment, of some kind on hand; no way to determine what it is—let it go. There's a bet on me; no way to find out what it is—let it go. That disposes of the indeterminable quantities; the remainder of the matter is tangible, solid, and may be classed and labeled with certainty. If I ask the Bank of England to place this bill to the credit of the man it belongs to, they'll do it, for they know him, although I don't; but they will ask me how I came in possession of it, and if I tell the truth, they'll put me in the asylum, naturally, and a lie will land me in jail. The same result would follow if I tried to bank the bill anywhere or to borrow money on it. I have got to carry this immense burden around until those men come back, whether I want to or not. It is useless to me, as useless as a handful of ashes, and yet I must take care of it, and watch over it, while I beg my living. I couldn't *give* it away, if I should try, for neither honest citizen nor highwayman would accept it or meddle with it for anything. Those brothers are safe. Even if I lose their bill, or burn it, they are still safe, because they can stop payment, and the Bank will make them whole; but meantime, I've got to do a month's suffering without wages or profit—unless I help win that bet, whatever it may be, and get that situation that I am promised. I *should* like to get that; men of their sort have situations in their gift that are worth having.

I got to thinking a good deal about the situation. My hopes began to rise high. Without doubt the salary would be large. It would begin in a month; after that I should be all right. Pretty soon I was feeling first rate. By this time I was tramping the streets again. The sight of a tailor shop gave me a sharp longing to shed my rags, and to clothe myself decently once more. Could I afford it? No; I had nothing in the world but a million pounds. So I forced myself to go on by. But soon I was drifting back again. The temptation persecuted me cruelly. I must have passed that shop back and forth six times during that manful struggle. At last I gave in; I had to. I asked if they had a misfit suit that had been thrown on their hands. The fellow I spoke to nodded his head toward another fellow, and gave me no answer. I went to the indicated fellow, and he indicated another fellow with *his* head, and no words. I went to him, and he said:

"'Tend to you presently."

I waited till he was done with what he was at, then he took me into a back room, and overhauled a pile of rejected suits, and selected the rattiest one for me. I put it on. It didn't fit, and wasn't in any way attractive, but it was new, and I was anxious to have it; so I didn't find any fault, but said with some diffidence:

"It would be an accommodation to me if you could wait some days for the money. I haven't any small change about me."

The fellow worked up a most sarcastic expression of countenance, and said:

"Oh, you haven't? Well, of course, I didn't expect it. I'd only expect gentlemen like you to carry large change."

I was nettled, and said:

"My friend, you shouldn't judge a stranger always by the clothes he wears. I am quite able to pay for this suit; I simply didn't wish to put you to the trouble of changing a large note."

He modified his style a little at that, and said, though still with something of an air:

"I didn't mean any particular harm, but as long as rebukes are going, I might say it wasn't quite your affair to jump to the conclusion that we couldn't change any note that you might happen to be carrying around. On the contrary, we *can.*"

I handed the note to him, and said:

"Oh, very well; I apologize."

He received it with a smile, one of those large smiles which goes all around over, and has folds in it, and wrinkles, and spirals, and looks like the place where you have thrown a brick in a pond; and then in the act of his taking a glimpse of the bill this smile froze solid, and turned yellow, and looked like those wavy, wormy spreads of lava which you find hardened on little levels on the side of Vesuvius. I never before saw a smile caught like that, and perpetuated. The man stood there holding the bill, and looking like that, and the proprietor hustled up to see what was the matter, and said briskly:

"Well, what's up? What's the trouble? What's the wanting?"

I said: "There isn't any trouble. I'm waiting for my change."

"Come, come; get him his change, Tod; get him his change."

Tod retorted: "Get him his change! It's easy to say, sir; but look at the bill yourself."

The proprietor took a look, gave a low, eloquent whistle, then made a dive for the pile of rejected clothing, and began to snatch it this way and that, talking all the time excitedly, and as if to himself:

"Sell an eccentric millionaire such an unspeakable suit as that! Tod's a fool—a born fool. Always doing something like this. Drives every millionaire away from this place, because he can't tell a millionaire from a tramp, and never could. Ah, here's the thing I'm after. Please get those things off, sir, and throw them in the fire. Do me the favor to put on this shirt and this suit; it's just the thing, the very thing—plain, rich, modest, and just ducally nobby; made to order for a foreign prince—you may know him, sir, his Serene Highness the Hospodar of Halifax; had to leave it with us and take a mourning suit because his mother was going to die—which she didn't. But that's all right; we can't always have things the way we—that is, the way they—there! Trousers all right, they fit you to a charm, sir; now the waist coat; aha, right again! Now the coat—lord! Look at that, now! Perfect—the whole thing! I never saw such a triumph in all my experience."

I expressed my satisfaction.

"Quite right, sir, quite right; it'll do for a makeshift, I'm bound to say. But wait till you see what we'll get up for you on your own measure. Come, Tod, book and pen; get at it. Length of leg, 32"—and so on. Before I could get in a word he had measured me, and was giving orders for dress suits, morning suits, shirts, and all sorts of things. When I got a chance I said:

"But my dear sir, I *can't* give these orders, unless you can wait indefinitely, or change the bill."

"Indefinitely! It's a weak word, sir, a weak word. Eternally—*that's* the word, sir. Tod, rush these things through, and send them to the gentleman's address without any waste of time. Let the minor customers wait. Set down the gentleman's address and— "

"I'm changing my quarters. I will drop in and leave the new address."

"Quite right, sir, quite right. One moment—let me show you out, sir. There—good day, sir, good day."

Well, don't you see what was bound to happen? I drifted naturally into buying whatever I wanted, and asking for change. Within a week I was sumptuously equipped with all needful comforts and luxuries, and was housed in an expensive private hotel in Hanover Square. I took my dinners there, but for breakfast I stuck by Harris's humble feeding house, where I had got my first meal on my million-pound bill. I was the making of Harris. The fact had gone all abroad that the foreign crank who carried million-pound bills in his vest-pocket was the patron saint of the place. That was enough. From being a poor, struggling, little hand-to-mouth enterprise, it had become celebrated, and overcrowded with customers. Harris was so grateful that he forced loans upon me, and would not be denied; and so, pauper as I was, I had money to spend, and was living like the rich and the great. I judged that there was going to be a crash by and by, but I was in, now, and must swim across or drown. You see there was just that element of impending disaster to give a serious side, a sober side, yes, a tragic side, to a state of things which would otherwise have been purely ridiculous. In the night, in the dark, the tragedy part was always to the front, and always warning, always threatening; and so I moaned and tossed, and sleep was hard to find. But in the cheerful daylight the tragedy element faded out and disappeared, and I walked on air, and was happy to giddiness, to intoxication, you may say.

And it was natural; for I had become one of the notorieties of the metropolis of the world, and it turned my head, not just a little, but a good deal. You could not take up a newspaper, English, Scotch, or Irish, without finding in it one or more references to the "vest-pocket million-pounder" and his latest doings and sayings. At first, in these mentions, I was at the bottom of the personal-gossip column; next, I was listed above the knights, next above the baronets, next above the barons, and so on, and so on, climbing steadily, as my notoriety augmented, until I reached the highest altitude possible, and there I remained, taking precedence of all dukes not royal, and of all ecclesiastics except the primate of all England. But mind, this was not fame; and yet I had achieved only notoriety. Then came the climaxing stroke—the accolade, so to speak—which in a single instance transmuted the perishable dross of notoriety into the enduring gold of fame: "Punch" caricatured me! Yes, I was a made man, now; my place was established. I might be joked about still, but reverently, not hilariously, not rudely; I could be smiled at, but not laughed at. The time for that had gone by. "Punch" pictured me all aflutter with rags, dickering with a beef-eater for the Tower of London. Well, you can imagine how it was with a young fellow who had never been taken notice of before, and now all of a sudden couldn't say a thing that wasn't taken up and repeated everywhere; couldn't stir abroad without constantly overhearing the remark flying from lip to lip, "There he goes; that's him!" couldn't take his breakfast without a crowd to look on; couldn't appear in an opera-box without concentrating there the fire of a thousand lorgnettes. Why, I just swam in the glory all day long—that is the amount of it.

You know, I even kept my old suit of rags, and every now and then appeared in them, so as to have the old pleasure of buying trifles, and being insulted, and then shooting the scoffer dead with the million-pound bill. But I couldn't keep that up. The illustrated papers made the outfit so familiar that when I went out in it I was at once recognized and followed by a crowd, and if I attempted a purchase the man would offer me his whole shop on credit before I could pull my note on him.

About the tenth day of my fame I went to fulfill my duty to my flag by paying my respects to the American minister. He received me with the enthusiasm proper in my case, upbraided me for being so tardy in my duty, and said that there was only one way to get his forgiveness, and that was to take the seat at his dinner party that night made vacant by the illness of one of his guests. I said I would, and we got to talking. It turned out that he and my father had been schoolmates in boyhood, Yale students together later, and always warm friends up to my father's death. So then he required me to put in at his house all the odd time I might have to spare, and I was very willing, of course.

In fact I was more than willing; I was glad. When the crash should come, he might somehow be able to save me from total destruction; I didn't know how, but he might think of a way, maybe. I couldn't venture to unbosom myself to him at this late date, a thing which I would have been quick to do in the beginning of this awful career of mine in London. No, I couldn't venture it now; I was in too deep; that is, too deep for me to be risking revelations to so new a friend, though not clear beyond my depth, as *I* looked at it. Because, you see, with all my borrowing, I was carefully keeping within my means—I mean within my salary. Of course I couldn't *know* what my salary was going to be, but I had a good enough basis for estimate in the fact that, if I won the bet, I was to have *choice* of any situation in that rich old gentleman's gift provided I was competent—and I should certainly prove competent; I hadn't any doubt about that; I had always been lucky. Now my estimate of the salary was six hundred to a thousand a year; say, six hundred for the first year, and so on up year by year, till I struck the upper figure by proved merit. At present I was only in debt for my first year's salary. Everybody had been trying to lend me money, but I fought off the most of them on one pretext or another; so this indebtedness represented only £300 borrowed money, the other £300 represented my keep and my purchases. I believed my second year's salary would carry me through the rest of the month if I went on being cautious and economical, and I intended to look sharply out for that. My month ended, my employer back from his journey, I should be all right once more, for I should at once divide the two years' salary among my creditors by assignment, and get right down to my work.

It was a lovely dinner party of fourteen. The Duke and Dutchess of Shoreditch, and their daughter Lady Anne-Grace-Eleanor-Celeste-and-so-forth-and so-forth-de-Bohun, the Earl and Countess of Newgate, Viscount Cheapside, Lord and Lady Blatherskite, some untitled people of both sexes, the minister and his wife and daughter, and his daughter's visiting friend, an English girl of twenty-two named Portia Langham, whom I fell in love with in two minutes, and she with me—I could see it without glasses. There was still another guest, an American—but I am a little ahead of my story. While the people were still in the drawing room, whetting up for dinner, and coldly inspecting the latecomers, the servant announced:

"Mr. Lloyd Hastings."

The moment the usual civilities were over, Hastings caught sight of me, and came straight with cordially outstretched hand; then stopped short when about to shake, and said with an embarrassed look:

"I beg your pardon, sir, I thought I knew you."

"Why, you do know me, old fellow."

"No! Are *you* the—the"

"Vest-pocket monster? I am, indeed. Don't be afraid to call me by my nickname; I'm used to it."

"Well, well, well, this is a surprise. Once or twice I've seen your own name coupled with the nickname, but it never occurred to me that *you* could be the Henry Adams referred to. Why, it isn't six months since you were clerking away for Blake Hopkins in Frisco on a salary, and sitting up nights on an extra allowance, helping me arrange and verify the Gould and Curry Extension papers and statistics. The idea of your being in London, and a vast millionaire, and a colossal celebrity! Why, it's the Arabian Nights come again. Man, I can't take it in at all; can't realize it; give me time to settle the whirl in my head."

The fact is, Lloyd, you are no worse off than I am.. I can't realize it myself."

"Dear me, it *is* stunning, now isn't it? Why, it's just three months today since we went to the Miners' restaurant—"

"No; the What Cheer."

"Right, it *was* the What Cheer; went there at two in the morning, and had a chop and coffee after a hard six hours' grind over those Extension papers, and I tried to persuade you to come to London with me, and offered to get leave of absence for you and pay all your expenses, and give you something over if I succeeded in making the sale; and you would not listen to me, said I wouldn't succeed, and you couldn't afford to lose the run of business and be no end of time getting the hang of things again when you got back home. And yet here you are. How odd it all is! How did you happen to come, and whatever *did* give you this incredible start?"

"Oh, just an accident. It's a long story—a romance, a body may say. I'll tell you all about it, but not now."

"When?"

"The end of this month."

"That's more than a fortnight yet. It's too much of a strain on a person's curiosity. Make it a week."

"I can't. You'll know why, by and by. But how's the trade getting along?"

His cheerfulness vanished like a breath, and he said with a sigh:

"You were a true prophet, Hal, a true prophet. I wish I hadn't come. I don't want to talk about it."

"But you must. You must come and stop with me tonight, when we leave here, and tell me all about it."

"Oh, may I? Are you in earnest?" and the water showed in his eyes.

"Yes, I want to hear the whole story, every word."

"I'm so grateful! Just to find a human interest once more, in some voice and in some eye, in me and affairs of mine, after what I've been through here—lord! I could go down on my knees for it!"

He gripped my hand hard, and braced up, and was all right and lively after that for the dinner—which didn't come off. No; the usual thing happened, the thing that is always happening under that vicious and aggravating English system—the matter of precedence couldn't be settled, and so there was no dinner. Englishmen always eat dinner before they go out to dinner because *they* know the risks they are running; but nobody ever warns the stranger, and so he walks placidly into the trap. Of course nobody was hurt this time, because we had all been to dinner, none of us being novices except Hastings, and he having been informed by the minister at the time that he invited him that in deference to the English custom he had not provided any dinner. Everybody took a lady and processioned down to the dining room, because it is usual to go through the motions; but there the dispute began. The Duke of Shoreditch wanted to take precedence, and sit at the head of the table, holding that he outranked a minister who represented merely a nation and not a monarch; but I stood for my rights, and refused to yield. In the gossip column I ranked all dukes not royal, and said so, and claimed precedence of this one. It couldn't be settled, of course, struggle as we might and did, he finally (and injudiciously) trying to play birth and antiquity, and I "seeing" his Conqueror and "raising" him with Adam, whose direct posterity I was, as shown by my name, while *he* was of a collateral branch, as shown by *his,* and by recent Norman origin; so we all processioned back to the drawing room again and had a perpendicular lunch plate of sardines and a strawberry, and you group yourself and stand up and eat it. Here the religion of precedence is not so strenuous; the two persons of highest rank chuck up a shilling, the one that wins has first go at his strawberry, and the loser gets the shilling. The next two chuck up, then the next two, and so on. After refreshment, tables were brought, and we all played cribbage, sixpence a game. The English never play any game for amusement. If they can't make something or lose something,—they don't care which,—they won't play.

We had a lovely time; certainly two of us had, Miss Langham and I. I was so bewitched with her that I couldn't count my hands if they went above a double sequence; and when I struck home I never discovered it, and started up the outside row again, and would have lost the game every time, only the girl did the same, she being in just my condition, you see; and consequently neither of us ever got out, or cared to wonder why we didn't want to be interrupted. And I *told* her—I did indeed—told her I loved her; and she—well, blushed till her hair turned red, but she liked it; she *said* she did. Oh, there was never such an evening! Every time I pegged I put on a postscript; every time she pegged she acknowledged receipt of it, counting the hands the same. Why, I couldn't even say "Two for his heels" without adding, "*My,* how sweet you do look!" and she would say, "Fifteen two, fifteen four, fifteen six, and a pair are eight, and eight are sixteen—*do* you think so?"—peeping out aslant from under her lashes, you know, so sweet and cunning. Oh, it was just *too*-too!

Well, I was perfectly honest and square with her; told her I hadn't a cent in the world but just the million-pound note she'd heard so much talk about, and *it* didn't belong to me; and that started her curiosity, and then I talked low, and told her the whole history right from the start, and it nearly killed her, laughing. What in the nation she could find to laugh about, *I* couldn't see, but there it was; every half minute some new detail would fetch her, and I would have to stop as much as a minute and a half to give her a chance to settle down again. Why, she laughed herself lame, she did indeed; I never saw anything like it. I mean I never saw a painful story—a story of a person's troubles and worries and fears—produce just *that* kind of effect before. So I loved her all the more, seeing she could be so cheerful when there wasn't anything to be cheerful about; for I might soon need that kind of wife, you know, the way things looked. Of course I told her we should have to wait a couple of years, till I could catch up on my salary; but she didn't mind that, only she hoped I would be as careful as possible in the matter of expenses, and not let them run the least risk of trenching on our third year's pay. Then she began to get a little worried, and wondered if we were making any mistake, and starting the salary on a higher figure for the first year than I would get. This was good sense, and it made me feel a little less confident than I had been feeling before; but it gave me a good business idea, and I brought it frankly out.

"Portia, dear, would you mind going with me that day, when I confront those old gentlemen?"

She shrank a little, but said:

"No; if my being with you would help hearten you. But—would it be quite proper, do you think?"

"No, I don't know that it would; in fact I'm afraid it wouldn't: but you see, there's so *much* dependent upon it that—"

"Then I'll go anyway, proper or improper," she said, with a beautiful and generous enthusiasm.

"Oh, I shall be so happy to think I'm helping."

"Helping, dear? Why, you'll be doing it all. You're so beautiful and so lovely and so winning, that with you there I can pile our salary up till I break those good old fellows, and they'll never have the heart to struggle."

Sho! You should have seen the rich blood mount, and her happy eyes shine!

"You wicked flatterer! There isn't a word of truth in what you say, but still I'll go with you. Maybe it will teach you not to expect other people to look with your eyes."

Were my doubts dissipated? Was my confidence restored? You may judge by this fact: privately I raised my salary to twelve hundred the first year on the spot. But I didn't tell her; I saved it for a surprise.

All the way home I was in the clouds, Hastings talking, I not hearing a word. When he and I entered my parlor, he brought me to myself with his fervent appreciations of my manifold comforts and luxuries.

"Let me just stand here a little and look my fill! Dear me, it's just a palace! And in it everything a body *could* desire, including cozy coal fire and supper standing ready. Henry, it doesn't merely make me realize how rich you are, it makes me realize, to the bone, to the marrow, how poor I am—how poor I am, and how miserable, how defeated, routed, annihilated!"

Plague take it! This language gave me the cold shudders. It scared me broad awake, and made me comprehend that I was standing on a half-inch crust, with a crater underneath. *I* didn't know I had been dreaming—that is, I hadn't been allowing myself to know it for a while back; but *now*—oh, dear! Deep in debt, not a cent in the world, a lovely girl's happiness or woe in my hands, and nothing in front of me but a salary which might never—oh, *would* never—materialize! Oh, oh, oh, I am ruined past hope; nothing can save me!

"Henry, the mere unconsidered drippings of your daily income would—"

"Oh, my daily income! Here, down with this hot Scotch, and cheer up your soul. Here's with you! Or, no—you're hungry; sit down and—"

"Not a bite for me; I'm past it. I can't eat, these days; but I'll drink with you till I drop. Come!"

"Barrel for barrel, I'm with you! Ready? Here we go! Now, then, Lloyd, unreel your story while I brew."

"Unreel it? What, again?"

"Again? What do you mean by that?"

"Why, I mean do you want to hear it *over* again?"

"Do I want to hear it *over* again? This *is* a puzzler. Wait; don't take any more of that liquid. You don't need it."

"Look here, Henry, you alarm me. Didn't I tell you the whole story on the way here?"

"You?"

"Yes, I."

"I'll be hanged if I heard a word of it."

"Henry, this is a serious thing. It troubles me. What did you take up yonder at the minister's?"

Then it all flashed on me, and I owned up, like a man.

"I took the dearest girl in this world—prisoner!"

So then he came with a rush, and we shook, and shook, and shook till our hands ached and he didn't blame me for not having heard a word of a story which had lasted while we walked three miles. He just sat down then, like the patient, good fellow he was, and told it all over again. Synopsized, it amounted to this: He had come to England with what he thought was a grand opportunity; he had an "option" to sell the Gould and Curry Extension for the "locators" of it, and keep all he could get over a million dollars. He had worked hard, had pulled every wire he knew of, had left no honest expedient untried, had spent nearly all the money he had in the world, had not been able to get a solitary capitalist to listen to him, and his option would run out at the end of the month. In a word, he was ruined. Then he jumped up and cried out:

"Henry, you can save me! You can save me, and you're the only man in the universe that can. Will you do it?"

"Tell me how. Speak out, my boy."

"Give me a million and my passage home for my 'option'! Don't, *don't* refuse!"

I was in a kind of agony. I was right on the point of coming out with the words, "Lloyd, I'm a pauper myself—absolutely penniless, and in *debt!*" But a white-hot idea came flaming through my head, and I gripped my jaws together, and calmed myself down till I was as cold as a capitalist. Then I said, in a commercial and self-possessed way:

"I will save you, Lloyd—"

"Then I'm already saved! God be merciful to you forever! If ever I—"

"Let me finish, Lloyd. I will save you, but not in that way; for that would not be fair to you, after your hard work, and the risks you've run. I don't need to buy mines; I can keep my capital moving, in a commercial centre like London without that; it's what I'm at, all the time; but here is what I'll do. I know all about that mine, of course; I know its immense value, and can swear to it if anybody wishes it. You shall sell out inside of the fortnight for three million in cash, using my name freely, and we'll divide, share and share alike."

Do you know, he would have danced the furniture to kindling-wood in his insane joy, and broken everything on the place, if I hadn't tripped him up and tied him.

Then he lay there, perfectly happy, saying:

"I may use your name! Your name—think of it! Man, they'll flock in droves, these rich Londoners; they'll *fight* for that stock! I'm a made man, I'm a made man forever, and I'll never forget you as long as I live!"

In less that twenty-four hours London was abuzz! I hadn't anything to do, day after day, but sit at home, and say to all comers:

"Yes; I told him to refer to me. I know the man, and I know the mine. His character is above reproach, and the mine is worth far more than he asks for it."

Meantime I spent all my evenings at the minister's with Portia. I didn't say a word to her about the mine; I saved it for a surprise. We talked salary; never anything but salary and love; sometimes love, sometimes salary, sometimes love and salary together. And my! The interest the minister's wife and daughter took in our little affair, and the endless ingenuities they invented to save us from interruption, and to keep the minister in the dark and unsuspicious—well, it was just lovely of them!

When the month was up, at last, I had a million dollars to my credit in the London and County Bank, and Hastings was fixed in the same way. Dressed at my level best, I drove by the house in Portland Place, judged by the look of things that my birds were home again, went on toward the minister's and got my precious, and we started back, talking salary with all our might. She was so excited and anxious that it made her just intolerably beautiful. I said:

"Dearie, the way you're looking it's a crime to strike for a salary a single penny under three thousand a year."

"Henry, Henry, you'll ruin us!"

"Don't you be afraid. Just keep up those looks, and trust to me. It'll all come out right."

So as it turned out, I had to keep bolstering up *her* courage all the way. She kept pleading with me, and saying:

"Oh, please remember that if we ask for too much we may get no salary at all; and then what will become of us, with no way in the world to earn our living?"

We were ushered in by that same servant, and there they were, the two old gentlemen. Of course they were surprised to see that wonderful creature with me, but I said:

"It's all right, gentlemen; she is my future stay and helpmate."

And I introduced them to her, and called them by name. It didn't surprise them; they knew I would know enough to consult the directory. They seated us, and were very polite to me, and very solicitous to relieve her from embarrassment, and put her as much at her ease as they could. Then I said:

"Gentlemen, I am ready to report."

"We are glad to hear it," said *my* man, "for now we can decide the bet which my brother Abel and I made. If you have won for me, you shall have any situation in my gift. Have you the million-pound note?"

"Here it is, sir," and I handed it to him.

"I've won!" he shouted, and slapped Abel on the back. "*Now* what do you say, brother?"

"I say he *did* survive, and I've lost twenty thousand pounds. I never would have believed it."

"I've a further report to make," I said, "and a pretty long one. I want you to let me come soon, and detail my whole month's history; and I promise you it's worth hearing. Meantime, take a look at that."

"What a man! Certificate of deposit for £200,000? Is it yours?"

"Mine. I earned it by thirty days' judicious use of that little loan you let me have. And the only use I made of it was to buy trifles and offer the bill in change."

"Come, this is astonishing! It's incredible, man!"

"Never mind, I'll prove it. Don't take my word unsupported."

But now Portia's turn was come to be surprised. Her eyes spread wide, and she said:

"Henry, is that really your money? Have you been fibbing to me?"

"I have indeed, dearie. But you'll forgive me, *I* know."

She put up an arch pout, and said:

"Don't you be so sure. You are a naughty thing to deceive me so!"

"Oh, you'll get over it, sweetheart, you'll get over it; it was only fun, you know. Come, let's be going."

"But wait, wait! The situation, you know. I want to give you the situation," said my man.

"Well," I said, "I'm just as grateful as I can be, but really I don't want one."

"But you can have the very choicest one in my gift."

"Thanks again, with all my heart; but I don't even want *that* one."

"Henry, I'm ashamed of you. You don't half thank the good gentleman. May I do it for you?"

"Indeed you shall, dear, if you can improve it. Let us see you try."

She walked to my man, got up in his lap, put her arm round his neck, and kissed him right on the mouth. Then the two old gentlemen shouted with laughter, but I was dumbfounded, just petrified, as you may say. Portia said:

"Papa, he has said you haven't a situation in your gift that he'd take; and I feel just as hurt as—"

"My darling! Is that your papa?"

"Yes; he's my steppapa, and the dearest one that ever was. You understand now, don't you, why I was able to laugh when you told me at the minister's, not knowing my relationships, what trouble and worry papa's and Uncle Abel's scheme was giving you?"

Of course I spoke right up, now, without any fooling, and went straight to the point.

"Oh, my dearest dear sir, I want to take back what I said. You *have* got a situation open that I want."

"Name it."

"Son-in-law."

"Well, well, well! But you know, if you haven't ever served in that capacity, you of course can't furnish recommendations of a sort to satisfy the conditions of the contract, and so—"

"Try me—oh, do, I beg of you! Only just try me thirty or forty years, and if—"

"Oh, well, all right; it's a little thing to ask. Take her along."

Happy, we too? There are not words enough in the unabridged to describe it. And when London got the whole history, a day or two later, of my month's adventures with that banknote, and how they ended, did London talk, and have a good time? Yes.

My Portia's papa took that friendly and hospitable bill back to the Bank of England and cashed it; then the Bank canceled it and made him a present of it, and he gave it to us at our wedding, and it has always hung in its frame in the sacredest place in our home, ever since. For it gave me my Portia. But for it I could not have remained in London, would not have appeared at the minister's, never should have met her. And so I always say, "Yes, it's a million-pounder, as you see; but it never made but one purchase in its life, and *then* got the article about a tenth part of its value."

THE DISAPPEARANCE OF CRISPINA UMBERLEIGH

SAKI

IN A FIRST-CLASS CARRIAGE OF A TRAIN speeding Balkanward across the flat, green Hungarian plain, two Britons sat in friendly, fitful converse. They had first foregathered in the cold grey dawn at the frontier line, where the presiding eagle takes on an extra head and Teuton lands pass from Hohenzollern to Habsburg keeping—and where a probing official beak requires to delve in polite and perhaps perfunctory, but always tiresome, manner into the baggage of sleep-hungry passengers. After a day's break of their journey at Vienna the travelers had again foregathered at the trainside and paid one another the compliment of settling instinctively into the same carriage. The elder of the two had the appearance and manner of a diplomat; in point of fact he was the well-connected foster-brother of a wine business. The other was certainly a journalist. Neither man was talkative and each was grateful to the other for not being talkative. That is why from time to time they talked.

One topic of conversation naturally thrust itself forward in front of all others. In Vienna the previous day they had learned of the mysterious vanishing of a world-famous picture from the walls of the Louvre.

"A dramatic disappearance of that sort is sure to produce a crop of imitations," said the Journalist.

"It has had a lot of anticipations, for the matter of that," said the Wine-brother.

"Oh, of course there have been thefts from the Louvre before."

"I was thinking of the spiriting away of human beings rather than pictures. In particular I was thinking of the case of my aunt, Crispina Umberleigh."

"I remember hearing something of the affair," said the Journalist, "but I was away from England at the time. I never quite knew what was supposed to have happened."

"You may hear what really happened if you will respect it as a confidence," said the Wine Merchant. "In the first place I may say that the disappearance of Mrs. Umberleigh was not regarded by the family entirely as a bereavement. My uncle, Edward Umberleigh, was not by any means a weak-kneed individual, in fact in the world of politics he had to be reckoned with more or less as a strong man, but he was unmistakably dominated by Crispina; indeed I never met any human being who was not frozen into subjection when brought into prolonged contact with her. Some people are born to command; Crispina Mrs. Umberleigh was born to legislate, codify, administrate, censor, license, ban, execute, and sit in judgment generally. If she was not born with that destiny she adopted it at an early age. From the kitchen regions upwards everyone in the household came under her despotic sway and stayed there with the submissiveness of molluscs involved in a glacial epoch. As a nephew on a footing of only occasional visits she affected me merely as an epidemic, disagreeable while it lasted, but without any permanent effect; but her own sons and daughters stood in mortal awe of her; their studies, friendships, diet, amusements, religious observances, and way of doing their hair were all regulated and ordained according to the august lady's will and pleasure. This will help you to understand the sensation of stupefaction which was caused in the family when she unobtrusively and inexplicably vanished. It was as though St. Paul's Cathedral or the Piccadilly Hotel had disappeared in the night, leaving nothing but an open space to mark where it had stood. As far as was known nothing was troubling her; in fact there was much before her to make life particularly well worth living. The youngest boy had come back from school with an unsatisfactory report, and she was to have sat in judgment on him the very afternoon of the day she disappeared—if it had been he who had vanished in a hurry one could have supplied the motive. Then she was in the middle of a newspaper correspondence with a rural dean in which she had already proved him guilty of heresy, inconsistency, and unworthy quibbling, and no ordinary consideration would have induced her to discontinue the controversy. Of course the matter was put in the hands of the police, but as far as possible it was kept out of the papers, and the generally accepted explanation of her withdrawal from her social circle was that she had gone into a nursing home."

"And what was the immediate effect on the home circle?" asked the Journalist.

"All the girls bought themselves bicycles; the feminine cycling craze was still in existence, and Crispina had rigidly vetoed any participation in it among the members of her household. The youngest boy let himself go to such an extent during his next term that it had to be his last as far as that particular establishment was concerned. The elder boys propounded a theory that their mother might be wandering somewhere abroad, and searched for her assiduously, chiefly, it must be admitted, in a class of Montmartre resort where it was extremely improbable that she would be found."

"And all this while couldn't your uncle get hold of the least clue?"

"As a matter of fact he had received some information, though of course I did not know of it at the time. He got a message one day telling him that his wife had been kidnapped and smuggled out of the country; she was said to be hidden away, in one of the islands off the coast of Norway I think it was, in comfortable surroundings and well cared for. And with the information came a demand for money; a lump sum was to be handed over to her kidnappers and a further sum of £2,000 was to be paid yearly. Failing this she would be immediately restored to her family."

The Journalist was silent for a moment, and then began to laugh quietly.

"It was certainly an inverted form of holding to ransom," he said.

"If you had known my aunt," said the Wine Merchant, "you would have wondered that they didn't put the figure higher."

"I realize the temptation. Did your uncle succumb to it?"

"Well, you see, he had to think of others as well as himself. For the family to have gone back into the Crispina thraldom after having tasted the delights of liberty would have been a tragedy, and there were even wider considerations to be taken into account. Since his bereavement he had unconsciously taken up a far bolder and more initiatory line in public affairs, and his popularity and influence had increased correspondingly. From being merely a strong man in the political world he began to be spoken of as *the* strong man. All this he knew would be jeopardized if he once more dropped into the social position of the husband of Mrs. Umberleigh. He was a rich man, and the £2,000 a year, though not exactly a fleabite, did not seem an extravagant price to pay for the boarding-out of Crispina. Of course, he had severe qualms of conscience about the arrangement. Later on, when he took me into his confidence, he told me that in paying the ransom, or hush-money as I should have called it, he was partly influenced by the fear that if he refused it the kidnappers might have vented their rage and disappointment on their captive. It was better, he said, to think of her being well cared for as a highly valued paying guest in one of the Lofoden Islands than to have her struggling miserably home in a maimed and mutilated condition. Anyway he paid the yearly installment as punctually as one pays a fire insurance, and with equal promptitude there would come an acknowledgment of the money and a brief statement to the effect that Crispina was in good health and fairly cheerful spirits. One report even mentioned that she was busying herself with a scheme for proposed reforms in Church management to be pressed on the local pastorate. Another spoke of a rheumatic attack and a journey to a 'cure' on the mainland, and on that occasion an additional eighty pounds was demanded and conceded. Of course it was to the interest of the kidnappers to keep their charge in good health, but the secrecy with which they managed to shroud their arrangements argued a really wonderful organization. If my uncle was paying a rather high price, at least he could console himself with the reflection that he was paying specialists' fees."

"Meanwhile had the police given up all attempts to track the missing lady?" asked the Journalist.

"Not entirely; they came to my uncle from time to time to report on clues which they thought might yield some elucidation as to her fate or whereabouts, but I think they had their suspicions that he was possessed of more information than he had put at their disposal. And then, after a disappearance of more than eight years, Crispina returned with dramatic suddenness to the home she had left so mysteriously."

"She had given her captors the slip?"

"She had never been captured. Her wandering away had been caused by a sudden and complete loss of memory. She usually dressed rather in the style of a superior kind of charwoman, and it was not so very surprising that she should have imagined that she was one, and still less that people should accept her statement and help her to get work. She had wandered as far afield as Birmingham, and found fairly steady employment there, her energy and enthusiasm in putting people's rooms in order counterbalancing her obstinate and domineering characteristics. It was the shock of being patronizingly addressed as 'my good woman' by a curate, who was disputing with her where the stove should be placed in a parish concert hall, that led to the sudden restoration of her memory. 'I think you forget who you are speaking to,' she observed crushingly, which was rather unduly severe, considering she had only just remembered it herself."

"But," exclaimed the Journalist, "the Lofoden Island people! Who had they got hold of?"

"A purely mythical prisoner. It was an attempt in the first place by someone who knew something of the domestic situation, probably a discharged valet, to bluff a lump sum out of Edward Umberleigh before the missing woman turned up; the subsequent yearly installments were an unlooked-for increment to the original haul.

"Crispina found that the eight years' interregnum had materially weakened her ascendency over her now grown-up offspring. Her husband, however, never accomplished anything great in the political world after her return; the strain of trying to account satisfactorily for an unspecified expenditure of sixteen thousand pounds spread over eight years sufficiently occupied his mental energies. Here is Belgrad and another custom house."

POISSON D'AVRIL

SOMERVILLE AND ROSS

THE ATMOSPHERE OF THE WAITING ROOM set at naught at a single glance the theory that there can be no smoke without fire. The stationmaster, when remonstrated with, stated, as an incontrovertible fact, that any chimney in the world would smoke in a south-easterly wind, and further, said there wasn't a poker, and that if you poked the fire the grate would fall out. He was, however, sympathetic, and went on his knees before the smouldering mound of slack, endeavouring to charm it to a smile by subtle proddings with the handle of the ticket-punch. Finally, he took me to his own kitchen fire and talked politics and salmon-fishing, the former with judicious attention to my presumed point of view, and careful suppression of his own, the latter with no less tactful regard for my admission that for three days I had not caught a fish, while the steam rose from my wet boots, in witness of the ten miles of rain through which an outside car had carried me.

Before the train was signalled I realised for the hundredth time the magnificent superiority of the Irish mind to the trammels of officialdom, and the inveterate supremacy in Ireland of the Personal Element.

"You might get a foot-warmer at Carrig Junction," said a species of lay porter in a knitted jersey, ramming my suitcase upside down under the seat. "Sometimes they're in it, and more times they're not."

The train dragged itself rheumatically from the station, and a cold spring rain—the time was the middle of a most inclement April—smote it in flank as it came into the open. I pulled up both windows and began to smoke; there is, at least, a semblance of warmth in a thoroughly vitiated atmosphere.

It is my wife's habit to assert that I do not read her letters, and being now on my way to join her and my family in Gloucestershire, it seemed a sound thing to study again her latest letter of instructions.

"I am starting today, as Alice wrote to say we must be there two days before the wedding, so as to have a rehearsal for the pages. Their dresses have come, and they look too delicious in them—"

(I omit here profuse particulars not pertinent to this tale)—

"It is sickening for you to have had such bad sport. If the worst comes to the worst couldn't you buy one?—"

I smote my hand upon my knee. I had forgotten the infernal salmon! What a score for Philippa! If these contretemps would only teach her that I was not to be relied upon, they would have their uses, but experience is wasted upon her; I have no objection to being called an idiot, but, that being so, I ought to be allowed the privileges and exemptions proper to idiots. Philippa had, no doubt, written to Alice Hervey, and assured her that Sinclair would be only too delighted to bring her a salmon, and Alice Hervey, who was rich enough to find much enjoyment in saving money, would reckon upon it, to its final fin in mayonnaise.

Plunged in morose meditations, I progressed through a country parcelled out by shaky and crooked walls into a patchwood of hazel scrub and rocky fields, veiled in rain. About every six miles there was a station, wet and windswept; at one the sole occurrence was the presentation of a newspaper to the guard by the stationmaster; at the next the guard read aloud some choice excerpts from the same to the porter. The Personal Element was potent on this branch of the Munster and Connaught Railways. Routine, abhorrent to all artistic minds, was sheathed in conversation; even the engine-driver, a functionary ordinarily as aloof as the Mikado, alleviated his enforced isolation by sociable shrieks to every level crossing, while the long row of public-houses that formed, as far as I could judge, the town of Carrig, received a special and, as it seemed, humorous salutation.

The Time-Table decreed that we were to spend ten minutes at Carrig Junction; it was fifteen before the crowd of market people on the platform had been assimilated; finally, the window of a neighbouring carriage was flung open, and a wrathful English voice asked how much longer the train was going to wait. The stationmaster, who was at the moment engrossed in conversation with the guard and a man who was carrying a long parcel wrapped in newspaper, looked round, and said gravely—

"Well, now, that's a mystery!"

The man with the parcel turned away, and convulsively studied a poster. The guard put his hand over his mouth.

The voice, still more wrathfully, demanded the earliest hour at which its owner could get to Belfast.

"Ye'll be asking me next when I take me breakfast," replied the stationmaster, without haste or palpable annoyance.

The window went up again with a bang, the man with the parcel dug the guard in the ribs with his elbow, and the parcel slipped from under his arm and fell on the platform.

"Oh my! oh my! Me fish!" exclaimed the man, solicitously picking up a remarkably good-looking salmon that had slipped from its wrapping of newspaper.

Inspiration came to me, and I, in my turn, opened my window and summoned the stationmaster.

Would his friend sell me the salmon? The stationmaster entered upon the mission with ardour, but without success.

No; the gentleman was only just after running down to the town for it in the delay, but why wouldn't I run down and get one for myself? There was half-a-dozen more of them below at Coffey's, selling cheap; there would be time enough, the mail wasn't signalled yet.

I jumped from the carriage and doubled out of the station at top speed, followed by an assurance from the guard that he would not forget me.

Congratulating myself on the ascendancy of the Personal Element, I sped through the soapy limestone and mud towards the public-houses. En route I met a heated man carrying yet another salmon, who, without preamble, informed me that there were three or four more good fish in it, and that he was after running down from the train himself.

"Ye have whips o' time!" he called after me. "It's the first house that's not a public-house. Ye'll see boots in the window—she'll give them for tenpence a pound if ye're stiff with her!"

I ran past the public-houses.

"Tenpence a pound!" I exclaimed inwardly, "at this time of year! That's good enough."

Here I perceived the house with boots in the window, and dived into its dark doorway.

A cobbler was at work behind a low counter. He mumbled something about Herself, through lengths of waxed thread that hung across his mouth, a fat woman appeared at an inner door, and at that moment I heard, appallingly near, the whistle of the incoming mail. The fat woman grasped the situation in an instant, and with what appeared but one movement, snatched a large fish from the floor of the room behind her and flung a newspaper round it.

"Eight pound weight!" she said, swiftly. "Ten Shillings!"

A convulsive effort of mental arithmetic assured me that this was more than tenpence a pound, but it was not the moment for stiffness. I shoved a half-sovereign into her fishy hand, clasped my salmon in my arms, and ran.

Needless to say it was uphill, and at the steepest gradient another whistle stabbed me like a spur; above the station roof successive and advancing puffs of steam warned me that the worst had probably happened, but still I ran. When I gained the platform my train was already clear of it, but the Personal Element held good. Every soul in the station, or so it seemed to me, lifted up his voice and yelled. The stationmaster put his fingers in his mouth and sent after the departing train an unearthly whistle, with a high trajectory and a serrated edge. It took effect; the train slackened, I plunged from the platform and followed it up the rail, and every window in both trains blossomed with the heads of deeply interested spectators. The guard met me on the line, very apologetic and primed with an explanation that the gentleman going for the boat-train wouldn't let him wait any longer, while from our rear came an exultant cry from the stationmaster.

"Ye *told* him ye wouldn't forget him!"

"There's a few countrywomen in your carriage, sir," said the guard, ignoring the taunt, as he shoved me and my salmon up the side of the train, "but they'll be getting out in a couple of stations. There wasn't another seat in the train for them!"

My sensational return to my carriage was viewed with the utmost sympathy by no less than seven shawled and cloaked countrywomen. In order to make room for me, one of them seated herself on the floor with her basket in her lap, another, on the seat opposite to me, squeezed herself under the central elbow flap that had been turned up to make room. The aromas of wet cloaks, turf smoke, and salt fish formed a potent blend. I was excessively hot, and the eyes of the seven women were fastened upon me with intense and unwearying interest.

"Move west a small piece, Mary Jack, if you please," said a voluminous matron in the corner, "I declare we're as throng as three in a bed this minute!"

"Why then Julia Casey, there's little throubling yourself," grumbled the woman under the flap. "Look at the way meself is! I wonder is it to be putting humps on themselves the gentry has them things down on top o' them! I'd sooner be carrying a basket of turnips on me back than to be scrooged this way!"

The woman on the floor at my feet rolled up at me a glance of compassionate amusement at this rustic ignorance, and tactfully changed the conversation by supposing that it was at Coffey's I got the salmon.

I said it was.

There was a silence, during which it was obvious that one question burned in every heart.

"I'll go bail she axed him tinpence!" said the woman under the flap, as one who touches the limits of absurdity.

"It's a beautiful fish!" I said defiantly. "Eight pounds weight. I gave her ten shillings for it."

What is described in newspapers as "sensation in court" greeted this confession.

"Look!" said the woman under the flap, darting her head out of the hood of her cloak, like a tortoise, "t' is what it is, ye haven't as much roguery in your heart as'd make ye a match for her!"

"Divil blow the ha'penny Eliza Coffey paid for that fish!" burst out the fat woman in the corner. "Thim lads o' her's had a creel full o' thim snatched this morning before it was making day!"

"How would the gentleman be a match for her!" shouted the woman on the floor through a long-drawn whistle that told of a coming station. "Sure a Turk itself wouldn't be a match for her! That one has a tongue that'd clip a hedge!"

At the station they clambered out laboriously, and with groaning. I handed down to them their monster baskets, laden, apparently, with ingots of lead; they told me in return that I was a fine *grauver* man, and it was a pity there weren't more like me; they wished, finally, that my journey might well thrive with me, and passed from my ken, bequeathing to me, after the agreeable manner of their kind, a certain comfortable mental sleekness that reason cannot immediately dispel. They also left me in possession of the fact that I was about to present the irreproachable Alice Hervey with a contraband salmon.

The afternoon passed cheerlessly into evening, and my journey did not conspicuously thrive with me. Somewhere in the dripping twilight I changed trains, and again later on, and at each change the salmon moulted some more of its damp raiment of newspaper, and I debated seriously the idea of interring it, regardless of consequences, in my portmanteau. A lamp was banged into the roof of my carriage, half an inch of orange flame, poised in a large glass globe, like a goldfish, and of about as much use as an illuminant. Here also was handed in the dinner basket that I had wired for, and its contents, arid though they were, enabled me to achieve at least some measure of mechanical distension, followed by a dreary lethargy that was not far from drowsiness.

At the next station we paused long; nothing whatever occurred, and the rain drummed patiently upon the roof. Two nuns and some schoolgirls were in the carriage next door, and their voices came plaintively and in snatches through the partition; after a long period of apparent collapse, during which I closed my eyes to evade the cold gaze of the salmon through the netting, a voice in the next carriage said resourcefully:

"Oh, girls, I'll tell you what we'll do! We'll say the Rosary!"

"Oh, that will be lovely!" said another voice; "well, who'll give it out? Theresa Condon, you'll give it out."

Theresa Condon gave it out, in a not unmelodious monotone, interspersed with the responses, always in a lower cadence; the words were indistinguishable, but the rise and fall of the western voices was lulling as the hum of bees. I fell asleep.

I awoke in total darkness; the train was motionless, and complete and profound silence reigned. We were at a station, that much I discerned by the light of the dim lamp at the far end of a platform glistening with wet. I struck a match and ascertained that it was eleven o'clock, precisely the hour at which I was to board the mail train. I jumped out and ran down the platform; there was no one in the train; there was no one even on the engine, which was forlornly hissing to itself in the silence. There was not a human being anywhere. Every door was closed, and all was dark. The nameboard of the station was faintly visible; with a lighted match I went along it letter by letter. It seemed as if the whole alphabet were in it, and by the time I had got to the end I had forgotten the beginning. One fact I had, however, mastered, that it was not the junction at which I was to catch the mail.

I was undoubtedly awake, but for a moment I was inclined to entertain the idea that there had been an accident, and that I had entered upon existence in another world. Once more I assailed the station house and the appurtenances thereof, the ticket office, the waiting room, finally, and at some distance, the goods store, outside which the single lamp of the station commented feebly on the drizzle and the darkness. As I approached it a crack of light under the door became perceptible, and a voice was suddenly uplifted within.

"Your best now agin that! Throw down your Jack!"

I opened the door with pardonable violence, and found the guard, the stationmaster, the driver, and the stoker, seated on barrels round a packing case, on which they were playing a game of cards.

To have too egregiously the best of a situation is not, to a generous mind, a source of strength. In the perfection of their overthrow I permitted the driver and stoker to wither from their places, and to fade away into the outer darkness without any suitable send-off; with the guard and the stationmaster I dealt more faithfully, but the pleasure of throwing water on drowned rats is not a lasting one. I accepted the statements that they thought there wasn't a Christian in the train, that a few minutes here or there wouldn't signify, that they would have me at the junction in twenty minutes, and it was often the mail was late.

Fired by this hope I hurried back to my carriage, preceded at an emulous gallop by the officials. The guard thrust in with me the lantern from the card table, and fled to his van.

"Mind the goods, Tim!" shouted the stationmaster, as he slammed my door, "she might be coming anytime now!"

The answer travelled magnificently back from the engine.

"Let her come! She'll meet her match!" A war-whoop upon the steam whistle fittingly closed the speech, and the train sprang into action.

We had about fifteen miles to go, and we banged and bucketed over it in what was, I should imagine, record time. The carriage felt as if it were galloping on four wooden legs, my teeth chattered in my head, and the salmon slowly churned its way forth from its newspaper, and moved along the netting with dreadful stealth.

All was of no avail.

"Well," said the guard, as I stepped forth onto the deserted platform of Loughranny, "that owld Limited Mail's th' unpunctualest thrain in Ireland! If you're a minute late she's gone from you, and maybe if you were early you might be half-an-hour waiting for her!"

On the whole the guard was a gentleman. He said he would show me the best hotel in the town, though he feared I would be hard set to get a bed anywhere because of the *"Feis"* (a Feis, I should explain, is a Festival, devoted to competitions in Irish songs and dances). He shouldered my portmanteau, he even grappled successfully with the salmon, and, as we traversed the empty streets, he explained to me how easily I could catch the morning boat from Rosslare, and how it was, as a matter of fact, quite the act of Providence that my original scheme had been frustrated.

All was dark at the uninviting portals of the hotel favoured by the guard. For a full five minutes we waited at them, ringing hard: I suggested that we should try elsewhere.

"He'll come," said the guard, with the confidence of the Pied Piper of Hamelin, retaining an implacable thumb upon the button of the electric bell. "He'll come. Sure it rings in his room!"

The victim came, half awake, half dressed, and with an inch of dripping candle in his fingers. There was not a bed there, he said, nor in the town neither.

I said I would sit in the dining room till the time for the early train.

"Sure there's five beds in the dining room," replied the boots, "and there's mostly two every bed."

His voice was firm, but there was a wavering look in his eye.

"What about the billiard room, Mike?" said the guard, in wooing tones.

"Ah, God bless you! We have a mattress on the table this minute!" answered the boots, wearily, "and the fellow that got the First Prize for Reels asleep on top of it!"

"Well, and can't ye put the palliasse on the floor under it, ye omadhawn?" said the guard, dumping my luggage and the salmon in the hall, "sure there's no snugger place in the house! I must run away home now, before Herself thinks I'm dead altogether!"

His retreating footsteps went lightly away down the empty street.

"Anything don't throuble *him!*" said the boots bitterly.

As for me, nothing save the Personal Element stood between me and destitution.

It was in the dark of the early morning that I woke again to life and its troubles. A voice, dropping, as it were, over the edge of some smothering over-world, had awakened me. It was the voice of the First Prize for Reels, descending through a pocket of the billiard table.

"I beg your pardon, sir, are ye going on the 5 to Cork?"

I grunted a negative.

"Well, if ye were, ye'd be late," said the voice.

I received this useful information in indignant silence, and endeavoured to wrap myself again in the vanishing skirts of a dream.

"I'm going on the 6:30 meself," proceeded the voice, "and it's unknown to me how I'll put on me boots. Me feet is swelled the size o' three-pound loaves with the dint of the little dancing-shoes I had on me in the competition last night. Me feet's delicate that way, and I'm a great epicure about me boots."

I snored aggressively, but the dream was gone. So, for all practical purposes, was the night.

The First Prize for Reels arose, presenting an astonishing spectacle of grass-green breeches, a white shirt, and pearl-grey stockings, and accomplished a toilet that consisted of removing these and putting on ordinary garments, completed by the apparently excruciating act of getting into his boots. At any other hour of the day I might have been sorry for him. He then removed himself and his belongings to the hall, and there entered upon a resounding conversation with the boots, while I crawled forth from my lair to renew the strife with circumstances and to endeavour to compose a telegram to Alice Hervey of explanation and apology that should cost less than seven and sixpence. There was also the salmon to be dealt with.

Here the boots intervened, opportunely, with a cup of tea, and the intelligence that he had already done up the salmon in straw bottle-covers and brown paper, and that I could travel Europe with it if I liked. He further informed me that he would run up to the station with the luggage now, and that maybe I wouldn't mind carrying the fish myself; it was on the table in the hall.

My train went at 6:15. The boots had secured for me one of many empty carriages, and lingered conversationally till the train started; he regretted politely my bad night at the hotel, and assured me that only for Jimmy Durkan having a little drink taken—Jimmy Durkan was the First Prize for Reels—he would have turned him off the billiard table for my benefit. He finally confided to me that Mr. Durkan was engaged to his sister, and was a rising baker in the town of Limerick, "indeed," he said, "any girl might be glad to get him. He dances like whale-bone, and he makes grand bread!"

Here the train started.

It was late that night when, stiff, dirty, with tired eyes blinking in the dazzle of electric lights, I was conducted by the Herveys' beautiful footman into the Herveys' baronial hall, and was told by the Herveys' imperial butler that dinner was over, and the gentlemen had just gone into the drawing room. I was in the act of hastily declining to join them there, when a voice cried—

"Here he is!"

And Philippa, rustling and radiant, came forth into the hall, followed in shimmers of satin, and flutterings of lace, by Alice Hervey, by the bride elect, and by the usual festive rout of exhilarated relatives, male and female, whose mission it is to keep things lively before a wedding.

"Is this a wedding present for me, Uncle Sinclair?" cried the bride elect, through a deluge of questions and commiserations, and snatched from under my arm the brown paper parcel that had remained there from force of direful habit.

"I advise you not to open it!" I exclaimed; "it's a salmon!"

The bride elect, with a shriek of disgust, and without an instant of hesitation, hurled it at her nearest neighbour, the head bridesmaid. The head bridesmaid, with an answering shriek, sprang to one side, and the parcel that I had cherished with a mother's care across two countries and a stormy channel, fell with a crash, on the flagged floor.

Why did it crash?

"A salmon!" screamed Philippa, gazing at the parcel, round which a pool was already forming, "why that's whisky! Can't you smell it?"

The footman here respectfully interposed, and kneeling down, cautiously extracted from folds of brown paper a straw bottle-cover full of broken glass and dripping with whisky.

"I'm afraid the other things are rather spoiled, sir," he said seriously, and drew forth, successively, a very large pair of high-low shoes, two long grey worsted stockings, and a pair of grass-green britches.

They brought the house down, in a manner doubtless familiar to them when they shared the triumphs of Mr. Jimmy Durkan, but they left Alice Hervey distinctly cold.

"You know, darling," she said to Philippa afterwards, "I don't think it was very clever of dear Sinclair to take the wrong parcel. I *had* counted on that salmon."

BABY SYLVESTER

BRET HARTE

IT WAS AT A LITTLE MINING CAMP in the California Sierras that he first dawned upon me in all his grotesque sweetness.

I had arrived early in the morning, but not in time to intercept the friend who was the object of my visit. He had gone "prospecting,"—so they told me on the river,—and would not probably return until late in the afternoon. They could not say what direction he had taken; they could not suggest that I would be likely to find him if I followed. But it was the general opinion that I had better wait.

I looked around me. I was standing upon the bank of the river; and apparently the only other human beings in the world were my interlocutors, who were even then just disappearing from my horizon, down the steep bank, toward the river's dry bed. I approached the edge of the bank.

Where could I wait?

Oh! anywhere,—down with them on the river-bar, where they were working, if I liked. Or I could make myself at home in any of those cabins that I found lying round loose. Or perhaps it would be cooler and pleasanter for me in my friend's cabin on the hill. Did I see those three large sugar-pines, and, a little to the right, a canvas roof and chimney, over the bushes? Well, that was my friend's,—that was Dick Sylvester's cabin. I could stake my horse in that little hollow, and just hang round there till he came. I would find some books in the shanty. I could amuse myself with them; or I could play with the baby.

Do what?

But they had already gone. I leaned over the bank, and called after their vanishing figures,—

"What did you say I could do?"

The answer floated slowly up on the hot, sluggish air,—

"Pla-a-y with the ba-by."

The lazy echoes took it up, and tossed it languidly from hill to hill, until Bald Mountain opposite made some incoherent remark about the baby; and then all was still.

I must have been mistaken. My friend was not a man of family; there was not a woman within forty miles of the river camp; he never was so passionately devoted to children as to import a luxury so expensive. I must have been mistaken.

I turned my horse's head toward the hill. As we slowly climbed the narrow trail, the little settlement might have been some exhumed Pompeiian suburb, so deserted and silent were its habitations. The open doors plainly disclosed each rudely-furnished interior,—the rough pine table, with the scant equipage of the morning meal still standing; the wooden bunk, with its tumbled and dishevelled blankets. A golden lizard, the very genius of desolate stillness, had stopped breathless upon the threshold of one cabin; a squirrel peeped impudently into the window of another; a woodpecker, with the general flavor of undertaking which distinguishes that bird, withheld his sepulchral hammer from the coffin lid of the roof on which he was professionally engaged, as we passed. For a moment I half regretted that I had not accepted the invitation to the riverbed; but, the next moment, a breeze swept up the long, dark canyon, and the waiting files of the pines beyond bent toward me in salutation. I think my horse understood, as well as myself, that it was the cabins that made the solitude human, and therefore unbearable; for he quickened his pace, and with a gentle trot brought me to the edge of the wood, and the three pines that stood like vedettes before the Sylvester outpost.

Unsaddling my horse in the little hollow, I unslung the long *riata* from the saddle-bow, and, tethering him to a young sapling, turned toward the cabin. But I had gone only a few steps, when I heard a quick trot behind me; and poor Pomposo, with every fibre tingling with fear, was at my heels. I looked hurriedly around. The breeze had died away; and only an occasional breath from the deep-chested woods, more like a long sigh than any articulate sound, or the dry singing of a cicala in the heated canyon, were to be heard. I examined the ground carefully for rattlesnakes, but in vain. Yet here was Pomposo shivering from his arched neck to his sensitive haunches, his very flanks pulsating with terror. I soothed him as well as I could, and then walked to the edge of the wood, and peered into its dark recesses. The bright flash of a bird's wing, or the quick dart of a squirrel, was all I saw. I confess it was with something of superstitious expectation that I again turned towards the cabin. A fairy-child, attended by Titania and her train, lying in an expensive cradle, would not have surprised me: a Sleeping Beauty, whose awakening would have repeopled these solitudes with life and energy, I am afraid I began to confidently look for, and would have kissed without hesitation.

But I found none of these. Here was the evidence of my friend's taste and refinement, in the hearth swept scrupulously clean, in the picturesque arrangement of the fur-skins that covered the floor and furniture, and the striped *serápe* lying on the wooden couch. Here were the walls fancifully papered with illustrations from "The London News"; here was the woodcut portrait of Mr. Emerson over the chimney, quaintly framed with blue-jays' wings; here were his few favorite books on the swinging-shelf; and here, lying upon the couch, the latest copy of "Punch." Dear Dick! The flour sack was sometimes empty; but the gentle satirist seldom missed his weekly visit.

I threw myself on the couch, and tried to read. But I soon exhausted my interest in my friend's library, and lay there staring through the open door on the green hillside beyond. The breeze again sprang up; and a delicious coolness, mixed with the rare incense of the woods, stole through the cabin. The slumbrous droning of bumblebees outside the canvas roof, the faint cawing of rooks on the opposite mountain, and the fatigue of my morning ride, began to droop my eyelids. I pulled the *serápe* over me, as a precaution against the freshening mountain breeze, and in a few moments was asleep.

I do not remember how long I slept. I must have been conscious, however, during my slumber, of my inability to keep myself covered by the *serápe;* for I awoke once or twice, clutching it with a despairing hand as it was disappearing over the foot of the couch. Then I became suddenly aroused to the fact that my efforts to retain it were resisted by some equally persistent force; and, letting it go, I was horrified at seeing it swiftly drawn under the couch. At this point I sat up, completely awake; for immediately after, what seemed to be an exaggerated muff began to emerge from under the couch. Presently it appeared fully, dragging the *serápe* after it. There was no mistaking it now: it was a baby bear,—a mere suckling, it was true, a helpless roll of fat and fur, but unmistakably a grizzly cub!

I cannot recall anything more irresistibly ludicrous than its aspect as it slowly raised its small, wondering eyes to mine. It was so much taller on its haunches than its shoulders, its forelegs were so disproportionately small, that, in walking, its hind feet invariably took precedence. It was perpetually pitching forward over its pointed, inoffensive nose, and recovering itself always, after these involuntary somersaults with the gravest astonishment. To add to its preposterous appearance, one of its hind feet was adorned by a shoe of Sylvester's, into which it had accidentally and inextricably stepped. As this somewhat impeded its first impulse to fly, it turned to me; and then, possibly recognizing in the stranger the same species as its master, it paused. Presently it slowly raised itself on its hind legs, and vaguely and deprecatingly waved a baby paw, fringed with little hooks of steel. I took the paw, and shook it gravely. From that moment we were friends. The little affair of the *serápe* was forgotten.

Nevertheless, I was wise enough to cement our friendship by an act of delicate courtesy. Following the direction of his eyes, I had no difficulty in finding on a shelf near the ridgepole the sugar box and the square lumps of white sugar that even the poorest miner is never without. While he was eating them, I had time to examine him more closely. His body was a silky, dark, but exquisitely modulated grey, deepening to black in his paws and muzzle. His fur was excessively long, thick, and soft as eiderdown; the cushions of flesh beneath perfectly infantine in their texture and contour. He was so very young, that the palms of his half-human feet were still tender as a baby's. Except for the bright blue, steely hooks, half sheathed in his little toes, there was not a single harsh outline or detail in his plump figure. He was as free from angles as one of Leda's offspring. Your caressing hand sank away in his fur with dreamy languor.

To look at him long was an intoxication of the senses; to pat him was a wild delirium; to embrace him, an utter demoralization of the intellectual faculties.

When he had finished the sugar, he rolled out of the door with a half-diffident, half-inviting look in his eyes as if he expected me to follow. I did so; but the sniffing and snorting of the keen-scented Pomposo in the hollow not only revealed the cause of his former terror, but decided me to take another direction. After a moment's hesitation, he concluded to go with me, although I am satisfied, from a certain impish look in his eye, that he fully understood and rather enjoyed the fright of Pomposo. As he rolled along at my side, with a gait not unlike a drunken sailor, I discovered that his long hair concealed a leather collar around his neck, which bore for its legend the single word "Baby!" I recalled the mysterious suggestion of the two miners. This, then, was the "baby" with whom I was to "play."

How we "played"; how Baby allowed me to roll him downhill, crawling and puffing up again each time with perfect good humor; how he climbed a young sapling after my Panama hat, which I had "shied" into one of the topmost branches; how, after getting it, he refused to descend until it suited his pleasure; how, when he did come down, he persisted in walking about on three legs, carrying my hat, a crushed and shapeless mass, clasped to his breast with the remaining one; how I missed him at last, and finally discovered him seated on a table in one of the tenantless cabins, with a bottle of syrup between his paws, vainly endeavoring to extract its contents,—these and other details of that eventful day I shall not weary the reader with now. Enough that, when Dick Sylvester returned, I was pretty well fagged out, and the baby was rolled up, an immense bolster, at the foot of the couch, asleep. Sylvester's first words after our greeting were,—

"Isn't he delicious?"

"Perfectly. Where did you get him?"

"Lying under his dead mother, five miles from here," said Dick, lighting his pipe. "Knocked her over at fifty yards: perfectly clean shot; never moved afterwards. Baby crawled out, scared, but unhurt. She must have been carrying him in her mouth, and dropped him when she faced me; for he wasn't more than three days old, and not steady on his pins. He takes the only milk that comes to the settlement, brought up by Adams

Express at seven o'clock every morning. They say he looks like me. Do you think so?" asked Dick with perfect gravity, stroking his hay-colored mustachios, and evidently assuming his best expression.

I took leave of the baby early the next morning in Sylvester's cabin, and, out of respect to Pomposo's feelings, rode by without any postscript of expression. But the night before I had made Sylvester solemnly swear, that, in the event of any separation between himself and Baby, it should revert to me. "At the same time," he had added, "it's only fair to say that I don't think of dying just yet, old fellow; and I don't know of anything else that would part the cub and me."

Two months after this conversation, as I was turning over the morning's mail at my office in San Francisco, I noticed a letter bearing Sylvester's familiar hand. But it was postmarked "Stockton," and I opened it with some anxiety at once. Its contents were as follows:—

"O Frank!—Don't you remember what we agreed upon anent the baby? Well, consider me as dead for the next six months, or gone where cubs can't follow me,—East. I know you love the baby; but do you think, dear boy,—now, really, do you think you *could* be a father to it? Consider this well. You are young, thoughtless, well-meaning enough; but dare you take upon yourself the functions of guide, genius, or guardian to one so young and guileless? Could you be the Mentor to this Telemachus? Think of the temptations of a metropolis. Look at the question well, and let me know speedily; for I've got him as far as this place, and he's kicking up an awful row in the hotel-yard, and rattling his chain like a maniac. Let me know by telegraph at once. Sylvester."

"P.S.—Of course he's grown a little, and doesn't take things always as quietly as he did. He dropped rather heavily on two of Watson's 'purps' last week, and snatched old Watson himself bald headed, for interfering. You remember Watson? For an intelligent man, he knows very little of California fauna. How are you fixed for bears on Montgomery Street, I mean in regard to corrals and things? S."

"P.P.S.—He's got some new tricks. The boys have been teaching him to put up his hands with them. He slings an ugly left. S."

I am afraid that my desire to possess myself of Baby overcame all other considerations; and I telegraphed an affirmative at once to Sylvester. When I reached my lodgings late that afternoon, my landlady was awaiting me with a telegram. It was two lines from Sylvester,—

"All right. Baby goes down on night-boat. Be a father to him. S."

It was due, then, at one o'clock that night. For a moment I was staggered at my own precipitation. I had as yet made no preparations, had said nothing to my landlady about her new guest. I expected to arrange everything in time; and now, through Sylvester's indecent haste, that time had been shortened twelve hours.

Something, however, must be done at once. I turned to Mrs. Brown. I had great reliance in her maternal instincts: I had that still greater reliance common to our sex in the general tenderheartedness of pretty women. But I confess I was alarmed. Yet, with a feeble smile, I tried to introduce the subject with classical ease and lightness. I even said, "If Shakespeare's Athenian clown, Mrs. Brown, believed that a lion among ladies was a dreadful thing, what must"— But here I broke down; for Mrs. Brown, with the awful intuition of her sex, I saw at once was more occupied with my manner than my speech. So I tried a business *brusquerie,* and, placing the telegram in her hand, said hurriedly, "We must do something about this at once. It's perfectly absurd; but he will be here at one tonight. Beg thousand pardons; but business prevented my speaking before"—and paused out of breath and courage.

Mrs. Brown read the telegram gravely, lifted her pretty eyebrows, turned the paper over, and looked on the other side, and then, in a remote and chilling voice, asked me if she understood me to say that the mother was coming also.

"Oh, dear no!" I exclaimed with considerable relief. "The mother is dead, you know. Sylvester, that is my friend who sent this, shot her when the baby was only three days old." But the expression of Mrs. Brown's face at this moment was so alarming, that I saw that nothing but the fullest explanation would save me. Hastily, and I fear not very coherently, I told her all.

She relaxed sweetly. She said I had frightened her with my talk about lions. Indeed, I think my picture of poor Baby, albeit a trifle highly colored, touched her motherly heart. She was even a little vexed at what she called Sylvester's "hard-heartedness." Still I was not without some apprehension. It was two months since I had seen him; and Sylvester's vague allusion to his "slinging an ugly left" pained me. I looked at sympathetic little Mrs. Brown; and the thought of Watson's pups covered me with guilty confusion.

Mrs. Brown had agreed to sit up with me until he arrived. One o'clock came, but no Baby. Two o'clock, three o'clock, passed. It was almost four when there was a wild clatter of horses' hoofs outside, and with a jerk a wagon stopped at the door. In an instant I had opened it, and confronted a stranger. Almost at the same moment, the horses attempted to run away with the wagon.

The stranger's appearance was, to say the least, disconcerting. His clothes were badly torn and frayed; his linen sack hung from his shoulders like a herald's apron; one of his hands was bandaged; his face scratched; and there was no hat on his dishevelled head. To add to the general effect, he had evidently sought relief from his woes in drink; and he swayed from side to side as he clung to the door-handle, and, in a very thick voice, stated that he had "suthin" for me outside. When he had finished, the horses made another plunge.

Mrs. Brown thought they must be frightened at something.

"Frightened!" laughed the stranger with bitter irony. "Oh, no! Hossish ain't frightened! On'y ran away four timesh comin' here. Oh, no! Nobody's frightened. Every thin's all ri'. Ain't it, Bill?" he said, addressing the driver. "On'y been overboard twish; knocked down a hatchway once. Thash nothin'! On'y two men unner doctor's han's at Stockton. Thash nothin'! Six hunner dollarsh cover all dammish."

I was too much disheartened to reply, but moved toward the wagon. The stranger eyed me with an astonishment that almost sobered him.

"Do you reckon to tackle that animile yourself?" he asked, as he surveyed me from head to foot.

I did not speak, but, with an appearance of boldness I was far from feeling, walked to the wagon, and called "Baby!"

"All ri'. Cash loose them straps, Bill, and stan' clear."

The straps were cut loose; and Baby, the remorseless, the terrible, quietly tumbled to the ground, and, rolling to my side, rubbed his foolish head against me.

I think the astonishment of the two men was beyond any vocal expression. Without a word, the drunken stranger got into the wagon, and drove away.

And Baby? He had grown, it is true, a trifle larger; but he was thin, and bore the marks of evident ill usage. His beautiful coat was matted and unkempt; and his claws, those bright steel hooks, had been ruthlessly pared to the quick. His eyes were furtive and restless; and the old expression of stupid good humor had changed to one of intelligent distrust. His intercourse with mankind had evidently quickened his intellect, without broadening his moral nature.

I had great difficulty in keeping Mrs. Brown from smothering him in blankets, and ruining his digestion with the delicacies of her larder; but I at last got him completely rolled up in the corner of my room, and asleep. I lay awake some time later with plans for his future. I finally determined to take him to Oakland—where I had built a little cottage, and always spent my Sundays—the very next day. And in the midst of a rosy picture of domestic felicity, I fell asleep.

When I awoke, it was broad day. My eyes at once sought the corner where Baby had been lying; but he was gone. I sprang from the bed, looked under it, searched the closet, but in vain. The door was still locked; but there were the marks of his blunted claws upon the sill of the window that I had forgotten to close. He had evidently escaped that way. But where? The window opened upon a balcony, to which the only other entrance was through the hall. He must be still in the house.

My hand was already upon the bell-rope; but I stayed it in time. If he had not made himself known, why should I disturb the house? I dressed myself hurriedly, and slipped into the hall. The first object that met my eyes was a boot lying upon the stairs. It bore the marks of Baby's teeth; and, as I looked along the hall, I saw too plainly that the usual array of freshly blackened boots and shoes before the lodgers' doors was not there. As I ascended the stairs, I found another, but with the blacking carefully licked off. On the third floor were two or three more boots, slightly mouthed; but at this point Baby's taste for blacking had evidently palled. A little farther on was a ladder, leading to an open scuttle. I mounted the ladder, and reached the flat roof, that formed a continuous level over the row of houses to the corner of the street. Behind the chimney on the very last roof, something was lurking. It was the fugitive Baby.

He was covered with dust and dirt and fragments of glass. But he was sitting on his hind legs, and was eating an enormous slab of peanut candy, with a look of mingled guilt and infinite satisfaction. He even, I fancied, slightly stroked his stomach with his disengaged forepaw as I approached. He knew that I was looking for him; and the expression of his eye said plainly, "The past, at least, is secure."

I hurried him, with the evidences of his guilt, back to the scuttle, and descended on tiptoe to the floor beneath. Providence favored us: I met no one on the stairs; and his own cushioned tread was inaudible. I think he was conscious of the dangers of detection; for he even forebore to breathe, or much less chew the last mouthful he had taken; and he skulked at my side with the syrup dropping from his motionless jaws. I think he would have silently choked to death just then, for my sake; and it was not until I had reached my room again, and threw myself panting on the sofa, that I saw how near strangulation he had been. He gulped once or twice apologetically, and then walked to the corner of his own accord, and rolled himself up like an immense sugarplum, sweating remorse and treacle at every pore.

I locked him in when I went to breakfast, when I found Mrs. Brown's lodgers in a state of intense excitement over certain mysterious events of the night before, and the dreadful revelations of the morning. It appeared that burglars had entered the block from the scuttles; that, being suddenly alarmed, they had quitted our house without committing any depredation, dropping even the boots they had collected in the halls; but that a desperate attempt had been made to force the till in the confectioner's shop on the corner, and that the glass showcases had been ruthlessly smashed. A courageous servant in No. 4 had seen a masked burglar, on his hands and knees, attempting to enter their scuttle; but, on her shouting, "Away wid yees!" he instantly fled.

I sat through this recital with cheeks that burned uncomfortably; nor was I the less embarrassed, on raising my eyes, to meet Mrs. Brown's fixed curiously and mischievously on mine. As soon as I could make my escape from the table, I did so, and, running rapidly upstairs, sought refuge from any possible inquiry in my own room. Baby was still asleep in the corner. It would not be safe to remove him until the lodgers had gone downtown; and I was revolving in my mind the expediency of keeping him until night veiled his obtrusive eccentricity from the public eye, when there came a cautious tap at my door. I opened it. Mrs. Brown slipped in quietly, closed the door softly, stood with her back against it, and her hand on the knob, and beckoned me mysteriously towards her. Then she asked in a low voice,—

"Is hair-dye poisonous?"

I was too confounded to speak.

"Oh, do! you know what I mean," she said impatiently. "This stuff." She produced suddenly from behind her a bottle with a Greek label so long as to run two or three times spirally around it from top to bottom. "He says it isn't a dye: it's a vegetable preparation, for invigorating"—

"Who says?" I asked despairingly.

"Why, Mr. Parker, of course!" said Mrs. Brown severely, with the air of having repeated the name a great many times,—"the old gentleman in the room above. The simple question I want to ask," she continued with the calm manner of one who has just convicted another of gross ambiguity of language, "is only this: If some of this stuff were put in a saucer, and left carelessly on the table, and a child, or a baby, or a cat, or any young animal, should come in at the window, and drink it up,—a whole saucer full,—because it had a sweet taste, would it be likely to hurt them?"

I cast an anxious glance at Baby, sleeping peacefully in the corner, and a very grateful one at Mrs. Brown, and said I didn't think it would.

"Because," said Mrs. Brown loftily as she opened the door, "I thought, if it was poisonous, remedies might be used in time. Because," she added suddenly, abandoning her lofty manner, and wildly rushing to the corner with a frantic embrace of the unconscious Baby, "because, if any nasty stuff should turn its booful hair a horrid green, or a naughty pink, it would break its own muzzer's heart, it would!"

But, before I could assure Mrs. Brown of the inefficiency of hair dye as an internal application, she had darted from the room.

That night, with the secrecy of defaulters, Baby and I decamped from Mrs. Brown's. Distrusting the too emotional nature of that noble animal, the horse, I had recourse to a handcart, drawn by a stout Irishman, to convey my charge to the ferry. Even then, Baby refused to go, unless I walked by the cart, and at times rode in it.

"I wish," said Mrs. Brown, as she stood by the door, wrapped in an immense shawl, and saw us depart, "I wish it looked less solemn,—less like a pauper's funeral."

I must admit, that, as I walked by the cart that night, I felt very much as if I were accompanying the remains of some humble friend to his last resting place; and that, when I was obliged to ride in it, I never could entirely convince myself that I was not helplessly overcome by liquor, or the victim of an accident, *en route* to the hospital. But at last we reached the ferry. On the boat, I think no one discovered Baby, except a drunken man, who approached me to ask for a light for his cigar, but who suddenly dropped it, and fled in dismay to the gentlemen's cabin, where his incoherent ravings were luckily taken for the earlier indications of *delirium tremens.*

It was nearly midnight when I reached my little cottage on the outskirts of Oakland; and it was with a feeling of relief and security that I entered, locked the door, and turned him loose in the hall, satisfied that henceforward his depredations would be limited to my own property. He was very quiet that night; and after he had tried to mount the hat-rack, under the mistaken impression that it was intended for his own gymnastic exercise, and knocked all the hats off, he went peaceably to sleep on the rug.

In a week, with the exercise afforded him by the run of a large, carefully boarded enclosure, he recovered his health, strength, spirits, and much of his former beauty. His presence was unknown to my neighbors, although it was noticeable that horses invariably "shied" in passing to the windward of my house, and that the baker and milkman had great difficulty in the delivery of their wares in the morning, and indulged in unseemly and unnecessary profanity in so doing.

At the end of the week, I determined to invite a few friends to see the Baby, and to that purpose wrote a number of formal invitations. After descanting, at some length, on the great expense and danger attending his capture and training, I offered a programme of the performance, of the "Infant Phenomenon of Sierran Solitudes," drawn up into the highest professional profusion of alliteration and capital letters. A few extracts will give the reader some idea of his educational progress:—

1. He will, rolled up in a Round Ball, roll down the Wood-Shed Rapidly, illustrating His manner of Escaping from His Enemy in His Native Wilds.
2. He will Ascend the Well-Pole, and remove from the Very Top a Hat, and as much of the Crown and Brim thereof, as May be Permitted.

3. He will perform in a pantomime, descriptive of the Conduct of the Big Bear, The Middle-Sized Bear, and The Little Bear of the Popular Nursery Legend.
4. He will shake his chain Rapidly, showing his Manner of striking Dismay and Terror in the Breasts of Wanderers in Ursine Wildernesses.

The morning of the exhibition came; but an hour before the performance the wretched Baby was missing. The Chinese cook could not indicate his whereabouts. I searched the premises thoroughly; and then, in despair, took my hat, and hurried out into the narrow lane that led toward the open fields and the woods beyond. But I found no trace nor track of Baby Sylvester. I returned, after an hour's fruitless search, to find my guests already assembled on the rear veranda. I briefly recounted my disappointment, my probable loss, and begged their assistance.

"Why," said a Spanish friend, who prided himself on his accurate knowledge of English, to Barker, who seemed to be trying vainly to rise from his reclining position on the veranda, "why do you not disengage yourself from the veranda of our friend? And why, in the name of Heaven, do you attach to yourself so much of this thing, and make to yourself such unnecessary contortion? Ah," he continued, suddenly withdrawing one of his own feet from the veranda with an evident effort, "I am myself attached! Surely it is something here!"

It evidently was. My guests were all rising with difficulty. The floor of the veranda was covered with some glutinous substance. It was—syrup!

I saw it all in a flash. I ran to the barn. The keg of "golden syrup," purchased only the day before, lay empty upon the floor. There were sticky tracks all over the enclosure, but still no Baby.

"There's something moving the ground over there by that pile of dirt," said Barker.

He was right. The earth was shaking in one corner of the enclosure like an earthquake. I approached cautiously. I saw, what I had not before noticed, that the ground was thrown up; and there, in the middle of an immense grave-like cavity, crouched Baby Sylvester, still digging, and slowly but surely sinking from sight in a mass of dust and clay.

What were his intentions? Whether he was stung by remorse, and wished to hide himself from my reproachful eyes, or whether he was simply trying to dry his syrup-besmeared coat, I never shall know; for that day, alas! was his last with me.

He was pumped upon for two hours, at the end of which time he still yielded a thin treacle. He was then taken, and carefully inwrapped in blankets, and locked up in the storeroom. The next morning he was gone! The lower portion of the window sash and pane were gone too. His successful experiments on the fragile texture of glass at the confectioner's, on the first day of his entrance to civilization, had not been lost upon him. His first essay at combining cause and effect ended in his escape.

Where he went, where he hid, who captured him, if he did not succeed in reaching the foothills beyond Oakland, even the offer of a large reward, backed by the efforts of an intelligent police, could not discover. I never saw him again from that day until—

Did I see him? I was in a horse-car on Sixth Avenue, a few days ago, when the horses suddenly became unmanageable, and left the track for the sidewalk, amid the oaths and execrations of the driver. Immediately in front of the car a crowd had gathered around two performing bears and a showman. One of the animals, thin, emaciated, and the mere wreck of his native strength, attracted my attention. I endeavored to attract his. He turned a pair of bleared, sightless eyes in my direction; but there was no sign of recognition. I leaned from the car window, and called softly, "Baby!" But he did not heed. I closed the window. The car was just moving on, when he suddenly turned, and, either by accident or design, thrust a callous paw through the glass.

"It's worth a dollar and half to put in a new pane," said the conductor, "if folks will play with bears!"—

LINGERING ENCOUNTERS

THE DOOR IN THE WALL

H. G. WELLS

One confidential evening, not three months ago, Lionel Wallace told me this story of the Door in the Wall. And at the time I thought that so far as he was concerned it was a true story.

He told it to me with such a direct simplicity of conviction that I could not do otherwise than believe in him. But in the morning, in my own flat, I woke to a different atmosphere, and as I lay in bed and recalled the things he had told me, stripped of the glamour of his earnest slow voice, denuded of the focussed shaded table light, the shadowy atmosphere that wrapped about him and the pleasant bright things, the dessert and glasses and napery of the dinner we had shared, making them for the time a bright little world quite cut off from everyday realities, I saw it all as frankly incredible. "He was mystifying!" I said, and then: "How well he did it!.... It isn't quite the thing I should have expected him, of all people, to do well."

Afterwards, as I sat up in bed and sipped my morning tea, I found myself trying to account for the flavour of reality that perplexed me in his impossible reminiscences, by supposing they did in some way suggest, present, convey—I hardly know which word to use—experiences it was otherwise impossible to tell.

Well, I don't resort to that explanation now. I have got over my intervening doubts. I believe now, as I believed at the moment of telling, that Wallace did to the very best of his ability strip the truth of his secret for me. But whether he himself saw, or only thought he saw, whether he himself was the possessor of an inestimable privilege, or the victim of a fantastic dream, I cannot pretend to guess. Even the facts of his death, which ended my doubts forever, throw no light on that. That much the reader must judge for himself.

I forget now what chance comment or criticism of mine moved so reticent a man to confide in me. He was, I think, defending himself against an imputation of slackness and unreliability I had made in relation to a great public movement in which he had disappointed me. But he plunged suddenly. "I have" he said, "a preoccupation—"

"I know," he went on, after a pause that he devoted to the study of his cigar ash, "I have been negligent. The fact is—it isn't a case of ghosts or apparitions—but—it's an odd thing to tell of, Redmond—I am haunted. I am haunted by something—that rather takes the light out of things, that fills me with longings. . . ."

He paused, checked by that English shyness that so often overcomes us when we would speak of moving or grave or beautiful things. "You were at Saint Athelstan's all through," he said, and for a moment that seemed to me quite irrelevant. "Well"—and he paused. Then very haltingly at first, but afterwards more easily, he began to tell of the thing that was hidden in his life, the haunting memory of a beauty and a happiness that filled his heart with insatiable longings that made all the interests and spectacle of worldly life seem dull and tedious and vain to him.

Now that I have the clue to it, the thing seems written visibly in his face. I have a photograph in which that look of detachment has been caught and intensified. It reminds me of what a woman once said of him—a woman who had loved him greatly. "Suddenly," she said, "the interest goes out of him. He forgets you. He doesn't care a rap for you—under his very nose. . . ."

Yet the interest was not always out of him, and when he was holding his attention to a thing Wallace could contrive to be an extremely successful man. His career, indeed, is set with successes. He left me behind him long ago; he soared up over my head, and cut a figure in the world that I couldn't cut—anyhow. He was still a year short of forty, and they say now that he would have been in office and very probably in the new Cabinet if he had lived. At school he always beat me without effort—as it were by nature. We were at school together at Saint Athelstan's College in West Kensington for almost all our school time. He came into the school as my co-equal, but he left far above me, in a blaze of scholarships and brilliant performance. Yet I think I made a fair average running. And it was at school I heard first of the Door in the Wall—that I was to hear of a second time only a month before his death.

To him at least the Door in the Wall was a real door leading through a real wall to immortal realities. Of that I am now quite assured.

And it came into his life early, when he was a little fellow between five and six. I remember how, as he sat making his confession to me with a slow gravity, he reasoned and reckoned the date of it. "There was," he said, "a crimson Virginia creeper in it—all one bright uniform crimson in a clear amber sunshine against a white wall. That came into the impression somehow, though I don't clearly remember how, and there were horse-chestnut leaves upon the clean pavement outside the green door. They were blotched yellow and green, you know, not brown nor dirty, so that they must have been new fallen. I take it that means October. I look out for horse-chestnut leaves every year, and I ought to know.

"If I'm right in that, I was about five years and four months old." He was, he said, rather a precocious little boy—he learned to talk at an abnormally early age, and he was so sane and "old-fashioned," as people say, that he was permitted an amount of initiative that most children scarcely attain by seven or eight. His mother died when he was born, and he was under the less vigilant and authoritative care of a nursery governess. His father was a stern, preoccupied lawyer, who gave him little attention, and expected great things of him. For all his brightness he found life a little grey and dull I think. And one day he wandered.

He could not recall the particular neglect that enabled him to get away, nor the course he took among the West Kensington roads. All that had faded among the incurable blurs of memory. But the white wall and the green door stood out quite distinctly.

As his memory of that remote childish experience ran, he did at the very first sight of that door experience a peculiar emotion, an attraction, a desire to get to the door and open it and walk in. And at the same time he had the clearest conviction that either it was unwise or it was wrong of him—he could not tell which—to yield to this attraction. He insisted upon it as a curious thing that he knew from the very beginning—unless memory has played him the queerest trick—that the door was unfastened, and that he could go in as he chose.

I seem to see the figure of that little boy, drawn and repelled. And it was very clear in his mind, too, though why it should be so was never explained, that his father would be very angry if he went through that door.

Wallace described all these moments of hesitation to me with the utmost particularity. He went right past the door, and then, with his hands in his pockets, and making an infantile attempt to whistle, strolled right along beyond the end of the wall. There he recalls a number of mean, dirty shops, and particularly that of a plumber and decorator, with a dusty disorder of earthenware pipes, sheet lead ball taps, pattern books of wallpaper, and tins of enamel. He stood pretending to examine these things, and coveting, passionately desiring the green door.

Then, he said, he had a gust of emotion. He made a run for it, lest hesitation should grip him again, he went plump with outstretched hand through the green door and let it slam behind him. And so, in a trice, he came into the garden that has haunted all his life.

It was very difficult for Wallace to give me his full sense of that garden into which he came.

There was something in the very air of it that exhilarated, that gave one a sense of lightness and good happening and well-being; there was something in the sight of it that made all its colour clean and perfect and subtly luminous. In the instant of coming into it one was exquisitely glad—as only in rare moments and when one is young and joyful one can be glad in this world. And everything was beautiful there....

Wallace mused before he went on telling me. "You see," he said, with the doubtful inflection of a man who pauses at incredible things, "there were two great panthers there.... Yes, spotted panthers. And I was not afraid. There was a long wide path with marble-edged flower borders on either side, and these two huge velvety beasts were playing there with a ball. One looked up and came towards me, a little curious as it seemed. It came right up to me, rubbed its soft round ear very gently against the small hand I held out and purred. It was, I tell you, an enchanted garden. I know. And the size? Oh! It stretched far and wide, this way and that. I believe there were hills far away. Heaven know where West Kensington had suddenly got to go. And somehow it was just like coming home.

"You know, in the very moment the door swung to behind me, I forgot the road with its fallen chestnut leaves, its cabs and tradesmen's carts, of home, I forgot all hesitations and fear, forgot discretion, forgot all the intimate realities of this life. I became in a moment a very glad and wonder-happy little boy—in another world. It was a world with a different quality, a warmer, more penetrating and mellower light, with a faint clear gladness in its air, and wisps of sun-touched cloud in the blueness of its sky. And before me ran this long wide path, invitingly, with weedless beds on either side, rich with untended flowers, and these two great panthers. I put my little hands fearlessly on their soft fur, and caressed their round ears and the sensitive corners under their ears, and played with them, and it was as though they welcomed me home. There was keen sense of homecoming in my mind, and when presently a tall, fair girl appeared in the pathway and came to meet me, smiling, and said 'Well?' to me, and lifted me, and kissed me, and put me down, and led me by the hand, there was no amazement, but only an impression of delightful rightness, of being reminded of happy things that had in some strange way been overlooked. There were broad steps, I remember, that came into view between spikes of delphinium, and up these we went to a great avenue between very old and shady dark trees. All down this avenue, you know, between the red chapped stems, were marble seats of honour and statuary, and very tame and friendly white doves....

"And along this avenue my girlfriend led me, looking down—I recall the pleasant lines, the finely-modelled chin of her sweet kind face—asking me questions in a soft, agreeable voice, and telling me things, pleasant things I know, though what they were I was never able to recall.... And presently a little Capuchin monkey, very clean, with a fur of ruddy brown and kindly hazel eyes, came down a tree to us and ran besides me, looking up at me and grinning, and presently leapt to my shoulder. So we went on our way in great happiness...."

He paused.

"Go on," I said

"I remember little things. We passed an old man musing among laurels, I remember, and a place gay with paroquets, and came through a broad shaded colonnade to a spacious cool palace, full of pleasant fountains, full of beautiful things, full of the quality and promise of heart's desire. And there were many things and many people, some that still seem to stand out clearly and some that are a little vague, but all these people were beautiful and kind. In some way—I don't know how—it was conveyed to me that they were kind to me, glad to have me there, and filling me with gladness by their gestures, by the touch of their hands, by the welcome and love in their eyes. Yes—"

He mused for a while. "Playmates I found there. That was very much to me, because I was a lonely little boy. They played delightful games in a grass-covered court where there was a sundial set about with flowers. And as one played one loved. . . .

"But—it's odd—there's a gap in my memory. I don't remember the games we played. I never remembered. Afterwards, as a child, I spent long hours trying, even with tears, to recall the form of that happiness. I wanted to play it all over again—in my nursery—by myself. No! All I remember is the happiness and two dear playfellows who were most with me. . . . Then presently came a sombre dark woman, with a grave, pale face and dreamy eyes, a sombre woman wearing a soft long robe of pale purple, who carried a book and beckoned and took me aside with her into a gallery above a hall—though my playmates were loathe to have me go, and ceased their game and stood watching as I was carried away. 'Come back to us!' they cried. 'Come back to us soon!' I looked up at her face, but she heeded them not at all. Her face was very gentle and grave. She took me to a seat in the gallery, and I stood beside her, ready to look at her book as she opened it upon her knee. The pages fell open. She pointed, and I looked, marvelling, for in the living pages of that book I saw myself; it was a story about myself, and in it were all the things that had happened to me since ever I was born. . . .

"It was wonderful to me, because the pages of that book were not pictures, you understand, but realities."

Wallace paused gravely—looked at me doubtfully.

"Go on," I said. "I understand."

"They were realities—yes, they must have been; people moved and things came and went in them; my dear mother, whom I had near forgotten; then my father, stern and upright, the servants, the nursery, all the familiar things of home. Then the front door and the busy streets, with traffic to and fro: I looked and marvelled, and looked half doubtfully again into the woman's face and turned the pages over, skipping this and that, to see more of this book, and more, and so at least I came to myself hovering and hesitating outside the green door in the long white wall, and felt again the conflict and the fear.

"'And next?' I cried, and would have turned on, but the cool hand of the grave woman delayed me.

"'Next?' I insisted, and struggled gently with her hand, pulling up her fingers with all my childish strength, and as she yielded and the page came over she bent down upon me like a shadow and kissed my brow.

"But the page did not show the enchanted garden, nor the panthers, nor the girl who had led me by the hand, nor the playfellows who had been so loathe to let me go. It showed a long grey street in West Kensington, on that chill hour of afternoon before the lamps are lit, and I was there, a wretched little figure, weeping aloud, for all that I could do to restrain myself, and I was weeping because I could not return to my dear playfellows who had called after me, 'Come back to us! Come back to us soon!' I was there. This was no page in a book, but harsh reality; that enchanted place and the restraining hand of the grave mother at whose knee I stood had gone—wither have they gone?"

He halted again, and remained for a time, staring into the fire.

"Oh! the wretchedness of that return!" he murmured.

"Well?" I said after a minute or so.

"Poor little wretch I was—brought back to this grey world again! As I realised the fullness of what had happened to me, I gave way to quite ungovernable grief. And the shame and humiliation of that public weeping and my disgraceful homecoming remain with me still. I see again the benevolent-looking old gentleman in gold spectacles who stopped and spoke to me—prodding me first with his umbrella. 'Poor little chap,' said he; 'and are you lost then?'—and me a London boy of five and more! And he must needs bring in a kindly young policeman and make a crowd of me, and so march me home. Sobbing, conspicuous and frightened, I came from the enchanted garden to the steps of my father's house.

"That is as well as I can remember my vision of that garden—the garden that haunts me still. Of course, I can convey nothing of that indescribable quality of translucent unreality, that difference from the common things of experience that hung about it all; but that—that is what happened. If it was a dream, I am sure it was a daytime and altogether extraordinary dream... H'm!—naturally there followed a terrible questioning, by my aunt, my father, the nurse, the governess—everyone....

"I tried to tell them, and my father gave me my first thrashing for telling lies. When afterwards I tried to tell my aunt, she punished me again for my wicked persistence. Then, as I said, everyone was forbidden to listen to me, to hear a word about it. Even my fairy-tale books were taken away from me for a time—because I was 'too imaginative.' Eh? Yes, they did that! My father belonged to the old school.... And my story was driven back upon myself. I whispered it to my pillow—my pillow that was often damp and salt to my whispering lips with childish tears. And I added always to my official and less fervent prayers this one heartfelt request: 'Please God I may dream of the garden. Oh! take me back to my garden! Take me back to my garden!'

"I dreamt often of the garden. I may have added to it, I may have changed it; I do not know.... All this you understand is an attempt to reconstruct from fragmentary memories a very early experience. Between that and the other consecutive memories of my boyhood there is a gulf. A time came when it seemed impossible I should ever speak of that wonder glimpse again."

I asked an obvious question.

"No," he said. "I don't remember that I ever attempted to find my way back to the garden in those early years. This seems odd to me now, but I think that very probably a close watch was kept on my movements after this misadventure to prevent my going astray. No, it wasn't until you knew me that I tried for the garden again. And I believe there was a period—incredible as it seems now—when I forgot the garden altogether—when I was about eight or nine it may have been. Do you remember me as a kid at Saint Athelstan's?"

"Rather!"

"I didn't show any signs did I in those days of having a secret dream?"

II

He looked up with a sudden smile.

"Did you ever play North-West Passage with me?... No, of course you didn't come my way!"

"It was the sort of game," he went on, "that every imaginative child plays all day. The idea was the discovery of a North-West Passage to school. The way to school was plain enough; the game consisted in finding some way that wasn't plain, starting off ten minutes early in some almost hopeless direction, and working one's way round through unaccustomed streets to my goal. And one day I got entangled among some rather low-class streets on the other side of Campden Hill, and I began to think that for once the game would be against me and that I should get to school late. I tried rather desperately a street that had seemed a *cul de sac,* and found a passage at the end. I hurried through that with renewed hope. 'I shall do it yet,' I said, and passed a row of frowsy little shops that were inexplicably familiar to me, and behold! There was my long white wall and the green door that led to the enchanted garden!

"The thing whacked upon me suddenly. Then, after all, that garden, that wonderful garden, wasn't a dream!"....

He paused.

"I suppose my second experience with the green door marks the world of difference there is between the busy life of a schoolboy and the infinite leisure of a child. Anyhow, this second time I didn't for a moment think of going in straightaway. You see.... For one thing my mind was full of the idea of getting to school in time—set on not breaking my record for punctuality. I must surely have felt *some* little desire at least to try the door—yes, I must have felt that.... But I seem to remember the attraction of the door mainly as another obstacle to my overmastering determination to get to school. I was immediately interested by this discovery I had made, of course—I went on with my mind full of it—but I went on. It didn't check me. I ran past tugging out my watch, found I had ten minutes still to spare, and then I was going downhill into familiar surroundings. I got to school, breathless, it is true, and wet with perspiration, but in time. I can remember hanging up my coat and hat.... Went right by it and left it behind me. Odd, eh?"

He looked at me thoughtfully. "Of course, I didn't know then that it wouldn't always be there. Schoolboys have limited imaginations. I suppose I thought it was an awfully jolly thing to have it there, to know my way back to it, but there was the school tugging at me. I expect I was a good deal distraught and inattentive that morning, recalling what I could of the beautiful strange people I should presently see again. Oddly enough I had no doubt in my mind that they would be glad to see me.... Yes, I must have thought of the garden that morning just as a jolly sort of place to which one might resort in the interludes of a strenuous scholastic career.

"I didn't go that day at all. The next day was a half holiday, and that may have weighed with me. Perhaps, too, my state of inattention brought down impositions upon me and docked the margin of time necessary for the detour. I don't know. What I do know is that in the meantime the enchanted garden was so much upon my mind that I could not keep it to myself.

"I told—What was his name?—a ferrety-looking youngster we used to call Squiff."

"Young Hopkins," said I.

"Hopkins it was. I did not like telling him, I had a feeling that in some way it was against the rules to tell him, but I did. He was walking part of the way home with me; he was talkative, and if we had not talked about the enchanted garden we should have talked of something else, and it was intolerable to me to think about any other subject. So I blabbed.

"Well, he told my secret. The next day in the play interval I found myself surrounded by half a dozen bigger boys, half teasing and wholly curious to hear more of the enchanted garden. There was that big Fawcett—you remember him?—and Carnaby and Morley Reynolds. You weren't there by any chance? No, I think I should have remembered if you were....

"A boy is a creature of odd feelings. I was, I really believe, in spite of my secret self-disgust, a little flattered to have the attention of these big fellows. I remember particularly a moment of pleasure caused by the praise of Crawshaw—you remember Crawshaw major, the son of Crawshaw the composer?—who said it was the best lie he had ever heard. But at the same time there was a really painful undertow of shame at telling what I felt was indeed a sacred secret. That beast Fawcett made a joke about the girl in green—."

Wallace's voice sank with the keen memory of that shame. "I pretended not to hear," he said. "Well, then Carnaby suddenly called me a young liar and disputed with me when I said the thing was true. I said I knew where to find the green door, could lead them all there in ten minutes. Carnaby became outrageously virtuous, and said I'd have to—and bear out my words or suffer. Did you ever have Carnaby twist your arm? Then perhaps you'll understand how it went with me. I swore my story was true. There was nobody in the school then to save a chap from Carnaby though Crawshaw put in a word or so. Carnaby had got his game. I grew excited and red-eared, and a little frightened, I behaved altogether like a silly little chap, and the outcome of it all was that instead of starting alone for my enchanted garden, I led the way presently—cheeks flushed, ears hot, eyes smarting, and my soul one burning misery and shame—for a party of six mocking, curious and threatening schoolfellows.

"We never found the white wall and the green door..."

"You mean?— "

"I mean I couldn't find it. I would have found it if I could. "

"And afterwards when I could go alone I couldn't find it. I never found it. I seem now to have been always looking for it through my schoolboy days, but I've never come upon it again."

"Did the fellows—make it disagreeable?"

"Beastly.... Carnaby held a council over me for wanton lying. I remember how I sneaked home and upstairs to hide the marks of my blubbering. But when I cried myself to sleep at last it wasn't for Carnaby, but for the garden, for the beautiful afternoon I had hoped for, for the sweet friendly women and the waiting playfellows and the game I had hoped to learn again, that beautiful forgotten game....

"I believed firmly that if I had not told—...I had bad times after that—crying at night and woolgathering by day. For two terms I slackened and had bad reports. Do you remember? Of course you would! It was *you*—your beating me in mathematics that brought me back to the grind again."

III

For a time my friend stared silently into the red heart of the fire. Then he said: "I never saw it again until I was seventeen.

"It leapt upon me for the third time—as I was driving to Paddington on my way to Oxford and a scholarship. I had just one momentary glimpse. I was leaning over the apron of my hansom smoking a cigarette, and no doubt thinking myself no end of a man of the world, and suddenly there was the door, the wall, the dear sense of unforgettable and still attainable things.

"We clattered by—I too taken by surprise to stop my cab until we were well past and round a corner. Then I had a queer moment, a double and divergent movement of my will: I tapped the little door in the roof of the cab, and brought my arm down to pull out my watch. 'Yes, sir!' said the cabman, smartly. 'Er—well—it's nothing,' I cried. '*My* mistake! We haven't much time! Go on!' and he went on . . .

"I got my scholarship. And the night after I was told of that I sat over my fire in my little upper room, my study, in my father's house, with his praise—his rare praise—and his sound counsels ringing in my ears, and I smoked my favourite pipe—the formidable bulldog of adolescence—and thought of that door in the long white wall. 'If I had stopped,' I thought, 'I should have missed my scholarship, I should have missed Oxford—muddled all the fine career before me! I begin to see things better!' I fell musing deeply, but I did not doubt then this career of mine was a thing that merited sacrifice.

"Those dear friends and that clear atmosphere seemed very sweet to me, very fine, but remote. My grip was fixing now upon the world. I saw another door opening—the door of my career."

He stared again into the fire. Its red lights picked out a stubborn strength in his face for just one flickering moment, and then it vanished again.

"Well," he said and sighed, "I have served that career. I have done—much work, much hard work. But I have dreamt of the enchanted garden a thousand dreams, and seen its door, or at least glimpsed its door, four times since then. Yes—four times. For a while this world was so bright and interesting, seemed so full of meaning and opportunity that the half-effaced charm of the garden was by comparison gentle and remote. Who wants to pat panthers on the way to dinner with pretty women and distinguished men? I came down to London from Oxford, a man of bold promise that I have done something to redeem. Something—and yet there have been disappointments. . . .

"Twice I have been in love—I will not dwell on that—but once, as I went to someone who, I know, doubted whether I dared to come, I took a shortcut at a venture through an unfrequented road near Earl's Court, and so happened on a white wall and a familiar green door. 'Odd!' said I to myself, 'but I thought this place was on Campden Hill. It's the place I never could find somehow—like counting Stonehenge—the place of that queer daydream of mine.' And I went by it intent upon my purpose. It had no appeal to me that afternoon.

"I had just a moment's impulse to try the door, three steps aside were needed at the most—though I was sure enough in my heart that it would open to me—and then I thought that doing so might delay me on the way to that appointment in which I thought my honour was involved. Afterwards I was sorry for my punctuality—I might at least have peeped in I thought, and waved a hand to those panthers, but I knew enough by this time not to seek again belatedly that which is not found by seeking. Yes, that time made me very sorry. . . .

"Years of hard work after that and never a sight of the door. It's only recently it has come back to me. With it there has come a sense as though some thin tarnish had spread itself over my world. I began to think of it as a sorrowful and bitter thing that I should never see that door again. Perhaps I was suffering a little from overwork—perhaps it was what I've heard spoken of as the feeling of forty. I don't know. But certainly the keen brightness that makes effort easy has gone out of things recently, and that just at a time with all these new political developments—when I ought to be working. Odd, isn't it? But I do begin to find life toilsome, its rewards, as I come near them, cheap. I began a little while ago to want the garden quite badly. Yes—and I've seen it three times."

"The garden?"

"No—the door! And I haven't gone in!"

He leaned over the table to me, with an enormous sorrow in his voice as he spoke. "Thrice I have had my chance—*thrice!* If ever that door offers itself to me again, I swore, I will go in out of this dust and heat, out of this dry glitter of vanity, out of these toilsome futilities. I will go and never return. This time I will stay.... I swore it and when the time came—*I didn't go.*

"Three times in one year have I passed that door and failed to enter. Three times in the last year.

"The first time was on the night of the snatch division on the Tenants' Redemption Bill, on which the Government was saved by a majority of three. You remember? No one on our side—perhaps very few on the opposite side—expected the end that night. Then the debate collapsed like eggshells. I and Hotchkiss were dining with his cousin at Brentford, we were both unpaired, and we were called up by telephone, and set off at once in his cousin's motor. We got in barely in time, and on the way we passed my wall and door—livid in the moonlight, blotched with hot yellow as the glare of our lamps lit it, but unmistakable. 'My God!' cried I. 'What?' said Hotchkiss. 'Nothing!' I answered, and the moment passed.

"'I've made a great sacrifice,' I told the whip as I got in. 'They all have,' he said, and hurried by.

"I do not see how I could have done otherwise then. And the next occasion was as I rushed to my father's bedside to bid that stern old man farewell. Then, too, the claims of life were imperative. But the third time was different; it happened a week ago. It fills me with hot remorse to recall it. I was with Gurker and Ralphs—it's no secret now you know that I've had my talk with Gurker. We had been dining at Frobisher's, and the talk had become intimate between us. The question of my place in the reconstructed ministry lay always just over the boundary of the discussion. Yes—yes. That's all settled. It needn't be talked about yet, but there's no reason to keep a secret from you.... Yes—thanks! thanks! But let me tell you my story.

"Then, on that night things were very much in the air. My position was a very delicate one. I was keenly anxious to get some definite word from Gruker, but was hampered by Ralphs' presence. I was using the best power of my brain to keep that light and careless talk not too obviously directed to the point that concerns me. I had to. Ralphs' behaviour since has more than justified my caution.... Ralphs, I knew, would leave us beyond the Kensington High Street, and then I could surprise Gurker by a sudden frankness. One has sometimes to resort to these little devices.... And then it was that in the margin of my field of vision I became aware once more of the white wall, the green door before us down the road.

"We passed it talking. I passed it. I can still see the shadow of Gurker's marked profile, his opera hat tilted forward over his prominent nose, the many folds of his neck wrap going before my shadow and Ralphs' as we sauntered past.

"I passed within twenty inches of the door. 'If I say good night to them, and go in,' I asked myself, 'what will happen?' And I was all atingle for that word with Gurker.

"I could not answer that question in the tangle of my other problems. 'They will think me mad,' I thought. 'And suppose I vanish now!—Amazing disappearance of a prominent politician!' That weighed with me. A thousand inconceivably petty worldlinesses weighed with me in that crisis."

Then he turned on me with a sorrowful smile, and, speaking slowly; "Here I am!" he said.

"Here I am!" he repeated, "and my chance has gone from me. Three times in one year the door has been offered me—the door that goes into peace, into delight, into a beauty beyond dreaming, a kindness no man on earth can know. And I have rejected it, Redmond, and it has gone—"

"How do you know?"

"I know. I know. I am left now to work it out, to stick to the tasks that held me so strongly when my moments came. You say, I have success—this vulgar, tawdry, irksome, envied thing. I have it." He had a walnut in his big hand. "If that was my success," he said, and crushed it, and held it out for me to see.

"Let me tell you something, Redmond. This loss is destroying me. For two months, for ten weeks nearly now, I have done no work at all, except the most necessary and urgent duties. My soul is full of inappeasable regrets. At nights—when it is less likely I shall be recognised—I go out. I wander. Yes. I wonder what people would think of that if they knew. A Cabinet Minister, the responsible head of that most vital of all departments, wandering alone—grieving—sometimes near audibly lamenting—for a door, for a garden!"

IV

I can see now his rather pallid face, and the unfamiliar sombre fire that had come into his eyes. I see him very vividly tonight. I sit recalling his words, his tones, and last evening's *Westminster Gazette* still lies on my sofa, containing the notice of his death. At lunch today the club was busy with him and the strange riddle of his fate.

They found his body very early yesterday morning in a deep excavation near East Kensington Station. It is one of two shafts that have been made in connection with an extension of the railway southward. It is protected from the intrusion of the public by a hoarding upon the high road, in which a small doorway has been cut for the convenience of some of the workmen who live in that direction. The doorway was left unfastened through a misunderstanding between two gangers, and through it he made his way. . . .

My mind is darkened with questions and riddles.

It would seem he walked all the way from the House that night—he has frequently walked home during the past Session—and so it is I figure his dark form coming along the late and empty streets, wrapped up, intent. And then did the pale electric lights near the station cheat the rough planking into a semblance of white? Did that fatal unfastened door awaken some memory?

Was there, after all, ever any green door in the wall at all?

I do not know. I have told this story as he told it to me. There are times when I believe that Wallace was no more than the victim of the coincidence between a rare but not unprecedented type of hallucination and a careless trap, but that indeed is not my profoundest belief. You may think me superstitious if you will, and foolish; but, indeed, I am more than half convinced that he had in truth, an abnormal gift, and a sense, something—I know not what—that in the guise of wall and door offered him an outlet, a secret and peculiar passage of escape into another and altogether more beautiful world. At any rate, you will say, it betrayed him in the end. But did it betray him? There you touch the inmost mystery of these dreamers, these men of vision and the imagination. We see our world fair and common, the hoarding and the pit. By our daylight standard he walked out of security into darkness, danger and death. But did he see like that?

THE MASTER OF THE INN

ROBERT HERRICK

It was a plain brick house, three full stories, with four broad chimneys, and overhanging eaves. The tradition was that it had been a colonial tavern—a dot among the fir-covered northern hills on the climbing post-road into Canada. The village scattered along the road below the inn was called Albany—and soon forgotten when the railroad sought an opening through a valley less rugged, eight miles to the west.

Rather more than thirty years ago the Doctor had arrived, one summer day, and opened all the doors and windows of the neglected old house, which he had bought from scattered heirs. He was a quiet man, the Doctor, in middle life then or nearly so; and he sank almost without remark into the world of Albany, where they raise hay and potatoes and still cut good white pine off the hills. Gradually the old brick tavern resumed the functions of life: many buildings were added to it as well as many acres of farm and forest to the Doctor's original purchase of intervale land. The new Master did not open his house to the public, yet he, too, kept a sort of Inn, where men came and stayed a long time. Although no sign now hung from the old elm tree in front of the house, nevertheless an ever-widening stream of humanity mounted the winding road from White River and passed through the doors of the Inn, seeking life....

That first summer the Doctor brought with him Sam, the Chinaman, whom we all came to know and love, and also a young man, who loafed much while the Doctor worked, and occasionally fished. This was John Herring—now a famous architect—and it was from his designs, sketched those first idle summer days, that were built all the additions to the simple old house—the two low wings in the rear for the "cells," with the Italian garden between them; the marble seat curving around the pool that joined the wings on the west; also the substantial wall that hid the Inn, its terraced gardens and orchards, from Albanian curiosity. Herring found a store of red brick in some crumbling buildings in the neighborhood, and he discovered the quarry whence came those thick slabs of purple slate. The blue-veined marble was had from a fissure in the hills, and the Doctor's School made the tiles.

I think Herring never did better work than in the making over of this old tavern: he divined that subtle affinity which exists between north Italy, with all its art, and our bare New England; and he dared to graft boldly one to the other, having the rear of the Inn altogether Italian with its portico, its dainty colonnades, the garden and the fountain and the pool. From all this one looked down on the waving grass of the Intervale, which fell away gently to the turbulent White River, then rose again to the wooded hills that folded one upon another, with ever deepening blue, always upward and beyond.

Not all this building at once, to be sure, as the millionaire builds; but a gradual growth over a couple of decades; and all built lovingly by the "Brothers," stone on stone, brick and beam and tile—many a hand taking part in it that came weak to the task and left it sturdy. There was also the terraced arrangement of gardens and orchards on either side of the Inn, reaching to the farm buildings on the one side and to the village on the other. For a time Herring respected the quaint old tavern with its small rooms and pine wainscot; then he made a stately two-storied hall out of one half where we dined in bad weather, and a pleasant study for the Doctor from the rest. The doors east and west always stood open in the summer, giving the rare passer-by a glimpse of that radiant blue heaven among the hills, with the silver flash of the river in the middle distance, and a little square of peaceful garden close at hand.... The tough northern grasses rustled in the breezes that always played about

Albany; and the scent of spruce drawn by the hot sun—the strong resinous breath of the north—was borne from the woods.

Thus it started, that household of men in the old Inn at the far end of Albany village among the northern hills, with the Doctor and Sam and Herring, who had been flung aside after his first skirmish with life and was picked up in pure kindness by the Doctor, as a bit of the broken waste of our modern world, and carried off with him out of the city. The young architect returning in due time to the fight—singing—naturally venerated the Doctor as a father; and when a dear friend stumbled and fell in the *via dura* of this life, he whispered to him word of the Inn and its Master—of the life up there among the hills where Man is little and God looks down on his earth.... "Oh, you'll understand when you put your eyes on White Face some morning! The Doctor? He heals both body and soul." And this one having heeded spoke the word in turn to others in need—"to the right sort, who would understand." Thus the custom grew like a faith, and a kind of brotherhood was formed, of those who had found more than health at the Inn—who had found themselves. The Doctor, every busy about his farms and his woods, his building, and above all his School, soon had on his hands a dozen or more patients or guests, as you might call them, and he set them to work speedily. There was little medicine to be found in the Inn: the sick labored as they could and thus grew strong....

And so, as one was added to another, they began to call themselves in joke "Brothers," and the Doctor, "Father." The older "Brothers" would return to the Inn from all parts of the land, for a few days or a few weeks, to grasp the Doctor's hand, to have a dip in the pool, to try the little brooks among the hills. Young men and middle-aged, and even the old, they came from the cities where the heat of living had scorched them, where they had faltered and doubted the goodness of life. In some way word of the Master had reached them, with this compelling advice—"Go! And tell him I sent you." So from the clinic or the lecture room, from the office or the mill—wherever men labor with tightening nerves—the needy one started on his long journey. Toward evening he was set down before the plain red face of the Inn. And as the Stranger entered the old hall, a voice was sure to greet him from within somewhere, the deep voice of a hearty man, and presently the Master appeared to welcome the newcomer, resting one hand on his guest's shoulder perhaps, with a yearning affection that ran before knowledge.

"So you've come, my boy," he said. "Herring [or some one] wrote me to look for you."

And after a few more words of greeting, the Doctor beckoned to Sam, and gave the guest over to his hands. Thereupon the Chinaman slippered through tiled passageways to the court, where the Stranger, caught by the beauty and peace so well hidden, lingered a while. The little space within the wings was filled with flowers as far as the yellow water of the pool and the marble bench. In the centre of the court was an old gray fountain—sent from Verona by a Brother—from which the water dropped and ran away among the flower beds to the pool. A stately elm tree shaded this place, flecking the water below. The sun shot long rays beneath its branches into the court, and over all there was an odor of blossoming flowers and the murmur of bees.

"Bath!" Sam explained, grinning toward the pool.

With the trickle of the fountain in his ears the Stranger looked out across the ripening fields of the Intervale to the noble skyline of the Stowe hills. Those little mountains of the north! Mere hills to all who know the giants of the earth—not mountains in the brotherhood of ice and snow and rock! But in form and color, in the lesser things that create the love of men for places, they rise nobly toward heaven, those little hills! On a summer day like this their broad breasts flutter with waving tree-tops, and at evening depth on depth of purple mist gathers over them, dropping into those soft curves where the little brooks flow, and mounting even to the skyline. When the sun has fallen, there rests a band of pure saffron, and in the calm and perfect peace of evening there is a hint of coming moonlight. Ah, they are of the fellowship of mountains, those little hills of Stowe! And when in winter their flanks are jewelled with ice and snow, then they raise their heads proudly to the stars, calling across the frozen valleys to their greater brethren in the midriff of the continent—"Behold, we also are hills, in the sight of the Lord!"...

Meantime Sam, with Oriental ease, goes slipping along the arcade until he comes to a certain oak door, where he drops your bag, and disappears, having saluted. It is an ample and lofty room, and on the outer side of it hangs a little balcony above the orchard, from which there is a view of the valley and the woods beyond, and from somewhere in the fields the note of the thrush rises. The room itself is cool, of a gray tone, with a broad fireplace, a heavy table, and many books. Otherwise there are bed and chairs and dressing-table, the necessities of life austerely provided. And Peace! God, what Peace to him who has escaped from the furnace men make! It is as if he had come all the way to the end of the world, and found there a great still room of peace.

Soon a bell sounds—with a strange vibration as though in distant lands it had summoned many a body of men together—and the household assembles under the arcade. If it is fair and not cold, Sam and his helpers bring out the long narrow table and place it, as Veronese places his feasters, lengthwise beneath the colonnade, and thus the evening meal is served. A fresh, coarse napkin is laid on the bare board before each man, no more than enough for all those present, and the Doctor sits in the middle, serving all. There are few dishes, and for the most part such as may be got at home there in the hills. There is a pitcher of cider at one end and a pitcher of mild white wine at the other, and the men eat and drink, with jokes and talk—the laughter of the day. (The Novice might feel only the harmony of it all, but later he will learn how many considered elements go to the making of Peace.) Afterward, when Sam has brought pipes and tobacco, the Master leads the way to the sweeping semicircle of marble seat around the pool with the leafy tree overhead; and there they sit into the soft night, talking of all things, with the glow of pipes, until one after another slips away to sleep. For as the Master said, "Talk among men in common softens the muscles of the mind and quickens the heart." Yet he loved most to hear the talk of others.

Thus insensibly for the Novice there begins the life of the place, opening in a gentle and persistent routine that takes him in its flow and carries him on with it. He finds Tradition and Habit all about him, in the ordered, unconscious life of the Inn, to which he yields without question.... Shortly after dawn the bell sounds, and then the men meet at the pool, where the Doctor is always first. A plunge into the yellow water which is flecked with the fallen leaves, and afterward to each man's room there is brought a large bowl of coffee and hot milk, with bread and eggs and fruit. What more he craves may be found in the hall.

Soon there is a tap on the newcomer's door, and a neighborly voice calls out—"We all go into the fields every morning, you know. You must earn your dinner, the Doctor says, or borrow it!" So the Novice goes forth to earn his first dinner with his hands. Beyond the gardens and the orchards are the barns and sheds, and a vista of level acres of hay and potatoes and rye, the bearing acres of the farm, and beyond these the woods on the hills. "Nearly a thousand acres, fields and woods," the neighbor explains. "Oh, there's plenty to do all times!" Meantime the Doctor strides ahead through the wet grass, his eyes roaming here and there, inquiring the state of his land. And watching him the newcomer believes that there is always much to be done wherever the Doctor leads.

It may be July and hay time—all the Intervale grass land is mowed by hand—there is a sweat-breaking task! Or it may be potatoes to hoe. Or later in the season the apples have to be gathered—a pleasant pungent job, filling the baskets and pouring them into the fat-bellied barrels. But whatever the work may be the Doctor keeps the Novice in his mind, and as the sun climbs high over the Stowe hills, he taps the new one on the shoulder—"Better stop here today, my boy! You'll find a good tree over there by the brook for a nap. . . ."

Under that particular tree in the tall timothy, there is the coolest spot, and the Novice drowses, thinking of those wonderful mowers in *Anna,* as he gazes at the marching files eating their way through the meadow until his eyelids fall and he sleeps, the ripple of waving timothy in ears. At noon the bell sounds again from the Inn, and the men come striding homeward wiping the sweat from their faces. They gather at the swimming pool, and still panting from their labor strip off their wet garments, then plunge one after another, like happy boys. From bath to room, and a few minutes for fresh clothes, and all troop into the hall, which is dark and cool. The old brick walls of the tavern never held a gayer lot of guests.

From this time on each one is his own master; there is no common toil. The farmer and his men take up the care of the farm, and the Master usually goes down to his School, in company with some of the Brothers. Each one finds his own way of spending the hours till sunset—some fishing or shooting, according to the season; others, in tennis or games with the boys of the School; and some reading or loafing—until the shadows begin to fall across the pool into the court, and Sam brings out the long table for dinner.

The seasons shading imperceptibly into one another vary the course of the day. Early in September the men begin to sit long about the hall-fire of an evening, and when the snow packs hard on the hills there is wood-cutting to be done, and in early spring it is the carpenter's shop. So the form alters, but the substance remains—work and play and rest....

To each one a time will come when the Doctor speaks to him alone. At some hour, before many days have passed, the Novice will find himself with those large eyes resting on his face, searchingly. It may be in the study after the others have scattered, or at the pool where the Master loved to sit beneath the great tree and hear his "confessions," as the men called these talks. At such times, when the man came to remember it afterward, the Doctor asked few questions, said little, but listened. He had the confessing ear! And as if by chance his hand would rest on the man's arm or shoulder. For he said—"Touch speaks: soul flows through flesh into soul."

Thus he sat and confessed his patients one after another, and his dark eyes seemed familiar with all man's woes, as if he had listened always. Men said to him what they had never before let pass their lips to man or woman, what they themselves scarce looked at in the gloom of their souls. Unawares it slipped from them, the reason within the reason for their ill, the ultimate cause of sorrow. From the moment they had revealed to him this hidden thing—had slipped the leash on their tongues—it seemed no longer to be feared. "Trouble evaporates, being properly aired," said the Doctor. And already in the troubled one's mind the sense of the confused snarl of life began to lessen and veils began to descend between him and it.... "For you must learn to forget," counseled the Doctor, "forget day by day until the recording soul beneath your mind is clean. Therefore—work, forget, be new!"....

A self-important young man, much concerned with himself, once asked the Master:

"Doctor, what is the regimen that you would recommend to me?"

And we all heard him say in reply—

"The potatoes need hilling, and then you'll feel like having a dip in the pool."

The young man, it seems, wrote back to the friend in the city who had sent him—"This Doctor cannot understand my case: he tells me to dig potatoes and bathe in a swimming pool. That is all! All!" But the friend, who was an old member of the Brotherhood, telegraphed back—"Dig and swim, you fool! Sam took the message at the telephone while we were dining, and repeated it faithfully to the young man within the hearing of all. A laugh rose that was hard in dying, and I think the Doctor's lips wreathed in smile.... In the old days they say the Master gave medicine like other doctors. That was when he spent part of the year in the city and had an office there and believed in drugs. But as he gave up going to the city, the stock of drugs in the cabinet at the end of the study became exhausted, and was never renewed. All who needed medicine were sent to an old Brother, who had settled down the valley at Stowe. "He knows more about pills than I do," the Doctor said. "At least he can give you the stuff with confidence." Few of the inmates of the Inn ever went to Stowe, though Dr. Williams was an excellent physician. And it was from about this time that we began to drop the title of doctor, calling him instead the Master; and the younger men sometimes, Father. He seemed to like these new terms, as denoting affection and respect for his authority.

By the time we called him Master, the Inn had come to its maturity. Altogether it could hold eighteen guests, and if more came, as in midsummer or autumn, they lived in tents in the orchard or in the hill camps. The Master was still adding to the forest land—fish and game preserve the village people called it; for the Master was a hunter and a fisherman. But up among those curving hills, when he looked out through the waving trees, measuring by eye a fir or a pine, he would say, nodding his head—"Boys, behold my heirs—from generation to generation!"

He was now fifty and had ceased altogether to go to the city. There were ripe men in the great hospitals that still remembered him as a young man in the medical school; but he had dropped out, they said—why? He might have answered that, instead of following the beaten path, he had spoken his word to the world through men—and spoken widely. For there was no break in the stream of life that flowed upward to the old Inn. The "cells" were always full, winter and summer. Now there were coming children of the older Brothers, and these, having learned the ways of the place from their fathers, were already housebroken, as we said, when they came. They knew that no door was locked about the Inn, but that if they returned after ten it behooved them to come in by the pool and make no noise. They knew that when the first ice formed on the pool, then they were not expected to get out of bed for the morning plunge. They knew that there was an old custom which no one ever forgot, and that was to put money in the house-box behind the hall door on leaving, at least something for each day of the time spent, and as much more as one cared to give. For, as everyone knew, all in the box beyond the daily expense went to maintain the School on the road below the village. So the books of the Inn were easy to keep—there was never a word about money in the place—but I know that many a large sum of money was found in this box, and the School never wanted means.

That I might tell more of what took place in the Inn, and what the Master said, and the sort of men one found there, and the talk we all had summer evenings beside the pool and winter nights in the hall! Winter, I think, was the best time of all the year, the greatest beauty and the greatest joy, from the first fall of the snow to the yellow brook water and the floating ice in White River. Then the broad velvety shadows lay on the hills between the stiff spruces, then came rosy mornings out of darkness when you knew that some good thing was waiting for you in the world. After you had drunk your bowl of coffee, you got your axe and followed the procession of choppers, who were carefully foresting the Doctor's woods. In the spring when the little brooks had begun to run down the slopes, there was road making and mending; for the Master kept in repair most of the roads about Albany, grinding the rock in his pit, saying that—"a good road is one sure blessing."

And the dusks I shall never forget—those gold and violet moments with the light of immortal heavens behind the rampart of hills; and the nights, so still, so still like everlasting death, each star set jewel-wise in a black sky above a white earth. How splendid it was to turn out of the warm hall where we had been reading and talking into the frosty court, with the thermometer at twenty below and still falling, and look down across the broad white valley, marked by the streak of bushy alders where the dumb river flowed, up to the little frozen water courses among the hills, up above where the stars glittered! You took your way to your room in the silence, rejoicing that it was all so, that somewhere in this tumultuous world of ours there was hidden all this beauty and the secret of living; and that you were of the brotherhood of those who had found it....

Thus was the Inn and its Master in the year when he touched sixty, and his hair and beard were more white than gray.

II

Then there came to the Inn one day in the early part of the summer a new guest—a man about fifty, with an aging, worldly face. Bill, the Albany stage man, had brought him from Island Junction, and on the way had answered all his questions, discreetly, reckoning in his wisdom that his passenger was "one of those queer folks that went up to the old Doctor's place." For there was something smart and fashionable about the stranger's appearance that made Bill uncomfortable.

"There," he said, as he pulled up outside the red brick house and pointed over the wall into the garden, "mos' likely you'll find the man fussin' 'round somewheres inside there, if he hain't down to the School," and he drove off with the people's mail.

The stranger looked back through the village street, which was as silent as a village street should be at four o'clock on a summer day. Then he muttered to himself, whimsically, "Mos' likely you'll find the old man fussin' 'round somewheres inside!" Well, *what next?* And he glanced at the homely red brick building with the cold eye of one who has made many goings out and comings in, and to whom novelty offers little entertainment. As he stood there (thinking possibly of that early train from the junction on the morrow) the hall door opened wide, and an oldish man with white eyebrows and black eyes appeared. He was dressed in a linen suit that deepened the dark tan of his face and hands. He said:

"You are Dr. Augustus Norton?"

"And you," the Stranger replied with a gracious smile, "are the Master—and this is the Inn!"

He had forgotten what Percival called the old boy—forgot everything these days—had tried to remember the name all the way up—nevertheless, he had turned it off well! So the two looked at each other—one a little younger as years go, but with lined face and shaking fingers; the other solid and self-contained, with less of that ready language which comes from always jostling with nimble wits. But as they stood there, each saw a Man and an Equal.

"The great surgeon of St. Jerome's," said our Master in further welcome.

"Honored by praise from your lips!" Thus the man of the city lightly turned the compliment, and extended his hand, which the Master took slowly, gazing meanwhile steadily at his guest.

"Pray come into my house," said the Master of the Inn, with more stateliness of manner than he usually had with a new Brother. But, it may be said, Dr. Augustus Norton had the most distinguished name of that day in his profession. He followed the Master to his study, with uncertain steps, and sinking into a deep chair before the smouldering ashes looked at his host with a sad grin—"Perhaps you'll give me something—the journey, you know?..."

Two years before the head surgeon of St. Jerome's had come to the hospital of a morning to perform some operation—one of those affairs for which he was known from coast to coast. As he entered the officers' room that day, with the arrogant eye of the commander-in-chief, one of his aides looked at him suspiciously, then glanced again—and the great surgeon felt those eyes upon him when he turned his back. And he knew why! Something was wrong with him. Nevertheless in glum silence he made ready to operate. But when the moment came, and he was about to take the part of God toward the piece of flesh lying in the ether sleep before him, he hesitated. Then, in the terrible recoil of Fear, he turned back.

"Macroe!" he cried to his assistant, "you will have to operate. I cannot—I am not well!"

There was almost panic, but Macroe was a man, too, and proceeded to do his work without a word. The great surgeon, his hands now trembling beyond disguise, went back to the officers' room, took off his white robes, and returned to his home. There he wrote his resignation to the directors of St. Jerome's, and his resignation from other offices of honor and responsibility. Then he sent for a medical man, an old friend, and held out his shaking hand to him:

"The damn thing won't go," he said, pointing also to his head.

"Too much work," the doctor replied, of course.

But the great surgeon, who was a man of clear views, added impersonally, "Too much everything, I guess!"

There followed the usual prescription, making the sick man a wanderer and pariah—first to Europe, "to get rid of me," the surgeon growled; then to Georgia for golf, to Montana for elk, to Canada for salmon, and so forth. Each time the sick man returned with a thin coat of tan that peeled off in a few days, and with those shaking hands that suggested immediately another journey to another climate. Until it happened finally that the men of St. Jerome's who had first talked of the date of their chief's return merely raised their eyebrows at the mention of his name.

"Done for, poor old boy!" and the great surgeon read it with his lynx eyes, in the faces of the men he met at his clubs. His mouth drew together sourly and his back sloped. "Fifty-two," he muttered. "God, this is too early—something ought to pull me together." So he went on trying this and that, while his friends said he was "resting," until he had slipped from men's thoughts.

One day Percival of St. Jerome's, one of those boys he had growled at and cursed in former times, met him crawling down the avenue to his quietest club, and the old surgeon took him by the arm—he was gray in face and his neck was wasting away—and told the story of his troubles—as he would to anyone these days. The young man listened respectfully. Then he spoke of the old Inn, of the Brotherhood, of the Master and what he had done for miserable men, who had despaired. The famous surgeon, shaking his head as one who has heard of these miracles many times and found them naught, was drinking it all in, nevertheless.

"He takes a man," said the young surgeon, "who doesn't want to live and makes him fall in love with life."

Dr. Augustus Norton sniffed.

"In love with life! That's good! If your Wonder of the Ages can make a man of fifty fall in love with anything, I must try him." He laughed a sneering laugh, the feeble merriment of doubt.

"Ah, Doctor!" cried the young man, "you must go and live with the Master. And then come back to us at St. Jerome's: for we need you!"

And the great surgeon, touched to the heart by these last words, said:

"Well, what's the name of your miracle-worker, and where is he to be found?... I might as well try all the cures—write a book on 'em one of these days!"...

So he came by the stage to the gate of the old Inn, and the Master, who had been warned by a telegram from the young doctor only that morning, stood at his door to welcome his celebrated guest.

He put him in the room of state above the study, a great square room at the southwest, overlooking the wings and the flower-scented garden, the pool, and the waving grass fields beyond, dotted with tall elms—all freshly green.

"Not a bad sort of place," murmured the weary man, "and there must be trout in those brooks up yonder. Well, it will do for a week or two, if there's fishing."... Then the bell sounded for dinner which was served for the first time that season out of doors in the soft twilight. The Brothers had gathered in the court beside the fountain, young men and middle-aged—all having bent under some burden, which they were now learning to carry easily. They stood about the hall door until the distinguished Stranger appeared, and he walked between them to the place of honor at the Master's side. Every one at the long table was named to the great surgeon, and then with the coming of the soup he was promptly forgotten, while the talk of the day's work and the morrow's rose vigorously from all sides. It was a question of the old mill, which had given way. An engineer among the company described what would have to be done to get at the foundations. And a young man who happened to sit next to the surgeon explained that the Master had reopened an old mill above the Inn in the Intervale, where he ground corn and wheat and rye with the old water-wheel; for the country people, who had always got their grain ground there, complained when the mill had been closed. It seemed to the Stranger that the dark coarse bread which was served was extraordinarily good, and he wondered if the ancient process had anything to do with it and he resolved to see the old mill. Then the young man said something about bass: there was a cool lake up the valley, which had been stocked. The surgeon's eye gleamed. Did he know how to fish for bass! Why, before this boy—yes, he would go at five in the morning, sharp.... After the meal, while the blue wreaths of smoke floated across the flowers and the talk rose and fell in the court, the Master and his new guest were seated alone beneath the great elm. The surgeon could trace the Master's face in the still waters of the pool at their feet, and it seemed to him like a finely cut cameo, with gentle lines about the mouth and eyes that relieved the thick nose. Nevertheless he knew by certain instinct that they were not of the same kind. The Master was very silent this night, and his guest felt that some mystery, some vacuum existed between them, as he gazed on the face in the water. It was as if the old man were holding him off at arm's length while he looked into him. But the great surgeon, who was used to the amenities of city life, resolved to make his host talk:

"Extraordinary sort of place you have here! I don't know that I have ever seen anything just like it. And what is your System?"

"What is my System?" repeated the Master wonderingly.

"Yes! Your method of building these fellows up—electricity, diet, massage, baths—what is your line?" An urbane smile removed the offence of the banter.

"I have no System!" the Master replied thoughtfully. "I live my life here with my work, and those you see come and live with me as my friends."

"Ah, but you have ideas . . . extraordinary success . . . so many cases," the great man muttered, confused by the Master's steady gaze.

"You will learn more about us after you have been here a little time. You will see, and the others will help you to understand. Tomorrow we work at the mill, and the next day we shall be in the gardens—but you may be too tired to join us. And we bathe here, morning and noon. Harvey will tell you all our customs."

The celebrated surgeon of St. Jerome's wrote that night to an old friend: "And the learned doctor's prescription seems to be to dig in the garden and bathe in a great pool! A daffy sort of place—but I am going bass fishing tomorrow at five with a young man, who is just the right age for a son! So to bed, but I suspect that I shall see you soon—novelties wear out quickly at my years."

Just here there entered that lovely night wind, rising far away beyond the low lakes to the south—it soughed through the room, swaying the draperies, sighing, sighing, and it blew out the candle. The sick man looked down on the court below, white in the moonlight, and his eyes roved farther to the dark orchard, and the great barns and the huddled cattle.

"Quite a bit of country here!" the surgeon murmured. As he stood there looking into the misty light which covered the Intervale, up to the great hills above which floated luminous cloud banks, the chorus of an old song rose from below where the pipes gleamed in the dark about the pool. He leaned out into the air, filled with all the wild scent of green fields, and added under a sort of compulsion—"And a good place, enough!"

He went to bed to a deep sleep, and over his tired, worldly face the night wind passed gently, stripping leaf by leaf from his weary mind that heavy coating of care which he had wrapped about him in the course of many years.

Dr. Augustus Norton did not return at the end of one week, nor of two. The city saw him, indeed, no more that year. It was said that a frisky, rosy ghost of the great surgeon had slipped into St. Jerome's near Christmas—had skipped through a club or two and shaken hands about pretty generally—and disappeared. Sometimes letters came from him with an out-of-the-way postmark on them, saying in a jesting tone that he was studying the methods of an extraordinary country doctor, who seemed to cure men by touch. "He lives up here among the hills in forty degrees of frost, and if I am not mistaken he is nearer the Secret than all of you pill slingers"—(for he was writing a mere doctor of medicine!). "Anyhow I shall stay on until I learn the Secret—or my host turns me out; for life up here seems as good to me as ice cream and kisses to a girl of sixteen.... Why should I go back mucking about with you fellows—just yet? I caught a five-pounder yesterday, and *ate* him!"

There are many stories of the great surgeon that have come to me from those days. He was much liked, especially by the younger men, after the first gloom had worn off, and he began to feel the blood run once more. He had a joking way with him that made him a good table companion, and the Brothers pretending that he would become the historian of the order taught him all the traditions of the place. "But the Secret, the Secret! Where is it?" he would demand jestingly. One night—it was at table and all were there—Harvey asked him:

"Has the Master confessed you?"

"'Confessed me'?" repeated the surgeon. "What's that?"

A sudden silence fell on all, because this was the one thing never spoken of, at least in public. Then the Master, who had been silent all that evening, turned the talk to other matters.

The Master, to be sure, gave this distinguished guest all liberties, and they often talked together as men of the same profession. And the surgeon witnessed all—the mending of the mill, the planting and the hoeing and the harvesting, the preparations for the long winter, the chopping and the road-making—all, and he tested it with his hands. "Not bad sport," he would say, "with so many sick-well young men about to help!"

But meanwhile the "secret" escaped the keen mind, though he sought for it daily.

"You give no drugs, Doctor," he complained. "You're a scab on the profession!"

"The drugs gave out," the Master explained, "and I neglected to order more. . . . There's always Bert Williams at Stowe, who can give you anything you might want—shall I send for him, Doctor?"

There was laughter all about, and when it died down the great surgeon returned to the attack.

"Well, come, tell us now what you do believe in? Magic, the laying on of hands? Come, there are four doctors here, and we have the right to know—or we'll report you!"

"I believe," said the Master solemnly, in reply to the banter, "I believe in Man and in God." And there followed such talk as had never been in the old hall; for the surgeon was, after his kind, a materialist and pushed the Master for definition. The Master believed, as I recall it, that Disease could not be cured, for the most part. No chemistry would ever solve the mystery of pain! But Disease could be ignored, and the best way to forget pain was through labor. Not labor merely for oneself; but also something for others. Wherefore the School, around which the Inn and the farm and all had grown. For he told us then that he had bought the Inn as a home for his boys, the waste product of the city. Finding the old tavern too small for his purpose and seeing how he should need helpers, he had encouraged ailing men to come to live with him and to cure themselves by curing others. Without that School below in the valley, with its workshops and cottages, there would have been no Inn!

As for God—that night he would go no further, and the surgeon said rather flippantly, we all thought, that the Master had left little room in his world for God, anyhow—he had made man so large. It was a stormy August evening, I remember, when we had been forced to dine within on account of the gusty rain that had come after a still, hot day. The valley seemed filled with murk, which was momentarily torn by fire, revealing the trembling leaves upon the trees. When we passed through the arcade to reach our rooms, the surgeon pointed out into this sea of fire and darkness, and muttered with a touch of irony—

"HE seems to be talking for himself this evening!"

Just then a bolt shot downward, revealing with large exaggeration the hills, the folded valleys—the descents.

"It's like standing on a thin plank in a turbulent sea!" the surgeon remarked wryly. "Ah, my boy, Life's like that!" and he disappeared into his room.

Nevertheless, it was that night he wrote to his friend: "I am getting nearer this Mystery, which I take to be, the inner heart of it, a mixture of the Holy Ghost and Sweat—with a good bath afterward! But the old boy is the mixer of the Pills, mind you, and he *is* a Master! Most likely I shall never get hold of the heart of it; for somehow, yet with all courtesy, he keeps me at a distance. I have never been 'confessed,' whatever that may be—an experience that comes to the youngest boy among them! Perhaps the Doctor thinks that old fellows like you and me have only dead sins to confess, which would crumble to dust if exposed. But there is a sting in very old sins, I think—for instance—oh! if you were here tonight, I should be as foolish as a woman. . . ."

The storm that night struck one of the school buildings and killed a lad. In the morning the Master and the surgeon set out for the School Village, which was lower in the valley beyond Albany. It was warm and clear at the Inn; but thick mist wreaths still lay heavily over the Intervale. The hills all about glittered as in October, and there was in the air that laughing peace, that breath of sweet plenty which comes the morning after a storm. The two men followed the footpath, which wound downward from the Inn across the Intervale. The sun filled the windless air, sucking up the spicy odors of the tangled path—fern and balsam and the mother scent of earth and rain and sun. The new green rioted over the dead leaves. . . . The Master, closely observing his guest, remarked:

"You seem quite well, Doctor. I suppose you will be leaving us soon?"

"Leaving?" the surgeon questioned slowly, as if a secret dread had risen at the Master's hint of departure. "Yes," he admitted, after a time, "I suppose I am what you would call well—well enough. But something still clogs within me. It may be the memory of Fear. I am afraid of myself!"

"Afraid? You need some test, perhaps. That will come sooner or later; we need not hurry it!"

"No, we need not hurry!"

Yet he knew well enough that the Inn never sheltered drones, and that many special indulgences had been granted him: he had borrowed freely from the younger Brothers—of their time and strength. He thought complacently of the large cheque which he should drop into the house-box on his departure. With it the Master would be able to build a new cottage or a small hospital for the School.

"Some of them," mused the Master, "never go back to the machine that once broke them. They stay about here and help me—buy a farm and revert! But for the most part they are keen to get back to the fight, as is right and best. Sometimes when they loiter too long, I shove them out of the nest!"

"And I am near the shoving point?" his companion retorted quickly. "So I must leave all your dear boys and Peace and Fishing and *you!* Suppose so, suppose so!. . . . Doctor, you've saved my life—oh, hang it, that doesn't tell the story. But even *I* can feel what it is to live at the Inn!"

Instinctively he grasped his host by the arm—he was an impulsive man. But the Master's arm did not respond to the clasp; indeed, a slight shiver seemed to shake it, so that the surgeon's hand fell away while the Master said:

"I am glad to have been of service—to you—yes, especially to *you*. . . ."

They came into the School Village, a tiny place of old white houses, very clean and trim, with a number of sweeping elms along the narrow road. A mountain brook turned an old waterwheel, supplying power for the workshops where the boys were trained. The great surgeon had visited the place many times in company with the Master, and though he admired the order and economy of the institution, and respected its purpose—that is, to create men out of the refuse of society—to tell the truth, the place bored him a trifle. This morning they went directly to the little cottage that served as infirmary, where the dead boy had been brought. He was a black-haired Italian, and his lips curved upward pleasantly. The Master putting his hand on the dead boy's brow as he might have done in life stood looking at the face.

"I've got a case in the next room, I'd like to have your opinion on, Doctor," the young physician said in a low tone to the surgeon, and the two crossed the passage into the neighboring room. The surgeon fastened his eyes on the sick lad's body: here was a case he understood, a problem with a solution. The old Master coming in from the dead stood behind the two.

"Williams," the surgeon said, "it's so, sure enough—you must operate—at once!"

"I was afraid it was that," the younger man replied. "But how can I operate here?"

The surgeon shrugged his shoulders—"He would never reach the city!"

"Then I must, you think—"

The shrewd surgeon recognized Fear in the young man's voice. Quick the thrill shot through his nerves, and he cried, "I will operate *now.*"

In half an hour it was over, and the Master and the surgeon were leaving the village, climbing up by the steep path under the blazing noon sun. The Master glanced at the man by his side, who strode along confidently, a trifle of a swagger in his buoyant steps. The Master remarked:

"The test came, and you took it—splendidly."

"Yes," the great surgeon replied, smiling happily, "it's all there, Doctor, the old power. I believe I am about ready to get into harness again!" After they had walked more of the way without speaking, the surgeon added, as to himself—"But there are other things to be feared!"

Though the Master looked at him closely he invited no explanation, and they finished their homeward walk without remark.

It soon got about among the inmates of the Inn what a wonderful operation the surgeon of St. Jerome's had performed, and it was rumored that at the beginning of autumn he would go back to his old position. Meantime the great surgeon enjoyed the homage that men always pay to power, the consideration of his fellows. He had been much liked; but now that the Brothers knew how soon he was to leave them, they surrounded him with those attentions that men most love, elevating him almost to the rank of the Master—and they feared him less. His fame spread, so that from some mill beyond Stowe they brought to the Inn a desperate case, and the surgeon operated again successfully, demonstrating that he was once more master of his art, and master of himself. So he stayed on merely to enjoy his triumph and escape the dull season in the city.

It was a wonderful summer, that! The fitful temper of the north played in all its moods. There were days when the sun shone tropically down into the valleys, without a breath of air, when the earthy, woodsy smells were strong—and the nights—perfect stillness and peace, as if some spirit of the air were listening for love words on the earth. The great elms along Albany road hung their branches motionless, and when the moon came over behind the house the great hills began to swim ghostly, vague—beyond, always beyond!... And then there were the fierce storms that swept up the valley and hung growling along the hills for days, and afterward, sky-washed and clear, the westerly breeze would come tearing down the Intervale, drying the earth before it. . . . But each day there was a change in the sound and the smell of the fields and the woods—in the quick race of the northern summer—a change that the surgeon, fishing up the tiny streams, felt and noted. Each day, so radiant with its abundant life, sounded some under-note of fulfillment and change—speaking beforehand of death to come.

Toward the end of August a snap of cold drove us indoors for the night meal. Then around the fire there was great talk between the Master and the surgeon, a sort of battle of the soul, to which we others paid silent attention. For wherever those nights the talk might rise, in the little rills of accidental words, it always flowed down to the deep underlying thoughts of men. And in those depths, as I said, these two wrestled with each other. The Master, who had grown silent of late years, woke once more with fire. The light, keen thrusts of the surgeon, who argued like a fencer, roused his whole being; and as day by day it went on we who watched saw that in a way the talk of these two men set forth the great conflict of conflicts, that deepest fissure of life and belief anent the Soul and the Body. And the Master, who had lived his faiths by his life before our eyes, was being worsted in the argument! The great surgeon had the better mind, and he had seen all of life that one may see with eyes. . . .

They were talking of the day of departure for the distinguished guest, and arranging for some kind of triumphal procession to escort him to White River. But he would not set the time, shrinking from this act, as if all were not yet done. There came a warm, glowing day early in September, and at night after the pipes were lighted the surgeon and the Master strolled off in the direction of the pool, arm in arm. There had been no talk that day, the surgeon apparently shrinking from coming to the last grapple with one whose faiths were so important to him as the Master's.

"The flowers are dying: they tell me it's time to move on," said the surgeon. "And yet, my dear host, I go without the Secret, without understanding All!"

"Perhaps there is no inner Secret," the Master smiled. "It is all here before you."

"I know that—you have been very good to me, shared everything. If I have not learned the Secret, it is my fault, my incapacity. But—" and the gay tone dropped quickly and a flash of bitterness succeeded—"I at least know that there *is* a Secret!"

They sat down on the marble bench and looked into the water, each thinking his thoughts. Suddenly the surgeon began to speak, hesitantly, as if there had long been something in his mind that he was compelled to say.

"My friend," he said, " I too have something to tell—the cause within the cause, the reason of the reason—at least, sometimes I think it is! The root reason for all—unhappiness, defeat, for the shaking hand and the jesting voice. And I want you to hear it—if you will."

The Master raised his face from the pool but said never a word. The surgeon continued, his voice trembling at times, though he spoke slowly evidently trying to banish all feeling.

"It is a common enough story at the start, at least among men of our kind. You know that I was trained largely in Europe. My father had the means to give me the best, and time to take it in. So I was over there, before I came back to St. Jerome's, three, four years at Paris, Munich, Vienna, all about.... While I was away I lived as the others, for the most part—you know our profession—and youth. The rascals are pretty much the same today, I judge from what my friends say of their sons! Well, at least I worked like the devil, and was decent.... Oh, it isn't for that I'm telling the tale! I was ambitious, then. And the time came to go back, as it does in the end, and I took a few weeks' run through Italy as a final taste of the lovely European thing, and came down to Naples to get the boat for New York. I've never been back to Naples since, and that was twenty-six years ago this autumn. But I can see the city always as it was then! The seething human hive—the fellows piling in the freight to the music of their songs—the fiery mouth of Vesuvius up above. And the soft, dark night with just a plash of waves on the quay!"

The Master listened, his eyes again buried in the water at their feet.

"Well, *she* was there on board, of course—looking out also into that warm dark night and sighing for all that was to be lost so soon. There were few passengers in those days.... She was my countrywoman, and beautiful, and there was something—at least so I thought then—of especial sweetness in her eyes, something strong in her heart. She was engaged to a man living somewhere in the States, and she was going back to marry him. Why she was over there then I forget, and it is of no importance. I think that the man was a doctor, too—in some small city... I loved her!"

The Master raised his eyes from the pool and leaning on his folded arms looked into the surgeon's face.

"I am afraid I never thought much about that other fellow—never have to this day! That was part of the brute I am—to see only what is before my eyes. And I knew by the time we had swung into the Atlantic that I wanted that woman as I had never wanted things before. She stirred me, mind and all. Of course it might have been someone else—anyone you will say—and if she had been an ordinary young girl, it might have gone differently? It is one of the things we can't tell in this life. There was something in that woman that was big all through and roused the spirit in me. I never knew man or woman who thirsted more for greatness, for accomplishment. Perhaps the man she was to marry gave her little to hope for—probably it was some raw boy-and-girl affair such as we have in America.... The days went by, and it was clearer to both of us what must be. But we didn't speak of it. She found in me, I suppose, the power, the sort of thing she had missed in the other. I was to do all those grand things she was so hot after. I have done some of them too. But that was when she had gone and I no longer needed her.... I needed her then, and I took her—that is all.

"The detail is old and dim—and what do you care to hear of a young man's loves! Before we reached port it was understood between us. I told her I wanted her to leave the other chap—he was never altogether clear to me—and to marry me as soon as she could. We did not stumble or slide into it, not in the least: we looked it through and through—that was her kind and mine. How she loved to look life in the face! I have found few women who like that.... In the end she asked me not to come near her the last day. She would write me the day after we had landed, either yes or no. So she kissed me, and we parted still out at sea."

All the Brothers had left the court and the arcades, where they had been strolling, and old Sam was putting out the Inn lights. But the two men beside the pool made no movement. The west wind still drew in down the valley with summer warmth and ruffled the water at their feet.

"My father met me at the dock—you know he was the first surgeon at St. Jerome's before me. My mother was with him.... But as she kissed me I was thinking of that letter.... I knew it would come. Some things must! Well, it came."

The silent listener bent his head, and the surgeon mused on his passionate memory. At last the Master whispered in a low voice that hardly reached into the night:

"Did you make her happy?"

The surgeon did not answer the question at once.

"Did you make her happy?" the old man demanded again, and his voice trembled this time with such intensity that his companion looked at him wonderingly. And in those dark eyes of the Master's he read something that made him shrink away. Then for the third time the old man demanded sternly:

"Tell me—did you make her happy?"

It was the voice of one who had a right to know, and the surgeon whispered back slowly:

"Happy? No, my God! Perhaps at first, in the struggle, a little. But afterward there was too much—too many things. It went, the inspiration and the love. I broke her heart—she left me! That—that is *my* Reason!"

"It *is* the Reason! For you took all, all—you let her give all, and you gave her—what?"

"Nothing—she died."

"I know—she died."

The Master had risen, and with folded arms faced his guest, a pitying look in his eyes. The surgeon covered his face with his hands, and after a long time said:

"So you knew this?"

"Yes, I knew!"

"And knowing you let me come here. You took me into your house, you healed me, you gave me back my life!"

And the Master replied with a firm voice:

"I knew, and I gave you back your life." In a little while he explained more softly: "You and I are no longer young men who feel hotly and settle such a matter with hate. We cannot quarrel now for the possession of a woman.... She chose: remember that!.... It was twenty-six years this September. We have lived our lives, you and I; we have lived out our lives, the good and the evil. Why should we now for the second time add passion to sorrow?"

"And yet knowing all you took me in!"

"Yes!" the old man cried almost proudly. "And I have made you again what you once were.... What *she* loved as you," he added to himself, "a man full of Power."

Then they were speechless in face of the fact: the one had taken all and the sweet love turned to acid in his heart, and the other had lost and the bitter turned to sweet! When a long time had passed the surgeon spoke timidly:

"It might have been so different for her with you! You loved her—more."

There was the light of a compassionate smile on the Master's lips as he replied:

"Yes, I loved her, too."

"And it changed things—for you!"

"It changed things. There might have been my St. Jerome's—my fame also. Instead, I came here with my boys. And here I shall die, please God."

The old Master then became silent, his face set in a dream of life, as it was, as it would have been; while the great surgeon of St. Jerome's thought such thoughts as had never passed before into his mind. The night wind had died at this late hour, and in its place there was a coldness of the turning season. The stars shone near the earth and all was silent with the peace of mysteries. The Master looked at the man beside him and said calmly:

"It is well as it is—all well!"

At last the surgeon rose and stood before the Master.

"I have learned the Secret," he said, "and now it is time for me to go."

He went up to the house through the little court and disappeared within the Inn, while the Master sat by the poll, his face graven like the face of an old man, who has seen the circle of life and understands.... The next morning there was much talk about Dr. Norton's disappearance, until someone explained that the surgeon had been suddenly called back to the city.

The news spread through the Brotherhood one winter that the old Inn had been burned to the ground, a bitter December night when all the water-taps were frozen. And the Master, who had grown deaf of late, had been caught in his remote chamber, and burned or rather suffocated. There were few men in the Inn at the time, it being the holiday season, and when they had fought their way to the old man's room, they found him lying on the lounge by the window, the lids fallen over the dark eyes and his face placid with sleep or contemplation.... They sought in vain for the reason of the fire—but why search for causes?

All those beautiful hills that we loved to watch as the evening haze gathered, the Master left in trust for the people of the State—many acres of waving forests. And the School continued in its old place, the Brothers looking after its wants and supplying it with means to continue its work. But the Inn was never rebuilt. The blackened ruins of buildings were removed and the garden in the court extended so that it covered the whole space where the Inn had stood. This was enclosed with a thick plantation of firs on all sides but that one which looked westward across the Intervale. The spot can be seen for miles around on the Albany hillside.

And when it was ready—all fragrant and radiant with flowers—they placed the Master there beside the pool, where he had loved to sit, surrounded by men. On the sunken slab his title was engraved—

THE MASTER OF THE INN

GREEN GARDENS

FRANCES NOYES HART

DAPHNE WAS SINGING TO HERSELF when she came through the painted gate in the back wall. She was singing partly because it was June, and Devon, and she was seventeen, and partly because she had caught a breathtaking glimpse of herself in the long mirror as she had flashed through the hall at home, and it seemed almost too good to be true that the radiant small person in the green muslin frock with the wreath of golden hair bound about her head, and the sea-blue eyes laughing back at her, was really Miss Daphne Chiltern. Incredible, incredible luck to look like that, half Dryad, half Kate Greenaway—she danced down the turf path to the herb-garden, swinging her great wicker basket and singing like a small mad thing.

"He promised to buy me a bonnie blue ribbon," carolled Daphne, all her own ribbons flying,

"He promised to buy me a bonnie blue ribbon,
He promised to buy me a bonnie blue ribbon
To tie up—"

The song stopped as abruptly as though someone had struck it from her lips. A strange man was kneeling by the beehive in the herb-garden. He was looking at her over his shoulder, at once startled and amused, and she saw that he was wearing a rather shabby tweed suit and that his face was oddly brown against his close-cropped, tawny hair. He smiled, his teeth a strong flash of white.

"Hello!" he greeted her, in a tone at once casual and friendly.

Daphne returned the smile uncertainly. "Hello," she replied gravely. The strange man rose easily to his feet, and she saw that he was very tall and carried his head rather splendidly, like the young bronze Greek in Uncle Roland's study at home. But his eyes—his eyes were strange—quite dark and burned out. The rest of him looked young and vivid and adventurous—but his eyes looked as though the adventure were over, though they were still questing.

"Were you looking for anyone?" she asked, and the man shook his head, laughing.

"No one in particular, unless it was you."

Daphne's soft brow darkened. "It couldn't possibly have been me," she said in a rather stately small voice, "because, you see, I don't know you. Perhaps you didn't know that there is no one living in Green Gardens now?"

"Oh, yes, I knew. The Fanes have left for Ceylon, haven't they?"

"Sir Harry left two weeks ago, because he had to see the old governor before he sailed, but Lady Audrey only left last week. She had to close the London house, too, so there was a great deal to do."

"I see. And so Green Gardens is deserted?"

"It is sold," said Daphne, with a small quaver in her voice, "just this afternoon. I came over to say goodbye to it, and to get some mint and lavender from the garden."

"Sold?" repeated the man, and there was an agony of incredulity in the stunned whisper. He flung out his arm against the sun-warmed bricks of the high wall as though to hold off some invader. "No, no; they'd never dare to sell it."

"I'm glad you mind so much," said Daphne softly. "It's strange that nobody minds but us, isn't it? I cried at first—and then I thought that it would be happier if it wasn't lonely and empty, poor dear—and then, it was such a beautiful day, that I forgot to be unhappy."

The man bestowed a wretched smile on her. "You hardly conveyed the impression of unrelieved gloom as you came around that corner," he assured her.

"I—I haven't a very good memory for being unhappy," Daphne confessed remorsefully, a lovely and guilty rose staining her to her brow at the memory of that exultant chant.

He threw back his head with a sudden shout of laughter.

"These are glad tidings! I'd rather find a pagan than a Puritan at Green Gardens any day. Let's both have a poor memory. Do you mind if I smoke?"

"No," she replied, "but do you mind if I ask you what you are doing here?"

"Not a bit." He lit the stubby brown pipe, curving his hand dexterously to shelter it from the little breeze. He had the most beautiful hands that she had ever seen, slim and brown and fine—they looked as though they would be miraculously strong—and miraculously gentle. "I came to see—I came to see whether there was 'honey still for tea,' Mistress Dryad!"

"Honey-–for tea?" she echoed wonderingly; "was that why you were looking at the hive?"

He puffed meditatively, "Well—partly. It's a quotation from a poem. Ever read Rupert Brooke?"

"Oh, yes, yes." Her voice tripped in its eagerness.

"I know one by heart—

" 'If I should die think only this of me:

(That there's some corner of a foreign field

(That is forever England. There shall be—"

He cut in on the magical little voice roughly.

"Ah, what damned nonsense! Do you suppose he's happy, in his foreign field, that golden lover? Why shouldn't even the dead be homesick? No, no—he was sick for home in Germany when he wrote that poem of mine—he's sicker for it in Heaven, I'll warrant." He pulled himself up swiftly at the look of amazement in Daphne's eyes. "I've clean forgotten my manners," he confessed ruefully. "No, don't get that flying look in your eyes—I swear that I'll be good. It's a long time—it's a long time since I've talked to anyone who needed gentleness. If you knew what need I had of it, you'd stay a little while, I think."

"Of course, I'll stay," she said. "I'd love to, if you want me to."

"I want you to more than I've ever wanted anything that I can remember." His tone was so matter-of-fact that Daphne thought that she must have imagined the words. "Now, can't we make ourselves comfortable for a little while? I'd feel safer if you weren't standing there ready for instant flight! Here's a nice bit of grass—and the wall for a back—"

Daphne glanced anxiously at the green muslin frock. "It's—it's pretty hard to be comfortable without cushions," she submitted diffidently.

The man yielded again to laughter. "Are even Dryads afraid to spoil their frocks? Cushions it shall be. There are some extra ones in the chest in the East Indian room, aren't there?"

Daphne let the basket slip through her fingers, her eyes black through sheer surprise.

"But how did you know—how did you know about the lacquer chest?" she whispered breathlessly.

"Oh, devil take me for a blundering ass!" He stood considering her forlornly for a moment, and then shrugged his shoulders, with the brilliant and disarming smile. "The game's up, thanks to my inspired lunacy! But I'm going to trust you not to say that you've seen me. I know about the lacquer chest because I always kept my marbles there."

"Are you—are you Stephen Fane?"

At the awed whisper the man bowed low, all mocking grace, his hand on his heart—the sun burnishing his tawny head.

"Oh-h!" breathed Daphne. She bent to pick up the wicker basket, her small face white and hard.

"Wait!" said Stephen Fane. His face was white and hard too. "You are right to go—entirely, absolutely right—but I am going to beg you to stay. I don't know what you've heard about me—however vile it is, it's less than the truth—"

"I have heard nothing of you," said Daphne, holding her gold-wreathed head high, "but five years ago I was not allowed to come to Green Gardens for weeks because I mentioned your name. I was told that it was not a name to pass decent lips."

Something terrible leaped in those burned-out eyes—and died.

"I had not thought they would use their hate to lash a child," he said. "They were quite right—and you, too. Good night."

"Good night," replied Daphne clearly. She started down the path, but at its bend she turned to look back—because she was seventeen, and it was June, and she remembered his laughter. He was standing quite still by the golden straw beehive, but he had thrown one arm across his eyes, as though to shut out some intolerable sight. And then, with a soft little rush she was standing beside him.

"How—how do we get the cushions?" she demanded breathlessly.

Stephen Fane dropped his arm, and Daphne drew back a little at the sudden blaze of wonder in his face.

"Oh," he whispered voicelessly. "Oh, you Loveliness!" He took a step toward her, and then stood still, clinching his brown hands. Then he thrust them deep in his pockets, standing very straight. "I do think," he said carefully, "I do think you had better go. The fact that I have tried to make you stay simply proves the particular type of rotter that I am. Good-by—I'll never forget that you came back."

"I am not going," said Daphne sternly. "Not if you beg me. Not if you are a devil out of hell. Because you need me. And no matter how many wicked things you have done, there can't be anything as wicked as going away when someone needs you. How do we get the cushions?"

"Oh, my wise Dryad!" His voice broke on laughter, but Daphne saw that his lashes were suddenly bright with tears. "Stay, then—why, even I cannot harm you. God himself can't grudge me this little space of wonder—he knows how far I've come for it—how I've fought and struggled and ached to win it—how in dirty lands and dirty places I've dreamed of summer twilight in a still garden—and England, England!"

"Didn't you dream of me?" asked Daphne wistfully, with a little catch of reproach.

He laughed again, unsteadily. "Why, who could ever dream of you, my Wonder? You are a thousand, thousand dreams come true."

Daphne bestowed on him a tremulous and radiant smile. "Please let us get the cushions. I think I am a little tired."

"And I am a graceless fool! There used to be a pane of glass cut out in one of the south casement windows. Shall we try that?"

"Please, yes. How did you find it, Stephen?" She saw again that thrill of wonder on his face, but his voice was quite steady.

"I didn't find it; I did it! It was uncommonly useful, getting in that way sometimes, I can tell you. And, by the Lord Harry, here it is. Wait a minute, Loveliness—I'll get through and open the south door for you—no chance that way of spoiling the frock." He swung himself up with the swift, sure grace of a cat, smiled at her—vanished—it was hardly a minute later that she heard the bolts dragging back in the south door, and he flung it wide.

The sunlight streamed into the deep hall and stretched hesitant fingers into the dusty quiet of the great East Indian room, gilding the soft tones of the faded chintz, touching very gently the polished furniture and the dim prints on the walls. He swung across the threshold without a word, Daphne tiptoeing behind him.

"How still it is," he said in a hushed voice. "How sweet it smells!"

"It's the potpourri in the Canton jars," she told him shyly. "I always made it every summer for Lady Audrey—she thought I did it better than anyone else. I think so too." She flushed at the mirth in his eyes, but held her ground sturdily. "Flowers are sweeter for you if you love them—even dead ones," she explained bravely.

"They would be dead indeed, if they were not sweet for you." Her cheeks burned bright at the low intensity of his voice, but he turned suddenly away. "Oh, there she sails—there she sails still, my beauty. Isn't she the proud one though—straight into the wind!" He hung over the little ship model, thrilled as any child. "*The Flying Lady*—see where it's painted on her? Grandfather gave it to me when I was seven—he had it from his father when he was six. Lord, how proud I was!" He stood back to see it better, frowning a little. "One of those ropes is wrong; any fool could tell that—" His hands hovered over it for a moment—dropped. "No matter—the new owners are probably not seafarers! The lacquer chest is at the far end, isn't it? Yes, here. Are three enough—four? We're off!" But still he lingered, sweeping the great room with his dark eyes.

"It's full of all kinds of junk—they never liked it—no period, you see. I had the run of it—I loved it as though it were alive; it was alive, for me. From Elizabeth's day down, all the family adventurers brought their treasures here—beaten gold and hammered silver—mother-of-pearl and peacock feathers, strange woods and stranger spices, porcelains and embroideries and blown glass. There was always an adventurer somewhere in each generation—and however far he wandered, he came back to Green Gardens to bring his treasures home. When I was a yellow-headed imp of Satan, hiding my marbles in the lacquer chest, I used to swear that when I grew up I would bring home the finest treasure of all, if I had to search the world from end to end. And now the last adventurer has come home to Green Gardens—and he has searched the world from end to end—and he is empty-handed."

"No, no," whispered Daphne. "He has brought home the greatest treasure of all, that adventurer. He has brought home the beaten gold of his love, and the hammered silver of his dreams—and he has brought them from very far."

"He had brought greater treasures than those to you, lucky room," said the last of the adventurers. "You can never be sad again—you will always be gay and proud—because for just one moment he brought you the gold of her hair and the silver of her voice."

"He is talking great nonsense, room," said a very small voice, "but it is beautiful nonsense, and I am a wicked girl, and I hope that he will talk some more. And please, I think we will go into the garden and see."

All the way back down the flagged path to the herb-garden they were quiet—even after he had arranged the cushions against the rose-red wall, even after he had stretched out at full length beside her and lighted another pipe.

After a while he said, staring at the straw hive: "There used to be a jolly little fat brown one that was a great pal of mine. How long do bees live?"

"I don't know," she answered vaguely, and after a long pause, full of quiet, pleasant odors from the bee-garden, and the sleepy happy noises of small things tucking themselves away for the night, and the faint but poignant drift of tobacco smoke, she asked: "What was it about 'honey still for tea'?"

"Oh, that!" He raised himself on one elbow so that he could see her better. "It was a poem I came across while I was in East Africa; someone sent a copy of Rupert Brooke's things to a chap out there, and this one fastened itself around me like a vise. It starts where he's sitting in a café in Berlin with a lot of German Jews around him, swallowing down their beer; and suddenly he remembers. All the lost, unforgettable beauty comes back to him in that dirty place; it gets him by the throat. It got me, too.

"'Ah, God! to see the branches stir
Across the moon at Grantchester!
To smell the thrilling-sweet and rotten
Unforgettable, unforgotten
River-smell, and hear the breeze
Sobbing in the little trees.
Oh, is the water sweet and cool,
Gentle and brown, above the pool?

And laughs the immortal river still
Under the mill, under the mill?
Say, is there Beauty yet to find?
And Certainty? And Quiet kind?
Deep meadows yet, for to forget
The lies, and truths, and pain?—oh, yet
Stands the Church clock at ten to three?
And is there honey still for tea?'"

"That's beautiful," she said, "but it hurts."

"Thank God you'll never know how it hurts, little Golden Heart in quiet gardens. But for some of us, caught like rats in the trap of the ugly fever we called living, it was black torture and yet our dear delight to remember the deep meadows we had lost—to wonder if there was honey still for tea."

"Stephen, won't you tell me about it—won't that help?"

And suddenly someone else looked at her through those haunted eyes—a little boy, terrified and forsaken. "Oh, I have no right to soil you with it. But I came back to tell someone about it—I had to, I had to. I had to wait until father and Audrey went away. I knew they'd hate to see me—she was my stepmother, you know, and she always loathed me, and he never cared. In East Africa I used to stay awake at night thinking that I might die, and that no one in England would ever care—no one would know how I had loved her. It was worse than dying to think that."

"But why couldn't you come back to Green Gardens—why couldn't you make them see, Stephen?"

"Why, what was there to see? When they sent me down from Oxford for that dirty little affair, I was only nineteen—and they told me I had disgraced my name and Green Gardens and my country—and I went mad with pride and shame, and swore I'd drag their precious name through the dirt of every country in the world. And I did—and I did."

His head was buried in his arms, but Daphne heard. It seemed strange indeed to her that she felt no shrinking and no terror; only great pity for what he had lost, great grief for what he might have had. For a minute she forgot that she was Daphne, the heedless and gay-hearted, and that he was a broken and an evil man. For a minute he was a little lad, and she was his lost mother.

"Don't mind, Stephen," she whispered to him, "don't mind. Now you have come home—now it is all done with, that ugliness. Please, please don't mind."

"No, no," said the stricken voice, "you don't know, you don't know, thank God. But I swear I've paid—I swear, I swear I have. When the others used to take their dirty drugs to make them forget, they would dream of strange paradises, unknown heavens—but through the haze and mist that they brought, I would remember—I would remember. The filth and the squalor and vileness would fade and dissolve—and I would see the sun-dial, with the yellow roses on it, warm in the sun, and smell the clove pinks in the kitchen border, and touch the cresses by the brook, cool and green and wet. All the sullen drums and whining flutes would sink to silence, and I would hear the little yellow-headed cousin of the vicar's singing in the twilight, singing, 'There is a lady, sweet and kind' and 'Weep you no more, sad fountains' and 'Hark, hark, the lark.' And the small painted yellow faces and the little wicked hands and perfumed fans would vanish and I would see again the gay beauty of the lady who hung above the mantel in the long drawing room, the lady who laughed across the centuries in her white muslin frock, with eyes that matched the blue ribbon in her wind-blown curls—the lady who was as young and lovely as England, for all the years! Oh, I would remember, I would remember! It was twilight, and I was hurrying home through the dusk after tennis at the rectory; there was a bell ringing quietly somewhere and a moth flying by brushed against my face with velvet—and I could smell the hawthorn hedge glimmering white, and see the first star swinging low above the trees, and lower still, and brighter still, the lights of home.—And then before my very eyes, they would fade, they would fade, dimmer and dimmer—they would flicker and go out, and I would be back again, with tawdriness and shame and vileness fast about me—and I would pay."

"But now you have paid enough," Daphne told him. "Oh, surely, surely—you have paid enough. Now you have come home—now you can forget."

"No," said Stephen Fane. "Now I must go."

"Go?" At the small startled echo he raised his head.

"What else?" he asked. "Did you think that I would stay?"

"But I do not want you to go." Her lips were white, but she spoke very clearly.

Stephen Fane never moved but his eyes, dark and wondering, rested on her like a caress.

"Oh, my little Loveliness, what dream is this?"

"You must not go away again, you must not."

"I am baser that I thought," he said, very low. "I have made you pity me, I who have forfeited your lovely pity this long time. It cannot even touch me now. I have sat here like a dark Othello telling tales to a small white Desdemona, and you, God help me, have thought me tragic and abused. You shall not think that. In a few minutes I will be gone—I will not have you waste a dream on me. Listen—there is nothing vile that I have not done—nothing, do you hear? Not clean sin like murder—I have cheated at cards, and played with loaded dice, and stolen the rings off the fingers of an Argentine Jewess who—" His voice twisted and broke before the lovely mercy in the frightened eyes that still met his so bravely.

"But why, Stephen?"

"So that I could buy my dreams. So that I could purchase peace with little dabs of brown in a pipe-bowl, little puffs of white in the palm of my hand, little drops of liquid on a ball of cotton. So that I could drug myself with dirt—and forget the dirt and remember England."

He rose to his feet with that swift grace of his, and Daphne rose too, slowly.

"I am going now; will you walk to the gate with me?"

He matched his long step to hers, watching the troubled wonder on her small white face intently.

"How old are you, my Dryad?"

"I am seventeen."

"Seventeen! Oh God be good to us, I had forgotten that one could be seventeen. What's that?"

He paused, suddenly alert, listening to a distant whistle, sweet on the summer air.

"Oh, that—that is Robin."

"Ah—" His smile flashed, tender and ironic. "And who is Robin?"

"He is—just Robin. He is down from Cambridge for a week, and I told him that he might walk home with me."

"Then I must be off quickly. Is he coming to this gate?"

"No, to the south one."

"Listen to me, my Dryad—are you listening?" For her face was turned away.

"Yes," said Daphne.

"You are going to forget me—to forget this afternoon—to forget everything but Robin whistling through the summer twilight."

"No," said Daphne.

"Yes; because you have a very poor memory about unhappy things! You told me so. But just for a minute after I have gone, you will remember that now all is very well with me, because I have found the deep meadows—and honey still for tea—and you. You are to remember that for just one minute—will you? And now good-by—"

She tried to say the words, but she could not. For a moment he stood staring down at the white pathos of the small face, and then he turned away. But when he came to the gate, he paused and put his arms about the wall, as though he would never let it go, laying his cheek against the sun-warmed bricks, his eyes fast closed. The whistling came nearer, and he stirred, put his hand on the little painted gate, vaulted across it lightly, and was gone. She turned at Robin's quick step on the walk.

"Ready, dear? What are you staring at?"

"Nothing! Robin—Robin, did you ever hear of Stephen Fane?"

He nodded grimly.

"Do you know—do you know what he is doing now?"

"Doing now?" He stared at her blankly. "What on earth do you mean? Why, he's been dead for months—killed in the campaign in East Africa—only decent thing he ever did in his life. Why?"

Daphne never stirred. She stood quite still, staring at the painted gate. Then she said, very carefully: "Someone thought—someone thought that they had seen him—quite lately."

Robin laughed comfortingly. "No use looking so scared about it, my blessed child. Perhaps they did. The War Office made all kinds of ghastly blunders—it was a quick step from 'missing in action' to 'killed.' And he probably would have been jolly glad of a chance to drop out quietly and have everyone think he was done for."

Daphne never took her eyes from the gate. "Yes" she said quietly, "I suppose he would. Will you get my basket, Robin? I left it by the beehive. There are some cushions that belong in the East Indian room, too. The south door is open."

When he had gone, she stood shaking for a moment, listening to his footsteps die away, and then she flew to the gate, searching the twilight desperately with straining eyes. There was no one there—no one at all—but then the turn in the lane would have hidden him by now. And suddenly terror fell from her like a cloak.

She turned swiftly to the brick wall, straining up, up on tiptoes, to lay her cheek against its roughened surface, to touch it very gently with her lips. She could hear Robin whistling down the path but she did not turn. She was bidding farewell to Green Gardens—and the last adventurer.

BUTTERCUP-NIGHT

JOHN GALSWORTHY

WHY IS IT THAT IN SOME PLACES there is such a feeling of life being all one; not merely a long picture-show for human eyes, but a single breathing, glowing, growing thing, of which we are no more important a part than the swallows and magpies, the foals and sheep in the meadows, the sycamores and ash trees and flowers in the fields, the rocks and little bright streams, or even the long fleecy clouds and their soft-shouting drivers, the winds?

True, we register these parts of being, and they—so far as we know—do not register us; yet it is impossible to feel, in such places as I speak of, the busy, dry, complacent sense of being all that matters, which in general we humans have so strongly.

In these rare spots, that are always in the remote country, untouched by the advantages of civilization, one is conscious of an enwrapping web or mist of spirit, the glamorous and wistful wraith of all the vanished shapes which once dwelt there in such close comradeship.

It was Sunday of an early June when I first came on one such, far down in the West country. I had walked with my knapsack twenty miles; and, there being no room at the tiny inn of the very little village, they directed me to a wicket gate, through which by a path leading down a field I would come to a farmhouse where I might find lodging. The moment I got into that field I felt within me a peculiar contentment, and sat down on a rock to let the feeling grow. In an old holly tree rooted to the bank about fifty yards away, two magpies evidently had a nest, for they were coming and going, avoiding my view as much as possible, yet with a certain stealthy confidence which made one feel that they had long prescriptive right to that dwelling-place.

Around, as far as one could see, there was hardly a yard of level ground; all was hill and hollow, that long ago had been reclaimed from the moor; and against the distant folds of the hills the farmhouse and its thatched barns were just visible, embowered amongst beeches and some dark trees, with a soft bright crown of sunlight over the whole. A gentle wind brought a faint rustling up from those beeches, and from a large lime tree that stood by itself; on this wind some little snowy clouds, very high and fugitive in that blue heaven, were always moving over. But what struck me most were the buttercups. Never was field so lighted up by those tiny lamps, those little bright pieces of flower china out of the Great Pottery. They covered the whole ground, as if the sunlight had fallen bodily from the sky, in tens of millions of gold patines; and the fields below as well, down to what was evidently a stream, were just as thick with the extraordinary warmth and glory of them.

Leaving the rock at last, I went toward the house. It was long and low and rather sad, standing in a garden all mossy grass and buttercups, with a few rhododendrons and flowery shrubs, below a row of fine old Irish yews. On the stone verandah a gray sheepdog and a very small golden-haired child were sitting close together, absorbed in each other. A pleasant woman came in answer to my knock, and told me, in a soft, slurring voice, that I might stay the night; and dropping my knapsack, I went out again.

Through an old gate under a stone arch I came on the farmyard, quite deserted save for a couple of ducks moving slowly down a gutter in the sunlight; and noticing the upper half of a stable-door open, I went across, in search of something living. There, in a rough loose-box, on thick straw, lay a long-tailed black mare with the skin and head of a thoroughbred. She was swathed in blankets, and her face, all cut about the cheeks and over the eyes, rested on an ordinary human's pillow, held by a bearded man in shirt-sleeves; while, leaning against the whitewashed walls, sat fully a dozen other men, perfectly silent, very gravely and intently gazing.

The mare's eyes were half closed, and what could be seen of them dull and blueish, as though she had been through a long time of pain. Save for her rapid breathing, she lay quite still, but her neck and ears were streaked with sweat, and every now and then her hind legs quivered spasmodically. Seeing me at the door, she raised her head, uttering a queer half-human noise, but the bearded man at once put his hand on her forehead, and with a "Whoa, my dear—whoa, my pretty!" pressed it down again, while with the other hand he plumped up the pillow for her cheek. And, as the mare obediently let fall her head, one of the men said in a low voice, "I never see anything so like a Christian—like a Christian!"

It went to one's heart to watch her, and I moved off down the farm lane into an old orchard, where the apple trees were still in bloom, with bees—very small ones—busy on the blossoms, whose petals were dropping on the dock leaves and buttercups in the long grass. Climbing over the bank at the far end, I found myself in a meadow the like of which—so wild and yet so lush—I think I have never seen. Along one hedge of its meandering length was a mass of pink mayflower; and between two little running streams grew quantities of yellow water-iris—"daggers," as they call them; the "print-frock" orchid, too, was everywhere in the grass, and always the buttercups. Great stones coated with yellowish moss were strewn among the ash trees and dark hollies; and through a grove of beeches on the far side, such as Corot might have painted, a girl was running, with a youth after her, who jumped down over the bank and vanished. Thrushes, blackbirds, yaffles, cuckoos, and one other very monotonous little bird were in full song; and this, with the sound of the streams and the wind, and the shapes of the rocks and trees, the colors of the flowers, and the warmth of the sun, gave one a feeling of being lost in a very wilderness of nature. Some ponies came slowly from the far end,—tangled, gypsy-headed little creatures,—stared, and went off again at speed. It was just one of those places where any day the Spirit of all Nature might start up in one of those white gaps that separate the trees and rocks. But though I sat a long time waiting—hoping—She did not come.

They were all gone from the stable when I went back up to the farm, except the bearded nurse and one tall fellow, who might have been the "Dying Gaul" as he crouched there in the straw; and the mare was sleeping—her head between her nurse's knees.

That night I woke at two o'clock to find it almost as bright as day, with moonlight coming in through the flimsy curtains. And, smitten with the felling that comes to us creatures of routine so rarely,—of what beauty and strangeness we let slip by without ever stretching out hand to grasp it,—I got up, dressed, stole downstairs, and out.

Never was such a night of frozen beauty, never such dream-tranquillity. The wind had dropped, and the silence was such that one hardly liked to tread even on the grass. From the lawn and fields there seemed to be a mist rising—in truth, the moonlight caught on the dewy buttercups; and across this ghostly radiance the shadows of the yew trees fell in dense black bars.

Suddenly I bethought me of the mare. How was she faring, this marvelous night? Very softly opening the door into the yard, I tiptoed across. A light was burning in her box. And I could hear her making the same half-human noise she had made in the afternoon, as if wondering at her feelings; and instantly the voice of the bearded man talking to her as one might talk to a child: "Oover, my darlin'; yu've a-been long enough o' that side. Wa-ay, my swate—yu let old Jack turn yu, then!" Then came a scuffling in the straw, a thud, that half-human sigh, and his voice again: "Putt your 'ead to piller, that's my dandy gel. Old Jack would n' 'urt yu; no more 'n if yu was the Queen!" Then only her quick breathing could be heard, and his cough and mutter, as he settled down once more to his long vigil.

I crept very softly up to the window, but she heard me at once; and at the movement of her head the old fellow sat up, blinking his eyes out of the bush of his grizzled hair and beard. Opening the door, I said,—

"May I come in?"

"Oo ay! Come in, zurr, if yu'm a mind tu."

I sat down beside him on a sack. And for some time we did not speak, taking each other in. One of his legs was lame, so that he had to keep it stretched out all the time; and awfully tired he looked, gray-tired.

"You're a great nurse!" I said at last. "It must be tiring work, watching out here all night."

His eyes twinkled; they were of that bright gray kind through which the soul looks out.

"Aw, no!" he said. "Ah, don't grudge it vur a dumb animal. Poor things they can't 'elp theirzelves. Many's the naight ah've zat up with 'orses and beast tu. 'T es en me—can't bear to zee dumb creatures zuffer."

And laying his hand on the mare's ears, "They zay 'orses 'aven't no souls. 'T es my belief they've souls zame as us. Many's the Christian ah've seen ain't got the soul of an 'orse. Same with the beasts—an' the ship; 't es only they'm can't spake their minds."

"And where," I said, "do you think they go to when they die?"

He looked at me a little queerly, fancying perhaps that I was leading him into some trap; making sure, too, that I was a real stranger, without power over his body or soul—for humble folk must be careful in the country; then, reassured, and nodding in his beard, he answered knowingly,—

"Ah don't think they goes so very far!"

"Why? Do you ever see their spirits?"

"Naw, naw; I never zeen none; but, for all they zay, ah, don't think none of us goes such a brave way off. There's room for all, dead or alive. An' there's Christians ah've zeen—well, ef they'm not dead for gude, then neither aren't dumb animals, for sure."

"And rabbits, squirrels, birds, even insects? How about them?"

He was silent, as if I had carried him a little beyond the confines of his philosophy; then shook his head.

"'T es all a bit dimsy. But you watch dumb animals, even the laste littlest one, an' yu'll zee they knows a lot more'n what we du; an' they du's things tu that putts shame on a man's often as not. They've a got that in them as passes show." Not noticing my stare at that unconscious plagiarism, he went on, "Ah'd zooner zet up of a naight with an 'orse than with an 'uman—they've more zense, and patience." And stroking the mare's forehead, he added, "Now, my dear, time for yu t' 'ave yure bottle."

I waited to see her take her draft, and lay her head down once more on the pillow. Then, hoping he would get a sleep, I rose to go.

"Aw, 't es nothin' much," he said, "this time o' year; not like in winter. 'T will come day before yu know, these buttercup-nights."

And twinkling up at me out of his kindly bearded face, he settled himself again into the straw.

I stole a look back at his rough figure propped against the sack, with the mare's head down beside his knee, at her swathed black body, and the gold of the straw, the white walls, and dusky nooks and shadows of that old stable illumined by the dimsy light of the old lantern. And with the sense of having seen something holy, I crept away up into the field where I had lingered the day before, and sat down on the same halfway rock.

Close on dawn it was, the moon still sailing wide over the moor, and the flowers of this "buttercup-night" fast closed, not taken in at all by her cold glory! Most silent hour of all the twenty-four—when the soul slips half out of sheath, and hovers in the cool; when the spirit is most in tune with what, soon or late, happens to all spirits; hour when a man cares least whether or no he be alive, as we understand the word.

"None of us goes such a brave way off—there's room for all, dead or alive." Though it was almost unbearably colorless, and quiet, there was warmth in thinking of those words of his; in the thought, too, of the millions of living things snugly asleep all round; warmth in realizing that unanimity of sleep. Insects and flowers, birds, men, beasts, the very leaves on the trees—away in slumberland.

Waiting for the first bird to chirrup, one had perhaps even a stronger feeling than in daytime of the unity and communion of all life, of the subtle brotherhood of living things that fall all together into oblivion, and, all together, wake. When dawn comes, while moonlight is still powdering the world's face, quite a long time passes before one realizes how the quality of the light has changed; so it was day before I knew it. Then the sun came up above the hills; dew began to sparkle, and color to stain the sky. That first praise of the sun from every bird and leaf and blade of grass, the tremulous flush and chime of dawn! One has strayed so far from the heart of things, that it comes as something strange and wonderful! Indeed, I noticed that the beasts and girds gazed at me as if I simply could not be there, at this hour that so belonged to them. And to me, too, they seemed strange and new—with that in them "that passed show," and as of a world where man did not exist, or existed only as just another form of life, another sort of beast. It was one of those revealing moments when we see our proper place in the scheme; go past our truly irreligious thought: "Man, hub of the Universe!" which has founded most religions. One of those moments when our supreme importance will not wash either in the bath of purest spiritual ecstasy, or in the clear fluid of scientific knowledge; and one sees clear, with the eyes of true religion, man playing his little, not unworthy, part in the great game of Perfection.

But just then began the crowning glory of that dawn—the opening and lighting of the buttercups. Not one did I actually see unclose, yet, all of a sudden, they were awake, the fields once more a blaze of gold.

CHERISHED FABLES

THE GRIFFIN AND THE MINOR CANON

FRANK R. STOCKTON

OVER THE GREAT DOOR of an old, old church which stood in a quiet town of a far-away land there was carved in stone the figure of a large griffin. The old-time sculptor had done his work with great care, but the image he had made was not a pleasant one to look at. It had a large head, with enormous open mouth and savage teeth; from its back arose great wings, armed with sharp hooks and prongs; it had stout legs in front, with projecting claws; but there were no legs behind,—the body running out into a long and powerful tail, finished off at the end with a barbed point. This tail was coiled up under him, the end sticking up just back of his wings.

The sculptor, or the people who had ordered this stone figure, had evidently been very much pleased with it, for little copies of it, also in stone, had been placed here and there along the sides of the church, not very far from the ground, so that people could easily look at them, and ponder on their curious forms. There were a great many other sculptures on the outside of this church,—saints, martyrs, grotesque heads of men, beasts, and birds, as well as those of other creatures which cannot be named, because nobody knows exactly what they were; but none were so curious and interesting as the great griffin over the door, and the little griffins on the sides of the church.

A long, long distance from the town, in the midst of dreadful wilds scarcely known to man, there dwelt the Griffin whose image had been put up over the church door. In some way or other, the old-time sculptor had seen him, and afterward, to the best of his memory, had copied his figure in stone. The Griffin had never known this, until, hundreds of years afterward, he heard from a bird, from a wild animal, or in some manner which it is not now easy to find out, that there was a likeness of him on the old church in the distant town. Now, this Griffin had no idea how he looked. He had never seen a mirror, and the streams where he lived were so turbulent and violent that a quiet piece of water, which would reflect the image of anything looking into it, could not be found. Being, as far as could be ascertained, the very last of his race, he had never seen another griffin. Therefore it was, that, when he heard of this stone image of himself, he became very anxious to know what he looked like, and at last he determined to go to the old church, and see for himself what manner of being he was. So he started off from the dreadful wilds, and flew on and on until he came to the countries inhabited by men, where his appearance in the air created great consternation; but he alighted nowhere, keeping up a steady flight until he reached the suburbs of the town which had his image on its church. Here, late in the afternoon, he alighted in a green meadow by the side of a brook, and stretched himself on the grass to rest. His great wings were tired, for he had not made such a long flight in a century, or more.

The news of his coming spread quickly over the town, and the people, frightened nearly out of their wits by the arrival of so extraordinary a visitor, fled into their houses, and shut themselves up. The Griffin called loudly for someone to come to him, but the more he called, the more afraid the people were to show themselves. At length he saw two laborers hurrying to their homes through the fields, and in a terrible voice he commanded them to stop. Not daring to disobey, the men stood, trembling.

"What is the matter with you all?" cried the Griffin. "Is there not a man in your town who is brave enough to speak to me?"

"I think," said one of the laborers, his voice shaking so that his words could hardly be understood, "that—perhaps—the Minor Canon—would come."

"Go, call him, then!" said the Griffin; "I want to see him."

The Minor Canon, who filled a subordinate position in the church, had just finished the afternoon services, and was coming out of a side door, with three aged women who had formed the weekday congregation. He was a young man of a kind disposition, and very anxious to do good to the people of the town. Apart from his duties in the church, where he conducted services every weekday, he visited the sick and the poor, counselled and assisted persons who were in trouble, and taught a school composed entirely of the bad children in the town with whom nobody else would have anything to do. Whenever the people wanted something difficult done for them, they always went to the Minor Canon. Thus it was that the laborer thought of the young priest when he found that someone must come and speak to the Griffin.

The Minor Canon had not heard of the strange event, which was known to the whole town except himself and the three old women, and when he was informed of it, and was told that the Griffin had asked to see him, he was greatly amazed, and frightened.

"Me!" he exclaimed. "He has never heard of me! What should he want with *me?*"

"Oh! you must go instantly!" cried the two men. "He is very angry now because he has been kept waiting so long; and nobody knows what may happen if you don't hurry to him."

The poor Minor Canon would rather have had his hand cut off than go out to meet an angry griffin; but he felt that it was his duty to go, or it would be a woeful thing if injury should come to the people of the town because he was not brave enough to obey the summons of the Griffin. So, pale and frightened, he started off.

"Well," said the Griffin, as soon as the young man came near, "I am glad to see that there is someone who has the courage to come to me."

The Minor Canon did not feel very courageous, but he bowed his head.

"Is this the town," said the Griffin, "where there is a church with a likeness of myself over one of the doors?"

The Minor Canon looked at the frightful creature before him and saw that it was, without doubt, exactly like the stone image on the church. "Yes," he said, "you are right."

"Well, then," said the Griffin, "will you take me to it? I wish very much to see it."

The Minor Canon instantly thought that if the Griffin entered the town without the people knowing what he came for, some of them would probably be frightened to death, and so he sought to gain time to prepare their minds.

"It is growing dark, now," he said, very much afraid, as he spoke, that his words might enrage the Griffin, "and objects on the front of the church cannot be seen clearly. It will be better to wait until morning, if you wish to get a good view of the stone image of yourself."

"That will suit me very well," said the Griffin. "I see you are a man of good sense. I am tired, and I will take a nap here on this soft grass, while I cool my tail in the little stream that runs near me. The end of my tail gets red-hot when I am angry or excited, and it is quite warm now. So you may go, but be sure and come early tomorrow morning, and show me the way to the church."

The Minor Canon was glad enough to take his leave, and hurried into the town. In front of the church he found a great many people assembled to hear his report of his interview with the Griffin. When they found that he had not come to spread ruin and devastation, but simply to see his stony likeness on the church, they showed neither relief nor gratification, but began to upbraid the Minor Canon for consenting to conduct the creature into the town.

"What could I do?" cried the young man. "If I should not bring him he would come himself and, perhaps, end by setting fire to the town with his red-hot tail."

Still the people were not satisfied, and a great many plans were proposed to prevent the Griffin from coming into the town. Some elderly persons urged that the young men should go out and kill him; but the young men scoffed at such a ridiculous idea. Then someone said that it would be a good thing to destroy the stone image so that the Griffin would have no excuse for entering the town; and this proposal was received with such favor that many of the people ran for hammers, chisels, and crowbars, with which to tear down and break up the stone griffin. But the Minor Canon resisted this plan with all the strength of his mind and body. He assured the people that this action would enrage the Griffin beyond measure, for it would be impossible to conceal from him that his image had been destroyed during the night. But the people were so determined to break up the stone griffin that the Minor Canon saw that there was nothing for him to do but stay there and protect it. All night he walked up and down in front of the church door, keeping away the men who brought ladders, by which they might mount to the great stone griffin, and knock it to pieces with their hammers and crowbars. After many hours the people were obliged to give up their attempts, and went home to sleep; but the Minor Canon remained at his post till early morning, and then he hurried away to the field where he had left the Griffin.

The monster had just awakened, and rising to his forelegs and shaking himself, he said that he was ready to go into the town. The Minor Canon, therefore, walked back, the Griffin flying slowly through the air, at a short distance above the head of his guide. Not a person was to be seen in the streets, and they proceeded directly to the front of the church, where the Minor Canon pointed out the stone griffin.

The real Griffin settled down in the little square before the church and gazed earnestly at his sculptured likeness. For a long time he looked at it. First he put his head on one side, and then he put it on the other; then he shut his right eye and gazed with his left, after which he shut his left eye and gazed with his right. Then he moved a little to one side and looked at the image, then he moved the other way. After a while he said to the Minor Canon, who had been standing by all this time:

"It is, it must be, an excellent likeness! That breadth between the eyes, that expansive forehead, those massive jaws! I feel that it must resemble me. If there is any fault to find with it, it is that the neck seems a little stiff. But that is nothing. It is an admirable likeness,—admirable!"

The Griffin sat looking at his image all the morning and all the afternoon. The Minor Canon had been afraid to go away and leave him, and had hoped all through the day that he would soon be satisfied with his inspection and fly away home. But by evening the poor young man was utterly exhausted, and felt that he must eat and sleep. He frankly admitted this fact to the Griffin, and asked him if he would not like something to eat. He said this because he felt obliged in politeness to do so, but as soon as he had spoken the words, he was seized with dread lest the monster should demand half a dozen babies, or some tempting repast of that kind.

"Oh, no," said the Griffin, "I never eat between the equinoxes. At the vernal and at the autumnal equinox I take a good meal, and that lasts me for half a year. I am extremely regular in my habits, and do not think it healthful to eat at odd times. But if you need food, go and get it, and I will return to the soft grass where I slept last night and take another nap."

The next day the Griffin came again to the little square before the church, and remained there until evening, steadfastly regarding the stone griffin over the door. The Minor Canon came once or twice to look at him, and the Griffin seemed very glad to see him; but the young clergyman could not stay as he had done before, for he had many duties to perform. Nobody went to the church, but the people came to the Minor Canon's house, and anxiously asked him how long the Griffin was going to stay.

"I do not know," he answered, "but I think he will soon be satisfied with regarding his stone likeness, and then he will go away."

But the Griffin did not go away. Morning after morning he came to the church, but after a time he did not stay there all day. He seemed to have taken a great fancy to the Minor Canon, and followed him about as he pursued his various avocations. He would wait for him at the side door of the church, for the Minor Canon held services every day, morning and evening, though nobody came now. "If anyone should come," he said to himself, "I must be found at my post." When the young man came out, the Griffin would accompany him in his visits to the sick and the poor, and would often look into the windows of the schoolhouse where the Minor Canon was teaching his unruly scholars. All the other schools were closed, but the parents of the Minor Canon's scholars forced them to go to school, because they were so bad they could not endure them all day at home,—griffin or no griffin. But it must be said they generally behaved very well when that great monster sat up on his tail and looked in at the schoolroom window.

When it was perceived that the Griffin showed no signs of going away, all the people who were able to do so left the town. The canons and the higher officers of the church had fled away during the first day of the Griffin's visit, leaving behind only the Minor Canon and some of the men who opened the doors and swept the church. All the citizens who could afford it shut up their houses and travelled to distant parts, and only the working people and the poor were left behind. After some days these ventured to go about and attend to their business, for if they did not work they would starve. They were getting a little used to seeing the Griffin, and having been told that he did not eat between equinoxes, they did not feel so much afraid of him as before.

Day by day the Griffin became more and more attached to the Minor Canon. He kept near him a great part of the time, and often spent the night in front of the little house where the young clergyman lived alone. This strange companionship was often burdensome to the Minor Canon; but, on the other hand, he could not deny that he derived a great deal of benefit and instruction from it. The Griffin had lived for hundreds of years, and had seen much; and he told the Minor Canon many wonderful things.

"It is like reading an old book," said the young clergyman to himself; "but how many books I would have had to read before I would have found out what the Griffin has told me about the earth, the air, the water, about minerals, and metals, and growing things, and all the wonders of the world!"

Thus the summer went on, and drew toward its close. And now the people of the town began to be very much troubled again.

"It will not be long," they said, "before the autumnal equinox is here, and then that monster will want to eat. He will be dreadfully hungry, for he has taken so much exercise since his last meal. He will devour our children. Without doubt, he will eat them all. What is to be done?"

To this question no one could give an answer, but all agreed that the Griffin must not be allowed to remain until the approaching equinox. After talking over the matter a great deal, a crowd of the people went to the Minor Canon, at a time when the Griffin was not with him.

"It is all your fault," they said, "that that monster is among us. You brought him here, and you ought to see that he goes away. It is only on your account that he stays here at all, for, although he visits his image every day, he is with you the greater part of the time. If you were not here, he would not stay. It is your duty to go away and then he will follow you, and we shall be free from the dreadful danger which hangs over us."

"Go away!" cried the Minor Canon, greatly grieved at being spoken to in such a way. "Where shall I go? If I go to some other town, shall I not take this trouble there? Have I a right to do that?"

"No," said the people, "you must not go to any other town. There is no town far enough away. You must go to the dreadful wilds where the Griffin lives; and then he will follow you and stay there."

They did not say whether or not they expected the Minor Canon to stay there also, and he did not ask them anything about it. He bowed his head, and went into his house, to think. The more he thought, the more clear it became to his mind that it was his duty to go away, and thus free the town from the presence of the Griffin.

That evening he packed a leathern bag full of bread and meat, and early the next morning he set out on his journey to the dreadful wilds. It was a long, weary, and doleful journey, especially after he had gone beyond the habitations of men, but the Minor Canon kept on bravely, and never faltered. The way was longer than he had expected, and his provisions soon grew so scanty that he was obliged to eat but a little every day, but he kept up his courage, and pressed on, and after many days of toilsome travel he reached the dreadful wilds.

When the Griffin found that the Minor Canon had left the town he seemed sorry, but showed no disposition to go and look for him. After a few days had passed, he became much annoyed, and asked some of the people where the Minor Canon had gone. But, although the citizens had been anxious that the young clergyman should go to the dreadful wilds, thinking that the Griffin would immediately follow him, they were now afraid to mention the Minor Canon's destination, for the monster seemed angry already, and, if he should suspect their trick, he would doubtless become very much enraged. So everyone said he did not know, and the Griffin wandered about disconsolate. One morning he looked into the Minor Canon's schoolhouse, which was always empty now, and thought that it was a shame that everything should suffer on account of the young man's absence.

"It does not matter so much about the church," he said, "for nobody went there; but it is a pity about the school. I think I will teach it myself until he returns."

It was the hour for opening the school, and the Griffin went inside and pulled the rope which rang the school bell. Some of the children who heard the bell ran in to see what was the matter, supposing it to be a joke of one of their companions; but when they saw the Griffin they stood astonished, and scared.

"Go tell the other scholars," said the monster, "that school is about to open, and that if they are not all here in ten minutes, I shall come after them."

In seven minutes every scholar was in place.

Never was seen such an orderly school. Not a boy or girl moved, or uttered a whisper. The Griffin climbed into the master's seat, his wide wings spread on each side of him, because he could not lean back in his chair while they stuck out behind, and his great tail coiled around, in front of the desk, the barbed end sticking up, ready to tap any boy or girl who might misbehave. The Griffin now addressed the scholars, telling them that he intended to teach them while their master was away. In speaking he endeavored to imitate, as far as possible, the mild and gentle tones of the Minor Canon, but it must be admitted that in this he was not very successful. He had paid a good deal of attention to the studies of the school, and he determined not to attempt to teach them anything new, but to review them in what they had been studying; so he called up the various classes, and questioned them upon their previous lessons. The children racked their brains to remember what they had learned. They were so afraid of the Griffin's displeasure that they recited as they had never recited before. One of the boys far down in his class answered so well that the Griffin was astonished.

"I should think you would be at the head," said he. "I am sure you have never been in the habit of reciting so well. Why is this?"

"Because I did not choose to take the trouble," said the boy, trembling in his boots. He felt obliged to speak the truth, for all the children thought that the great eyes of the Griffin could see right through them, and that he would know when they told a falsehood.

"You ought to be ashamed of yourself," said the Griffin. "Go down to the very tail of the class, and if you are not at the head in two days, I shall know the reason why."

The next afternoon the boy was number one.

It was astonishing how much these children now learned of what they had been studying. It was as if they had been educated over again. The Griffin used no severity toward them, but there was a look about him which made them unwilling to go to bed until they were sure they knew their lessons for the next day.

The Griffin now thought that he ought to visit the sick and the poor; and he began to go about the town for this purpose. The effect upon the sick was miraculous. All, except those who were very ill indeed, jumped from their beds when they heard he was coming, and declared themselves quite well. To those who could not get up, he gave herbs and roots, which none of them had ever before thought of as medicines, but which the Griffin had seen used in various parts of the world; and most of them recovered. But, for all that, they afterward said that no matter what happened to them, they hoped that they should never again have such a doctor coming to their bedsides, feeling their pulses and looking at their tongues.

As for the poor, they seemed to have utterly disappeared. All those who had depended upon charity for their daily bread were now at work in some way or other; many of them offering to do odd jobs for their neighbors just for the sake of their meals,—a thing which before had been seldom heard of in the town. The Griffin could find no one who needed his assistance.

The summer had now passed, and the autumnal equinox was rapidly approaching. The citizens were in a state of great alarm and anxiety. The Griffin showed no signs of going away, but seemed to have settled himself permanently among them. In a short time, the day for his semi-annual meal would arrive, and then what would happen? The monster would certainly be very hungry, and would devour all their children.

Now they greatly regretted and lamented that they had sent away the Minor Canon; he was the only one on whom they could have depended in this trouble, for he could talk freely with the Griffin, and so find out what could be done. But it would not do to be inactive. Some step must be taken immediately. A meeting of the citizens was called, and two old men were appointed to go and talk to the Griffin. They were instructed to offer to prepare a splendid dinner for him on equinox day,—one which would entirely satisfy his hunger. They would offer him the fattest mutton, the most tender beef, fish, and game of various sorts, and anything of the kind that he might fancy. If none of these suited, they were to mention that there was an orphan asylum in the next town.

"Anything would be better," said the citizens, "than to have our dear children devoured."

The old men went to the Griffin, but their propositions were not received with favor.

"From what I have seen of the people of this town," said the monster, "I do not think I could relish anything which was prepared by them. They appear to be all cowards, and, therefore, mean and selfish. As for eating one of them, old or young, I could not think of it for a moment. In fact, there was only one creature in the whole place for whom I could have had any appetite, and that is the Minor Canon, who has gone away. He was brave, and good, and honest, and I think I should have relished him."

"Ah!" said one of the old men very politely, "in that case I wish we had not sent him to the dreadful wilds!"

"What!" cried the Griffin. "What do you mean? Explain instantly what you are talking about!"

The old man, terribly frightened at what he had said, was obliged to tell how the Minor Canon had been sent away by the people, in the hope that the Griffin might be induced to follow him.

When the monster heard this, he became furiously angry. He dashed away from the old men and, spreading his wings, flew backward and forward over the town. He was so much excited that his tail became red-hot, and glowed like a meteor against the evening sky. When at last he settled down in the little field where he usually rested, and thrust his tail into the brook, the steam arose like a cloud, and the water of the stream ran hot through the town. The citizens were greatly frightened, and bitterly blamed the old man for telling about the Minor Canon.

"It is plain," they said, "that the Griffin intended at last to go and look for him, and we should have been saved. Now who can tell what misery you have brought upon us."

The Griffin did not remain long in the little field. As soon as his tail was cool he flew to the town hall and rang the bell. The citizens knew that they were expected to come there, and although they were afraid to go, they were still more afraid to stay away; and they crowded into the hall. The Griffin was on the platform at one end, flapping his wings and walking up and down, and the end of his tail was still so warm that it slightly scorched the boards as he dragged it after him.

When everybody who was able to come was there the Griffin stood still and addressed the meeting.

"I have had a contemptible opinion of you," he said, "ever since I discovered what cowards you are, but I had no idea that you were so ungrateful, selfish, and cruel as I now find you to be. Here was your Minor Canon, who labored day and night for your good, and thought of nothing else but how he might benefit you and make you happy; and as soon as you imagine yourselves threatened with a danger,—for well I know you are dreadfully afraid of me,—you send him off, caring not whether he returns or perishes, hoping thereby to save yourselves. Now, I had conceived a great liking for that young man, and had intended, in a day or two, to go and look him up. But I have changed my mind about him. I shall go and find him, but I shall send him back here to live among you, and I intend that he shall enjoy the reward of his labor and his sacrifices. Go, some of you, to the officers of the church who so cowardly ran away when I first came here, and tell them never to return to this town under penalty of death. And if, when your Minor Canon comes back to you, you do not bow yourselves before him, put him in the highest place among you, and serve and honor him all his life, beware of my terrible vengeance! There were only two good things in this town: the Minor Canon and the stone image of myself over your church door. One of these you have sent away, and the other I shall carry away myself."

With these words he dismissed the meeting, and it was time, for the end of his tail had become so hot that there was danger of its setting fire to the building.

The next morning, the Griffin came to the church, and tearing the stone image of himself from its fastenings over the great door, he grasped it with his powerful forelegs and flew up into the air. Then, after hovering over the town for a moment, he gave his tail an angry shake and took up his flight to the dreadful wilds. When he reached this desolate region, he set the stone Griffin upon a ledge of a rock which rose in front of the dismal cave he called his home. There the image occupied a position somewhat similar to that it had had over the church door; and the Griffin, panting with the exertion of carrying such an enormous load to so great a distance, lay down upon the ground, and regarded it with much satisfaction. When he felt somewhat rested he went to look for the Minor Canon. He found the young man, weak and half-starved, lying under the shadow of a rock. After picking him up and carrying him to his cave, the Griffin flew away to a distant marsh, where he procured some roots and herbs which he well knew were strengthening and beneficial to man, though he had never tasted them himself. After eating these the Minor Canon was greatly revived, and sat up and listened while the Griffin told him what had happened in the town.

"Do you know," said the monster, when he had finished, "that I have had, and still have, a great liking for you?"

"I am very glad to hear it," said the Minor Canon, with his usual politeness.

"I am not at all sure that you would be," said the Griffin, "if you thoroughly understood the state of the case, but we will not consider that now. If some things were different, other things would be otherwise. I have been so enraged by discovering the manner in which you have been treated that I have determined that you shall at last enjoy the rewards and honors to which you are entitled. Lie down and have a good sleep, and then I will take you back to the town."

As he heard these words, a look of trouble came over the young man's face.

"You need not give yourself any anxiety," said the Griffin, "about my return to the town. I shall not remain there. Now that I have that admirable likeness of myself in front of my cave, where I can sit at my leisure, and gaze upon its noble features and magnificent proportions, I have no wish to see that abode of cowardly and selfish people."

The Minor Canon, relieved from his fears, lay back, and dropped into a doze; and when he was sound asleep the Griffin took him up, and carried him back to the town. He arrived just before daybreak, and putting the young man gently on the grass in the little field where he himself used to rest, the monster, without having been seen by any of the people, flew back to his home.

When the Minor Canon made his appearance in the morning among the citizens, the enthusiasm and cordiality with which he was received were truly wonderful. He was taken to a house which had been occupied by one of the vanished high officers of the place, and everyone was anxious to do all that could be done for his health and comfort. The people crowded into the church when he held services, so that the three old women who used to be his weekday congregation could not get to the best seats, which they had always been in the habit of taking; and the parents of the bad children determined to reform them at home, in order that he might be spared the trouble of keeping up his former school. The Minor Canon was appointed to the highest office of the old church, and before he died, he became a bishop.

During the first years after his return form the dreadful wilds, the people of the town looked up to him as a man to whom they were bound to do honor and reverence; but they often, also, looked up to the sky to see if there were any signs of the Griffin coming back. However, in the course of time, they learned to honor and reverence their former Minor Canon without the fear of being punished if they did not do so.

But they need never have been afraid of the Griffin. The autumnal equinox day came round, and the monster ate nothing. If he could not have the Minor Canon, he did not care for anything. So, lying down, with his eyes fixed upon the great stone griffin, he gradually declined, and died. It was a good thing for some people of the town that they did not know this.

If you should ever visit the old town, you would still see the little griffins on the sides of the church; but the great stone griffin that was over the door is gone.

THE REMARKABLE ROCKET

OSCAR WILDE

THE KING'S SON WAS GOING TO BE MARRIED, so there were general rejoicings. He had waited a whole year for his bride, and at last she had arrived. She was a Russian Princess, and had driven all the way from Finland in a sledge drawn by six reindeer. The sledge was shaped like a great golden swan, and between the swan's wings lay the little Princess herself. Her long ermine cloak reached right down to her feet, on her head was a tiny cap of silver tissue, and she was as pale as the Snow Palace in which she had always lived. So pale was she that as she drove through the streets all the people wondered. "She is like a white rose!" they cried, and they threw down flowers on her from the balconies.

At the gate of the Castle the Prince was waiting to receive her. He had dreamy violet eyes, and his hair was like fine gold. When he saw her he sank upon one knee, and kissed her hand.

"Your picture was beautiful," he murmured, "but you are more beautiful than your picture;" and the little Princess blushed.

"She was like a white rose before," said a young Page to his neighbour, "but she is like a red rose now;" and the whole Court was delighted.

For the next three days everybody went about saying "White rose, Red rose, Red rose, White rose," and the King gave orders that the Page's salary was to be doubled. As he received no salary at all this was not of much use to him, but it was considered a great honour and was duly published in the Court Gazette.

When the three days were over the marriage was celebrated. It was a magnificent ceremony, and the bride and bridegroom walked hand in hand under a canopy of purple velvet embroidered with little pearls. Then there was a State Banquet, which lasted for five hours. The Prince and Princess sat at the top of the Great Hall and drank out of a cup of clear crystal. Only true lovers could drink out of this cup, for if false lips touched it, it grew grey and dull and cloudy.

"It is quite clear that they loved each other," said the little Page, "as clear as crystal!" and the King doubled his salary a second time.

"What an honour!" cried all the courtiers.

After the banquet there was to be a Ball. The bride and bridegroom were to dance the Rose dance together, and the King had promised to play the flute. He played very badly, but no one had ever dared to tell him so, because he was the King. Indeed, he knew only two airs, and was never quite certain which one he was playing; but it made no matter, for, whatever he did, everybody cried out, "Charming! Charming!"

The last item on the programme was a grand display of fireworks, to be let off exactly at midnight. The little Princess had never seen a firework in her life, so the King had given orders that the Royal Pyrotechnist should be in attendance on the day of her marriage.

"What are fireworks like?" she had asked the Prince, one morning, as she was walking on the terrace.

"They are like the Aurora Borealis," said the King, who always answered questions that were addressed to other people, "only much more natural. I prefer them to stars myself, as you always know when they are going to appear, and they are as delightful as my own flute-playing. You must certainly see them."

So at the end of the King's garden a great stand had been set up, and as soon as the Royal Pyrotechnist had put everything in its proper place, the fireworks began to talk to each other.

"The world is certainly very beautiful," cried a little Squib. "Just look at those yellow tulips. Why! if they were real crackers they could not be lovelier. I am very glad I have travelled. Travel improves the mind wonderfully, and does away with all one's prejudices."

"The King's garden is not the world, you foolish Squib," said a big Roman Candle; "the world is an enormous place, and it would take you three days to see it thoroughly."

"Any place you love is the world to you," exclaimed the pensive Catherine Wheel, who had been attached to an old deal box in early life, and prided herself on her broken heart; "but love is not fashionable anymore, the poets have killed it. They wrote so much about it that nobody believed them, and I am not surprised. True love suffers, and is silent. I remember myself once—But no matter now. Romance is a thing of the past."

"Nonsense!" said the Roman Candle, "Romance never dies. It is like the moon, and lives forever. The bride and bridegroom, for instance, love each other very dearly. I heard all about them this morning from a brown-paper cartridge, who happened to be staying in the same drawer as myself, and he knew the latest Court news."

But the Catherine Wheel shook her head. "Romance is dead, Romance is dead, Romance is dead," she murmured. She was one of those people who think that, if you say the same thing over and over a great many times, it becomes true in the end.

Suddenly, a sharp, dry cough was heard, and they all looked around.

It came from a tall, supercilious-looking Rocket, who was tied to the end of a long stick. He always coughed before he made any observations, so as to attract attention.

"Ahem! Ahem!" he said, and everybody listened except the poor Catherine Wheel, who was still shaking her head, and murmuring, "Romance is dead."

"Order! order!" cried out a Cracker. He was something of a politician, and had always taken a prominent part in the local elections, so he knew the proper Parliamentary expressions to use.

"Quite dead," whispered the Catherine Wheel, and she went off to sleep.

As soon as there was perfect silence, the Rocket coughed a third time and began. He spoke with a very slow, distinct voice, as if he were dictating his memoirs, and always looked over the shoulder of the person to whom he was talking. In fact, he had a most distinguished manner.

"How fortunate it is for the King's son," he remarked, "that he is to be married on the very day on which I am to be let off! Really, if it had not been arranged beforehand, it could not have turned out better for him; but Princes are always lucky."

"Dear me!" said the little Squib, "I thought it was quite the other way, and that we were to be let off in the Prince's honour."

"It may be so with you," he answered; "indeed, I have no doubt that it is, but with me it is different. I am a very remarkable Rocket, and come of remarkable parents. My mother was the most celebrated Catherine Wheel of her day, and was renowned for her graceful dancing. When she made her great public appearance she spun round nineteen times before she went out, and each time that she did so she threw into the air seven pink stars. She was three feet and a half in diameter, and made of the very best gunpowder. My father was a Rocket like myself, and of French extraction. He flew so high that the people were afraid that he would never come down again. He did, though, for he was of a kind disposition, and he made a most brilliant descent in a shower of golden rain. The newspapers wrote about his performance in very flattering terms. Indeed, the Court Gazette called him a triumph of Pylotechnic art."

"Pyrotechnic, Pyrotechnic, you mean," said a Bengal Light; "I know it is Pyrotechnic, for I saw it written on my own canister."

"Well, I said Pylotechnic," answered the Rocket, in a severe tone of voice, and the Bengal Light felt so crushed that he began at once to bully the little Squibs, in order to show that he was still a person of some importance.

"I was saying," continued the Rocket, "I was saying—What was I saying?"

"You were talking about yourself," replied the Roman Candle.

"Of course; I knew I was discussing some interesting subject when I was so rudely interrupted. I hate rudeness and bad manners of every kind, for I am extremely sensitive. No one in the whole world is so sensitive as I am, I am quite sure of that."

"What is a sensitive person?" said the Cracker to the Roman Candle.

"A person who, because he has corns himself, always treads on other people's toes," answered the Roman Candle in a low whisper; and the Cracker nearly exploded with laughter.

"Pray, what are you laughing at?" inquired the Rocket; "I am not laughing."

"I am laughing because I am happy," replied the Cracker.

"That is a very selfish reason,' said the Rocket angrily. "What right have you to be happy? You should be thinking about others. In fact, you should be thinking about me. I am always thinking about myself, and I expect everybody else to do the same. That is what is called sympathy. It is a beautiful virtue, and I possess it in a high degree. Suppose, for instance, anything happened to me tonight, what a misfortune that would be for everyone! The Prince and Princess would never be happy again, their whole married life would be spoiled; and as for the King, I know he would not get over it. Really, when I begin to reflect on the importance of my position, I am almost moved to tears."

"If you want to give pleasure to others," cried the Roman Candle, "you had better keep yourself dry."

"Certainly," exclaimed the Bengal Light, who was now in better spirits; "that is common sense."

"Common sense, indeed!" said the Rocket indignantly; "you forget that I am very uncommon, and very remarkable. Why, anybody can have common sense, provided that they have no imagination. But I have imagination, for I never think of things as they really are; I always think of them as being quite different. As for keeping myself dry, there is evidently no one here who can at all appreciate an emotional nature. Fortunately for myself, I don't care. The only thing that sustains one through life is the consciousness of the immense inferiority of everybody else, and this is a feeling I have always cultivated. But none of you have any hearts. Here you are laughing and making merry just as if the Prince and Princess had not just been married."

"Well, really," exclaimed a small Fire-balloon, "why not? It is a most joyful occasion, and when I soar up into the air I intend to tell the stars all about it. You will see them twinkle when I talk to them about the pretty bride."

"Ah, what a trivial view of life!" said the Rocket; "but it is only what I expected. There is nothing in you; you are hollow and empty. Why, perhaps the Prince and Princess may go to live in a country where there is a deep river, and perhaps they may have one only son, a little fair-haired boy with violet eyes like the Prince himself; and perhaps some day he may go out to walk with his nurse; and perhaps the nurse may go to sleep under a great elder-tree; and perhaps the little boy may fall into the deep river and be drowned. What a terrible misfortune! Poor people, to lose their only son! It is really too dreadful! I shall never get over it."

"But they have not lost their only son," said the Roman Candle; "no misfortune has happened to them at all."

"I never said that they had," replied the Rocket; "I said that they might. If they had lost their only son there would be no use in saying anymore about the matter. I hate people who cry over spilt milk. But when I think that they might lose their only son, I certainly am very much affected."

"You certainly are!" cried the Bengal Light. "In fact, you are the most affected person I ever met."

"You are the rudest person I ever met," said the Rocket, "and you cannot understand my friendship for the Prince."

"Why, you don't even know him," growled the Roman Candle.

"I never said I knew him," answered the Rocket. "I dare say that if I knew him I should not be his friend at all. It is a very dangerous thing to know one's friends."

"You had really better keep yourself dry," said the Fire-balloon. "That is the important thing."

"Very important for you, I have no doubt," answered the Rocket, "but I shall weep if I choose;" and he actually burst into real tears, which flowed down his stick like raindrops, and nearly drowned two little beetles, who were just thinking of setting up house together, and were looking for a nice dry spot to live in.

"He must have a truly romantic nature," said the Catherine Wheel, "for he weeps when there is nothing at all to weep about;" and she heaved a deep sigh and thought about the deal box.

But the Roman Candle and the Bengal Light were quite indignant, and kept saying, "Humbug! Humbug!" at the top of their voices. They were extremely practical, and whenever they objected to anything they called it humbug.

Then the moon rose like a wonderful silver shield; and the stars began to shine, and a sound of music came from the palace.

The Prince and Princess were leading the dance. They danced so beautifully that the tall white lilies peeped in at the window and watched them, and the great red poppies nodded their heads and beat time.

Then ten o'clock stuck, and then eleven, and then twelve, and at the last stroke of midnight everyone came out on the terrace, and the King sent for the Royal Pyrotechnist.

"Let the fireworks begin," said the King; and the Royal Pyrotechnist made a low bow, and marched down to the end of the garden. He had six attendants with him, each of whom carried a lighted torch at the end of a long pole.

It was certainly a magnificent display.

Whizz! Whizz! went the Catherine Wheel, as she spun round and round. Boom! Boom! went the Roman Candle. Then the Squibs danced all over the place, and the Bengal Lights made everything look scarlet. "Good-bye," cried the Fire-balloon, as he soared away, dropping tiny blue sparks. Bang! Bang! answered the Crackers, who were enjoying themselves immensely. Everyone was a great success except the Remarkable Rocket. He was so damped with crying that he could not go off at all. The best thing in him was the gunpowder, and that was so wet with tears that it was of no use. All his poor relations, to whom he would never speak, except with a sneer, shot up into the sky like wonderful golden flowers with blossoms of fire. Huzza! Huzza! cried the Court; and the little Princess laughed with pleasure.

"I suppose they are reserving me for some grand occasion," said the Rocket; "no doubt that is what it means," and he looked more supercilious than ever.

The next day the workmen came to put everything tidy. "This is, evidently, a deputation," said the Rocket; "I will receive them with becoming dignity:" so he put his nose in the air, and began to frown severely, as if he were thinking about some very important subject. But they took no notice of him at all till they were just going away. Then one of them caught sight of him. "Hallo!" he cried, "what a bad rocket!" and he threw him over the wall into the ditch.

"Bad Rocket? Bad Rocket?" he said, as he whirled through the air; "impossible! Grand Rocket, that is what the man said. Bad and Grand sound very much the same, indeed they often are the same;" and he fell into the mud.

"It is not comfortable here," he remarked, "but no doubt it is some fashionable watering-place, and they have sent me away to recruit my health. My nerves are certainly very much shattered, and I require rest."

Then a little Frog, with bright jewelled eyes, and a green mottled coat, swam up to him.

"A new arrival, I see!" said the Frog. "Well, after all there is nothing like mud. Give me rainy weather and a ditch, and I am quite happy. Do you think it will be a wet afternoon? I am sure I hope so, but the sky is quite blue and cloudless. What a pity!"

"Ahem! Ahem!" said the Rocket, and he began to cough.

"What a delightful voice you have!" cried the Frog. "Really it is quite like a croak, and croaking is, of course, the most musical sound in the world. You will hear our glee-club this evening. We sit in the old duck-pond close by the farmer's house, and as soon as the moon rises we begin. It is so entrancing that everybody lies awake to listen to us. In fact, it was only yesterday that I heard the farmer's wife say to her mother that she could not get a wink of sleep at night on account of us. It is most gratifying to find oneself so popular."

"Ahem! Ahem!" said the Rocket angrily. He was very much annoyed that he could not get a word in.

"A delightful voice, certainly," continued the Frog; "I hope you will come over to the duck-pond. I am off to look for my daughters. I have six beautiful daughters, and I am so afraid the Pike might meet them. He is a perfect monster, and would have no hesitation in breakfasting off them. Well, good-bye; I have enjoyed our conversation very much, I assure you."

"Conversation, indeed!" said the Rocket. "You have talked the whole time yourself. That is not conversation."

"Somebody must listen," answered the Frog, "and I like to do all the talking myself. It saves time, and prevents arguments."

"But I like arguments," said the Rocket.

"I hope not," said the Frog complacently. "Arguments are extremely vulgar, for everybody in good society holds exactly the same opinions. Good-bye a second time; I see my daughters in the distance;" and the little Frog swam away.

"You are a very irritating person," said the Rocket, "and very ill-bred. I hate people who talk about themselves, as you do, when one wants to talk about oneself, as I do. It is what I call selfishness, and selfishness is a most detestable thing, especially to anyone of my temperament, for I am well known for my sympathetic nature. In fact, you should take example by me; you could not possibly have a better model. Now that you have the chance you had better avail yourself of it, for I am going back to Court almost immediately, I am a great favourite at Court; in fact, the Prince and Princess were married yesterday in my honour. Of course, you know nothing of these matters, for you are a provincial."

"There is no good talking to him," said a Dragonfly, who was sitting on the top of a large brown bulrush; "no good at all, for he has gone away."

"Well, that is his loss, not mine," answered the Rocket. "I am not going to stop talking to him merely because he pays no attention. I like hearing myself talk. It is one of my greatest pleasures. I often have long conversations all by myself, and I am so clever that sometimes I don't understand a single word of what I am saying."

"Then you should certainly lecture on Philosophy," said the Dragonfly, and he spread a pair of lovely gauze wings and soared away into the sky.

"How very silly of him not to stay here!" said the Rocket. "I am sure that he has not often got such a chance of improving his mind. However, I don't care a bit. Genius like mine is sure to be appreciated some day;" and he sank down a little deeper into the mud.

After some time a larger White Duck swam up to him. She had yellow legs, and webbed feet, and was considered a great beauty on account of her waddle.

"Quack, quack, quack," she said. "What a curious shape you are! May I ask were you born like that, or is it the result of an accident?"

"It is quite evident that you have always lived in the country," answered the Rocket, "otherwise you would know who I am. However, I excuse your ignorance. It would be unfair to expect other people to be as remarkable as oneself. You will no doubt be surprised to hear that I can fly up into the sky, and come down in a shower of golden rain."

"I don't think much of that," said the Duck, "as I cannot see what use it is to anyone. Now, if you could plough the fields like the ox, or draw a cart like the horse, or look after the sheep like the collie-dog, that would be something."

"My good creature," cried the Rocket in a very haughty tone of voice, "I see that you belong to the lower orders. A person of my position is never useful. We have certain accomplishments, and that is more than sufficient. I have no sympathy myself with industry of any kind, least of all with such industries as you seem to recommend. Indeed, I have always been of opinion that hard work is simply the refuge of people who have nothing whatever to do."

"Well, well," said the Duck, who was of a very peaceful disposition, and never quarrelled with anyone, "everybody has different tastes. I hope, at any rate, that you are going to take up your residence here."

"Oh! dear no," cried the Rocket. "I am merely a visitor, a distinguished visitor. The fact is that I find this place rather tedious. There is neither society here, nor solitude. In fact, it is essentially suburban. I shall probably go back to Court, for I know that I am destined to make a sensation in the world."

"I had thoughts of entering public life once myself," remarked the Duck; "there are so many things that need reforming. Indeed, I took the chair at a meeting some time ago, and we passed resolutions condemning everything that we did not like. However, they did not seem to have much effect. Now I go in for domesticity, and look after my family."

"I am made for public life," said the Rocket, "and so are all my relations, even the humblest of them. Whenever we appear we excite great attention. I have not actually appeared myself, but when I do so it will be a magnificent sight. As for domesticity, it ages one rapidly, and distracts one's mind from higher things."

"Ah! The higher things of life, how fine they are!" said the Duck; "and that reminds me how hungry I feel;" and she swam away down the stream, saying, "Quack, quack, quack."

"Come back! Come back!" screamed the Rocket, "I have a great deal to say to you;" but the Duck paid no attention to him. "I am glad that she has gone," he said to himself, "she had a decidedly middle-class mind;" and he sank a little deeper still into the mud, and began to think about the loneliness of genius, when suddenly two little boys in white smocks came running down the bank, with a kettle and some faggots.

"This must be the deputation," said the Rocket, and he tried to look very dignified.

"Hallo!" cried one of the boys, "look at this old stick; I wonder how it came here;" and he picked the Rocket out of the ditch.

"Old Stick!" said the Rocket, "impossible! Gold Stick, that is what he said. Gold Stick is very complimentary. In fact, he mistakes me for one of the Court dignitaries!"

"Let us put it into the fire!" said the other boy, "it will help to boil the kettle."

So they piled the faggots together, and put the Rocket on top, and lit the fire.

"This is magnificent," cried the Rocket, "they are going to let me off in broad daylight, so that everyone can see me."

"We will go to sleep now," they said, "and when we wake up the kettle will be boiled;" and they lay down on the grass, and shut their eyes.

The Rocket was very damp, so he took a long time to burn. At last, however, the fire caught him.

"Now I am going off!" he cried, and he made himself very stiff and straight. "I know I shall go much higher than the stars, much higher than the moon, much higher than the sun. In fact, I shall go so high that—"

Fizz! Fizz! Fizz! and he went straight up into the air.

"Delightful!" he cried, "I shall go on like this forever. What a success I am!"

But nobody saw him.

Then he began to feel a curious tingling sensation all over him.

"Now I am going to explode," he cried. "I shall set the whole world on fire, and make such a noise that nobody will talk about anything else for a whole year." And he certainly did explode. Bang! Bang! Bang! went the gunpowder. There was no doubt about it.

But nobody heard him, not even the two little boys, for they were sound asleep.

Then all that was left of him was the stick, and this fell down the back of Goose who was taking a walk by the side of the ditch.

"Good heavens!" cried the Goose. "It is going to rain sticks;" and she rushed into the water.

"I knew I should create a great sensation," gasped the Rocket, and he went out.

HAPPY RETURNS

LAURENCE HOUSMAN

By the side of a great river, whose stream formed the boundary to two countries, lived an old ferryman and his wife. All the day, while she minded the house, he sat in his boat by the ferry, waiting to carry travellers across; or, when no travellers came, and he had his boat free, he would cast dragnets along the bed of the river for fish. But for the food which he was able thus to procure at times, he and his wife might well have starved, for travellers were often few and far between, and often they grudged him the few pence he asked for ferrying them; and now he had grown so old and feeble that when the river was in flood he could scarcely ferry the boat across; and continually he feared lest a younger and stronger man should come and take his place, and the bread from his mouth.

But he had trust in Providence. "Will not God," he said, "who has given us no happiness in this life, save in each other's help and companionship, allow us to end our days in peace?"

And his wife answered, "Yes, surely, if we trust Him enough He will."

One morning, it being the first day of the year, the ferryman going down to his boat, found that during the night it had been loosed from its moorings and taken across the river, where it now lay fastened to the further bank.

"Wife," said he, "I can remember this same thing happening a year ago, and the year before also. Who is this traveller who comes once a year, like a thief in the night, and crosses without asking me to ferry him over?"

"Perhaps it is the good folk," said his wife. "Go over and see if they have left no coin behind them in the boat."

The old man got on to a log and poled himself across, and found, down in the keel of the boat, the mark of a man's bare foot driven deep into the wood; but there was no coin or other trace to show who it might be.

Time went on; the old ferryman was all bowed down with age, and his body was racked with pains. So slow was he now in making the passage of the stream, that all travellers who knew those parts took a road higher up the bank, where a stronger ferryman plied.

Winter came; and hunger and want pressed hard at the old man's door. One day while he drew his net along the stream, he felt the shock of a great fish striking against the meshes down below, and presently, as the net came in, he saw a shape like living silver, leaping and darting to and fro to find some way of escape. Up to the bank he landed it, a great gasping fish.

When he was about to kill it, he saw, to his astonishment, tears running out of its eyes, that gazed at him and seemed to reproach him for his cruelty. As he drew back, the Fish said: "Why should you kill me, who wish to live?"

The old man, altogether bewildered at hearing himself thus addressed, answered: "Since I and my wife are hungry, and God gave you to be eaten, I have good reason for killing you."

"I could give you something worth far more than a meal," said the Fish, "if you would spare my life."

"We are old," said the ferryman, "and want only to end our days in peace. Today we are hungry; what can be more good for us than a meal which will give us strength for the morrow, which is the new year?"

The Fish said: "Tonight someone will come and unfasten your boat, and ferry himself over, and you know nothing of it till the morning, when you see the craft moored out yonder by the further bank."

The old man remembered how the thing had happened in previous years, directly the Fish spoke. "Ah, you know that then! How is it?" He asked.

"When you go back to your hut at night to sleep, I am here in the water," said the Fish. "I see what goes on."

"What goes on, then?" asked the old man, very curious to know who the strange traveller might be.

"Ah," said the Fish, "if you could only catch him in your boat, he could give you something you might wish for! I tell you this: do you and your wife keep watch in the boat all night, and when he comes, and you have ferried him into midstream, where he cannot escape, then throw your net over him and hold him till he pays you for all your ferryings."

"How shall he pay me? All my ferryings of a lifetime!"

"Make him take you to the land of Returning Time. There, at least, you can end your days in peace."

The old man said: "You have told me a strange thing; and since I mean to act on it, I suppose I must let you go. If you have deceived me, I trust you may yet die a cruel death."

The Fish answered: "Do as I tell you, and you shall die a happy one." And, saying this, he slipped down into the water and disappeared.

The ferryman went back to his wife supperless, and said to her: "Wife, bring a net, and come down into the boat!" And he told her the story of the Fish and of the yearly traveller.

They sat long together under the dark bank, looking out over the quiet and cold moonlit waters, till the midnight hour. The air was chill, and to keep themselves warm they covered themselves over with the net and lay down in the bottom of the boat. It was the very hour when the old year dies and the new year is born.

Before they well knew that they had been asleep, they started to feel the rocking of the boat, and found themselves out upon the broad waters of the river. And there in the fore-part of the boat, clear and sparkling in the moonlight, stood a naked man of shining silver. He was bending upon the pole of the boat, and his long hair fell over it right down into the water.

The old couple rose up quietly, and unwinding themselves from the net, threw it over the Silver Man, over his head and hands and feet, and dragged him down into the bottom of the boat.

The old man caught the ferry pole, and heaved the boat still into the middle of the stream. As he did so a gentle shock came to the heart of each; feebly it fluttered and sank low. "Oh, wife!" sighed the old man, and reached out his hand for hers.

The Silver Man lay still in the folds of the net, and looked at them with a wise and quiet gaze. "What would you have of me?" he said, and his voice was far off and low.

They said, "Bring us into the land of Returning Time."

The Silver Man said: "Only once can you go there, and once return."

They both answered, "We wish once to go there, and once return."

So he promised them that they should have the whole of their request; and they unloosed him from the net, and landed all together on the further bank.

Up the hill they went, following the track of the Silver Man. Presently they reached its crest; and there before them lay all the howling winter of the world.

The Silver Man turned his face and looked back; and looking back it became all young, and ruddy, and bright. The ferryman and his wife gazed at him, both speechless at the wonderful change. He took their hands, making them turn the way by which they had come; below their feet was a deep black gulf, and beyond and away lay nothing but a dark starless hollow of air.

"Now," said their guide, "you have but to step forward one step, and you shall be in the land of Retuning Time."

They loosed hold of his hands, joined clasp, husband with wife, and at one step upon what seemed gulf beneath their feet, found themselves in a green and flowery land. There were perfumed valleys and grassy hills, whose crops stretched down before the breeze; thick fleecy clouds crossed their tops, and overhead, amid a blue air rang the shrill trilling of birds. Behind lay, fading mistily as a dream, the bare world they had left; and fast on his forward road, growing small to them from a distance, went the Silver Man, a shining point on the horizon.

The ferryman and his wife looked, and saw youth in each other's faces beginning to peep out through the furrows of age; each step they took made them grow younger and stronger; years fell from them like worn-out rags as they went down into the valleys of the land of Returning Time.

How fast Time returned! Each step made the change of a day, and every mile brought them five years back toward youth. When they came down to the streams that ran in the bed of each valley, the ferryman and his wife felt their prime return to them. He saw the gold come back into her locks, and she the brown into his. Their lips became open to laughter and song. "Oh, how good," they cried, "to have lived all our lives poor, to come at last to this!"

They drank water out of the streams, and tasted the fruit from the trees that grew over them; till presently, being tired for mere joy, they lay down in the grass to rest. They slept hand within hand and cheek against cheek, and, when they woke, found themselves quite young again, just at the age when they were first married in the years gone by.

The ferryman started up and felt the desire of life strong in his blood. "Come!" he said to his wife, "or we shall become too young with lingering here. Now we have regained our youth, let us go back into the world once more!"

His wife hung upon his hand, "Are we not happy enough," she asked, "as it is? Why should we return?"

"But," he cried, "we shall grow too young; now we have youth and life at its best let us return! Time goes too fast with us; we are in danger of it carrying us away."

She said no further word, but followed up toward the way by which they had entered. And yet, in spite of her wish to remain, as she went her young blood frisked. Presently coming to the top of a hill, they set off running and racing; at the bottom they looked at each other, and saw themselves boy and girl once more.

"We have stayed here too long!" said the ferryman, and pressed on.

"Oh, the birds," sighed she, "and the flowers, and the grassy hills to run on, we are leaving behind!" But still the boy had the wish for a man's life again, and urged her on; and still with every step they grew younger and younger. At length, two small children, they came to the border of that enchanted land, and saw beyond the world bleak and wintry and without leaf. Only a further step was wanted to bring them face to face once more with the hard battle of life.

Tears rose in the child-wife's eyes: "If we go," she said, "we can never return!" Her husband looked long at her wistful face; he, too, was more of a child now, and was forgetting his wish to be a man again.

He took hold of her hand and turned round with her, and together they faced once more the flowery orchards, and the happy watered valleys.

Away down there light streams tinkled, and birds called. Downwards they went, slowly at first, then with dancing feet, as with shoutings and laughter they ran.

Down into the level fields they ran; their running was turned to a toddling; their toddling to a tumbling; their tumbling to a slow crawl upon hands and feet among the high grass and flowers; till at last they were lying side by side, curled up into a cuddly ball, chuckling and dimpling and crowing to the insects and birds that passed over them.

Then they heard the sweet laughter of Father Time; and over the hill he came, young, ruddy, and shining, and gathered them up sound asleep on the old boat by the ferry.

"POET, TAKE THY LUTE!"

RICHARD LE GALLIENNE

All the rest of the village of Twelvetrees was asleep, and only the moon looked on, with natural sympathy one must believe, at what was taking place in a little house on the hillside, somewhat lonely in situation—in fact, the last house, as the highroad began to breast the hill and seriously settle down to the King's business of reaching the next market-town.

It lacked an hour of midnight, and, for some long time before, the moon had been aware of the noise of altercation inside that lonely house. A stern voice, heated with anger, had been mightily pounding at a boyish voice of much sweetness, which was occasionally able to interject a pleading sentence here and there into the thundercloud of the darker voice.

Suddenly the door of the cottage flashed open, and a frail, boyish figure was hurled into the garden, and the door shut again. Almost immediately it was again opened, and an object which the ejected one eagerly recognized as his lute was thrown after him.

"Take your toy with you!" said the voice, "and never let me see either of you again."

The lad seized his lute with loving anxiety, and stood up in the light of the moon to examine it—lest it should have suffered hurt. It had fared better than he could have hoped. Only one of the strings had been cut upon a stone. Involuntarily he tried the others, a proceeding which, being mistaken by his angered father for bravado, provoked a fiercely opened window and a volley of books.

"Take these, too," shouted the father; "till you read these you were of some use in the world. . . ."

The boy calmly and gently examined the books, and then, turning to his father, he said:

"Father, will you do me one last favor? You have thrown me out the wrong books. I shall be able to carry only one upon my journey—and it is not here. . . ."

"Well?" bellowed the father.

"It is a little vellum-bound duodecimo of the poems of Catullus, printed by the brothers Elzevir of Amsterdam, father dear—and it is more precious to me than any other book in the world. . . . If you will but give me that—you will find it, I think, on the right-hand corner of the fourth shelf—I will go away this moment, and trouble you no more as long as I live. . . ."

There was something so irresistible in the combined gentleness and self-command of the boy that he was able to win this concession, and, grimly leaving the window, his father examined the shelves a moment, and then, finding the volume, threw it out to his son, who caught it in his waiting hands with the skill of a juggler.

"Is that the nonsense you want?" growled the father.

"It is, indeed. Thank you with all my heart!" answered the son, affectionately placing the book in his doublet. "And now good-by, father. I am very, very sorry to have been such a disappointment to you, but really I could not help being born a poet . . . really I couldn't. I would be a cobbler if I only could; indeed, I have been trying my best. . . ."

The father was curiously softened.

"Hadn't you better come in, and try again?" he said.

"No, thank you, father! I have tried all I can. I had better go. Good-by."

"Don't you want any money?" called the father.

"No, thank you," said the boy proudly. "I have my lute"—and therewith he flung out of the garden and up the hill on the way to the moon.

So soon as he felt himself at a safe distance, he put down his lute softly on the grass, and throwing his hat into the air, danced an elfish *pas seul,* expressive of wild delight.

"Free, free!" he shouted aloud. "Free! Think of it! No more cobbling anymore forever!"

"But now to business," he said, when he had finished his dance; "where shall we sleep, O Jacobus Rossignol, and where shall we eat, and where is the money to come from to do either!"

As he spoke, he turned out his pockets to the moon. They were quite empty, except for a little medal of Our Lady of Consolation, which had been given him by a pretty village girl who had fallen in love with his singing.

Not a sou! However, that was no surprise, and no great worry. As for sleep—how often had he slept under the stars, lying on his back listening to their music, and been beaten by his father for his truancy. A bed of fern, with the firmament for a bed-curtain—there you had a bedchamber for a king.

But our poor Jacobus suddenly realized that he was hungry. Indeed, his purse was no emptier than his stomach, and there was a pain in one which he didn't feel—or care about—in the other.

Yes! He must eat! Otherwise he could not appreciate his starry bedroom as he would wish to. Even a poet must be fed.

He looked up at the moon. He judged by her position that it was not yet midnight.

"Four miles," he said to himself. "Four miles to the inn of 'The Flaming Sword!'—and on the way I will make a song wherewith to buy a supper!"

So with a brave heart little Jacobus Rossignol picked up his lute and stoutly footed the high road.

In spite of his two emptinesses, his heart beat high. How could it be otherwise with him, on so fragrant a night, and with such a moon! Indeed, his whole nature was so full of music that anything he looked at or thought of turned immediately into a song. Need I say that it was with no thought of his supper that he made this song to the moon, as he walked with his lute pressed close to his heart? You must sing about something nearer than the moon if you expect a supper in exchange for your song. But poor Rossignol had never been practical—he could only sing just what he wanted to sing at the moment; and, although he was so very hungry, he wasted those four miles in making this song to the moon:

"Sweet mother moon! for am I not your child?
  Kind mother moon! what is your child to do?
For surely there is in me something wild—
  And they all tell me that it comes from you.

"Here am I lonely as a babe new-born,—
  Nothing to bring the world in hard exchange;
A ray too delicate to live till morn,
  A phantom in the daylight, lost and strange.

"Oh, put a dream into my lunar head—
  That I may sell its silver as I sing,
And earn a meal, moon-mother, and a bed,
  And buy my bruised lute another string."

Though "The Flaming Sword" was still open when Rossignol arrived there, it was evidently all but gone to bed. The landlord was just awake in a corner, and close by him there snored in company a heavy-looking ploughman and a big soldier.

As Rossignol pushed open the door and looked in, the landlord sat up, and eyed his guest with no affectionate regard. At first sight, poor little Rossignol was not prepossessing—not, at all events, to landlords—with his thread of a body and his white wisp of a face; and then he looked worn, and poor as well, and he had not had the forethought to remove the dirt from his clothes consequent upon his father's precipitation of him into the garden. Surely, his appearance was not that of a profitable visitor.

"Well," shouted the landlord, in a voice as near thunder as he could make it, "well, what do you want?"

Rossignol was so tired that he had not his customary nerve about him, so he answered promptly from his heart:

"Supper!"

"Supper.... You are a likely one to order supper at this time of night, aren't you? Let me see your purse, and then, perhaps, you shall see—your supper.... What say you! Master Weevil?" and he nudged the snoring ploughman at his side. "Supper! Lord 'a' mercy! What do you think of that, Corporal!" and he appealed to the sleeping soldier—but the corporal was too fast asleep to hear him.

Seeing that his humor was somewhat wasted, he again turned to Rossignol.

"Let me see your purse, young man," he said, "and then we will see about supper."

"I have no purse," answered Rossignol, seeing that ready words could alone help him. "I threw it away four miles back. It was too heavy to carry—with nothing in it. Is there anything so heavy, Master Hirondelle—for though you know nothing of me, I know you for the best arm at bowls in six counties—is there anything so heavy as an empty purse?..."

But the innkeeper was too important a character in that countryside to be softened with so worn a compliment.

"That is all very well," he said, "but supper costs me money—why should I give it to you for nothing?..."

"I will sing you a song in exchange," answered Rossignol, shouldering his lute, as though he would play.

"A song...a nice time to sing," answered the landlord. "Why! You would rouse the house. There is a company upstairs of ladies and gentlemen worth more money to me than I could make out of fellows like you, if I kept this inn for a thousand years...."

But it was somehow evident in the landlord's expression that he had a kind ear for music, and at that moment the big soldier suddenly sat up with a yawn.

"Who said a song?" he roared, "a song! That's just what I want. Who said a song?..."

The corporal was evidently a man of some importance in those parts, and the landlord turned to him with respect.

"This ragamuffin here," he answered.

The soldier rubbed his eyes, and looked at Rossignol, with sleepy fierceness.

"What can you sing?" he said presently.

"Anything," answered Rossignol, on his mettle.

"Can you sing a soldier's song?"

"Can I?"

"So! Well, sing us 'The Three Jolly Corporals.'"

"That I cannot do, for I do not know it, but if Master Landlord will give me some refreshment—for I have walked a long way and am tired—I will sing you a soldier's song of my own making."

"No, no," interrupted the landlord bruskly. "I am here to sell, not to give.... Let us have your song, and we will then see...."

"I am sorry," answered Rossignol. "I would do as you ask, if I had the strength, but as I said I am very tired, and I am too faint to sing without some food...."

"Give him what he wants," said the soldier commandingly to the landlord. "You know me. Give him something good.... I like the boy; there is a brave light in his face...."

And the soldier being, as I said, a great man in those parts, the landlord scuttled off immediately, and in a moment or two placed a dish in front of little Rossignol, almost as big as himself.

"Now, sir," said the soldier, addressing Rossignol, "allow me to salute you. You carry a lute, I see; I carry a sword. They have always been old friends. Men like our host here, a good fellow in his way, don't understand these matters. They merely sell...and look narrowly at their returns, but the soldier and the poet give, give for the joy of giving; the soldier gives his life, the poet gives his song; and asks nothing more in return than you asked just now."

Rossignol was naturally much cheered by this address, and he looked at the corporal with a smile so winning, so full of naïve gratitude, that the corporal's heart was his from that moment.

"My name, Corporal," he said, "is Jacobus Rossignol; if I had a sword, how proud it would be to be the younger brother of your sword. As it is, I have nothing but a lute. Would it were worthier of being at your service...."

Thereon Rossignol took his lute and pulled here and there at its strings.

"It has had an accident tonight," he explained; "one of its strings is broken...but I will do what I can."

"No hurry!" said the soldier. "The night is still young."

Rossignol took up his lute in good earnest, and sang:

"Soldier, going to the war—
  Will you take my heart with you,
So that I may share a little
  In the famous things you do?

"Soldier, going to the war,
If in battle you must fall,
Will you, among all the faces,
See my face the last of all?

"Soldier, coming from the war,
Who shall bind your sunburnt brow
With the laurel of the hero,
Soldier, soldier—vow to vow!

"Soldier, coming from the war,
When the street is one wild sea,
Flags and streaming eyes and glory—
Soldier, will you look for me?"

The corporal expressed his appreciation of Rossignol's ballad with such heartiness that the ploughman, who had slept peacefully through the singing, woke up....

"You have missed a good song, Master Weevil," said the corporal; "but perhaps Master Rossignol will sing it over again for your benefit...."

To this Rossignol readily assented, once more to the corporal's great satisfaction.

"The sword is all very well in its way," said the ploughman, after a pause, "but I am a man of peace, a man of the fields and the plough. I suppose you have no quiet song for a countryman like me."

"Have I not?" said Rossignol. "Listen," and once more he took up his lute and sang:

"Let whoso will sing towns and towers,
'Tis not so that my heart is made,
My world is a wide world of flowers,
Leaf upon leaf and blade on blade.

"Of buds and butterflies and birds
I ponder, lying in the grass,
For company, the quiet herds,
And the slow clouds that pass and pass

"Safe in the leafy arms of trees,
I watch, through many a Summer noon,
The silken shadows of the breeze,
Till the stars come and bring the moon.

"To silent talk of growing things
I hearken with a loving ear,
And all that buds or builds or sings,
Is to my heart beloved and near.

"O meadows of the earth so green!
O meadows of the sky so blue!
How happy have these sad eyes been
Just looking, my great love, at you!"

So sweet was the sound of Rossignol's voice that it presently came about as the landlord feared. One by one the guests rose from their beds and stole along the corridor, and hung over the staircases, forgetful of one another, if only they might hear more clearly that unexpected music. Like bees on a blossom, so the landlord's guests clung to the balustrade. Rossignol had but finished "The Countryman's Song," when a woman's voice haughtily summoned the landlord into the hall. It was the Princess Bellefleur speaking for all the rest.

"Who is it that sings so sweetly at midnight, Mr. Landlord," she asked, as M. Hirondelle came out, with an apologetic mien.

"I am sure," answered M. Hirondelle, "I beg your pardon, Princess; I beg of all you lords and ladies, but—"

"Stop!" said the Princess. "Man or nightingale, give him this, and beg him sing another song"; and she flung down a gold piece as big as a rose.

"Let us see him, too," she cried; and thereon the whole company on a sudden impulse streamed laughing down the stairs into the tap-room, bidding the landlord bring them refreshment, and there were Rossignol and the corporal smiling and wishing each other good health.

The landlord of "The Flaming Sword" was so impressed by the reception given to his vagabond guest that, when Rossignol made ready to leave the next morning, he begged him think twice before setting out, for, he added, so long as he was landlord of "The Flaming Sword," Mr. Jacobus

Rossignol might count on it as his home. In fact, if he would only consent to make "The Flaming Sword" his cage, he, the landlord, was willing to pay him many gold pieces a month in exchange for his song.

But "No! No!" laughed Rossignol, as he stepped out once more upon the road. "Make *me* a slave if you will, . . . but my lute shall be always free. . . ."

As Rossignol walked along in the morning air, he tossed his lute up toward the sun.

"Why! I believe you and I together could win a kingdom," he said, apostrophizing it, as he caught it in his arms as tenderly as if it had been a flower; "that is, if either of us were foolish enough to care about a kingdom!"

"Yes, indeed," Rossignol continued, "who would care to be a king, when he could make songs like you and me, and fill beautiful eyes with tears, and draw lords and ladies from their beds, and make strong soldiers our friends—all for a handful of butterflies."

Indeed, little Master Rossignol, without being foolishly arrogant, was very satisfied with himself and his lute and life in general, this fine morning; and he was more glad than ever that his father had cast him out to the care of the moon.

"Think of it!" he exclaimed, keeping himself company with conversation, as was his dramatic habit, "think of it! Who in the world is so free as I am. Now, other men walking this road would have business great or small that demanded their arrival here or there. A mitred abbot, travelling luxuriously with his kitchen, must needs take a certain turning of the road. He may not wander away into yonder fairy-lane of hawthorn. He is due on a grave mission at the Monastery of the Five Streams and the Fat Meadows. The good monks are already *en fête* in anticipation of his coming. He cannot, merely as a gentleman, disappoint them . . . but you and I, my lute, have no such obligations. No one expects us. It matters to no one but ourselves what road we take, and yet our wandering music will always find kind ears to listen wherever we go. . . ."

"Besides, my lute, we have forgotten . . . we have money as well," and plunging his hand into his pocket, he drew forth the rose-noble which the Princess had thrown down for him to the landlord, and which the landlord had been too flurried to rob him of.

"Did you ever see such pretty money!" said poor Rossignol, and he spun it after a lark just then climbing his ladder of dew, and caught it again with his usual elfish dexterity. "Yes! it is too beautiful almost for money. It is almost big enough to be beaten out into a crown...."

At this moment his soliloquy was interrupted by his becoming aware that he no longer had the road to himself; for there suddenly faced him, moving slowly between the trees, a small dilapidated cart drawn sullenly by a not-too-well-conditioned donkey, and it rattled rustily as it crawled along.

But immediately his eyes forgot the donkey and the cart, as they fell upon the ragged, barefooted apparition of a beautiful girl, who, with one hand at the donkey's bit, held in her other hand a long wand of hazel, with a few leaves at its top.

Presently the tinker's cavalcade came within speech of Rossignol—for it was just a tinker's cart rattling with pots and pans; and as the girl drew nearer to him he saw that hers was at once the saddest and the loveliest face he had ever seen. Her poor clothes seemed rather to set off her beauty than to mar it, and as Rossignol looked upon her face, his heart sank with joy and sorrow; for he knew that he was no longer free.

Taking his hat from his head, he bowed to her very reverently and low.

"You seem weary," he said. "May I not be of some trifling service to you? Let me drive your donkey for you, at least... or will you not rest here a little and eat some cherries with me, and refresh yourself"—for Rossignol, in addition to his gold piece, had set out from "The Flaming Sword" with his wallet comfortably packed with good things to eat.

"Hush!" she said. "Your face is gentle. But I dare not speak to you, for my master is close behind. I left him but now in the village, and he will follow me in a moment. He is very strong, and his heart is very hard."

"Are you his slave?" asked Rossignol, wondering at the beauty of the girl.

"Yes! I am his niece, whom he has fed and clothed from my cradle. He has been very good to me, but he is often very cruel...."

"But see," said Rossignol, taking his lute in his hand, "with this I can do anything—give me leave, and I will soften his heart with a song...."

"Hush!" said the girl. "I hear him coming. Leave me, for he must not see us talking together."

But, almost before Rossignol could answer, a lumbering giant of a man had overtaken them, and loudly demanded of his niece why she thus loitered to talk with strangers upon the road, keeping back the donkey, which was slower than a snail, anyway.

Rossignol had barely time to whisper to her, "I will love you as long as I live. I would die for you," when he found himself caught roughly by the shoulders, and whizzed off so forcibly that it was all he could do to remain standing at the end of his surprise. But, though he had almost lost his feet, he had lost neither his courage nor his tongue, both of which asserted themselves together, and very swiftly and strongly.

"You brute!" he shouted at his enemy, with his heart on fire, "you brute!"

There were blades of grass on the wayside there which were almost as tall as Rossignol, as he stood up so absurdly ready to fight the impossible, but there was such a fierceness in his white face that even the giant paused a moment, not out of pity, but from sheer admiration of such a fighting soul in so tiny a thing; but the giant was only a common creature, after all; his purse was light, and he was in haste to reach the next town where there was business to be had.

So, with the least trouble in the world, he took the wriggling wight of poor little Jacobus by the collar, and boxing his ears in some such fashion as an elephant might admonish a fly, flung him, as carelessly and easily as he might have flung a nut, down into the underbrush at the edge of the road.

When Rossignol sat up, the road was empty of travellers once more.

"Faith!" he said, ruefully picking up his lute, "we are not so powerful as we flattered ourselves. . . . But no! I forgot. It was I that failed, not you! If only I had been given the chance to sing him my song of 'The Green Leaves and the Blue Sky,' I am sure he would have listened—and, who knows, he might have given me his niece for my wife. . . ."

He looked down the long road sadly. It was still rainbowed for him with the remembrance of that beautiful face.

"If only he could have heard me sing!" said little Rossignol.

So, somewhat downcast, Rossignol picked himself up out of the fern and walked the high road once more; nor did he or his lute say a word one to the other for many days. Instead of singing, he paid his way with the gold piece, for he was so sad that he told himself over and over that he would never sing again. He told himself that his life henceforward was to be a lonely pilgrimage to that beautiful face. His wanderings now had but one object—to look upon it again. He pictured it to himself moving down the lanes like some holy light, and he shuddered to think of so fair a creature in so cruel and sordid a bondage. But whither in the maze of this world had it wandered!

One day, about noon, having thrown himself down under a hawthorn, with all its fragrant clouds for a canopy, he remembered the friend he had in his pocket, and, taking out his little Catullus, began to read about Lesbia's sparrow for the thousandth time. The day was heavy with all the honey and the heat of the Summer, and, as he read, the book fell from his hand, and he slept there on the grass underneath the hawthorn, the forefinger of his left hand in his book, and his right arm thrown lightly over the back of his lute.

"What, after all, is he but a child?" said the Princess Bellefleur, as by chance passing that way in search of silence and wild flowers, she found him lying asleep, with his small white face among his red curls, like an egg in a nest.

"Just a child!... I wonder what his mother was like," said the Princess softly, as she sat down close by him under the hawthorn; proposing to herself to cross-examine him, for her amusement, as great ladies may, when he awoke.

It was a full hour before he even stirred in his sleep, and, meanwhile, the Princess watched him with a very gentle look. At last he opened his eyes, just as he lay, and, while they were still half asleep, they fell upon the Princess. Dreamily he looked at her, without a word. He was too sleepy yet to distinguish between dream and daylight. At length the Princess spoke:

"You remember me?" she said.

"No, I do not," he answered, with the simplicity of a boy; and he added immediately:

"I remember only one woman. You are very beautiful, but you are not that woman."

"And who, I wonder, was she?" asked the Princess.

"I hardly know, for I saw her but for a moment. She was the niece of a tinker, and I saw her for a moment on the high road.... I do not even know her name, for I had hardly spoken to her before her uncle came upon me, and beat me so that when I came back to myself—her face had gone—as you might pluck a rose from a tree. Ever since we have gone seeking her, my lute and I, but caught no glimpse of her face. O Princess, she was more beautiful than water-lilies in the starlight."

"A tinker's niece!" said the Princess, half to herself, "think of it—you love a tinker's niece!"

"Why not!" exclaimed the poet, suddenly leaping up, wide awake.

"Why not, indeed," answered the Princess, with diplomacy, and, her eye falling upon the open book, she turned their talk a safer way.

"You are a scholar, too, I see! Will you not read to me out of your book.... How pretty this Latin looks!" she added. "If only I could read it. Tell me what this means, dear poet...."

"Alas! I am no scholar," answered Rossignol, his thoughts momentarily diverted. "I am too idle. I am afraid I guess at the meaning of words by their looks, as I guess at the meaning of beautiful faces,... yet this surely I can spell out for you. I was trying to make a song of it just now as I fell asleep. My words are poor, indeed, in exchange... what words have I for words like these?... Ah! to think that a spray of this hawthorn is not so fresh as a line of Catullus after two thousand years! Just listen:

"Passer mortuus est meæ puellæ,
Passer, deliciæ meæ puellæ,
Quem plus illa oculis suis amabat....

"The tenderness of it! Isn't it strange that words of so long ago should mean so much to me today, sitting here under a comparatively recent hawthorn! What words have I, or any other man... but listen again:

"Nec sese a gremio illius movebat,
Sed circumsiliens modo huc modo illuc
Ad solam dominam usque pipilabat....

"*Pipilabat,*" he repeated, "doesn't it break your heart—just one word—*pipilabat!* O Princess, you are very wonderful, but you are not so wonderful as a word like that—you are not so wonderful as *pipilabat.*"

"I am quite sure that I am not," said the Princess, smiling; "and I am the more certain, as I will confess that I am no scholar, and that I have as little idea of the meaning '*pipilabat*' as yonder crow. Tell me what it all means, you wandering boy; and, if you will only sing it to me, I will listen—yes! I will listen, you strange boy, as long as you will sing," and she laid her hand lightly and tenderly upon his for a moment. Her heart, which many had called cold and selfish, merely because they had not the power to touch its secret spring, was strangely stirred by this enthusiastic lad.

"You are very gracious, Princess," answered Rossignol, "but, indeed, it is preposterous to attempt to put such words as these in any other tongue. . . . You might as well ask me to translate a wild rose. However, I will do the little that I can"; and Rossignol took up his lute and sang to her:

"Weep, Mother of Love! Weep, Baby-Boy of Arrows!
And weep all men that have a tear to shed!
Because—alas!—the sparrow of all sparrows,
The sparrow of my little girl, is dead.

"Oh, it was sweet to hear him twitter—twitter
In the dear bosom where he made his nest!
Lesbia, sweetheart, who shall say how bitter
This grief to us—so small to all the rest.

"For Lesbia loved no less that little bird,
Nor less was loved, than mother loves her daughter,
Or daughter mother; would you could have heard
His tiny voice, pretty as falling water!

"And in no other bosom would he sing,
But sometimes, sitting here and sometimes there,
On one bough and another, would he sing,—
Faithful to Lesbia—as I am to her.

"He, little bird, must go, as go the flowers,
Down the dark road by which no man returns;
Oh, curses on the black strength that devours
The beauty of life, and all its music burns!

"Foul shades of Orcus, evil you befall!
 'Tis true you smote her little sparrow dead—
But this you did to Lesbia worse than all:
 You made her eyes with weeping—oh, so red!"

"I would you were not so much in love with the tinker's niece," said the Princess, as he finished.

"Why do you say that," asked Rossignol.

"Because," she answered, rising and making ready to return to her castle close by in the woods, "because, I am inclined to think you might have married a king's daughter. . . ."

And thereupon she left him.

"A king's daughter!" said Rossignol to himself, still only half awake.

"What could she mean? Anyhow, it is no matter; for am I not in love with the tinker's niece?"

"Think of it, lute," he said, as he once more started along the road. "Think of it—we are great people, after all. . . . We might have married the king's daughter."

"But ah!" he added, "have we not seen the tinker's niece?"

"It is a sweet life we lead, you and I," said Rossignol one day to his lute, "a wonderful life! Do you think we are quite as grateful for it as we ought to be? Think how little we give—and all they give us in exchange! What am I? Now look at me, a mere imp of a man, one half rags and the other wrinkles; and come, now, what are you? A frail shell of rather cheap wood, with almost all your varnish rubbed away, cracked as well in two places, and subsisting on charity for your strings. If anyone else were to play upon you but me, me with these fingers"— Rossignol's fingers were his only personal vanities—"me, too, with my love, do you think he would be able to wring a tune out of you? But ah!" he added, "forgive me, little brother, my fingers could make music with no other strings. We are neither of us anything without the other. I could play upon no other lute—and no other musician—shall we not say, 'master!'—could play upon you. Am I not right?"

"That being agreed upon between us," Rossignol went on again, "I mean that we two good-for-nothings, of no value apart, are able in our affectionate combination, with no trouble in the world, indeed, with the mere self-indulgence of our united gifts, to do—well, to do as we please. We are our own masters and heed no one's bidding, having stored here in our common pouch all the gold pieces we can conveniently carry, and certainly more that you and I could spend in a twelve-month."

"I wonder who found the last overflow," continued Rossignol, "when our purse was so full that it burst, and we left gold pieces lying like king cups along the road. I wonder who found them and what they did with them."

"Do you see those arrowheads down there in the stream," said Rossignol presently. "You and I have time enough to gather them if we care—but the soldier riding past may not stop, and the mail-coach is too much behind time already to waste any time upon flowers. Even the little stream, leisurely as it is, must go on—only you and I, my lute, may sit here and be as lazy as we please, and watch the clouds moving like white cows through the blue pastures of heaven, and listen, if we will, to yonder bird—listen to it, if it sings well enough—and long enough, till the evening star.... Yes! our life is very wonderful...but, O lute, you shall sup as lute never supped before, you shall sleep in a bed of down, with silk curtains woven on Flemish looms; and your dreams shall be as sweet as a meadow of daisies:—if only...if only you will take me to the tinker's niece!"

Day after day, Summer and Winter, Rossignol and his lute walked and sang together, and there was no foot of the way that did not seem to them a-flower with kindness and wonder. And it was not only by his singing that Rossignol won his way. There was something good about his young-old little face, something that took you right away with its kindness. You couldn't say that it was beautiful—in the usual sense—but there was something about it that made beautiful faces look silly. Besides, he seemed to love and understand everything and everybody. Nothing ever happened but he knew all about it, and knew the only thing there was to do; no one ever got into trouble without his seeing why—indeed, there was nothing else for him to do—and seeing in an instant the way out.

He was, in fact, almost inhumanly clever, but one was compelled to remark that he was never clever merely for himself. There seemed nothing he could not do. Challenged not infrequently, as he was, to conform to the foolish excitement of the world, he could in mere child's play do so marvelously with a borrowed sword—for he had none of his own, being so small a man, his lute was heavy enough—that he made many another soldier his friend; and he could play such tricks with a pack of cards, that a whole city devoted to the curing of hides, and dumbly indifferent to his song, begged him to live there forever.

Once on his way he came upon a wandering clock-maker fast asleep. The clock-maker's cart was drawn under the hedge, and a spirited dog, fastened to it, barked an alarm at his sleeping master. But Rossignol silenced him so completely with a touch of his hand, that he licked his fingers lavishly in token of friendship: for Rossignol had never yet met with a dog, cat or horse that he could not with some kindness of his hands, or some friendship in his voice, turn into his devoted slave.

The clock-maker's dog was evidently wild for a run among the possible game of the adjacent fields, for there was a strain of an old hunting grandsire in his lowly blood, and, seeing that the clock-maker was not likely to wake up for some time, Rossignol released the poor soul, and applied himself to an old clock with a pretty brass face, which it was evident the clock-maker had been trying to mend as he had fallen asleep.

Very soon Rossignol, delighting in all its delicate mechanism, had started the old clock ticking again; and, wondering why anybody should care to keep account of time, he went upon his way.

He was the friend, too, of all the children along the roads. When some tired mother had given up her querulous infant in despair, he would take it in his arms, and in a few moments put it to sleep with a soothing murmur mysteriously his own—or with the sprightly imitation of some homely animal, so entertaining that the child's thoughts were diverted from its sorrow.

And so the years went by, and the people along the roads began to understand that the odd little vagabond with his kind eyes and his sweet voice, and that old lute of his, was what is known as a great man. There was hardly any need for him to sing his songs himself, as he passed along, for mothers sang them to their children, and lovers sang them to one another; indeed, the very birds sang them from the trees. Yes, Jacobus Rossignol and his lute became at length so famous that universities met him with laurel as he entered the city gates, dusty from the road, and with the same old lute on his arm; and made him Doctor of Laws—in spite of his old clothes.

Kings invited him to make his home at their courts, and sometimes he smiled to himself as he thought of—that king's daughter!

But fame had no power over his simplicity.

The world had still nothing more to give him than it gave the night his father cast him out-of-doors. And, speaking of his father—well, the lute he had used so despitefully had long since made him so rich and at ease in the world that the village of Twelvetrees had proved too small for him, and his mere stables resembled a village. His son knew life too well to feel any triumph over the old man in all this, and, in every way he could, he tried to persuade him that, if his father had not shot him through the door that night, he would never have been a real poet at all....

"I needed to face the world for myself, dear father," he said, "and I knew nothing about it till that night. Indeed, I never knew that the moon even was so beautiful, till you threw me out into the moonlight...."

But, for all his honors, Rossignol and his lute continued their simple way about the world. Rossignol gave his money day by day to the poor, reserving no more for himself than sufficed for food and clothes and lodging, and an occasional new string for his old lute, and still, as when a boy, he could not be persuaded that the world could give him anything better worth having than: The Spring, A Hawthorn in Blossom, A Copy of Catullus, An Old Lute, and The Face of the Tinker's Niece.

But, though he tramped many a dusty road, and read Catullus under many a vernal bush, he looked in vain for that little rusty cavalcade. Oh, to hear again the clanking of those pots and pans. Oh, again to be pitched headlong into the fern!

But it was fated that Rossignol should never see or hear those pots and pans again; and only by accident, in one of his wanderings, did he at last come upon the tinker's niece, as she was starting on a long journey.

Rossignol was still quite a boy to look at, though, indeed, the years had perhaps seemed more and longer to him than to other people—for other, wiser people had so many other things to do. He had been doing nothing all this time but walking through lanes, looking for the tinker's niece. He had seemed to be looking for her for years upon years; and actually she was little more than a woman when he saw her for the last time—suddenly, one morning, all covered with flowers, in a little churchyard, just as he and his lute were going by, without a thought of his coming upon her like that.

There were sad voices and solemn music about her, as Rossignol entered the churchyard gate, with a strange sinking in his heart. Gently making his way through the dark crowd, Rossignol caught sight once more of her lovely face, but her eyes were fast closed, and her brows were wreathed with lilies.

"At last!" he cried out, in a voice that made the mourners stand still in astonishment. "At last!"

And then, standing as one with authority by the bier, he turned to the priest, taking his lute in his hands, and thus asserted himself, for the first time in his modest life. "Your pardon, Father," he said, "but I am the poet, Jacobus Rossignol. I love this lady, and either I will sing her awake again, or I and my lute shall be buried in her grave."

So sudden and strange was his apparition, that his hands were on the strings and his voice among the words, before anyone had thought of hindering him—and, so soon as he began to sing, no one had a thought except for his song—and his sorrow.

"Poor soul," said some under their breath, "his grief has broken his heart."

And this was the song that Rossignol sang to the tinker's niece, as she lay with closed eyes among the lilies:

"This is my lady—pray you wait a while,
  Before you lock such beauty underground,
Shut in this dungeon that immortal smile,
  And plunder music of its sweetest sound.

"This is my lady! Ah! I never told
  All that I dare speak now that she is dead;
This is my lady! She who lies so cold,
  White as the flowers that wither on her head.

"This is my lady! She will never know
  How my heart breaks because my heart is hers;

I am the nightingale, she was the rose!
Oh, give me leave to sing to her, fair sirs!

"Ah! Rose untimely smitten of the cold,
I bring my burning lute afire with Spring—
So young 'twould turn to blossom faces old!
For thee to listen—scarce is need to sing!

"Love, sleeping on with such a silent air—
Awake, for all the land is flower and bird;
What dost thou, little sluggard, sleeping there,
Sleeping as sound as though thou hadst not heard!

"Oh, raise thy head!—or, if too weary thou,
Open thine eyes and nod a little smile,
And in my arms, ah! Love, I'll take thee now
And carry thee to God each shining mile."

But the tinker's niece lay there as if she had never heard a word of the song that made the tears stream from all other eyes in the churchyard except hers—as they had not even streamed for her.

"It is strange that she should sleep like this," said Rossignol to himself. "She cannot have heard my voice. I will sing to her my song of 'The Coming of Spring,' and then, surely, when she remembers the gladness of the green world, she will awake." And, taking up his lute once more, Rossignol sang:

"Heart, have you heard the news?
The Spring has come back—have you heard?
With little green shoot and little pink bud, and the little new-hatched bird;

"And the Rose—yes! yes! the Rose—
Nightingale, have you heard the news?
The Rose has come back, and the green and the blue,
And everything is as new as the dew—
New nightingale, new rose.

"Wind of the east, flower-footed breeze,
Oh, take my love to the budding trees,
To the cypress take it, and take it, too,
To the tender nurslings of meadows and leas,
To the basil take it, messenger breeze,
And I send it, my love, to you.

"O April skies!
The Winter's done,
O April skies!
The Spring's begun;
And honey—humming
Summer's coming—
O April skies!"

But the tinker's niece lay there in her shroud of flowers, and never stirred, and the priests and the mourners looked on at the strange grief of Rossignol, ignorantly awed.

"It is strange," said Rossignol, and he stood pondering in silence a long while.

Then again he spoke:

"Perhaps it is her will to sleep," he said; "perhaps she is weary and would rest. Let us not call her again, my lute; let us rather sing low to her, that she may indeed sleep."

And taking his lute in his hand for the last time, Rossignol sang softly this lullaby of death:

"Vain, all in vain! O love, thou dost not hear;
Thou art too lost in sleep to wake again;
In vain my song, in vain the falling tear,
Vain, all in vain!

"She will not wake again till Gabriel sings;
For any mortal music we can make,
My lute and I, with these heartbroken strings,
She will not wake.

"Sleep then, ah! sleep—if slumber be thy will;
We would not vex thee, though we needs must weep;
Of slumber everlasting take thy fill—
Sleep then, ah! sleep."

As he finished his song, Rossignol bent his head over his breast, and burst into tears. Then, gaining command of himself, he stood up before the people, and turning to that grim uncle whom he loved now because he had thrown him among the ferns:

"Will you do this for me?" he said. "Will you bury my lute with her—for what to me is the music she cannot hear!"

And as Rossignol left the churchyard in a dream, he laughed sadly to himself:

"O my lute—my lute! We were nothing, after all!"

FAMILY REVELATIONS

AN OLD WIFE'S TALE

ELLEN T. FOWLER

Though harps be dumb and crowns be dim,
I care not, if I comfort him.

NOT FORSAKEN

"RACHEL, MY LOVE," said old Mr. Weatherley, "perhaps Ethel would take a dish of tea with us, if we could induce our hyperpunctual handmaid to bring it before the appointed time."

Mrs. Weatherley smiled. "I will ring, dear, and see what we can do," she replied in her gentle voice; "but, as you know, our good Martha cannot endure an irregularity."

"Oh! the land of bondage that we live in—we unfortunate men whose homes are ruled by women," cried the dear old gentleman, gleefully rubbing his hands together.

But here I chimed in. "Please don't order tea any earlier on my account, Mrs. Weatherley, for I really am not in the slightest hurry. I was only afraid you might find the 'linked sweetness' of my visitation 'drawn out' a little too long, and that is why I made attempts at departure."

"Sit down, my dear Ethel, sit down," cried Mr. Weatherley; "do we ever find the sunset comes too late even on the longest day?"

"That is very pretty of you!" I replied; "now I shall stay and enjoy myself. But what a pity that you rang to order tea earlier!"

"Not at all, not at all! It will not make a shadow of difference. My wife may order the tea—as King Canute ordered the tide—at whatsoever hour seemeth good to her; but the tea and the tide will still come in at the time appointed to them by Nature and Martha respectively. Great laws, my dear young lady, are not set aside to please every careless petitioner."

I laughed. "You knock-under shockingly to Martha," I said.

"Nay; I wisely submit to the inevitable, and bow before a power greater than myself. And so does my wife. We never dare to defy Martha, do we dear?" he said, taking Mrs. Weatherley's withered hand in his.

Mrs. Weatherley smiled without speaking. She never spoke unless she was compelled to do so; but the cheerful, garrulous old gentleman talked enough for both.

I do not think I ever saw a more devoted couple than the Weatherleys. Fortunatus Weatherley was still a handsome man, and must have been a perfect demigod in his youth; but, alas! an accident, which occurred shortly before his marriage, had rendered him stone blind. His wife was a gentle, faded, elegant woman, whose whole nature seemed to be absorbed by her intense passion for her husband. Verily she was eyes to the blind; for she read to him, listened to him, tended him, with unceasing care. And although she was so quiet, one felt it was not because she had nothing to say. She was one of the women who remind one of Elise's shop window: not much show, but any amount of prestige. There was nothing modern about the Weatherleys—they would have scorned the idea; he cared for Addison and old port, and she for real lace and gardening; but, above all, they cared for each other—perhaps an equally old-fashioned taste.

Reading aloud to Mr. Weatherley was a liberal education to me, who, alas! in those days was terribly up-to-date. He would not listen to modern novels, which were as meat and drink to my intellectual palate; he preferred style to plot, and good English to mental analysis. He would rather discover the origin of a word than vivisect a woman's feelings; and he appeared to regard the fathers and schoolmen as greater authorities than the leader-writers of the daily papers. He was a most cultured old gentleman.

"Do you ever wonder what people's minds would look like if you could see inside them?" I asked one day.

"No, my dear, no; what a very peculiar idea!"

"Well, I know what yours is like," I continued.

"Do you indeed? Pray tell me," he requested politely.

"Your mind is exactly like an old library; it is full of books bound in vellum and written in Latin, and its air is the atmosphere of culture and refinement. But it is just a bit—a very little bit—stuffy, don't you know? It wants to have its windows opened to let in the fresh breezes of today."

Mr. Weatherley laughed. "Very good, very good indeed! Now shall I tell you what your mind is like, my dear young lady?"

"Certainly; I am dying to hear."

"It is like a newspaper stall: here a bit of news, and there a piece of gossip; here the review of some fresh book, and there the description of some fashionable costume; first one thing and then another, and the whole superstructure new every day."

"You are rather hard on me, Mr. Weatherley!"

"No, my dear, I am not. Remember that, nowadays, for one man that reads a book fifty read the newspaper; so you are on the winning side."

"Now Mrs. Weatherley's mind," I continued thoughtfully, "is like a picture-gallery in some grand old château; but when one comes to examine the pictures they are all portraits of you."

"Very neat, my dear, very neat indeed. You have a wonderful power of observation, Ethel, and a most happy gift of putting that which you see into words; a gift, my child, which is no less a source of pleasure to yourself than to those who have the privilege of enjoying your friendship, I should imagine."

"I'm glad that my chatter amuses you, Mr. Weatherley."

"It does so to a very great extend. I have always felt a sincere interest in young people; and as I have never had a child of my own, I delight to surround myself with young persons not of my own household. My quarrel with the young people of today is that they are not young enough."

"Do you think that we are too advanced?"

"Quite so, quite so. Nowadays younger women are always bothering their pretty heads about abstruse social problems or the higher mathematics; but when I was young they had more important things to think of—such as their latest sweethearts and their newest bonnets."

"But we still have bonnets and sweethearts, as well as social problems and higher mathematics," I argued. "We may love Rome more than we used to do, but not Caesar less."

"Perhaps so, perhaps so, my dear. You doubtless still go in for bonnets and sweethearts, but what bonnets!—and what sweethearts!—compared with those the girls had in my young days."

"Do you think them so very inferior?"

"Inferior beyond expression! Of course I cannot see these things for myself; but my Rachel reads to me descriptions of the same now and again in some modern book or newspaper, and they make me feel positively unwell."

I laughed.

"When I was young," continued Mr. Weatherley, "a bonnet was—well, a bonnet; and I can assure you that it placed an almost insurmountable barrier betwixt one's self and the young woman concealed in the depths of it."

"Like Truth at the bottom of a well."

"Precisely. Today, as far as I can gather, an impossible butterfly makes a nest of lace under the shadow of an artificial rose; and there is your bonnet!"

"It seems like a falling off, I confess," I said, "And what about the sweethearts?"

"There, my dear Ethel, the decadence is even more lamentable. In my time a young man fell in love with a young woman, and never rested till he had made a suitable home for her. Now a young man makes—at his leisure—a suitable home; and then, when he is middle-aged, furnishes it with the woman of his acquaintance who bores him the least."

"What an awful description!"

"But," he continued, "to make up for not feeling love, modern people talk about it; just as they indulge in senseless conversation about medical science to make up for their lack of health and strength. We have more love stories than we used to have, but less love; just as we have more dentists than we used have, but fewer teeth."

"Tell me your love story, please," I coaxed.

"Oh! that is an old story, Ethel, a very old story; but it is always new to me."

"I do *so* want to hear it," I urged.

"Then, my dear, I will tell it to you with pleasure. When I was very young I went to Canada, and there met two most charming orphan sisters, Naomi and Rachel Lestrange. Naomi, the elder, was a quiet, unobtrusive woman, with nothing distinctive about either her character or her appearance; but Rachel was the most beautiful and loveable creature I ever saw in my life."

And the old man smiled with tender pride as he recalled the love of his youth.

"I daresay," he continued, "that now it is difficult for you to realize how very lovely my wife was when she was young. I have never seen her since, so she is still beautiful Rachel Lestrange to me; but I suppose her pretty hair is grey, and her dear face aged now."

"Her hair is grey and her face worn," I admitted; "but she is still a most elegant woman, with a wonderful air of distinction."

"She always had that," he said, looking pleased. "It was a characteristic of all the Lestranges that they had the grand air, I believe. She is very proud of her family, you know; it was one of the best French families in Canada."

"She always shows by every movement that she is well-born," I replied; "but please go on with your story."

"Well, of course I fell over head and ears in love with Rachel as soon as I set eyes on her; and to let you into an open secret, my dear, I have been in that state ever since. But before I dared to ask her to be my wife, the great catastrophe of my life occurred."

"What was that?"

"One bitter winter's night the Lestranges' house caught fire, and was burnt to the ground. Fire, as you know, spreads very rapidly in that dry climate, and is most difficult to extinguish. When I appeared on the scene the staircase had already fallen in ruins, and the two sisters were standing at their bedroom window shrieking for help."

"How terrible!" I exclaimed.

"Quick as thought," continued Mr. Weatherley, "I placed a ladder against the wall of the burning house, and ascended it; though already the walls scorched my hands, and the smoke was so dense that I could hardly see. On reaching the sisters' room I seized Rachel—who happened to be nearest to the window—in my arms, carried her down the ladder, and resigned her to the crowd of friendly hands below. Then I reascended the ladder in order to save Naomi; but, alas! ere I was half-way up, the side of the house fell in, and I was precipitated into the burning ruins. Poor Naomi, of course, perished in the flames; but I was saved, though as by a miracle."

"Were you much hurt?" I asked in breathless interest.

"Terribly. For many years I hung between life and death; and when at last I did recover, it was to the sad consciousness that I should be hopelessly blind to the end of my life."

"How sad!" I whispered.

"Through all that long illness my Rachel nursed me with indefatigable skill and unwearying tenderness, and it was to her care that I really owned my recovery. Of course I felt that a blind man, such as I then found myself, had no right to ask any woman to link her lot with his; nor should I ever have done such a thing."

"Not even if you knew she loved you?"

"No; her love would be no excuse for my selfishness."

"But," I argued, "a woman, who really loved you, would only love you the more for your blindness; women are made like that."

"I know they are, my dear, and men are made like this. But there was no need for me to ask Rachel anything, for during my illness—as I learnt afterwards—her name was ever on my lips, and I told her over and over again the story of my love for her."

"And, when you were well enough to listen to her, she told you the story of her love for you, I suppose."

"She did, bless her! she did. And I have been well enough for that ever since, thank Heaven! and have found increasing pleasure in the exercise."

"And were you married soon afterwards?"

"Immediately that I was able to be moved, Rachel brought me to Halifax, away from the scene of our great catastrophe: there we were quietly married, and thence we sailed for England as soon as I was strong enough for the voyage."

"Poor Mrs. Weatherley! Did she feel her sister's death very much?" I asked.

"Sadly, my dear, sadly! In fact, I do not think she has ever been the same woman since. They were the most devoted pair of sisters I ever saw; but, between ourselves, I used to think that Naomi was just a little hard and severe on my sweet, loving Rachel, and domineered over her too much. But you, who have seen something of my darling's intensely sensitive and loving nature, can understand that a cold and stern and unsympathetic woman, such as Naomi was, might easily wound her without knowing it."

"That is very likely," I said, "for I think it is quite impossible for those cold, calm natures to enter into the feelings of so passionately loving a woman as Mrs. Weatherley."

"But what distressed my poor Rachel so much," added he, "was that she felt that her sister's life had been, so to speak, sacrificed for hers; and she has an idea that perhaps she ought to have made me save Naomi first and then come back for her."

"But in that case Rachel would have been burnt to death."

"Of course she would. One of them must have perished anyhow, and I cannot cease to feel thankful that the one that was spared was my darling wife. But Rachel was always so utterly unselfish—as you see she is now in all her dealings with me—that she would rather suffer herself to any extent than let suffering fall on those whom she loved. As I hinted to you before, I think that poor Naomi—who was the older and the least affectionate—sometimes took advantage of this; but I would not suggest such a thing to Rachel for worlds. She would not allow me—even in Naomi's lifetime—to suggest to her that there was a flaw in her idolized elder sister; and I should not be likely to do such a thing now that the poor woman has been in her grave these forty years and more."

"It seems to me that Mrs. Weatherley has a perfect genius for loving," I said softly.

"She has, my dear, she has; but I sometimes fear that it takes too much out of her. Her body is so frail, and her heart so strong."

Life passed on like an old-world dream in the quiet home of Fortunatus Weatherley. It was a perfect idyl to see these two old sweethearts together, and to guess at the love beyond all words which existed between them. But it grieved me to perceive that they both grew feebler as the days went by, and that their years were beginning to tell upon them.

"Ethel," said Mrs. Weatherley to me one day when her husband was out of earshot, "don't you think that Fortunatus is looking less vigorous than he did some time ago?"

"You see, dear Mrs. Weatherley, the weather is rather trying just now," I replied evasively.

She gave a sad little laugh. "Think of any weather's being trying to my Fortunatus! Why, Ethel, he has always been so splendidly strong that he never knew if the days were cold or hot, and he has never allowed a thermometer inside his house; he regarded them as what he calls modern medical rubbish."

"But don't you think he is well?"

"No, I don't. I have shut my eyes to it as long as I could, but now they will not keep shut any longer. I can't help seeing it, though it almost kills me to do so."

"Dear Mrs. Weatherley," I said, kissing her, because I did not know what else to say; and I find, in my dealings with my own sex, that kisses are as useful as asterisks in filling up inconvenient spaces.

"My child," she said tenderly, her large blue eyes filling with tears, "I hope you will fall in love some day, for no woman can be happy until she does. But pray that you may never love as much as I do! It is killing work."

"Yet it means great joy."

"And great sorrow. Surely the woman who feels "within her eyes the tears of two" has more than her share of weeping."

"But she has the smiles of two as well."

"Perhaps. And, Ethel, also pray that you and your sister may never fall in love with the same man. That is what I and my sister did, and it was the first cloud that ever came between us. The servant who described a cloud of the size of a man's hand as only a small cloud was very young and inexperienced, for a cloud of that size and shape is large enough to throw an unlifting shadow over the lives of countless women."

"And did your sister love him very much?" I asked in youthful curiosity.

"I think she loved him as much as she was capable of loving anybody. But she had not the intense and concentrated power of loving, nor of feeling, nor of suffering, that I have. I have loved Fortunatus too much, Ethel; it would have been better for him and better for me if I had widened the circle of our life, and taken in more friends and broader interests. I see it all, now that it is too late."

"Dear Mrs. Weatherley, you are wrong."

"No, child, I am right. Being a woman, the man I loved was quite enough for me, and filled every crevice of my life. But men are different. No woman—however much he loves her—is enough to fill a man's life and be his whole world, in the same way that men are everything to us.

And I ought to have remembered this, seeing that my Fortunatus was blind, and could not make fresh interests for himself."

"Yet he has been very happy," I urged.

"Yes, he has; but he would have been happier had he lived in a larger world, and his hold on life would have been stronger. People who are moped die more easily than people who have plenty of interests."

"But you did it because you loved much," I said by way of comfort.

"Surely," she answered with her sad smile, "that plea for forgiveness can always be mine, whatever sins, negligences, and ignorances are brought up against me."

Mrs. Weatherley was right. Fortunatus was breaking up. Day by day he grew frailer and frailer, and even his wife's great love could not hold him back from the unknown bourne, whither he was journeying so quickly. Within a few months of my conversation with Mrs. Weatherley, Fortunatus was dead; he died holding his wife's hand, and the last word he said was "Rachel."

But—to everyone's surprise, her own included—the blow did not kill Mrs. Weatherley. Those slim, fragile creatures have often more latent strength than their robuster sisters, and it was so in her case. Strong, hearty women in the village fell and died, and still the thin, delicate-looking old lady lived on and on at the Manor House, not caring for her life in the very least. I never saw Mrs. Weatherley smile after her husband's death, and I do not believe anyone else ever did. Poor old Martha finished her work and went to her place, but her mistress lived on and on, taking no notice of anything or anybody.

One day, when she was very old indeed, Mrs. Weatherley said to me—

"Ethel, now that my life is over I see that it has all been a mistake."

"How?" I asked.

"I cannot forgive myself for letting Fortunatus save me, and leave my poor sister to be burnt to death."

"But, dear Mrs. Weatherley," I argued, "you did not know that he would not be able to come back and fetch her also."

"Of course, child, I did not. Had I thought so, nothing would have induced me not to stay behind. But, though it was all unintentional, my life really was saved at the sacrifice of my sister's."

"But otherwise hers would have been saved at the expense of yours, which comes to the same thing. And if that had been the case, and she had lived and you had died, think what a difference it would have made to your husband!"

"I know; I have often thought of that, and it is my one comfort. Even had they married each other (which is doubtful, as my sister had a great horror of anyone with a physical infirmity), she could never have loved and cared for Fortunatus as I have done; it wasn't in her. And suppose—which is far more likely—that they had not married each other, what woman could have ever been to Fortunatus what I was?"

"No one, I am sure."

"My sister loved him then because she always adored strength and beauty; but she would not have had the patience to wait on a blind man all her life, which to me was perfect bliss," continued the old lady.

"Don't be unhappy about it, dear," I said, trying in vain to soothe her.

She took no notice of me, but went on: "You see, Ethel, it was all done in such a hurry I had not time to think. Fortunatus appeared at the window, and took me in his arms and carried me down through the blinding smoke, before I had time to realize what was happening. If I had known my sister would die I would never have left her, never. We had better have died together; though that would have been dreary for Fortunatus."

"It would indeed. He could not have lived without you, Mrs. Weatherley. Believe me, it is all for the best. I am sure that Naomi herself would forgive you, and understand."

She looked at me with sorrowful eyes. "I am Naomi," she said; "but he never found it out."

THE PRELIMINARIES

CORNELIA A. P. COMER

I

YOUNG OLIVER PICKERSGILL was in love with Peter Lannithorne's daughter. Peter Lannithorne was serving a six-year term in the penitentiary for embezzlement.

It seemed to Ollie that there was only one right-minded way of looking at these basal facts of his situation. But this simple view of the matter was destined to receive several shocks in the course of his negotiations for Ruth Lannithorne's hand. I say negotiations advisedly. Most young men in love have only to secure the consent of the girl and find enough money to go to housekeeping. It is quite otherwise when you wish to marry into a royal family, or to ally yourself with a criminal's daughter. The preliminaries are more complicated.

Ollie thought a man ought to marry the girl he loves, and prejudices be hanged! In the deeps of his soul, he probably knew this to be the magnanimous, manly attitude, but certainly there was no condescension in his outward bearing when he asked Ruth Lannithorne to be his wife. Yet she turned on him fiercely, bristling with pride and tense with over-wrought nerves.

"I will never marry anyone," she declared, "who doesn't respect my father as I do!"

If Oliver's jaw fell, it is hardly surprising. He had expected her to say she would never marry into a family where she was not welcome. He had planned to get around the natural objection of his parents somehow—the details of this were vague in his mind—and then he meant to reassure her warmly, and tell her that personal merit was the only thing that counted with him or his. He may have visualized himself as wiping away her tears and gently raising her to share the safe social pedestal whereon the Pickersgills were firmly planted. The young do have these visions not infrequently. But to be asked to respect Peter Lannithorne, about whom he knew practically nothing save his present address!

"I don't remember that I ever saw your father, Ruth," he faltered.

"He was the best man," said the girl excitedly, "the kindest, the most indulgent—That's another thing, Ollie. I will never marry an indulgent man, nor one who will let his wife manage him. If it hadn't been for mother—" She broke off abruptly.

Ollie tried to look sympathetic and not too intelligent. He had heard that Mrs. Lannithorne was considered difficult.

"I oughtn't to say it, but can't explain father unless I do. Mother nagged; she wanted more money than there was; she made him feel her illnesses, and our failings, and the overdone beefsteak, and the underdone bread,—everything that went wrong, always, was his fault. His fault—because he didn't make more money. We were on the edge of things, and she wanted to be in the middle, as she was used to being. Of course, she really hasn't been well, but I think it's mostly nerves," said Ruth, with the terrible hardness of the young. "Anyhow, she might just as well have stuck knives into him as to say the things she did. It hurt him—like knives, I could see him wince—and try harder—and get discouraged—and then, at last—" The girl burst into a passion of tears.

Oliver tried to soothe her. Secretly he was appalled at these squalid revelations of discordant family life. The domestic affairs of the Pickersgills ran smoothly, in affluence and peace. Oliver had never listened to a nagging woman in his life. He had an idea that such phenomena were confined to the lower classes.

"Don't you care for me at all, Ruth?"

The girl crumpled her wet handkerchief. "Ollie, you're the most beautiful thing that ever happened—except my father. He was beautiful, too; indeed, indeed, he was. I'll never think differently. I can't. He tried so hard."

All the latent manlines in the boy came to the surface and showed itself.

"Ruth, darling, I don't want you to think differently. It's right for you to be loyal and feel as you do. You see, you know, and the world doesn't. I'll take what you say and do as you wish. You mustn't think I'm on the other side. I'm not. I'm on your side, wherever that is. When the time comes I'll show you. You may trust me, Ruth."

He was eager, pleading, earnest. He looked at the moment so good, so loving and sincere, that the girl, out of her darker experience of life, wondered wistfully if it were really true that Providence ever let people just live their lives out like that—being good, and prosperous, and generous, advancing from happiness to happiness, instead of stubbing along painfully as she felt she had done, from one bitter experience to another, learning to live by failures.

It must be beautiful to learn from successes instead, as it seemed to her Oliver had done. How could any one refuse to share such a radiant life when it was offered? As for loving Oliver, that was a foregone conclusion. Still, she hesitated.

"You're awfully dear and good to me, Ollie," she said. "But I want you to see father. I want you to go and talk to him about this, and know him for yourself. I know I'm asking a hard thing of you, but, truly, I believe it's best. If *he* says it's all right for me to marry you, I will—if your family want me, of course," she added as an afterthought.

"Oughtn't I to speak to your mother?" hesitated Oliver.

"Oh,—mother? Yes, I suppose she'd like it," said Ruth, absent-mindedly. "Mother has views about getting married, Ollie. I dare say she'll want to tell you what they are. You mustn't think they're my views, though."

"I'd rather hear yours, Ruth."

She flashed a look at him that opened from him the heavenly deeps that lie before the young and the loving, and he had a sudden vision of their life as a long sunlit road, winding uphill, winding down, but sunlit always—because looks like that illumine any dusk.

"I'll tell you my views—some day," Ruth said softly. "But first—"

"First I must talk to my father, your mother, your father." Oliver checked them off on his fingers. "Three of them. Seems to me that's a lot of folks to consult about a thing that doesn't really concern anybody but you and me!"

II

After the fashion of self-absorbed youth, Oliver had never noticed Mrs. Lannithorne especially. She had been to him simply a sallow little figure in the background of Ruth's vivid young life; someone to be spoken to very politely, but otherwise of no particular moment.

If his marital negotiations did nothing else for him, they were at least opening his eyes to the significance of the personalities of older people.

The things Ruth said about her mother had prepared him to find that lady querulous and difficult, but essentially negligible. Face to face with Mrs. Lannithorne, he had a very different impression. She received him in the upstairs sitting room to which her semi-invalid habits usually confined her. Wrapped in a white wool shawl and lying in a long Canton lounging-chair by a sunshiny window, she put out a chilly hand in greeting, and asked the young man to be seated.

Oliver, scanning her countenance, received an unexpected impression of dignity. She was thin and nervous, with big dark eyes peering out of a pale, narrow face; she might be a woman with a grievance, but he apprehended something beyond mere fretfulness in the discontent of her expression. There was suffering and thought in her face, and even when the former is exaggerated and the latter erroneous, these are impressive things.

"Mrs. Lannithorne, have you any objection to letting Ruth marry me?"

"Mr. Pickersgill, what are your qualifications for the care of a wife and family?"

Oliver hesitated. "Why, about what anybody's are, I think," he said, and was immediately conscious of the feebleness of this response. "I mean," he added, flushing to the roots of his blond hair, "that my prospects in life are fair. I am in my father's office, you know. I am to have a small share in the business next year. I needn't tell you that the firm is a good one. If you want to know about my qualifications as a lawyer—why, I can refer you to people who can tell you if they think I am promising."

"Do your family approve of this marriage?"

"I haven't talked to them about it yet."

"Have you ever saved any money of your own earning, or have you any property in your own name?"

Oliver thought guiltily of his bank account, which had a surprising way of proving, when balanced, to be less than he expected.

"Well,—not exactly."

"In other words, then, Mr. Pickersgill, you are a young and absolutely untried man; you are in your father's employ and practically at his mercy; you propose a great change in your life of which you do not know that he approves; you have no resources of your own, and you are not even sure of your earning capacity if your father's backing were withdrawn. In these circumstances you plan to double your expenses and assume the whole responsibility of another person's life, comfort, and happiness. Do you think that you have shown me that your qualifications are adequate?"

All this was more than a little disconcerting. Oliver was used to being accepted as old Pickersgill's only son—which meant a cheerfully accorded background of eminence, ability, and comfortable wealth. It had not occurred to him to detach himself from that background and see how he looked when separated from it. He felt a little angry, and also a little ashamed of the fact that he did not bulk larger as a personage, apart from his environment. Nevertheless, he answered her question honestly.

"No, Mrs. Lannithorne, I don't think that I have."

She did not appear to rejoice in his discomfiture. She even seemed a little sorry for it, but she went on quietly: —

"Don't think I am trying to prove that you are the most ineligible young man in the city. But it is absolutely necessary that a man should stand on his own feet, and firmly, before he undertakes to look after other lives than his own. Otherwise there is nothing but misery for the woman and children who depend upon him. It is a serious business, getting married."

"I begin to think it is," muttered Oliver blankly.

"I don't *want* my daughters to marry," said Mrs. Lannithorne. "The life is a thousand times harder than that of the self-supporting woman—harder work, fewer rewards, less enjoyment, less security. That is true even of an ordinarily happy marriage. And if they are not happy—Oh, the bitterness of them!"

She was speaking rapidly now, with energy, almost with anguish. Oliver, red in the face, subdued, but eager to refute her out of the depths and heights of his inexperience, held himself rigidly still and listened.

"Did you ever hear that epigram of Disraeli—that all men should marry, but no women? That is what I believe! At least, if women must marry, let others do it, not my children, not my little girls!—It is curious, but that is how we always think of them. When they are grown they are often uncongenial. My daughter Ruth does not love me deeply, nor am I greatly drawn to her now, as an individual, a personality,—but Ruth was such a dear baby! I can't bear to have her suffer."

Oliver started to protest, hesitated, bit his lip, and subsided. After all, did he dare say that his wife would never suffer? The woman opposite looked at him with hostile, accusing eyes, as if he incarnated in his youthful person all the futile masculinity in the world.

"Do you think a woman who has suffered willingly gives her children over to the same fate?" she demanded passionately. "I wish I could make you see it for five minutes as I see it, you, young, careless, foolish! Why, you know nothing—nothing! Listen to me. The woman who marries gives up everything, or at least jeopardizes everything: her youth, her health, her life perhaps, certainly her individuality. She acquires the permanent possibility of self-sacrifice. She does it gladly, but she does not know what she is doing. In return, is it too much to ask that she be assured a roof over her head, food to her mouth, clothes to her body? How many men marry without being sure that they have even so much to offer? You yourself, of what are you sure? Is your arm strong? Is your heart loyal? Can you shelter her soul as well as her body? I know your father has money. Perhaps you can care for her creature needs, but that isn't all. For some women life is one long affront, one slow humiliation. How do I know you are not like that?"

"Because I'm not, that's all!" said Oliver Pickersgill abruptly, getting to his feet.

He felt badgered, baited, indignant, yet he could not tell this frail, excited woman what he thought. There were things one didn't say, although Mrs. Lannithorne seemed to ignore the fact. She went on ignoring it.

"I know what you are thinking," she said, "that I would regard these matters differently if I had married another man. That is not wholly true. It is because Peter Lannithorne was a good man at heart, and tried to play the man's part as well as he knew how, and because it was partly my own fault that he failed so miserably, that I have thought of it all so much. And the end of all my thinking is that I don't want my daughters to marry."

Oliver was white now, and a little unsteady. He was also confused. There was the note of truth in what she said, but he felt that she said it with too much excitement, with too great facility. He had the justified masculine distrust of feminine fluency as hysterical. Nothing so presented could carry full conviction. And he felt physically bruised and battered, as if he had been beaten with actual rods instead of stinging words; but he was not yet defeated.

"Mrs. Lannithorne, what do you wish me to understand from all this. Do you forbid Ruth and me to marry—is that it?"

She looked at him dubiously. She felt so fiercely the things she had been saying that she could not feel them continuously. She, too, was exhausted.

Oliver Pickersgill had a fine head, candid eyes, a firm chin, strong capable hands. He was young, and the young know nothing, but it might be that there was the making of a man in him. If Ruth must marry, perhaps him as well as another. But she did not trust her own judgment, even of such hands, such eyes, and such a chin. Oh, if the girls would only believe her, if they would only be content to trust the wisdom she had distilled from the bitterness of life! But the young know nothing, and believe only the lying voices in their own hearts!

"I wish you would see Ruth's father," she said suddenly. "I am prejudiced. I ought not to have to deal with these questions. I tell you, I pray Heaven none of them may marry—ever; but, just the same, they will! Go ask Peter Lannithorne if he thinks his daughter Ruth has a fighting chance for happiness as your wife. Let him settle it. I have told you what I think. I am done."

"I shall be very glad to talk with Ruth's father about the matter," said Oliver with a certain emphasis on *father.* "Perhaps he and I shall be able to understand each other better. Good-morning, Mrs. Lannithorne!"

III

Oliver Pickersgill Senior turned his swivel-chair about, bit hard on the end of his cigar, and started at his only son.

"What's that?" he said abruptly. "Say that again."

Oliver Junior winced, not so much at the words as at his father's face.

"I want to marry Ruth Lannithorne," he repeated steadily.

There was a silence. The elder Pickersgill looked at his son long and hard from under lowered brows. Oliver had never seen his father look at him like that before: as if he were a rank outsider, some detached person whose doings were to be scrutinized coldly and critically, and judged on their merits. It is a hard hour for a beloved child when he first sees that look in heretofore indulgent parental eyes. Young Oliver felt a weight at his heart, but he sat the straighter, and did not flinch before the appraising glance.

"So you want to marry Peter Lannithorne's daughter, do you? Well, now what is there in the idea of marrying a jail-bird's child that you find especially attractive?"

"Of course I might say that I've seen something of businessmen in this town, Ross, say, and Worcester, and Jim Stone, and that if it came to a choice between their methods and Lannithorne's, his were the squarer, for he settled up, and is paying the price besides. But I don't know that there's any use saying that. I don't want to marry any of their daughters—and you wouldn't want me to. You know what Ruth Lannithorne is as well as I do. If there's a girl in town that's finer-grained, or smarter, or prettier, I'd like to have you point her out! And she has a sense of honor like a man's. I don't know another girl like her in that. She knows what's fair," said the young man.

Mr. Pickersgill's face relaxed a little. Oliver was making a good argument with no mushiness about it, and he had a long-settled habit of appreciating Ollie's arguments.

"She knows what's fair, does she? Then what does she say about marrying you?"

"She says she won't marry anybody who doesn't respect her father as she does!"

At this the parent grinned a little, grimly it is true, but appreciatively. He looked past Oliver's handsome, boyish head, out of the window, and was silent for a time. When he spoke, it was gravely, not angrily.

"Oliver, you're young. The things I'm as sure of as two and two, you don't yet believe at all. Probably you won't believe 'em if I put them to you, but it's up to me to do it. Understand, I'm not getting angry and doing the heavy father over this. I'm just telling you how some things are in this world,—facts, like gravitation and atmospheric pressure. Ruth

Lannithorne is a good girl, I don't doubt. This world is chuck full of good girls. It makes *some* difference which one of 'em you marry, but not nearly so much difference as you think it does. What matters, from forty on, for the rest of your life, is the kind of inheritance you've given your children. You don't know it yet, but the thing that's laid on men and women to do is to give their children as good an inheritance as they can. Take it from me that this is Gospel truth, can't you? Your mother and I have done the best we can for you and your sisters. You come from good stock, and by that I mean honest blood. You've got to pass it on untainted. Now—hold on!" he held up a warning hand as Oliver was about to interrupt hotly. "Wait till I'm through—and then think it over. I'm not saying that Peter Lannithorne's blood isn't as good as much that passes for untainted, or that Ruth isn't a fine girl. I'm only telling you this: when first you look into your son's face, every failing of your own will rise up to haunt you because you will wish for nothing on God's earth so much as that that boy shall have a fair show in life and be a better man than you. You will thank Heaven for every good thing you know of in your blood and in your wife's, and you will regret every meanness, every weakness, that he may inherit, more than you knew it was in you to regret anything. Do you suppose when that hour comes to you that you'll want to remember his grandfather was a convict? How will you face that down?"

Young Oliver's face was pale. He had never thought of things like this. He made no response for a while. At least he asked,—

"What kind of a man is Peter Lannithorne?"

"Eh? What kind of—? Oh, well, as men go, there have been worse ones. You know how he came to get sent up. He speculated, and he borrowed some of another man's money without asking, for twenty-four hours, to protect his speculation. He didn't lose it, either! There's a point where his case differs from most. He pulled the thing off and made enough to keep his family going in decent comfort, and he paid the other money back; but they concluded to make an example of him, so they sent him up. It was just, yes, and he said so himself. At the same time there are a great many more dishonest men out of prison than Peter Lannithorne, though he is in it. I meet 'em every day, and I ought to know. But that's not the point. As you said yourself, you don't want to marry their daughters. Heaven forbid that you should! You want to marry his daughter. And he was weak. He was tempted and fell—and got found out. He is a convict, and the taint sticks. The Lord knows why the stain of unsuccessful dishonesty should stick longer than the stain of successful dishonesty. I don't. But we know it does. That is the way things are. Why not marry where there is no taint?"

"Father—?"

"Yes, Ollie."

"Father, see here. He was weak and gave way—*once!* Are there any men in the world who haven't given way at least *once* about something or other?—Are there, Father?"

There was a note of anguish in the boys' voice. Perhaps he was being pushed too far. Oliver Pickersgill Senior cleared his throat, paused, and at last answered sombrely,—

"God knows, Ollie. I don't. I won't say there are."

"Well, then—"

"See here!" his father interrupted sharply. "Of course I see your argument. I won't meet it. I shan't try. It doesn't change my mind even if it is a good argument. We'll never get anywhere, arguing along those lines. I'll propose something else. Suppose you go ask Peter Lannithorne whether you shall marry his daughter or not. Yes, ask him. He knows what's what as well as the next man. Ask Peter Lannithorne what a man wants in the family of the woman he marries."

There was a note of finality in the older man's voice. Ollie recognized it drearily. All roads led to Lannithorne, it seemed. He rose, oppressed with the sense that hence-forward life was going to be full of unforeseen problems; that things which, from afar, looked simple, and easy, and happy, were going to prove quite otherwise. Mrs. Lannithorne had angered rather than frightened him, and he had held his own with her; but this was his very own father who was piling the load on his shoulders and filling his heart with terror of the future. What was it, after all, this adventure of the married life whereof these seasoned travelers spoke so dubiously? Could it really be that it was not the divine thing it seemed when he and Ruth looked into each other's eyes?

He crossed the floor dejectedly, with the step of an older man, but at the door he shook himself and looked back.

"Say, Dad!"

"Yes, Ollie."

"Everybody is so terribly depressing about this thing, it almost scares me. Aren't there really any happy times for married people, ever? You and Mrs. Lannithorne make me feel there aren't; but somehow I have a hunch that Ruth and I know best! Own up now! Are you and mother miserable? You never looked it!"

His father surveyed him with an expression too wistful to be complacent. Ah, those broad young shoulders that must be fitted to the yoke! Yet for what other end was their strength given them? Each man must take his turn.

"It's not a soft snap. I don't know anything worth while that is. But there are compensations. You'll see what some of them are when your boys begin to grow up."

IV

Across Oliver's young joy fell the shadow of fear. If, as his heart told him, there was nothing to be afraid of, why were his elders thus cautious and terrified? He felt himself affected by their alarms all the more potently because his understanding of them was vague. He groped his way in fog. How much ought he to be influenced by Mrs. Lannithorne's passionate protests and his father's stern warnings? He realized all at once that the admonitory attitude of age to youth is rooted deep in immortal necessity. Like most lads, he had never thought of it before save as an unpleasant parental habit. But fear changes the point of view, and Oliver had begun to be afraid.

Then again, before him loomed the prospect of his interview with Peter Lannithorne. This was a very concrete unpleasantness. Hang it all! Ruth was worth any amount of trouble, but still it was a tough thing to have to go down to the state capital and seek one's future father-in-law in his present boarding-place! One oughtn't to have to plough through that particular kind of difficulty on such an errand. Dimly he felt that the path to the Most Beautiful should be rose-lined and soft to the feet of the approaching bridegroom. But, apparently, that wasn't the way such paths were laid out. He resented this bitterly, but he set his jaws and proceeded to make his arrangements.

It was not difficult to compass the necessary interview. He knew a man who knew the warden intimately. It was quickly arranged that he was to see Peter Lannithorne in the prison library, quite by himself.

Oliver dragged himself to that conference by the sheer strength of his developing will. Every fibre of his being seemed to protest and hold back. Consequently he was not in the happiest imaginable temper for important conversation.

The prison library was a long, narrow room, with bookcases to the ceiling on one side and windows to the ceiling on the other. There were red geraniums on brackets up the sides of the windows, and a canary's cage on a hook gave the place a false air of domesticity, contradicted by the barred sash. Beneath, there was a window-seat, and here Oliver Pickersgill awaited Lannithorne's coming.

Ollie did not know what he expected the man to be like, but his irritated nerves were prepared to resent and dislike him, whatever he might prove. He held himself rigidly as he waited, and he could feel the muscles of his face setting themselves into hard lines.

When the door opened and some one approached him, he rose stiffly and held out his hand like an automation.

"How do you do, Mr. Lannithorne? I am Oliver Pickersgill, and I have come—I have come—"

His voice trailed off into silence, for he had raised his eyes perfunctorily to Peter Lannithorne's face, and the things printed there made him forget himself and the speech he had prepared.

He saw a massive head topping an insignificant figure. A fair man was Peter Lannithorne, with heavy reddish hair, a bulging forehead, and deep-set gray eyes with a light behind them. His features were irregular and unnoticeable, but the sum-total of them gave the impression of force. It was a strong face, yet you could see that it had once been a weak one. It was a tremendously human face, a face like a battle-ground, scarred and seamed and lined with the stress of invisible conflicts. There was so much of struggle and thought set forth in it that one involuntarily averted one's gaze. It did not seem decent to inspect so much of the soul of a man as was shown in Peter Lannithorne's countenance. Not a triumphant face at all, and yet there was peace in it. Somehow, the man had achieved something, arrived somewhere, and the record of the journey was piteous and terrible. Yet it drew the eyes in awe as much as in wonder, and in pity not at all!

These things were startlingly clear to Oliver. He saw them with a vividness not to be overestimated. This was a prison. This might be a convict, but he was a man. He was a man who knew things and would share his knowledge. His wisdom was as patent as his suffering, and both stirred young Oliver's heart to its depths. His pride, his irritation, his rigidity vanished in a flash. His fears were in abeyance. Only his wonder and his will to learn were left.

Lannithorne did not take the offered hand, yet did not seem to ignore it. He came forward quietly and sat down on the window-seat, half turning so that he and Oliver faced each other.

"Oliver Pickersgill?" he said. "Then you are Oliver Pickersgill's son."

"Yes, Mr. Lannithorne. My father sent me here—my father, and Mrs. Lannithorne, and Ruth."

At his daughter's name a light leaped into Peter Lannithorne's eyes that made him look even more acutely and painfully alive than before.

"And what have you to do with Ruth, or her mother?" the man asked.

Here it was! The great moment was facing him. Oliver caught his breath, then went straight to the point.

"I want to marry your daughter, Mr. Lannithorne. We love each other very much. But—I haven't quite persuaded her, and I haven't persuaded Mrs. Lannithorne and my father at all. They don't see it. They say things—all sorts of dreadful things," said the boy. "You would think they had never been young and—cared for anybody. They seem to have forgotten what it means. They try to make us afraid—just plain afraid. How am I to suppose that they know best about Ruth and me?"

Lannithorne looked across at the young man long and fixedly. Then a great kindliness came into his beaten face, and a great comprehension.

Oliver, meeting his eyes, had a sudden sense of shelter, and felt his haunting fears allayed. It was absurd and incredible, but this man made him feel comfortable, yes, and eager to talk things over.

"They all said you would know. They sent me to you."

Peter Lannithorne smiled faintly to himself. He had not left his sense of humor behind him in the outside world.

"They sent you to me, did they, boy? And what did they tell you to ask me? They had different motives, I take it."

"Rather! Ruth said you were the best man she had ever known, and if you said it was right for her to marry me, she would. Mrs. Lannithorne said I should ask you if you thought Ruth had a fighting chance for happiness with me. She doesn't want Ruth to marry anybody, you see. My father—my father"—Oliver's voice shook with his consciousness of the cruelty of what was to follow, but he forced himself to steadiness and got the words out—"said I was to ask you what a man wants in the family of the woman he marries. He said you knew what was what, and I should ask you what to do."

Lannithorne's face was very grave, and his troubled gaze sought the floor. Oliver, convicted of brutality and conscience-smitten, hurried on, "And now that I've seen you, I want to ask you a few things for myself, Mr. Lannithorne. I—I believe you know."

The man looked up and held up an arresting hand. "Let me clear the way for you a little," he said. "It was a hard thing for you to come and seek me out in this place. I like your coming. Most young men would have refused, or come in a different spirit. I want you to understand that if in Ruth's eyes, and my wife's, and your father's, my counsel has value, it is because they think I see things as they are. And that means, first of all, that I know myself for a man who committed a crime, and is paying the penalty. I am satisfied to be paying it. As I see justice, it is just. So, if I seem to wince at your necessary allusions to it, that is part of the price. I don't want you to feel that you are blundering or hurting me more than is necessary. You have got to lay the thing before me as it is."

Something in the words, in the dry, patient manner, in the endurance of the man's face, touched Oliver to the quick and made him feel all manner of new things; such as a sense of the moral poise of the universe, acquiescence in its retributions, and a curious pride, akin to Ruth's own, in a man who could meet him after this fashion, in this place.

"Thank you, Mr. Lannithorne," he said. "You see, it's this way, sir. Mrs. Lannithorne says—"

And he went on eagerly to set forth his new problems as they had been stated to him.

"Well, there you have it," he concluded at last. "For myself, the things they said opened chasms and abysses. Mrs. Lannithorne seemed to think I would hurt Ruth. My father seemed to think Ruth would hurt me. *Is* married life something to be afraid of? When I look at Ruth, I am sure everything is all right. It may be miserable for other people, but how could it be miserable for Ruth and me?"

Peter Lannithorne looked at the young man long and thoughtfully again before he answered. Oliver felt himself measured and estimated, but not found wanting. When the man spoke, it was slowly and with difficulty, as if the habit of intimate, convincing speech had been so long discussed that the effort was painful. The sentences seemed wrung out of him, one by one.

"They haven't the point of view," he said. "It is life that is the great adventure. Not love, not marriage, not business. They are just chapters in the book. The main thing is to take the road fearlessly,—to have courage to live one's life.

"Courage?"

Lannithorne nodded.

"That is the great word. Don't you see what ails your father's point of view, and my wife's? One wants absolute security in one way for Ruth; the other wants absolute security in another way for you. And security—why, it's just the one thing a human being can't have, the thing that's the damnation of him if he gets it! The reason it is so hard for a rich man to enter the kingdom of Heaven is that he has that false sense of security. To demand it just disintegrates a man. I don't know why. It does."

Oliver shook his head uncertainly.

"I don't quite follow you, sir. Oughtn't one to try to be safe?"

"One ought to try, yes. That is common prudence. But the point is that, whatever you do or get, you aren't after all secure. There is no such condition, and the harder you demand it, the more risk you run. So it is up to a man to take all reasonable precautions about his money, or his happiness, or his life, and trust the rest. What every man in the world is looking for is the sense of having the mastery over life. But I tell you, boy, there is only one thing that really gives it!"

"And that is—?"

Lannithorne hesitated perceptibly. For the thing he was about to tell this undisciplined lad was his most precious possession; it was the piece of wisdom for which he had paid with the years of his life. No man parts lightly with such knowledge.

"It comes," he said, with an effort, "with the knowledge of our power to endure. That's it. *You are safe only when you can stand everything that can happen to you.* Then and then only! Endurance is the measure of a man."

Oliver's heart swelled within him as he listened, and his face shone, for these words found his young soul where it lived. The chasms and abysses in his path suddenly vanished, and the road lay clear again, winding uphill, winding down, but always lit for Ruth and him by the light in each other's eyes. For surely neither Ruth nor he could ever fail in courage!

"Sometimes I think it is harder to endure what we deserve, like me," said Lannithorne, "than what we don't. I was afraid, you see, afraid for my wife and all of them. Anyhow, take my word for it. Courage is security. There is no other kind."

"Then—Ruth and I—"

"Ruth is the core of my heart!" said Lannithorne thickly. "I would rather die than have her suffer more than she must. But she must take her chances like the rest. It is the law of things. If you know yourself fit for her, and feel reasonably sure you can take care of her, you have a right to trust the future. Myself, I believe there is Some One to trust it to. As for the next generation, God and the mothers look after that! You may tell your father so from me. And you may tell my wife I think there is the stuff of a man in you. And Ruth—tell Ruth—"

He could not finish. Oliver reached out and found his hand and wrung it hard.

"I'll tell her, sir, that I feel about her father as she does! And that he approves of our venture. And I'll tell myself, always, what you've just told me. Why, it *must* be true! You needn't be afraid I'll forget—when the time comes for remembering."

Finding his way out of the prison yard a few minutes later, Oliver looked, unseeing, at the high walls that soared against the blue spring sky. He could not realize them, there was such a sense of light, air, space, in his spirit.

Apparently, he was just where he had been an hour before, with all his battles still to fight, but really he knew they were already won, for his weapon had been forged and put in his hand. He left his boyhood behind him as he passed that stern threshold, for the last hour had made a man of him, and a prisoner had given him the master-key that opens every door.

THE HEART OF RACHEL

ELEANOR MERCEIN KELLY

THE NEW TEACHER WATCHED SCHOOL "LET OUT" with a sigh of weary thanksgiving. April had come to Misty Top, and with it the season's vague, yearning restlessness, a wonder whether the sacrifice of her youth and her energy were after all a vain oblation. To teach dirty, stolid little mountaineers to spell cat, and add figures, and bound Brazil—surely there were higher things in life than this?

The last pupil to leave was Bud Hardy, who sidled past her, as she stood at the door, with such evident wish to escape detection that Teacher looked in spite of herself.

Then her lips twitched. Yes, there it was again, its outlines plainly visible beneath his store shirt—a book which she recognized from long familiarity with its shape as a First Reader.

It was not the first time she had caught the boy smuggling away some book, to which he was quite welcome, with the air of one compounding a felony. His passion for books touched and rather surprised her, for in school hours it was not evident. She had tactfully forborne comment, respecting a reserve typical of the mountaineer, and for that matter of boyhood itself; which never willingly confesses to a thirst for learning.

But as he mounted the family mule, upon which his small sister was already perched, waiting, Bud was overtaken by fate. A button of the store shirt gave; the First Reader came to earth at Teacher's very feet. With one look of agonized mortification, Bud whipped up the mule.

"Wait a minute, boy; you've dropped something," a voice called after him. He looked back, miserably. Teacher was laughing!

"He never tookn hit fer hisself," flashed out Sis, small womanhood to the rescue. "He wouldn't do no sich a thing! Hit were ol' Miz' Tolliver—"

"You shut up, Sis," growled the boy.

"I won't do hit, shut up. He allus brings 'em back agin, Teacher; he allus does! An' he jes' borries 'em for ol' Miz' Tolliver, kase him an' me is l'arnin her to read. Thar now!" finished the little girl, quite breathless with pride and trepidation.

"Why," said the teacher softly—"why, bless your hearts!" She was not laughing now. "Couldn't you persuade Mrs. Tolliver to come down to school with you?"

The boy shook his head, grinning a little. "She don't aim to look like no fool. Besides, she's plowin' now," he said, briefly.

The name Tolliver was associated in more minds than the teacher's with lawlessness and bloodshed, with feuds, with illicit stills, with everything of hopeless, ignorant defiance of the civilization that yearly threatens more closely the freedom of the mountain fastnesses. Once the Tollivers had been a clan to be reckoned with. Now there were only two left on Misty to bear the name—a man reputed less lawless than his kin, although even he was "hiding out" because of the recent killing of a revenue officer; and his mother, who tilled her steep and meager fields alone, since there were no men left to help her.

Once, passing a little clearing just beneath the sky, the teacher had seen this woman, an unforgettable figure, gaunt, gnarled, aged before her time, with eyes so suspicious and fierce, and withal so piteous, that the girl from a gentler world thought of Longfellow's "Resignation" lines:

> The heart of Rachel, for her children crying,
> Will not be comforted.

And it was she, this savage old fighting dam of a fighting brood, who at sixty wanted to learn to read!

The lassitude was gone from Teacher's face. She was like a cavalry horse that has heard the bugle. "How can I get up there?" she thought, aloud.

The little girl answered, eagerly, "You kin ride with we-uns!"

She eyed the mule with some misgiving. It looked patient, and a mountain school-teacher acquires many accomplishments besides mere book learning. But mule-riding had not hitherto been included in her growing experience. "Do you think there's room on him?" she asked.

"Ef they ain't, I kin walk," replied Bud, simply.

It was not gallantry; among his kind, as among animals, the female is distinctly a lesser order of being. It was mere mountain hospitality. He offered her his place on the mule as he would have offered her his bed, or his last piece of corn-pone with drippings.

But the mule's back proved unexpectedly capacious. Along the steep and winding trail they jogged for many a mile, Sis and the teacher behind Bud, sitting modestly sidewise as became females, with legs hanging down on opposite sides to balance. So jogging, they came at last to the highest clearing, where a figure that appeared to be a scarecrow come to life was turning the soil with an ancient hand-plow.

"Thar she be. Better take keer, Teacher; she's mighty servigrous with strangers," warned Bud. "I hope she won't set the dawg on ye!"

"I hope she won't, indeed," murmured the girl, and approached with some nervousness. "Howdy, Miz' Tolliver?" she called. "A fine day for planting, isn't it?"

The woman turned slowly, took her pipe from her mouth, and stared. "I ain't plantin'," she remarked, and turned her back again.

Somewhat daunted, the teacher said, in good mountainese, "I thought I'd come and set a spell."

To this, Mrs. Tolliver vouchsafed no reply whatever.

The teacher seated herself on the cabin doorstep, after one glance within—one only. The poverty of it was too appalling. She had no money to give these people, only her youth and her energy.

A slender hog and some bedraggled hens wandered in and out of the door at will, and a bulldog of sorts, chained in the lean-to, lunged at her now and then to the full length of his tether. She waited, hoping that the chain was strong.

She held on her knees a black leather bag that looked like a surgeon's case of instruments—and so it was; instruments for operating on ignorance.

Whenever the woman in the field reached the end of a furrow, she paused and stared at this bag. At last curiosity conquered. She left her plow.

"What air you-all totin' in that theer satchel, anyhow?" she demanded, gruffly.

"Books!" The teacher's smile had done much to thaw the shyness of Misty Top. "I thought you'd like some new books to read."

"Who, me?" The old woman shot her a quick, suspicious glance, and her chin lifted. "Us Tollivers don't hold much with book l'arnin' and sich-like foolishness. 'Cep'n my boy Benjy. I 'low Benjy kin read and write as good as what you kin," she added, with inconsistent pride.

"Good for Benjy! Where did he go to school?"

"He never. He done got l'arnin' when he as in jail onct, down to the settlemints. They was a preacher what l'arnt him."

"I see," said the girl, in some haste. "What a pity he did not teach you, when he came home!"

"What fer? Anyhow, I 'low I'm too old to l'arn new tricks," muttered the old woman, with a curiously appealing glance. "I'm sixty, come July."

"Why, so much the better. If little Sis Hardy can learn at six, surely you can at sixty."

"Naw, I cain't. I've done tried, and I cain't, I tell ye! They ain't no *sense* to them letters and figgers and curlycues. Hit's all plumb foolishness."

But despite its gruffness, there was a sort of desperation in her voice not lost upon the sensitive teacher. "Mrs. Tolliver," she said, earnestly, "I give you my word of honor that you can learn to read and write in five days, if you really want to."

"Ef I want to! Say, looka here." All pretense at indifference suddenly vanished. "I got to read—I plumb *got* to!"

Her fierce intensity startled the girl. Evidently there was more in this than met the eye. "I'll teach you. I'll come up every day after school until you have learned," she offered.

The eagerness of the old face was pathetic; but she shook her head. "I ain't got no money to pay ye," she said.

"Never mind that. The state pays me."

"Not fer me, hit don't," said the other, shrewdly. "Only fer chillun. 'Pears like the state ain't got much use fer ol' folks."

"But I don't want to be paid! It's my work, I'm only too glad—" She stopped short, warned by the stiffening of the woman's features.

She had forgotten the pride of the mountain people, inherited with their fine names and their hospitality and their invincible honesty from some earlier, nobler race of men. Her quick brain sought for an idea that would lead out of this impasse.

The few poor hens, the one pig, the meager little fields—evidently no payment could be made in produce. Then her eyes chanced upon a half-knit stocking that lay on a bench just inside the door. The idea came.

"What wonderful knitting!" she exclaimed, taking up the clumsy woolen thing to examine it with admiration. "I wish I knew how to knit."

"Don't ye?" asked the woman, incredulously. "How do you make out fer stockin's, then?"

"I have to buy them." The girl examined her neat lisle-clad ankle ruefully: "Pretty flimsy, aren't they?"

"They shore do be," admitted Mrs. Tolliver, with interest. "Now what would you be givin' at the store fer them things?"

"Thirty-five cents."

"*Thirty-five cents!*" Mrs. Tolliver was horrified. "Why, they ain't no warmth to 'em, and no w'ar, neither. Looka here!" she cried, suddenly. "S'posin' I was to l'arn you knittin' while you l'arn me readin'?"

"Done!" laughed the girl; and thanked God.

During the rest of that week, there was no well-earned leisure for Teacher. As soon as school was over, the Hardys and their long-suffering mule conveyed her proudly up the mountain-side, down which she walked again, some hours later, through the blossomy April twilight. On Saturday, there being no school and no mule, she walked both up and down the mountain, and did not sleep that night from sheer exhaustion. But the eagerness with which Mrs. Tolliver awaited her, the fierce, wistful determination to conquer "l'arnin'" by main force, were things she could not have thwarted so long as she had legs to carry her.

Often there was a lump in her throat as she watched her pupil; straggling gray hair bent over a child's slate, gnarled hand gripping the pencil as if it were a plow handle, tongue well out and working with the desperate effort of transcribing: "The cat runs after the rat." "Why does the dog bark at the cow?" etc.

The old woman seemed in dire haste. This was no leisurely progress of culture, but a forced march against the enemy, Time.

"Cain't ye make me l'arn no faster?" was her constant demand; and again, "I don't keer nothing' about writing'—hit's readin' I got ter have. Why must I l'arn 'em both to onct? Hit's wastin' time!"

Despite her hurry, she stopped at conscientious intervals to superintend the progress of the teacher's stockings; which, it must be confessed, was not rapid. "You-all ain't very peart with yore hands, be ye? But then yo're just a gal yit—you ain't had to do fer a lot of men-chillun," she said once, tolerantly.

The girl realized that she had never had so apt a pupil. It was as if an intelligence that had been dammed for years had found an outlet, and was flowing toward the accomplishment of its purpose with the driving force of a mill stream. She found herself mentally breathless with the effort to keep up.

"And on the seventh day He rested—" but not so Teacher. The Sabbath simply meant to her that she could give Mrs. Tolliver some extra hours of instruction.

She was about to start her climb up the mountain on foot when she saw a familiar figure hurrying down the trail—familiar and yet unfamiliar; a gnarled, bent figure, with the stride of a man somewhat hampered by the skirts of a woman, clad further in a tight and pointed basque and the ballooning sleeves of a long-past era. It was Mrs. Tolliver, dressed for meetin'.

"Howdy, Teacher!" she cried as she came. Her face was no longer stolid, but working with some long-pent emotion, and the eager words tumbled over each other. "I done hit, Teacher! I read hit yistiddy, every word, by myself! Every *word* of hit!"

"Every word of what?"

"My Benjy's letter!" Triumphantly she drew from that straining basque a crumpled, unstamped envelope that had evidently come to its address through many and dirty hands. "They was a feller done fotched hit to me, 'long about Christmas time, an' 'lowed hit was from Benjy. Teacher, I bin afeared. I thought he was in trouble somewhere—sick an' dyin', mebbe—an' I couldn't git to read hit, nowhow! Hit were like he was a-callin' me, the last of my boys callin' fer his mammy, like they done when they was little fellers; an' I couldn't git to go to him."

The teacher cried out in pity. "But why didn't you bring me the letter to read?"

"I darsn't trust ye," answered the mother, simply. "I darsn't trust nobody. The law's after Benjy. I was feared hit might say in the letter whar he was at. But I might 'a' knowed better," she added, proudly, "I might 'a' knowed he'd suckled mo' hoss sense from his mammy than that! Teacher, he ain't in trouble, ner sick; he ain't even in jail! Teacher, he's *all right,*" she said; and wept in her happiness after the fashion of women, civilized or uncivilized.

The girl's own eyes were blurred as she read the scrawl held out to her:

> Deer Mammy
> Here I be down in the settlements agin an I got me a good job an I lik it fine ony i git lonesome fer you-all wishin i knowed how yore gittin on an ef you got the misry in yore back agin. ef you kin git me word someways i got a fren wud git it fer me at the p.o. in lexinton Gen'l delivery name of E. Jones. Maw i never done it *you know what* ony i was with the feller what did an i seen him so ef the law ketches me i will have to tell an i caint do that, tell on a naybor. so i will stay hid till he gits cotched annyhow wich i hope will be soon cos i am homesik and he is a fule, so no more at present from your Trewly.
>
> Benjy

"Why," exclaimed the teacher, "do you mean to say he is *innocent?* He's hiding out rather than betray a friend?"

"In co'se," said the mother, "Benjy couldn't tell the law on a neighbor!"

The old face was quite transfigured, almost beautiful with happiness; and for months this happiness had lain within her reach, if she had but known how to take it.

"There's something else in the envelope," murmured the girl. "Why, it's money—it's ten dollars!"

Mrs. Tolliver stared at the postal order with awe. "Funniest-lookin' ten dollars ever I see—but thar now! Come to think of it, I ain't never seed ten dollars before, nohow."

Teacher's face was almost as radiant as her own. "To think that you can thank him for it!" she cried. "To think that you can write to him yourself, and tell him all about the book l'arnin', and the mis'ry in your back, and everything!

The old woman's eyes widened. She had not thought of that. "I kin," she said, slowly, "an' I will!"

For a moment or two Mrs. Tolliver paused, and with uncertainty surveyed the piece of paper and the fountain pen which the teacher handed to her. Then she seated herself rather heavily at Bud Harvey's little desk, and sighed—sighed as one sighs when confronted by a terrific task, aware that it must be done. There was another short pause. At last, with tongue out, brows heavily wrinkled, and feet drawn up tightly under her, she began.

The fountain pen spluttered and scratched in her agitated grasp, but she wrote on and on, without assistance or advice—wrote for two hours, two hours of the hardest work she had ever done in all her hard-working sixty years; at the end of which she heaved another mighty sigh, and surveyed her first love letter.

"Thar now!" she said at last. "Want to read hit, Teacher?"

"Why, no," said the girl, softly. "That's Benjy's letter."

"I ain't so sure about the spellin'. That word lovin', now—oughtn't thar to be a g in it somewhars?"

"Never mind, I'm sure Benjy will understand. Will you trust me to mail it for you?"

"Yes!" said the old woman, and bestowed the letter upon her as a queen might bestow an accolade.

Long after the ungainly figure had disappeared up the trail, Teacher stood smiling down at the queerly scrawled envelope in her hand. She was tasting, for the first time, power. She was sharing with her Creator the feeling He must have known when, after the seven days' labor, He looked upon the work of His hands and found it good.

MISS BECKY'S PILGRIMAGE

SARAH ORNE JEWETT

I

BEFORE HER BROTHER, the Rev. Mr. Parsons, died, Miss Becky and he had often talked about going back to Maine, to visit their old friends; but somehow the right time had never come, and now, when she thought of going all by herself, she felt as if it were her duty to carry out this cherished wish.

To be sure, it would be sad to go alone. They had often said that there would be many changes, and they should find few persons who remembered them; and so it would not have been altogether cheerful, at any rate. The minister and his sister had had few relatives, and most of those were dead, except a cousin in Brookfield, whom they had heard from now and then, but, though they reminded each other of the changes that had taken place, they still instinctively thought of their native town as if it were very nearly the same as it used to be when they had last seen it, thirty or forty years before. Their father and mother had died when they were very young, and Miss Becky had lived with an old aunt. Her brother had early shown unmistakable proofs of his calling to the ministry, and had used most of his share of their small fortune for his education; and he had been settled in his first parish only two or three years when Miss Becky went to live with him, her aunt having suddenly died and Mr. Parsons being in distress for a housekeeper. It proved a most judicious arrangement, for neither of them ever married, and they were capitally suited to each other, having that difference of disposition and similarity of tastes which make it possible for two people to live together without being too often reminded of the fact that we are in this world for the sake of discipline, and not enjoyment. It was always said that Mr. Parsons had been disappointed in love while he was pursuing his studies at the theological school, and whether he took this for an indication that he would be more useful as a single man I do not know; but, at any rate, in spite of frequent good chances and the way to seize them being made easy for him by members of his parishes, he never fell in love again and seemed to grow better satisfied with life year by year. He was a handsome man, and Miss Becky was proud of him. He was to her not only the best of preachers and kindest of men, but the most admirable of gentlemen. She had a thoroughly English respect for the cloth, and she had been born in the days when, in her native New England town, the league of Church and State was powerful and prominent, and the believers in the Congregational mode of worship and church government were able to look down upon other sects as dissenters. She had left Brookfield with great regret, though she had not known how dear the old place was to her until she came to leave it. She had never been very happy at her aunt's, for she never had liked her uncle very well, and his wife was a fretful, tiresome sort of woman, who made it so uncomfortable for every one, when she was not pleased, that her household became cowards in never daring to take their own way or to have minds of their own about even their own affairs; and it seemed a bright future to Miss Parsons to have a home of her own, as she knew her brother's house would be, for she was to have all the good fortune of a minister's wife,—the glory and honor and pride of it, with none of the responsibility of suiting herself to the parish, which in a country town is sometimes no light weight to carry.

It was a long journey to take, for Mr. Parsons had been called to a church in Western New York, which seemed to Miss Becky like a foreign country. It was known throughout Brookfield that she was to start one Monday morning, and on Sunday her departure was referred to in the long prayer before the morning sermon, and in the evening meeting both deacons and some other pillars of the church prayed devoutly that she might be kept from danger and peril on her journey, and that she might help to scatter the good seed among the far-away people with whom she was to make her home. It was almost the same thing as if she were going to be a foreign missionary, and she was very solemn about it; but after she reached Alton it seemed as civilized and as home-like as Brookfield itself, and any sacrifice she had gloried in making proved to have been only in her imagination. Twice since then Mr. Parsons had accepted calls to other parishes, farther West, and for the last twenty-seven or twenty-eight years they had been in Devonport, which had started to be a rival to New York city itself. It had been disappointed and left at one side by the railroads, which presently put an end to the usefulness of a canal which had brought some business to the little town, and it had grown very dull and a good deal less important in its own mind. The minister and his sister had lived on year after year in comfortable fashion. The salary was small, but, fortunately, certain, and Miss Becky had a little income which relieved her from any feeling of dependence or uncomfortable humility toward the parishioners. Her hand had been asked in marriage more than once; but she never had thought it best to change her situation, for in neither case had it appeared likely that she should better herself, and she felt that there could be no reproach attached to single-blessedness while she kept her brother's house, and he was a minister of the gospel. It gave her a position and duty for which one must have a vocation.

But, as I have said, as years went on, Miss Becky's heart and thoughts were oftener and oftener turned toward Brookfield; and the minister himself, from hearing her say so much about it, came to have as great a wish as she to go back to New England. It is always home to all the people who go away from it to the westward. As they grow older they love it better and better, and it is a strong bond between the older settlers if in their youth they had some knowledge of each other's neighborhoods. The hearts of New England travelers are often touched at being asked to visit some old people, because they came from the Eastern States, and with all the Westener's pride in his new country his thoughts often turn fondly toward the rising sun. There is in this generation an instinctive homesickness that will probably be outgrown in the next. To any subject of the Queen England is always home, and a Canadian or a New Zealander is first of all and last of all an Englishman.

Miss Becky's brother, for some months before his death, had not seemed so strong as usual. He was several years older than she, and seemed very old in the part of the country where most of the people are young or, at furthest, middle-aged. He had never been in the habit of taking stated vacations (in fact, it had been a matter of pride and principle with him not to do so); but early in the summer he had said he should take a rest of a month when September came, and then they would go to Brookfield. He wished to verify some dates and records, and, though there were few people he cared much to see, there were a good many tombstones, and the old town itself was dearer to him then he ever used to believe. He had been hardly more than a boy when he left it, and it was his long-lost boyhood that he hoped to find again. They would go to the seashore for a little while—he should like to get a whiff of salt air; and on their way home they would stop in New York, where there was to be a general meeting of the churches that was of great interest to him.

They talked about their plans like two children; but they never carried them out, for, as I have said, the minister died. It was a great shock to Miss Becky, who until the very last was sure that a change of air was all that her brother needed to make him well and strong again; but he only went on a last short journey instead, and all the clergy in that corner of the world assembled to follow him, and they preached about him, and wrote about him in the religious newspapers, and said how sadly he would be missed and what a pillar had fallen. And then the world went on very much the same as ever, except to Miss Becky, who felt as if it had come to an end.

She stayed on in Devonport for a while, until she began to be very unhappy. The parish was hearing candidates with a view to settling a successor to Mr. Parsons, and they seemed so unfit for his place (as, indeed, they were, being mostly young and puffed up with pride) that she listened to them with great impatience and distress, and she made up her mind, by little and little, that as soon as the spring opened she would go to Brookfield and make a long visit. After all, there were a good many people in that place and its neighboring towns whom she wished to see, and whom she thought would be glad to see her; and, if she did not care to visit, she had it in her power to board for a while, and the more she thought about it the more in a hurry she felt to be on the way. She was by no means a rich woman; but, if she lost nothing, she would have enough to live on comfortably, since she spent but little and had an uncommon faculty for making that little go a long way.

The journey to Boston was bewildering and tiresome to her, for the most part; but when she was fairly started one morning to take the last half-day's car-ride, she was much delighted, and looked out of the window eagerly, and examined the faces in the car, to see if there might not possibly be one that was familiar. The very names of the stations were delightful to her ears, and after a while she felt as if she were traveling in disguise and as if everybody would be overjoyed if she only told them who she was. "I haven't been here for forty years," she told the conductor, after he had answered some question she had put to him; and he looked at her curiously (as if to see whether she was an old acquaintance, she thought), and said that she must find things a good deal changed. She heard a gentleman in front call him Mr. Prescott, and, if he had not hurried on, she would have asked him if he were not one of the sons of an old schoolmate of hers, who had married a Prescott and gone to live in Portland. She was sure he had a look of Adaline Emery.

It was a great pleasure that at one of the stations a new-comer took a seat beside her, the cars being full. She was a woman of about her own age, and evidently a journey was a matter of great importance to her. So Miss Becky felt a sympathy for her, and ventured to say that she had been in the cars for nearly two days and nights, after her companion had asked the name of one of the stations which she had failed to hear.

"I want to know if you have!" said she, looking at Miss Becky with respect. "Seems to me I couldn't stand it, noways; but then it ain't come in my lot to be much of a traveler. Was you ever this way before?"

"I was born and brought up down in Brookfield," answered Miss Becky; "but I have been away pretty near forty years. I wonder if you are acquainted about there any."

"Why, I was raised in Brookfield," said the woman, "and I've got a brother and sister living there. I'm just going to Brookfield now, to stop with them. I thought it was a great while since I was there; but you beat me. I was there nine years ago, and I expect I shall find a good many changes." And our two friends looked at each other searchingly, and in a minute a glimmer of satisfaction overspread Miss Becky's face. "I declare to my heart if you aren't Mahaly Robinson! I thought you looked sort of natural when I see you come into the cars. I s'pose you must have forgot all about Rebecca Parsons by this time." But her friend had not, and they grasped each other's hand and kissed each other at once, and the sudden outburst of affection was not amusing to the neighboring passengers.

"Why, I feel as if I had got home, seeing you," said Miss Becky, thinking how dreadfully old her friend looked, while the friend thought exactly the same thing of her, and each flattered herself that in her case time had left but little trace of its flight. "I forget your married name?" inquired Miss Becky. "I did know it at the time. You know you wrote me just after I went out West; but I always think of you as Mahaly Robinson—same's when we went to school together."

"I married first with a Sands; but I lost him when we had only been married three years," said Mahala, without any appearance of regret, "and then I married Joshua Parker, of Gloucester. I've been a widow now these fourteen years. He was a ship-master and used to sail out o' Salem when I first met with him; and after that he was master of the Fleetwing, out o' Boston for a good many years. He was lost at sea. She was never heard from after they left Callao. I wa'n't left very well off; we'd had considerable sickness, and his father and mother and a foolish sister made it their home with us and was considerable expense. I always set a great deal by Father Parker, though. He was a real good man and he always did what he could. He got frost-bit down to the Banks, one winter, and his hands and feet were crippled. We had hard scratchin' one spell: but my boys and girls got so's they could work, and then there wa'n't any more trouble. I've had a good deal to be thankful for; but I've seen the time I'd a-laid down and died, I was so discouraged. I live with my youngest daughter now, and she's got a handsome a little farm as you ever see and a good husband. He's doing well, too. They are always thinking o' things to please me, both of 'em. I ain't got a child I've been sorry for, and that's a good deal to say. There's a sight of risk in fetchin' up six of 'em. But I want to know how it's been with you. I see by 'The Congregationalist' that your brother had been taken away."

"Yes," said Miss Becky, with a sigh. "He was a dreadful loss to me. We'd been together so many years, and there never was a man like Joseph, any way. He was known all through that part of the West. We'd talked about coming on, and it's real sad to come without him; but I feel's if it was just what he'd want me to do, if he knew it. I hoped I should see him stand up and preach in the old meeting-house. Some of his sermons were thought a great deal of. I couldn't always understand the deeper thought in 'em," said Miss Becky, proudly. "We set a good many times to come on; and we did get as far as New York once, to the meetings of the American Board, and then somehow there was always some place we thought we must go to first, out West. It ain't that we've stayed right in the same place all these years," she explained. "My brother used to travel about a good deal. Seems to me, coming back this way, I miss him more than ever. I keep thinking o' things I ought to tell him when I get back to Devonport. It's been right hard to get reconciled."

"Then you're not coming back to settle?" asked Mrs. Parker. "I thought first that perhaps you was. There, we're a getting into Portsmouth; but I don't suppose I should know my way round. I lived here 'long of my first husband, and I always liked the place."

"I remember coming, when I was a young girl, to stop with my aunt Dennett for a spell, over on the Kittery shore. We've got to go across the river, haven't we? I shouldn't wonder if you could see the house. My sakes alive, how good and fresh the salt water smells! Don't it? I declare, how it carries me back!" exclaimed Miss Becky.

"The wind must have come round into the east," said Mrs. Parker, wisely. "It was a little north of west when I started this morning, and I thought I should have a good day; but then we're going right back into the country. Who are you expecting to stop with?"

"I wrote to Cousin Sophy Annis, because I've been in the habit of hearing from her every year, and one of her sons is living West, and has stopped with us several times. I didn't get any answer, for I started off pretty sudden. I found I was going to have company as far as Syracuse. I can go to the tavern, if it don't seem to be convenient for Sophia. I don't know but it would be just as well, any way, for I feel as if I was almost a stranger. I shouldn't mind the expense," she added, with a good deal of satisfaction.

"I know they won't let you go to no tavern; Brookfield folks will have altered a good deal if they have come to that!" exclaimed Mrs. Parker, in a way that was gratifying. "You'll find more that is glad to see you than you've any idea of. If you don't find anybody a-waiting for you, you come right home with me to Sister Phebe's; and then they'll take you over to Sophy's, after tea or in the morning, just as you are a mind to. You know it's right on the way there, and Sophy won't think nothing of your stopping 'long of me, as we fell in with each other in the cars."

But it seemed very lonely to Miss Becky, who was tired with her long journey; and she became uncertain of her reception, and almost wished she had not undertaken the pilgrimage. She began to understand how changed the place must be, and how little it would be like the Brookfield she had left. And when Mrs. Parker remembered that she had spoken of her brother's preaching in the old meeting-house, and explained that it had been torn down, to make place for a new one, the year before, it was really a great sorrow to our friend. She felt that if it were not for visiting the burying-ground it would not have been worth while to go at all.

"I did think it would be so pleasant to set in the old pew again, where I used to set when I was a girl," she said, sadly. "I have thought just how it all looked so many times!" As they neared Brookfield, the country grew more and more familiar, and Miss Becky looked out of the car-window all the time, and was again in high spirits. She told the names of the hills, and when she saw a farm-house that she remembered, not far from the railway, she was perfectly overjoyed, and hurriedly collected her carpet-bag, and her basket, and her big pasteboard box, that held some treasures which she had been afraid to trust to her trunk. "Do tell me if I look all right, Mahaly," she said, quickly passing her hand, in its loose black-thread glove, over the front of her bonnet and her neat frisett. "I don't s'pose I am fit to look at. I've always had to keep myself looking nice, on Joseph's account, being a minister, and we were always subject to a good deal o' company," she remarked; but Widow Parker said she looked as if she had only traveled from the next town, and in a few minutes more they were standing on the platform of the Brookfield station.

There were only strangers waiting there, and they were mostly little boys, and Miss Becky felt a strange sense of desolation; but presently some one greeted Mrs. Parker (who was much flustered) with great cordiality, and she walked off, without given a thought to her fellow-traveler, who stood still, looking anxiously at every face that passed, as if she hoped to find it familiar. She held the box and the bag and the basket, and suddenly wondered if her trunk had come, and looked down the platform the wrong way, and distressed herself with the thought that it had not been put off the train, since it was not in sight. The little boys strolled away, and the rest of the people began to disappear also, and Miss Becky remembered her companion, and wondered what could have become of Mrs. Parker, who had seemed so friendly; and just then some one came driving up to the platform. It was a young woman, and she jumped out quickly and came toward our friend.

"I wonder if you are Miss Parsons?" asked the girl, pleasantly.

"Why, yes, dear," said poor Miss Becky, who had been almost ready to cry.

"Grandmother said that I had better come round by the depot, but the rest of us were certain you wouldn't be here until tomorrow. How do you do?" and she kissed the old lady as if she really cared something about her. "We are all so pleased because you are coming. Now let me see to your baggage. We can take the trunk right into the back of the wagon."

"I was just feeling afraid it hadn't come," said Miss Becky; but the station-master asked if that were not the one which he was just going to drag into the depot, and in a few minutes more they were in the wagon, driving away.

"I hope you won't be too tired," said the girl. "We shall have to ride three or four miles; but then it is nice and cool."

"I always liked to ride," said Miss Becky, "and it is so refreshing to get out of the cars. There! you don't know what a difference there is between the air here and out West; but now I want you to tell me who you are?"

"I forgot you didn't know," said the girl, laughing. "We have talked so much about you that I forgot you didn't know me just as well as I do you. I'm Annie Downs, and my mother was Julia Annis."

"I can't believe Sophy Annis has got a granddaughter as old as you!" exclaimed Miss Becky. "Why, I don't feel any older than ever I did, but she was four or five years older than I."

"I have a brother and sister older than I," said Annie; "but they're both married. We lived at Freeport, but I suppose you knew that father died some years ago, and grandmother was getting feeble, so she wanted mother and me to break up and come to live with her. I have been keeping the town school for two years. It's very near, you know. Mother's brother carries on the farm—Uncle Daniel. He says he remembers you, and your coming to say good-by just before you went West; but grandmother says he was too young."

"I guess he does remember me," said Miss Becky, with a sudden affection for this relative of hers. "I know he was a dear little fellow, running round the kitchen. It was in cold weather, I know. I was going to kiss him, and he hid under the table." This was very pleasant and seemed to bring the strange relatives much nearer. "Your mother was the oldest, and was quite a girl then. I remember hearing of your father's being taken away; but I always thought of you all as little bits of children."

"There, I did feel so lonesome today!" said Miss Becky to old Mrs. Annis and her daughter, that evening; "but I feel now as if I had got back among my own folks. I like out West; but somehow I never have felt at home there as I do here, and after Joseph's death I saw it was being with him that had kept me from feeling strange. And I don't know why it is, either, for there are a good many people in our place from New England and everybody is free and neighborly."

Nothing could have pleased Miss Becky more than the welcome she received from the townspeople. She said over and over again that she had no idea she should find so many people who remembered her, and the excitement her visit seemed to make was deeply gratifying. It was exactly the way her brother was treated when he went back to visit one of his old parishes, and she accepted invitations to spend the day or to make a week's visit after haying until she was entirely confused at the thought of her engagements. It was very pleasant; but sometimes, when she was tired, the future suggested itself for her decision, and she wondered what she had better do when the visits were over, for there was all the rest of her life to be lived, and she ought to be making some plans.

II

It would not be fair to withhold an account of the wretchedness of poor Mrs. Mahala Parker when she remembered, on the evening after her arrival at her sister's, that she had meant to bring with her another guest. Something happened to remind her of their conversation in the cars, and she suddenly looked gray for a minute, while a chill crept over her. "Oh! my good land o' compassion!" she groaned. "What have I been and done? I believe my mind's a-failing of me." And her amazed companions asked what could be the matter.

"I met Rebecca Parsons in the cars," said she, "coming on from the West. We happened to sit in the same seat; but I never should have known her if she hadn't called me by name and told me who she was. She said she had been gone forty years. I shouldn't have said it was more than thirty, if it was that; but time does go so fast! She didn't seem certain about anybody's coming to meet her, and I told her I'd fetch her along with me, and then you'd send her over to the Annises, where she expected to stop; and I come right off without ever even saying Good-by to her. I don't know what she will think. I never felt so in my life. I don't remember to have seen no other conveyance there, and she must ha' been real put to it to know what to do. I got sort of excited, it's so long since I went anywhere before. It must have looked just as if I wanted to get rid of her. There was something on my mind all the way here; but I kept thinking it was because I had left something in the cars."

"Well, right after breakfast one of the girls shall take you over to the Annises, Sister Mahaly," said Mrs. Littlefield. "You'd feel better to see her yourself than to send word. I suppose she will be there, or she may have stopped up to the tavern, and they ought to know it. And you may as well ask them all to come over and take tea tomorrow and spend a good long afternoon. I sha'n't have another chance for some time, on account of haying. I was calculating to ask our minister, any way; and when I got your letter I thought I would wait until you was here."

"Adaline sent to Boston by one of our neighbors, who is real tasty and got me a beautiful cap, just before I came away," mentioned Mrs. Parker. "She said I'd be likely to want it, and those I had were getting a little past; but I told her I wished she hadn't. It will be just what I need, though, won't it? Rebecca was dressed real plain; but everything seemed to be of good quality. I dare say she put on what was old and wouldn't hurt, she had so far to come."

Miss Becky had been a little angry at being deserted; but she took a grim satisfaction in thinking Mrs. Parker's mind was not what it used to be, and when she made her appearance in the morning, entirely pentinent and armed with an invitation to tea, she was forgiven in full. The tea-party was a great success, and Miss Becky was the centre of attraction. There were so many questions to be asked and answered, wherever she went; the fates and fortunes of so many families had to be recounted for her satisfaction; and she made herself very agreeable by giving interesting reminiscences of her own life, and telling of the strange customs of some Westerners and the contrasts she noticed in the fashions of living East and West. She felt herself to be a person of great interest and consequence.

You may be sure that she wore her best black silk, and that she succeeded in leaving an impression on the minister's mind of her being well posted on clerical and religious questions. She told the Annis family, complacently, as they drove home together in the two-seated wagon, after the tea-party was over, that she always felt at home with ministers and knew their ways better than she did anybody's.

Cousin Sophia was pleased at being the owner of such an attractive and satisfactory guest. "I don't think I ever saw Mr. Beachman appear to enjoy himself better," she said. "He isn't much of a talker, as a general thing; but you brought him out right off. I tell you, Rebeccy, you ought to set your cap for the parson. He is well off. We give him eight hundred dollars, and he's got means beside. I think he's been a widower long enough; but folks here has got tired setting their caps for him, 'less it's old Cynthy Rush, and she 'pears to think that while there's life there's hope."

"He seems to be an excellent Christian man," said Miss Becky, flushing a little; but it was too dark for anybody to notice it.

"I'm going to have him to our house to tea," said Mrs. Annis, giving her daughter a suggestive poke. "He always likes to come in strawberry time."

Annie Downs had been much amused that evening at the evident interest which Mr. Beacham and Miss Becky took in each other. It was a funny, sedate likeness of a mild flirtation between two young people. They were mindful of the respect due to their own advanced years and the properties of a tea-party; but they found each other very attractive. They were both fine-looking. Mr. Beacham would have been fairly imposing in even a gown and bands, but in a surplice he would have been magnificent. One longed to see him in a ruffled shirt and small-clothes, instead of his plain black garments; but his solemn countenance bore on it the stamp of ecclesiastical dignity. "Anybody would know he was a minister," said Miss Becky, decidedly, and she had had vast experience among the Western clergy.

The June days went by quickly, and Miss Parsons enjoyed her visit more and more, and felt less and less inclination to go back to her Devonport life. She had not supposed that people would be so glad to see her; but, having once welcomed her, they never were made sorry, for our friend was really a good and pleasant person to know. The young people found her full of sympathy and kind-heartedness, and she gave a great deal of pleasure wherever she went. It was easy to see that she did not think only of how her friends greeted her and what they did for her, for she was as anxious to help and to give, in her turn, and she could be as amusing as heart could wish. There was an unfaded girlishness about her yet, in spite of the fallen snows of so many winters. She was very happy in Brookfield, and there was a companionship to be had even in the cypress-grown burying-ground, which was dearer to her than she had dreamed it would be. The people in the church on Sundays soon felt as if she were again their neighbor and friend, and Mr. Beacham found himself looking often toward the Annis pew, as he preached; and he selected his best sermon the next Sunday after he met Miss Parsons, and repeated it for her benefit, and was rewarded by her telling him, as he gravely shook hands with her on his way out of church, that it reminded her of one of her dear brother's on the same text, but Mr. Beacham had expanded the subject much more fully. "You know how to make things very clear," Miss Becky said, with a sudden brightening of her eyes and a simple frankness, that he thought extremely desirable. "It is something to be most grateful for, if a word we speak reaches and helps another struggling soul," he said, and shook hands absently with a parishioner in the next pew.

"Did you see poor Mary Ann Dean at church, today?" some one asked, as they drove home after meeting. And Mrs. Annis answered that she doubted if the poor soul ever got out to church again. "I haven't told you about her, have I, R'becky? She was a daughter of Susan Beckett, who used to be at your aunt's a good deal; but it may have been after you went West. She has had about the hardest time of anybody I know. Their house burnt down, and they lost most everything; and four of the family died within sixteen months. Mary Ann was left all alone, with one brother that drank like a fish, and she had to earn what she could and bear the brunt of everything. She was a good deal younger than the rest of the children. She has been failing this good while; but she wouldn't give up. She's always reminded me of a flower in the road that every wheel goes over. There ain't a better young woman anywhere in Brookfield. I set everything by Mary Ann."

"I do feel sorry," said Miss Becky. "I had it on my mind in meeting to ask you if any of Susan's folks were about here; and I noticed that poor, sick-looking girl. I'll go to see her the first of the week, if she don't live too far off, on her mother's account, if nothing else."

"It is only a little way," said Annie Downs. "I'll go with you tomorrow afternoon, if you will come along to the school-house after school, Cousin Becky."

Miss Becky was very kind to this new friend, who soon grew more ill and quite depended upon the kindness of her neighbors, and our heroine, having no family cares, was with her a good deal for the next fortnight. Haying had begun, and it was lucky that so good a nurse was for the most of the time at leisure, since the other women were all so busy, and, indeed, at any time had their hands full with their own work.

It happened that two or three times Mr. Beacham came to visit his sick parishioner; and it must be confessed that Miss Becky did not show her usual composure in the presence of the clergy, and that she began to feel uncomfortably self-conscious and to insist upon it to herself that she took no interest in the man whatever. She openly said (feeling all the time that she might be sorry for it) that she did not entertain each other; and Daniel wished that some of the women would come back. He thought of the unfailing resource of all farmers, and longed to ask the minister to come out and have a look at the hogs; but, being a minister, he feared it might not be the proper thing.

Happily, Mr. Beacham himself suggested that they should take a walk down to the bee-hives, and presently they fell into easy discourse together on some parish matters. And after a little while Miss Becky reappeared, and mentioned that some one wished to see Daniel at the barn, about pressing the hay; and while he hurried back to the house our friend and the minister strolled along together slowly.

It was a pleasant old garden, and in the middle path there was a long, rickety arbor, covered thick with grape-vines. The sun was getting low; but, for all that, the shade was pleasant, and Mr. Beacham stopped for a minute, but Miss Becky was uneasy and wished he would go on.

"Since I laid away my dear companion, now seven years ago," he said, in a tone that made Miss Beckys' heart thump dreadfully, "I have had no desire to fill her place in my home, solitary though it has been, but I find that I am no longer contented with my situation, and that you possess all the qualifications to make me happy. We are not young; but the Lord may continue our lives for many years yet, and I believe that we should enjoy a united home. You already know the responsibilities and cares of a minister's life, and it seems to me unwise that you should return to the

West permanently, though I do not doubt you have formed many associations which are dear to you and which it will be hard to sever. Permit me to say that you have already become very dear to me, and that I can assure you of a most heart-felt and enduring affection. I hope you will take the matter, as I have, into serious and prayerful consideration."

Miss Parsons felt for her handkerchief; but she mistook the way to her pocket, and fumbled at her dress without finding it, while the tears were ready to fall from her eyes, and Mr. Beacham and the grape-leaves and a red hollyhock that had pushed through the trellis were all in a dazzle together. She had somehow expected to have the solemn little speech followed by the benediction; but the minister stood there as if he expected her to say something. So she put out her left hand toward him, and covered her face with the other, and the handkerchief, which was found, at last, just in time. And Annie Downs, who was in the strawberry bed not a dozen feet away, hardly daring to breathe lest they should notice her, heard a resounding kiss, and then stole softly away among the pear-trees, and told her mother she need not be worried any more because supper would be so late.

They went out on wedding journey to Devonport, where Miss Becky was so much older than most people in town that her returning to them a bride caused great fun and astonishment; but everybody was very glad. She seemed so happy herself and she did not look a day over fifty-five. She carried back to the East some household goods that were dear to her, and she gave away the rest most generously.

But she felt very sad when she paid a last visit to her brother's grave, and as she came away she noticed some trees he had planted and tended with great care, and she felt as if she were taking a sad farewell of all her happy life with him. She was very contented in Brookfield and was looked up to by the whole parish, and she made Mr. Beacham an excellent wife; but she thought, with all her admiration for him, that, although an uncommon writer, he never could quite equal her brother's great sermon on Faith and Works. Dear Miss Becky! She often thought that her life had been most wonderfully ordered. Everything had happened just right, and she did not see how it was that all the events of life, other people's affairs, and things that seemed to have no connection with her, all matched her needs and fitted in at just the right time. If she had come to Brookfield the year before she was sure that she should have had no temptation to stay there, though she and Mr. Beacham did seem to have been made for each other. Mr. Beacham would have said that it was the unfailing wisdom of Providence; but she wondered at it none the less and was very grateful. Perhaps her life would seem dull, and not in the least conspicuous or interesting to most people; but for the dullest life how much machinery is put in motion and how much provision is made, while to its possible success the whole world will minister and be laid under tribute.

THRILLING INTRIGUES

A PRINCESS'S VENGEANCE

C. L. PIRKIS

"THE GIRL IS YOUNG, pretty, friendless and a foreigner, you say, and has disappeared as completely as if the earth had opened to receive her," said Miss Brooke, making a résumé of the facts that Mr. Dyer had been relating to her. "Now, will you tell me why two days were allowed to elapse before the police were communicated with?"

"Mrs. Druce, the lady to whom Lucie Cunier acted as amanuensis," answered Mr. Dyer, "took the matter very calmly at first and said she felt sure that the girl would write to her in a day or so, explaining her extraordinary conduct. Major Druce, her son, the gentleman who came to me this morning, was away from home, on a visit, when the girl took flight. Immediately on his return, however, he communicated the fullest particulars to the police."

"They do not seem to have taken up the case very heartily at Scotland Yard."

"No, they have as good as dropped it. They advised Major Druce to place the matter in my hands, saying that they considered it a case for private rather than a police investigation."

"I wonder what made them come to that conclusion."

"I think I can tell you, although the Major seemed quite at a loss on the matter. It seems he had a photograph of the missing girl, which he kept in a drawer of his writing-table. (By-the-way, I think the young man is a good deal 'gone' on this Mdlle. Cunier, in spite of his engagement to another lady.) Well, this portrait he naturally thought would be most useful in helping to trace the girl, and he went to his drawer for it, intending to take it with him to Scotland Yard. To his astonishment, however, it was nowhere to be seen, and, although he at once instituted a rigorous search, and questioned his mother and the servants, one and all, on the matter, it was all to no purpose."

Loveday thought for a moment.

"Well, of course," she said presently, "that photograph must have been stolen by someone in the house, and, equally of course, that someone must know more on the matter than he or she cares to avow, and, most probably, has some interest in throwing obstacles in the way of tracing the girl. At the same time, however, the fact in no way disproves the possibility that a crime, and a very black one, may underlie that girl's disappearance."

"The Major himself appears confident that a crime of some sort has been committed, and he grew very excited and a little mixed in his statements more than once just now."

"What sort of woman is the Major's mother?"

"Mrs. Druce? She is rather a well-known personage in certain sets. Her husband died about ten years ago, and since his death she has posed as promoter and propagandist of all sorts of benevolent, though occasionally somewhat visionary, ideas; theatrical missions, magic-lantern and playing cards missions, societies for providing perpetual music for the sick poor, for supplying cabmen with comforters, and a hundred other similar schemes have in turn occupied her attention. Her house is a rendezvous for faddists of every description. The latest fad, however, seems to have put all others to flight; it is a scheme for alleviating the condition of 'our sisters in the East,' so she puts it in her prospectus; in other words a Harem Mission on somewhat similar, but I suppose broader lines than the old-fashioned Zenana Mission. This Harem Mission has gathered about her a number of Turkish and Egyptian potentates resident in or visiting London, and has thus incidentally brought about the engagement of her son, Major Druce, with the Princess Dullah-Veih. This

Princess is a beauty and an heiress, and although of Turkish parentage, has been brought up under European influence in Cairo."

"Is anything known of the antecedents of Mdlle. Cunier?"

"Very little. She came to Mrs. Druce from a certain Lady Gwynne, who had brought her to England from an orphanage for the daughters of jewellers and watchmakers at Echallets, in Geneva. Lady Gwynne intended to make her governess to her young children, but when she saw that the girl's good looks had attracted her husband's attention, she thought better of it, and suggested to Mrs. Druce that Mademoiselle might be useful to her in conducting her foreign correspondence. Mrs. Druce accordingly engaged the young lady to act as her secretary and amanuensis, and appears, on the whole, to have taken to the girl, and to have been on a pleasant, friendly footing with her. I wonder if the Princess Dullah-Veih was on an equally pleasant footing with her when she saw, as no doubt she did, the attention she received at the Major's hands." (Mr. Dyer shrugged his shoulders.) "The Major's suspicions do not point in that direction, in spite of the fact which I elicited from him by judicious questioning, that the Princess has a violent and jealous temper, and has at times made his life a burden to him. His suspicions centre solely upon a certain Hafiz Cassimi, son of the Turkish-Egyptian banker of that name. It was at the house of these Cassimis that the Major first met the Princess, and he states that she and young Cassimi are like brother and sister to each other. He says that this young man has had the run of his mother's house and made himself very much at home in it for the past three weeks, ever since, in fact, the Princess came to stay with Mrs. Druce, in order to be initiated into the mysteries of English family life. Hafiz Cassimi, according to the Major's account, fell desperately in love with the little Swiss girl almost at first sight and pestered her with his attentions, and off and on there appear to have passed hot words between the two young men."

"One could scarcely expect a princess with Eastern blood in her veins to sit a quiet and passive spectator to such a drama of cross-purposes."

"Scarcely. The Major, perhaps, hardly takes the Princess sufficiently into his reckoning. According to him, young Cassimi is a thorough-going Iago, and he begs me to concentrate attention entirely on him. Cassimi, he says, has stolen the photograph. Cassimi has inveigled the girl out of the house on some pretext—perhaps out of the country also, and he suggests that it might be as well to communicate with the police at Cairo, with as little delay as possible."

"And it hasn't so much as entered his mind that his Princess might have a hand in such a plot as that!"

"Apparently not. I think I told you that Mademoiselle had taken no luggage—not so much as a handbag—with her. Nothing, beyond her coat and hat, has disappeared from her wardrobe. Her writing-desk, and, in fact, all her boxes and drawers have been opened and searched, but no letters or papers of any sort have been found that throw any light upon her movements."

"At what hour in the day is the girl supposed to have left the house?"

"No one can say for certain. It is conjectured that it was some time in the afternoon of the second of this month—a week ago today. It was one of Mrs. Druce's big reception days, and with a stream of people going and coming, a young lady, more or less, leaving the house would scarcely be noticed."

"I suppose," said Loveday, after a moment's pause, "this Princess Dullah-Veih has something of a history. One does not often get a Turkish princess in London."

"Yes, she has a history. She is only remotely connected with the present reigning dynasty in Turkey, and I dare say her princess-ship has been made the most of. All the same, however, she has had an altogether exceptional career for an Oriental lady. She was left an orphan at an early age, and was consigned to the guardianship of the elder Cassimi by her relatives. The Cassimis, both father and son, seem to be very advanced and European in their ideas, and by them she was taken to Cairo for her education. About a year ago they 'brought her out' in London, where she made the acquaintance of Major Druce. The young man, by-the-way, appears to be rather hot-headed in his lovemaking, for within six weeks of his introduction to her their engagement was announced. No doubt it had Mrs. Druce's fullest approval, for knowing her son's extravagant habits and his numerous debts, it must have patent to her that a rich wife was a necessity to him. The marriage, I believe, was to have taken place this season; but taking into consideration the young man's ill-advised attentions to the little Swiss girl, and the fervour he is throwing into the search for her, I should say it was exceedingly doubtful whether—"

"Major Druce, sir, wishes to see you," said a clerk at that moment, opening the door leading from the outer office.

"Very good; show him in," said Mr. Dyer. Then he turned to Loveday. "Of course I have spoken to him about you, and he is very anxious to take you to his mother's reception this afternoon, so that you may have a look round and—"

He broke off, having to rise and greet Major Druce, who at that moment entered the room.

He was a tall, handsome young fellow of about seven or eight and twenty, "well turned out" from head to foot, moustache waxed, orchid in button-hole, light kid gloves, and patent leather boots. There was assuredly nothing in his appearance to substantiate his statement to Mr. Dyer that he "hadn't slept a wink all night, that in fact another twenty-four hours of this terrible suspense would send him into his grave."

Mr. Dyer introduced Miss Brooke, and she expressed her sympathy with him on the painful matter that was filling his thoughts.

"It is very good of you, I'm sure," he replied, in a slow, soft drawl, not unpleasant to listen to. "My mother receives this afternoon from half past four to half past six, and I shall be very glad if you will allow me to introduce you to the inside of our house, and to the very ill-looking set that we have somehow managed to gather about us."

"The ill-looking set?"

"Yes; Jews, Turks, heretics and infidels—all there. And they're on the increase too, that's the worst of it. Every week a fresh importation from Cairo."

"Ah, Mrs. Druce is a large-hearted, benevolent woman," interposed Mr. Dyer; "all nationalities gather within her walls."

"Was your mother a large-hearted, benevolent woman?" said the young man, turning upon him. "No! well then, thank Providence that she wasn't; and admit that you know nothing at all on the matter. Miss Brooke," he continued, turning to Loveday, "I've brought round my hansom for you; it's nearly half past four now, and it's a good twenty minutes' drive from here to Portland Place. If you're ready, I'm at your service."

Major Druce's hansom was, like himself, in all respects "well turned out," and the indiarubber tires round its wheels allowed an easy flow of conversation to be kept up during the twenty minutes' drive from Lynch Court to Portland Place.

The Major led off the talk in frank and easy fashion.

"My mother," he said, "prides her self on being cosmopolitan in her tastes, and just now we are very cosmopolitan indeed. Even our servants represent divers nationalities: the butler is French, the two footmen Italians, the maids, I believe, are some of them German, some Irish; and I've no doubt if you penetrated to the kitchen-quarters, you'd find the staff there composed in part of South Sea Islanders. The other quarters of the globe you will find fully represented in the drawing room."

Loveday had a direct question to ask.

"Are you certain that Mdlle. Cunier had no friends in England?" she said.

"Positive. She hadn't a friend in the world outside my mother's four walls, poor child! She told me more than once that she was 'seule sur la terre.'" He broke off for a moment, as if overcome by a sad memory, then added: "But I'll put a bullet into him, take my word for it, if she isn't found within another twenty-four hours. Personally I should prefer settling the brute in that fashion to handing him over to the police."

His face flushed a deep red, there came a sudden flash to his eye, but for all that, his voice was as soft and slow and unemotional, as though he were talking of nothing more serious than bringing down a partridge.

There fell a brief pause; then Loveday asked another question.

"Is Mademoiselle Catholic or Protestant, can you tell me?"

The Major thought for a moment, then replied:

" 'Pon my word, I don't know. She used sometimes to attend a little church in South Savile Street—I've walked with her occasionally to the church door—but I couldn't for the life of me say whether it was a Catholic, Protestant, or Pagan place of worship. But—but you don't think those confounded priests have—"

"Here, we are in Portland Place," interrupted Loveday. "Mrs. Druce's rooms are already full, to judge from that long line of carriages!"

"Miss Brooke," said the Major suddenly, bethinking himself of his responsibilities, "how am I to introduce you? what role will you take up this afternoon? Pose as faddist of some sort, if you want to win my mother's heart. What do you say to having started a grand scheme for supplying Hottentots and Kaffirs with eyeglasses? My mother would swear eternal friendship with you at once."

"Don't introduce me at all that first," answered Loveday. "Get me into some quiet corner, where I can see without being seen. Later on in the afternoon, when I have had time to look round a little, I'll tell you whether it will be necessary to introduce me or not."

"It will be a mob this afternoon, and no mistake," said Major Druce, as, side by side, they entered the house. "Do you hear that fizzing and clucking just behind us? That's Arabic; you'll get it in whiffs between gusts of French and German all the afternoon. The Egyptian contingent seems to be in full force today. I don't see any Choctaw Indians, but no doubt they'll send their representatives later on. Come in at this side door, and we'll work our way round to that big palm. My mother is sure to be at the principal doorway."

The drawing rooms were packed from end to end, and Major Druce's progress, as he headed Loveday through the crowd, was impeded by handshaking and the interchange of civilities with his mother's guests.

Eventually the big palm standing in a Chinese cistern was reached, and there, half screened from view by its graceful branches, he placed a chair for Miss Brooke.

From this quiet nook, as now and again the crowd parted, Loveday could command a fair view of both drawing rooms.

"Don't attract attention to me by standing at my elbow," she whispered to the Major.

He answered her whisper with another.

"There's the Beast—Iago, I mean," he said; "do you see him? He's standing talking to that fair, handsome woman in pale green, with a picture hat. She's Lady Gwynne. And there's my mother, and there's Dolly—the Princess I mean—alone on the sofa. Ah! you can't see her now for the crowd. Yes, I'll go, but if you want me, just nod to me and I shall understand."

It was easy to see what had brought such a fashionable crowd to Mrs. Druce's rooms that afternoon. Every caller, as soon as she had shaken hands with the hostess, passed on to the Princess's sofa, and there waited patiently till opportunity presented itself for an introduction to her Eastern Highness.

Loveday found it impossible to get more than the merest glimpse of her, and so transferred her attention to Mr. Hafiz Cassimi, who had been referred to in such unceremonious language by Major Druce.

He was a swarthy, well-featured man, with bold, black eyes, and lips that had the habit of parting now and again, not to smile, but as if for no other purpose than to show a double row of gleaming white teeth. The European dress he wore seemed to accord ill with the man; and Loveday could fancy that those black eyes and that double row of white teeth would have shown to better advantage beneath a turban or a fez cap.

From Cassimi, her eye wandered to Mrs. Druce—a tall, stout woman, dressed in black velvet, and with hair mounted high on her head, that had the appearance of being either bleached or powdered. She gave Loveday the impression of being that essential modern product of modern society—the woman who combines in one person that hard-working philanthropist with the hard-working woman of fashion. As arrivals began to slacken, she left her post near the door and began to make the round of the room. From snatches of talk that came to her where she sat, Loveday could gather that with one hand, as it were, this energetic lady was organizing a grand charity concert, and with the other pushing the interests of a big ball that was shortly to be given by the officers of her son's regiment.

It was a hot June day. In spite of closed blinds and open windows, the rooms were stifling to a degree. The butler, a small, dark, slight Frenchman, made his way through the throng to a window at Loveday's right hand, to see if a little more air could be admitted.

Major Druce followed on his heels to Loveday's side.

"Will you come into the next room and have some tea?" he asked; "I'm sure you must feel nearly suffocated here." He broke off, then added in a lower tone; "I hope you have kept your eyes on the Beast. Did you ever in your life see a more repulsive-looking animal?"

Loveday took his questions in their order.

"No tea, thank you," she said, "but I shall be glad if you will tell your butler to bring me a glass of water—there he is, at your elbow. Yes, off and on I have been studying Mr. Cassimi, and I must admit I do not like his smileless smile."

The butler brought the water. The Major, much to his annoyance, was seized upon simultaneously by two ladies, one eager to know if any tiding had been received of Mdlle. Cunier, the other anxious to learn if a distinguished president to the Harem Mission had been decided upon.

Soon after six the rooms began to thin somewhat, and presentations to the Princess ceasing, Loveday was able to get a full view of her.

She presented a striking picture, seated, half-reclining, on a sofa, with two white-robed, dark-skinned Egyptian maidens standing behind it. A more unfortunate sobriquet than "Dolly" could scarcely have been found by the Major for this Oriental beauty, with her olive complexion, her flashing eyes and extravagant richness of attire.

"'Queen of Sheba' would be fare more appropriate," thought Loveday. "She turns the commonplace sofa into a throne, and, I should say, makes every one of those ladies feel as if she ought to have donned court dress and plumes for the occasion."

It was difficult for her, from where she sat, to follow the details of the Princess's dress. She could only see that a quantity of soft orange-tinted silk was wound about the upper part of her arms and fell from her shoulders like drooping wings, and that here and there jewels flashed out from its folds. Her thick black hair was loosely knotted, and kept in its place by jewelled pins and a bandeau of pearls; and similar bandeaus adorned her slender throat and wrists.

"Are you lost in admiration?" said the Major, once more at her elbow, in a slightly sarcastic tone. "That sort of thing is very taking and effective at first, but after a time—"

He did not finish his sentence, shrugged his shoulders and walked away. Half-past six chimed from a small clock on a bracket. Carriage after carriage was rolling away from the door now, and progress on the stairs was rendered difficult by a descending crowd.

A quarter to seven struck, the last handshaking had been gone through, and Mrs. Druce, looking hot and tired, had sunk into a chair at the Princess's right hand, bending slightly forward to render conversations with her easy.

On the Princess's left hand, Lady Gwynne had taken a chair, and sat in converse with Hafiz Cassimi, who stood beside her.

Evidently these four were on very easy and intimate terms with each other. Lady Gwynne had tossed her big picture hat on a chair at her left hand, and was fanning herself with a palm-leaf. Mrs. Druce, beckoning to the butler, desired him to bring them some claret-cup from the refreshment room.

No one seemed to observe Loveday seated still in her nook beside the big palm.

She signalled to the Major, who stood looking discontentedly from one of the windows.

"That is a most interesting group," she said; "now, if you like, you may introduce me to your mother."

"Oh, with pleasure—under what name?" he asked.

"Under my own," she answered, "and please be very distinct in pronouncing it, raise your voice slightly so that everyone of those persons may hear it. And then, please add my profession, and say I am here at your request to investigate the circumstances connected with Mdlle. Cunier's disappearance."

Major Druce looked astounded.

"But—but," he stammered, "have you seen anything—found out anything? If not, don't you think it will be better to preserve your incognita a little longer."

"Don't stop to ask questions," said Loveday sharply; "now, this very minute, do what I ask you, or the opportunity will be gone."

The Major without further demur, escorted Loveday across the room. The conversation between the four intimate friends had now become general and animated, and he had to wait for a minute or so before he could get an opportunity to speak to his mother.

During that minute Loveday stood a little in his rear, with Lady Gwynne and Cassimi at her right hand.

"I want to introduce this lady to you," said the Major, when a pause in the talk gave him his opportunity. "This is Miss Loveday Brooke, a lady detective, and she is here at my request to investigate the circumstances connected with the disappearance of Mdlle. Cunier."

He said the words slowly and distinctly.

"There!" he said to himself complacently, as he ended; "if I had been reading the lessons in church, I couldn't have been more emphatic."

A blank silence for a moment fell upon the group, and even the butler, just then entering with the claret-cup, came to a standstill at the door.

Then, simultaneously, a glance flashed from Mrs. Druce to Lady Gwynne, from Lady Gwynne to Mrs. Druce, and then, also simultaneously, the eyes of both ladies rested, though only for an instant, on the big picture hat lying on the chair.

Lady Gwynne started to her feet and seized her hat, adjusting it without so much as a glance at a mirror.

"I must go at once; this very minute," she said. "I promised Charlie I would be back soon after six, and now it is past seven. Mr. Cassimi, will you take me down to my carriage?" And with the most hurried of leave-takings to the Princess and her hostess, the lady swept out of the room, followed by Mr. Cassimi.

The butler still standing at the door, drew back to allow the lady to pass, and then, claret-cup and all, followed her out of the room.

Mrs. Druce drew a long breath and bowed formally to Loveday.

"I was a little taken by surprise," she began—

But here the Princess rose suddenly from the sofa.

"Moi, je suis fatiguée," she said in excellent French to Mrs. Druce, and she too swept out of the room, throwing, as she passed, what seemed to Loveday a slightly scornful glance towards the Major.

Her two attendants, one carrying her fan, and the other her reclining cushions, followed.

Mrs. Druce again turned to Loveday.

"Yes, I confess I was taken a little by surprise," she said, her manner thawing slightly. "I am not accustomed to the presence of detectives in my house; but now tell me what do you propose doing; how do you mean to begin your investigations—by going over the house and looking in all the corners, or by cross-questioning the servants? Forgive my asking, but really I am quite at a loss; I haven't the remotest idea how such investigations are generally conducted."

"I do not propose to do much in the way of investigation tonight," answered Loveday as formally as she had been addressed, "for I have very important business to transact before eight o'clock this evening. I shall ask you to allow me to see Mdlle. Cunier's room—ten minutes there will be sufficient—after that, I do not think I need further trouble you."

"Certainly; by all means," answered Mrs. Druce; "you'll find the room exactly as Lucie left it, nothing has been disturbed."

She turned to the butler, who had by this time returned and stood presenting the claret-cup, and, in French, desired him to summon her maid, and tell her to show Miss Brooke to Mdlle. Cunier's room.

The ten minutes that Loveday had said would suffice for her survey of this room extended themselves to fifteen, but the extra five minutes assuredly were not expended by her in the investigation of drawers and boxes. The maid, a pleasant, well-spoken young woman, jingled her keys, and opened every lock, and seemed not at all disinclined to enter into the light gossip that Loveday contrived to set going.

She answered freely a variety of questions that Loveday put to her respecting Mademoiselle and her general habits, and from Mademoiselle, the talk drifted to other members of Mrs. Druce's household.

If Loveday had, as she had stated, important business to transact that evening, she certainly set about it in a strange fashion.

After she quitted Mademoiselle's room, she went straight out of the house, without leaving a message of any sort for either Mrs. or Major Druce. She walked the length of Portland Place in leisurely fashion, and then, having first ascertained that her movements were not being watched, she called a hansom, and desired the man to drive her to Madame Céline's, a fashionable milliner's in Old Bond Street.

At Madame Céline's she spent close upon half-an-hour giving many and minute directions for the making of a hat, which assuredly, when finished, would compare with nothing in the way of millinery that she had ever before put upon her head.

From Madame Céline's the hansom conveyed her to an undertaker's shop, at the corner of South Savile Street, and here she spent a brief ten minutes in conversation with the undertaker himself in his little back parlour.

From the undertaker's she drove home to her rooms in Gower Street, and then, before she divested herself of hat and coat, she wrote a brief note to Major Druce, requesting him to meet her on the following morning at Eglacé's, the confectioner's, in South Savile Street, at nine o'clock punctually.

This note she committed to the charge of the cab-driver, desiring him to deliver it at Portland Place on his way back to his stand.

"They've queer ways of doing things—these people!" said the Major, as he opened and read the note. "Suppose I must keep the appointment though, confound it. I can't see that she can possibly have found out anything by just sitting still in a corner for a couple of hours! And I'm confident she didn't give that beast Cassimi one quarter the attention she bestowed on other people."

In spite of his grumbling, however, the Major kept his appointment, and nine o'clock the next morning saw him shaking hands with Miss Brooke on Eglacé's doorstep.

"Dismiss your hansom," she said to him. "I only want you to come a few doors down the street, to the Swiss Protestant church, to which you have sometimes escorted Mdlle. Cunier."

At the church door Loveday paused a moment.

"Before we enter," she said, "I want you to promise that whatever you may see going on there—however greatly you may be surprised—you will make no disturbance, not so much as open your lips till we come out."

The Major, not a little bewildered, gave the required promise; and, side by side, the two entered the church.

It was little more than a big room; at the farther end, in the middle of the nave, stood the pulpit, and immediately behind this was a low platform, enclosed by a brass rail.

Behind this brass rail, in a black Geneva gown, stood the pastor of the church, and before him, on cushions, kneeled two persons, a man and a woman.

These two persons and an old man, the verger, formed the whole of the congregation. The position of the church, amid shops and narrow backyards, had necessitated the filling in of every one of its windows with stained glass; it was, consequently, so dim that, coming in from the outside glare of sunlight, the Major found it difficult to make out what was going on at the farther end.

The verger came forward and offered to show them to a seat. Loveday shook her head—they would be leaving in a minute, she said, and would prefer standing where they were.

The Major begin to take in the situation.

"Why, they're being married!" he said in a loud whisper. "What on earth have you brought me in here for?"

Loveday laid her finger on her lips and frowned severely at him.

The marriage service came to an end, the pastor extended his black-gowned arms like the wings of a bat and pronounced the benediction; the man and woman rose from their knees and proceeded to follow him into the vestry.

The woman was neatly dressed in a long dove-coloured travelling cloak. She wore a large hat, from which fell a white gossamer veil that completely hid her face from view. The man was small, dark and slight, and as he passed on to the vestry beside his bride, the Major at once identified him as his mother's butler.

"Why, that's Lebrun!" he said in a still louder whisper than before. "Why, in the name of all that's wonderful, have you brought me here to see that fellow married?"

"You'd better come outside if you can't keep quiet," said Loveday severely, and leading the way out of the church as she spoke.

Outside, South Savile Street was busy with early morning traffic.

"Let us go back to Eglacé's," said Loveday, "and have some coffee. I will explain to you there all you are wishing to know."

But before the coffee could be brought to them, the Major had asked at least a dozen questions.

Loveday put them all on one side.

"All in good time," she said. "You are leaving out the most important question of all. Have you no curiosity to know who was the bride that Lebrun has chosen?"

"I don't suppose it concerns me in the slightest degree," he answered indifferently; "but since you wish me to ask the question—Who was she?"

"Lucie Cunier, lately your mother's amanuensis."

"The—!" cried the Major, jumping to his feet and uttering an exclamation that must be indicated by a blank.

"Take it calmly," said Loveday; "don't rave. Sit down and I'll tell you all about it. No, it is not the doing of your friend Cassimi, so you need not threaten to put a bullet into him; the girl has married Lebrun of her own free will—no one has forced her into it."

"Lucie has married Lebrun of her own free will!" he echoed, growing very white and taking the chair which faced Loveday at the little table.

"Will you have sugar?" asked Loveday, stirring the coffee, which the waiter at the moment brought.

"Yes, I repeat," she presently resumed, "Lucie has married Lebrun of her own free will, although I conjecture she might not perhaps have been quite so willing to crown his happiness if the Princess Dullah-Veih had not made it greatly to her interest to do so."

"Dolly made it to her interest to do so?" again echoed the Major.

"Do not interrupt me with exclamations; let me tell the story my own fashion, and then you may ask as many questions as you please. Now, to begin at the beginning, Lucie became engaged to Lebrun within a month of her coming to your mother's house, but she carefully kept the secret from everyone, even from the servants, until about a month ago, when she mentioned the fact in confidence to Mrs. Druce in order to defend herself from the charge of having sought to attract your attention. There was nothing surprising in this engagement; they were both lonely and in a foreign land, spoke the same language, and no doubt had many things in common; and although chance has lifted Lucie somewhat out of her station, she really belongs to the same class in life as Lebrun. Their love-making appears to have run along smoothly enough until you came home on leave, and the girls' pretty face attracted your attention. Your evident admiration for her disturbed the equanimity of the Princess, who saw your devotion to herself waning; of Lebrun, who fancied Lucie's manner to him had changed; of your mother, who was anxious that you should make a suitable marriage. Also additional complications arose from the fact that your attentions to the little Swiss girl had drawn Mr. Cassimi's notice to her numerous attractions, and there was the danger of you two young men posing as rivals. At this juncture Lady Gwynne, as an intimate friend, and one who had herself suffered a twinge of heartache on Mademoiselle's account, was taken into your mother's confidence, and the three ladies in council decided that Lucie, in some fashion, must be got out of the way before you and Mr. Cassimi came to an open breach, or you had spoilt your matrimonial prospects."

Here the Major made a slightly impatient movement.

Loveday went on: "It was the Princess who solved the question how this was to be done. Fair Rosamonds are no longer put out of the way by 'a cup of cold poison'—golden guineas do the thing far more easily and innocently. The Princess expressed her willingness to bestow a thousand pounds on Lucie on the day that she married Lebrun, and to set her up afterwards as a fashionable milliner in Paris. After this munificent offer, everything else became mere matter of detail. The main thing was to get the damsel out of the way without your being able to trace her—perhaps work on her feelings, and induce her, at the last moment, to throw over Lebrun. Your absence from home, on a three days' visit, gave them the wished-for opportunity. Lady Gwynne took her milliner into her confidence. Madame Céline consented to receive Lucie into her house, seclude her in a room on the upper floor, and at the same time give her an insight into the profession of a fashionable milliner. The rest I think you know. Lucie quietly walks out of the house one afternoon, taking no luggage, calling no cab, and thereby cutting off one very obvious means of being traced. Madame Céline receives and hides her—not a difficult feat to accomplishment in London, more especially if the one to be hidden is a foreign amanuensis, who is seldom seen out of doors, and who leaves no photograph behind her."

"I suppose it was Lebrun who had the confounded cheek to go to my drawer and appropriate that photograph. I wish it had been Cassimi—I could have kicked him, but—but it makes one feel rather small to have posed as rival to one's mother's butler."

"I think you may congratulate yourself that Lebrun did nothing worse than go to your drawer and appropriate that photograph. I never saw a man bestow a more deadly look of hatred than he threw at you yesterday afternoon in your mother's drawing room; it was that look of hatred that first drew my attention to the man and set me on the track that has ended in the Swiss Protestant church this morning."

"Ah! Let me hear about that—let me have the links in the chain, one by one, as you came upon them," said the Major.

He was still pale—almost as the marble table at which they sat, but his voice had gone back to its normal slow, soft drawl.

"With pleasure. The look that Lebrun threw at you, as he crossed the room to open the window, was link number one. As I saw that look, I said to myself there is someone in that corner whom that man hates with a deadly hatred. Then you came forward to speak to me, and I saw that it was you that the man was ready to murder, if opportunity offered. After this, I scrutinised him closely—not a detail of his features or his dress escaped me, and I noticed, among other things, that on the fourth finger of his left hand, half hidden by a more pretentious ring, was an old fashioned curious looking silver one. That silver ring was link number two in the chain."

"Ah, I suppose you asked for that glass of water on purpose to get a closer view of the ring?"

"I did, I found it was a Genevese ring of ancient make, the like of which I had not seen since I was a child and played with one, that my old Swiss bonne used to wear. Now I must tell you a little bit of Genevese history before I can make you understand how important a link that silver ring was to me. Echallets, the town in which Lucie was born, and her father had kept a watchmaker's shop, has long been famous for its jewellery and watchmaking. The two trades, however, were not combined in one until about a hundred years ago, when the corporation of the town passed a law decreeing that they should unite in one guild for their common good. To celebrate this amalgamation of interests, the jewellers fabricated a certain number of silver rings, consisting of a plain band of silver, on which two hands, in relief, clasped each other. These rings were distributed among the members of the guild, and as time has gone on they have become scarce and valuable as relics of the past. In certain families, they have been handed down as heirlooms, and have frequently done duty as betrothal rings—the clasped hands no doubt suggesting their suitability for this purpose. Now, when I saw such a ring on Lebrun's finger, I naturally guessed from whom he had received it, and at once classed his interests with those of your mother and the Princess, and looked upon him as their possible coadjutor."

"What made you throw the brute Cassimi altogether out of your reckoning?"

"I did not do so at this stage of events; only, so to speak, marked him as 'doubtful' and kept my eye on him. I determined to try an experiment that I have never before attempted in my work. You know what that experiment was. I saw five persons, Mrs. Druce, the Princess, Lady Gwynne, Mr. Cassimi and Lebrun all in the room within a few yards of each other, and I asked you to take them by surprise and announce my name and profession, so that every one of those five persons could hear you."

"You did. I could not, for the life of me, make out what was your motive for so doing."

"My motive for so doing was simply, as it were, to raise the sudden cry, 'The enemy is upon you,' and to set every one of those five persons guarding their weak point—that is, if they had one. I'll draw your attention to what followed. Mr. Cassimi remained nonchalant and impassive; your mother and Lady Gwynne exchanged glances, and then both simultaneously threw a nervous look at Lady Gwynne's hat lying on the chair. Now as I had stood waiting to be introduced to Mrs. Druce, I had casually read the name of Madame Céline on the lining of the hat and I at once concluded that Madame Céline must be a very weak point indeed; a conclusion that was confirmed when Lady Gwynne hurriedly seized her hat and as hurriedly departed. Then the Princess scarcely less abruptly rose and left the room, and Lebrun, on the point of entering, quitted it also. When he returned five minutes later, with the claret-cup, he had removed the ring from his finger, so I had now little doubt where his weak point lay."

"It's wonderful; it's like a fairy tale," drawled the Major. "Pray, go on."

"After this," continued Loveday, "my work became very simple. I did not care two straws for seeing Mademoiselle's room, but I cared very much to have a talk with Mrs. Druce's maid. From her I elicited the important fact that Lebrun was leaving very unexpectedly on the following day, and that his boxes were packed and labelled for Paris. After I left your house, I drove to Madame Céline's, and there, as a sort of entrance fee, ordered an elaborate hat. I praised freely the hats they had on view, and while giving minute directions as to the one I required, I extracted the information that Madame Céline had recently taken on a new milliner who had very great artistic skill. Upon this, I asked permission to see this new milliner and give her special instructions concerning my hat. My request was referred to Madame Céline, who appeared much ruffled by it, and informed me that it would be quite useless for me to see this new milliner; she could execute no more orders, as she was leaving the next day for Paris, where she intended opening an establishment on her own account.

"Now you see the point at which I had arrived. There was Lebrun and there was this new milliner each leaving for Paris on the same day; it was not unreasonable to suppose that they might start in company, and that before so doing, a little ceremony might be gone through in the Swiss Protestant church that Mademoiselle occasionally attended. This conjecture sent me to the undertaker in South Savile Street, who combines with his undertaking the office of verger to the little church. From him I learned that a marriage was to take place at the church at a quarter to nine the next morning and that the names of contracting parties were Pierre Lebrun and Lucie Cuénin."

"Cuénin!"

"Yes, that is the girl's real name; it seems Lady Gwynne re-christened her Cunier, because she said the English pronunciation of Cuénin grated on her ear—people would insist upon adding a *g* after the *n*. She introduced her to Mrs. Druce under the name of Cunier, forgetting, perhaps, the girl's real name, or else thinking it a matter of no importance. This fact, no doubt, considerably lessened Lebrun's fear of detection in procuring his licence and transmitting it to the Swiss pastor. Perhaps you are a little surprised at my knowledge of the facts I related to you at the beginning of our conversation. I got at them through Lebrun this morning. At half-past eight I went down to the church and found him there, waiting for his bride. He grew terribly excited at seeing me, and thought I was going to bring you down on him and upset his wedding arrangements at the last moment. I assured him to the contrary, and his version of the facts I have handed on to you. Should, however, any details of the story seem to you to be lacking, I have no doubt that Mrs. Druce or the Princess will supply them, now that all necessity for secrecy has come to an end."

The Major drew on his gloves; his colour had come back to him; he had resumed his easy suavity of manner.

"I don't think," he said slowly, "I'll trouble my mother or the Princess; and I shall be glad, if you have the opportunity, if you will make people understand that I only moved in the matter at all out of—of mere kindness to a young and friendless foreigner."

THE MONKEY AND THE BOX

EDGAR WALLACE

When Christopher Angle went to school he was very naturally called "Angel" by his fellows. When, in after life, he established a reputation for tact, geniality and a remarkable equability of temper, he became "Angel, Esquire," and as Angel, Esquire, he went through the greater portion of his adventurous life, so that on the coast and in the islands and in the wild lands that lie beyond the Ituri forest, where Mr. C Angle is unknown, the remembrance of Angel, Esquire, is kept perennially green.

In what department of the Government he was before he took up a permanent suite of offices at New Scotland Yard it is difficult to say.

All that is known is that when the "scientific expedition" of Dr. Kauffhaus penetrated to the head waters of the Kasa-kasa River, Angel, Esquire, was in the neighbourhood shooting elephants. A native messenger *en route* to the nearest post, carrying a newly-ratified treaty, countersigned by the native chief, can vouch for Angel's presence, because Angel's men fell upon him and beat him, and Angel took the newly-sealed letter and calmly tore it up.

When, too, yet another "scientific expedition" were engaged in making elaborate soundings in a neutral port in the Pacific, it was his steam launch that accidentally upset the boat of the men of science, and many invaluable instruments and drawings were irretrievably lost in the deeps of the rocky inlet.

Following, however, upon some outrageous international incident, no less than the—but perhaps it would be wiser not to say—Angel was transferred bodily to Scotland Yard, undisguisedly a detective, and was placed in charge of the Colonial Department, which deals with all matters in those countries—British or otherwise—where the temperature rises above 103° Fahrenheit.

His record in this department was one of unabated success, and the inter-departmental criticism which was aroused by its creation, and his appointment, have long since been silenced by the remarkable success that attended, amongst others, his investigations into the strange disappearance of the Corringham Mine, the discovery of the Third Slave, and his brilliant and memorable work in connection with the Croupier's Safe.

To Angel, Esquire, in the early spring, came an official of the Criminal Investigation Department.

"Do you know Congoland at all, Angel?" he asked.

"Little bit of it," said Angel modestly.

"Well, here's a letter that the Chief wants you to deal with—the writer is the daughter of an old friend, and he would like you to give the matter your personal attention."

Angel's insulting remark about corruption in the public service need not be placed on record.

The letter was written on notepaper of unusual thinness.

"A lady who has had or is having correspondence with somebody in a part of the world where the postage rate is high," he said to himself, and the first words of the letter confirmed this view.

> My husband, who was just returned from the Congo, where he has been on behalf of a Belgian firm to report on alluvial gold discoveries, has become strange in his manner, and there are, moreover, such curious circumstances in connection with his conduct, that I am taking this course, knowing that as a friend of my dear father's you will not place any unkind construction upon it, and that you will help me to get at the bottom of this mystery.

The letter was evidently hurriedly written. There were words crossed out and written in.

"Humph," said Angel; "rather a miserable little domestic drama—I trust I shall not be called in to investigate every family jar that occurs in the homes of the Chief's friends."

But he wrote a polite little note to the lady on his "unofficial" paper, asking for an appointment and telling her that he had been asked to make the necessary inquiries.

The next morning he received a wire inviting him to go to Dulwich to the address that had appeared at the head of the note. Accordingly, he started that afternoon, with the irritating sense that his time was being wasted.

Nine hundred and three Lordship Lane was a substantial looking house, standing back from the road, and a trim maid opened the door to him and ushered him into the drawing room.

He was waiting impatiently for the lady, when the door was flung open, and a man staggered in. He had an opened letter in his hand, and there was a look on his face that shocked Angel. It was the face of a soul in torment—drawn, haggard, and white.

"My God! My God!" he muttered; then he saw Angel, and straightened himself for a moment. It was only for a moment, for he started forward and seized the detective by the arm eagerly.

"You—you," he gasped; "are you from Liverpool?—have they sent you down to say it was a mistake?"

There was a rustle of a dress, and a girl came into the room. She was little more than a girl, but the traces of suffering that Angel saw had aged her.

She came quickly to the side of the man and laid her hand on his arm.

"What is it—oh, what is it, Jack?" she entreated.

The man stepped back, shaking his head.

"I'm sorry—ver' sorry," he said dully, and Angel noticed that he clipped his words. "I thought—I mistook this gentleman for someone else."

Angel explained his identity to the girl in a swift glance.

"This—this is a friend of mine," she faltered, "a friend of my father's," she went on hesitatingly, "who has called to see me."

"Sorry—sorry," he said stupidly. He stumbled to the door and went out, leaving it open. They heard him blundering up the stairs, and after a while a door slammed, and there came a faint "click" as he locked it.

"Oh, *can* you help me?" cried the girl in distress. "I am beside myself with anxiety—"

"Please sit down, Mrs. Farrow," said Angel hastily, but kindly. A woman on the verge of tears always alarmed him. Already he felt an unusual interest in the case. "Just tell me from the beginning."

"My husband is a metallurgist, and a year ago he was commissioned by a Belgian company interested in gold mining to go to the Congo and report on some property there."

"Had he ever been there before?"

"No; he had never been to Africa before. It was against my wish that he went at all, but the fee was so temptingly high and the opportunities so great that I yielded to his persuasion, and allowed him to go."

"How did he leave you?"

"As he had always been: bright, optimistic, and full of good spirits. We were very happily married, Mr. Angel—" she stopped, and her lips quivered.

"Yes, yes," said the alarmed detective; "please go on."

"He wrote by every mail, and even sent natives in their canoes hundreds of miles to connect with the mail steamers, and his letters were bright and full of particulars about the country and the people. Then, quite suddenly, they changed. From being the cheery, long letters they had been, they became almost notes, telling me just the bare facts of his movements. They worried me a little, because I thought it meant that he was ill, had fever, and did not want me to know."

"And had he?"

"No. A man who was with him said he was never once down with fever. Well, I cabled to him, but cabling to the Congo is a heartbreaking business, and there was fourteen days' delay on the wire."

"I know," said Angel sympathetically, "the land wire down to Brazzaville."

"Then, before my cable could reach him, I received a brief telegram from him saying he was coming home."

"Yes?"

"There was a weary month of waiting, and then he arrived. I went to Southampton to meet him."

"To Southampton, not to Liverpool?"

"To Southampton. He met me on the deck, and I shall never forget the look of agony in his eyes when he saw me. It struck me dumb. 'What is the matter, Jack?' I asked. 'Nothing,' he said, in, oh, such a listless, hopeless way. I could get nothing from him. Almost as soon as he got home he went to his room and locked the door."

"When was this?"

"A month ago."

"And what has happened since?"

"Nothing; except that he has got steadily more and more depressed, and—and—"

"Yes?" asked Angel.

"He gets letters—letters that he goes to the door to meet. Sometimes they make him worse, sometimes he gets almost cheerful after they arrive; but he had his worst bout after the arrival of the box."

"What box?"

"It came whilst I was dressing for dinner one night. All that afternoon he had been unusually restless, running down from his room at every ring of the bell. I caught a glance of it through his half-opened door."

"Do you not enter his room occasionally?"

She shook her head.

"Nobody has been into his room since his return—he will not allow the servants in, and sweeps and tidies it himself."

"Well, and the box?"

"It was about eighteen inches high, and twelve inches square. It was of polished yellow wood."

"Did it remind you of anything?"

"Of an electric battery," she said slowly. "One of those big portable things that you can buy at an electrician's."

Angel thought deeply.

"And the letters—have you seen them?" he asked.

"Only once, when the postman overlooked a letter, and came back with it. I saw it for a moment only, because my husband came down immediately and took it from me."

"And the postmark?"

"It looked like Liverpool," she said.

He questioned her again on one or two aspects that interested him.

"I must see into your husband's room," he said decisively.

She shook her head.

"I am afraid it will be impossible," she said.

"We shall see," said Angel cheerfully.

Then an unearthly chattering and screeching met their ears, and the girl turned pale.

"Oh, I had forgotten the most unpleasant thing—the monkey!" she said, and beckoned him from the room. He passed through the house to the garden at the back. Well sheltered from the road was a big iron cage, wherein sat a tiny Congo monkey, shivering in the chill spring air, and drawing about his hairy shoulders the torn half of a blanket.

"My husband brought one home with him," she said, "but it died. This is the fifth monkey we have had in a month, and he, poor beastie, does not look as if he were long for life."

The little animal fixed his bright eyes on Angel, and chattered dismally.

"They get ill, and my husband shoots them," the girl went on "I wanted him to let a veterinary surgeon see the last one, but he would not."

"Curious," said Angel musing; and after making arrangements to call the next morning, he went back to his office in a puzzled frame of mind.

He duly reported to his Chief the substance of his interview.

"It isn't drink, and it isn't drugs," he said. "To me it looks like sheer panic. If that man is not in mortal fear of somebody or something, I am very much mistaken.

The girl had given him some of the earlier letters she had received from Africa, and after dinner that night Angel sat down in his little flat in Jermyn Street to read them.

In the first letter (it was dated Boma) occurred a passage that gave him pause. After telling how he had gone ashore at Flagstaff, and had made a little excursion up one of the rivers, the letter went on to say:—

> ...Apparently, I have quite unwillingly given deep offence to one of the secret societies—if you can imagine a native secret society—by buying from a native a most interesting Ju-ju, or idol. The native, poor beggar, was found dead on the beach this morning; and although the official view is that he was bitten by a poisonous snake, I feel that his death had something to do with the selling of the idol—which, by the way, resembles nothing so much as a decrepit monkey...

In his search through the letters he could find no other references to the incident, except in one of the last of the longer epistles, where he found:—

> . . . the canoe overturned, and we were struggling in the water. To my intense annoyance, amongst other personal effects lost, was the Coast Ju-ju I wrote to you about. A missionary who lives close at hand said the current not being strong about here, the idol is recoverable, and has promised to send a boy down first, and if he finds it to send it on to me. I have given him our address at home in case it turns up. . . .

"In case it turns up!" repeated Angel. "I wonder—"

He knew of these extraordinary societies. He knew, too, how strong a hold they had in the country that lay behind Flagstaff. These dreadful organisations were not to be lightly dismissed. Their power was indisputable.

"The questions is, how far are they responsible for the present trouble," he said, discussing the affair with his Chief the next morning, "how far the arm of the offended Ju-ju can reach. If we were on the Coast, I should not be surprised to find our young friend dead in his bed any morning. But we are in England—and in Dulwich to boot!"

"The yellow box may explain everything," said his Chief thoughtfully.

"And I mean to see it today," said Angel determinedly.

He did not see it that day, for on his return to his office he found a telegram awaiting him from Mrs. Farrow:

> Please come at once. My husband disappeared last night, and has not returned; he has taken with him the box and the monkey.

He was ringing at the door of the house within an hour after receiving the telegram. Her eyes were red with weeping, and it was a little time before she could speak. Then, brokenly, she told the story of her husband's disappearance. It was after the household had retired for the night, she thought she heard a vehicle draw up to the door. She was half asleep, but the sound of voices roused her, and she got out of bed and looked through the venetian blinds. Her room faced the road, and she could see a carriage drawn up opposite the gate. A man was walking beside her husband, who carried a box, which she recognised as the yellow box, and in the strange man's arms she could discern, by the light of the street lamp, a quivering bundle, which proved to be the monkey.

Before she could move or raise the window, her husband entered the carriage taking with him the monkey, and the other man jumped up by the side of the driver as the vehicle drove off; and, as he did, she saw his face. It was that of a negro.

Angel suppressed the exclamation that sprang to his lips as he heard this. It was evident that she had not attached any importance to the story of the Ju-ju, and he did not wish to alarm her.

"Did he leave a message?"

She handed him a sheet of paper, without replying. Only a few lines were scrawled on the sheet:—

> I am a moral coward, darling, and dare not tell you. If I come back, you will know why I have left you. If not, pray for me, and remember me kindly. I have placed all my money to the credit of your banking account.

The girl was crying quietly.

"Let me see his room," said Angel; and she conducted him to the little apartment that was half laboratory and half study. A truckle bed ran lengthways beneath the window, and a heap of blackened ashes were piled up in the fireplace.

"Nothing has been touched," said the girl.

Gingerly Angel lifted the curling ashes one by one.

"I've known burnt paper to"—he was going to say "hang a man," but altered it to—"be of great service." There were one or two pieces that the fire had not burnt, and some on which the letters were still discernible. One of these he lifted and carried to the window.

"Hullo!" he muttered.

He could not find a complete sentence, but as he read it it ran:—

> . . . very bad . . . sign . . . monkey . . . take you away your own fault . . .

There was a blotting pad upon the little table, and a square dust mark, where, he surmised, the mysterious box had stood. He lifted the pad; underneath were a number of strips of paper.

He glanced at them carelessly, then:

"What on earth—?" he said.

Indelibly printed on the slips before him were a dozen red thumb prints.

He looked at them closely.

The thumb prints were blood!

Then, in the midst of his mystification a light dawned on Angel, and he turned to the girl.

"Has your husband bought a methylated spirit lamp lately?" he asked.

She looked at him in astonishment.

"Why, yes," she said, "a fortnight ago he bought one."

"And has he been asking for needles?"

She almost gasped.

"Yes, yes, almost every day!"

Angel looked again at the charred paper, and smiled.

"Of course, this may be serious," he said; "but really I think it isn't at all. If you will content your mind for a day, I will tell how serious it is; if you will extend your content for four days, I would almost undertake to promise to restore him to you."

He left her that afternoon in an agony of suspense, and three hours afterwards she received a telegram:

Found your husband—expect him home tomorrow.

To his Chief, Angel explained the mystery in three minutes.

"I thought the Ju-ju had nothing to do with it," he said cheerfully. "The whole thing illustrates the folly of a man who has never been farther from home than Wiesbaden penetrating God's primeval forest. Farrow, on the Congo, surrounded on all sides by the disease, must needs be suddenly obsessed by the belief that he has sleeping-sickness. So home he comes, filled with dread forebodings and visions of the madness that comes to people with hypnosomiasis. Buys microscopes (our yellow box!), and jabs his finger day by day to examine his blood for microbes! As soon as I heard he had got the approved spirit lamp for sterilising purposes, I knew *that.* He corresponds with the Tropical School of Medicine in London and Liverpool, boring those poor people to death with his outrageous symptoms. Jabs his blood into monkeys, and when they die—of cold and bad feeding—fears the worst. So, at last, some wise doctor at the London School, after writing and telling him that he was an ass, that he couldn't be very bad, and that the monkey's death wasn't any sign—except of cruelty to animals—offers to take him into hospital for a few days and put him under observation. So along comes the hospital carriage, with their black porter, and away goes our foolish hypochondriac, with his monkey and his box of tricks. They are turning him out of hospital tomorrow."

A SCANDAL IN BOHEMIA

SIR ARTHUR CONAN DOYLE

I

To Sherlock Holmes she is always *the* woman. I have seldom heard him mention her under any other name. In his eyes she eclipses and predominates the whole of her sex. It was not that he felt any emotion akin to love for Irene Adler. All emotions, and that one particularly, were abhorrent to his cold, precise but admirably balanced mind. He was, I take it, the most perfect reasoning and observing machine that the world has seen, but as a lover he would have placed himself in a false position. He never spoke of the softer passions, save with a gibe and a sneer. They were admirable things for the observer—excellent for drawing the veil from men's motives and actions. But for the trained reasoner to admit such intrusions into his own delicate and finely adjusted temperament was to introduce a distracting factor which might throw a doubt upon all his mental results. Grit in a sensitive instrument, or a crack in one of his own high-power lenses, would not be more disturbing than a strong emotion in a nature such as his. And yet there was but one woman to him, and that woman was the late Irene Adler, of dubious and questionable memory.

I had seen little of Holmes lately. My marriage had drifted us away from each other. My own complete happiness, and the home-centred interests which rise up around the man who first finds himself master of his own establishment, were sufficient to absorb all my attention, while Holmes, who loathed every form of society with his whole Bohemian soul, remained in our lodgings in Baker Street, buried among his old books, and alternating from week to week between cocaine and ambition, the drowsiness of the drug, and the fierce energy of his own keen nature. He was still, as ever, deeply attracted by the study of crime, and occupied his immense faculties and extraordinary powers of observation in following out those clues, and clearing up those mysteries which had been abandoned as hopeless by the official police. From time to time I heard some vague account of his doings: of his summons to Odessa in the case of the Trepoff murder, of his clearing up of the singular tragedy of the Atkinson brothers at Trincomalee, and finally of the mission which he had accomplished so delicately and successfully for the reigning family of Holland. Beyond these signs of his activity, however, which I merely shared with all the readers of the daily press, I knew little of my former friend and companion.

One night—it was on the 20th of March, 1888—I was returning from a journey to a patient (for I had now returned to civil practice), when my way led me through Baker Street. As I passed the well-remembered door, which must always be associated in my mind with my wooing, and with the dark incidents of the Study in Scarlet, I was seized with a keen desire to see Holmes again, and to know how he was employing his extraordinary powers. His rooms were brilliantly lit, and, even as I looked up, I saw his tall, spare figure pass twice in a dark silhouette against the blind. He was pacing the room swiftly, eagerly, with his head sunk upon his chest and his hands clasped behind him. To me, who knew his every mood and habit, his attitude and manner told their own story. He was at work again. He had risen out of his drug-created dreams and was hot upon the scent of some new problem. I rang the bell and was shown up to the chamber which had formerly been in part my own.

His manner was not effusive. It seldom was; but he was glad, I think, to see me. With hardly a word spoken, but with a kindly eye, he waved me to an armchair, threw across his case of cigars, and indicated a spirit case and a gasogene in the corner. Then he stood before the fire and looked me over in his singular introspective fashion.

"Wedlock suits you," he remarked. "I think, Watson, that you have put on seven and a half pounds since I saw you."

"Seven," I answered.

"Indeed, I should have thought a little more. Just a trifle more, I fancy, Watson. And in practice again, I observe. You did not tell me that you intended to go into harness."

"Then, how do you know?"

"I see it, I deduce it. How do I know that you have been getting yourself very wet lately, and that you have a most clumsy and careless servant girl?"

"My dear Holmes," said I, "this is too much. You would certainly have been burned, had you lived a few centuries ago. It is true that I had a country walk on Thursday and came home in a dreadful mess, but as I have changed my clothes I can't imagine how you deduce it. As to Mary Jane, she is incorrigible, and my wife has given her notice; but there, again, I fail to see how you work it out."

He chuckled to himself and rubbed his long, nervous hands together.

"It is simplicity itself," said he; "my eyes tell me that on the inside of your left shoe, just where the firelight strikes it, the leather is scored by six almost parallel cuts. Obviously they have been caused by someone who has very carelessly scraped round the edges of the sole in order to remove crusted mud from it. Hence, you see, my double deduction that you had been out in vile weather, and that you had a particularly malignant boot-slitting specimen of the London slavey. As to your practice, if a gentleman walks into my rooms smelling of iodoform, with a black mark of nitrate of silver upon his right forefinger, and a bulge on the right side of his top-hat to show where he has secreted his stethoscope, I must be dull, indeed, if I do not pronounce him to be an active member of the medical profession."

I could not help laughing at the ease with which he explained his process of deduction. "When I hear you give your reasons," I remarked, "the thing always appears to me to be so ridiculously simple that I could easily do it myself, though at each successive instance of your reasoning I am baffled until you explain your process. And yet I believe that my eyes are as good as yours."

"Quite so," he answered, lighting a cigarette, and throwing himself down into an armchair. "You see, but you do not observe. The distinction is clear. For example, you have frequently seen the steps which lead up from the hall to this room."

"Frequently."

"How often?"

"Well, some hundreds of times."

"Then how many are there?"

"How many! I don't know."

"Quite so! You have not observed. And yet you have seen. That is just my point. Now, I know that there are seventeen steps, because I have both seen and observed. By the way, since you are interested in these little problems, and since you are good enough to chronicle one or two of my trifling experiences, you may be interested in this." He threw over a sheet of pink-tinted notepaper which had been lying open upon the table. "It came by the last post," said he. "Read it aloud."

The note was undated, and without either signature or address.

"There will call upon you tonight, at a quarter to eight o'clock," it said, "a gentleman who desires to consult you upon a matter of the very deepest moment. Your recent services to one of the royal houses of Europe have shown that you are one who may safely be trusted with matters which are of an importance which can hardly be exaggerated. This account of you we have from all quarters received. Be in your chamber then at that hour, and do not take it amiss if your visitor wear a mask."

"This is indeed a mystery," I remarked. "What do you imagine that it means?"

"I have no data yet. It is a capital mistake to theorize before one has data. Insensibly one begins to twist facts to suit theories, instead of theories to suit facts. But the note itself. What do you deduce from it?"

I carefully examined the writing, and the paper upon which it was written.

"The man who wrote it was presumably well to do," I remarked, endeavouring to imitate my companion's processes. "Such paper could not be bought under half a crown a packet. It is peculiarly strong and stiff."

"Peculiar—that is the very word," said Holmes. "It is not an English paper at all. Hold it up to the light."

I did so, and saw a large *E* with a small *g,* a *P,* and a large *G* with a small *t* woven into the texture of the paper.

"What do you make of that?" asked Holmes.

"The name of the maker, no doubt; or his monogram, rather."

"Not at all. The *G* with the small *t* stands for 'Gesellschaft,' which is the German for 'Company.' It is a customary contraction like our 'Co.' *P,* of course, stands for 'Papier.' Now for the *Eg.* Let us glance at our Continental Gazetteer." He took down a heavy brown volume from his shelves. "Eglow, Eglonitz—here we are, Egria. It is in a German-speaking country—in Bohemia, not far from Carlsbad. 'Remarkable as being the scene of the death of Wallenstein, and for its numerous glass-factories and paper-mills.' Ha, ha, my boy, what do you make of that?" His eyes sparkled, and he sent up a great blue triumphant cloud from his cigarette.

"The paper was made in Bohemia," I said.

"Precisely. And the man who wrote the note is a German. Do you note the peculiar construction of the sentence—'This account of you we have from all quarters received.' A Frenchman or Russian could not have written that. It is the German who is so uncourteous to his verbs. It only remains, therefore, to discover what is wanted by this German who writes upon Bohemian paper and prefers wearing a mask to showing his face. And here he comes, if I am not mistaken, to resolve all our doubts."

As he spoke there was the sharp sound of horses' hoofs and grating wheels against the curb, followed by a sharp pull at the bell. Holmes whistled.

"A pair, by the sound," said he. "Yes," he continued, glancing out of the window. "A nice little brougham and a pair of beauties. A hundred and fifty guineas apiece. There's money in this case, Watson, if there is nothing else."

"I think that I had better go, Holmes."

"Not a bit, Doctor. Stay where you are. I am lost without my Boswell. And this promises to be interesting. It would be a pity to miss it."

"But your client—"

"Never mind him. I may want your help, and so may he. Here he comes. Sit down in that armchair, Doctor, and give us your best attention."

A slow and heavy step, which had been heard upon the stairs and in the passage, paused immediately outside the door. Then there was a loud and authoritative tap.

"Come in!" said Holmes.

A man entered who could hardly have been less than six feet six inches in height, with the chest and limbs of a Hercules. His dress was rich with a richness which would, in England, be looked upon as akin to bad taste. Heavy bands of Astrakhan were slashed across the sleeves and fronts of his double-breasted coat, while the deep blue cloak which was thrown over his shoulders was lined with flame-coloured silk and secured at the neck with a brooch which consisted of a single flaming beryl. Boots which extended halfway up his calves, and which were trimmed at the tops with rich brown fur, completed the impression of barbaric opulence which was suggested by his whole appearance. He carried a broad-brimmed hat in his hand, while he wore across the upper part of his face, extending down past the cheekbones, a black vizard mask, which he had apparently adjusted that very moment, for his hand was still raised to it as he entered. From the lower part of the face he appeared to be a man of strong character, with a thick, hanging lip, and a long, straight chin suggestive of resolution pushed to the length of obstinacy.

"You had my note?" he asked with a deep harsh voice and a strongly marked German accent. "I told you that I would call." He looked from one to the other of us, as if uncertain which to address.

"Pray take a seat," said Holmes. "This is my friend and colleague, Dr. Watson, who is occasionally good enough to help me in my cases. Whom have I the honour to address?"

"You may address me as the Count Von Kramm, a Bohemian nobleman. I understand that this gentleman, your friend, is a man of honour and discretion, whom I may trust with a matter of the most extreme importance. If not, I should much prefer to communicate with you alone."

I rose to go, but Holmes caught me by the wrist and pushed me back into my chair. "It is both, or none," said he. "You may say before this gentleman anything which you may say to me."

The Count shrugged his broad shoulders. "Then I must begin," said he, "by binding you both to absolute secrecy for two years; at the end of that time the matter will be of no importance. At present it is not too much to say that it is of such weight it may have an influence upon European history."

"I promise," said Holmes.

"And I."

"You will excuse this mask," continued our strange visitor. "The august person who employs me wishes his agent to be unknown to you, and I may confess at once that the title by which I have just called myself is not exactly my own."

"I was aware of it," said Holmes dryly.

"The circumstances are of great delicacy, and every precaution has to be taken to quench what might grow to be an immense scandal and seriously compromise one of the reigning families of Europe. To speak plainly, the matter implicates the great House of Ormstein, hereditary kings of Bohemia."

"I was also aware of that," murmured Holmes, settling himself down in his armchair and closing his eyes.

Our visitor glanced with some apparent surprise at the languid, lounging figure of the man who had been no doubt depicted to him as the most incisive reasoner and most energetic agent in Europe. Holmes slowly reopened his eyes and looked impatiently at his gigantic client.

"If your Majesty would condescend to state your case," he remarked, "I should be better able to advise you."

The man sprang from his chair and paced up and down the room in uncontrollable agitation. Then, with a gesture of desperation, he tore the mask from his face and hurled it upon the ground. "You are right," he cried, "I am the King. Why should I attempt to conceal it?"

"Why, indeed?" murmured Holmes. "Your Majesty had not spoken before I was aware that I was addressing Wilhelm Gottsreich Sigismond von Ormstein, Grand Duke of Cassel-Felstein, and hereditary King of Bohemia."

"But you can understand," said our strange visitor, sitting down once more and passing his hand over his high white forehead, "you can understand that I am not accustomed to doing such business in my own person. Yet the matter was so delicate that I could not confide it to an agent without putting myself in his power. I have come *incognito* from Prague for the purpose of consulting you."

"Then, pray consult," said Holmes, shutting his eyes once more.

"The facts are briefly these: Some five years ago, during a lengthy visit to Warsaw, I made the acquaintance of the well-known adventuress, Irene Adler. The name is no doubt familiar to you."

"Kindly look her up in my index, Doctor," murmured Holmes without opening his eyes. For many years he had adopted a system of docketing all paragraphs concerning men and things, so that it was difficult to name a subject or a person on which he could not at once furnish information. In this case I found her biography sandwiched in between that of a Hebrew rabbi and that of a staff-commander who had written a monograph upon the deep-sea fishes.

"Let me see?" said Holmes. "Hum! Born in New Jersey in the year 1858. Contralto—hum! La Scala, hum! Prima donna Imperial Opera of Warsaw—Yes! Retired from operatic stage—ha! Living in London—quite so! Your Majesty, as I understand, became entangled with this young person, wrote her some compromising letters, and is now desirous of getting those letters back."

"Precisely so. But how—"

"Was there a secret marriage?"

"None."

"No legal papers or certificates?"

"None."

"Then I fail to follow your Majesty. If this young person should produce her letters for blackmailing or other purposes, how is she to prove their authenticity?"

"There is the writing."

"Pooh, pooh! Forgery."

"My private notepaper."

"Stolen."

"My own seal."

"Imitated."

"My photograph."

"Bought."

"We were both in the photograph."

"Oh, dear! That is very bad! Your Majesty has indeed committed an indiscretion."

"I was mad—insane."

"You have compromised yourself seriously."

"I was only Crown Prince then. I was young. I am but thirty now."

"It must be recovered."

"We have tried and failed."

"Your Majesty must pay. It must be bought."

"She will not sell."

"Stolen, then."

"Five attempts have been made. Twice burglars in my pay ransacked her house. Once we diverted her luggage when she travelled. Twice she has been waylaid. There has been no result."

"No sign of it?"

"Absolutely none."

Holmes laughed. "It is quite a pretty little problem," said he.

"But a very serious one to me," returned the King reproachfully.

"Very, indeed. And what does she propose to do with the photograph?"

"To ruin me."

"But how?"

"I am about to be married."

"So I have heard."

"To Clotilde Lothman von Saxe-Meningen, second daughter of the King of Scandinavia. You may know the strict principles of her family. She is herself the very soul of delicacy. A shadow of a doubt as to my conduct would bring the matter to an end."

"And Irene Adler?"

"Threatens to send them the photograph. And she will do it. I know that she will do it. You do not know her, but she has a soul of steel. She has the face of the most beautiful of women, and the mind of the most resolute of men. Rather than I should marry another woman, there are no lengths to which she would not go—none."

"You are sure that she has not sent it yet?"

"I am sure."

"And why?"

"Because she has said that she would send it on the day when the betrothal was publicly proclaimed. That will be next Monday."

"Oh, then, we have three days yet," said Holmes with a yawn. "That is very fortunate, as I have one or two matters of importance to look into just at present. Your Majesty will, of course, stay in London for the present?"

"Certainly. You will find me at the Langham under the name of the Count Von Kramm."

"Then I shall drop you a line to let you know how we progress."

"Pray do so. I shall be all anxiety."

"Then, as to money?"

"You have *carte blanche.*"

"Absolutely?"

"I tell you that I would give one of the provinces of my kingdom to have that photograph."

"And for present expenses?"

The King took a heavy chamois leather bag from under his cloak, and laid it on the table.

"There are three hundred pounds in gold, and seven hundred in notes," he said.

Holmes scribbled a receipt upon a sheet of his notebook and handed it to him.

"And Mademoiselle's address?" he asked.

"Is Briony Lodge, Serpentine Avenue, St. John's Wood."

Holmes took a note of it. "One other question," said he. "Was the photograph a cabinet?"

"It was."

"Then, goodnight, your Majesty, and I trust that we shall soon have some good news for you. And goodnight, Watson," he added, as the wheels of the royal brougham rolled down the street. "If you will be good enough to call tomorrow afternoon at three o'clock I should like to chat this little matter over with you."

II

At three o'clock precisely I was at Baker Street, but Holmes had not yet returned. The landlady informed me that he had left the house shortly after eight o'clock in the morning. I sat down beside the fire, however, with the intention of awaiting him, however long he might be. I was already deeply interested in his inquiry, for, though it was surrounded by none of the grim and strange features which were associated with the two crimes which I have already recorded, still, the nature of the case and the exalted station of his client gave it a character of its own. Indeed, apart from the nature of the investigation which my friend had on hand, there was something in his masterly grasp of a situation, and his keen, incisive reasoning, which made it a pleasure to me to study his system of work, and to follow the quick, subtle methods by which he disentangled the most inextricable mysteries. So accustomed was I to his invariable success that the very possibility of his failing had ceased to enter into my head.

It was close upon four before the door opened, and a drunken-looking groom, ill-kempt and side-whiskered, with an inflamed face and disreputable clothes, walked into the room. Accustomed as I was to my friend's amazing powers in the use of disguises, I had to look three times before I was certain that it was indeed he. With a nod he vanished into the bedroom, whence he emerged in five minutes tweed-suited and respectable, as of old. Putting his hands into his pockets, he stretched out his legs in front of the fire and laughed heartily for some minutes.

"Well, really!" he cried, and then he choked and laughed again until he was obliged to lie back, limp and helpless, in the chair.

"What is it?"

"It's quite too funny. I am sure you could never guess how I employed my morning, or what I ended by doing."

"I can't imagine. I suppose that you have been watching the habits, and perhaps the house, of Miss Irene Adler."

"Quite so; but the sequel was rather unusual. I will tell you, however. I left the house a little after eight o'clock this morning in the character of a groom out of work. There is a wonderful sympathy and freemasonry among horsey men. Be one of them, and you will know all that there is to know. I soon found Briony Lodge. It is a *bijou* villa, with a garden at the back, but built out in front right up to the road, two stories. Chubb lock to the door. Large sitting room on the right side, well furnished, with long windows almost to the floor, and those preposterous English window fasteners which a child could open. Behind there was nothing remarkable, save that the passage window could be reached from the top of the coach-house. I walked round it and examined it closely from every point of view, but without noting anything else of interest.

"I then lounged down the street, and found, as I expected, that there was a mews in a lane which runs down by one wall of the garden. I lent the ostlers a hand in rubbing down their horses, and received in exchange twopence, a glass of half-and-half, two fills of shag tobacco, and as much information as I could desire about Miss Adler, to say nothing of half a dozen other people in the neighbourhood in whom I was not in the least interested, but whose biographies I was compelled to listen to."

"And what of Irene Adler?" I asked.

"Oh, she has turned all the men's heads down in that part. She is the daintiest thing under a bonnet on this planet. So say the Serpentine Mews, to a man. She lives quietly, sings at concerts, drives out at five every day, and returns at seven sharp for dinner. Seldom goes out at other times, except when she sings. Has only one male visitor, but a good deal of him. He is dark, handsome, and dashing, never calls less than once a day, and often twice. He is a Mr. Godfrey Norton, of the Inner Temple. See the advantages of a cabman as a confidant. They had driven him home a dozen times from Serpentine Mews, and knew all about him. When I had listened to all they had to tell, I began to walk up and down near Briony Lodge once more, and to think over my plan of campaign.

"This Godfrey Norton was evidently an important factor in the matter. He was a lawyer. That sounded ominous. What was the relation between them, and what the object of his repeated visits? Was she his client, his friend, or his mistress? If the former, she had probably transferred the photograph to his keeping. If the latter, it was less likely. On the issue of this question depended whether I should continue my work at Briony Lodge, or turn my attention to the gentleman's chambers in the Temple. It was a delicate point, and it widened the field of my inquiry. I fear that I bore you with these details, but I have to let you see my little difficulties, if you are to understand the situation."

"I am following you closely," I answered.

"I was still balancing the matter in my mind when a hansom cab drove up to Briony Lodge, and a gentleman sprang out. He was a remarkably handsome man, dark, aquiline, and moustached—evidently the man of whom I had heard. He appeared to be in a great hurry, shouted to the cabman to wait, and brushed past the maid who opened the door with the air of a man who was thoroughly at home.

"He was in the house about half an hour, and I could catch glimpses of him, in the windows of the sitting room, pacing up and down, talking excitedly, and waving his arms. Of her I could see nothing. Presently he emerged, looking even more flurried than before. As he stepped up to the cab, he pulled a gold watch from his pocket and looked at it earnestly. 'Drive like the devil,' he shouted, 'first to Gross & Hankey's in Regent Street, and then to the church of St. Monica in the Edgeware Road. Half a guinea if you do it in twenty minutes!'

"Away they went, and I was just wondering whether I should not do well to follow them when up the lane came a neat little landau, the coachman with his coat only half-buttoned, and his tie under his ear, while all the tags of his harness were sticking out of the buckles. It hadn't pulled up before she shot out of the hall door and into it. I only caught a glimpse of her at the moment, but she was a lovely woman, with a face that a man might die for.

"'The Church of St. Monica, John,' she cried, 'and half a sovereign if you reach it in twenty minutes.'

"This was quite too good to lose, Watson. I was just balancing whether I should run for it, or whether I should perch behind her landau when a cab came through the street. The driver looked twice at such a shabby fare, but I jumped in before he could object. 'The Church of St. Monica,' said I, 'and half a sovereign if you reach it in twenty minutes.' It was twenty-five minutes to twelve, and of course it was clear enough what was in the wind.

"My cabby drove fast. I don't think I ever drove faster, but the others were there before us. The cab and the landau with their steaming horses were in front of the door when I arrived. I paid the man and hurried into the church. There was not a soul there save the two whom I had followed and a surpliced clergyman, who seemed to be expostulating with them. They were all three standing in a knot in front of the altar. I lounged up the side aisle like any other idler who has dropped into a church. Suddenly, to my surprise, the three at the altar faced round to me, and Godfrey Norton came running as hard as he could towards me."

"Thank God," he cried. "You'll do. Come! Come!"

"What then?" I asked.

"Come, man, come, only three minutes, or it won't be legal."

I was half-dragged up to the altar, and before I knew where I was, I found myself mumbling responses which were whispered in my ear, and vouching for things of which I knew nothing, and generally assisting in the secure tying up of Irene Adler, spinster, to Godfrey Norton, bachelor. It was all done in an instant, and there was the gentleman thanking me on the one side and the lady on the other, while the clergyman beamed on me in front. It was the most preposterous position in which I ever found myself in my life, and it was the thought of it that started me laughing just now. It seems that there had been some informality about their license, that the clergyman absolutely refused to marry them without a witness of some sort, and that my lucky appearance saved the bridegroom from having to sally out into the streets in search of a best man. The bride gave me a sovereign, and I mean to wear it on my watch-chain in memory of the occasion."

"This is a very unexpected turn of affairs," said I; "and what then?"

"Well, I found my plans very seriously menaced. It looked as if the pair might take an immediate departure, and so necessitate very prompt and energetic measures on my part. At the church door, however, they separated, he driving back to the Temple, and she to her own house. 'I shall drive out in the park at five as usual,' she said as she left him. I heard no more. They drove away in different directions, and I went off to make my own arrangements."

"Which are?"

"Some cold beef and a glass of beer," he answered, ringing the bell. "I have been too busy to think of food, and I am likely to be busier still this evening. By the way, Doctor, I shall want your co-operation."

"I shall be delighted."

"You don't mind breaking the law?"

"Not in the least."

"Nor running a chance of arrest?"

"Not in a good cause."

"Oh, the cause is excellent!"

"Then I am your man."

"I was sure that I might rely on you."

"But what is it you wish?"

"When Mrs. Turner has brought in the tray I will make it clear to you. Now," he said, as he turned hungrily on the simple fare that our landlady had provided, "I must discuss it while I eat, for I have not much time. It is nearly five now. In two hours we must be on the scene of action. Miss Irene, or Madame, rather, returns from her drive at seven. We must be at Briony Lodge to meet her."

"And what then?"

"You must leave that to me. I have already arranged what is to occur. There is only one point on which I must insist. You must not interfere, come what may. You understand?"

"I am to be neutral?"

"To do nothing whatever. There will probably be some small unpleasantness. Do not join in it. It will end in my being conveyed into the house. Four or five minutes afterwards the sitting room window will open. You are to station yourself close to that open window."

"Yes."

"You are to watch me, for I will be visible to you."

"Yes."

"And when I raise my hand—so—you will throw into the room what I give you to throw, and will, at the same time, raise the cry of fire. You quite follow me?"

"Entirely."

"It is nothing very formidable," he said, taking a long cigar-shaped roll from his pocket. "It is an ordinary plumber's smoke-rocket, fitted with a cap at either end to make it self-lighting. Your task is confined to that. When you raise your cry of fire, it will be taken up by quite a number of people. You may then walk to the end of the street, and I will rejoin you in ten minutes. I hope that I have made myself clear?"

"I am to remain neutral, to get near the window, to watch you, and at the signal to throw in this object, then to raise the cry of fire, and to wait you at the corner of the street."

"Precisely."

"Then you may entirely rely on me."

"That is excellent. I think, perhaps, it is almost time that I prepare for the new *role* I have to play."

He disappeared into his bedroom and returned in a few minutes in the character of an amiable and simple-minded Nonconformist clergyman. His broad black hat, his baggy trousers, his white tie, his sympathetic smile, and general look of peering and benevolent curiosity were such as Mr. John Hare alone could have equalled. It was not merely that Holmes changed his costume. His expression, his manner, his very soul seemed to vary with every fresh part that he assumed. The stage lost a fine actor, even as science lost an acute reasoner, when he became a specialist in crime.

It was a quarter past six when we left Baker Street, and it still wanted ten minutes to the hour when we found ourselves in Serpentine Avenue. It was already dusk, and the lamps were just being lighted as we paced up and down in front of Briony Lodge, waiting for the coming of its occupant. The house was just such as I had pictured it from Sherlock Holmes's succinct description, but the locality appeared to be less private than I expected. On the contrary, for a small street in a quiet neighbourhood, it was remarkably animated. There was a group of shabbily dressed men smoking and laughing in a corner, a scissors-grinder with his wheel, two guardsmen who were flirting with a nurse-girl, and several well-dressed young men who were lounging up and down with cigars in their mouths.

"You see," remarked Holmes, as we paced to and fro in front of the house, "this marriage rather simplifies matters. The photograph becomes a double-edged weapon now. The chances are that she would be as averse to its being seen by Mr. Godfrey Norton, as our client is to its coming to the eyes of his princess. Now the question is—Where are we to find the photograph?"

"Where, indeed?"

"It is most unlikely that she carries it about with her. It is cabinet size. Too large for easy concealment about a woman's dress. She knows that the King is capable of having her waylaid and searched. Two attempts of the sort have already been made. We may take it, then, that she does not carry it about with her."

"Where, then?"

"Her banker or her lawyer. There is that double possibility. But I am inclined to think neither. Women are naturally secretive, and they like to do their own secreting. Why should she hand it over to anyone else? She could trust her own guardianship, but she could not tell what indirect or political influence might be brought to bear upon a business man. Besides, remember that she had resolved to use it within a few days. It must be where she can lay her hands upon it. It must be in her own house."

"But it has twice been burgled."

"Pshaw! They did not know how to look."

"But how will you look?"

"I will not look."

"What then?"

"I will get her to show me."

"But she will refuse."

"She will not be able to. But I hear the rumble of wheels. It is her carriage. Now carry out my orders to the letter."

As he spoke the gleam of the sidelights of a carriage came round the curve of the avenue. It was a smart little landau which rattled up to the door of Briony Lodge. As it pulled up, one of the loafing men at the corner dashed forward to open the door in the hope of earning a copper, but was elbowed away by another loafer, who had rushed up with the same intention. A fierce quarrel broke out, which was increased by the two guardsmen, who took sides with one of the loungers, and by the scissors-grinder, who was equally hot upon the other side. A blow was struck, and in an instant the lady, who had stepped from her carriage, was the centre of a little knot of flushed and struggling men, who struck savagely at each other with their fists and sticks. Holmes dashed into the crowd to protect the lady; but, just as he reached her, he gave a cry and dropped to the ground, with the blood running freely down his face. At his fall the guardsmen took to their heels in one direction and the loungers in the other, while a number of better-dressed people, who had watched the scuffle without taking part in it, crowded in to help the lady and to attend to the injured man. Irene Adler, as I will still call her, had hurried up the steps; but she stood at the top with her superb figure outlined against the lights of the hall, looking back into the street.

"Is the poor gentleman much hurt?" she asked.

"He is dead," cried several voices.

"No, no, there's life in him," shouted another. "But he'll be gone before you can get him to hospital."

"He's a brave fellow," said a woman. "They would have had the lady's purse and watch if it hadn't been for him. They were a gang, and a rough one, too. Ah, he's breathing now."

"He can't lie in the street. May we bring him in, marm?"

"Surely. Bring him into the sitting room. There is a comfortable sofa. This way, please!"

Slowly and solemnly he was borne into Briony Lodge and laid out in the principal room, while I still observed the proceedings from my post by the window. The lamps had been lit, but the blinds had not been drawn, so that I could see Holmes as he lay upon the couch. I do not know whether he was seized with compunction at that moment for the part he was playing, but I know that I never felt more heartily ashamed of myself in my life than when I saw the beautiful creature against whom I was conspiring, or the grace and kindliness with which she waited upon the injured man. And yet it would be the blackest treachery to Holmes to draw back now from the part which he had intrusted to me. I hardened my heart, and took the smoke-rocket from under my ulster. After all, I thought, we are not injuring her. We are but preventing her from injuring another.

Holmes had sat up upon the couch, and I saw him motion like a man who is in need of air. A maid rushed across and threw open the window. At the same instant I saw him raise his hand, and at the signal I tossed my rocket into the room with a cry of "Fire." The word was no sooner out of my mouth than the whole crowd of spectators, well dressed and ill—gentlemen, ostlers, and servant-maids—joined in a general shriek of "Fire." Thick clouds of smoke curled through the room and out at the open window. I caught a glimpse of rushing figures, and a moment later the voice of Holmes from within assuring them that it was a false alarm. Slipping through the shouting crowd I made my way to the corner of the street, and in ten minutes was rejoiced to find my friend's arm in mine, and to get away from the scene of uproar. He walked swiftly and in silence for some few minutes until we had turned down one of the quiet streets which lead towards the Edgeware Road.

"You did it very nicely, Doctor," he remarked. "Nothing could have been better. It is all right."

"You have the photograph!"

"I know where it is."

"And how did you find out?"

"She showed me, as I told you she would."

"I am still in the dark."

"I do not wish to make a mystery," said he, laughing. "The matter was perfectly simple. You, of course, saw that everyone in the street was an accomplice. They were all engaged for the evening."

"I guessed as much."

"Then, when the row broke out, I had a little moist red paint in the palm of my hand. I rushed forward, fell down, clapped my hand to my face, and became a piteous spectacle. It is an old trick."

"That also I could fathom."

"Then they carried me in. She was bound to have me in. What else could she do? And into her sitting room, which was the very room which I suspected. It lay between that and her bedroom, and I was determined to see which. They laid me on a couch, I motioned for air, they were compelled to open the window, and you had your chance."

"How did that help you?"

"It was all-important. When a woman thinks that her house is on fire, her instinct is at once to rush to the thing which she values most. It is a perfectly overpowering impulse, and I have more than once taken advantage of it. In the case of the Darlington substitution scandal it was of use to me, and also in the Arnsworth Castle business. A married woman grabs at her baby—an unmarried one reaches for her jewel-box. Now it was clear to me that our lady of today had nothing in the house more precious to her than what we are in quest of. She would rush to secure it. The alarm of fire was admirably done. The smoke and shouting were enough to shake nerves of steel. She responded beautifully. The photograph is in a recess behind a sliding panel just above the right bell-pull. She was there in an instant, and I caught a glimpse of it as she half-drew it out. When I cried out that it was a false alarm, she replaced it, glanced at the rocket, rushed from the room, and I have not seen her since. I rose, and, making my excuses, escaped from the house. I hesitated whether to attempt to secure the photograph at once; but the coachman had come in, and as he was watching me narrowly it seemed safer to wait. A little over-precipitance may ruin all."

"And now?" I asked.

"Our quest is practically finished. I shall call with the King tomorrow, and with you, if you care to come with us. We will be shown into the sitting room to wait for the lady, but it is probable that when she comes she may find neither us nor the photograph. It might be a satisfaction to His Majesty to regain it with his own hands."

"And when will you call?"

"At eight in the morning. She will not be up, so that we shall have a clear field. Besides, we must be prompt, for this marriage may mean a complete change in her life and habits. I must wire to the King without delay."

We had reached Baker Street and had stopped at the door. He was searching his pockets for the key when someone passing said:—

"Good-night, Mister Sherlock Holmes."

There were several people on the pavement at the time, but the greeting appeared to come from a slim youth in an ulster who had hurried by.

"I've heard that voice before," said Holmes, staring down the dimly lit street. "Now, I wonder who the deuce that could have been."

III

I slept at Baker Street that night, and we were engaged upon our toast and coffee in the morning when the King of Bohemia rushed into the room.

"You have really got it!" he cried, grasping Sherlock Holmes by either shoulder and looking eagerly into his face.

"Not yet."

"But you have hopes?"

"I have hopes."

"Then, come. I am all impatience to be gone."

"We must have a cab."

"No, my brougham is waiting."

"Then that will simplify matters." We descended and started off once more for Briony Lodge.

"Irene Adler is married," remarked Holmes.

"Married! When?"

"Yesterday."

"But to whom?"

"To an English lawyer named Norton."

"But she could not love him?"

"I am in hopes that she does."

"And why in hopes?"

"Because it would spare your Majesty all fear of future annoyance. If the lady loves her husband, she does not love your Majesty. If she does not love your Majesty, there is no reason why she should interfere with your Majesty's plan."

"It is true. And yet—! Well! I wish she had been of my own station! What a queen she would have made!" He relapsed into a moody silence, which was not broken until we drew up in Serpentine Avenue.

The door of Briony Lodge was open, and an elderly woman stood upon the steps. She watched us with a sardonic eye as we stepped from the brougham.

"Mr. Sherlock Holmes, I believe?" said she.

"I am Mr. Holmes," answered my companion, looking at her with a questioning and rather startled gaze.

"Indeed! My mistress told me that you were likely to call. She left this morning with her husband by the 5.15 train from Charing Cross for the Continent."

"What!" Sherlock Holmes staggered back, white with chagrin and surprise. "Do you mean that she has left England?"

"Never to return."

"And the papers?" asked the King, hoarsely. "All is lost."

"We shall see." He pushed past the servant and rushed into the drawing room, followed by the King and myself. The furniture was scattered about in every direction, with dismantled shelves and open drawers, as if the lady had hurriedly ransacked them before her flight. Holmes rushed at the bell-pull, tore back a small sliding shutter, and, plunging in his hand, pulled out a photograph and a letter. The photograph was of Irene Adler herself in evening dress, the letter was superscribed to "Sherlock Holmes, Esq. To be left till called for." My friend tore it open, and we all three read it together. It was dated at midnight of the preceding night, and ran in this way:—

> "My Dear Mr. Sherlock Holmes,—:
> You really did it very well. You took me in completely. Until after the alarm of fire, I had not a suspicion. But then, when I found how I had betrayed myself, I began to think. I had been warned against you months ago. I had been told that if the King employed an agent it would certainly be you. And your address had been given me. Yet, with all this, you made me reveal what you wanted to know. Even after I became suspicious, I found it hard to think evil of such a dear, kind old clergyman. But, you know, I have been trained as an actress myself. Male costume is nothing new to me. I often take advantage of the freedom which it gives. I sent John, the coachman, to watch you, ran upstairs, got into my walking-clothes, as I call them, and came down just as you departed.
>
> "Well, I followed you to your door, and so made sure that I was really an object of interest to the celebrated Mr. Sherlock Holmes. Then I, rather imprudently, wished you good-night, and started for the Temple to see my husband.
>
> "We both thought the best resource was flight, when pursued by so formidable an antagonist; so you will find the nest empty when you call tomorrow. As to the photograph, your client may rest in peace. I love and am loved by a better man than he. The King may do what he will without hindrance from one whom he has cruelly

wronged. I keep it only to safeguard myself, and to preserve a weapon which will always secure me from any steps which he might take in the future. I leave a photograph which he might care to possess; and I remain, dear Mr. Sherlock Holmes, very truly yours,

"IRENE NORTON, *née* ADLER."

"What a woman—oh, what a woman!" cried the King of Bohemia, when we had all three read this epistle. "Did I not tell you how quick and resolute she was? Would she not have made an admirable queen? Is it not a pity that she was not on my level?"

"From what I have seen of the lady she seems indeed to be on a very different level to your Majesty," said Holmes coldly. "I am sorry that I have not been able to bring your Majesty's business to a more successful conclusion."

"On the contrary, my dear sir," cried the King; "nothing could be more successful. I know that her word is inviolate. The photograph is now as safe as if it were in the fire."

"I am glad to hear your Majesty say so."

"I am immensely indebted to you. Pray tell me in what way I can reward you. This ring—." He slipped an emerald snake ring from his finger, and held it out upon the palm of his hand.

"Your Majesty has something which I should value even more highly," said Holmes.

"You have but to name it."

"This photograph!"

The King stared at him in amazement.

"Irene's photograph!" he cried. "Certainly, if you wish it."

"I thank your Majesty. Then there is no more to be done in the matter. I have the honour to wish you a very good morning." He bowed, and, turning away without observing the hand which the King had stretched out to him, he set off in my company for his chambers.

And that was how a great scandal threatened to affect the kingdom of Bohemia, and how the best plans of Mr. Sherlock Holmes were beaten by a woman's wit. He used to make merry over the cleverness of women, but I have not heard him do it of late. And when he speaks of Irene Adler, or when he refers to her photograph, it is always under the honourable title of *the* woman.

MISS HINCH

HENRY SYDNOR HARRISON

IN GOING FROM A GIVEN POINT on One Hundred and Twenty-Sixth Street to a subway station at One Hundred and Twenty-Fifth, it is not usual to begin by circling the block to One Hundred and Twenty-Seventh Street, especially in sleet, darkness, and deadly cold. When two people pursue such a course at the same time, moving unobtrusively on opposite sides of the street, in the nature of things the coincidence is likely to attract the attention of one or the other of them.

In the bright light of the entrance to the tube they came almost face to face, and the clergyman took a good look at her. Certainly she was a decent-looking old body, if any woman was: white-haired, wrinkled, spectacled, and stooped. A poor but thoroughly respectable domestic servant of the better class she looked, in her black hat, neat veil, and nondescript gray cloak; and her brief glance at the reverend gentleman was precisely what it should have been from her to him—deference itself. Nevertheless, he, going more slowly down the draughty steps, continued to study her from behind with a singular intentness.

An express was just thundering in, which the clergyman, handicapped as he was by his clubfoot and stout cane, was barely in time to catch. He entered the same car with the woman, and took a seat directly across from her. It must have been then well past midnight, and the wildness of the weather was discouraging to travel. The car was almost deserted. Even here under the earth the bitter breath of the night blew and bit, and the old woman shivered under her cloak. At last, her teeth chattering, she got up in an apologetic sort of way, and moved toward the rear of the car, feeling the empty seats as she went, in a palpable search for hot pipes. The clergyman's eyes followed her; he watched her sink down, presently into a seat on his own side of the car. A young couple sat between them now; he could no longer see the woman, beyond glimpses of her black knees and her faded bonnet, fastened on with a long steel hatpin.

Nothing could have seemed more natural or more trivial than this change of seats on the part of the thin-blooded and half-frozen passenger. But it happened to be a time of mutual doubts and general suspiciousness, when men looked askance into every strange face, and the smallest incidents might take on an hysterical importance. Through days of intense searching for a fugitive outlaw of extraordinary gifts, the nerves of the city had been visibly strained. All jumped now when anybody cried "Boo!" and the hue and cry went up falsely twenty times a day.

The clergyman pondered; mechanically he turned up his coat-collar and fell to stamping his feet. He was an Episcopal clergyman, by his garb—rather short, very full-bodied, not to say fat, bearded, and somewhat puffy faced, with heavy cheeks cut by deep creases. Well lined against the cold though he was, however, he, too, began to show signs of suffering, and presently rose and moved in his turn, seeking out a new place where the chilled heating apparatus might give a better account of itself. He found a seat just beyond the old serving woman, limped into it, and relapsed into his own thoughts.

The young couple, half a dozen seats away, appeared thoroughly absorbed in each other's society. The fifth traveler, a withered old gentleman sitting across and down the aisle, napped fitfully upon his cane. The woman in the shapeless cloak sat in a sad kind of silence; and the train hurled itself roaring through the tube. After a time, she glanced through her spectacles at the meditating clergyman, and her look fell swiftly from his face to the "ten-o'clock extra" in his hand. She removed her gaze and let it travel casually about the car; but before long it returned again, as if magnetized, to the newspaper. Then, with some obvious hesitation, she bent forward and said, above the noises of the train:

"Excuse me, Father, but would you please let me look at your paper a minute, sir?"

The clergyman came out of his reverie instantly, and looked at her with a quick smile.

"Certainly. Keep it, if you like: I am quite through with it. But," he said, in a pleasant deep voice, "I am an Episcopal minister, not a priest."

"Oh, sir—I beg your pardon! I thought—"

He dismissed the apology with a nod and a good-natured hand.

The woman opened the paper with the decent cotton-gloved fingers. The garish headlines told all the story: "Earth Opened and Swallowed Miss Hinch, Says Inspector—Police Confess 'Practically No Clue'—Even Jessie Dark"—so the bold capitals ran on—"Seems 'Stumped.'" Below the spread was a luridly written but flimsy narrative, "By Jessie Dark," which at once confirmed the odd implications of the caption. "Jessie Dark," it appeared, was one of those most extraordinary of the products of yellow journalism, a woman "crime expert" to be taken seriously, it seemed—no mere office-desk sleuth, but an actual performer with, unexpectedly enough, a somewhat formidable list of notches on her gun. So much, at least, was to be gathered from her paper's boxed display of "Jessie Dark's Triumphs":

March 2, 1901. Caught Julia Victorian, *alias* Gregory, the brains of the "Healy Ring" kidnappers.

October 7–29, 1903. Found Mrs. Trotwood and secured the letter that convicted her of the murder of her lover, Ellis E. Swan.

December 17, 1903. Ran down Charles Bartsch in a Newark laundry and trapped a confession from him.

July 4, 1904. Caught Hélène Gray, "Blackmail Queen," and recovered the Stratford jewels.

And so on—nine "triumphs" in all; and nearly every one of them, as the least observant reader could hardly fail to notice, involved the capture of a woman.

Nevertheless, it could not be pretended that the "snappy" paragraphs in this evening's extra seemed to foreshadow a new or tenth triumph for Jessie Dark at an early date; and the old serving-woman in the car presently laid down the sheet with a look of marked depression.

The clergyman glanced at her again. Her expression was so speaking that it seemed almost an invitation; moreover, public interest in the curious case had created a freemasonry which made conversation between total strangers the rule wherever two or three were gathered.

"You were reading about this strange mystery, I suppose?" he said as the train momentarily paused.

The woman with a sharp intake of breath, answered: "Yes, sir, it seems as if I couldn't think of anything else."

"Ah?" he said calmly. "It certainly appears to be a remarkable affair."

Remarkable, indeed, the affair seemed. In a tiny little room within ten steps of Broadway, at half-past nine o'clock on a fine evening, Miss Hinch had killed John Catherwood with the light sword she used in her famous representation of the Father of his Country. Catherwood, it was known, had come to tell her of his approaching marriage; and ten thousand amateur detectives, stimulated by the unprecedented "rewards," had required no further motive of a creature already notorious for fierce jealousy. So far the tragedy was commonplace enough, and even vulgar. What had redeemed it to romance from this point on was the extraordinary faculty of the woman, which had made her celebrated while she was still in her teens. Violent, unmoral, criminal she might be, but she happened also to be the most astonishing impersonator of her time. Her brilliant act consisted of a series of character changes, many of them done "in full view of audience" with the assistance only of a small table of properties half concealed under a net. Some of these transformations were so amazing as to be beyond belief, even after one had sat and watched them. Not the woman's appearance only, but voice, speech, manner, carriage, all shifted incredibly to fit the new part; so that she appeared to have no permanent form or fashion of her own, but to be only so much plastic human material out of which her cunning could mould at will man, woman, or child, great lady of the Louisan court, or Tammany chieftain with the modernest of East Side modernisms upon his lips.

With this strange gift, hitherto used only to enthrall audiences and wring extortionate contracts from managers, the woman known as Miss Hinch—she appeared to be without first name—was now fighting for her life somewhere against the police of the whole world. Without artifice, she was a tall, thin-chested young woman with strongly marked features and considerable beauty of a bold sort. What she would look like at the present moment nobody could venture a guess. Having stabbed John Catherwood in her dressing room at the Coliseum, she had donned hat and coat, dropped two wigs and her make-up kit into a handbag, and walked out into Broadway. Within ten minutes the dead body of Catherwood was found and the chase begun. At the stage door, as she passed out, Miss Hinch had met an acquaintance, a young comedian named Dargis, and exchanged a word of greeting with him. That had been ten days ago. After Dargis, no one had seen her. The earth, indeed, seemed to have opened and swallowed her. Yet her natural features were almost as well known as a President's, and the newspapers of a continent were daily reprinting them in a hundred variations.

"A very remarkable case," repeated the clergyman, rather absently; and his neighbor, the old woman, agreed mournfully that it was. Then, as the train slowed and quieted for the stop at Eighty-Sixth Street, she spoke again, with sudden bitterness:

"Oh, they'll never catch her, sir—never! She's too smart for 'em all, Miss Hinch is."

Attracted by her tone, the stout divine inquired if she was particularly interested in the case.

"Yes, sir—I got reason to be. Jack Catherwood's mother and me was at school together, and great friends all our life long. Oh, sir," she went on, as if in answer to his look of faint surprise, "Jack was a fine gentleman, with manners and looks and all beyond his people. But he never grew away from his old mother—no, sir, never! And I don't believe ever a Sunday passed that he didn't go up and set the afternoon away with her, talking and laughing just like he was a little boy again. Maybe he done things he hadn't ought, as high-spirited lads will, but oh, sir, he was a good boy at heart—a good boy. And it does seem too hard for him to die like that—and that hussy free to go her way, ruinin' and killin'—"

"My good woman," said the clergyman presently, after glancing about, "compose yourself. No matter how diabolical this woman's skill is, her sin will assuredly find her out."

The woman dutifully lowered her handkerchief and tried to compose herself, as bidden.

"But oh, she's that clever—diabolical, just as ye say, sir. Through poor Jack we of course heard much gossip about her, and they do say that her best tricks was not done on the stage at all. They say, sir, that, sittin' around a table with her friends, she could begin and twist her face so strange and terrible that they would beg her to stop, and jump up and run from the table—frightened out of their lives, sir, grown-up people, by the terrible faces she could make. And let her only step behind her screen for a minute—for she kept her secrets well, Miss Hinch did—and she'd come walking out to you, and you could go right up to her in the full light and take her hand, and still you couldn't make yourself believe that it was her."

"Yes," said the clergyman, "I have heard that she is remarkably clever—though, as a stranger in this part of the world, I, of course, never saw her. I must say, it is all very interesting and strange."

The express had started again with a jolt, and the rumbling and roaring all but drowned out his voice. He turned his head and stared through the window at the dark flying walls. At the same moment the woman turned her head and stared full at him. When he turned back, her gaze had gone off toward the door.

The clergyman picked up the paper thoughtfully and read for a while. But when, just outside of Grand Central station, the train came to a nameless halt, he at once resumed the conversation.

"I'm a visitor in the city, from Denver, Colorado," he explained in an easy way, "and knew little or nothing about the case until an evening or two ago, when I attended a meeting of gentlemen here. The Men's Club at Saint Matthias's Church—perhaps you know the place? Upon my word, they talked of nothing else. I confess they got me quite interested in their gossip. So tonight I bought this paper to see what this extraordinary woman detective it employs had to say about it. We don't have such things in the West, you know. But I must say I was disappointed, after all the talk about her."

"Yes, sir, indeed, and no wonder, for she's told Mrs. Catherwood herself that she's never made such a failure as this, so far. It seemed like she could always catch women, up to this. It seemed like she knew in her own mind just what a woman would do, where she'd try to hide, and all, and so she could find them time and time again when the men detectives didn't know where to look. But oh, sir, she's never had to hunt for such a woman as Miss Hinch before!"

"No? I suppose not," said the clergyman. "Her theorizing here certainly seems very sketchy."

"*Theorizing,* sir! Bless my soul!" suddenly exploded the old gentleman across the aisle, to the surprise of both. "You don't suppose the clever little woman is going to show her hand in those newspaper stories, with Miss Hinch in the city and reading every line of them! In the city, sir—such is my positive conviction!"

He had roused from his nap, it seemed, just in time to overhear the episcopate criticism. Now he answered the looks of the old woman and the clergyman with an elderly cackle.

"Excuse my intrusion, I'm sure! But I can't sit silent and hear anybody run down Jessie Dark—Miss Matthewson in private life, as perhaps you don't know. No, sir! Why, there's a man at my boarding-place—remarkable fellow named Hardy, Tom Hardy—whose known her for *years!* As to those *theorizings,* sir, I can assure you she puts in there *exactly the opposite of what she really thinks!*"

"You don't tell me!" said the clergyman.

"Yes, sir! Oh, she plays the game! She has her private ideas, her clues, her schemes. The woman doesn't live who is clever enough to hoodwink Jessie Dark. I look for developments any day, sir!"

"Grand Central!" cried the guard for the second time.

Doors rolled shut, and the train flung itself on its way. Within the car, a silence ensued. The clergyman stared at the floor, and the old woman fell back upon the borrowed "extra." She appeared to be rereading the observations of Jessie Dark with considerable care. Presently she lowered the paper and began a quiet search for something under the folds of her cloak; and at length, her hands emerging empty, she broke the silence, in a lifted voice:

"Oh, sir—have you a pencil you could lend me, please? I'd like to mark something in the piece to send to Mrs. Catherwood. It's what she says here about their hideouts, as she terms them."

The obliging divine felt in his pockets, and, after a good deal of hunting, produced a pencil—a white one, with thick blue lead. She thanked him gratefully.

"How is Mrs. Catherwood bearing all this strain and anxiety?" he asked suddenly, in the loud empty car. "Have you seen her today?"

"Oh, yes, sir. I've been spending the evening with her since nine o'clock, and am just back from there now. Oh, she's dreadful broke up, sir."

She glanced at him with an uncertain air. He stared straight in front of him, saying nothing, though conceivably he had learned, in common with the rest of the world, that Jack Catherwood's mother lived, not on One Hundred and Twenty-Sixth Street, but on West Eighth Street. Possibly his silence had been an error of judgment? Perhaps that misstatement of hers had not been a slip, but something cleverer?

The woman went on, rather easily: "Oh, sir, I only hope and pray those gentlemen may be right, but it does look to Mrs. Catherwood, and me too, that if Jessie Dark was going to catch her at all, she'd have done it before now. Look at those big, bold, blue eyes she had, sir, with lashes an inch long, they say, and that terrible long chin of hers. They do say she can change the color of her eyes, not forever, of course, but put a few drops into them and make them look entirely different for a time. But that chin, ye'd say—"

She broke off; for the clergyman, without preliminaries of any sort, had picked up his heavy stick and suddenly risen.

"Why!—here we are at Fourteenth Street!" he said, quite astonished. "I must change here—well, well! You go farther, perhaps? Good night! Success to Jessie Dark, I say."

He was watching the woman's sad, faded face, and he saw break into it a look of quick surprise which, it may be, was just what he had expected.

"Fourteenth Street, sir! I'd no notion at all—for I've paid no notice to the stops. It's where I change too, sir, the expresses not stopping at my station."

"Ah?" said the clergyman, smiling a little.

He led the way, limping and leaning on his stick. They emerged upon the chill and cheerless platform, not exactly together, yet still with some reference to their acquaintanceship on the car. But the clergyman, after stumping along a few steps, all at once realized that he was walking alone, and turned. The woman had halted. Over the intervening space their eyes met.

"Come," said the man gently. "Come, let us walk about a little to keep warm."

"Oh, sir—it's too kind of you," said the woman, slowly coming forward.

From other cars two or three chilled travelers had got off to make the change; one or two more came straggling in from the street; but, scattered over the bleak, narrow expanse, they detracted little from the isolation that seemed to surround the woman and the clergyman. Step for step, the odd pair made their way to the extreme northern end of the platform.

"By the way," said the clergyman, halting abruptly, "may I see that paper again for a moment?"

"Oh, yes, sir—of course," said the woman, producing it from under her cloak. "I thought you had finished with it, and I—"

He said that he wanted only to glance at it for a moment; but he fell to looking through it page by page, with rather a searching scrutiny. The woman glanced at him several times. At last she said hesitatingly:

"I thought, sir, I'd ask the ticket-chopper could he say how often the trains run at this time of night. I'm very late as it is, sir, and I still must stop to get something to eat before I go to bed."

"An excellent idea," said the clergyman, putting the newspaper in his pocket. Side by side, they retraced their steps down the platform, questioned the chopper with scant results, and then, as by tacit consent, started slowly back again. However, before they had gone very far, the woman all at once stopped short and, with a drawn face, leaned against a pillar.

"Oh, sir, I'm afraid I'll just have to stop and get a bite somewhere before I go on. You'll think me foolish, sir, but I missed my supper entirely tonight, and there is quite a faint feeling coming over me."

The clergyman eyed her with apparent concern. He said: "Do you know, your mentioning something to eat a moment ago reminded me that I myself am all but famishing." He glanced at his watch, appearing to deliberate. "Yes—it will not take long. Come, we will find some modest eating-place together."

"Oh, sir," she stammered, "but—you wouldn't want to eat with a poor old woman like me, sir."

"Why not? Are we not all equal in the sight of God?"

They ascended the stairs together, like any prosperous parson and his poor parishioner, and, coming out into Fourteenth Street, started west. On the first block the came to a little restaurant, a brilliantly lighted, tiled and polished place of the quick-lunch sort, well filled with late patrons. But the woman timidly preferred not to stop here, saying that the glare of such places was very bad for her old eyes. The divine accepted the objection, without comment. A block farther on they found on a corner a quieter resort, and old-fashioned establishment which boasted a "Ladies' Entrance" down the side street.

They entered, and sat down at a table, facing each other. The woman read the menu through, and finally, after some embarrassed uncertainty, ordered poached eggs on toast. The clergyman ordered the same. The simple meal was soon served. Just as they were finishing it, the woman said apologetically:

"If you'll excuse me, sir—could I see the bill of fare a minute? I think I'd best take a little pot of tea to warm me up, if they do not charge too high."

"I haven't the bill of fare," said the clergyman.

They looked diligently for the cardboard strip but it was nowhere to be seen. The waiter drew near.

"Yes, sir! I left it right there when I took the order."

"I'm sure I can't imagine what's become of it," repeated the clergyman.

He looked rather hard at the woman, and found that she was looking hard at him. Both pairs of eyes turned instantly.

The waiter brought another bill of fare; the woman ordered tea; the waiter came back with it. The clergyman paid for both orders with a bill that looked hard-earned.

The tea was very hot; it could not be drunk down at a gulp. The clergyman, watching the woman sidewise as she sipped, seemed to grow more and more restless. His agile fingers drummed the tablecloth; he could hardly sit still. All at once he said: "What is that calling in the street? It sounds like newsboys."

The woman put her old head on one side and listened. "Yes, sir. There seems to be an 'extra' out."

"Upon my word," he said, after a pause. "I believe I'll go get one. Good gracious! Crime is a very interesting thing to be sure!"

He rose slowly, took down his shovel-hat from the rack near him, and, grasping his heavy stick, limped to the door. Leaving it open behind him, much to the annoyance of the proprietor in the cashier's cage, he stood for a moment, looking up and down the street. Then he took a few slow steps eastward, beckoning with his hand as he went, and so passed out of sight of the woman at the table.

The eating-place was on the corner, and, outside, the clergyman paused for half a breath. North, east, south, and west he looked, and nowhere he found what his flying glance sought. He turned the corner into the cross-street, and began to walk, at first slowly, continually looking about him. Presently his pace quickened, quickened so that he no longer even stayed to use his stout cane. In another moment he was all but running, his club-foot pounding the sidewalk heavily as he went. A newsboy thrust a paper under his nose, and he did not see it.

Far down the street, nearly two blocks away, a tall figure in a blue coat stood and stamped in the freezing sleet; and the divine was speeding straight toward him. But he did not get very near. For, as he passed the side entrance at the extreme rear of the restaurant, a departing guest dashed out so recklessly as to run full into him, stopping him dead.

Without looking at her, he knew who it was. In fact, he did not look at her at all, but turned his head hurriedly up and down, sweeping the dark street with a swift eye. But the old woman, having drawn back with a sharp exclamation as they collided, rushed breathlessly into apologies:

"Oh, sir—excuse me! A newsboy popped his head into the side door just after you went out, and I ran to him to get you the paper. But he got away too quick for me, sir. I—"

"Exactly," said the clergyman in his quiet, deep voice. "That must have been the very boy I myself was after."

On the other side, two men had just turned into the street, well muffled against the night, talking cheerfully as they trudged along. Now the clergyman looked full at the woman, and she saw that there was a smile on his face.

"Well! As he seems to have eluded us both, suppose we now return to the subway?"

"Yes, sir; it's full time I—"

"The sidewalk is so slippery," he went on gently. "Perhaps you had better take my arm."

Behind the pair in the dingy restaurant, the waiter came forward to shut the door, and lingered to discuss with the proprietor the sudden departure of his two patrons. After listening to some unfavorable comments on the ways of the clergy, the waiter returned to his table to set it in order.

On the floor in the carpeted aisle between tables lay a white piece of cardboard, which his familiar eye recognized as a torn scrap of one of his own bills of fare, face downward. He stooped and picked it up. On the back of it was some scribbling, made with a blue lead-pencil.

The handwriting was very loose and irregular, as if the writer had had his eyes elsewhere while he wrote, and it was with some difficulty that the waiter deciphered this message:

Miss Hinch 14th St. subway Get police quick

The waiter carried this curious document to the proprietor, who read it over a number of times. He was a dull man, and had a dull man's suspiciousness of a practical joke. However, after a good deal of irresolute discussion, he put on his overcoat and went out for a policeman. He turned west, and halfway up the block spied an elderly bluecoat standing in a vestibule. The policeman looked at the scribbling, and dismissed it profanely as a wag's foolishness of the sort that was bothering the life out of him a dozen times a day. He walked along with the proprietor, and, as they drew near to the latter's establishment, both became aware of footsteps thudding nearer up the cross-street from the south. As they looked, two young policemen, accompanied by a man in a uniform like a streetcar conductor's, raced around the corner and dashed into the restaurant.

The first policeman and the proprietor ran in after them, and found them staring about rather vacantly. One of the arms of the law demanded if any suspicious characters had been seen about the place, and the dull proprietor said no. The officers, looking rather flat, explained their errand. It seemed that a few moments before, the third man, who was a ticket-chopper at the subway station, had found a mysterious message lying on the floor by his box. Whence it had come, how long it had lain there, he had not the slightest idea. However, there it was. The policeman exhibited a crumpled strip torn from a newspaper, on which was scrawled in blue pencil:

Miss Hinch Miller's Restaurant police quick

The first policeman, who was both the oldest and the fattest of the three, produced the message on the bill of fare, so utterly at odds with this. The dull proprietor, now bethinking himself, mentioned the clergyman and the old woman who had taken poached eggs and tea together, called for a second bill of fare, and departed so unexpectedly by different doors. The ticket-chopper gasped out that he had seen the same pair at his station; they had come up, he said, and questioned him about trains. The three policemen were momentarily puzzled by this testimony. However, it was soon plain to them that if either the woman or the clergy really had any information about Miss Hinch—a high improbable supposition in itself—they would never have stopped with peppering the neighborhood with silly, contradictory messages.

"They're a pair of old fools tryin' to have sport with the police, and if I catch 'em, I'll run 'em in for it," growled the fattest of the officers; and this was the general verdict.

The conference broke up. The dull proprietor returned to his cage, the waiter to his table; the chopper, crestfallen, departed on the run for his chopping-box; the three policemen passed out into the bitter night. They walked together, grumbling, and their feet, perhaps by some subconscious impulse, turned eastward toward the subway. And in the middle of the next block a man came running up to them.

"Mister! Look what I picked off'n the sidewalk!"

He held up a white slab which proved to be half of a bill of fare from Miller's Restaurant. On the back of it the three peering officers saw, almost illegibly scrawled in blue pencil:

Police! Miss Hinch 14th subw

The hand trailed off on the *w* as though the writer had been suddenly interrupted. The fat policeman blasphemed and threatened arrests. But the second policeman, who was young and wiry, raised his head from the bill of fare and said suddenly: "Tim, I believe there's something in this."

"There'd ought to be thirty days on the Island in it for them," growled Tim.

"Suppose, now," said the other policeman, staring intently at him, "the old woman was Miss Hinch herself, f'r instance, and the parson was shadowing her while pretendin' he never suspicioned her, and Miss Hinch not darin' to cut and run for it till she was sure she had a clean getaway. Well, now, lissen, what better could he do—"

"That's right!" exclaimed the third policeman. "'Specially when ye think that Hinch carries a gun, an'll use it, too! Why not have a look in at the subway station, anyway, the three of us?"

The proposal carried the day. The three officers started for the subway, the citizen following. They walked at a good pace and without more talk; and both their speed and their silence had a subtle psychological reaction. As the minds of the men turned inward upon the odd behavior of the pair in Miller's Restaurant, the conviction that, after all, something important might be afoot grew and strengthened within each one of them. Unconsciously their pace quickened. It was the young, wiry policeman who first broke into an open run, but the two others had been for twenty paces on the verge of it, and followed at a rapid pace.

However, these consultation and vacillations had taken time. The stout clergyman and the poor old woman had five minutes' start on the officers of the law, and that, as it fell out, was all that the occasion required. On the street, as they made their way arm in arm to the station, they were seen, and remembered, by several belated pedestrians. It was observed by more than one that the woman lagged as if she were tired, while the club-footed cleric, supporting her on his arm, steadily kept her up to his own brisk gait.

So walking, the pair descended the subway steps, came out upon the bleak platform again, and presently stood once more at the extreme uptown end of it, just where they had waited three quarters of an hour before. Nearby, a porter had at some time overturned a bucket of water, and a splotch of thin ice ran out and over the edge of the concrete. Two young men, taking turns up and down, distinctly heard the clergyman warn the woman to look out for this ice. Far away to the north was to be heard the faint roar of an approaching train.

The woman stood nearest the track, and the clergyman stood in front of her. In the vague light their looks met, and each must have been struck by the pallor of the other's face. In addition, the woman was breathing hard, and her hands and feet betrayed some nervousness. It was, of course, difficult now to ignore the fact that for an hour they had been clinging rather desperately to each other, at all cost; but the clergyman made a creditable effort to do so. He talked without ceasing, in a voice sounding only a little unnatural, for the most part of the deplorable weather, with a good deal about a train to Jersey, which he had not previously mentioned. And all the time both of them kept turning their heads toward the station entrances, as if expecting some arrival.

As he talked, the clergyman kept his hands quietly busy. From the bottom edge of his black sack-coat he drew a pin, and stuck it deep into the ball of his middle finger. He took out his handkerchief to dust the hard sleet from his hat; and under his overcoat he pressed the handkerchief against his bleeding finger. While making these small arrangements, he held the woman's eyes with his own, talking on; and, still holding them, he suddenly broke off his random talk and peered at her cheek with concern.

"My good woman, you've scratched your cheek somehow! Why, bless me, it's bleeding quite badly."

"Never mind,—never mind," said the woman, hurriedly, and swept her eyes toward the steps.

"But good gracious—Just allow me—Ah!"

Too quick for her, he leaned forward and, through the thin veil, brushed her cheek hard with the handkerchief; removing it, he held it up so that she might see the blood for herself. But she did not glance at the handkerchief, and neither did he. His gaze was riveted upon her cheek, which looked so smooth and clear where he had smudged the clever wrinkles away.

Down the steps and upon the platform pounded the feet of the three hurrying policemen. But it was evident now that the oncoming train would thunder in just ahead of them. The clergyman, standing close in front of the woman, took a firmer grip on his heavy stick and a look of stern triumph came into his face.

"You're not so terribly clever, after all!"

The woman had sprung back from him with an irrepressible exclamation; and in that instant she was aware of the police.

However, her foot slipped on the treacherous ice—or it may have tripped on the stout cane, when the clergyman suddenly shifted his position. In the next breath the train roared past.

By a curious chance, the body of the woman was not mangled or mutilated at all. There was a deep blue bruise on the left temple, but apparently that was all; even the old black hat remained on her head, skewered fast by the long pin. It was the clergyman who first made out the body, huddled at the side of the dark track where the train had flung it—he covered the still face and superintended the removal to the platform. Two eyewitnesses pointed out the ice on which the unfortunate woman had slipped and described their horror as they saw her companion spring forward just too late to save her.

Not wishing to bring on a delirium of excitement among the clustered bystanders, the oldest policeman drew the clergyman aside and showed him the three mysterious messages. Much affected by the shocking end of his sleuthery as he was, he readily admitted having written them. He briefly recounted how the woman's strange movements on One Hundred and Twenty-Sixth Street had arrested his attention, and how, watching her closely on the car, while encouraging every opportunity for conversation, he had finally detected that she wore a wig. Unfortunately, however, her suspicions had been aroused by his interest in her, and thereafter a long battle of wits had ensued between them—he trying to summon the police without her knowledge, she dogging him close to prevent that, and at the same time watching her chance to give him the slip. He rehearsed how, in the restaurant, when he had invented an excuse to leave her for a minute, she had made a bolt and narrowly missed getting away; and finally how, having brought her back to the subway, and seeing the police at last near, he had decided to risk exposing her make-up, with this unexpectedly shocking result.

"And now," he concluded in a shaken voice, "I am naturally most anxious to know whether I am right—or have made some terrible mistake. Will you take a look at her, officer, and tell me if it is indeed—she?"

But the old policeman shook his head over the well-known ability of Miss Hinch to look like everybody else in the world but herself.

"It'll take God Almighty to tell us that, sir—saving your presence. I'll leave it f'r Headquarters," he continued, as if that were the same thing. "But, if it is her, she's gone to her reward!"

"God pity her!" said the clergyman.

"Amen! Give me your name, sir. They'll likely want you in the morning."

The clergyman gave it: Reverend Theodore Shaler, of Denver; city address, a street and number near Washington Square. Having thus discharged his duty in the affair, he started sadly to go away; but, passing by the silent figure stretched on a bench under the ticket-sellers overcoat, he bared his head and stopped for one last look at it.

The parson's gentleness and efficiency had already won favorable comments from the bystanders, and of the first quality he now gave a final proof. The dead woman's little handbag, which somebody had recovered from the track and laid at her side, had slipped to the floor;

and the clergyman, observing it, stooped silently to restore it. This last small service chanced to bring his head close to the drooped head of the dead woman; and, as he straightened up, her projecting hatpin struck his cheek and ripped a straight line down it. This in itself would have been a trifle, since the scratches soon heal. But it happened that the point of the hatpin caught under the lining of the clergyman's perfect beard and stripped it clean from him; so that, as he rose, with a sudden shrilled cry, he turned upon the astonished onlookers the bare, smooth chin of a woman, curiously long and pointed.

There were not many such chins in the world, and the urchins in the street would have recognized this one. Amid a sudden uproar which ill became the presence of the dead, the police closed in on Miss Hinch and handcuffed her with violence, fearing suicide, if not some new witchery; and at the station-house an unemotional matron divested her of the last and best of all her many disguises.

This much the police did. But it was everywhere understood that it was Jessie Dark who had really made the capture, and all the papers next morning printed pictures of the unconquerable woman, and of the hatpin with which she had reached back from another world to bring her greatest—and her last—adversary to justice.

ROMANTIC EPISODES

FOUNTAINBLUE

JOHN BUCHAN

ONCE UPON A TIME, as the storybooks say, a boy came over a ridge of hill, from which a shallow vale ran out into the sunset. It was a high, wind-blown country, where the pines had a crook in their backs and the rocks were scarred and bitten with winter storms. But below was the beginning of pastoral. Soft birch-woods, shady beeches, meadows where cattle had browsed for generations, fringed the little brown river as it twined to the sea. Farther, and the waves broke on white sands, the wonderful billows of the West which cannot bear to be silent. And between, in a garden wilderness, with the evening flaming in its windows, stood Fountainblue, my little four-square castle which guards the valley and the beaches.

The boy had torn his clothes, scratched his face, cut one finger deeply, and soaked himself with bogwater, but he whistled cheerfully and his eyes were happy. He had had an afternoon of adventure, startling emprises achieved in solitude; assuredly a day to remember and mark with a white stone. And the beginning had been most unpromising. After lunch he had been attired in his best raiment, and, in the misery of a broad white collar, despatched with his cousins to take tea with the small lady who domineered in Fountainblue. The prospect had pleased him greatly, the gardens fed his fancy, the hostess was an old confederate, and there were sure to be excellent things to eat. But his curious temper had arisen to torment him. On the way he quarrelled with his party, and in a moment found himself out of sympathy with the future. The enjoyment crept out of the prospect. He knew that he did not shine in society, he foresaw an afternoon when he would be left out in the cold and his hilarious cousins treated as the favoured guests. He reflected that tea was a short meal at the best, and that games on a lawn were a poor form of sport. Above all, he felt the torture of his collar and the straitness of his clothes. He pictured the dreary return in the twilight, when the afternoon, which had proved, after all, such a dismal failure, had come to a weary end. So, being a person of impulses, he mutinied at the gates of Fountainblue and made for the hills. He knew he should get into trouble, but trouble, he had long ago found out, was his destiny, and he scorned to avoid it. And now, having cast off the fear of God and man, he would for some short hours do exactly as he pleased.

Half-crying with regret for the delights he had forsworn, he ran over the moor to the craggy hills which had always been forbidden him. When he had climbed among the rocks awe fell upon the desolate little adventurer, and he bewailed his choice. But soon he found a blue hawk's nest, and the possession of a coveted egg inspired him to advance. By-and-by he had climbed so high that he could not return, but must needs scale Stob Ghabhar itself. With a quaking heart he achieved it, and then, in the pride of his heroism, he must venture down the Grey Correi where the wild goats lived. He saw a bearded ruffian, and pursued him with stones, stalking him cunningly till he was out of breath. Then he found odd little spleenwort ferns, which he pocketed, and high up in the rocks a friendly raven croaked his encouragement. And then, when the shadows lengthened, he set off cheerily homewards, hungry, triumphant, and very weary.

All the way home he flattered his soul. In one afternoon he had been hunter and trapper, and what to him were girls' games and pleasant things to eat? He pictured himself the hardy outlaw, feeding on oatmeal and goat's-flesh, the terror and pride of his neighbourhood. Could the little mistress of Fountainblue but see him now, how she would despise his prosaic cousins! And then, as he descended on the highway, he fell in with his forsaken party.

For a wonder they were in good spirits—so good that they forgot to remind him, in their usual way, of the domestic terrors awaiting him. A man had been there who had told them stories and shown them tricks, and there had been coconut cake, and Sylvia had a new pony on which they had ridden races. The children were breathless with excitement, very much in love with each other as common sharers in past joys. And as they talked all the colour went out of his afternoon. The blue hawk's egg was cracked, and it looked a stupid, dingy object as it lay in his cap. His rare ferns were crumpled and withered, and who was to believe his stories of Stob Ghabhar and the Grey Correi? He had been a fool to barter ponies and tea and a man who knew tricks for the barren glories of following his own fancy. But at any rate he would show no sign. If he was to be an outlaw, he would carry his outlawry well; so with a catch in his voice and tears in his eyes he jeered at his inattentive companions, upbraiding himself all the while for his folly.

II

The sun was dipping behind Stob Ghabhar when Maitland drove over the ridge of hill, whence the moor-road dips to Fountainblue. Twenty long miles from the last outpost of railway to the western sea-loch, and twenty of the barest, steepest miles in the bleak north. And all the way he had been puzzling himself with the half-painful, half-pleasing memories of a childhood which to the lonely man still overtopped the present. Every wayside bush was the home of recollection. In every burn he had paddled and fished; here he had found the jacksnipe's nest, there he had hidden when the shepherds sought him for burning the heather in May. He lost for a little the burden of his years and cares, and lived again in that old fresh world which had no boundaries, where sleep and food were all his thought at night, and adventure the sole outlook of the morning. The western sea lay like a thin line of gold beyond the moorland, and down in the valley in a bower of trees lights began to twinkle from the little castle. The remote mountains, hiding deep corries and woods in their bosom, were blurred by twilight to a single wall of hazy purple, which shut off this fairy glen impenetrably from the world. Fountainblue—the name rang witchingly in his ears. Fountainblue, the last home of the Good Folk, the last hold of the vanished kings, where the last wolf in Scotland was slain, and, as stories go, the last saint of the Great Ages taught the people,—what had Fountainblue to do with his hard world of facts and figures? The thought woke him to a sense of the present, and for a little he relished the paradox. He had left it long ago, an adventurous child; now he was returning with success behind him and a portion of life's good things his own. He was rich, very rich and famous. Few men of forty had his power, and he had won it all in fair struggle with enemies and rivals and a niggardly world. He had been feared and hated, as he had been extravagantly admired; he had been rudely buffeted by fortune, and had met the blows with a fighter's joy. And out of it all something hard and austere had shaped itself, something very much a man, but a man with little heart and a lack of kindly human failings. He was master of himself in a curious degree, but the mastery absorbed his interests. Nor had he ever regretted it, when suddenly in this outlandish place the past swept over him, and he had a vision of a long avenue of vanished hopes. It pleased and disquieted him, and as the road dipped into the valley he remembered the prime cause of this mood of vagaries.

He had come up into the north with one purpose in view, he frankly told himself. The Etheridges were in Fountainblue, and ever since, eight months before, he had met Clara Etheridge, he had forgotten his ambitions. A casual neighbour at a dinner-party, a chance partner at a ball,—and then he had to confess that this slim, dark, bright-eyed girl had broken in irrevocably upon his contentment. At first he hated it for a weakness, then he welcomed the weakness with feverish ecstasy. He did nothing by halves, so he sought her company eagerly, and, being a great man in his way, found things made easy for him. But the girl remained shy and distant, flattered doubtless by his attention, but watching him curiously as an intruder from an alien world. It was characteristic of the man that he never thought of a rival. His whole aim was to win her love; for rivalry with other men he had the contempt of a habitual conqueror. And so the uneasy wooing went on till the Etheridges left town, and he found himself a fortnight later with his work done and a visit before him to which he looked forward with all the vehemence of a nature whose strong point had always been its hope. As the road wound among the fir-trees, he tried to forecast the life at Fountainblue, and map out the future in his usual business-like way. But now the future refused to be thus shorn and parcelled: there was an unknown quantity in it which defied his efforts.

The house-party were sitting round the hall-fire when he entered. The high-roofed place, the flagged floor strewn with rugs, and its walls bright with the glow of fire on armour; gave him a boyish sense of comfort. Two men in knickerbockers were lounging on a settle, and at his entrance came forward to greet him. One was Sir Hugh Clanroyden, a follower of his own; the other he recognised as a lawyer named Durward. From the circle of women Miss Etheridge rose and welcomed him. Her mother was out, but would be back for dinner; meantime he should be shown his room. He noticed that her face was browner, her hair a little less neat, and there seemed something franker and kindlier in her smile. So in a very good humour he went to rid himself of the dust of the roads.

Durward watched him curiously, and then turned, laughing, to his companion, as the girl came back to her friends with a heightened colour in her cheeks.

"Romeo the second," he said. "We are going to be spectators of a comedy. And yet, heaven knows! Maitland is not cast for comedy."

The other shook his head. "It will never come off. I've known Clara Etheridge most of my life, and I would as soon think of marrying a dancing-girl to a bishop. She is a delightful person, and my very good friend, but how on earth is she ever to understand Maitland? And how on earth can he see anything in her? Besides, there's another man."

Durward laughed. "Despencer! I suppose he will be a serious rival with a woman; but imagine him Maitland's rival in anything else! He'd break him like a rotten stick in half an hour. I like little Despencer, and I don't care about Maitland; but all the same it is absurd to compare the two, except in lovemaking."

"Lord, it will be comic," and Clanroyden stretched his long legs and lay back on a cushion. The girls were still chattering beside the fire, and the twilight was fast darkening into evening.

"You dislike Maitland?" he asked, looking up. "Now, I wonder why?"

Durward smiled comically at the ceiling. "Oh, I know I oughtn't to. I know he's supposed to be a man's man, and that it's bad form for a man to say he dislikes him, but I'm honest enough to own to detesting him. I suppose he's great, but he's not great enough yet to compel one to fall down and worship him, and I hate greatness in the making. He goes through the world with his infernal arrogance and expects everybody to clear out of his way. I am told we live in an age of reason, but that fellow has burked reason. He never gives a reason for a thing he does, and if you try to argue he crushes you. He has killed good talk for ever with his confounded rudeness. All the little sophistries and conventions which make life tolerable are so much rubbish to him, and he shows it. The plague of him is that he can never make believe. He is as hard as iron, and as fierce as the devil, and about as unpleasant. You may respect the sledge-hammer type, but it's confoundedly dull. Why, the man has not the imagination of a rabbit, except in his description of people he dislikes. I liked him when he said that Layden reminded him of a dissipated dove, because I disliked Layden; but when Freddy Alton played the fool and people forgave him, because he was a good sort, Maitland sent him about his business, saying he had no further use for weaklings. He is so abominably cold-blooded and implacable that every one must fear him, and yet most people can afford to despise him. All the kind simple things of life are shut out of his knowledge. He has no nature, only a heart of stone and an iron will and a terribly subtle brain. Of course he is a great man—in a way, but at the best he is only half a man. And to think that he should have fallen in love, and be in danger of losing to Despencer! It's enough to make one forgive him."

Clanroyden laughed. "I can't think of Despencer. It's too absurd. But, seriously, I wish I saw Maitland well rid of this mood, married or cured. That sort of a man doesn't take things easily."

"It reminds one of Theocritus and the Cyclops in love. Who would have thought to see him up in this moorland place, running after a girl? He doesn't care for sport."

"Do you know that he spent most of his childhood in this glen, and that he *is* keen about sport? He is too busy for many holidays, but he once went with Burton to the Caucasus, and Burton said the experience nearly killed him. He said that the fellow was tireless, and as mad and reckless as a boy with nothing to lose."

"Well, that simply bears out what I say of him. He does not understand the meaning of sport. When he gets keen about anything he pursues it as carefully and relentlessly as if it were something on the Stock Exchange. Now little Despencer is a genuine sportsman in his canary-like way. He loves the art of the thing and the being out of doors. Maitland, I don't suppose, ever thinks whether it is a ceiling or the sky above his august head. Despencer—"

But at the moment Clanroyden uncrossed his legs, bringing his right foot down heavily upon his companion's left. Durward looked up and saw a young man coming towards him, smiling.

The newcomer turned aside to say something to the girls round the fire, and then came and sat on an arm of the settle. He was a straight, elegant person, with a well-tanned, regular face, and very pleasant brown eyes.

"I've had such an afternoon," he said. "You never saw a place like Cairnlora. It's quite a little stone tower all alone in a fir-wood, and nothing else between the moor and the sea. It is furnished as barely as a prison, except for the chairs, which are priceless old Dutch things. Oh, and the silver at tea was the sort of thing that only South Africans can buy nowadays. Mrs. Etheridge is devoured with envy. But the wonder of the house is old Miss Elphinstone. She must be nearly seventy, and she looks forty-five, except for her hair. She speaks broad Scots, and she has the manners of a *marquise.* I would give a lot to have had Raeburn paint her. She reminded me of nothing so much as a hill-wind with her keen high-coloured old face. Yes, I have enjoyed the afternoon."

"Jack has got a new enthusiasm," said Durward. "I wish I were like you to have a new one once a-week. By the way, Maitland has arrived at last."

"Really!" said Despencer. "Oh, I forgot to tell you something which you would never have guessed. Miss Elphinstone is Maitland's aunt, and he was brought up a good deal at Cairnlora. He doesn't take his manners from her, but I suppose he gets his cleverness from that side of the family. She disapproves of him strongly, so of course I had to defend him. And what do you think she said? 'He has betrayed his tradition. He has sold his birthright for a mess of pottage, and I wish him joy of his bargain!' Nice one for your party, Hugh."

Miss Etheridge had left the group at the fire and was sanding at Despencer's side. She listened to him with a curious air of solicitude, like an affectionate sister. At the mention of Maitland's name Clanroyden had watched her narrowly, but her face did not change. And when Despencer asked, "Where is the new arrival?" she talked of him with the utmost nonchalance.

Maitland came down to dinner, ravenously hungry and in high spirits. Nothing was changed in this house since he had stared at the pictures and imagined terrible things about the armour and broken teacups with childish impartiality. His own favourite seat was still there, where, hidden by a tapestry screen, he had quarrelled with Sylvia while their elders gossiped. This sudden flood of memories mellowed him towards the world. He was cordial to Despencer, forbore to think Durward a fool, and answered every one of Mr. Etheridge's many questions. For the first time he felt the success of his life. The old house recalled his childhood, and the sight of Clanroyden, his devoted follower, reminded him of his power. Somehow the weariful crying for the moon, which had always tortured him, was exchanged for a glow of comfort, a shade of complacency in his haggard soul.... And then the sight of Clara dispelled his satisfaction.

Here in this cheerful homely party of friends he found himself out of place. On state occasions he could acquit himself with credit, for the man had a mind. He could make the world listen to him when he chose, and the choice was habitual. But now his loneliness claimed its lawful consequences, and he longed for the little friendly graces which he had so often despised. Despencer talked of scenery and weather with a tenderness to which this man, who loved nature as he loved little else, was an utter stranger. This elegant and appropriate sentiment would have worried him past endurance, if Miss Clara had not shared it. It was she who told some folktale about the Grey Correi with the prettiest hesitancy which showed her feeling. And then the talk drifted to books and people, fitting airily about their petty world. Maitland felt himself choked by their accomplishments. Most of the subjects were ones no sane man would trouble to think of, and yet here were men talking keenly about trifles and disputing with nimble-witted cleverness on the niceties of the trivial. Feeling miserably that he was the only silent one, he plunged desperately into the stream, found himself pulled up by Despencer and deftly turned. The event gave him the feeling of having been foiled by a kitten.

Angry with the world, angrier with his own angularity, he waited for the end of the meal. Times had not changed in this house since he had been saved by Sylvia from social disgrace. But when the women left the room he found life easier. His host talked of sport, and he could tell him more about Stob Ghabhar than any keeper. Despencer, victorious at dinner, now listened like a docile pupil. Durward asked a political question, and the answer came sharp and definite. Despencer demurred gently, after his fashion. "Well, but surely—" and a grimly smiling "What do you know about it?" closed the discussion. The old Maitland had returned for the moment.

The night was mild and impenetrably dark, and the fall of waters close at hand sounded like a remote echo. An open hall-door showed that some of the party had gone out to the garden, and the men followed at random. A glimmer of white frocks betrayed the women on the lawn, standing by the little river which slipped by cascade and glide from the glen to the low pasture-lands. In the featureless dark there was no clue to locality. The place might have been Berkshire or a suburban garden.

Suddenly the scream of some animal came from the near thicket. The women started and asked what it was.

"It was a hill-fox," said Maitland to Clara. "They used to keep me awake at nights on the hill. They come and bark close to your ear and give you nightmare."

The lady shivered. "Thank Heaven for the indoors," she said. "Now, if I had been the daughter of one of your old Donalds of the Isles, I should have known that cry only too well. Wild nature is an excellent background, but give me civilisation in front."

Maitland was looking into the wood. "You will find it creep far into civilisation if you look for it. There is a very narrow line between the warm room and the savage out-of-doors."

"There are miles of luxuries," the girl cried, laughing. "People who are born in the wrong century have to hunt over half the world before they find their savagery. It is all very tame, but I love the tameness. You may call yourself primitive, Mr. Maitland, but you are the most complex and modern of us all. What would Donald of the Isles have said to politics and the Stock Exchange?"

They had strolled back to the house. "Nevertheless I maintain my belief," said the man. "You call it miles of rampart; I call the division a line, a thread, a sheet of glass. But then, you see, you only know one side, and I only know the other."

"What preposterous affectation!" the girl said, as with a pretty shiver she ran indoors. Maitland stood for a moment looking back at the darkness. Within the firelit hall, with its rugs and little tables and soft chairs, he had caught a glimpse of Despencer smoking a cigarette. As he looked towards the hills he heard the fox's bark a second time, and then somewhere from the black distance came a hawk's scream, hoarse, lonely, and pitiless. The thought struck him that the sad elemental work of wood and mountain was far more truly his own than this cosey and elegant civilisation. And, oddly enough, the thought pained him.

III

The day following was wet and windy, when a fire was grateful, and the hills, shrouded in grey mist, had no attractions. The party read idly in arm-chairs during the morning, and in the afternoon Maitland and Clanroyden went down to the stream-mouth after sea-trout. So Despencer remained to talk to Clara, and, having played many games of picquet and grown heartily tired of each other, as tea-time approached they fell to desultory comments on their friends. Maitland was beginning to interest the girl in a new way. Formerly he had been a great person who was sensible enough to admire her, but something remote and unattractive, for whom friendship (much less love) was impossible. But now she had begun to feel his power, his manhood. The way in which other men spoke of him impressed her unconsciously, and she began to ask Despencer questions which were gall and wormwood to that young man. But he answered honestly, after his fashion.

"Isn't he very rich?" she asked. "And I suppose he lives very plainly?"

"Rich as Crœsus, and he sticks in his ugly rooms in the Albany because he never thinks enough about the thing to change. I've been in them once, and you never saw such a place. He's a maniac for fresh air, so they're large enough, but they're littered like a stable with odds and ends of belongings. He must have several thousand books, and yet he hasn't a decent binding among them. He hasn't a photograph of a single soul, and only one picture, which, I believe, was his father. But you never saw such a collection of whips and spurs and bits. It smells like a harness room, and there you find Maitland, when by any chance he is at home, working half the night and up to the eyes in papers. I don't think the man has any expenses except food and rent, for he wears the same clothes for years. And he has given up horses."

"Was he fond of horses?" Miss Clara asked.

"Oh, you had better ask him. I really can't tell you any more about him."

"But how do his friends get on with him?"

"He has hardly any, but his acquaintances, who are all the world, say he is the one great man of the future. If you want to read what people think of him, you had better look at the 'Monthly.'"

Under cover of this one ungenerous word Despencer made his escape, for he hated the business, but made it the rule of his life "never to crab a fellow." Miss Clara promptly sought out the "Monthly," and found twenty pages of superfine analysis and bitter, grudging praise. She read it with interest, and then lay back in her chair and tried to fix her thoughts. It is only your unhealthy young woman who worships strength in the abstract, and the girl tried to determine whether she admired the man as a power or disliked him as a brute. She chose a compromise, and the feeling which survived was chiefly curiosity.

The result of the afternoon was that when the fishermen returned, and Maitland, in dry clothes, appeared for tea, she settled herself beside him and prepared to talk. Maitland, being healthily tired, was in an excellent temper, and he found himself enticed into what for him was a rare performance—talk about himself. They were sitting apart from the others, and, ere ever he knew, he was answering the girl's questions with an absent-minded frankness. In a little she had drawn from him the curious history of his life, which most men knew, but never from his own lips.

"I was at school for a year," he said, "and then my father died and our affairs went to pieces. I had to come back and go into an office, a sort of bank. I hated it, but it was good for me, for it taught me something, and my discontent made me ambitious. I had about eighty pounds a-year, and I saved from that. I worked too at books incessantly, and by-and-by I got an Oxford scholarship at an obscure college. I went up there, and found myself in a place where every one seemed well-off, while I was a pauper. However, it didn't trouble me much, for I had no ambition to play the fool. I only cared about two things—horses and metaphysics. I hated all games, which I thought only fit for children. I daresay it was foolish, but then you see I had had a queer upbringing. I managed to save a little money, and one vacation when I was wandering about in Norfolk, sleeping under haystacks and working in harvest-fields when my supplies ran down, I came across a farmer. He was a good fellow and a sort of sportsman, and I took a fancy to him. He had a colt to sell which I fancied more, for I saw it had blood in it. So I bought it for what seemed a huge sum to me in those days, but I kept it at his farm and I superintended its education. I broke it myself and taught it to jump, and by-and-by in my third year I brought it to Oxford and entered for the Grind on it. People laughed at me, but I knew my own business. The little boys who rode in the thing knew nothing about horses, and not one in ten could ride; so I entered and won. It was all I wanted, for I could sell my horse then, and the fellow who rode second bought it. It was decent of him, for I asked a big figure, and I think he had an idea of doing me a kindness. I made him my private secretary the other day."

"You mean Lord Drapier?" she asked.

"Yes—Drapier. That gave me money to finish off and begin in town. Oh, and I had got a first in my schools. I knew very little about anything except metaphysics, and I never went to tutors. I suppose I knew a good deal more than the examiners in my own subject, and anyhow they felt obliged to give me my first after some grumbling. Then I came up to town with just sixty pounds in my pocket, but I had had the education of a gentleman."

Maitland looked out of the window, and the sight of the mist-clad hills recalled him to himself. He wondered why he was telling the girl this story, and he stopped suddenly.

"And what did you do in town?" she asked, with interest.

"I hung round and kept my eyes open. I nearly starved, for I put half my capital on a horse which I thought was safe, and lost it. By-and-by, quite by accident, I came across a curious fellow, Ransome—you probably have heard his name. I met him in some stables where he was buying a mare, and he took a fancy to me. He made me his secretary, and then, because I liked hard work, he let me see his business. It was enormous, for the man was a genius after a fashion; and I slaved away in his office and down at the docks for about three years. He paid me just enough to keep body and soul together and cover them with clothes; but I didn't grumble, for I had a sort of idea that I was on my probation. And then my apprenticeship came to an end."

"Yes," said the girl.

"Yes; for you see Ransome was an odd character. He had a sort of genius for finance, and within his limits he was even a great administrator. But in everything else he was as simple as a child. His soul was idyllic: he loved green fields and Herrick and sheep. So it had always been his fancy to back out some day and retire with his huge fortune to some country place and live as he pleased. It seemed that he had been training me from the first day I went into the business, and now he cut the rope and left the whole enormous concern in my hands. I needed every atom of my wits, and the first years were a hard struggle. I became of course very rich; but I had to do more, I had to keep the thing at its old level. I had no natural turn for the work, and I had to acquire capacity by sheer grind. However, I managed it, and then, when I felt my position sure, I indulged myself with a hobby and went into politics."

"You call it a hobby?"

"Certainly. The ordinary political career is simply a form of trifling. There's no trade on earth where a man has to fear so few able competitors. Of course it's very public and honourable and that sort of thing, and I like it; but sometimes it wearies me to death."

The girl was looking at him with curious interest. "Do you always get what you want?" she asked.

"Never," he said.

"Then is your success all disappointment?"

"Oh, I generally get a bit of my ambitions, which is all one can hope for in this world."

"I suppose your ambitions are not idyllic, like Mr. Ransome's?"

He laughed. "No. I suppose not. I never could stand your Corot meadows and ivied cottages and village church bells. But I am at home in this glen, or used to be."

"You said that last night, and I thought it was affectation," said the girl; "but perhaps you are right. I'm not at home in this scenery, at any rate in this weather. Ugh, look at that mist driving and that spur of Stob Ghabbar! I really must go and sit by the fire."

IV

The next day dawned clear and chill, with a little frost to whiten the heather; but by midday the sun had turned August to June, and sea and land drowsed in a mellow heat. Maitland was roused from his meditations with a pipe on a garden-seat by the appearance of Miss Clara, her eyes bright with news. He had taken her in to dinner the night before, and for the first time in his life had found himself talking easily to a woman. Her interest of the afternoon had not departed; and Despencer in futile disgust shunned the drawing room, his particular paradise, and played billiards with Clanroyden in the spirit of an unwilling martyr.

"We are going out in the yacht," Miss Clara cried, as she emerged from the shadow of a fuchsia-hedge, "to the Isles of the Waves, away beyond the Seal's Headland. Do you know the place, Mr. Maitland?"

"Eilean na Cille? Yes. It used to be dangerous for currents, but a steam-yacht does not require to fear them."

"Well, we'll be ready to start at twelve, and I must go in to give orders about lunch."

A little later she came out with a bundle of letters in her hands. "Here are your letters, Mr. Maitland; but you mustn't try to answer them, or you'll be late." He put the lot in his jacket pocket and looked up at the laughing girl. "My work is six hundred miles behind me," he said, "and today I have only the Eilean na Cille to think of." And, as she passed by, another name took the place of the Eilean, and it seemed to him that at last he had found the link which was to bind together the two natures—his boyhood and his prime.

Out on the loch the sun was beating with that steady August blaze which is more torrid than mid-summer. But as the yacht slipped between the horns of the land, it came into a broken green sea with rollers to the north where the tireless Atlantic fretted on the reefs. In a world of cool salt winds and the golden weather of afternoon, with the cries of tern and gull about the bows and the foam and ripple of green water in the wake, the party fell into a mood of supreme contentment. The restless Miss Clara was stricken into a figure of contemplation, which sat in the bows and watched the hazy blue horizon and the craggy mainland hills in silent delight. Maitland was revelling in the loss of his isolation. He had ceased to be alone, a leader, and for the moment felt himself one of the herd, a devotee of humble pleasures. His mind was blank, his eyes filled only with the sea, and the lady of his devotion, in that happy moment of romance, seemed to have come at last within the compass of his hopes.

The Islands of the Waves are low green ridges which rise little above the highest tide-mark. The grass is stiff with salt, the sparse heather and rushes are crooked with the winds, but there are innumerable little dells where a light wild scrub flourishes, and in one a spring of sweet water sends a tiny stream to the sea. The yacht's company came ashore in boats, and tea was made with a great bustle beside the well, while the men lay idly in the bent and smoked. All wind seemed to have died down, a soft, cool, airless peace like a June evening was abroad, and the heavy surging of the tides had sunk to a distant whisper. Maitland lifted his head, sniffed the air, and looked uneasily to the west, meeting the eye of one of the sailors engaged in the same scrutiny. He beckoned the man to him.

"What do you make of the weather?" he asked.

The sailor, an East-coast man from Arbroath, shook his head. "It's ower lown a' of a sudden," he said. "It looks like mair wind nor we want, but I think it'll haud till the morn."

Maitland nodded and lay down again. He smiled at the return of his old sea craft and weather-lore, on which he had prided himself in his boyhood; and when Miss Clara came up to him with tea she found him grinning vacantly at the sky.

"What a wonderful lull in the wind," she said. "When I was here last these were real isles of the waves, with spray flying over them and a great business to land. But now they might be the island in Fountainblue lake."

"Did you ever hear of the Ocean Quiet?" he asked. "I believe it to be a translation of a Gaelic word which is a synonym for death, but it is also a kind of natural phenomenon. Old people at Cairnlora used to talk of it. They said that sometimes fishermen far out at sea in blowing weather came into a place of extraordinary peace, where the whole world was utterly still and they could hear their own hearts beating."

"What a pretty fancy!" said the girl.

"Yes; but it had its other side. The fishermen rarely came home alive, and if they did they were queer to the end of their days. Another name for the thing was the Breathing of God. It is an odd idea, the passing from the wholesome turmoil of nature to the uncanny place where God crushes you by His silence."

"All the things to eat are down by the fire," she said, laughing. "Do you know, if you weren't what you are, people might think you a poet, Mr. Maitland. I thought you cared for none of these things."

"What things?" he asked. "I don't care for poetry. I am merely repeating the nonsense I was brought up on. Shall I talk to you about politics?"

"Heaven forbid! And now I will tell you my own story about these isles. There is a hermit's cell on one of them and crosses, like Iona. The hermit lived alone all winter, and was fed by boats from the shore when the weather was calm. When one hermit died another took his place, and no one knew where he came from. Now one day a great lord in Scotland disappeared from his castle. He was the King's Warden of the Marches and the greatest soldier of his day, but he disappeared utterly out of men's sight, and people forgot about him. Long years after the Northmen in a great fleet came down upon these isles, and the little chiefs fled before them. But suddenly among them there appeared an old man, the hermit of the Wave Islands, who organised resistance and gathered a strong army. No one dared oppose him, and the quarrelsome petty chiefs forgot their quarrels under his banner, for he had the air of one born to command. At last he met the invaders in the valley of Fountainblue, and beat them so utterly that few escaped in their ships. He fell himself in the first charge, but not before his followers had heard his battle-cry of 'Saint Bride,' and known that the Hermit of the Isles and the great King's Warden were the same."

"That was a common enough thing in wild times. Men grew tired of murder and glory and waving banners, and wanted quiet to make their peace with their own souls. I should have thought the craving scarcely extinct yet."

"Then here is your chance, Mr. Maitland," said the girl, laughing. "A little trouble would make the hut habitable, and you could simply disappear, leaving no address to forward your letters to. Think of the sensation, 'Disappearance of a Secretary of State,' and the wild theories and the obituaries. Then some day when the land question became urgent on the mainland, you would turn up suddenly, settle it with extraordinary wisdom, and die after confiding your life-story to some country reporter. But I am afraid it would scarcely do, for you would be discovered by Scotland Yard, which would be ignominious."

"It is a sound idea, but the old device is too crude. However, it could be managed differently. Some day, when civilisation grows oppressive, Miss Clara, I will remember your advice."

The afternoon shadows were beginning to lengthen, and from the west a light sharp wind was crisping the sea. The yacht was getting up steam, and boats were coming ashore for the party. The deep blue waters were flushing rose-pink as the level westering sun smote them from the summit of a cloud-bank. The stillness had gone, and the air was now full of sounds and colour. Miss Clara, with an eye on the trim yacht, declared her disapproval. "It is an evening for the cutter," she cried, and in spite of Mrs. Etheridge's protests she gave orders for it to be made ready. Then the self-willed young woman looked round for company. "Will you come, Mr. Maitland?" she said. "You can sail a boat, can't you? And Mr. Despencer, I shall want you to talk to me when Mr. Maitland is busy. We shall race the yacht, for we ought to be able to get through the Scart's Neck with this wind."

"I am not sure if you are wise, Miss Clara," and Maitland pulled down his brows as he looked to the west. "It will be wind—in a very little, and you stand the chance of a wetting."

"I don't mind. I want to get the full good of such an evening. You want to be near the water to understand one of our sunsets. I can be a barbarian too, you know."

It was not for Maitland to grumble at this friendliness; so he followed her into the cutter with Despencer, who had no love for the orders but much for her who gave them. He took the helm and steered, with directions from the lady, from his memory of the intricate coast. Despencer with many rugs looked to Miss Clara's comfort, and, having assured his own, was instantly entranced with the glories of the evening.

The boat tripped along for a little in a dazzle of light into the silvery grey of the open water. Far in front lay the narrow gut called the Scart's Neck, which was the by-way to the loch of Fountainblue. Then Maitland at the helm felt the sheets suddenly begin to strain, and, looking behind, saw that the Isles of the Waves were almost lost in the gloom, and that the roseate heavens were quickly darkening behind. The wind which he had feared was upon them; a few seconds more and it was sending the cutter staggering among billows. He could hardly make himself heard in the din, as he roared directions to Despencer about disposing of his person in another part of the boat. The girl with flushed face was laughing in pure joy of the storm. She caught a glimpse of Maitland's serious eye and looked over the gunwale at the threatening west. Then she too became quiet, and meekly sat down on the thwart to which he motioned her.

The gale made the Scart's Neck impossible, and the murky sky seemed to promise greater fury ere the morning. Twilight was falling, and the other entrance to the quiet loch meant the rounding of a headland and a difficult course through a little archipelago. It was the only way, for return was out of the question, and it seemed vain to risk the narrow chances of the short cut. Maitland looked down at his two companions, and reflected with pleasure that he was the controller of their fates. He had sailed much as a boy, and he found in this moment of necessity that his old lore returned to him. He felt no mistrust of his powers: whatever the gale he could land them at Fountainblue, though it might take hours and involve much discomfort. He remembered the coast like his own name; he relished the grim rage of the elements, and he kept the cutter's head out to sea with a delight in the primeval conflict.

The last flickering rays of light, coming from the screen of cloud, illumined the girl's pale face, and the sight disquieted him. There was a hint of tragedy in this game. Despencer, nervously self-controlled, was reassuring Clara. Ploughing onward in the blackening night in a frail boat on a wind-threshed sea was no work for a girl. But it was Despencer who was comforting her! Well, it was his proper work. He was made for the business of talking soft things to women. Maitland, his face hard with spray, looked into the darkness with a kind of humour in his heart. And then, as the boat shore and dipped into the storm, its human occupants seemed to pass out of the picture, and it was only a shell tossed on great waters in the unfathomable night. The evening had come, moonless and starless, and Maitland steered as best he could by the deeper blackness which was the configuration of the shore. Something loomed up that he knew for the headland, and they were drifting in a quieter stretch of sea, with the breakers grumbling ahead from the little tangle of islands.

Suddenly he fell into one of the abstractions which had always dogged him through his strenuous life. His mind was clear, he chose his course with a certain precision, but the winds and waves had become to him echoes of echoes. Wet with spray and shifting his body constantly with the movement of the boat, it yet was all a phantasmal existence, while his thoughts were following an airy morrice in a fairyland world. The motto of his house, the canting motto of old reivers, danced in his brain—"Parmi ceu haut bois conduyrai m'amie"—"Through the high wood I will conduct my love"—and in a land of green forests, dragon-haunted, he was piloting Clara robed in a quaint mediaeval gown, himself in speckless plate-armour. His fancy fled through a score of scenes, sometimes on a dark heath, or by a lonely river, or among great mountains, but always the lady and her protector. Clara, looking up from Despencer's side, saw his lips moving, noted that his eyes were glad, and for a moment hoped better things of their chances.

Then suddenly she was numb with alarm, for the cutter heeled over, and but that Maitland woke to clear consciousness and swung the sheet loose, all would have been past. The adventure nerved him and quickened his senses. The boat seemed to move more violently than the wind drove her, and in the utter blackness he felt for the first time the grip of the waters. The ugly cruel monster had wakened, and was about to wreak its anger on the toy. And then he remembered the currents which raced round Eilean Righ and the scattered isles. Dim shapes loomed up, shapes strange and unfriendly, and he felt miserably that he was as helpless now as Despencer. To the left night had wholly shut out the coast; his one chance was to run for one of the isles and risk a landing. It would be a dreary waiting for the dawn, but safety had come before any comfort. And yet, he remembered, the little islands were rock-bound and unfriendly, and he was hurrying forward in the grip of a black current with a gale behind and unknown reefs before.

And then he seemed to remember something of this current which swept along the isles. In a little—so he recalled a boyish voyage in clear weather—they would come to a place where the sea ran swift and dark beside a kind of natural wharf. Here he had landed once upon a time, but it was a difficult enterprise, needing a quick and a far leap at the proper moment, for the stream ran very fast. But if this leap were missed there was still a chance. The isle was the great Eilean Righ, and the current swung round its southern end, and then, joining with another stream, turned up its far side, and for a moment washed the shore. But if this second chance were missed, then nothing remained but to fall into the great sea-going stream and be carried out to death in the wide Atlantic. He strained his eyes to the right for Eilean Righ. Something seemed to approach, as they bent under an access of the gale. They bore down upon it, and he struggled to keep the boat's head away, for at this pace to grate upon rock would mean upsetting. The sail was down, fluttering amidships like a captive bird, and the gaunt mast bowed with the wind. A horrible fascination, the inertia of nightmare, seized him. The motion was so swift and beautiful; why not go on and onward, listlessly? And then, conquering the weakness, he leaned forward and called to Clara. She caught his arm like a child, and he pulled her up beside him. Then he beckoned Despencer, and, shrieking against the din, told him to follow him when he jumped. Despencer nodded, his teeth chattering with cold and the novel business. Suddenly out of the darkness, a yard on the right, loomed a great flat rock along which the current raced like a mill-lade. The boat made to strike, but Maitland forced her nose out to sea, and then as the stern swung round he seized his chance. Holding Clara with his left arm he stood up, balanced himself for a moment on the gunwale, and jumped. He landed sprawling on his side on some wet seaweed, over which the sea was lipping, but undeniably on land. As he pulled himself up he had a vision of the cutter, dancing like a cork, vanishing down the current into the darkness.

Holding the girl in his arms he picked his way across the rock pools to the edge of the island heather. For a moment he thought Clara had fainted. She lay still and inert, her eyes shut, her hair falling foolishly over her brow. He sprinkled some water on her face, and she revived sufficiently to ask her whereabouts. He was crossing the island to find Despencer, but he did not tell her. "You are safe," he said, and he carried her over the rough ground as lightly as a child. An intense exhilaration had seized him. He ran over the flats and strode up the low hillocks with one thought possessing his brain. To save Despencer, that of course was the far-off aim on his mind's horizon, but all the foreground was filled with the lady. "Parmi ceu haut bois"—the old poetry of the world had penetrated to his heart. The black night and the wild wind and the sea were the ministrants of love. The hollow shams of life with their mincing conventions had departed, and in this savage out-world a man stood for a man. The girl's light tweed jacket was no match for this chill gale, so he stopped for a moment, took off his own shooting-coat and put it round her. And then, as he came over a little ridge, he was aware of a grumbling of waters and the sea.

The beach was hidden in a veil of surf which sprinkled the very edge of the bracken. Beyond, the dark waters were boiling like a cauldron, for the tides in this little bay ran with the fury of a river in spate. A moon was beginning to struggle through the windy clouds, and surf, rock, and wave began to shape themselves out of the night. Clara stood on the sand, a slim, desolate figure, and clung to Maitland's arm. She was still dazed with the storm and the baffling suddenness of change. Maitland, straining his eyes out to sea, was in a waking dream. With the lady no toil was too great, no darkness terrible; for her he would scale the blue air and plough the hills and do all the lover's feats of romance. And then suddenly he shook her hand roughly from his arm and ran forward, for he saw something coming down the tide.

Before he left the boat he had lowered the sail, and the cutter swung to the current, an odd amorphous thing, now heeling over with a sudden gust and now pulled back to balance by the strong grip of the water. A figure seemed to sit in the stern, making feeble efforts to steer. Maitland knew the coast and the ways of the sea. He ran through the surf-ring into the oily-black eddies, shouting to Despencer to come overboard. Soon he was not ten yards from the cutter's line, where the current made a turn towards the shore before it washed the iron rocks to the right. He found deep water, and in two strokes was in the grip of the tides and borne wildly towards the reef. He prepared himself for what was coming, raising his feet and turning his right shoulder to the front. And then with a shock he was pinned against the rock-wall, with the tides tugging at his legs, while his hands clung desperately to a shelf. Here he remained, yelling directions to the coming boat. Surf was in his eyes, so that at first he could not see, but at last in a dip of the waves he saw the cutter, a man's form in the stern, plunging not twenty yards away. Now was his chance or never, for while the tide would take a boat far from his present place of vantage, it would carry a lighter thing, such as a man's body, in a circle nearer to the shore. He yelled again, and the world seemed to him quiet for a moment, while his voice echoed eerily in the void. Despencer must have heard it, for the next moment he saw him slip pluckily overboard, making the cutter heel desperately with his weight. And then—it seemed an age—a man, choking and struggling weakly, came down the current, and, pushing his right arm out against the rush of water, he had caught the swimmer by the collar and drawn him in to the side of the rock.

Then came the harder struggle. Maitland's left hand was numbing, and though he had a foothold, it was too slight to lean on with full weight. A second lassitude oppressed him, a supreme desire to slip into those racing tides and rest. He was in no panic about death, but he had the practical man's love of an accomplished task, and it nerved him to the extreme toil. Slowly by inches he drew himself up the edge of the reef, cherishing jealously each grip and foothold, with Despencer, half-choked and all but fainting, hanging heavily on his right arm. Blind with spray, sick with sea-water, and aching with his labours, he gripped at last the tangles of seaweed, which meant the flat surface, and with one final effort raised himself and Despencer to the top. There he lay for a few minutes with his head in a rock-pool till the first weariness had passed.

He staggered with his burden in his arms along the ragged reef to the strip of sand where Clara was weeping hysterically. The sight of her restored Maitland to vigour, the appeal of her lonely figure there in the wet brackens. She must think them all dead, he reflected, and herself desolate, for she could not have interpreted rightly his own wild rush into the waves. When she heard his voice she started, as if at a ghost, and then seeing his burden, ran towards him. "Oh, he is dead!" she cried. "Tell me! tell me!" and she clasped the inert figure so that her arm crossed Maitland's. Despencer, stupefied and faint, was roused to consciousness by a woman's kisses on his cheek, and still more by his bearer abruptly laying him on the heather. Clara hung over him like a mother, calling him by soft names, pushing his hair from his brow, forgetful of her own wet and sorry plight. And meanwhile Maitland stood watching, while his palace of glass was being shivered about his ears.

Aforetime his arrogance had kept him from any thought of jealousy; now the time and place were too solemn for trifling, and facts were laid bare before him. Sentiment does not bloom readily in a hard nature, but if it once comes to flower it does not die without tears and lamentation. The wearied man, who stood quietly beside the hysterical pair, had a moment of peculiar anguish. Then he conquered sentiment, as he had conquered all other feelings of whose vanity he was assured. He was now, as he was used to be, a man among children; and as a man he had his work. He bent over Clara. "I know a hollow in the middle of the island," he said, "where we can camp the night. I'll carry Despencer, for his ankle is twisted. Do you think you could try to walk?"

The girl followed obediently, her eyes only on her lover. Her trust in the other was infinite, her indifference to him impenetrable; while he, hopelessly conscious of his fate, saw in the slim dishevelled figure at his side the lost lady, the mistress for him of all romance and generous ambitions. The new springs in his life were choked; he had still his work, his power, and, thank God, his courage; but the career which ran out to the horizon of his vision was black and loveless. And he held in his arms the thing which had frustrated him, the thing he had pulled out of the deep in peril of his body; and at the thought life for a moment seemed to be only a comic opera with tragedy to shift the scenes.

He found a cleft between two rocks with a soft floor of heather. There had been no rain, so the bracken was dry, and he gathered great armfuls and driftwood logs from the shore. Soon he had a respectable pile of timber, and then in the nick of the cleft he built a fire. His matches, being in his jacket pocket, had escaped the drenchings of salt water, and soon with a smoke and crackling and sweet scent of burning wood, a fire was going cheerily in the darkness. Then he made couch of bracken, and laid there the still feeble Despencer. The man was more weak than ill; but for his ankle he was unhurt; and a little brandy would have brought him to himself. But this could not be provided, and Clara saw in his condition only the sign of mortal sickness. With haggard eyes she watched by him, easing his head, speaking soft kind words, forgetful of her own cold and soaking clothes. Maitland drew her gently to the fire, shook down the bracken to make a rest for her head, and left a pile of logs ready for use. "I am going to the end of the island," he said, "to light a fire for a signal. It is the only part which they can see on the mainland, and if they see the blaze they will come off for us as soon as it is light." The pale girl listened obediently. This man was the master, and in his charge was the safety of her lover and herself.

Maitland turned his back upon the warm nook, and stumbled along the ridge to the northern extremity of the isle. It was not a quarter of a mile away, but the land was so rough with gullies and crags that the journey took him nearly an hour. Just off the extreme point was a flat rock, sloping northward to a considerable height, a place from which a beacon could penetrate far over the mainland. He gathered brackens for kindling, and driftwood which former tides had heaped on the beach; and then with an armful he splashed through the shallow surf to the rock. Scrambling to the top, he found a corner where a fire might be lit, a place conspicuous and yet sheltered. Here he laid his kindling, and then in many wet journeys he carried his stores of firewood from the mainland to the rock. The lighting was nervous work, for he had few matches; but at last the dampish wood had caught, and tongues of flame shot up out of the smoke. Meantime the wind had sunk lower, the breakers seemed to have been left behind, and the eternal surge of the tides became the dominant sound to the watcher by the beacon.

And then, it seemed to him, the great convulsions of the night died away, and a curious peace came down upon the waters. The fire leaped in the air, the one living thing in a hushed and expectant world. It was not the quiet of sleep but of a sudden cessation, like the lull after a great floop or a snowslip. The tides still eddied and swayed, but it was noiselessly; the world moved, yet without sound or friction. The bitter wind which chilled his face and stirred up the red embers was like a phantom blast, without the roughness of a common gale. For a moment he seemed to be set upon a huge mountain with the world infinitely remote beneath his feet. To all men there come moments of loneliness of body, and to some few the mingled ecstasy and grief of loneliness of soul. The child-tale of the Ocean Quiet came back to him, the hour of the Breathing of God. Surely the great silence was now upon the world. But it was an evil presage, for all who sailed into it were homeless wanderers for ever after. Ah well! he had always been a wanderer, and the last gleam of home had been left behind, where by the firelight in the cold cranny a girl was crooning over her lover.

His past, his monotonous, brilliant past, slipped by with the knotless speed of a vision. He saw a boy, haunted with dreams, chafing at present delights, clutching evermore at the faint things of fancy. He saw a man, playing with the counters which others played with, fighting at first for bare existence and then for power and the pride of life. Success came over his path like a false dawn, but he knew in his heart that he had never sought it. What was that remote ineffable thing he had followed? Here in the quiet of the shadowy waters he had the moment of self-revelation which comes to all, and hopes and dim desires seemed to stand out with the clearness of accomplished facts. There had always been something elect and secret at the back of his fiercest ambitions. The ordinary cares of men had been to him but little things to be played with; he had won by despising them; casting them from him, they had fallen into the hollow of his hand. And he had held them at little, finding his rewards in his work, and in a certain alertness and freshness of spirit which he had always cherished. There is a story of island-born men who carry into inland places and the streets of cities the noise of sea-water in their ears, and hear continually the tern crying and the surf falling. So from his romantic boyhood this man had borne an arrogance towards the things of the world which had given him a contemptuous empire over a share of them. As he saw the panorama of his life no place or riches entered into it, but only himself, the haggard, striving soul, growing in power, losing, perhaps, in wisdom. And then, at the end of the way, Death, to shrivel the power to dust, and with the might of his sunbeam to waken to life the forgotten world of the spirit.

In the hush he seemed to feel the wheel and the drift of things, the cosmic order of nature. He forgot his weariness and his plashing clothes as he put more wood on the beacon and dreamed into the night. The pitiless sea, infinite, untamable, washing the Poles and hiding Earth's secrets in her breast, spoke to him with a far-remembered voice. The romance of the remote isles, the homes of his people, floating still in a twilight of old story, rose out of the darkness. His life, with its routine and success, seemed in a moment hollow, a child's game, unworthy of a man. The little social round, the manipulation of half-truths, the easy victories over fools—surely this was not the task for him. He was a dreamer, but a dreamer with an iron hand; he was scarcely in the prime of life; the world was wide and his chances limitless. One castle of cards had already been overthrown; the Ocean Quiet was undermining another. He was sick of domesticity of every sort—of town, of home, of civilisation. The sad elemental world was his, the fury and the tenderness of nature, the piece of the wilds which old folk had called the Breathing of God. *Parmi ceu haut bois conduyrai m'amie*—this was still his motto, to carry untarnished to the end an austere and beautiful dream. His little ambitions had been but shreds and echoes and shadows of this supreme reality. And his love had been but another such simulacrum; for what he had sought was no foolish, laughing girl, but the Immortal Shepherdess, who, singing the old songs of youth, drives her flocks to the hill in the first dewy dawn of the world.

Suddenly he started and turned his head. Day was breaking in a red windy sky, and somewhere a boat's oars were plashing in the sea. And then he realised for the first time that he was cold and starving and soaked to the bone.

V

MR. HENRY DURWARD TO
LADY CLAUDIA ETHERIDGE

"...Things have happened, my dear Clo, since I last wrote; time has passed; tomorrow I leave this place and go to stalk with Drapier; and yet in the stress of departure I take time to answer the host of questions with which you assailed me. I am able to give you the best of news. You have won your bet. Your prophecy about the conduct of the 'other Etheridge girl' has come out right. They are both here, as it happens, having come on from Fountainblue,—both the hero and heroine, I mean, of this most reasonable romance. You know Jack Despencer, one of the best people in the world, though a trifle given to chirping. But I don't think the grasshopper will become a burden to Miss Clara, for she likes that sort of thing. She must, for there is reason to believe that she refused for its sake the greatest match—I speak with all reverence—which this happy country could offer. I know you like Maitland as little as I do, but we agree in admiring the Colossus from a distance. Well, the Colossus has, so to speak, been laid low by a frivolous member of your sex. It is all a most romantic tale. Probably you have heard the gist of it, but here is the full and circumstantial account.

"We found Maitland beside the fire he had been feeding all night, and I shall never forget his figure alone in the dawn on that rock, drenched and dishevelled, but with his haggard white face set like a Crusader's. He took us to a kind of dell in the centre of the island, where we found Clara and Despencer shivering beside a dying fire. He had a twisted ankle and had got a bad scare, while she was perfectly composed, though she broke down when we got home. It must have been an awful business for both, but Maitland never seems to have turned a hair. I want to know two things. First, how in the presence of great danger he managed to get his dismissal from the lady,—for get it he assuredly did, and Despencer at once appeared in the part of the successful lover; second, what part he played in the night's events. Clara remembered little, Despencer only knew that he had been pulled out of the sea, but over all Maitland seems to have brooded like a fate. As usual he told us nothing. It was always his way to give the world results and leave it to find out his methods for itself....

"Despencer overwhelmed him with gratitude. His new happiness made him in love with life, and he included Maitland in the general affection. The night's events seemed to have left their mark on the great man also. He was very quiet, forgot to be rude to anybody, and was kind to both Clara and Despencer. It is his way of acknowledging defeat, the great gentleman's way, for, say what we like about him, he is a tremendous gentleman, one of the last of the breed....

"And then he went away—two days later. Just before he went Hugh Clanroyden and myself were talking in the library, which has a window opening on a flower-garden. Despencer was lying in an invalid's chair under a tree and Clara was reading to him. Maitland was saying good-bye, and he asked for Despencer. We told him that he was with Clara in the garden. He smiled one of those odd scarce smiles of his, and went out to them. When I saw his broad shoulders bending over the chair and the strong face looking down at the radiant Jack with his amiable good looks, confound it, Clo, I had to contrast the pair, and admit with Shakespeare the excellent foppery of the world. Well-a-day! 'Smooth Jacob stills robs homely Esau.' And perhaps it is a good thing, for we are most of us Jacobs, and Esau is an uncomfortable fellow in our midst.

"A week later came the surprising, the astounding news that he had taken the African Governorship. A career ruined, every one said, the finest chance in the world flung away; and then people speculated, and the story came out in bits, and there was only one explanation. It is the right one, as I think you will agree, but it points to some hidden weakness in that iron soul that he could be moved to fling over the ambitions of years because of a girl's choice. He will go and bury himself in the wilds, and our party will have to find another leader. Of course he will do his work well, but it is just as if I were to give up my chances of the Woolsack for a county-court judgeship. He will probably be killed, for he has a million enemies; he is perfectly fearless, and he does not understand the arts of compromise. It was a privilege, I shall always feel, to have know him. He was a great man, and yet—intellect, power, character, were at the mercy of a girl's caprice. As I write, I hear Clara's happy laugh below in the garden, probably at some witticism of the fortunate Jack's. Upon which, with my usual pride in the obvious, I am driven to reflect that the weak things in life may confound the strong, and that, after all, the world is to the young. . . ."

VI

SIR HUGH CLANROYDEN TO MR. HENRY DURWARD. SOME YEARS LATER

". . . I am writing this on board ship, as you will see from the heading, and shall post it when I get to the Cape. You have heard of my appointment, and I need not tell you how deep were my searchings of heart before I found courage to accept. Partly I felt that I had got my chance; partly I thought—an inconsequent feeling—that Maitland, if he had lived, would have been glad to see me in the place. But I am going to wear the Giant's Robe, and Heaven knows I have not the shoulders to fill it. Yet I am happy in thinking that I am in a small sense faithful to his memory.

"No further news, I suppose, has come of the manner of his death? Perhaps we shall never know, for it was on one of those Northern expeditions with a few men by which he held the frontier. I wonder if anyone will ever write fully the history of all that he did? It must have been a titanic work, but his methods were always so quiet that people accepted his results like a gift from Providence. He was given, one gathers, a practically free hand, and he made the country—four years' work of a man of genius. They wished to bring his body home, but he made them bury him where he fell—a characteristic last testament. And as he has gone out of the world into the world's history.

"I am still broken by his death, but, now that he is away, I begin to see more clearly. Most people, I think, misunderstood him. I was one of his nearest friends, and I only knew bits of the man. For one thing—and I hate to use the vulgar word—he was the only aristocrat I ever heard of. Our classes are three-fourths of them of yesterday's growth, without the tradition, character, manner, or any trait of an aristocracy. And the few, who are nominally of the blood, have gone to seed in mind, or are spoilt by coarse marriages, or, worst of all, have the little trifling superior airs of incompetence. But he, he had the most transcendent breeding in mind and spirit. He had no need for self-assertion, for his most casual acquaintances put him at once in a different class from all other men. He had never a trace of a vulgar ideal; men's opinions, worldly honour, the common pleasures of life, were merely degrees of the infinitely small. And yet he was no bloodless mystic. If race means anything, he had it to perfection. Dreams and fancies to him were the realities, while facts were the shadows which he made dance as it pleased him.

"The truth is, that he was the rarest of mortals, the iron dreamer. He thought in aeons and cosmic cycles, and because of it he could do what he pleased in life. We call a man practical if he is struggling in the crowd with no knowledge of his whereabouts, and yet in our folly we deny the name to the clear-sighted man who can rule the crowd from above. And here I join issue with you and everybody else. You thought it was Miss Clara's refusal which sent him abroad and interrupted his career. I read the thing otherwise. His love for the girl was a mere accident, a survival of the domestic in an austere spirit. Something, I do not know what, showed him his true desires. She may have rejected him; he may never have spoken to her; in any case the renunciation had to come. You must remember that that visit to Fountainblue was the first that he had paid since his boyhood to his boyhood's home. Those revisitings have often a strange trick of self-revelation. I believe that in that night on the island he saw our indoor civilisation and his own destiny in so sharp a contrast that he could not choose but make the severance. He found work where there could be small hope of honour or reward, but many a chance for a hero. And I am sure that he was happy, and that it was the longed-for illumination that dawned on him with the bullet which pierced his heart.

"But, you will say, the fact remains that he was once in love with Miss Clara, and that she would have none of him. I do not deny it. He was never a favourite with women; but, thank Heaven, I have better things to do than study their peculiarities...."

WHILE THE AUTO WAITS

O. HENRY

PROMPTLY AT THE BEGINNING OF TWILIGHT, came again to that quiet corner of that quiet, small park the girl in gray. She sat upon a bench and read a book, for there was yet to come a half hour in which print could be accomplished.

To repeat: Her dress was gray, and plain enough to mask its impeccancy of style and fit. A large-meshed veil imprisoned her turban hat and a face that shone through it with a calm and unconscious beauty. She had come there at the same hour on the day previous, and on the day before that; and there was one who knew it.

The young man who knew it hovered near, relying upon burnt sacrifices at the great joss, Luck. His piety was rewarded for, in turning a page, her book slipped from her fingers and bounded from the bench a full yard away.

The young man pounced upon it with instant avidity, returning it to its owner with the air that seems to flourish in parks and public places—a compound of gallantry and hope, tempered with respect for the policeman on the beat. In a pleasant voice, he risked an inconsequent remark upon the weather—that introductory topic responsible for so much of the world's unhappiness—and stood poised for a moment, awaiting his fate.

The girl looked him over leisurely; at his ordinary, neat dress and his features distinguished by nothing particular in the way of expression.

"You may sit down, if you like," she said, in a full, deliberate contralto. "Really, I would like to have you do so. The light is too bad for reading. I would prefer to talk."

The vassal of Luck slid upon the seat by her side with complaisance.

"Do you know," he said, speaking the formula with which park chairmen open their meetings, "that you are quite the stunningest girl I have seen in a long time? I had my eye on you yesterday. Didn't know somebody was bowled over by those pretty lamps of yours, did you, honeysuckle?"

"Whoever you are," said the girl, in icy tones, "you must remember that I am a lady. I will excuse the remark you have just made because the mistake was, doubtless, not an unnatural one—in your circle. I asked you to sit down; if the invitation must constitute me your honeysuckle, consider it withdrawn."

"I earnestly beg your pardon," pleaded the young man. His expression of satisfaction had changed to one of penitence and humility. "It was my fault, you know—I mean, there are girls in parks, you know—that is, of course, you don't know, but—"

"Abandon the subject, if you please. Of course I know. Now tell me about these people passing and crowding, each way, along these paths. Where are they going? Why do they hurry so? Are they happy?"

The young man had promptly abandoned his air of coquetry. His cue was now for a waiting part; he could not guess the role he would be expected to play.

"It *is* interesting to watch them," he replied, postulating her mood. "It is the wonderful drama of life. Some are going to supper and some to—er—other places. One wonders what their histories are."

"I do not," said the girl; "I am not so inquisitive. I come here to sit because here, only, can I be near the great, common, throbbing heart of humanity. My part in life is cast where its beats are never felt. Can you surmise why I spoke to you, Mr.—?"

"Parkenstacker," supplied the young man. Then he looked eager and hopeful.

"No," said the girl, holding up a slender finger, and smiling slightly. "You would recognize it immediately. It is impossible to keep one's name out of print. Or even one's portrait. This veil and this hat of my maid furnished me with an *incog.* You should have seen the chauffeur stare at it when he thought I did not see. Candidly, there are five or six names that belong in the holy of holies, and mine, by the accident of birth, is one of them. I spoke to you, Mr. Stackenpot—"

"Parkenstacker," corrected the young man, modestly.

"—Mr. Parkenstacker, because I wanted to talk, for once, with a natural man—one unspoiled by the despicable gloss of wealth and supposed social superiority. Oh! you do not know how weary I am of it—money, money, money! And of the men who surround me, dancing like little marionettes all cut by the same pattern. I am sick of pleasure, of jewels, of travel, of society, of luxuries of all kinds."

"I always had an idea," ventured the young man, hesitatingly, "that money must be a pretty good thing."

"A competence is to be desired. But when you have so many millions that—!" She concluded the sentence with a gesture of despair. "It is the monotony of it," she continued, "that palls. Drives, dinners, theatres, balls, suppers, with the gliding of superfluous wealth over it all. Sometimes the very tinkle of the ice in my champagne glass nearly drives me mad."

Mr. Parkenstacker looked ingenuously interested.

"I have always liked," he said, "to read and hear about the ways of wealthy and fashionable folks. I suppose I am a bit of a snob. But I like to have my information accurate. Now, I had formed the opinion that champagne is cooled in the bottle and not by placing ice in the glass."

The girl gave a musical laugh of genuine amusement.

"You should know," she explained, in an indulgent tone, "that we of the non-useful class depend for our amusement upon departure from precedent. Just now it is a fad to put ice in champagne. The idea was originated by a visiting Prince of Tartary while dining at the Waldorf. It will soon give way to some other whim. Just as at a dinner party this week on Madison Avenue a green kid glove was laid by the plate of each guest to be put on and used while eating olives."

"I see," admitted the young man, humbly. "These special diversions of the inner circle do not become familiar to the common public."

"Sometimes," continued the girl, acknowledging his confession of error by a slight bow, "I have thought that if I ever should love a man it would be one of lowly station. One who is a worker and not a drone.

But, doubtless, the claims of caste and wealth will prove stronger than my inclination. Just now I am besieged by two. One is a Grand Duke of a German principality. I think he has, or has had, a wife, somewhere, driven mad by his intemperance and cruelty. The other is an English Marquis, so cold and mercenary that I even prefer the diabolism of the Duke. What is it that impels me to tell you these things, Mr. Packenstacker?"

"Parkenstacker," breathed the young man. "Indeed, you cannot know how much I appreciate your confidences."

The girl contemplated him with a calm, impersonal regard that befitted the difference in their stations.

"What is your line of business, Mr. Parkenstacker?" she asked.

"A very humble one. But I hope to rise in the world. Were you really in earnest when you said that you could love a man of lowly position?"

"Indeed I was. But I said 'might.' There is the Grand Duke and the Marquis, you know. Yes; no calling could be too humble were the man what I would wish him to be."

"I work," declared Mr. Parkenstacker, "in a restaurant."

The girl shrank slightly.

"Not as a waiter?" she said, a little imploringly. "Labor is noble, but—personal attendance, you know—valets and—"

"I am not a waiter. I am cashier in"—on the street they faced that bounded the opposite side of the park was the brilliant electric sign "RESTAURANT"—"I am cashier in that restaurant you see there."

The girl consulted a tiny watch set in a bracelet of rich design upon her left wrist, and rose, hurriedly. She thrust her book into a glittering reticule suspended from her waist, for which, however, the book was too large.

"Why are you not at work?" she asked.

"I am on the night turn," said the young man; "it is yet an hour before my period begins. May I not hope to see you again?"

"I do not know. Perhaps—but the whim may not seize me again. I must go quickly now. There is a dinner, and a box at the play—and, oh! the same old round. Perhaps you noticed an automobile at the upper corner of the park as you came. One with a white body."

"And red running gear?" asked the young man, knitting his brows reflectively.

"Yes. I always come in that. Pierre waits for me there. He supposes me to be shopping in the department store across the square. Conceive of the bondage of the life wherein we must deceive even our chauffeurs. Good-night."

"But it is dark now," said Mr. Parkenstacker, "and the park is full of rude men. May I not walk—?"

"If you have the slightest regard from my wishes," said the girl, firmly, "you will remain at this bench for ten minutes after I have left. I do not mean to accuse you, but you are probably aware that autos generally bear the monogram of their owner. Again, good-night."

Swift and stately she moved away through the dusk. The young man watched her graceful form as she reached the pavement at the park's edge, and turned up along it toward the corner where stood the automobile. Then he treacherously and unhesitatingly began to dodge and skim among the park trees and shrubbery in a course parallel to her route, keeping her well in sight.

When she reached the corner she turned her head to glance at the motor car, and then passed it, continuing on across the street. Sheltered behind a convenient standing cab, the young man followed her movements closely with his eyes. Passing down the sidewalk of the street opposite the park, she entered the restaurant with the blazing sign. The place was one of those frankly glaring establishments, all white paint and glass, where one may dine cheaply and conspicuously. The girl penetrated the restaurant to some retreat at its rear, whence she quickly emerged without her hat and veil.

The cashier's desk was well to the front. A red-haired girl on the stool climbed down, glancing pointedly at the clock as she did so. The girl in gray mounted in her place.

The young man thrust his hands into his pockets and walked slowly back along the sidewalk. At the corner his foot struck a small, paper-covered volume lying there, sending it sliding to the edge of the turf. By its picturesque cover he recognized it as the book the girl had been reading. He picked it up carelessly, and saw that its title was "New Arabian Nights," the author being of the name of Stevenson. He dropped it again upon the grass, and lounged, irresolute, for a minute. Then he stepped into the automobile, reclined upon the cushions, and said two words to the chauffeur:

"Club, Henri."

BETWEEN TWO SHORES

ELLEN GLASGOW

SHE WAS LEANING AGAINST THE RAILING of the deck, gazing wistfully down upon the sea of faces on the landing below. She wore a skirt and coat of brown cloth, and her veil was raised in a white film above her small hat.

In the crowd clustering about her eager for the last glimpse of friends, she looked shy and nervous, and her brown eyes were dilated in alarm. Despite her thirty years, there was something girlish in her shrinking figure—a suggestion of the incipient emotions of youth. The fine line that time had set upon brow and lips were results of the flight of undifferentiated days, and lacked the intensity of experimental records. One might have classified her in superficial survey as a woman in whom temperamental fires had been smothered, rather than extinguished, by the ashes of unfulfilment. To existence, which is a series of rhythmic waves of the commonplace, she offered facial serenity; to life, which is a clash of opposing passions, she turned the wishful eyes of ignorance.

A tall girl, carrying an armful of crimson roses, pressed against her, and waved a heavily scented handkerchief to some one upon the landing. On the other side, a man was shouting directions in regard to a missing piece of baggage. "I marked it myself," he declared frantically. "It was to have been shipped from New Orleans to the Cunard dock. I marked it 'Not Wanted' with my own hands, and, by Jove, those dirty creoles have taken me at my word."

She rested her hand upon the railing, and leaned far over. Down below, a pretty girl in a pink shirt waist was kissing her gloved finger tips to a stout gentleman on deck. An excited group were waving congratulations to a bride and groom, who looked fatigued and slightly bored. She yawned and bowed her head to avoid the spoke of a black parasol sheltering the lady on her right. For the first time she recognized in this furtive shrinking a faint homesickness, and her thoughts recoiled to the dull Southern home, to the sisters-in-law who made her life burdensome, and to the little graveyard where the husband she had never loved lay buried. The girl with the crimson roses jostled her rudely, and from behind, some one was treading upon her gown. The insipid heat of the July sun flashed across her face, and in a vision she recalled the sweeping pastures of the old plantation, with the creek where the willows grew and the thrushes sang. Then the odor of the heavily scented handkerchief half sickened her. From the crowd some one was calling to the girl in tones of reassurance: "See you in London? Of course. Booked for 'Campania,' sailing twenty-sixth."

Suddenly the steamer gave a tremor of warning, and a volley of farewells ascended from below.

"Pleasant voyage!" called the man to the girl beside her. "Pleasant voyage!" called some one to the lady on her right. Then she realized that she was alone, and for the first time regretted that her father-in-law had not come. When the news of his delay had first reached her and she had volunteered to start alone, she had experienced a vivid elation. There was delight in the idea of freedom—of being accountable to no one, of being absolutely independent of advice. Now she wished that she had an acquaintance who would wish her godspeed, or shout an indistinct pleasantry from the crowded landing.

The steamer moved slowly out into the harbor, and the shore was white with fluttering good-byes. The girl still waved the scented cambric. Then the distance lapsed into gradual waves of blue.

She left the railing, and stumbled over a group of steamer chairs placed midway of the deck. She descended to her stateroom, which was in the center of the ship. At the door she found the stewardess, who inquired if she was "Mrs. L. Smith."

"That is my name, and I am going to be ill. I know it."

"Lie down at once. And about this bag? I thought it would give you more space if I put it in the gentleman's room. He hasn't much baggage."

Lucy Smith looked up in mystification. "But it is mine," she explained, "and I want it."

Then the boat gave a lurch, and she undressed and climbed into her berth.

The next day, after a sleepless night, she struggled up and left her stateroom, the stewardess following with her wraps. At the foot of the stairs she swayed, and fell upon the lowest step. "It's no use," she said plaintively, "I can't go up. I can't indeed."

The stewardess spoke with professional encouragement. "Oh, you're all right," she remonstrated. "Here's the gentleman now. He'll help you."

"Isn't there but one gentleman on board?" Mrs. Smith began, but her words failed.

Some one lifted her, and in a moment she was on deck and in her chair, while the stewardess wrapped rugs about her and a strange man arranged the pillows under her head. Then they both left her, and she lay with closed eyes.

"Perhaps you would like yesterday's 'Herald'?" said a voice.

She started from an uncertain doze, and looked around her. Hours had passed, and since closing her eyes the sea had grown bluer and the sun warmer. A pearl-colored foam was glistening on the waves. "I beg your pardon," she replied, turning in the direction whence the words came, "did you speak?"

The man in the next chair leaned towards her, holding a paper in his hand. He was tall and angular with commonplace features, lighted by the sympathetic gleam in his eyes.

"I asked if you would like a 'Herald'?" he repeated.

She looked at him reproachfully. "I am ill," she answered.

He smiled. "Oh, I beg your pardon," he said. "You didn't look it, and it is so hard to tell. I offered a lemon to that gray-green girl over there, and she flew into a rage. But *are* you ill in earnest?"

"I shouldn't exactly choose it for jest," she returned; "though, some how, it does make time pass. One forgets that there are such divisions as days and weeks. It all seems a blank."

"But it is very calm."

"So the stewardess says," she answered aggrievedly, "but the boat rocks dreadfully."

He did not reply, and in a moment his glance wandered to the card upon her chair. "Odd, isn't it?" he questioned.

She followed his gaze, and colored faintly. The card read: "Mrs. L. Smith." Then he pointed to a similar label upon his own chair, bearing in a rough scrawl the name, "L. Smith."

"It is a very common name," she remarked absently.

He laughed. "Very," he admitted.

"Perhaps your husband is Lawrence Smith also."

The smile passed from her lips.

"My husband is dead," she answered; "but his name was Lucien."

He folded the newspaper awkwardly. Then he spoke. "Nicer name than Lawrence," he observed.

She nodded. "A name is of very little consequence," she rejoined. "I have always felt that about every name in the world except Lucy. Lucy is mine."

He looked into her eyes. Despite her illness, they shone with a warm, fawn-like brown. "I think it is a pretty name," he said. "It is so soft."

"It has no character," she returned. "I have always known that life would have been different for me if I hadn't been called Lucy. People would not treat me like a child if I were Augusta or even Agnes—but *Lucy!*"

"People change their names sometimes," he suggested.

She laughed softly. "I tried to. I tried to become Lucinda, but I couldn't. Lucy stuck to me."

"It wouldn't be so bad without Smith," he remarked smiling.

"That was a horrible cross," she returned. "I wonder if you mind Smith as much as I do."

At first he did not answer. To her surprise his face grew grave, and she saw the haggard lines about his mouth which his smile had obscured. "It was a deuced good chance that I struck it," he said shortly, and opened his paper.

For a time they sat silent. Then, as the luncheon gong sounded and the passengers flocked past, he rose and bent over her chair. "You will have chicken broth?" he said distinctly. "I will send the steward." And before she recovered from her surprise he left her.

A little later the broth was brought, and soon after the steward reappeared bearing iced prunes. "The gentleman sent you word that you were to eat these," he said. And she sat up in bewilderment, and ate the prunes silently.

"You are very kind," she remarked timidly, when he came up from the dining-salon and threw himself into the chair beside her.

For an instant he looked at her blankly, his brow wrinkling. She saw that he was not thinking of her, and reddened.

"You were kind—about the prunes," she explained.

"The prunes?" he repeated vaguely. Then he brought himself together with a jerk. "Oh, you are the little woman who was sick—yes—I remember."

"They were very nice," she said more firmly.

"I am glad you liked them," he rejoined, and was silent. Then he broke into an irrelevant laugh, and the lines upon his forehead deepened. She saw that he carried an habitual sneer upon his lips. With a half-frightened gesture she drew from him.

"I am glad that you find life amusing," she observed stiffly. "I don't."

He surveyed her with a dogged humor. "It is not life, my dear lady, it is—you."

She spoke more stiffly still. "I don't catch your meaning," she said. "Is my hat on one side?"

He laughed again. "It is perfectly balanced, I assure you."

"Is my hair uncurled?"

"Yes, but I shouldn't have noticed it. It is very pretty."

She sat up in offended dignity. "I do not desire compliments," she returned. "I wish merely information."

Half closing his eyes, he leaned back in his chair, looking at her from under the brim of his cap. "Well, without comment, I will state that your hair has fallen upon your forehead and that a loosened lock is lying upon your check—no, don't put it back. I beg your pardon—"

A pink spot appeared in the cheek next to him. Her eyes flashed. "How intolerable you are!" she said.

The smile in his eyes deepened. "How delicious you are!" he retorted.

She rose from her chair, drawing herself to her full stature. "I shall change my seat," she began.

Then the steamer lurched, and she swayed and grasped the arm he held out. "I—I am so dizzy," she finished appealingly.

He put her back into her chair, and wrapped the rugs about her. As she still shivered, he added his own to the pile. When he placed the pillow beneath her head, she noticed that his touch was as tender as a woman's. The sneer was gone from his lips.

"But you will be cold," she remonstrated from beneath his rug.

"Not I," he responded. "I am a tough knot. If the fiery furnace has left me unscathed, a little cold wind won't do more than chap me."

His voice had grown serious, and she looked up inquiringly. "The fiery furnace?" she repeated.

"Oh, predestined damnation, if you prefer. Are you religious?"

"Don't," she pleaded, a tender light coming into her eyes, and she added: "The damned are not kind—and you are very kind."

"Kind?" he returned. "I wonder how many men we left in America would uphold that—that verdict—or how many women, for that matter?"

Her honest eyes did not waver. "I will stand by it," she replied simply.

A sudden illumination leaped to his face. "Against twelve good and true men?" he demanded daringly.

"Against a thousand—and the President thrown in."

He laughed a little bitterly. "Because of the prunes?" He was looking down into her face.

She reddened. "Because of the prunes and—and other things," she answered.

A ghost of the sneer awoke about his mouth. "I never did a meaner thing than about the prunes," he said hotly. Then he turned from her, and strode with swinging strides along the deck.

That evening he did not speak to her. They lay side by side in their steamer chairs, watching the gray mist that crept over the amber line of the horizon. She looked at his set and sallow face, where the grim line of the jaw was overcast by the constant sneer upon his reckless lips. It was not a good face, this she knew. It was the face of a man of strong will and stronger passion, who lived hard and fast. She wondered vaguely at the furrowed track he must have made of his past years. The wonder awed her, and she felt half afraid of his grimness, growing grimmer in the gathering dusk. If one were in his power, how quietly he might bend and break mere flesh and bone. But across the moodiness of his face she caught the sudden warmth of his glance, and she remembered the touch of his hands—tender as it was strong. She moved nearer, laying her fragile fingers on the arm of his chair. "I am afraid you are unhappy," she said.

He started nervously, and faced her almost roughly. "Who is happy?" he demanded sneeringly. "Are you?"

She shrank slightly. "Somehow I think that a woman is never happy," she responded gently; "but you—"

He leaned towards her, a swift change crossing his face, his keen glance softening to compassion. "Then it is dastardly unfair," he said. "What is goodness for, if it does not make one happy? I am a rough brute, and I get my desserts, but the world should be gentle to a thing like you."

"No, no," she protested, "I am not good."

His eyes lightened. "Any misdemeanors punishable by law?"

"I am discontented," she went on. "I rage when things go wrong. I am not a saint."

"I might have known it," he remarked, "or you wouldn't have spoken to me. I have known lots of saints—mostly women—and they always look the other way when a sinner comes along. The reputation of a saint is the most sensitive thing on earth. It should be kept in a glass case."

"Are you so very wicked?" she asked frankly.

He was gazing out to sea, where the water broke into waves of deepening gray. In the sky a single star shone like an emerald set in a fawn-colored dome. The lapping sound of the waves at the vessel's sides came softly through the stillness. Suddenly he spoke, his voice ringing like a jarring discord in a harmonious whole.

"Five days ago a man called me a devil," he said, "and I guess he wasn't far wrong. Only, if I was a single devil, he was a legion steeped in one. What a scoundrel he was!"

The passion in his tones caused her to start quickly. The words were shot out with the force of balls from a cannon, sustained by the impulse of evil. "Don't," she said pleadingly, "please, please don't."

"Don't what?" he demanded roughly. "Don't curse the blackest scoundrel that ever lived—and died?" Over the last word his voice weakened as if in appeal.

"Don't curse anybody," she answered. "It is not like you."

He turned upon her suspiciously. "Pshaw! How do you know?"

"I don't know. I only believe."

"I never had much use for belief," he returned; "it is a poor sort of thing."

She met his bitter gaze with one of level calm. "And yet men have suffered death for it."

Above her head an electric jet was shining, and it cast a white light upon her small figure buried under the mass of rugs. Her eyes were glowing. There was a soft suffusion upon her lashes, whether from the salt spray or from unshed tears, he could not tell.

"Well, believe in me if you choose," he said; "it won't do any harm, even if it doesn't do any good."

During the next few days he nursed her with constant care. When she came out in the morning, she found him waiting at the foot of the stairs ready to assist her on deck. When she went down at night, it was his arm upon which she leaned and his voice that wished her "Good-night" before her stateroom door. Her meals were served outside, and she soon found that his watchfulness extended to a host of trivialities.

It was not a confidential companionship. Sometimes they sat for hours without speaking, and again he attacked her with aggressive irony. At such times she smarted beneath the sting of his sneers, but it was more in pity for him than for herself. He seemed to carry in his heart a seething rage of cynicism, impassioned if impotent. When it broke control, as it often did, it lashed alike the just and the unjust, the sinner and the sinned against. It did not spare the woman for whose comfort he sacrificed himself daily in a dozen minor ways. It was as if he hated himself for the interest she inspired and hated her for inspiring it. He appeared to resent the fact that the mental pressure under which he labored had not annihilated all possibility of purer passion. And he often closed upon a gentler mood with burning bitterness.

"How about your faith?" he inquired one day, after a passing tenderness. "Is it still the evidence of virtues not visible in me?"

She flinched, as she always did at his flippancy. "There is circumstantial evidence of those," she replied, "sufficient to confound a jury."

There was a cloud upon his face. "Of the 'ministering angel' kind, I suppose," he suggested.

"Yes."

"Your judgment is warped," he went on. "Do you expect to convince by such syllogisms as: It is virtuous to make presents of prunes. He makes me presents of prunes. Therefore his is virtuous."

She looked at him with wounded eyes. "That is not kind of you," she said.

"But, my dear lady, I am not kind. That is what I am arguing for."

Her lips closed firmly. She did not answer.

"Is the assertion admitted?" he inquired.

Her mouth quivered. He saw it, and his mood melted.

"Do you mean to say," he asked, adjusting the rug about her shoulders and regarding her with an intent gaze, "that it makes any difference to you?"

The fragment of a sob broke from her. "Of course it makes a difference," she answered, "to—to be treated so."

His hand closed firmly over the rug, and rested against her shoulder.

"Why does it make a difference?" he demanded.

She stammered confusedly. "Because—because it does," she replied.

His face was very grave; the hand upon her shoulder trembled. "I hope to God it does not make a difference," he said. "Look! There is a sail."

They rose and went to the railing, following with unseeing eyes a white sail that skirted the horizon. At the vessel's side porpoises were leaping on the waves. She leaned over, her eyes brightening, her loosened hair blowing about her face in soft, brown strands. There was a pink flush in her cheeks. "I should like to be a porpoise," she said, "and to skim that blue water in the sunshine. How happy they are!"

"And you are not?"

The flush died from her cheeks. "I? Oh, no," she answered.

He leaned nearer; his hand brushed hers as it lay upon the railing.

"Did love make you happy?" he asked suddenly.

She raised her lashes, and their eyes met. "Love?" she repeated vaguely.

"That husband of yours," he explained almost harshly, "did you love him?"

Her gaze went back to the water. A wistful tremor shook her lips. "He was very good to me," she replied.

"And I suppose you loved him because he was good. Well, the reason suffices."

She looked at him steadily. "Because he was good to me," she corrected. Then she hesitated. "But I did not love him in the way you mean," she added slowly. "I know now that I did not."

"Eh!" he ejaculated half absently; and then: "How do you know it?"

She turned from him, looking after the vanishing sail, just visible in the remote violet of the distance. "There are many ways—"

His eyes rested upon the soft outline of her ear, half hidden in her blown hair. "What are they?"

She turned her face still further from him. "It made no difference to me," she said, "whether he came or went. It wearied me to be with him—and I was very selfish. When he kissed me it left me cold."

His gaze stung her sharply. "And if you loved some one," he said, "it would make great difference to you whether he came or went? It would gladden you to be with him, and when he kissed you it would not leave you cold?"

"I—I think so," she answered.

He bent towards her swiftly; then checked himself with a sneering laugh. "I'll give you a piece of valuable advice," he said; "don't allow yourself to grow sentimental. It is awful rot."

And he threw himself into his chair. He drew a note-book from his pocket, and when she seated herself he did not look up. There was a gray cast about his face, and his lips were compressed. She noticed that he was older than she at first supposed and that the hand with which he held the pencil twitched nervously. Then she lay watching him idly from beneath lowered lids.

An hour later he looked up, and their glances met. With sudden determination he closed the book and replaced it in his pocket. "You look pale," he remarked abruptly.

"Do I?" she questioned inanimatedly. "I do not see any reason why I should not."

"Perhaps—so long as it is not unbecoming to you."

"Why will you say such things?" she demanded angrily. "I detest them."

"Indeed? Yes, pallor is not unbecoming to you. It gives you an interesting look."

She rubbed the cheek next him with the edge of her rug until it glowed scarlet. "There!" she exclaimed in resentment.

"That gives you a radiant look," he remarked composedly.

Her eyes flashed. "You will make me hate you," she retorted.

He smiled slightly, his eyes half sad. "I am trying to," he responded.

She stamped her foot with impatience. "Then you won't succeed. I will not hate you. Do you hear? I will not!"

"Is it a question of will?"

"In this case, yes."

"Do you hate as you choose—and love?" he asked.

"I don't know," she replied. "I hardly think I could hate you if I would. Despite your—your hatefulness."

"Not though it were a part of wisdom?"

"Wisdom has nothing to do with—"

"With what?" he questioned.

"With hate."

"Nor with love?"

"Nor with love."

He shook himself free from an imaginary weight, passing his hand across his contracted brow. "Then so much the worse for hate," he responded, "and for love."

As she did not answer he spoke fiercely. "When you love, love a virtuous, straightaway plodder," he said. "Love a man because he is decent and plain and all the things that the romancers laugh at. Love a fool, if you will, but let him be a fool who goes to his office at nine and leaves it at six; who craves no more exciting atmosphere than the domestic one of house-girl worries and teething babies. If you ever find yourself loving a man like me, you had better make for the nearest lamp-post and—hang—"

"Hush!" she cried, her cheeks flaming. "How—how dare you?" Her voice broke sharply, and she fell to sobbing behind her raised hands.

"My God!" he said softly. She felt his breath upon her forehead, and a tremor passed over her. Then his hands fastened upon hers and drew them from her eyes. He was panting like a man who has run a race.

She was looking straight before her. A small homing bird alighted for a swift instant on the railing near them, scanning suspiciously the deserted corner—and she knew that that bird would be blazoned on her memory forever after. Then she felt the man's lips close upon her own.

"You shall love me," he said, "and right be damned!"

II

She stepped out upon the deck, her eyes shining. He met her moodily. "Shall we walk up into the bow?" he asked.

She nodded. "This is our last evening," she said. "We will make it long."

"However long we make it, there is always tomorrow."

Her face clouded. "Yes, there is tomorrow," she admitted.

She fell into step with him, and they walked the length of the deck. Once she lost her balance, and he laid his hand upon her arm. When she recovered herself, he did not remove it.

"Can we forget it?" he asked gloomily.

She smiled into his face. "I will make you," she answered. "Put your hands upon the railing—so—and watch the boat as it cuts the waves. Is it not like a bird? And see, the stars are coming out."

The salt spray dashed into their faces as they leaned far over. A wet wind blew past them, and she put up her hand to hold her hat. Her skirts were wrapped closely about her, and her figure seemed to grow taller in the gray fog that rose from the sea. The ethereal quality in her appearance was emphasized.

He drew away from her. "You are too delicate for my rough hands," he said.

"Am I?" she laughed softly; then a rising passion swelled in her voice: "I should choose to be broken by you to being caressed by any other man—"

His face whitened. "Don't say that," he protested hoarsely.

"Why not, since it is true?"

A half-moon was mounting into the heavens, and it lit the sea with a path of silver. The pearl-colored mist floated ahead of the steamer, fluttering like the filmy garments of a water sprite. A dozen stars hung overhead.

"But it is true," she answered. Her words rang clearly, with a triumphant note. For a time he did not speak. In the light of the half-moon she saw the deepening furrows upon his face. His hands were clenched.

"There is time yet," he said at last, "to withdraw a false play. Take your love back."

She trembled, and her lips parted. “I cannot,” she replied, “and I would not.”

He stretched out his arms, as if to draw her towards him, and she faltered before the passion in his glance. Then he fell back. “What a mess you are making of your life!” he said.

But his warming eyes had reassured her. “The mess is already made,” she responded.

“But it is not,” he returned. Then he summoned his flagging force. “And it shall not be.”

“How will you prevent it?”

“By an appeal to reason—”

She laughed. “What love was ever ruled by reason?”

“By proofs.”

She laughed again: “What proof ever shattered faith?”

“Great God!” he retorted passionately. “Stop! Think a moment! Look things in the face. What do you know of me?”

“I know that I love you.”

“I tell you I am a devil—”

“And I do not believe you.”

“Go back to America, and ask the first man you meet.”

“Why should I respect his opinion?”

“Because it is the opinion of the respectable public—”

“Then I don’t respect the respectable public.”

“You ought to.”

“I don’t agree with you.”

Again he was silent, and again he faced her. “What is it that you love in me?” he demanded. “It is not my face.”

“Certainly not.”

“Nor my manners?”

“Hardly.”

“Is there anything about me that is especially attractive?”

“I have not observed it.”

“Then I’ll be hanged if I know what it is!”

“So will I.”

He sighed impatiently. “No woman ever discovered it before,” he said, “though I’ve known all sorts and conditions. But then I never knew a woman like you.”

"I am glad of that," she responded.

"I would give two-thirds of my future—such as it is—if I had not known you."

"And yet you love me."

He made a step towards her, his face quivering. But his words were harsh. "My love is a rotten reed," he said. Then he turned from her, gazing gloomily out to sea. Across the water the path of moonlight lay unrolled. Small brisk waves were playing around the flying steamer. Suddenly he faced her. "Listen!" he said.

She bent her head.

"From the beginning I have lied to you—lied, do you hear? I singled you out for my own selfish ends. All my kindness, as you call it, was because of its usefulness to me. While you looked on in innocence I made you a tool in my hands for the furtherance of my own purposes. Even those confounded prunes were sent to you from any other motive than sympathy for you—"

She shivered, supporting herself against the railing. "I—I don't understand," she stammered.

"Then listen again: I needed you, and I used you. There is not a soul in this boat but believes me to be your husband. I have created the impression because I was a desperate man, and it aided me. My name is not even Lawrence Smith—"

"Stop!" she said faintly. For an instant she staggered towards him; then her grasp upon the railing tightened. "Go on," she added.

His face was as gray as the fog which shrouded it. "I left America a hunted man. When I reach the other side, I shall find them still upon my tracks. It is for an act which they call by an ugly name; and yet I would do it over again. It was justice."

She was shivering as from a strong wind. "I—I don't think I understand yet," she said.

"I have led a ruined life," he went on hurriedly. "My past record is not a pretty one—and yet there is no act of my life which I regret so little as the one for which they are running me down. It was a deed of honor, though it left blood upon my hands—"

Her quivering face was turned from him.

"I reached New York with the assistance of a friend—the only man on earth who knows and believes in me. He secured a stateroom from an L. Smith, who was delayed. I took his name as a safeguard, and when I saw yours beside me at a table, I concluded he was your husband, and I played his part in the eyes of the passengers. It succeeded well." He laughed bitterly. "Lawrence was a guess," he added.

Then before her stricken eyes his recklessness fell from him. "Oh, if I could undo this," he said, "I would go back gladly to stand my chances of the gallows—"

A sob broke from her. "Hush," she said wildly. "Have you no mercy—none?"

"You must believe this," he went on passionately, "that at the last I loved you. You must believe it."

She shook her head almost deliriously.

"You must believe it," he repeated savagely. "If I could make you believe it, I would lie down to let you walk over me. You must believe that I have loved you as I have loved no other woman in my life—as I could love no other woman but you. You must believe that, evil as I am, I am not evil enough to lie to you now. You must believe it." He put out his hands as if to touch her, but she shrank away.

"No—No!" she cried. And she fled from him into the obscurity of the deck.

All that night she sat up on the edge of her berth. Her eyes were strained, and she stared blankly at the foam breaking against the port-hole. Thought hung suspended, and she felt herself rocking mentally like a ship in open sea. She saw her future brought to bay before the threatening present, and she glanced furtively around in search of some byway of escape. The walls of the little stateroom seemed closing upon her, and she felt the upper berth bearing down. She sobbed convulsively. "It was so short," she said.

When she came up on deck next day, it was high tide and the steamer was drawing into Liverpool. She wore a closely fitting jacket, and carried a small bag in her hand. Through her lowered veil her eyes showed with scarlet lids as if she had been weeping. The crowd of passengers, leaning eagerly over the railing, parted slightly, and she caught a glimpse of the English landing, peopled by strange English faces. A sob stuck in her throat, and she fell hastily into a corner. She dreaded setting foot upon a strange shore. She heard the excited voices vaguely, as she had heard them seven days ago upon sailing. They grated upon her ears with the harsh insistence of unshared gaiety, and made her own unhappiness the more poignant.

"Why, there is Jack!" rang out the voice of a woman in front of her. "Lend me the glasses. Yes, it is Jack! And he came up from London to meet me."

Then the steamer drifted slowly to the landing, and the voyage was over. She saw the gangways swung across, and she saw a dozen men stroll leisurely aboard. Yes; the end had come. "There is no harm in good-bye," said a voice at her side.

She turned hastily. He was looking down upon her, his eyes filled with the old haunting gloom. "Good-bye," she answered.

He held out his hand. "And you will go home like a sensible woman and forget?"

"I will go home."

His face whitened. "And forget?"

"Perhaps."

"It is wise."

She looked up at him, her eyes wet with tears. "Oh, how could you?" she cried brokenly. "How could you?"

He shook his head. "Don't think of me," he responded; "it is not worth the trouble."

The hand that held her bag shook nervously. "I wish I had never seen you," she said.

Then a voice startled them.

"So you have got your wife safely across, Mr. Smith," it said, "and no worse for the voyage. May I have the pleasure?"

It was the ship's surgeon, a large man with a jovial face. "I am afraid it was not the brightest of honeymoons," he added with attempted facetiousness. She looked up, her face paling, a sudden terror in her eyes.

A man with a telegram in his hand passed them, glancing from right to left. He stopped suddenly, wheeled round, and came towards them.

All at once her voice rang clear. She laid her hand upon the arm of the man beside her. "It is a honeymoon," she said, and she smiled into the surgeon's face, "so bright that even seasickness couldn't dim it. You know it has lasted eight years—"

The surgeon smiled, and the strange man passed on.

Some one took her hand, and they descended the gangway together. As she stepped upon the landing, he looked down at her, his eyes aflame.

"For God's sake," he said, "tell me what it means?"

Her glance did not waver. "It means," she answered, "that I am on your side forever."

His hand closed over the one he held. "I ought to send you back," he said, "but I cannot."

"You cannot," she repeated resolutely.

Then her voice softened. "God bless that detective," she added fervently.

Across the passion in his eyes shot a gleam of his old reckless humor. "It was Cook's man after a tourist," he said, "but God bless him."

SOMETHING TO WORRY ABOUT

P. G. WODEHOUSE

A GIRL STOOD ON THE SHINGLE that fringes Millbourne Bay, gazing at the red roofs of the little village across the water. She was a pretty girl, small and trim. Just now some secret sorrow seemed to be troubling her, for on her forehead were wrinkles and in her eyes a look of wistfulness. She had, in fact, all the distinguishing marks of one who is thinking of her sailor lover.

But she was not. She had no sailor lover. What she was thinking of was that at about this time they would be lighting up the shop windows in London, and that of all the deadly, depressing spots she had ever visited this village of Millbourne was the deadliest.

The evening shadows deepened. The incoming tide glistened oilily as it rolled over the mud flats. She rose and shivered.

"Goo! What a hole!" she said, eyeing the unconscious village morosely. "*What* a hole!"

This was Sally Preston's first evening in Millbourne. She had arrived by the afternoon train from London—not of her own free will. Left to herself, she would not have come within sixty miles of the place. London supplied all that she demanded from life. She had been born in London; she had lived there ever since—she hoped to die there. She liked fogs, motor-buses, noise, policemen, paper boys, shops, taxi cabs, artificial light, stone pavements, houses in long, grey rows, mud, banana skins, and moving-picture exhibitions. Especially moving-pictures exhibitions. It was, indeed, her taste for these that had caused her banishment to Millbourne.

The great public is not yet unanimous on the subject of moving-picture exhibitions. Sally, as I have said, approved of them. Her father, on the other hand, did not. An austere ex-butler, who let lodgings in Ebury Street and preached on Sundays in Hyde Park, he looked askance at the "movies." It was his boast that he had never been inside a theatre in his life, and classed cinema palaces with theatres as wiles of the devil. Sally, suddenly unmasked as an habitual frequenter of these abandoned places, sprang with one bound into prominence as the Bad Girl of the Family. Instant removal from the range of temptation being the only possible plan, it seemed to Mr. Preston that a trip to the country was indicated.

He selected Millbourne because he had been butler at the Hall there, and because his sister Jane, who had been a parlour maid at the Rectory, was now married and living in the village.

Certainly he could not have chosen a more promising reformatory for Sally. Here, if anywhere, might she forget the heady joys of the cinema. Tucked away in the corner of its little bay, which an accommodating island converts into a still lagoon, Millbourne lies dozing. In all sleepy Hampshire there is no sleepier spot. It is a place of calm-eyed men and drowsy dogs. Things crumble away and are not replaced. Tradesmen book orders, and then lose interest and forget to deliver the goods. Only centenarians die, and nobody worries about anything—or did not until Sally came and gave them something to worry about.

Next door to Sally's Aunt Jane, in a cozy little cottage with a wonderful little garden, lived Thomas Kitchener, a large, grave, self-sufficing young man, who, by sheer application to work, had become already, though only twenty-five, second gardener at the Hall. Gardening absorbed him. When he was not working at the Hall he was working at home. On the morning following Sally's arrival, it being a Thursday and his day off, he was crouching in a constrained attitude in his garden, every fibre of his being concentrated on the interment of a plump young bulb. Consequently, when a chunk of mud came sailing over the fence, he did not notice it.

A second, however, compelled attention by bursting like a shell on the back of his neck. He looked up, startled. Nobody was in sight. He was puzzled. It could hardly be raining mud. Yet the alternative theory, that someone in the next garden was throwing it, was hardly less bizarre. The nature of his friendship with Sally's Aunt Jane and old Mr. Williams, her husband, was comfortable rather than rollicking. It was inconceivable that they should be flinging clods at him.

As he stood wondering whether he should go the fence and look over, or simply accept the phenomenon as one of those things which no fellow can understand, there popped up before him the head and shoulders of a girl. Poised in her right hand was a third clod, which, seeing that there was now no need for its services, she allowed to fall to the ground.

"Halloa!" she said. "Good morning."

She was a pretty girl, small and trim. Tom was by way of being the strong, silent man with a career to think of and no time for bothering about girls, but he saw that. There was, moreover, a certain alertness in her expression rarely found in the feminine population of Millbourne, who were apt to be slightly bovine.

"What do you think *you're* messing about at?" she said, affably.

Tom was a slow-minded young man, who liked to have his thoughts well under control before he spoke. He was not one of your gay rattlers. Besides, there was something about this girl which confused him to an extraordinary extent. He was conscious of new and strange emotions. He stood staring silent.

"What's your name, anyway?"

He could answer that. He did so.

"Oh! Mine's Sally Preston. Mrs. Williams is my aunt. I've come from London."

Tom had no remarks to make about London.

"Haved you lived here all your life?"

"Yes," said Tom.

"My goodness! Don't you ever feel fed up? Don't you want a change?"

Tom considered the point.

"No," he said.

"Well, *I* do. I want one now."

"It's a nice place," hazarded Tom.

"It's nothing of the sort. It's the beastliest hole in existence. It's absolutely chronic. Perhaps you wonder why I'm here. Don't think I *wanted* to come here. Not me! I was sent. It was like this." She gave him a rapid summary of her troubles. "There! Don't you call it a bit thick?" she concluded.

Tom considered this point, too.

"You must make the best of it," he said, at length.

"I won't! I'll make father take me back."

Tom considered this point also. Rarely, if ever, had he been given so many things to think about in one morning.

"How?" he inquired, at length.

"I don't know. I'll find some way. You see if I don't. I'll get away from here jolly quick, I give you *my* word."

Tom bent low over a rose bush. His face was hidden, but the brown of his neck seemed to take on a richer hue, and his ears were undeniably crimson. His feet moved restlessly, and from his unseen mouth there proceeded the first gallant speech his lips had ever framed. Merely considered as a speech, it was, perhaps, nothing wonderful; but from Tom it was a miracle of chivalry and polish.

What he said was: "I hope not."

And instinct telling him that he had made his supreme effort, and that anything further must be bathos, he turned abruptly and stalked into his cottage, where he drank tea and ate bacon and thought chaotic thoughts. And when his appetite declined to carry him more than half way through the third rasher, he understood. He was in love.

These strong, silent men who mean to be head gardeners before they are thirty, and eliminate women from their lives as a dangerous obstacle to the successful career, pay a heavy penalty when they do fall in love. The average irresponsible young man who has hung about North Street on Saturday nights, walked through the meadows and round by the mill and back home past the creek on Sunday afternoons, taken his seat in the brake for the annual outing, shuffled his way through the polka at the tradesmen's ball, and generally seized all legitimate opportunities for sporting with Amaryllis in the shade, has a hundred advantages which your successful careerer lacks. There was a hardly a moment during the days which followed when Tom did not regret his neglected education.

For he was not Sally's only victim in Millbourne. That was the trouble. Her beauty was not of that elusive type which steals imperceptibly into the vision of the rare connoisseur. It was sudden and compelling. It hit you. Bright brown eyes beneath a mass of fair hair, a determined little chin, a slim figure—these are disturbing things; and the youths of peaceful Millbourne sat up and took notice as one youth. Throw your mind back to the last musical comedy you saw. Recall the leading lady's song with chorus of young men, all proffering devotion simultaneously in a neat row? Well, that was how the lads of the village comported themselves towards Sally.

Mr. and Mrs. Williams, till then a highly-esteemed but little-frequented couple, were astonished at the sudden influx of visitors. The cottage became practically a *salon.* There was not an evening when the little sitting room looking out on the garden was not packed. It is true that the conversation lacked some of the sparkle generally found in the better class of *salon.* To be absolutely accurate, there was hardly any conversation. The youths of Millbourne were sturdy and honest. They were the backbone of England. England, in her hour of need, could have called upon them with the comfortable certainty that, unless they happened to be otherwise engaged, they would leap to her aid.

But they did not shine at small talk. Conversationally they were a spent force after they had asked Mr. Williams how his rheumatism was. Thereafter they contented themselves with sitting massively about in corners, glowering at each other. Still, it was all very jolly and sociable, and helped to pass the long evenings. And, as Mrs. Williams pointed out, in reply to some rather strong remarks from Mr. Williams on the subject of packs of young fools who made it impossible for a man to get a quiet smoke in his own home, it kept them out of the public houses.

Tom Kitchener, meanwhile, observed the invasion with growing dismay. Shyness barred him from the evening gatherings, and what was going on in that house, with young bloods like Ted Pringle, Albert Parsons, Arthur Brown, and Joe Blossom (to name four of the most assiduous) exercising their fascinations at close range, he did not like to think. Again and again he strove to brace himself up to join the feasts of reason and flows of soul which he knew were taking place nightly around the object of his devotions, but every time he failed. Habit is a terrible thing; it shackles the strongest, and Tom had fallen into the habit of inquiring after Mr. Williams' rheumatism over the garden fence first thing in the morning.

It was a civil, neighbourly thing to do, but it annihilated the only excuse he could think of for looking in at night. He could not help himself. It was like some frightful scourge—the morphine habit, or something of that sort. Every morning he swore to himself that nothing would induce him to mention the subject of rheumatism, but no sooner had the stricken old gentleman's head appeared above the fence than out it came.

"Morning, Mr. Williams."

"Morning, Tom."

Pause, indicative of a strong man struggling with himself; then:—

"How's the rheumatism, Mr. Williams?"

"Better, thank'ee, Tom."

And there he was, with his guns spiked.

However, he did not give up. He brought to his wooing the same determination which had made him second gardener at the Hall at twenty-five. He was a novice at the game, but instinct told him that a good line of action was to shower gifts. He did so. All he had to shower was vegetables, and he showered them in a way that would have caused the goddess Ceres to be talked about. His garden became a perfect crater, erupting vegetables. Why vegetables? I think I hear some heckler cry. Why not flowers—fresh, fair, fragrant flowers? You can do a lot with flowers. Girls love them. There is poetry in them. And, what is more, there is a recognised language of flowers. Shoot in a rose, or a calceolaria, or an herbaceous border, or something, I gather, and you have made a formal proposal of marriage without any of the trouble of rehearsing a long speech and practising appropriate gestures in front of your bedroom looking glass. Why, then, did not Thomas Kitchener give Sally Preston flowers? Well, you see, unfortunately, it was now late autumn, and there were no flowers. Nature had temporarily exhausted her floral blessings, and was jogging along with potatoes and artichokes and things. Love is like that. It invariably comes just at the wrong time. A few months before there had been enough roses in Tom Kitchener's garden to win the hearts of a dozen girls. Now there were only vegetables. 'Twas ever thus.

It was not to be expected that a devotion so practically displayed should escape comment. This was supplied by that shrewd observer, old Mr. Williams. He spoke seriously to Tom across the fence on the subject of his passion.

"Young Tom," he said, "drop it."

Tom muttered unintelligibly. Mr. Williams adjusted the top hat without which he never stirred abroad, even into his garden. He blinked benevolently at Tom.

"You're making up to that young gal of Jane's," he proceeded. "You can't deceive *me.* All these p'taties, and what not. *I* seen your game fast enough. Just you drop it, young Tom."

"Why?" muttered Tom, rebelliously. A sudden distaste for old Mr. Williams blazed within him.

"Why? 'Cos you'll only burn your fingers if you don't, that's why. I been watching this young gal of Jane's, and I seen what sort of a young gal she be. She's a flipperty piece, that's what she be. You marry that young gal, Tom, and you'll never have no more quiet and happiness. She's just take and turn the place upsy-down on you. The man as marries that young gal has got to be master in his own home. He's got to show her what's what. Now, you ain't got the devil in you to do that, Tom. You're what I might call a sort of a sheep. I admires it in you, Tom. I like to see a young man steady and quiet, same as what you be. So that's how it is, you see. Just you drop this foolishness, young Tom, and leave that young gal be, else you'll burn your fingers, same as what I say."

And, giving his top hat a rakish tilt, the old gentleman ambled indoors, satisfied that he had dropped a guarded hint in a pleasant and tactful manner.

It is to be supposed that this interview stung Tom to swift action. Otherwise, one cannot explain why he should not have been just as reticent on the subject nearest his heart when bestowing on Sally the twenty-seventh cabbage as he had been when administering the hundred and sixtieth potato. At any rate, the fact remains that, as that fateful vegetable changed hands across the fence, something resembling a proposal of marriage did actually proceed from him. As a sustained piece of emotional prose it fell short of the highest standard. Most of it was lost at the back of his throat, and what did emerge was mainly inaudible. However, as she distinctly caught the word "love" twice, and as Tom was shuffling his feet and streaming with perspiration, and looking everywhere at once except at her, Sally grasped the situation. Whereupon, without any visible emotion, she accepted him.

Tom had to ask her to repeat her remark. He could not believe his luck. It is singular how diffident a normally self-confident man can become, once he is in love. When Colonel Milvery, of the Hall, had informed him of his promotion to the post of second gardener, Tom had demanded no *encore.* He knew his worth. He was perfectly aware that he was a good gardener, and official recognition of the fact left him gratified, but unperturbed. But this affair of Sally was quite another matter. It had revolutionised his standards of value—forced him to consider himself as a man, entirely apart from his skill as a gardener. And until this moment he had had grave doubts as to whether, apart from his skill as a gardener, he amounted to much.

He was overwhelmed. He kissed Sally across the fence humbly. Sally, for her part, seemed very unconcerned about it all. A more critical man than Thomas Kitchener might have said that, to all appearances, the thing rather bored Sally.

"Don't tell anybody just yet," she stipulated.

Tom would have given much to be allowed to announce his triumph defiantly to old Mr. Williams, to say nothing of making a considerable noise about it in the village; but her wish was law, and he reluctantly agreed.

There are moments in a man's life when, however enthusiastic a gardener he may be, his soul soars above vegetables. Tom's shot with a jerk into the animal kingdom. The first present he gave Sally in his capacity of fiancé was a dog.

It was a half-grown puppy with long legs and a long tail, belonging to no one species, but generously distributing itself among about six. Sally loved it, and took it with her wherever she went. And on one of these rambles down swooped Constable Cobb, the village policeman, pointing out that, contrary to regulations, the puppy had no collar.

It is possible that a judicious meekness on Sally's part might have averted disaster. Mr. Cobb was human, and Sally was looking particularly attractive that morning. Meekness, however, did not come easily to Sally. In a speech which began as argument and ended (Mr. Cobb proving solid and unyielding) as pure cheek, she utterly routed the constable. But her victory was only a moral one, for as she turned to go Mr. Cobb, dull red and puffing slightly, was already entering particulars of the affair in his note book, and Sally knew that the last word was with him.

On her way back she met Tom Kitchener. He was looking very tough and strong, and at the sight of him a half-formed idea, which she had regretfully dismissed as impracticable, of assaulting Constable Cobb, returned to her in an amended form. Tom did not know it, but the reason why she smiled so radiantly upon him at that moment was that she had just elected him to the post of hired assassin. While she did not want Constable Cobb actually assassinated, she earnestly desired him to have his helmet smashed down over his eyes; and it seemed to her that Tom was the man to do it.

She poured out her grievance to him and suggested her scheme. She even elaborated it.

"Why shouldn't you wait for him one night and throw him into the creek? It isn't deep, and it's jolly muddy. "

"Um!" said Tom, doubtfully.

"It would just teach him," she pointed out.

But the prospect of undertaking the higher education of the police did not seem to appeal to Tom. In his heart he rather sympathised with Constable Cobb. He saw the policeman's point of view. It is all very well to talk, but when you are stationed in a sleepy village where no one ever murders, or robs, or commits arson, or even gets drunk and disorderly in the street, a puppy without a collar is simply a godsend. A man must look out for himself.

He tried to make this side of the question clear to Sally, but failed signally. She took a deplorable view of his attitude.

"I might have known you'd have been afraid," she said, with a contemptuous jerk of her chin. "Good morning."

Tom flushed. He knew he had never been afraid of anything in his life, except her; but nevertheless the accusation stung. And as he was still afraid of her he stammered as he began to deny the charge.

"Oh, leave off!" said Sally, irritably. "Suck a lozenge."

"I'm not afraid," said Tom, condensing his remarks to their minimum as his only chance of being intelligible.

"You are."

"I'm not. It's just that I—"

A nasty gleam came into Sally's eyes. Her manner was haughty.

"It doesn't matter." She paused. "I've no doubt Ted Pringle will do what I want."

For all her contempt, she could not keep a touch of uneasiness from her eyes as she prepared to make her next remark. There was a look about

Tom's set jaw which made her hesitate. But her temper had run away with her, and she went on.

"I am sure he will," she said. "When we became engaged he said that he would do anything for me."

There are some speeches that are such conversational knock-out blows that one can hardly believe that life will ever pick itself up and go on again after them. Yet it does. The dramatist brings down the curtain on such speeches. The novelist blocks his reader's path with a zareba of stars. But in life there are no curtains, no stars, nothing final and definite—only ragged pauses and discomfort. There was such a pause now.

"What do you mean?" said Tom at last. "You promised to marry me."

"I know I did—and I promised to marry Ted Pringle!"

That touch of panic which she could not wholly repress, the panic that comes to everyone when a situation has run away with them like a strange, unmanageable machine, infused a shade too much of the defiant into Sally's manner. She had wished to be cool, even casual, but she was beginning to be afraid. Why, she could not have said. Certainly she did not anticipate violence on Tom's part. Perhaps that was it. Perhaps it was just because he was so quiet that she was afraid. She had always looked on him contemptuously as an amiable, transparent lout, and now he was puzzling her. She got an impression of something formidable behind his stolidity, something that made her feel mean and insignificant.

She fought against the feeling, but it gripped her; and, in spite of herself, she found her voice growing shrill and out of control.

"I promised to marry Ted Pringle, and I promised to marry Joe Blossom, and I promised to marry Albert Parsons. And I was going to promise to marry Arthur Brown and anybody else who asked me. So now you know! I told you I'd make father take me back to London. Well, when he hears that I've promised to marry four different men, I bet he'll have me home by the first train."

She stopped. She had more to say, but she could not say it. She stood looking at him. And he looked at her. His face was grey and his mouth oddly twisted. Silence seemed to fall on the whole universe.

Sally was really afraid now, and she knew it. She was feeling very small and defenceless in an extremely alarming world. She could not have said what it was that had happened to her. She only knew that life had become of a sudden very vivid, and that her ideas as to what was amusing had undergone a striking change. A man's development is a slow and steady process of the years—a woman's a thing of an instant. In the silence which followed her words Sally had grown up.

Tom broke the silence.

"Is that true?" he said.

His voice made her start. He had spoken quietly, but there was a new note in it, strange to her. Just as she could not have said what it was that had happened to her, so now she could not have said what had happened to Tom. He, too, had changed, but how she did not know. Yet the explanation was simple. He also had, in a sense, grown up. He was no longer afraid of her.

He stood thinking. Hours seemed to pass.

"Come along!" he said, at last, and he began to move off down the road.

Sally followed. The possibility of refusing did not enter her mind.

"Where are you going?" she asked. It was unbearable, this silence.

He did not answer.

In this fashion, he leading, she following, they went down the road into a lane, and through a gate into a field. They passed into a second field, and as they did so Sally's heart gave a leap. Ted Pringle was there.

Ted Pringle was a big young man, bigger even than Tom Kitchener, and, like Tom, he was of silent habit. He eyed the little procession inquiringly, but spoke no word. There was a pause.

"Ted," said Tom, "there's been a mistake."

He stepped quickly to Sally's side, and the next moment he had swung her off her feet and kissed her.

To the type of mind that Millbourne breeds actions speak louder than words, and Ted Pringle, who had gaped, gaped no more. He sprang forward, and Tom, pushing Sally aside, turned to meet him.

I cannot help feeling a little sorry for Ted Pringle. In the light of what happened, I could wish that it were possible to portray him as a hulking brute of evil appearance and worse morals—the sort of person concerning whom one could reflect comfortably that he deserved all he got. I should like to make him an unsympathetic character, over whose downfall the reader would gloat. But honesty compels me to own that Ted was a thoroughly decent young man in every way. He was a good citizen, a dutiful son, and would certainly have made an excellent husband. Furthermore, in the dispute on hand he had right on his side fully as much as Tom. The whole affair was one of those elemental clashings of man and man where the historian cannot sympathise with either side at the expense of the other, but must confine himself to a mere statement of what occurred. And, briefly, what occurred was that Tom, bringing to the fray a pent-up fury which his adversary had had no time to generate, fought Ted to a complete standstill in the space of two minutes and a half.

Sally had watched the proceedings, sick and horrified. She had never seen men fight before, and the terror of it overwhelmed her. Her vanity received no pleasant stimulation from the thought that it was for her sake that this storm had been let loose. For the moment her vanity was dead, stunned by collision with the realities. She found herself watching in a dream. She saw Ted fall, rise, fall again, and lie where he had fallen; and then she was aware that Tom was speaking.

"Come along!"

She hung back. Ted was lying very still. Gruesome ideas presented themselves. She had just accepted them as truth when Ted wriggled. He wriggled again. Then he sat up suddenly, looked at her with unseeing eyes, and said something in a thick voice. She gave a little sob of relief. It was ghastly, but not so ghastly as what she had been imagining.

Somebody touched her arm. Tom was by her side, grim and formidable. He was wiping blood from his face.

"Come along!"

She followed him without a word. And presently, behold, in another field, whistling meditatively and regardless of impending ill, Albert Parsons.

In everything that he did Tom was a man of method. He did not depart from his chosen formula.

"Albert," he said, "there's been a mistake."

And Albert gaped, as Ted had gaped.

Tom then kissed Sally with the gravity of one performing a ritual.

The uglinesses of life, as we grow accustomed to them, lose their power to shock, and there is no doubt that Sally looked with a different eye upon this second struggle. She was conscious of a thrill of excitement, very different from the shrinking horror which had seized her before. Her stunned vanity began to tingle into life again. The fight was raging furiously over the trampled turf, and quite suddenly, as she watched, she was aware that her heart was with Tom.

It was no longer two strange brutes fighting in a field. It was her man battling for her sake.

She desired overwhelmingly that he should win, that he should not be hurt, that he should sweep triumphantly over Albert Parsons as he had swept over Ted Pringle.

Unfortunately, it was evident, even to her, that he was being hurt, and that he was very far from sweeping triumphantly over Albert Parsons. He had not allowed himself time to recover from his first battle, and his blows were slow and weary. Albert, moreover, was made of sterner stuff than Ted. Though now a peaceful tender of cows, there had been a time in his hot youth when, travelling with a circus, he had fought, week in, week out, relays of just such rustic warriors as Tom. He knew their methods—their headlong rushes, their swinging blows. They were the merest commonplaces of life to him. He slipped Tom, he sidestepped Tom, he jabbed Tom; he did everything to Tom that a trained boxer can do to a reckless novice, except knock the fight out of him, until presently, through the sheer labour of hitting, he, too, grew weary.

Now in the days when Albert Parsons had fought whole families of Toms in an evening, he had fought in rounds, with the boss holding the watch, and half-minute rests, and water to refresh him, and all orderly and proper. Today there were no rounds, no rests, no water, and the peaceful tending of cows had caused flesh to grow where there had been only muscle. Tom's headlong rushes became less easy to side-step, his swinging blows more swift than the scientific counter that shot out to check them. As he tired Tom seemed to regain strength. The tide of battle began to ebb. He clinched, and Tom threw him off. He feinted, and while he was feinting Tom was on him. It was the climax of battle—the last rally. Down went Albert, and stayed down. Physically, he was not finished; but in his mind a question had framed itself—the question, "Was it worth it?"—and he was answering, "No." There were other girls in the world. No girl was worth all this trouble.

He did not rise.

"Come along!" said Tom.

He spoke thickly. His breath was coming in gasps. He was a terrible spectacle, but Sally was past the weaker emotions. She was back in the Stone Age, and her only feeling was one of passionate pride. She tried to speak. She struggled to put all she felt into words, but something kept her dumb, and she followed him in silence.

In the lane outside his cottage, down by the creek, Joe Blossom was clipping a hedge. The sound of footsteps made him turn.

He did not recognise Tom till he spoke.

"Joe, there's been a mistake," said Tom.

"Been a gunpowder explosion, more like," said Joe, a simple, practical man. "What you been doin' to your face?"

"She's going to marry me, Joe."

Joe eyed Sally inquiringly.

"Eh? You promised to marry *me.*"

"She promised to marry all of us. You, me, Ted Pringle, and Albert Parsons."

"Promised—to—marry—all—of—us!"

"That's where the mistake was. She's only going to marry me. I—I've arranged it with Ted and Albert, and now I've come to explain to you, Joe."

"You promised to marry—!"

The colossal nature of Sally's deceit was plainly troubling Joe Blossom. He expelled his breath in a long note of amazement. Then he summed up.

"Why, you're nothing more nor less than a Joshua!"

The years that had passed since Joe had attended the village Sunday school had weakened his once easy familiarity with the characters of the Old Testament. It is possible that he had somebody else in his mind.

Tom stuck doggedly to his point.

"You can't marry her, Joe."

Joe Blossom raised his shears and clipped a protruding branch. The point under discussion seemed to have ceased to interest him.

"Who wants to?" he said. "Good riddance!"

They went down the lane. Silence still brooded over them. The words she wanted continued to evade her.

They came to a grassy bank. Tom sat down. He was feeling unutterably tired.

"Tom!"

He looked up. His mind was working dizzily.

"You're going to marry me," he muttered.

She sat down beside him.

"I know," she said. "Tom dear, lay your head on my lap and go to sleep."

If this story proves anything (beyond the advantage of being in good training when you fight), it proves that you cannot get away from the moving pictures even in a place like Millbourne; for as Sally sat there, nursing Tom, it suddenly struck her that this was the very situation with which that "Romance of the Middle Ages" film ended. You know the one I mean. Sir Percival Ye Something (which has slipped my memory for the moment) goes out after the Holy Grail; meets damsel in distress; overcomes her persecutors; rescues her; gets wounded, and is nursed back to life in her arms. Sally had seen it a dozen times. And every time she had reflected that the days of romance are dead, and that that sort of thing can't happen nowadays.

THE SHRINKING SHOE

WALTER BESANT

I

"OH YOU POOR DEAR!" said the two Elder Sisters in duet, "you've got to stay at home while we go to the ball. Good night, then. We *are* so sorry for you! We did hope that you were going too!"

"Good night, Elder Sisters," said the youngest, with a tear just showing in either eye, but not rolling down her cheek. "Go and be happy. If you *should* see the Prince you may tell him that I am waiting for the Fairy and the Pumpkin and the Mice."

The Elder Sisters fastened the last button—the sixth, was it? or the tenth perhaps—took one last critical, and reassuring, look at the glass, and departed.

When the door shut the Youngest Sister sat down by the fire; and one, two, three tears rolled down her cheeks.

Mind you, she had very good cause to cry. Many girls cry for much less. She was seventeen: she had understood that she would come out at this visit to London. Coming out, to this country girl, meant just this one dance and nothing more. But no—her sisters were invited and she was not. She was left alone at the house. And she sat down by the fire and allowed herself to be filled with gloom and sadness, and with such thoughts as, in certain antiquated histories, used to be called rebellious. In short, she was in a very bad temper indeed. Never before had she been in such a bad temper. As a general rule she was sweet-tempered as the day is long. But—which is a terrible thing to remember—there are always the possibilities of bad temper in every one: even in Katharine—Katie—Kitty, who generally looked as if she could never, never, never show by any outward sign that she was vexed, or cross, or put out, or rebellious. And now, alas! she was in a bad temper. No hope, no sunshine, no future prospects; her life was blasted—her young spring life. Disaster irretrievable had fallen upon her. She could not go to the ball. What made things worse was, the more angry she grew the louder she heard the dance music, though the band was distant more than a mile. Quite plainly she heard the musicians. They were playing a valse which she knew—a delicious, delirious, dreamy, swinging valse. She saw her sisters among a crowd of the most lovely girls in the world, whirling in the cadence that she loved upon a floor as smooth as ice, with cavaliers gallant and gay. The room was filled with maidens beautifully dressed, like her sisters, and with young men come to meet and greet them on their way. Oh, happy young men! Oh, happy girls! Katie had been brought up with such simplicity that she envied no other girl, whether for her riches or for her dresses; and was always ready to acknowledge the loveliness and the sweetness and the grace of any number of girls—even of her own age. As regards her own sex, indeed, this child of seventeen but had one fault; she considered twenty as already a serious age, and wondered how anybody could possibly laugh after five-and-twenty. And, as many, or most, girls believe, she thought that beauty was entirely a matter of dress; and that, except on state occasions, no one should think of beauty—*i.e.*, of fine dress.

She sat there for half an hour. She began to think that it would be best to go to bed and sleep off her chagrin, when a rat-tat-tat at the door roused her. Who was that? Could it—could it—could it be the Fairy with the Pumpkin and the Mice?

"My dear Katie"—it was not the Fairy, but it was the Godmother—"how sorry I am! Quick—lay out the things, Ladbrooke." Ladbrooke was a maid, and she bore a parcel. "It's not my fault. The stupid people only brought the things just now. It was my little surprise, dear. We will dress her here, Ladbrooke. I was going to bring the things in good time, to surprise you at the last moment. Never mind: you will only be a little late. I hope and trust the things will fit. I got one of your frocks, and Ladbrooke here can, if necessary——There, Katie! What do you think of that for your first ball dress?"

Katie was so astonished that she could say nothing, not even to thank her godmother. Her heart beat and her hands trembled; the maid dressed her and did her hair; her godmother gave her a necklace of pearls and a little bunch of flowers: she put on the most charming pair of white satin shoes: she found in the parcel a pair of white gloves with ever so many buttons, and a white fan with painted flowers. When she looked at the glass she could not understand it at all; for she was transformed. But never was any girl dressed so quickly.

"Oh!" she cried. "You *are* a Fairy. And you've got a Pumpkin as well?"

"The Pumpkin is at the door with the Mice. Come, dear. I shall be proud of my *débutante.*"

The odd thing was that all the time she was dressing, and all the time she sat in the carriage, Katie heard that valse tune ringing in her ears, and when they entered the ballroom that very same identical valse was being played, and the smooth floor was covered with dancers, gallant young men and lovely maidens—all she had seen and heard in her vision. Oh! there is something in the world more than coincidence. There must be; else, why did Katie . . .

"Oh, my dear," said the Elder Sisters, stopping in their dance, "you have come at last! We knew you were coming, but we couldn't tell. Shall we tell the Prince you are here?"

Then a young gentleman was presented to her. But Katie was too nervous to look up when he bowed and begged. After a little, Katie found that his step went very well with hers. She was able to consider things a little. Her first partner in her first ball was quite a young man—she had not caught his name, Mr. Geoffrey something—a handsome young man, she thought, but rather shy. He began to talk about the usual things.

"I live in the country," she said, to explain her ignorance. "And this is my first ball. So, you see, I do not know any people or anything."

He danced with her again: she was a wonderfully light dancer; she was strangely graceful; he found her, also, sweet to look at; she had soft eyes and a curiously soft voice, which was as if all the sympathy in all the world had been collected together and deposited in that little brain. He had the good fortune to take her in to supper; and, being a young man at this time singularly open to the charms of maidens, he lavished upon her all the attentions possible. Presently he was so far subdued by her winning manner that he committed the foolishness of Samson with his charmer. He told his secret. Just because she showed a little interest in him, and regarded him with eyes of wonder, he told her the great secret of his life—his ambition, the dream of his youth, his purpose. Next morning he felt he had been a fool. The girl would tell other girls, and they would all laugh together. He felt hot and ashamed for a moment. Then he thought of her eyes, and how they lightened when he whispered; and of her voice, and how it sank when she murmured sympathy and hope and faith. No—with such a girl his secret was safe.

So it was. But for her, if you think of it, was promotion indeed! For a girl who a few days before had been at school, under rules and laws, hardly daring to speak—certainly not daring to have an opinion of her own—now receiving deferential homage from a young man at least four years her senior, and actually being entrusted with his secret ambitions! More; there were other young men waiting about, asking for a dance; all treating her as if—well, modern manners do not treat young ladies with the old reverential courtesy—as if she were a person of considerable importance. But she liked the first young man the best. He had such an honest face, this young man. It was a charming supper, and, with her charming companion, Katie talked quite freely and at her ease. How nice to begin with a partner with whom one could be quite at one's ease! But everything at this ball was delightful.

After the young man had told his secret, blushing profoundly, Katie told hers—how she had nearly as possible missed her first ball; and how her sisters had gone without her and left her in the cinders, crying.

"Fairy Godmother turned up at the last moment, and when I was dressed we went out," she laughed merrily, "we found the Pumpkin and the Mice turned into lovely carriage and pair."

"It is a new version of the old story," said the young man.

"Yes," she replied thoughtfully, "and now all I want is to find the Prince."

The young man raised his eyes quickly. They said, with great humility, "If I could only be the Prince!" She read those words, and she blushed and became confused, and they talked no more that night.

"It was lovely," she said in the carriage going home. "All but one thing—one thing that I said—oh, such a stupid thing!"

"What was it you said, Katie?"

"No: I could never tell anybody. It was *too* stupid. Oh! To think of it makes me turn red. It almost spoiled the evening. And he saw it too."

"What was it, Katie?"

But she would not tell the Elder Sisters.

"Who was it," asked one of them, "that took Katie in to supper?"

"A young man named Armiger, I believe. Horace told me," said the other Elder. Horace was a cousin. "Horace says he is a cousin of a Sir Roland Armiger, about whom I know nothing. Horace says he is a good fellow—very young yet—an undergraduate somewhat. He is a nice-looking boy."

Then the Elder Sisters began to talk about matters really serious—namely, themselves and their own engagements—and Katie was forgotten.

Two days after the ball there arrived a parcel addressed to the three sisters collectively—"The Misses De Lisle." The three sisters opened it together, with Evelike curiosity.

It contained a white satin shoe; a silver buckle set with pearls adorned it, and a row of pearls ran round the open part. A most dainty shoe; a most attractive shoe; a most bewildering shoe.

"This," said the Elder Sisters, solemnly, "must be tried on by all of us in succession."

The Elder Sisters began: it was too small for either, though they squeezed and made faces and an effort and a fuss, and everything that could be made except making the foot go into the shoe. Then Katie tried it on. Wonderful to relate, the foot slipped in quite easily. Yet they say that there is nothing but coincidence in the world.

Katie blushed and laughed and blushed again. Then she folded up the shoe in its silver paper and carried it away; and nobody ever heard her mention the shoe again. But everybody knew that she kept it, and the Elder Sisters marvelled because the young prince did not come to see that shoe she tried on. He did not appear. Why not? Well—because he was too shy to call.

There are six thousand five hundred and sixty-three variants of this story, as has been discovered through the invaluable researches of the Folk-Lore Society, and it would be strange if they all ended in the same way.

II

The young man told his secret; he revealed what he had never before whispered to any living person; he told his ambition—the most sacred thing a young man possesses or can reveal.

There are many kinds of ambition; many of them are laudable; we are mostly ambitious of those things which seem to the lowest imagination to be within our reach—such, for instance, as the saving of money. Those who aspire to things which seem out of reach suffer the pain and the penalty of the common snub. This young man aspired to things which seemed to other people quite beyond his reach; for he had no money, and his otherwise highly respectable family had no political influence, and such a thing had never been heard of among his people that one of themselves should aspire to greater greatness than the succession to the family title with the family property. As a part of the new Revolution, which is already upon us, there will be few things indeed which an ambitious young man will consider beyond his reach. At the present moment, if I were to declare my ambition to become, when I grow up, Her Britannic Majesty's Ambassador at Paris, the thing would be actually received with derision. My young life would be blasted with contempt. Wait, however, for fifty years: you shall then see to what heights I will reach out my climbing hands.

Geoffrey Armiger would have soared. He saw before him the cases of Canning, of Burke, of Disraeli, of Robert Lowe, and of many others who started without any political influence and with no money, and he said to himself, "I, too, will become a Statesman."

That was the secret which he confined into Katie's ear; it was in answer to a question of hers, put quite as he could have wished, as to his future career. "I have told no one," he replied in a low voice, and with conscious flush. "I have never ventured to tell any one, because my people would not understand; they are not easily moved out of the ordinary groove. There is a family living, and I am to have it: that is the fate to which I am condemned, But—" his lips snapped; resolution flamed in his eyes.

"Oh!" cried Katie. "It is splendid! You must succeed. Oh! To be a great Statesman. Oh! There is only one thing better—to be a great Poet. You might be both."

Geoffrey replied modestly that, although he had written verse, he hardly expected to accomplish both greatness in poetry and greatness as a legislator. The latter, he declared, would be good enough for him.

That was the secret which this young man confided to the girl. You must own that, for such a young man to reveal such a secret to this girl, on the very first evening that he met her, argues for the maiden the possession of sympathetic qualities quite above the common.

III

Five years change a boy of twenty into a mature man of twenty-five, and a *débutante* of seventeen into an old woman of twenty-two. The acknowledgment of such a fact may save the historian a vast quantity of trouble.

It was five years after the great event of the ball. The family cousin, Horace, of whom mention has been already made, was sitting in his chambers at ten or eleven in the evening. With him sat his friend Sir Geoffrey Armiger, a young man whom you have already met. The death of his cousin had transformed him from a penniless youth into a baronet with a great estate (which might have been in Spain or Ireland for all the good it was), and with a great fortune in stocks. There was now no occasion for him to take the family living: that had gone to a deserving stranger; a clear field lay open for his wildest ambitions. This bad fortune to the cousin, who was still quite young, happened the year after the ball. Of course, therefore, the young man of vast ambition had already both feet on the ladder? You shall see.

"What are you going to do all summer?" asked the family cousin, Horace.

"I don't know," Geoffrey replied languidly. "Take the yacht somewhere, I suppose. Into the Baltic, perhaps. Will you come too?"

"Can't. I have work to do. I shall run over to Switzerland for three weeks perhaps. Better come with me and do some climbing."

Geoffrey shook his head.

"Man!" cried the other impatiently, "you want something to do. Doesn't it bore you—just going on day after day, day after day, with nothing to think of but your own amusement?"

Geoffrey yawned. "The Profession of Amusement," he said, "is, in fact, deadly dull."

"Then why follow it?"

"Because I am so rich. You fellows who've got nothing *must* work. When a man is not obliged to work, there are a thousand excuses. I don't believe that I *could* work now if I wanted to. Yet I used to have ambitions."

"You did. When it was difficult to find a way to live while you worked, you had enormous ambitions. 'If only I was not obliged to provide for the daily bread'; that was what you used to say. Well, now the daily bread is provided, what excuse have you?"

"I tell you a thousand excuses present themselves the moment I think of doing any work. Besides, the ambitions are dead!"

"Dead! And at five-and-twenty! They can't be dead."

"They are. Dead and buried. Killed by five years' racket. Profession of Pleasure—Pleasure, I believe they call it. No man can follow more than one profession."

"Well, old man, if the world's pleasures are already rather dry in the mouth, what will they be when you've been running after them for fifty years?"

"There are cards, I believe. Cards are always left. No,"—he got up and leaned over the mantelshelf,—"I can't say that the fortune has brought much happiness with it. That's the worst of being rich. You see very well that you are not half as happy as the fellows who are making their own way, and yet you can't give up your money and start fair with the rest. I always think of that story of the young man who was told to give up all he had to the poor. He couldn't, you see. He saw very clearly that it would be best for him; but he couldn't. I am that young man. If I was like you, with all the world to conquer, I should be ten times as strong and a hundred times as clever. I know it—yet I cannot give up the money."

"Nobody wants you to give it up. But surely you could go on like other fellows—as if you hadn't got it, I mean."

"No—you don't understand. It's like a millstone tied round your neck. It drags you down, and keeps you down,"

"Why don't you marry?"

"Why don't I? Well, when I meet the girl I fancy I will marry if she will have me. I suppose I'm constitutionally cold, because as yet—Who is this girl?" He took up a cabinet photograph which stood on the mantelshelf. "I seem to know her face. It's a winning kind of face—what they call a beseeching face. Where have I seen it?"

"That? It is the portrait of a cousin of mine. I don't think you can have met her anywhere, because she lives entirely in the country."

"I have certainly seen her somewhere. Perhaps in a picture. Beatrice, perhaps. It is the face of an angel. Faces sometime deceive, though: I know a girl in quite the smartest set who can assume the most saintly face when she pleases. She puts it on when she converses with the curate; when she goes to church she becomes simply angelic. At other times—Your cousin does not, however, I should say, follow the Profession of Amusement."

"Not exactly. She lives in a quiet little seaside place where they've got a convalescent home, and she slaves for the patients."

"It is a beautiful face," Geoffrey repeated. "But I seem to know it." He looked at the back of the photograph. "What are these lines written at the back?"

"They are some nonsense rhymes written by herself. There is a little family tradition that Katie is waiting for her Prince—she says to herself—she has refused a good many men. I think she will never marry, because she certainly will not find the man she dreams of."

"May I read the lines?" He read them aloud:—

Oh! tell me, Willow-wren and White-throat, beating
The sluggish breeze with eager homeward wing,
Beat you no message for me—not a greeting
From him you left behind—my Prince and my King?

You come from far—from south and east and west;
Somewhere you left him, daring some great thing,
I know not what, save that is the best:
Somewhere you saw him—saw my Prince and King.

You cannot choose but know him: by the crown
They placed upon his head—the crown and the ring;
And by the loud and many-voiced renown
After the footsteps of my Prince and King.

He speaks, and lo! the listening world obeys;
He leads, and all the men follow; and they cling,
And hang around the words and works and ways,
As of a Prophet—of my Prince and King.

What matter if he comes not, though I wait?
Bear you no greeting for me, birds of spring?
Again—what matter, since his work is great,
And greater grows his name—my Prince and King.

"You see," said the cousin, "she has set up an ideal man."

"Yes. Why does she call him her Prince?"

The cousin laughed. "There is a story about a ball—her first ball—her last too, poor child, because—well, there were losses, you know. Like the landlady, Katie has known better days; and friends died, and so she lives by herself in this little village, and looks after her patient convalescents."

"What about her first ball?"

"Well, she nearly missed it, because her godmother, who meant to give her a surprise, lost a train or got late somehow. So her Elder Sisters went without her, and she arrived late; and they said that, to complete the story, nothing was wanted but the Prince."

Geoffrey started and changed colour.

"That's all. She imagined a Prince, and goes on with her dream. She enacts a novel which never comes to an end, and has no situations, and has an invisible hero."

Geoffrey laid down the photograph. He now remembered everything, including the sending of the slipper. But the cousin had quite forgotten his own part in the story.

"I must go," he said. "I think I shall take the yacht somewhere round the coast. You say your cousin lives at—"

"Oh! Yes, she lives at Shellacomb Bay, near Torquay. Sit down again."

"No. Dull place, Shellacomb Bay: I've been there, I think." He was rather irresolute, but that was his way. "I must go. I rather think there are some men coming into my place about this time. There will be no nap. All professionals, you know—Professors of Amusement. It's dull work. I say, if your cousin found her Prince, what an awful, awful disappointment it would be!"

IV

At five in the morning Geoffrey was left alone. The night's play was over. He turned back the curtains and opened the windows, letting in the fresh morning air of April. He leaned out and took a deep breath. Then he returned to the room. The table was littered with packs of cards. There was a smell of a thousand cigarettes. It is an acrid smell, not like the honest downright smell of pipes and cigars; the board was covered with empty soda-water and champagne bottles.

"The Professional Pursuer of Pleasure," he murmured. "It's a learned profession, I suppose. Quite a close profession. Very costly to get into, and beastly stupid and dull when you are in it. A learned profession, certainly."

He sat down, and his thoughts returned to the girl who had made for herself a Prince. "Her Prince!" he said bitterly. And then the words came back to him—

> Daring some great thing,
> I know not what, save that it is the best:
> Somewhere you saw him—saw my Prince and King.

"For one short night I was her Prince and King," he murmured. "And I sent her the slipper—was stone-broke a whole term after through buying that slipper. And after all I was afraid to call at the house. Her Prince and King. I wonder—" He looked about him again—looked at the empty bottles. "*What* a Prince and King!" he laughed bitterly.

Then he sprang to his feet; he opened a drawer and took from it a bundle of letters, photographs, cards of invitation which were lying there piled up in confusion. He threw these on the fire in a heap; he opened another drawer and pulled out another bundle of notes and papers. These also he threw on the fire. "There!" he said resolutely. What he meant I know not, for he did not wait to see them burned, but went into his bedroom and so to bed.

V

Geoffrey spoke no more than the simple truth when he said that Katie De Lisle had a saintly face—the face of an angel. It was a lovely face when he first saw it—the face of a girl passing into womanhood. Five years of tranquil life, undisturbed by strong emotions, devoted to unselfish labours and to meditation, had now made that face saintly indeed. It was true that she had created for herself a Prince, one who was at once a Galahad of romance and a leader of the present day, chivalrous knight and Paladin of Parliament. What she did with her Prince I do not know. Whether she thought of him continually or only seldom, whether she believed in him or only hoped for him, no one can tell. When a man proposed to her—which happened whenever a man was presented to her—she refused him graciously, and told her sisters, who were now matrons, that another person had come representing himself to be the Prince, but that she had detected an impostor, for he was not the Prince. And it really seemed as if she never would find this impossible Prince, which was a great pity, if only because she had a very little income, and the Elder Sisters, who lived in great houses, desired her also to have a great house. Of course, every Prince who regards his own dignity must have a big house of his own.

Now, one afternoon in April, when the sun sets about a quarter-past seven and it is light until eight, Katie was sitting on one of the benches placed on the shore for the convenience of the convalescents, two or three of whom were strolling along the shore. The sun was getting low; a warmth and glow lay upon the bay like an illuminated mist. Katie had a book in her hand, but she let it drop into her lap, and sat watching the beauty and the splendour and the colour of the scene before her. Then there came, rounding the southern headland, a steam yacht, which slowly crept into the bay, and dropped anchor and let off steam: a graceful little craft, with her slender spars and her dainty curves. The girl watched with a little interest. Not often did craft of any kind put into that bay. There were bays to the east and bays to the west, where ships, boats, fishing smacks, and all kind of craft put in; but not in that bay, where there was no quay, or port, or anything but the convalescents, and Katie the volunteer nurse. So she watched, sitting on the bench, with the western sun falling upon her face.

After a little a boat was lowered, and a man and a boy got into it. The boy took the sculls and rowed the man ashore. The man jumped out, stood irresolutely looking about him, observed Katie on the bench, looked at her rather rudely it seemed, and walked quickly towards her. What made her face turn pale? What made her cheek turn red and pale? Nothing less that the appearance of her Prince—her Prince. She knew him at once. Her Prince! It was her Prince come to her at last.

But the Prince did not hold out both hands and cry, "I have come." Not at all. He gravely and politely took off his hat. "Miss De Lisle," he said. "I cannot hope that you remember me. I only met you once. But I—I heard that you were here, and I remembered your face at once."

"I seldom forget people," she replied, rising and giving him her hand. "You are Mr. Geoffrey Armiger. We danced together one night. I remember it especially, because it was my first ball."

"Which you nearly missed, and were left at home like Cinderella, till the fairy godmother came. I—I am cruising about here. I learned that you were living here from your cousin in the Temple, and—and I thought that, if we put in here, I might, perhaps, venture to call."

"Certainly. I shall be very glad to see you, Mr. Armiger. It is seven o'clock now. Will you come to tea tomorrow afternoon?"

"With the greatest pleasure. May I walk with you—in your direction?"

The situation was delicate. What Geoffrey wanted to convey was this: "You once received the confidences of a young man who hoped to do great things in the world. You have gone on believing that he would do great things. You have built up an ideal man, before whom all other men are small creatures. Well, that ideal must be totally disconnected with the young fellow who started it, because he has gone to the bad. He is only a Professor of Amusement, and idle killer of time, a man who wastes all his gifts and powers." A difficult thing to say, because it involved charging the girl with, or telling her he knew that she had been, actually thinking of him for five years.

That evening he got very little way. He reminded her again of the ball. He said that she had altered very little, which was true; for at twenty-two Katie preserved much the same ethereal beauty that she had at seventeen. That done, his jaws stuck, to use a classical phrase. He could say no more. He left her at the door of her cottage,—she lived in a cottage in the midst of tree fuchsias and covered with roses,—and went back to his yacht, where he had a solitary dinner and passed a morose evening.

At five o'clock in the afternoon next day he called again. Miss De Lisle was at the Home, but would come back immediately. The books on the girl's table betrayed the character of her mind. Katie's books showed the level of her thoughts and the standard of her ideals. They were the books of a girl who meditates. There are such people, even in this busy and noisy age. Geoffrey took them up with a sinking heart. Professors of Amusement never read such books.

Then she came in, quiet, serene; and they sat down, and the tea was brought in.

"Now, tell me," she said abruptly. "I see by your card that you have a title. What did you do to get it?"

"Nothing. I succeeded."

"Oh!" Her face fell a little. "When I saw you—the only time that I saw you—I remember that you had great ambitions. What have you done?"

"Nothing. Nothing at all. I have wasted my time. I have lived a life of what they call pleasure. I don't know that I ought to have called upon you at all."

"Is it possible? Oh! Can it be possible? Only a life of pleasure? And you—you with your noble dreams? Oh! Is it possible?"

"It is possible. It is quite true. I am the prodigal son, who has so much money that he cannot get through it. But do you remember the silly things I said? Why, you see, what happened was, that when the temptation came all the noble dreams vanished?"

"Is it possible?" she repeated. "Oh! I am very, very sorry!"—in fact, the tears came into her eyes. 'You have destroyed the one illusion that I nourished." Every one thinks that he has only one illusion and a clear eye for everything else. That is the Great, the Merciful, Illusion. "I thought that there was one true man at least in the world, fighting for the right. I had been honoured as a girl with the noble ambitions of that man when he was quite young. I thought I should hear of him from time to time winning recognition, power, and authority. It was a beautiful dream. It made me feel almost as if I were myself taking part in that great career, even from this obscure corner in the country. No one knows the pleasure that a woman has in watching the career of a brave and wise man. And now it is gone. I am sorry you called,"—her voice became stony and her eyes hard: even an angel or a saint has moments of righteous indignation,—"I am very sorry, Sir Geoffrey Armiger, that you took the trouble to call."

Her visitor rose. "I am also very sorry," he said, "that I have said or done anything to pain you. Forgive me: I will go."

But he lingered. He took up a paper-knife, and considered it as if it were something rare and curious. He laid it down. Then he laughed a little short laugh, and turned to Katie with smiling lips and solemn eyes.

"Did that slipper fit?" he asked, abruptly.

She blushed. But she answered him.

"It was too small for my Elder Sisters, but it fitted me."

"Will you try it on again?"

She went out of the room and presently returned with the pretty, jewelled, little slipper. She took off her shoe, sat down, and tried it on.

"You see," she said, "it is now too small for my foot. Oh! my foot has not changed in the least. It has grown too small."

"Try again." The Prince looked on anxiously. "Perhaps, with a little effort, a little goodwill—"

"No; it is quite hopeless. The slipper has shrunk; you can see for yourself, if you remember what it was like when you bought it. See, it is ever so much smaller that it was, Sir Geoffrey." She looked up, gravely. "See for yourself. And the silver buckle is black, and even the pearls are tarnished. See!" There was a world of meaning in her words.

"Think what it was five years ago."

He took it from her hand and turned it round and round disconsolately.

"You remember it—five years ago—when it was new?" the girl asked again.

"I remember. Oh! yes, I remember. A pretty thing it was then, wasn't it? A world of promise in it, I remember. Hope, and courage, and—and all kinds of possibilities. Pity—silver gone black, pearls tarnished, colour faded, the thing itself shrunken. Yes." He gave it back to her. "I'm glad you've kept it."

"Of course I kept it."

"Yes, of course. Will you go on keeping it?"

"I think so. One likes to remember a time of promise, and of hope, and courage, and, as you say, all kinds of possibilities."

He sighed.

"Slippers are so. There are untold sympathies in slippers. I call this the Oracle of the slipper. Not that I am in the least surprised. I came here, in fact, on purpose to ascertain, if I could, the amount of shrinkage. It would be interesting to return every five years or so, just to see how much it shrinks every year. Next time it would be a doll's shoe, for instance. Well, now"—again he fell back upon the paper-knife—"there was something else I had to say; something else—" He dropped his eyes and examined the paper-knife closely. "The other day in your cousin's rooms I saw your photograph; and I remembered the kind of young fellow I was when we talked about ambitions and you sympathized with me. I think I should like to take up those ambitions again, if it is not too late. I am sick and weary of the Profession of Pleasure. I have wasted five good years, but perhaps they can be retrieved. Let me, if possible, burnish up that silver, expand the shrinking shoe, renew those dreams."

"Do you mean it? Are you strong enough? Oh! You have fallen so low. Are you strong enough to rise?"

"I don't know. If the event should prove—if that slipper should enlarge again—if it should once more fit your foot—"

"If! Oh! how can a man say *if*, when he ought to say *shall?*"

"The slipper *shall* enlarge," he said quietly, but with as much determination as one can expect from an Emeritus Professor of Pleasure.

"When it does, then come again. Till then, do not, if you please, seek me out in my obscurity. It would only be the final destruction of a renewed hope. Farewell, Sir Geoffrey."

"*Au revoir.* Not farewell."

He stooped and kissed her hand and left her.

THE MAGIC OF A VOICE

WILLIAM DEAN HOWELLS

THERE WAS A FULL MOON, and Langbourne walked about the town, unable to come into the hotel and go to bed. The deep yards of the houses gave out the scent of syringas and June roses; the light of lamps came through the fragrant bushes from the open doors and windows, with the sound of playing and singing and bursts of young laughter. Where the houses stood near the street, he could see people lounging on the thresholds, and their heads silhouetted against the luminous interiors. Other houses, both those which stood further back and those that stood nearer, were dark and still, and to those he attributed the happiness of love in fruition, safe from unrest and longing.

His own heart was tenderly oppressed, not with desire, but with the memory of desire. It was almost as if in his faded melancholy he were sorry for the disappointment of someone else.

At last he turned and walked back through the streets of dwellings to the business centre of the town, where a gush of light came from the veranda of his hotel, and the druggist's window cast purple and yellow blurs out upon the footway. The other stores were shut, and he alone seemed to be abroad. The church clock struck ten as he mounted the steps of his hotel and dropped the remnants of his cigar over the side.

He had slept badly on the train the night before, and he had promised himself to make up his lost sleep in the good conditions that seemed to offer themselves. But when he sat down in the hotel office he was more wakeful than he had been when he started to walk himself drowsy.

The clerk gave him the New York paper which had come by the evening train, and he thanked him, but remained musing in his chair. At times he thought he would light another cigar, but the hand that he carried to his breast pocket dropped nervelessly to his knee again, and he did not smoke. Through his memories of disappointment pierced a self-complacency of regret; and yet he could not have been sure, if he had asked himself, that this pang did not heighten the luxury of his psychological experience.

He rose and asked the clerk for a lamp, but he turned back from the stairs to inquire when there would be another New York mail. The clerk said there was a train from the south due at eleven-forty, but it seldom brought any mail; the principal mail was as seven. Langbourne thanked him, and came back to beg the clerk to be careful and not have him called in the morning, for he wished to sleep. Then he went up to his room, where he opened his window to let in the night air. He heard a dog barking, a cow lowed; from a stable somewhere the soft thumping of horses' feet came at intervals lullingly.

II

Langbourne fell asleep so quickly that he was aware of no moment of waking after his head touched the fragrant pillow. He woke so much refreshed by his first sound, soft sleep that he thought it must be nearly morning. He got his watch into a ray of the moonlight and made out that it was only a little after midnight, and he perceived that it must have been the sound of low murmuring voices and broken laughter in the next room which had wakened him. But he was rather glad to have been roused to a sense of his absolute comfort, and he turned unresentfully to sleep again. All the heaviness of heart was gone; he felt curiously glad and young; he had somehow forgiven the wrong he had suffered and the wrong he had done. The subdued murmuring went on in the next room, and he kept himself awake to enjoy it for a while. Then he let himself go, and drifted away into gulfs of slumber, where, suddenly, he seemed to strike against something, and started up in bed.

A laugh came from the next room. It was not muffled, as before, but frank and clear. It was a woman's laughter, and Langbourne easily inferred girlhood as well as womanhood from it. His neighbors must have come by the late train, and they had probably begun to talk as soon as they got into their room. He imagined their having spoken low at first for fear of disturbing some one, and then, in their forgetfulness, or their belief that there was no one near, allowed themselves greater freedom. There were survivals of their earlier caution at times, when their voices sank so low as scarcely to be heard; then there was a break in it when they rose clearly distinguishable from each other. They were never so distinct that he could make out what was said; but each voice unmistakably conveyed character.

Friendship between girls is never equal; they may equally love each other, but one must worship and one must suffer worship. Langbourne read the differing temperaments necessary to this relation in the differing voices. That which bore mastery was a low, thick murmur, coming from deep in the throat, and flowing out in a steady stream of indescribable coaxing and drolling. The owner of that voice had imagination and humor which could charm with absolute control her companion's lighter nature, as it betrayed itself in a gay tinkle of amusement and succession of nervous whispers. Langbourne did not wonder at her subjection; with the first sounds of that rich, tender voice, he had fallen under its spell too; and he listened intensely, trying to make out some phrase, some word, some syllable. But the talk kept its subaudible flow, and he had to content himself as he could with the sound of the voice.

As he lay eavesdropping with all his might he tried to construct an image of the two girls from their voices. The one with the crystalline laugh was little and lithe, quick in movement, of a mobile face, with gray eyes and fair hair; the other was tall and pale, with full, blue eyes and a regular face, and lips that trembled with humor; very demure and yet very honest; very shy and yet very frank; there was something almost mannish in her essential honesty; there was nothing of feminine coquetry in her, though everything of feminine charm. She was a girl who looked like her father, Langbourne perceived with a flash of divination. She dressed simply in dark blue, and her hair was of a dark mahogany color.

The smaller girl wore light gray checks or stripes, and the shades of silver.

The talk began to be less continuous in the next room, from which there came the sound of sighs and yawns, and then of mingled laughter at these. Then the talk ran unbrokenly for a while, and again dropped into laughs that recognized the drowse creeping upon the talkers. Suddenly it stopped altogether, and left Langbourne, as he felt, definitively awake for the rest of the night.

He had received an impression which he could not fully analyze. With some inner sense he kept hearing that voice, low and deep, and rich with whimsical suggestion. Its owner must have a strange, complex nature, which would perpetually provoke and satisfy. Her companionship would be as easy and reasonable as a man's, while it had the charm of a woman's. At the moment it seemed to him that life without this companionship would be something poorer and thinner than he had yet known, and that he could not endure to forego it. Somehow he must manage to see the girl and make her acquaintance. He did not know how it could be contrived, but it could certainly be contrived, and he began to dramatize their meeting on these two various terms. It was interesting and it was delightful, and it always came, in its safe impossibility, to his telling her that he loved her, and to her consenting to be his wife. He resolved to take no chance of losing her, but to remain awake, and somehow see her before she could leave the hotel in the morning. The resolution gave him calm; he felt that the affair was so far settled.

Suddenly he started from his pillow; and again he heard that mellow laugh, warm and rich as the cooing of doves on sunlit eaves. The sun was shining through the crevices of his window-blinds; he looked at his watch; it was half-past eight. The sound of fluttering skirts and flying feet in the corridor shook his heart. A voice, the voice of the mellow laugh, called as if to someone on the stairs, "I must have put it in my bag. It doesn't matter, anyway."

He hurried on his clothes, in the vain hope of finding his neighbors before breakfast; but before he had finished dressing he heard wheels before the veranda below, and he saw the hotel barge* drive away as if to

*According to *Webster's*, "a large horse-drawn omnibus usually used for excursions or the transportation of groups (as from a railroad station to a hotel)"; the term was chiefly of New England usage.

the station. There were two passengers in it; two women, whose faces were hidden by the fringe of the barge-roof, but whose slender figures showed themselves from their necks down. It seemed to him that one was tall and slight, the other slight and little.

III

He stopped in the hall, and then, tempted by his despair, he stepped within the open door of the next room and looked vaguely over it, with shame at being there. What was it that the girl had missed, and had come back to look for? Some trifle, no doubt, which she had not cared to lose, and yet had not wished to leave behind. He failed to find anything in the search, which he could not make very thorough, and he was going guiltily out when his eye fell upon an envelope, perversely fallen beside the door and almost indiscernible against the white paint, with the addressed surface inward.

This must be the object of her search, and he could understand why she was not very anxious when he found it a circular from a nurseryman, containing nothing more than a list of flowering shrubs. He satisfied himself that this was all without satisfying himself that he had quite a right to do so; and he stood abashed in the presence of the superscription on the envelope somewhat as if Miss Barbara F. Simpson, Upper Ashton Falls, N.H., were there to see him tampering with her correspondence. It was indelicate, and he felt that his whole behavior had been indelicate, from the moment that her laugh had wakened him in the night till now, when he had invaded her room. He had no more doubt that she was the taller of the two girls than that this was her name on the envelope. He liked Barbara; and Simpson could be changed. He seemed to hear her soft throaty laugh in response to the suggestion, and with a leap of the heart he slipped the circular into his breast pocket.

After breakfast he went to the hotel office, and stood leaning on the long counter and talking with the clerk till he could gather courage to look at the register, where he knew the names of the girls must be written. He asked where Upper Ashton Falls was, and whether it would be a good place to spend a week.

The clerk said that it was about thirty miles up the road, and was one of the nicest places in the mountains; Langbourne could not go to a nicer; and there was a very good little hotel. "Why," he said, "there were two ladies here overnight that just left for there, on the seven-forty. Odd you should ask about it."

Langbourne owned that it was odd, and then he asked if the ladies lived at Upper Ashton Falls, or were merely summer folks.

"Well, a little of both," said the clerk. "They're cousins, and they've got an aunt living there that they stay with. They used to go away winters,—teaching, I guess,—but this last year they stayed right through. Been down to Springfield, they said, and just stopped the night because the accommodation don't go any farther. Wake you up last night? I had to put 'em into the room next to yours, and girls usually talk."

Langbourne answered that it would have taken a good deal of talking to wake him the night before, and then he lounged across to the timetable hanging on the wall, and began to look up the trains for Ashton Falls.

"If you want to go to the Falls," said the clerk, "there's a through train at four, with a drawing room on it, that will get you there by five."

"Oh, I fancy I was looking up the New York trains," Langbourne returned. He did not like these evasions, but in his consciousness of Miss Simpson he seemed unable to avoid them. The clerk went out on the veranda to talk with a farmer bringing supplies, and Langbourne ran to the register, and read there the names of Barbara F. Simpson and Juliet D. Bingham. It was Miss Simpson who had registered for both, since her name came first, and the entry was in a good, simple hand, which was like a man's in its firmness and clearness. He turned from the register decided to take the four-o'clock train for Upper Ashton Falls, and met a messenger with a telegram which he knew was for himself before the boy could ask his name. His partner had suddenly fallen sick; his recall was absolute, his vacation was at an end; nothing remained for him but to take the first train back to New York. He thought how little prescient he had been in his pretence that he was looking the New York trains up; but the need of one had come already, and apparently he should never have any use for a train to Upper Ashton Falls.

IV

All the way back to New York Langbourne was oppressed by a sense of loss such as his old disappointment in love now seemed never to have inflicted. He found that his whole being had set toward the unseen owner of the voice which had charmed him, and it was like a stretching and tearing of the nerves to be going from her instead of going toward her. He was as much under duress as if he were bound by a hypnotic spell. The voice continually sounded, not in his ears, which were filled with the noises of the train, as usual, but in the inmost of his spirit, where it was a low, cooing coaxing murmur. He realized now how intensely he must have listened for it in the night, how every tone of it must have pervaded him and possessed him. He was in love with it, he was as entirely fascinated by it as if it were the girl's whole presence, her looks, her qualities.

The remnant of the summer passed in the fret of business which was doubly irksome through his feeling of being kept from the girl whose personality he constructed from the sound of her voice, and set over his fancy in an absolute sovereignty. The image he had created of her remained a dim and blurred vision through the day, but by night it became distinct and compelling. One evening, late in the fall, he could endure the stress no longer, and he yielded to the temptation which had beset him from the first moment he renounced his purpose of returning in person the circular addressed to her as a means of her acquaintance. He wrote to her, and in terms as dignified as he could contrive, and as free from any ulterior import, he told her he had found it in the hotel hallway and had meant to send it to her at once, thinking it might be of some slight use to her. He had failed to do this, and now, having come upon it among some other papers, he sent it with an explanation which he hoped she would excuse him for troubling her with.

This was not true, but he did not see how he could begin with her by saying that he had found the circular in her room, and had kept it by him ever since, looking at it every day, and leaving it where he could see it last thing before he slept every night and the first thing after he woke in the morning. As to her reception of the story, he had to trust his knowledge that she was, like himself, of country birth and breeding, and to his belief that she would not take alarm at his overture. He did not go much into the world and was little acquainted with its usages, yet he knew enough to suspect that a woman of the world would either ignore his letter, or would return a cold and snubbing expression of Miss Simpson's thanks for Mr. Stephen M. Langbourne's kindness.

He had not only signed his name and given his address carefully in hopes of a reply, but he had enclosed the business card of his firm as a token of his responsibility. The partner in a wholesale stationery house ought to be an impressive figure in the imagination of a village girl; but it was some weeks before any answer came to Langbourne's letter. The reply began with an apology for the delay, and Langbourne perceived that he had gained rather than lost by the writer's hesitation; clearly she believed that she had put herself in the wrong, and that she owed him a certain reparation. For the rest, her letter was discreetly confined to an acknowledgment of the trouble he had taken.

But this spare return was richly enough for Langbourne; it would have sufficed, if there had been nothing in the letter, that the handwriting proved Miss Simpson to have been the one who had made the entry of her name and her friend's in the hotel register. This was most important as one step in corroboration of the fact that he had rightly divined her; that the rest should come true was almost a logical necessity. Still, he was puzzled to contrive a pretext for writing again, and he remained without one for a fortnight. Then, in passing a seedsman's store which he used to pass every day without thinking, he one day suddenly perceived his opportunity. He went in and got a number of the catalogues and other advertisements, and addressed them then and there, in a wrapper the seedsman gave him, to Miss Barbara F. Simpson, Upper Ashton Falls, N.H.

Now the response came with a promptness which at least testified of the lingering compunction of Miss Simpson. She asked if she were right in supposing that the seedsman's catalogues and folders had come to her from Langbourne and whether the seedsman in question was reliable; it was so difficult to get garden seeds that one could trust.

The correspondence now established itself, and with one excuse or another it prospered throughout the winter. Langbourne was not only willing, he was most eager, to give her proof of his reliability; he spoke of stationers in Springfield and Greenfield to whom he was personally known; and he secretly hoped she would satisfy herself through friends in those places that he was an upright and trustworthy person.

Miss Simpson wrote delightful letters, with that whimsical quality which had enchanted him in her voice. The coaxing and caressing was not there, and could not be expected to impart itself, unless in those refuges of deep feeling supposed to lurk between the lines. But he hoped to provoke it from these in time, and his own letters grew the more earnest the more ironical hers became. He wrote to her about a book he was reading, and when she said she had not seen it, he sent it her; in one of her letters she casually betrayed that she sang contralto in the choir, and then he sent her some new songs, which he had heard in the theatre, and which he had informed himself from a friend were contralto. He was always tending to the expression of the feeling which swayed him; but on her part there was no sentiment. Only in the fact that she was willing to continue this exchange of letters with a man personally unknown to her did she betray that romantic tradition which underlies all our young life, and in those unused to the world tempts to things blameless in themselves, but of the sort shunned by the worldlier wise. There was no great wisdom in Miss Simpson's letters, but Langbourne did not miss it; he was content with her mere words, as they related the little events of her simple daily life. These repeated themselves from the page in the tones of her voice and filled him with a passionate intoxication.

Towards spring he had his photograph taken, for no reason that he could have given; but since it was done he sent one to his mother in Vermont, and then he wrote his name on another, and sent it to Miss Simpson in New Hampshire. He hoped, of course, that she would return a photograph of herself; but she merely acknowledged his with some dry playfulness. Then, after disappointing him so long that he had ceased to expect anything, she enclosed a picture. The face was so far averted that Langbourne could get nothing but the curve of a longish cheek, the point of a nose, the segment of a crescent eyebrow. The girl said that as they should probably never meet, it was not necessary that he should know her when he saw her; she explained that she was looking away because she had been attracted by something on the other side of the photograph gallery just at the moment the artist took the cap off the tube of his camera, and she could not turn back without breaking the plate.

Langbourne replied that he was going up to Springfield on business the first week in May, and that he thought he might push on as far north as Upper Ashton Falls. To this there came no rejoinder whatever, but he did not lose courage. It was now the end of April, and he could not bear to wait for a further verification of his ideal; the photograph had confirmed him in its evasive fashion at every point of his conjecture concerning her. It was the face he had imagined her having, or so he now imagined, and it was just such a long oval face as would go with the figure he attributed to her. She must have the healthy pallor of skin which associates itself with masses of dark, mahogany-colored hair.

V

It was so long since he had know a Northern spring that he had forgotten how much later the beginning of May was in New Hampshire; but as his train ran up from Springfield he realized the difference of the season from that which he had left in New York. The meadows were green only in the damp hollows; most of the trees were as bare as in midwinter; the willows in the swamplands hung out their catkins, and the white birches showed faint signs of returning life. In the woods were long drifts of snow, though he knew that in the brown leaves along the edges the pale pink flowers of the trailing arbutus were hiding their wet faces. A vernal mildness overhung the landscape. A blue haze filled the distances and veiled the hills; from the farm door-yards the smell of burning leaf-heaps and garden-stalks came through the window which he lifted to let in the dull, warm air. The sun shone down from a pale sky, in which the crows called to one another.

By the time he arrived in Upper Ashton Falls the afternoon had waned so far towards evening that the first robins were singing their vespers from the leafless choirs of the maples before the hotel. He indulged the landlord in his natural supposition that he had come up to make a timely engagement for summer board; after supper he even asked what the price of such rooms as his would be by the week in July, while he tried to lead the talk round to the fact which he wished to learn.

He did not know where Miss Simpson lived; and the courage with which he set out on his adventure totally lapsed, leaving in its place an accusing sense of silliness. He was where he was without reason, and in defiance of the tacit unwillingness of the person he had come to see; she certainly had given him no invitation, she had given him no permission to come. For the moment, in his shame, it seemed to him that the only thing for him was to go back to New York by the first train in the morning. But then what would the girl think of him? Such an act must forever end the intercourse which had now become an essential part of his life. That voice which had haunted him for so long, was he never to hear it again? Was he willing to renounce forever the hope of hearing it?

He sat at his supper so long, nervelessly turning his doubts over in his mind, that the waitress came out of the kitchen and drove him from the table with her severe, impatient stare.

He put on his hat, and with his overcoat on his arm he started out for a walk which was hopeless, but not so aimless as he feigned to himself. The air was lullingly warm still as he followed the long village street down the hill toward the river, where the lunge of rapids filled the dusk with a sort of humid uproar; then he turned and followed it back past the hotel as far as it led towards the open country. At the edge of the village he came to a large, old-fashioned house, which struck him as typical, with its outward swaying fence of the Greek border pattern, and its gate-posts topped by tilting urns of painted wood. The house itself stood rather far back from the street, and as he passed it he saw that it was approached by a pathway of brick which was bordered with box. Stalks of last year's hollyhocks and lilacs from garden beds on either hand lifted their sharp points, here and there broken and hanging down. It was curious how these details insisted through the twilight.

He walked on until the wooden village pathway ended in the country mud, and then again he returned up upon his steps. As he reapproached the house he saw lights. A brighter radiance streamed from the hall door, which was apparently open, and a softer glow flushed the windows of one of the rooms that flanked the hall.

As Langbourne came abreast of the gate the tinkle of a gay laugh rang out to him; then ensued a murmur of girls' voices in the room, and suddenly this stopped, and the voice that he knew, the voice that seemed never to have ceased to sound in his nerves and pulses, rose in singing words set to the Spanish air of *La Paloma.*

It was one of the songs he had sent to Miss Simpson, but he did not need this material proof that it was she whom he now heard. There was no question of what he should do. All doubt, all fear, had vanished; he had again but one impulse, one desire, one purpose. But he lingered at the gate till the song ended, and then he unlatched it and started up the walk towards the door. It seemed to him a long way; he almost reeled as he went; he fumbled tremulously for the bell-pull beside the door, while a confusion of voices in the adjoining room—the voices which had waked him from his sleep, and which now sounded like voices in a dream—came to him.

The light from the lamp hanging in the hall shone full in his face, and the girl who came from that room beside it to answer his ring gave a sort of conscious jump at sight of him as he uncovered and stood bareheaded before her.

VI

She must have recognized him from the photograph he had sent, and in stature and figure he recognized her as the ideal he had cherished, though her head was gilded with the light from the lamp, and he could not make out whether her hair was dark or fair; her face was, of course, a mere outline, without color or detail against the luminous interior.

He managed to ask, dry-tongued and with a heart that beat into his throat, "Is Miss Simpson at home?" and the girl answered, with a high, gay tinkle:

"Yes, she's at home. Won't you walk in?"

He obeyed, but at the sound of her silvery voice his heart dropped back into his breast. He put his hat and coat on an entry chair, and prepared to follow her into the room she had come out of. The door stood ajar, and he said, as she put out her hand to push it open, "I am Mr. Langbourne."

"Oh, yes," she answered in the same high, gay tinkle, which he fancied had now a note of laughter in it.

An elderly woman of a ladylike village type was sitting with some needlework beside a little table, and a young girl turned on the piano-stool and rose to receive him. "My aunt, Mrs. Simpson, Mr. Langbourne," said the girl who introduced him to these presences, and she added, indicating the girl at the piano, "Miss Simpson."

They all three bowed silently, and in the hush the sheet on the music frame slid from the piano with a sharp clash, and skated across the floor to Langbourne's feet. It was the song of *La Paloma* which she had been singing; he picked it up, and she received it with a drooping head, and an effect of guilty embarrassment.

She was short and of rather a full figure, though not too full. She was not plain, but she was by no means the sort of beauty who had lived in Langbourne's fancy for the year past. The oval of her face was squared; her nose was arched; she had a pretty, pouting mouth, and below it a deep dimple in her chin; her eyes were large and dark, and they had the questioning look of near-sighted eyes; her hair was brown. There was a humorous tremor in her lips, even with the prim stress she put upon them in saying, "Oh, thank you," in a thick whisper of the voice he knew.

"And I," said the other girl, "am Juliet Bingham. Won't you sit down, Mr. Langbourne?" She pushed towards him the arm-chair before her, and he dropped into it. She took her place on the hair-cloth sofa, and Miss Simpson sank back upon the piano stool with a painful provisionality, while her eyes sought Miss Bingham's in a sort of admiring terror.

Miss Bingham was easily mistress of the situation; she did not try to bring Miss Simpson into the conversation, but she contrived to make Mrs. Simpson ask Langbourne when he arrived at Upper Ashton Falls; and she herself asked him when he had left New York, with many apposite suppositions concerning the difference in the season in the two latitudes. She presumed he was staying at the Falls house, and she said, always in her high, gay tinkle, that it was very pleasant there in the summer time. He did not know what he answered. He was aware that from time to time Miss Simpson said something in a frightened undertone. He did not know how long it was before Mrs. Simpson made an errand out of the room, in the abeyance which age practices before youthful society in this country; he did not know how much longer it was before Miss Bingham herself jumped actively up, and said, Now she would run over to Jenny's, if Mr. Langbourne would excuse her, and tell her that they could not go the next day.

"It will do just as well in the morning," Miss Simpson pitifully entreated.

"No, she's got to know tonight," said Miss Bingham, and she said she should find Mr. Langbourne there when she got back. He knew that in compliance with simple village tradition he was being purposely left alone with Miss Simpson, as rightfully belonging to her. Miss Bingham betrayed no intentionality to him, but he caught a glimpse of mocking consciousness in the sidelong look she gave Miss Simpson as she went out; and if he had not known before he perceived then, in the vanishing oval of her cheek, the corner of her arched eyebrow, the point of her classic nose, the original of the photograph he had been treasuring as Miss Simpson's.

VII

"It was *her* picture I sent you," said Miss Simpson. She was the first to break the silence to which Miss Bingham abandoned them, but she did not speak till her friend had closed the outer door behind her and was tripping down the brick wall to the gate.

"Yes," said Langbourne, in a dryness which he could not keep himself from using.

The girl must have felt it, and her voice faltered a very little as she continued. "We—I—did it for fun. I meant to tell you. I—"

"Oh, that's all right," said Langbourne. "I had no business to expect yours, or to send you mine." But he believed that he had; that his faithful infatuation had somehow earned him the right to do what he had done, and to hope for what he had not got; without formulating the fact, he divined that she believed it too. Between the man-soul and the woman-soul it can never go so far as it had done in their case without giving them claims upon each other which neither of them can justly deny.

She did not attempt to deny it. "I oughtn't to have done it, and I ought to have told you at once—the next letter—but I—you said you were coming, and I thought if you did come—I didn't really expect you to; and it was all a joke,—off-hand."

It was very lame, but it was true, and it was piteous; yet Langbourne could not relent. His grievance was not with what she had done, but what she was; not what she really was, but what she materially was; her looks, her figure, her stature, her whole presence, so different from that which he had been carrying in his mind, and adoring for a year past.

If it was ridiculous, and if with her sense of the ridiculous she felt it so, she was unable to take it lightly, or to make him take it lightly. At some faint gleams which passed over her face he felt himself invited to regard it less seriously; but he did not try, even provisionally, and they fell into a silence that neither seemed to have the power of breaking.

It must be broken, however; something must be done; they could not sit there dumb forever. He looked at the sheet of music on the piano and said, "I see you've been trying that song. Do you like it?"

"Yes, very much," and now for the first time she got her voice fairly above a whisper. She took the sheet down from the music-rest and looked at the picture of the lithographed title. It was of a tiled roof lifted among cypresses and laurels with pigeons strutting on it and sailing over it.

"It was that picture," said Langbourne, since he must say something, "that I believe I got the song for; it made me think of the roof of an old Spanish house I saw in Southern California."

"It must be nice, out there," said Miss Simpson, absently staring at the picture. She gathered herself together to add, pointlessly, "Juliet says she's going to Europe. Have you ever been?"

"Not to Europe, no. I always feel as if I wanted to see my own country first. Is she going soon?"

"Who? Juliet? Oh, no! She was just saying so. I don't believe she's engaged her passage yet."

There was invitation to greater ease in this, and her voice began to have the tender, coaxing quality which had thrilled his heart when he heard it first. But the space of her variance from his ideal was between them, and the voice reached him faintly across it.

The situation grew more and more painful for her, he could see, as well as for him. She too was feeling the anomaly of their having been intimates without having been acquaintances. They necessarily met as strangers after the exchange of letters in which they had spoken with the confidence of friends.

Langbourne cast about in his mind for some middle ground where they could come together without that effect of chance encounter which had reduced them to silence. He could not recur to any of the things they had written about; so far from wishing to do this, he almost had a terror of touching upon them by accident, and he felt that she shrank from them too, as if they involved a painful misunderstanding which could not be put straight.

He asked questions about Upper Ashton Falls, but these led up to what she had said of it in her letters; he tried to speak of the winter in

New York, and he remembered that every week he had given her a full account of his life there. They must go beyond their letters or they must fall far back of them.

VIII

In their attempts to talk he was aware that she was seconding all his endeavors with intelligence, and with a humorous subtlety to which he could not pretend. She was suffering from their anomalous position as much as he, but she had the means of enjoying it while he had not. After half an hour of these defeats Mrs. Simpson operated a diversion by coming in with two glasses of lemonade on a tray and some slices of sponge-cake. She offered this refreshment first to Langbourne and then to her niece, and they both obediently took a glass, and put a slice of cake in the saucer which supported the glass. She said to each in turn, "Won't you take some lemonade? Won't you have a piece of cake?" and then went out with her empty tray, and the air of having fulfilled the duties of hospitality to her niece's company.

"I don't know," said Miss Simpson, "but it's rather early in the season for *cold* lemonade," and Langbourne, instead of laughing, as her tone invited him to do, said:

"It's very good, I'm sure." But this seemed too stiffly ungracious, and he added: "What delicious sponge-cake! You never get this out of New England."

"We have to do something to make up for our doughnuts," Miss Simpson suggested.

"Oh, I like doughnuts, too" said Langbourne. "But you can't get the right kind of doughnuts, either, in New York."

They began to talk about cooking. He told her of the tamales which he had first tasted in San Francisco, and afterward found superabundantly in New York; they both made a great deal of the topic; Miss Simpson had never heard of tamales. He became solemnly animated in their exegesis, and she showed a resolute interest in them.

They were in the midst of the forced discussion when they heard a quick foot on the brick walk, but they had both fallen silent when Miss

Bingham flounced elastically in upon them. She seemed to take in with a keen glance which swept them from her lively eyes that they had not been getting on, and she had the air of taking them at once in hand.

"Well, it's all right about Jenny," she said to Miss Simpson. "She'd a good deal rather go day after tomorrow, anyway. What have you been talking about? I don't want to make you go over the same ground. Have you got through with the weather? The moon's out, and it feels more like the beginning of June than the last of April. I shut the front door against dor-bugs; I couldn't help it, though they won't be here for another six weeks yet. Do you have dor-bugs in New York, Mr. Langbourne?"

"I don't know. There may be some in the Park," he answered.

"We think a great deal of our dor-bugs in Upper Ashton," said Miss Simpson demurely, looking down. "We don't know what we should do without them."

"Lemonade!" exclaimed Miss Bingham, catching sight of the glasses and saucers on the corner of the piano, where Miss Simpson had allowed Langbourne to put them. "Has Aunt Elmira been giving you lemonade while I was gone? I will just see about that!" She whipped out of the room, and was back in a minute with a glass in one hand and a bit of sponge-cake between the fingers of the other. "She had kept some for me! Have you sung *Paloma* for Mr. Langbourne, Barbara?"

"No," said Barbara. "We hadn't gone around to it, quite."

"Oh, do!" Langbourne entreated, and he wondered that he had not asked her before; it would have saved them from each other.

"Wait a moment," cried Juliet Bingham, and she gulped the last draught of her lemonade upon a final morsel of sponge-cake, and was down at the piano while still dusting the crumbs from her fingers. She struck the refractory sheet of music flat upon the rack with her palm, and then tilted her head over her shoulder towards Langbourne, who had risen with some vague notion of turning the sheets of the song. "Do you sing?"

"Oh, no. But I like—"

"Are you ready, Bab?" she asked, ignoring him; and she dashed into the accompaniment.

He sat down in his chair behind the two girls, where they could not see his face.

Barbara began rather weakly, but her voice gathered strength, and then poured full volume to the end, where it weakened again. He knew that she was taking refuge from him in the song, and in the magic of her voice he escaped from the disappointment he had been suffering. He let his head drop and his eyelids fall, and in the rapture of her singing he got back what he had lost; or rather, he lost himself again to the illusion which had grown so precious to him.

Juliet Bingham sounded the last note almost as she rose from the piano; Barbara passed her handkerchief over her forehead, as if to wipe the heat from it, but he believed that this was a ruse to dry her eyes in it: they shone with a moist brightness in the glimpse he caught of them. He had risen, and they all stood talking; or they all stood, and Juliet talked. She did not offer to sit down again, and after stiffly thanking them both, he said he must be going, and took leave of them. Juliet gave his hand a nervous grip; Barbara's hand was lax and cold; the parting with her was painful; he believed that she felt it so much as he.

The girl's voices followed him down the walk,—Juliet's treble, and Barbara's contralto,—and he believed that they were making talk purposely against a pressure of silence, and did not know what they were saying. It occurred to him that they had not asked how long he was staying, or invited him to come again: he had not thought to ask if he might; and in the intolerable inconclusiveness of this ending he faltered at the gate till the lights in the window of the parlor disappeared, as if carried into the hall, and then they twinkled into darkness. From an upper entry window, which reddened with a momentary flush and was then darkened, a burst of mingled laughter came. The girls must have thought him beyond hearing, and he fancied the laugh a burst of hysterical feeling in them both.

IX

Langbourne went to bed as soon as he reached his hotel because he found himself spent with the experience of the evening; but as he rested from his fatigue he grew wakeful, and he tried to get its whole measure and meaning before him. He had a methodical nature, and he now balanced one fact against another none the less passionately because the process was a series of careful recognitions. He perceived that the dream in which he had lived for the year past was not wholly an illusion. One of the girls whom he had heard but not seen was what he had divined her to be: a dominant influence, a control to which the other was passively obedient. He had not erred greatly as to the face or figure of the superior, but he had given all the advantages to the wrong person. The voice, indeed, the spell which had bound him, belonged with the one to whom he had attributed it, and the qualities with which it was inextricably blended in his fancy were hers; she was more like his ideal than the other, though he owned that the other was a charming girl too, and that in the thin treble of her voice lurked a potential fascination which might have made itself ascendently felt if he had happened to feel it first.

There was a dangerous instant in which he had a perverse question of changing his allegiance. This passed into another moment, almost as perilous, of confusion through a primal instinct of the man's by which he yields a double or divided allegiance and simultaneously worships at two shrines; in still another breath he was aware that this was madness.

If he had been younger, he would have had no doubt as to his right in the circumstances. He had simply corresponded all winter with Miss Simpson; but though he opened his heart freely and had invited her to the same confidence with him, he had not committed himself, and he had a right to drop the whole affair. She would have no right to complain; she had not committed herself either: they could both come off unscathed. But he was now thirty-five, and life had taught him something concerning the rights of others which he could not ignore. By seeking her confidence and by offering her his, he had given her a claim which was none the less binding because it was wholly tacit. There had been a time when he might have justified himself in dropping the affair; that was when she had failed to answer his letter; but he had come to see her in defiance of her silence, and now he could not withdraw, simply because he was disappointed, without cruelty, without atrocity.

This was what the girl's wistful eyes said to him; this was the reproach of her trembling lips; this was the accusation of her dejected figure, as she drooped in vision before him on the piano-stool and passed her hand soundlessly over the key-board. He tried to own to her that he was disappointed, but he could not get the words out of his throat; and now in her presence, as it were, he was not sure that he was disappointed.

X

He woke late, with a longing to put his two senses of her to the proof of the day; and as early in the fore-noon as he could hope to see her, he walked out towards her aunt's house. It was a mild, dull morning, with a misted sunshine; in the little crimson tassels of the budded maples overhead the bees were droning.

The street was straight, and while he was yet a good way off he saw the gate open before the house, and a girl whom he recognized as Miss Bingham close it behind her. She then came down under the maples towards him, at first swiftly, and then more and more slowly, until finally she faltered to a stop. He quickened his own pace and came up to her with a "Good-morning" called to her and a lift of his hat. She returned neither salutation, and said, "I was coming to see you, Mr. Langbourne." Her voice was still a silver bell, but it was not gay, and her face was severely unsmiling.

"To see *me?*" he retuned. "Has anything—"

"No, there's nothing the matter. But—I should like to talk with you." She held a little packet, tied with blue ribbon, in her intertwined hands, and she looked urgently at him.

"I shall be very glad," Langbourne began, but she interrupted,—

"Should you mind walking down to the Falls?"

He understood that for some reason she did not wish him to pass the house, and he bowed. "Wherever you like. I hope Mrs. Simpson is well. And Miss Simpson?"

"Oh, perfectly," said Miss Bingham, and they fenced with some questions and answers of no interest till they had walked back through the village to the Falls at the other end of it, where the saw in a mill was whirring through a long pine log, and the water, streaked with sawdust, was spreading over the rocks below and flowing away with a smooth swiftness. The ground near the mill was piled with fresh-sawed, fragrant lumber and strewn with logs.

Miss Bingham found a comfortable place on one of the logs, and began abruptly:

"You may think it's pretty strange, Mr. Langbourne, but I want to talk to you about Miss Simpson." She seemed to satisfy a duty of convention by saying Miss Simpson at the outset, and after that she called her friend Barbara. "I've brought you your letters to her," and she handed him the packet she had been holding. "Have you got hers with you?"

"They are at the hotel," answered Langbourne.

"Well, that's right, then. I thought perhaps you had brought them. You see," Miss Bingham continued, much more cold-bloodedly than Langbourne thought she need, "we talked it over last night, and it's too silly. That's the way Barbara feels herself. The fact is," she went on confidingly, and with the air of saying something that he might appreciate, "I always thought it was some *young* man, and so did Barbara; or I don't believe she would ever have answered your first letter."

Langbourne knew he was not a young man in a young girl's sense; but no man likes to have it said that he is old. Besides, Miss Bingham herself was not apparently in her first quarter of a century, and probably Miss Simpson would not see the earliest twenties again. He thought none the worse of her for that; but he felt that he was not so unequally matched in time with her that she need take the attitude with regard to him which Miss Bingham indicated. He was not in the least gray nor the least bald, and his tall figure kept his youthful lines.

Perhaps his face manifested something of his suppressed resentment. At any rate, Miss Bingham said apologetically, "I mean that if we had known that it was a *serious* person we should have acted differently. I oughtn't to have let her thank you for those seedsman's catalogues; but I thought it couldn't do any harm. And then, after your letters had begun to come, we didn't know just when to stop them. To tell you the truth, Mr. Langbourne, we got so interested we couldn't *bear* to stop them. You wrote so much about your life in New York, that it was like a visit there every week; and it's pretty quiet at Upper Ashton in the winter time."

She seemed to refer this fact to Langbourne for sympathetic appreciation; he said mechanically, "Yes."

She resumed: "But when your picture came, I said it had *got* to stop; and so we just sent back my picture,—or I don't know but what Barbara did it without asking me,—and we did suppose that would be the last of it; when you wrote back that you were coming here, we didn't believe you really would unless we said so. That's all there is about it; and if there is anybody to blame, I am the one. Barbara would never have done it in the world if I hadn't put her up to it."

In these words the implication that Miss Bingham had operated the whole affair finally unfolded itself. But distasteful as the fact was to Langbourne, and wounding as was the realization that he had been led on by this witness of his infatuation for the sake of the entertainment which his letters gave two girls in the dull winter of a mountain village, there was still greater pain, with an additional embarrassment, in the regret which his words conveyed. It appeared that it was not he who had done the wrong; he had suffered it, and so far from having to offer reparation to a young girl for having unwarrantably wrought her up to expect of him a step from which he afterwards recoiled, he had a duty of forgiving her a trespass on his own invaded sensibilities. It was humiliating to his vanity; it inflicted a hurt to something better than his vanity. He began very uncomfortably: "It's all right, as far as I'm concerned. I had no business to address Miss Simpson in the first place—"

"Well," Miss Bingham interrupted, "that's what I told Barbara; but she got to feeling badly about it; she thought if you had taken the trouble to send back the circular that she dropped in the hotel, she couldn't do less than acknowledge it, and she kept on so about it that I had to let her. That was the first false step."

These words, while they showed Miss Simpson in a more amiable light, did not enable Langbourne to see Miss Bingham's merit so clearly. In the methodical and consecutive working of his emotions, he was aware that it was no longer a question of divided allegiance, and that there could never be any such question again. He perceived that Miss Bingham had not such a good figure as he had fancied the night before, and that her eyes were set rather too near together. While he dropped his own eyes, and stood trying to think what he should say in answer to her last speech, her high, sweet voice tinkled out in gay challenge, "How do, John?"

He looked up and saw a square-set, brown-faced young man advancing towards them in his shirt-sleeves; he came deliberately, finding his way in and out among the logs, till he stood smiling down, through a heavy moustache and thick black lashes, into the face of the girl, as if she were some sort of joke. The sun struck into her face as she looked up at him, and made her frown with a knot between her brows that pulled her eyes still closer together, and she asked, with no direct reference to his shirt-sleeves,—"A'n't you forcing the season?"

"Don't want to let the summer get the start of you," the young man generalized, and Miss Bingham said,—

"Mr. Langbourne, Mr. Dickery." The young man silently shook hands with Langbourne, whom he took into the joke of Miss Bingham with another smile; and she went on: "Say, John, I wish you'd tell Jenny I don't see why we shouldn't go this afternoon, after all."

"All right," said the young man.

"I suppose you're coming too?" she suggested.

"Hadn't heard of it," he returned.

"Well, you have now. You've got to be ready at two o'clock."

"That so?" the young fellow inquired. Then he walked away among the logs, as casually as he had arrived, and Miss Bingham rose and shook some bits of bark from her skirt.

"Mr. Dickery is the owner of the mills," she explained, as she explored Langbourne's face for an intelligence which she did not seem to find there. He thought, indifferently enough, that this young man had heard the two girls speak of him, and had satisfied a natural curiosity in coming to look him over; it did not occur to him that he had any especial relationship to Miss Bingham.

She walked up into the village with Langbourne, and he did not know whether he was to accompany her home or not. But she gave him no sign of dismissal till she put her hand upon her gate to pull it open without asking him to come in. Then he said, "I will send Miss Simpson's letters to her at once."

"Oh, any time will do, Mr. Langbourne," she returned sweetly. Then, as if it had just occurred to her, she added, "We're going after May-flowers this afternoon. Wouldn't you like to come too?"

"I don't know," he began, "whether I shall have the time—"

"Why, you're not going away today!"

"I expected—I—But if you don't think I shall be intruding—"

"Why, *I* should be delighted to have you. Mr. Dickery's going, and Jenny Dickery, and Barbara. I don't *believe* it will rain."

"Then, if I may," said Langbourne.

"Why, certainly, Mr. Langbourne!" she cried, and he started away. But he had gone only a few rods away when he wheeled about and hurried back. The girl was going up the walk to the house, looking over her shoulder after him; at his hurried return she stopped and came back to the gate again.

"Miss Bingham, I think—I think I had better not go."

"Why, just as you feel about it, Mr. Langbourne," she assented.

"I will bring the letters this evening, if you will let me—if Miss Simpson—if you will be at home."

"We shall be very happy to see you, Mr. Langbourne," said the girl formally, and then he went back to his hotel.

XI

Langbourne could not have told just why he had withdrawn his acceptance of Miss Bingham's invitation. If at the moment it was the effect of quite reasonless panic, he decided later that it was because he wished to think. It could not be said, however, that he did think, unless thinking consists of a series of dramatic representations which the mind makes to itself from a given impulse, and which it is quite powerless to end. All the afternoon, which Langbourne spent in his room, his mind was the theatre of scenes with Miss Simpson, in which he perpetually evolved the motives governing him from the beginning, and triumphed out of his difficulties and embarrassments. Her voice, as it acquiesced in all, no longer related itself to that imaginary personality which had inhabited his fancy. That was gone irrevocably; and the voice belonged to the likeness of Barbara, and no other; from her similitude, little, quaint, with her hair of cloudy red and her large, dim-sighted eyes, it played upon the spiritual sense within him with the coaxing, drolling, mocking charm which he had felt from the first. It blessed him with intelligent and joyous forgiveness. But as he stood at her gate that evening this unmerited felicity fell from him. He now really heard her voice, through the open doorway, but perhaps because it was mixed with other voices—the treble of Miss Bingham, and the bass of a man who must be the Mr. Dickery he had seen at the saw mills—he turned and hurried back to his hotel, where he wrote a short letter saying that he had decided to take the express for New York that night. With an instinctive recognition of her authority in the affair, or with a cowardly shrinking from direct dealing with Barbara, he wrote to Juliet Bingham, and he addressed to her the packet of letters which he sent for Barbara. Superficially, he had done what he had no choice but to do. He had been asked to return her letters, and he returned them, and brought the affair to an end.

In his long ride to the city he assured himself in vain that he was doing right if he was not sure of his feelings towards the girl. It was quite because he was not sure of his feeling that he could not be sure he was not acting falsely and cruelly.

The fear grew upon him through the summer, which he spent in the heat and stress of the town. In his work he could forget a little the despair in which he lived; but in a double consciousness like that of a hypochondriac, the girl whom it seemed to him he had deserted was visibly and audibly present with him. Her voice was always in his inner ear, and it visualized her looks and movements to his inner eye.

Now he saw and understood at last that what his heart had more than once misgiven him might be the truth, and that though she had sent back his letters, and asked her own in return, it was not necessarily her wish that he should obey her request. It might very well have been an experiment of his feelings towards her, a mute quest of the impression she had made upon him, a test of his will and purpose, an overture to a clearer and truer understanding between them. This misgiving became a conviction from which he could not escape.

He believed too late that he had made a mistake, that he had thrown away the supreme chance of his life. But was it too late? When he could bear it no longer, he began to deny that it was too late. He denied it even to the pathetic presence which haunted him, and in which the magic of her voice itself was merged at last, so that he saw her more than he heard her. He overbore her weak will with his stronger will, and set himself strenuously to protest to her real presence what now he always said to her phantom. When his partner came back from vacation, Langbourne told him that he was going to take a day or two off.

XII

He arrived at Upper Ashton Falls long enough before the early autumnal dusk to note that the crimson buds of the maples were now their crimson leaves, but he kept as close to the past as he could by not going to find Barbara before the hour of the evening when he had turned from her gate without daring to see her. It was a soft October evening now, as it was a soft May evening then; and there was a mystical hint of unity in the like feel of the dull, mild air. Again voices were coming out of the open doors and windows of the house, and they were the same voices that he had last heard there.

He knocked, and after a moment of startled hush within Juliet Bingham came to the door. "Why, Mr. Langbourne!" she screamed.

"I—I should like to come in, if you will let me," he gasped out.

"Why, certainly, Mr. Langbourne," she returned.

He had not dwelt so long and so intently on the meeting at hand without considering how he should account for his coming, and he had formulated a confession of his motives. But he had never meant to make it to Juliet Bingham, and now he found himself unable to allege a word in explanation of his presence. He followed her into the parlor. Barbara silently gave him her hand and then remained passive in the background, where Dickery held aloof, smiling in what seemed his perpetual enjoyment of the Juliet Bingham joke. She at once put herself in authority of the situation; she made Langbourne let her have his hat; she seated him when and where she chose; she removed and put back the lampshades; she pulled up and pulled down the window blinds; she shut the outer door because of the night air, and opened it because of the unreasonable warmth within. She excused Mrs. Simpson's absence on account of a headache, and asked him if he would have a fan; when he refused it she made him take it, and while he sat helplessly dangling it from his hand, she asked him about the summer he had had, and whether he had passed it in New York. She was very intelligent about the heat in New York, and tactful in keeping the one-sided talk from falling. Barbara said nothing after a few faint attempts to take part in it, and Langbourne made briefer and briefer answers. His reticence seemed only to heighten Juliet Bingham's satisfaction, as she said, with a final supremacy, that she had been intending to go out with Mr. Dickery to a business meeting of the book club, but they would be back before Langbourne could get away; she made him promise to wait for them. He did not know if Barbara looked any protest,—at least she spoke none,—and Juliet went out with Dickery. She turned at the door to bid Barbara say, if anyone called, that she was at the book-club meeting. Then she disappeared, but reappeared and called, "See here, a minute, Bab!" and at the outer threshold she detained Barbara in vivid whisper, ending aloud, "Now you be sure to do both, Bab! Aunt Elmira will tell you where the things are." Again she vanished, and was gone long enough to have reached the gate and come back from it. She was renewing all her whispered and out-spoken charges when Dickery showed himself at her side, put his hand under her elbow, and wheeled her about, and while she called gayly over her shoulder to the others, "Did you ever?" walked her definitively out of the house.

Langbourne did not suffer the silence which followed her going to possess him. What he had to do he must do quickly, and he said, "Miss Simpson, may I ask you one question."

"Why, if you won't expect me to answer it," she suggested quaintly.

"You must do as you please about that. It has to come before I try to excuse myself for being here; it's the only excuse I can offer. It's this: Did you send Miss Bingham to get back your letters from me last spring?"

"Why, of course!"

"I mean, was it your idea?"

"We thought it would be better."

The evasion satisfied Langbourne, but he asked, "Had I given you some cause to distrust me at that time?"

"Oh, no," she protested. "We got to talking it over, and—and we thought we had better."

"Because I had come here without being asked?"

"No, no; it wasn't that," the girl protested.

"I know I oughtn't to have come. I know I oughtn't to have written to you in the beginning, but you had let me write, and I thought you would let me come. I always tried to be sincere with you; to make you feel that you could trust me. I believe that I am an honest man; I thought I was a better man for having known you through the letters. I couldn't tell you how much they had been to me. You seemed to think, because I lived in a large place, that I had a great many friends; but I have very few; I might say I hadn't any—such as I thought I had when I was writing to you. Most of the men I know belong to some sort of clubs; but I don't. I went to New York when I was feeling alone in the world,—it was from something that had happened to me partly through my own fault,—and I've never got over being alone there. I've never gone into society; I don't know what society is, and I suppose that's why I'm acting differently than a society man now. The only change I ever had from business was reading at night; I've got a pretty good library. After I began to get your letters, I went out more—to the theatre, and lectures, and concerts, and all sorts of things—so that I could have something interesting to write about; I thought you'd get tired of always hearing about me. And your letters filled up my life, so that I didn't seem alone anymore. I read them all hundreds of times; I should have said that I knew them by heart, if they had not been as fresh at last as they were at first. I seemed to hear you talking in them." He stopped as if withholding himself from what he had nearly said without intending, and resumed: "It's some comfort to know that you didn't want them back because you doubted me, or my good faith."

"Oh, no, indeed," said Barbara compassionately.

"Then why did you?"

"I don't know. We—"

"No; *not* 'we.' *You!*"

She did not answer for so long that he believed she resented his speaking so peremptorily and was not going to answer him at all. At last she said, "I thought you would rather give them back." She turned and looked at him, with the eyes which he knew saw his face dimly, but saw his thought clearly.

"What made you think that?"

"Oh, I don't know. Didn't you want to?"

He knew that the fact which their words veiled was now in their mutual consciousness. He spoke the truth in saying, "No, I never wanted to," but this was only a mechanical truth, and he knew it. He had an impulse to put the burden of the situation on her, and press her to say why she thought he wished to do so; but his next emotion was shame for this impulse. A thousand times, in these reveries in which he had imagined meeting her, he had told her first of all how he had overheard her talking in the room next to his own in the hotel, and of the power her voice had instantly and lastingly had upon him. But now, with a sense spiritualized by her presence, he perceived that this, if it was not unworthy, was secondary, and that the right to say it was not yet established. There was something that must come before this,—something that could alone justify him in any further step. If she could answer him first as he wished, then he might open his whole heart out, at whatever cost; he was not greatly to blame, if he did not realize that the cost could not be wholly his, as he asked, remotely enough from her question, "After I wrote that I was coming up here, and you did not answer me, did you think I was coming?"

She did not answer, and he felt that he had been seeking a mean advantage. He went on: "If you didn't expect it, if you never thought I was coming, there's no need for me to tell you anything else."

Her face turned towards him a very little, but not so much as even to get a sidelong glimpse at him; it was as if it were drawn by a magnetic attraction; and she said, "I didn't know but you would come."

"Then I will tell you why I came—the only thing that gave me the right to come against your will, if it *was* against it. I came to ask you to marry me. Will you?"

She now turned to look fully at him, though he was aware of being a mere blur in her near-sighted vision.

"Do you mean to ask it now?"

"Yes."

"And have you wished to ask it ever since you first saw me?"

He tried to say that he had, but he could not; he could only say, "I wish to ask it now more than ever."

She shook her head slowly. "I'm not sure how you want me to answer you."

"Not sure?"

"No. I'm afraid I might disappoint you again."

He could not make out whether she was laughing at him. He sat, not knowing what to say, and he blurted out, "Do you mean that you won't?"

"I shouldn't want you to make another mistake."

"I don't know what you"—he was going to say "mean," but he substituted "wish. If you wish for more time, I can wait as long as you choose."

"No, I might wish for time, if there was anything more. But if there's nothing else you have to tell me—then no, I cannot marry you."

Langbourne rose, feeling justly punished, somehow, but bewildered as much as humbled, and he stood stupidly unable to go. "I don't know what you could expect me to say after you've refused me—"

"Oh, I don't expect anything."

"But there *is* something I should like to tell you. I know that I behaved that night as if—as if I hadn't come to ask you—what I have; I don't blame you for not trusting me now. But it is no use to tell you what I intended if it is all over."

He looked down into his hat, and she said in a low voice, "I think I ought to know. Won't you—sit down?"

He sat down again. "Then I will tell you at the risk of—But there's nothing left to lose! You know how it is, when we think about a person or a place before we see them: we make some sort of picture of them, and expect them to be like it. I don't know how to say it; you do look more like what I thought than you did at first. I suppose I must seem a fool to say it; but I thought you were tall, and that you were—well!—rather masterful—"

"Like Juliet Bingham?" she suggested, with a gleam in the eye next to him.

"Yes, like Juliet Bingham. It was your voice made me think—it was your voice that first made me want to see you, that made me write to you, in the beginning. I heard you talking that night in the hotel, where you left that circular; you were in the room next to mine; and I wanted to come right up here then; but I had to go back to New York, and so I wrote to you. When your letters came, I always seemed to hear you speaking in them."

"And when you saw me you were disappointed. I knew it."

"No; not disappointed—"

"Why not? My voice didn't go with my looks; it belonged to a tall, strong-willed girl."

"No," he protested. "As soon as I got away it was just as it always had been. I mean that your voice and looks went together again."

"As soon as you got away?" the girl questioned.

"I mean—What do you care for it, anyway!" he cried, in self-scornful exasperation.

"I know," she said thoughtfully, "that my voice isn't like me; I'm not good enough for it. It ought to be Juliet Bingham's—"

"No, no!" he interrupted, with a sort of disgust that seemed not to displease her, "I can't imagine it!"

"But we can't any of us have everything, and she's got enough as it is. She's a head higher than I am, and she wants to have her way ten times as bad."

"I didn't mean that," Langbourne began. "I—but you must think me enough of a simpleton already."

"Oh, no, not near," she declared. "I'm a good deal of a simpleton myself at times."

"It doesn't matter," he said desperately; "I love you."

"Ah, that belongs to the time when you thought I looked differently."

"I don't want you to look differently. I—"

"You can't expect me to believe that now. It will take time for me to do that."

"I will give you time," he said, so simply that she smiled.

"If it was my voice you cared for I should have to live up to it, somehow, before you cared for me. I'm not certain that I ever could. And if I couldn't? You see, don't you?"

"I see that I was a fool to tell you what I have," he so far asserted himself. "But I thought I ought to be *honest.*"

"Oh, you've been honest!" she said.

"You have a right to think that I am a flighty, romantic person," he resumed, "and I don't blame you. But if I could explain, it has been a very real experience for me. It was your nature that I cared for in your voice. I can't tell you just how it was; it seemed to me that unless I could hear it again, and always, my life would not be worth much. This was something deeper and better than I could make you understand. It wasn't merely a fancy; I do not want you to believe that."

"I don't know whether fancies are such very bad things. I've had some of my own," Barbara suggested.

He sat still with his hat between his hands, as if he could not find a chance of dismissing himself, and she remained looking down at her skirt where it tented itself over the toe of her shoe. The tall clock in the hall ticked second after second. It counted thirty of them at least before he spoke, after a preliminary noise in his throat.

"There is one thing I should like to ask: If you had cared for me, would you have been offended at my having thought you looked differently?"

She took some time to consider this. "I might have been vexed, or hurt, I suppose, but I don't see how I could really have been offended."

"Then I understand," he began, in one of his inductive emotions; but she rose nervously, as if she could not sit still, and went to the piano. The Spanish song he had given her was lying open upon it, and she struck some of the chords absently, and then let her fingers rest on the keys.

"Miss Simpson," he said, coming stiffly forward, "I should like to hear you sing that song once more before I—Won't you sing it?"

"Why, yes," she said, and she slipped laterally into the piano-seat.

At the end of the first stanza he gave a long sigh, and then he was silent to the close.

As she sounded the last notes of the accompaniment Juliet Bingham burst into the room with somehow the effect to Langbourne of having lain in wait outside for that moment.

"Oh, I just *knew* it!" she shouted, running upon them. "I bet John anything! Oh, I'm so happy it's come out all right and now I'm going to have the first—"

She lifted her arms as if to put them round his neck; he stood dazed, and Barbara rose from the piano-stool and confronted her with nothing less than horror in her face.

Juliet Bingham was beginning again, "Why, haven't you—"

"*No!*" cried Barbara. "I forgot all about what you said! I just happened to sing it because he asked me," and she ran from the room.

"Well, if I ever!" said Juliet Bingham, following her with astonished eyes. Then she turned to Langbourne. "It's perfectly ridiculous, and I don't see how I can ever explain it. I don't think Barbara has shown a great deal of tact," and Juliet Bingham was evidently prepared to make up the defect by a diplomacy which she enjoyed. "I don't know where to begin exactly; but you must certainly excuse my—manner, when I came in."

"Oh, certainly," said Langbourne in polite mystification.

"It was all through a misunderstanding that I don't think *I* was to blame for, to say the least; but I can't explain it without making Barbara appear perfectly—Mr. Langbourne, *will* you tell me whether you are engaged?"

"No! Miss Simpson has declined my offer," he answered.

"Oh, then it's all right," said Juliet Bingham, but Langbourne looked as if he did not see why she should say that. "Then I can understand; I see the whole thing now; and I didn't want to make *another* mistake. Ah—won't you sit down?"

"No. Thank you. I believe I will go."

"But you have a right to know—"

"Would my knowing alter the main facts?" he asked dryly.

"Well, no, I can't say it would," Juliet Bingham replied with an air of candor. "And, as you *say,* perhaps it's just as well," she added with an air of relief. Langbourne had not said it, but he acquiesced with a faint sigh, and absently took the hand of farewell which Juliet Bingham gave him. "I know Barbara will be very sorry not to see you; but I guess it's better."

In spite of the supremacy which the turn of affairs had given her, Juliet Bingham looked far from satisfied, and she let Langbourne know with a sense of inconclusiveness which showed in the parting inclination towards him; she kept the effect of this after he turned from her.

He crept light-headedly down the brick walk with a feeling that the darkness was not half thick enough, though it was so thick that it hid a figure that leaned upon the gate and held it shut, as if forcibly to interrupt his going.

"Mr. Langbourne," said the voice of this figure, which, though so unnaturally strained, he knew for Barbara's voice, "you have got to *know!* I'm ashamed to tell you, but I should be more ashamed not to, after what's happened. Juliet made me promise when she went out to the book-club meeting that if I—if—if it turned out as *you* wanted, I would sing that song as a sign—It was a joke—like my sending her picture. It was my mistake and I am sorry, I beg your pardon—I—"

She stopped with a quick catch in her breath, and the darkness round them seemed to become luminous with the light of hope that broke upon him within.

"But if there really was no mistake," he began. He could not get further. She did not answer, and for the first time her silence was sweeter than her voice. He lifted her tip-toe in his embrace, but he did not wish her taller; her yielding spirit lost itself in his own, and he did not regret the absence of the strong will which he had once imagined hers.

ABOUT THE AUTHORS

J. M. BARRIE (1860–1937) was a popular Scottish playwright and novelist whose *Peter Pan,* or *The Boy Who Wouldn't Grow Up* (1902) has been one of literature's best-loved classics since it was first introduced on the London stage a century ago. Awarded a baronetcy in 1913, Barrie also delighted theatergoers with such plays as *Quality Street* (1901), *The Admirable Crichton* (1902), *What Every Woman Knows* (1908), and *Dear Brutus* (1917). The best-known novels of Sir J. M. Barrie, who in his will left all royalties from *Peter Pan* to London's Great Ormond Street Hospital, are *The Little Minister* (1891), *Sentimental Tommy* (1896), and its sequel, *Tommy and Grizel* (1900).

SIR WALTER BESANT (1836–1901) was an English historian, novelist, and social reformer. Educated at King's College, London, and Christ's College, Cambridge, he helped found the influential Society of Authors in 1884 and later served as editor of its journal, *The Author.* Besant has been called "one of the most widely read novelists of the late nineteenth century," and among his works are *All Sorts and Conditions of Men* (1882), which helped draw attention to the plight of the poor in London's slum-ridden East End; *Dorothy Forster* (1884), and *The Orange Girl* (1898). In 1890 he finished Wilkie Collins's *Blind Love,* which had been left uncompleted at the time of Collins's death, and in 1895 he received a knighthood.

There are numerous familiar quotes attributed to Besant, including "England and America are two countries separated by the same language" and "Youth is a wonderful thing; what a crime to waste it on children."

JOHN BUCHAN (1875–1940), the first Baron Tweedsmuir, saw service in South Africa during the Boer War, worked in British military intelligence during the First World War, and throughout World War II served as Governor General of Canada. He began his writing career as a very young man, publishing regularly when he was barely out of his teens, and had his first great success with *The Thirty-Nine Steps* (1915), a still-mesmerizing tale of pursuit and flight, centering upon one man's attempt to thwart a diabolical conspiracy. Other books featuring the same hero, Richard Hannay, are *Greenmantle* (1916) and *The Three Hostages* (1924).

The Thirty-Nine Steps has been filmed three times, but it is the 1935 version, directed by Alfred Hitchcock and starring Robert Donat, that is a classic of the cinema. The story "Fountainblue" is taken from a 1912 John Buchan collection, *The Moon Endureth: Tales and Fancies.*

CORNELIA A. P. COMER (1867?–1929) is the author of the collection *The Preliminaries and Other Stories* (1912). A graduate of Vassar College, she contributed both fiction and non-fiction pieces to the *Atlantic Monthly* and *Harper's Monthly* magazines. (One of her *Atlantic* essays elicited an enthusiastic note of appreciation from reader Theodore Roosevelt.) Among her other books are *Daughter of a Stoic* (1896) and *A Book of Martyrs* (1896).

SIR ARTHUR CONAN DOYLE (1859–1930) was born in Edinburgh and received his medical degree there in 1885. Three years later, *A Study in Scarlet,* the first case featuring the immortal Sherlock Holmes—certainly the most famous detective in all of literature—was published in the pages of the *Strand* magazine. Its success caused the young doctor, who had been seeking to supplement his income, to produce further mysteries set in the environs of Holmes's Baker Street domicile, including *The Sign of Four* (1891), *The Hound of the Baskervilles* (1902), and such casebooks as *The Adventures of Sherlock Holmes* (1892), *The Memoirs of Sherlock Holmes* (1894), and *The Return of Sherlock Holmes* (1905). (Doyle's exasperated attempt to kill off Holmes, for once and for all, by sending him plunging over the Reichenbach Falls, lasted only as long as the author could withstand the incredible public clamor to bring his beloved character back, hence the eleven-year hiatus between *The Memoirs of Sherlock Holmes* and *The Return of Sherlock Holmes.*)

His other works of fiction include the historical novel, *The White Company* (1891), and the fantasy *The Lost World* (1912). Doyle received his knighthood in 1902.

ELLEN T. FOWLER (1860–1929), the daughter of an English viscount and member of Parliament, began her writing life as a poet, with *Verses Grave and Gay* (1891) and *Verses Wise and Otherwise* (1895). Her novels, however, brought her popular success, and one, *Her Ladyship's Conscience* (1913), with its story of the love affair between a younger man and an older woman, earned her a feminist reputation. A Fellow of the Royal Society of Literature, she wrote numerous novels that, in fact, featured independent-minded heroines, including *Concerning Isabel Carnaby,* a best-seller in 1898, and *Miss Fallowfield's Fortune* (1908).

JOHN GALSWORTHY (1867–1933) was an English novelist and dramatist whose most celebrated work, a group of three linked trilogies known as *The Forsyte Saga,* was published between 1906 and 1933. Of his works for the stage, which often addressed social problems of his era, probably the best known today is *The Skin Game* (1931). In the 1960s, a popular television adaptation introduced his chronicle of the intertwined personal dramas of successive generations of one upper-middle-class family, the Forsytes, to a new and appreciative audience; now, just over three decades later, it has once again been produced for the small screen.

Educated at Oxford and afterward trained in law, Galsworthy had refused a knighthood in 1918, but two decades later, he accepted the Order of Merit from George V. In 1932, he was awarded the Nobel Prize for Literature.

ELLEN GLASGOW (1873–1945) was the daughter of a prominent family in Richmond, Virginia, and except for trips abroad, spent her entire life as a pillar of society in this southern state capital. Yet, according to one critic, "her conventional exterior was at odds with her unconventional novels, with their enduring feminist and radical demands for an end to hypocrisy." Glasgow's first novel, *The Descendant,* was published in 1897, and her subsequent works include *The Voice of the People* (1900), *Virginia* (1913), *Barren Ground* (1925), and *The Romantic Comedians* (1926). She was awarded the Pulitzer Prize for fiction for her last novel, *This Is Our Life* (1941).

HENRY SYDNOR HARRISON (1880–1930) was a Tennessee native whose short stories appeared in *The Saturday Evening Post* and other magazines. Two of his novels were best-sellers—*Queed* (1911) and *Angela's Business* (1915)—and praised by contemporary critics for their realistic portrayal of the middle-class southern milieu Harrison knew well. The film made from another of this author's novels, *Captivating Mary Carstairs* (1910), gave early screen great Norma Talmadge her first starring role. Henry Harrison also wrote *When I Come Back* (1919), a nonfiction account of a soldier killed in the First World War. Harrison died in Atlantic City, New Jersey.

FRANCES NOYES HART (1890–1943) was an American novelist whose greatest success was the classic courtroom mystery, *The Bellamy Trial* (1927), based loosely on the notorious Hall-Mills murders and serialized initially in *The Saturday Evening Post.* Born outside of Washington, D.C., she was the daughter of Frank Noyes, who owned and edited *The Washington Star* and was president of the Associated Press. Her short stories were collected in *Contact* (1923), and her account of a leisurely trip through France with her husband was published as *Pigs in Clover* (1931).

Referring to herself "a great reader and small writer," Hart enthusiastically championed women's magazines and the cultural value of women's popular literature, in general.

BRET HARTE (1836–1902) headed west to seek his fortune in California when he was only nineteen. Briefly a miner, then a schoolteacher, and finally, a magazine editor, he achieved his greatest success in the late 1860s with his sentimental tales of colorful frontier characters, of which "The Luck of Roaring Camp" (1868) and "The Outcasts of Poker Flat" (1869) are two of the best known. With Mark Twain, he wrote a play, *Ah Sin,* in 1877; however, it was an effort that failed to revive his writing career, and soon after, he chose to move abroad. As U.S. consul in Germany and Scotland, Harte found himself in demand in European literary circles.

O. HENRY (1862–1910) is the pseudonym of William Sydney Porter, an American writer whose name has become synonymous with the form in which he chose to work: the short story. Born in North Carolina, he was editing a humor magazine in Texas before the moment came when he chose to flee to Central America, intending to escape charges of embezzlement. After his eventual return, he served three years in federal prison; it was in 1899, while he was behind bars, that Porter published his first tale as "O. Henry" in *McClure's* magazine. "The Last Leaf" (1907) and "The Gift of the Magi" (1906) are his two most famous stories, each perfectly illustrating the author's gift for the surprise ending. The title of his celebrated collection *The Four Million* (1906)—containing twenty-five stories about life on the streets and in the tenements of New York City—is a reference to the actual metropolitan population at the time.

ROBERT HERRICK (1868–1938) was a patrician New Englander born in Cambridge, Massachusetts, and educated at Harvard. He taught first at the Massachusetts Institute of Technology and then at the University of Chicago, where he originated a special program focusing on composition and rhetoric. Widely published in the prestigious magazines of his day, he also penned numerous novels, including *The Memoirs of an American Citizen* (1905), *One Woman's Life* (1913), and *Chimes* (1926).

"The Master of the Inn," which appeared originally in *Scribner's Magazine* in 1907, served as the basis the following year for the best loved of Herrick's full-length fictions, which bore the same title.

ANTHONY HOPE (1863–1933) was the pen name of an Oxford-educated English barrister, Sir Anthony Hope Hawkins. *The Dolly Dialogues,* a series of witty sketches published in the *Westminster Gazette* in 1894, brought him sufficient acclaim to cause him to leave the bar and devote himself to writing. His best-selling novel of royal impersonation and romantic intrigue, *The Prisoner of Zenda* (1894), added to the language the name of the imaginary middle-European kingdom, Ruritania, where it was set. A sequel, *Rupert of Hentzau,* published four years later, was, unfortunately, less successful. *Zenda* was filmed at least three times; the 1937 version, produced by David O. Selznick, starred Ronald Colman, Douglas Fairbanks, Jr., and David Niven.

LAURENCE HOUSMAN (1865–1959) was the younger brother of poet A. E. Housman and made his own career as a novelist, dramatist, and illustrator. He achieved his first celebrity with the anonymous publication, *An Englishwoman's Love Letters* (1900), a work the public accepted as real until the unmasking of a thirty-five-year-old male writer as its author. A different sort of scandal occurred when his most famous play, *Victoria Regina* (1934), was banned from the London stage because it dared to depict still-living members of the royal family; it was, however, produced successfully in New York the following year, with Helen Hayes triumphant in the lead.

WILLIAM DEAN HOWELLS (1837–1920) was an American editor, novelist, and critic who, though he received little education during his Ohio boyhood, rose to the highest ranks of the late nineteenth-century literary scene and became editor of the distinguished Boston magazine, the *Atlantic Monthly,* in 1871. (His ascendance had begun with an early book of poetry and a campaign biography of Abraham Lincoln. For this latter effort, he was rewarded with the U.S. consulship in Venice, where he spent the years of the Civil War.) Howells was a close friend of Mark Twain's and a mentor to many writers, including Henry James, Stephen Crane, and Sarah Orne Jewett, and he served as president of the American Academy of Arts and Letters.

Among his many novels, which are still today both relevant and readable as they examine the strains of upwardly mobile American life, are *A Modern Instance* (1881), *The Rise of Silas Lapham* (1885), and *A Hazard of New Fortunes* (1890).

SARAH ORNE JEWETT (1849–1909) took her inspiration from the Maine coastal countryside in which she lived. She was the daughter of a prosperous doctor and published her first short story in the *Atlantic Monthly* when she was only nineteen. Encouraged in her writing career by its editor, William Dean Howells, she later went on, briefly, to mentor the young Willa Cather. (In 1925, contributing an introduction to a new edition of Jewett's most celebrated book, *The Country of the Pointed Firs,* Cather described the 1896 collection of tales and regional sketches as "almost flawless examples of literary art.") Jewett's other novels are *Deephaven* (1877) and *A Country Doctor* (1884).

ELEANOR MERCEIN KELLY (1880–1968) was a novelist and short-story writer who married and moved to Louisville, Kentucky, in 1901, after being educated at a convent school in Washington, D.C. Her first book was *Toya the Unlike* (1913), and between 1916 and 1925, she published three novels set in her adopted state—*The Kildares of Storm, Why Joan?,* and *The Mansion House*—all featuring strong women protagonists. She received an O. Henry Prize for her tale, "Basquerie," in 1925 and two years later published a longer version as a novel of the same name. She traveled widely, especially in southern and eastern Europe; her last book, *Proud Castle* (1951), was set among the Magyars of Hungary.

RICHARD LE GALLIENNE (1866–1947) was an English man of letters who, after settling in the United States, continued to contribute to the leading periodicals on both sides of the Atlantic. Early in his career he had been associated with *The Yellow Book,* the notorious fin de siècle literary quarterly, and later, in the books *The Romantic '90s* (1925) and *From a Paris Garrett* (1936), he set down his reminiscences of those Bohemian years. A poet himself, he edited the anthologies *Le Gallienne's Book of American Verse* and *Le Gallienne's Book of English Verse.* Of his novels, one of the better known is *Quest of the Golden Girl* (1896). His daughter, Eva Le Gallienne, became a well-known actress, especially acclaimed for her interpretations of Ibsen, whom she translated.

C. L. PIRKIS (?–1910) was a granddaughter of the English clergyman Richard Lyne, who wrote both a popular Latin grammar and a primer. She was married to a naval officer and wrote a total of fourteen novels, of which *The Experiences of Loveday Brooke, Lady Detective* (1894) was the last. She lived in London and, as her writing career waned, began to devote herself to good works. Along with her husband, she founded the National Canine Defense League, an organization still active in Great Britain.

SAKI (1870–1916) is the pen name of Hector Hugh Munro, a Scottish-born writer whose eccentric and droll short stories have delighted readers for over a century. His best-known tale is undoubtedly the heavily anthologized "The Open Window"—in which a mischievous young woman chooses to tell a visitor a highly dubious ghost story—but "Sredni Vashtar," about a small boy's cool revenge, is a close runner-up. *The Unbearable Bassington* (1912) is, according to some critics, a long-underrated novel, while it is upon such story collections as *The Chronicles of Clovis* (1912) and *Beasts and Super Beasts* (1914) that the reputation of Saki rests. Saki died while fighting in World War I.

SOMERVILLE AND ROSS were two cousins, Edith Oenone Somerville (1858–1949) and Violet Florence Martin (1862–1915), who collaborated on a variety of books with Irish subjects. Both campaigned for the cause of female suffrage, and Somerville, an ardent hunter, had the distinction in 1903 of becoming the first woman ever to be named a Master of Fox Hounds. Their works include novels, among them *The Real Charlotte* (1894), as well as a series of droll sketches portraying the Irish rural gentry entitled *Some Experiences of an Irish R.M.* (1899)—"Poisson d'Avril" is taken from its sequel, *Further Experiences* *of an Irish R.M.* (1908)—and travel memoirs, such as *Through Connemara in a Governess Cart* (1893).

F. J. STIMSON (1855–1943) was a distinguished Boston lawyer who wrote novels and short stories as well as legal textbooks. He published his earliest fiction under the pseudonym, "J. S. of Dale." He was assistant attorney general of the state of Massachusetts in the 1880s and later a Democratic candidate for Congress.

"Our Consul at Carlsruhe," a story of thwarted love that will undoubtedly remind many readers of Edith Wharton's *The Age of Innocence* (1920), may, in fact, have inspired her. It appeared in Stimson's 1886 collection, *The Sentimental Calendar,* and twenty years later was already being selected for inclusion in a volume of *American Short Story Classics.* It is interesting to note that Stimson's 1906 novel, *In Cure of Her Soul,* took for its hero Austin Pinckney, a son of the "Consul at Carlsruhe."

FRANK R. STOCKTON (1834–1902) was the son of a Philadelphia clergyman who entered the engraving trade at the behest of his father. But he loved making up stories, particularly for children, and soon turned to literature as his life's work. He served on the staff at *Scribner's Monthly* and at *St. Nicholas Magazine,* quitting to write full-time only after the commercial success of his first adult novel, *Rudder Grange* (1878). His most famous story (even, perhaps, one of the most famous stories ever written by anyone), "The Lady or the Tiger?" (1882), was originally titled "The King's Arena" and was read aloud first by Stockton to friends at a party, then published in the *Century Magazine.* Stockton's comic novel *The Casting Away of Mrs. Lecks and Mrs. Aleshine* (1886) followed the adventures of two shipwrecked New England widows, and his complete works were collected in twenty-three volumes.

MARK TWAIN (1835–1910), literary alter ego to Samuel Langhorne Clemens, has long been one of the most cherished of American voices. After working as a Mississippi River pilot, the Missouri-born writer began to make his career as a lecturer and a roving correspondent, gaining wide recognition with the success of his 1865 story, "The Celebrated Jumping Frog of Calaveras County." Among his many celebrated creations: *The Adventures of Tom Sawyer* (1876), *The Prince and the Pauper* (1881), *The Adventures of Huckleberry Finn* (1884), and *A Connecticut Yankee in King Arthur's Court* (1889).

The pen name "Mark Twain" was taken from the river slang for "two fathoms deep." A master of tongue-in-cheek techniques—including mock reverence and deadpan exaggeration—Twain is credited as the author responsible for making colloquial speech a part of American fiction.

EDGAR WALLACE (1875–1932) was a prolific journalist and author of best-selling fiction who produced more than 170 books, the majority of which were highly colorful mysteries and thrillers. Perhaps his most famous title is *The Four Just Men* (1905), an early tale of international terrorism, but he is also admired as the creator of J. G. Reeder, a deceptively meek bureaucrat who sleuths his way through one novel and three collections of ingenious short stories beginning with *The Mind of Mr. J. G. Reeder* (1925). Wallace frequently created works for stage and screen, and was one of the writers of the screenplay for the classic *King Kong* (1933).

Reported to have dashed off a play, *On the Spot* (1930), in four days and a novel, *The Coat of Arms* (1931), in a single weekend, Wallace regarded himself, above all, as an entertainer, and once summed up his career to an interviewer by stating, "I write to amuse." In London, there is a popular Fleet Street pub that bears his name.

H. G. WELLS (1866–1946) was a prolific English writer whose many passionately held social, political, and scientific theories informed his novels and short stories as well his non-fiction work. His science-fiction fantasies, among them *The Time Machine* (1895), *The Invisible Man* (1897), and *The War of the Worlds* (1898), though published in the waning years of the nineteenth century, are thrilling enough to continue to entertain readers on into the twenty-first. Of his other novels, *Kipps* (1905), *Tono-Bungay* (1909), and *The History of Mr. Polly* (1910) are some of the best known.

An energetic popularizer, Wells also strove to educate the public with ambitious volumes, such as the *Outline of History* and *Mankind in the Making.*

EDITH WHARTON (1862–1937) made her debut as a short story writer in 1891. The earliest of her novels, *The Valley of Decision,* appeared eleven years later, and in 1906, *The House of Mirth* was one of the year's top ten best-sellers. She was the first woman to win a Pulitzer Prize, awarded for her novel, *The Age of Innocence* in 1921.

Wharton also produced influential works on design, including *The Decoration of Houses* (1897, with Ogden Codman, Jr.) and *Italian Villas and Their Gardens*

(1904). Born a member of old New York society, she lived abroad for much of her life. After the First World War, she was made a Chevalier of the Legion of Honor by the French government for her efforts on behalf of refugees and displaced children.

OSCAR WILDE (1854–1900) was an Irish-born, Oxford-educated poet, playwright, and novelist celebrated for his aphoristic wit. His engagingly cynical drawing room comedies, among them *Lady Windemere's Fan* (1892), *The Importance of Being Earnest* (1895), and *An Ideal Husband* (1895), have remained widely performed and seen in the century following his death. His other best-known works include the novel, *The Picture of Dorian Gray* (1891); the poem, "The Ballad of Reading Gaol" (1898); and his collection of original fairy stories, *The Happy Prince, and Other Tales* (1888).

The aesthetic movement ("Art for art's sake" was its motto) that the flamboyant Wilde helped found during his undergraduate years was later satirized by Gilbert and Sullivan in their operetta, *Patience.*

P. G. WODEHOUSE (1881–1975), born in Great Britain, was knighted by Queen Elizabeth II for his services to literature shortly before his death. Yet for many years he had been, in fact, both a resident in the United States and an American citizen. That said, it is also true that the popularity of his much-adored creation, the Honorable Bertie Wooster—a lovably dimwitted English aristocrat whose escapades are invariably held in check, if only barely, by his long-suffering valet, Jeeves—has never been subject to national boundaries. Among the many titles featuring Bertie and Jeeves are *Leave It to Psmith* (1923), *The Code of the Woosters* (1938), and *French Leave* (1956).

Performing Flea (1953) and *Over Seventy* (1957) are two of Wodehouse's autobiographical works, and *Sunset at Blandings* (1977), his unfinished last novel, was published posthumously.